Rave reviews for
LORD VALENTINE'S CASTLE:

"A SUREFIRE PAGETURNER . . . The giant
planet of Majipoor is a brilliant concept of the imagination. There is a lot of good reading here."
— *Chicago Sun-Times*

"DESERVES TO BE ONE OF THE YEAR'S
HITS . . . This absorbing book is more successful
in creating a wildly imaginative universe than
Heinlein's *Stranger in a Strange Land.*"
— *People*

"A HANDSOME, WELL-WRITTEN ADVEN-
TURE . . . an epic quest in the grandest tradition,
full of strange adventures and stranger sights."
— *Future Life*

"SILVERBERG HAS DONE THE ROPE TRICK
WITH THIS ONE—pulled you into a superbly con-
structed world-system-ecology-history."
— *Anne McCaffrey*

"A GRAND, PICARESQUE TALE . . . by one of
the great storytellers of the century. *Lord Valentine's
Castle* has everything—action, intrigue, a horde of
interesting characters."
— *Roger Zelazny*

Lord Valentine's Castle

Robert Silverberg

For David Hartwell
Page Cuddy
John Bush

they pushed very gently

This low-priced Bantam Book
has been completely reset in a type face
designed for easy reading, and was printed
from new plates. It contains the complete
text of the original hard-cover edition.
NOT ONE WORD HAS BEEN OMITTED.

LORD VALENTINE'S CASTLE
A Bantam Book/published by arrangement with
Harper & Row, Publishers Inc.

PRINTING HISTORY
This work originally appeared in somewhat different form in
THE MAGAZINE OF FANTASY AND SCIENCE FICTION
Harper & Row edition published April 1980
A Selection of Doubleday Science Fiction Book Club June 1980
Bantam edition/July 1981

ISBN 0-553-14428-6

Published simultaneously in the United States and Canada

PRINTED IN THE UNITED STATES OF AMERICA

0 9 8 7 6 5 4 3 2 1

Contents

Acknowledgments

For assistance with the technical aspects of juggling in this novel I am indebted to Catherine Crowell of San Francisco and to those extraordinary performers the Flying Karamazov Brothers, who may not be aware until this moment of just how much help they rendered. However, the concepts of the theory and practice of juggling as expressed herein are primarily my own, especially as regards the capabilities of four-armed jugglers, and neither Ms. Crowell nor the Karamazovs should be held responsible for any implausibilities or impossibilities in these pages.

Invaluable assistance in other aspects of writing this book was provided by Marta Randall. Among Ms. Randall's contributions are the texts of some of the songs found herein.

For additional criticism of the manuscript in its troublesome early stages I am grateful to Barbara Silverberg and Susanne L. Houfek, and I owe thanks to Ted Chichak of the Scott Meredith Literary Agency for his support and encouragement and professional acumen.

—ROBERT SILVERBERG

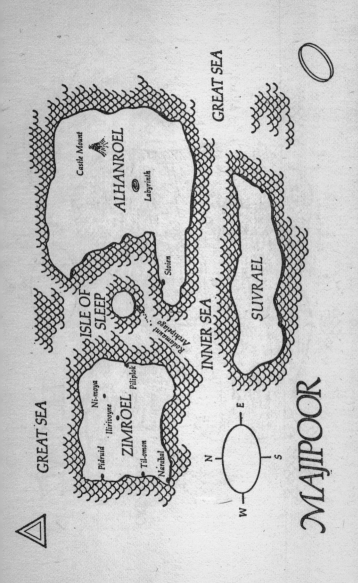

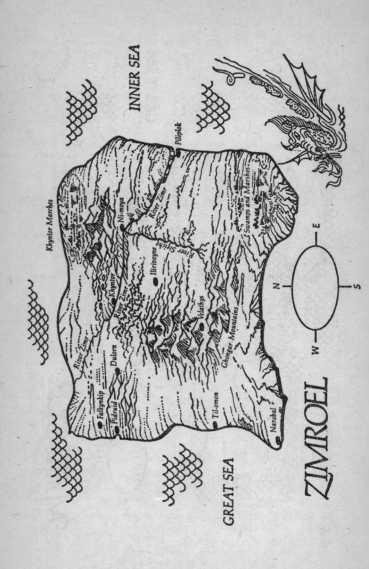

INNER SEA

GREAT SEA

Khyntor Marches

River Zimr

Falkynkip

Dulorn

Pidruid

Khyntor

River Zimr

Ni-moya

Piliplok

River Zimr

Ilirivoyne

River Strait

Swamps and Marshes

Velalisys

Ghongar Mountains

Til-omon

Narabal

ZIMROEL

N

W   E

S

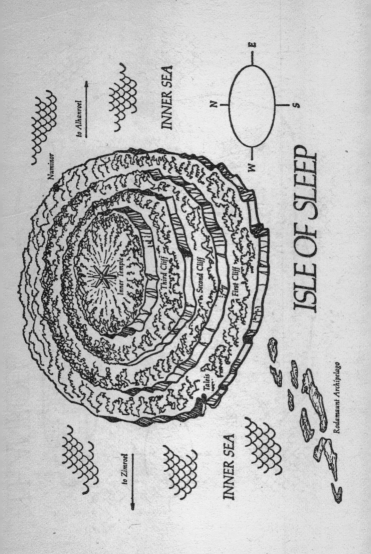

ISLE OF SLEEP

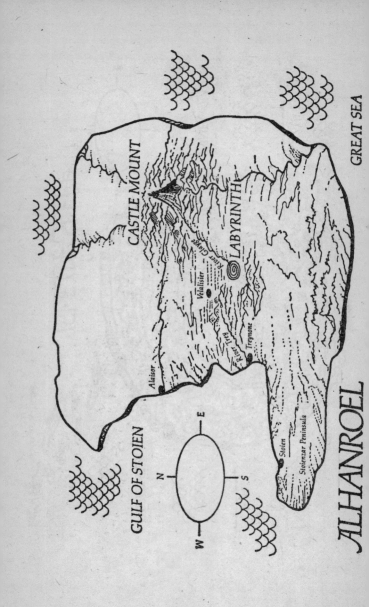

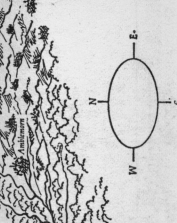

GLAYGE VALLEY AND CASTLE MOUNT

CASTLE

Amblemorn

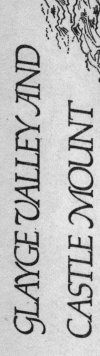

Velalisier

Makroprosopos

Pendiwane Ti

River Glayge

Lake Roghoiz

LABYRINTH

N
W — E
S

I

The Book of the King of Dreams

And then, after walking all day through a golden haze of humid warmth that gathered about him like fine wet fleece, Valentine came to a great ridge of outcropping white stone overlooking the city of Pidruid. It was the provincial capital, sprawling and splendid, the biggest city he had come upon since—since?—the biggest in a long while of wandering, at any rate.

There he halted, finding a seat at the edge of the soft, crumbling white ridge, digging his booted feet into the flaking ragged stone, and he sat there staring down at Pidruid, blinking as though newly out of sleep. On this summer day twilight was still some hours away, and the sun hung high to the southwest beyond Pidruid, out over the Great Sea. I will rest here for a while, Valentine thought, and then I will go down into Pidruid and find lodging for the night.

As he rested he heard pebbles tumbling past him from a higher point on the ridge. Unhurriedly he looked back the way he had come. A young herdsman had appeared, a boy with straw-colored hair and a freckled face, leading a train of fifteen or twenty mounts down the hill road. They were fat sleek purple-skinned beasts, obviously well looked after. The boy's own mount looked older and less plump, a wise and toughened creature.

"Hoy!" he called down to Valentine. "Where are you bound?"

"Pidruid. And you?"

"The same. Bringing these mounts to market. Thirsty work it is, too. Do you have wine?"

1

"Some," Valentine said. He tapped the flask at his hip, where a fiercer man might wear a weapon. "Good red mid-country wine. I'll be sorry to see the last of it."

"Give me a drink and I'll let you ride into town with me."

"Done," said Valentine.

He got to his feet as the boy dismounted and scrambled down the ridge toward him. Valentine offered him the flask. The boy was no more than fourteen or fifteen, he guessed, and small for his age, though deep through the chest and brawny. He came hardly elbow-high to Valentine, who was tall but not unusually so, a sturdy man just above middle height, with wide flat shoulders and big capable hands.

The boy swirled the wine in the flask, inhaled in a knowing way, nodded his approval, took a deep gulp, sighed. "I've been eating dust all the way from Falkynkip! And this sticky heat—it chokes you! Another dry hour and I'd have been a dead one." He returned the wine to Valentine. "You live in town?"

Valentine frowned. "No."

"Here for the festival, then?"

"Festival?"

"You don't know?"

Valentine shook his head. He felt the pressure of the boy's bright, mocking eyes, and was confused. "I've been traveling. I haven't followed the news. Is this festival time in Pidruid?"

"This week it is," said the boy. "Beginning on Starday. The grand parade, the circus, the royal celebration. Look down there. Don't you see *him* entering the city even now?"

He pointed. Valentine sighted along the boy's outstretched arm and squinted, peering at Pidruid's southern corner, but all he saw was a jumble of green-tiled rooftops and a tangle of ancient streets following no rational plan. Again he shook his head. "There," the boy said impatiently. "Down by the harbor. See? The ships? The five tremendous ones, with *his* banner flying from the rigging? And there's the procession, coming through Dragon Gate, just beginning to march Black Highway. I think that's his chariot, coming up now by the Arch of Dreams. Don't you see? Is there something wrong with your eyes?"

"I don't know the city," said Valentine mildly. "But yes, I see the harbor, the five ships."

"Good. Now follow along inland a little way—the big stone gate? And the wide highway running through it? And that ceremonial arch, just this side of—"

"I see it now, yes."

2

"And his banner over the chariot?"

"Whose banner? If I sound dim, forgive me, but—"

"Whose? Whose? Lord Valentine's banner! Lord Valentine's chariot! Lord Valentine's bodyguard marching through the streets of Pidruid! Don't you know the Coronal has arrived?"

"I didn't."

"And the festival! Why do you think there's a festival at this time of summer, if not to welcome the Coronal?"

Valentine smiled. "I've been traveling and I haven't followed the news. Would you like more wine?"

"There's not much left," the boy said.

"Go on. Finish it. I'll buy more in Pidruid."

He handed over the flask and turned toward the city again, letting his gaze travel down the slope and across the woodsy suburbs to the dense and teeming city, and outward toward the waterfront, and to the great ships, the banners, the marching warriors, the chariot of the Coronal. This must be a great moment in the history of Pidruid, for the Coronal ruled from far-off Castle Mount, all the way on the other side of the world, so distant that he and it were almost legendary, distances being what they were on this world of Majipoor. Coronals of Majipoor did not come often to the western continent. But Valentine was oddly unmoved by the knowledge of the presence of his glittering namesake down below there. I am here and the Coronal is here, he thought, and he will sleep tonight in some splendid palace of the masters of Pidruid, and I will sleep in some pile of hay, and then there will be a grand festival, and what is that to me? He felt almost apologetic, being so placid in the face of the boy's excitement. It was a discourtesy.

He said, "Forgive me. I know so little of what's been happening in the world these past months. Why is the Coronal here?"

"He makes the grand processional," said the boy. "To every part of the realm, to mark his coming to power. This is the new one, you know. Lord Valentine, only two years on his throne. The brother to Lord Voriax who died. You knew that, that Lord Voriax was dead, that Lord Valentine was our Coronal?"

"I had heard," said Valentine vaguely.

"Well, that's he, down there in Pidruid. Touring the realm for the first time since he got the Castle. He's been down south all month, in the jungle provinces, and yesterday he sailed up the coast to Pidruid, and tonight he enters the city, and in a few days there'll be the festival, and food and drink

3

for everyone, games, dancing, delights, a great market too where I'll sell these animals for a fortune. Afterward he travels overland through the whole continent of Zimroel, from capital to capital, a journey of so many thousands of miles it makes my head ache to think of it, and from the eastern shore he'll sail back to Alhanroel and Castle Mount, and none of us in Zimroel will see him again for twenty years or more. A fine thing it must be to be Coronal!" The boy laughed. "That was good wine. My name's Shanamir. What's yours?"

"Valentine."

"Valentine? *Valentine?* An auspicious name!"

"A common one, I'm afraid."

"Put *Lord* in front of it and you'd be the Coronal!"

"It's not as easy as that. Besides, why would I want to be Coronal?"

"The power," said Shanamir, wide-eyed. "The fine clothes, the food, the wine, the jewels, the palaces, the women—"

"The responsibility," Valentine said somberly. "The burden. Do you think a Coronal does nothing but drink golden wine and march in grand processions? Do you think he's put there just to enjoy himself?"

The boy considered. "Perhaps not."

"He rules over billions upon billions of people, across territories so huge we can't comprehend them. Everything falls on his shoulders. To carry out the decrees of the Pontifex, to sustain order, to support justice in every land—it tires me to think of it, boy. He keeps the world from collapsing into chaos. I don't envy him. Let him have the job."

Shanamir said, after a moment, "You're not as stupid as I first thought, Valentine."

"Did you think I was stupid, then?"

"Well, simple. Easy of mind. Here you are a grown man, and you seem to know so little of certain things, and I half your age and I have to explain. But perhaps I misjudge you. Shall we go down into Pidruid?"

2

Valentine had his pick of the mounts the boy was taking to market; but they all seemed alike to him, and after making a pretense of choosing he picked one at random, vaulting lightly into the creature's natural saddle. It was good to ride, after so long on foot. The mount was comfortable, as well it might be,

4

for they had been bred for comfort for thousands of years, these artificial animals, these witchcraft-creatures out of the old days, strong and tireless and patient, able to convert any sort of trash into food. The skill of making them was long forgotten, but now they bred of themselves, like natural animals, and it would be a slow business getting about on Majipoor without them.

The road to Pidruid led along the high ridge for more than a mile, then began sudden sharp switchbacks down into the coastal plain. Valentine let the boy do most of the talking as they made the descent. Shanamir came, he said, from a district two and a half days' journey inland, to the northeast; there he and his brothers and his father raised mounts for sale at Pidruid market, and turned a good living at it; he was thirteen years old, and had a high opinion of himself; he had never been outside the province of which Pidruid was the capital, but someday he meant to go abroad, to travel everywhere on Majipoor, to make the pilgrimage to the Isle of Sleep and kneel before the Lady, to cross the Inner Sea to Alhanroel and achieve the ascent of Castle Mount, even to go down south, maybe, beyond the steaming tropics, into the burnt and barren domain of the King of Dreams, for what was the use of being alive and healthy on a world as full of wonders as Majipoor if you did not journey hither and thither about on it?

"And you, Valentine?" he asked suddenly. "Who are you, where from, whither bound?"

Valentine was caught by surprise, lulled by the boy's prattle and the steady gentle rhythm of the mount as it padded down the broad twisting road, and the burst of jabbing questions left him unprepared. He said only, "I come from the eastern provinces. I have no plans beyond Pidruid. I'll stay here until I have reason to leave."

"Why have you come?"

"Why not?"

"Ah," said Shanamir. "All right. I know purposeful evasion when I hear it. You're the younger son of a duke in Ni-moya or Piliplok, and you sent someone a mischievous dream and were caught at it, and your father gave you a pouch of money and told you to vanish to the far side of the continent. Right?"

"Precisely," Valentine said, with a wink.

"And you're loaded with royals and crowns and you're going to set yourself up like a prince in Pidruid and drink and dance until your last coin is gone, and then you'll hire aboard a seagoing vessel and ship out for Alhanroel, and you'll take me with you as your squire. Isn't that so?"

5

"You have it exactly, my friend. Except for the money. I neglected to provide for that part of your fantasy."

"But you have *some* money," said Shanamir, not so playfully now. "You aren't a beggar, are you? They're very hard on beggars in Pidruid. They don't allow any sort of vagrancy down there."

"I have a few coins," Valentine said. "Enough to carry me through festival time and a bit beyond. And then I'll see."

"If you do go to sea, take me with you, Valentine!"

"If I do, I will," he promised.

They were halfway down the slope now. The city of Pidruid lay in a great basin along the coast, rimmed by low gray hills on the inland side and along much of the shore, save only where a break in the outer range allowed the ocean to spill through, forming a blue-green bay that was Pidruid's magnificent harbor. As he approached sea level here in late afternoon Valentine felt the offshore breezes blowing toward him, cool, fragrant, breaking the heat. Already white shoals of fog were rolling toward the shore out of the west, and there was a salty tang to the air, thick as it was now with water that had embraced the fishes and sea-dragons only hours before. Valentine was awed by the size of the city that lay before him. He could not remember ever having seen a larger one; but there was so much, after all, that he could not remember.

This was the edge of the continent. All of Zimroel lay at his back, and for all he knew he had walked it from end to end, from one of the eastern ports indeed, Ni-moya or Piliplok, except that he knew himself to be a young man, not very young but young enough, and he doubted that it was possible to have made such a journey on foot in one lifetime, and he had no recollection of having been on any sort of mount until this afternoon. On the other hand, he seemed to know how to ride, he had lifted himself knowledgeably into the beast's broad saddle, and that argued that he must have ridden at least part of the way before. It did not matter. He was here now, and he felt no restlessness; since Pidruid was where he had somehow arrived, Pidruid was where he would stay, until there was reason to go elsewhere. He lacked Shanamir's hunger for travel. The world was so big it did not bear thinking about, three great continents, two enormous seas, a place that one could comprehend fully only in dreams, and even then not bring much of the truth of it away into the waking world. They said this Lord Valentine the Coronal lived in a castle eight thousand years old, with five rooms for every year of its existence, and that the castle sat upon a mountain so tall it

6

pierced the sky, a colossal peak thirty miles high, on whose slopes were fifty cities as big as Pidruid. Such a thing as that did not bear much thought either. The world was too big, too old, too populous for one man's mind. I will live in this city of Pidruid, Valentine thought, and I will find a way to pay for my food and lodging, and I will be happy.

"Naturally you don't have a bed reserved in an inn," Shanamir said.

"Of course not."

"It stands to reason you wouldn't. And naturally everything in town is full, this being festival time and the Coronal already here. So where will you sleep, Valentine?"

"Anywhere. Under a tree. On a mound of rags. In the public park. That looks like a park there, over to the right, that stretch of green with the tall trees."

"You remember what I told you about vagrants in Pidruid? They'll find you and lock you deep for a month, and when they let you out they'll have you sweeping dung until you can buy your way out of your fine, which at the pay of a dung-sweeper will take you the rest of your life."

"At least dung-sweeping's steady work," Valentine said.

Shanamir didn't laugh. "There's an inn the mount-sellers stay at. I'm known there, or rather my father is. We'll get you in somehow. But what would you have done without me?"

"Become a dung-sweeper, I suppose."

"You sound as though you really wouldn't mind." The boy touched his mount's ear, halting it, and looked closely at him. "Doesn't *anything* matter to you, Valentine? I don't understand you. Are you a fool, or simply the most carefree man on Majipoor?"

"I wish I knew," said Valentine.

At the foot of the hill the ridge road joined with a grand highway that came running down out of the north and curved westward toward Pidruid. The new road, wide and straight along the valley floor, was rimmed with low white markers stamped with the double crest of Pontifex and Coronal, the labyrinth and the starburst, and was paved in smooth blue-gray stuff of light resiliency, a springy, flawless roadbed that probably was of great antiquity, as were so many of the best things of this world. The mounts plodded tirelessly. Synthetic things that they were, they scarcely understood fatigue, and would clop from Pidruid to Piliplok without resting and without complaining. From time to time Shanamir glanced back, checking for strays, since the beasts were not tied; but they remained blandly in their places, one after another, blunt

7

snout of one close behind coarse ropy tail of another, along the flank of the highway.

Now the sun was faintly tinged with late-day bronze, and the city lay close before them. A stunning sight presented itself in this part of the road: on both shoulders of it had been planted noble trees, twenty times the height of a man, with slim tapering trunks of dark bluish bark and mighty crowns of glistening greenish-black leaves sharp as daggers. Out of those crowns burst astounding clusters of bloom, red tipped with yellow, that blazed like beacons as far as Valentine could see.

"What are those trees?" he asked.

"Fireshower palms," Shanamir said. "Pidruid is famous for them. They grow only near the coast and flower just one week a year. In the winter they drop sour berries, that make a strong liquor. You'll drink it tomorrow."

"The Coronal has picked a good moment to come here, then."

"Not by chance, I imagine."

On and on the twin column of brilliant trees stretched, and they followed along, until open fields yielded to the first country villas, and then suburban tracts thick with more modest homes, and then a dusty zone of small factories, and finally the ancient wall of Pidruid itself, half as high as a fireshower tree, pierced by a pointed arch set with archaic-looking battlements. "Falkynkip Gate," Shanamir announced. "The eastern entrance to Pidruid. Now we enter the capital. Eleven million souls here, Valentine, and all the races of Majipoor to be found, not just humans, no, everything here, all mixed together, Skandars and Hjorts and Liimen and all the rest. Even, so they say, a little group of Shapeshifters."

"Shapeshifters?"

"The old race. The first natives."

"We call them something else," Valentine said vaguely. "*Metamorphs*, is it?"

"The same. Yes. I've heard they're called that in the east. You have a strange accent, do you know that?"

"No stranger than yours, friend."

Shanamir laughed. "To me your accent's strange. And I have no accent at all. I speak normal speech. You shape your words with fancy sounds. '*We call them Metamorphs*,' " he said, mimicking. "That's how you sound to me. Is that Nimoyan talk?"

Valentine replied only with a shrug.

Shanamir said, "They frighten me, Shapeshifters. Metamorphs. This would be a happier planet without them. Sneak-

8

ng around, imitating others, working mischief. I wish they would keep to their own territory."

"Mostly they do, is that not so?"

"Mostly. But they say a few live in each city. Plotting who knows what kind of trouble for the rest of us." Shanamir leaned across toward Valentine, caught his arm, peered solemnly into his face. "One might meet one anywhere. Sitting on a ridge looking out toward Pidruid on a hot afternoon, for example."

"So you think I'm a Metamorph in masquerade?"

The boy cackled. "Prove that you aren't!"

Valentine groped for some way to demonstrate his authenticity, found none, and made a terrifying face instead, stretching his cheeks as though they were rubber, twisting his lips in opposite directions, rolling his eyeballs high. "My true visage," he said. "You have discovered me." And they laughed, and passed on through Falkynkip Gate into the city of Pidruid.

Within the gate everything seemed much older, the houses built in a curious angular style, humpbacked walls swelling outward and upward to tiled roofs, and the tiles themselves often chipped and broken, and interspersed with heavy clumps of low fleshy-leaved roof-weeds that had gained footholds in cracks and earthy pockets. A heavy layer of fog hovered over the city, and it was dark and cool beneath it, with lights glowing in almost every window. The main highway split, and split again, until now Shanamir was leading his animals down a much narrower street, though still a fairly straight one, with secondary streets coiling off from it in every direction. The streets were thick with folk. Such crowds made Valentine obscurely uncomfortable; he could not recall having had so many others so close about him at once, almost at his elbow, smack up against his mount, pushing, darting about, a jostling mob of porters, merchants, mariners, vendors, people from the hill country like Shanamir bringing animals or produce to the market, tourists in fine robes of glowing brocades, and little boys and girls underfoot everywhere. Festival time in Pidruid! Gaudy banners of scarlet cloth were strung across the street from the upper stories of buildings, two and three on every block, emblazoned with the starburst crest, hailing in bright green lettering Lord Valentine the Coronal, bidding him be welcome to this his westernmost metropolis.

"Is it far to your inn?" Valentine asked.

"Halfway across town. Are you hungry?"

"A little. More than a little."

Shanamir signaled to his beasts and they marched obedi- ently into a cobbled cul-de-sac between two arcades, where he left them. Then, dismounting, he pointed out a tiny grimy booth across the street. Skewered sausages hung grilling over a charcoal flame. The counterman was a Liiman, squat and hammerheaded, with pocked gray-black skin and three eyes that glowed like coals in a crater. The boy pantomimed, and the Liiman passed two skewers of sausages to them, and poured tumblers of pale amber beer. Valentine produced a coin and laid it on the counter. It was a fine thick coin, bright and gleaming, with a milled edge, and the Liiman looked at it as though Valentine had offered him a scorpion. Hastily Shanamir scooped up the piece and put down one of his own, a squarish coppery coin with a triangular hole punched in the center. The other he returned to Valentine. They retreated to the cul-de-sac with their dinner.

"What did I do wrong?" Valentine asked.

"With that coin you could buy the Liiman and all his sau- sages, and a month of beer! Where did you get it?"

"Why, from my purse."

"Are there more like that in there?"

"It could be," said Valentine. He studied the coin, which bore on one face the image of an old man, gaunt and with- ered, and on the other the visage of a young and vigorous one. The denomination was fifty royals. "Will this be too valuable to use anywhere?" he asked. "What will it buy, in truth?"

"Five of my mounts," Shanamir said. "A year's lodgings in princely style. Transportation to Alhanroel and back. Any of those. Perhaps even more. To most of us it would be many months' wages. You have no idea of the value of things?"

Valentine looked abashed. "It would seem that way."

"These sausages cost ten weights. A hundred weights make a crown, ten crowns make a royal, and this is fifty of those. Now do you follow? I'll change it for you at the market. Meanwhile keep it to yourself. This is an honest city and a safe one, more or less, but with a purse full of those you tempt fate. Why didn't you tell me you were carrying a fortune?" Shanamir gestured broadly. "Because you didn't know, I sup- pose. There's such a strange innocence about you, Valentine. You make me feel like a man, and I'm only a boy. You seem so much like a child. Do you know anything? Do you even know how old you are? Finish your beer and let's move along."

Valentine nodded. One hundred weights to a crown, he thought, ten crowns to a royal, and he wondered what he would have said had Shanamir pressed him on the matter of his age. Twenty-eight? Thirty-two? He had no idea. What if he were asked in earnest? Thirty-two, he decided. That had a good sound to it. Yes, I am thirty-two years old, and ten crowns make a royal, and the shining piece that shows the old man and the young one is worth fifty of those.

3

The road to Shanamir's inn led squarely through the heart of Pidruid, across districts that even at this late hour were crowded and hectic. Valentine asked if that was on account of the visit of the Coronal, but Shanamir said no, the city was like this all the time, for it was the major port of the western coast of Zimroel. From here went vessels to every major part of Majipoor: up and down this busy coast, but also across the Inner Sea on the enormous journey to Alhanroel, a voyage requiring the better part of a year, and there was even some commerce with the sparsely populated southern continent, Suvrael, the sun-blasted lair of the King of Dreams. When Valentine thought of the totality of Majipoor he felt oppressed by the weight of the world, the sheer mass of it, and yet he knew that was foolish, for was not Majipoor a light and airy place, a giant bubble of a planet, huge but without much substance, so that one felt forever buoyant, forever afloat? Why this leaden sense of pressure across his back, why these moments of unfounded dismay? He led himself quickly back to an easier mood. Soon he would sleep, and the morning would be a day of new marvels.

"We cross the Golden Plaza," said Shanamir, "and on the far side of it we take Water Road, that leads to the piers, and our inn is ten minutes out that way. You'll find the plaza amazing."

Indeed it was, such of it as Valentine was able to see: a vast rectangular space, wide enough to drill two armies in, bordered on all four sides by immense square-topped buildings on whose broad flat faces were inlaid dazzling designs in gold leaf, so that by the evening's torchlight the great towers blazed with reflected light and were more brilliant than the fire-shower trees. But there was no crossing the plaza tonight. A hundred paces from its eastern entrance it was roped off with thick braided cord of red plush, behind which stood troops in the uniform of the Coronal's bodyguard, smug, impassive,

11

arms folded across their green-and-gold jerkins. Shanamir leaped from his mount and trotted forward, and spoke quickly with a vendor. When he returned he said angrily, "They have it entirely blocked. May the King of Dreams send them prickly sleep tonight!"

"What's happening?"

"The Coronal has taken lodging in the mayor's palace—that's the tallest building, with the jagged golden swirls on its walls, on the far side over there—and nobody can get near it tonight. We can't even go around the plaza's inner rim, because there's such a mob piled up there, waiting for a glimpse of Lord Valentine. So it's a detour for us, an hour or more the long way around. Well, sleep isn't that important, I suppose. Look, there he is!"

Shanamir indicated a balcony high on the façade of the mayor's palace. Figures had emerged on it. At this distance they were no larger than mice, but mice of dignity and grandeur, clad in sumptuous robes; Valentine could see at least that much. There were five of them, and the central personage was surely the Coronal. Shanamir was straining and standing on tiptoe for a better view. Valentine could make out very little: a dark-haired man, possibly bearded, in a heavy white steetmoy-fur robe over a doublet in green or light blue. The Coronal stood at the front of the balcony, spreading his arms toward the crowd, who made the starburst symbol with their outstretched fingers and shouted his name again and again: "Valentine! Valentine! Lord Valentine!"

And Shanamir, at Valentine's side, cried out too: "Valentine! Lord Valentine!"

Valentine felt a fierce shudder of revulsion. "Listen to them!" he muttered. "Yelling as if he's the Divine Itself, come down for dinner in Pidruid. He's only a man, isn't he? When his bowels are full he empties them, yes?"

Shanamir blinked in shock. "He's the Coronal!"

"He means nothing to me, even as I mean less than nothing to him."

"He governs. He administers justice. He holds back chaos. You said those things yourself. Aren't such things worthy of your respect?"

"Respect, yes. But not my worship."

"To worship the king is nothing new. My father has told me of olden times. They had kings as far back as Old Earth itself, and I'll bet they were worshiped, Valentine, in scenes far more wild than what you see here tonight."

12

"And some were drowned by their own slaves, and some were poisoned by their chief ministers, and some were smothered by their wives, and some were overthrown by the people they pretended to serve, and every last one was buried and forgotten." Valentine felt himself growing surprisingly warm with anger. He spat in disgust. "And many lands on Old Earth got along without kings altogether. Why do we need them on Majipoor? These expensive Coronals, and the weird old Pontifex hiding in his Labyrinth, and the sender of bad dreams out of Suvrael— No, Shanamir, I may be too simple to understand it, but it makes no sense to me. This frenzy! These screams of delight! No one screams delight, I'll wager, when the Mayor of Pidruid rides through the streets."

"We need kings," Shanamir insisted. "This world is too big to be ruled by mayors alone. We need great and potent symbols, monarchs who are almost like gods, to hold things together. Look. Look." The boy pointed toward the balcony. "Up there, that little figure in the white robe: the Coronal of Majipoor. You feel nothing go shivering down your back when I say that?"

"Nothing."

"You get no thrill, knowing that there are twenty billion people on this world and only one is Coronal, and that tonight you behold him with your own eyes, something which you will never do again? You feel no awe?"

"None."

"You're a strange one, Valentine. I've never met anyone like you at all. How could anyone be untouched by the sight of the Coronal?"

"I am," said Valentine, shrugging, a little puzzled by it himself. "Come, let's get out of here. This mob tires me. Let's find the inn."

It was a long journey around the plaza, for all streets ran into it but few ran parallel to it, and Valentine and Shanamir had to move in ever-widening circles while trying to proceed westward, with the train of mounts clopping placidly wherever Shanamir led. But at last they emerged from a district of hotels and fine shops into one of warehouses and lofts, and approached the edge of the waterfront, and came finally to a weatherbeaten inn of warped black timbers and frayed thatching, with stables to the rear. Shanamir housed his beasts and went through a courtyard to the innkeeper's quarters, leaving Valentine alone in the shadows. He waited a long while. It seemed to him that even here he could hear the blurred and muffled cries: *"Valentine . . . Valentine . . . Lord Valen tine!"* But it meant nothing whatever to him that multitude were crying his name, for it was the name of another.

Shanamir returned in time, sprinting lightly and silentl across the yard.

"It's arranged. Give me some money."

"The fifty?"

"Smaller. Much smaller. A half-crown or so."

Valentine groped for coins, sorted through them by dim lamplight, handed several well-worn pieces to Shanamir. "Fo the lodging?" he asked.

"To bribe the doorkeeper," Shanamir replied. "Places t sleep are hard to come by tonight. Crowding in one mor means less room for everybody, and if someone counts head and complains, it's the doorkeeper must back us up. Follo me and say nothing."

They went in. The place smelled of salt air and mildew Just within, a fat grayish-faced Hjort sat like an enormou toad at a desk, arranging playing-cards in patterns. Th rough-skinned creature barely looked up. Shanamir laid th coins before him and the Hjort signaled with an almost imper ceptible flicker of its head. Onward, to a long narrow window less room, lit by three widely spaced glowfloats that yielded hazy reddish light. A row of mattresses spanned the length o the room, one close by the next on the floor, and nearly all o them were occupied. "Here," Shanamir said, nudging on with the tip of his boot. He stripped off his outer clothes an lay down, leaving room for Valentine. "Dream well," the bo said.

"Dream well," said Valentine, and kicked off his boots an shed his top-garments, and dropped down beside him. Distan shouts echoed in his ears, or perhaps in his mind. It astonishe him how weary he was. There might be dreams tonight, yes and he would watch carefully for them so that he could sif them for meaning, but first there would be deep sleep, th sleep of the utterly exhausted. And in the morning? A nev day. Anything might befall. Anything.

4

There was a dream, of course, somewhere toward the depth o the night. Valentine placed himself at a distance from it an watched it unfold, as he had been taught from childhood

14

Dreams held great significance; they were messages from the Powers that ruled the world, by which one was to guide one's life; they were ignored only at one's peril, for they were manifestations of the deepest truth. Valentine saw himself crossing a vast purple plain under a baleful purple sky and a swollen amber sun. He was alone and his face was drawn, his eyes were tense and strained. As he marched, ugly fissures opened in the ground, gaping cracks that were bright orange within, and things popped forth like children's toys popping from a box, laughing shrilly at him and swiftly retreating into the fissures as they closed.

That was all. Not a full dream, then, for it had no story, no pattern of conflicts and resolution. It was only an image, a bizarre scene, a slice from some larger canvas not yet revealed to him. He could not even tell whether it was a sending from the Lady, the blessed Lady of the Isle of Sleep, or from the malevolent King of Dreams. He lay half awake, pondering it awhile, and decided at last to give it no deeper consideration. He felt oddly adrift, cut free from his own inner self: it was as though he had not even existed the day before yesterday. And even the wisdom of dreams was concealed from him now.

He slept again, a sleep unbroken except when a light patter of rain fell briefly but noisily, and he was unaware of further dreams. Early light woke him: warm golden-green light pouring in through the far end of the long narrow hall. The door stood open. Shanamir was nowhere about. Valentine was alone, except for a couple of snorers deeper into the room.

Valentine rose, stretched, flexed his arms and legs, dressed. He washed at a basin against the wall, and stepped out into the courtyard, feeling alert, energetic, ready for whatever this day might bring. The morning air was thick with moisture, but warm and bright, and last night's fog had altogether burned off; out of a clear sky came the throbbing heat of the summer sun. In the courtyard grew three great vines, one along each wall, with gnarled woody trunks broader than a man's waist, and shovel-shaped glossy leaves of a deep bronze hue, the new growth bright red. The vine was abloom with showy yellow blossoms like little trumpets, but also it bore ripened fruit, heavy blue-white berries glistening with beads of wetness. Valentine plucked one boldly and ate it: sweet, tart as well, with the headiness of very young wine. He had another, then reached for a third and thought better of it.

Circling the courtyard, he peered into the stables and saw Shanamir's mounts munching quietly on bits of straw, but no

Shanamir. Off on business, perhaps. Onward now around a bend, and the odor of grilled fish came to him and made him tingle with sudden hunger. He pushed open a rickety door and found himself in a kitchen where a small weary-looking man was cooking breakfast for half a dozen lodgers of several races. The cook looked at Valentine without interest.

"Am I too late to eat?" Valentine asked softly.

"Take a seat. Fish and beer, thirty weights."

He found a half-crown piece and laid it on the stove. The cook pushed a few coppers back at him and threw another fillet onto his griddle. Valentine took a seat against the wall. Several of the diners got up to depart, and one, a slender, lithe young woman with close-clipped black hair, paused near him. "The beer's in that pitcher," she said. "You help yourself around here."

"Thank you," said Valentine, but she was already out the door.

He poured a mugful—it was heavy, tangy stuff, thick against his tongue. In a minute he had his fish, crisply cooked and sweet. He ate it swiftly. "Another?" he said to the cook, who eyed him sourly but complied.

As he ate, Valentine became aware that a lodger at the next table—a Hjort, thick-bodied and puffy-faced, with pebble-textured ashen skin and big bulging eyes—was peering intently at him. The strange surveillance made Valentine uncomfortable. After a time he glanced directly back at the Hjort, who blinked and looked quickly away.

Some moments later the Hjort turned to Valentine again and said, "Just got here, did you?"

"Last night."

"Staying long?"

"Through the festival, at least," Valentine said.

Definitely there was something about the Hjort that he instinctively disliked. Perhaps it was merely his looks, for Valentine found Hjorts unattractive, coarse and bloated creatures. But that was unkind, he knew. Hjorts bore no responsibility for the way they looked, and they probably found humans equally disagreeable, pale scrawny things with disgustingly smooth skins.

Or possibly it was the intrusion on his privacy that bothered him, the staring, the questions. Or maybe just the way the Hjort was decorated with fleshy daubs of orange pigment. Whatever it was, it made him feel queasy and bothered.

But he felt mild guilt for such prejudices and he had no wish to be unsociable. By way of atoning he offered a luke-

16

warm smile and said, "My name's Valentine. I'm from Ni-moya."

"Long way to come," said the Hjort, chewing noisily.

"You live near here?"

"Little way south of Pidruid. Name's Vinorkis. Dealer in haigus hides." The Hjort sliced fussily at his food. After a moment he returned his attention to Valentine, letting his great fishy eyes rest fixedly on him. "You traveling with that boy?"

"Not really. I met him on my way into Pidruid."

The Hjort nodded. "Going back to Ni-moya after the festival?"

The flow of questions was becoming an annoyance. But Valentine still hesitated to be impolite even in the face of this impoliteness. "I'm not sure yet," he said.

"Thinking of staying here, then?"

Valentine shrugged. "I really have no plans at all."

"Mmm," the Hjort said. "Fine way to live."

It was impossible to tell, from the Hjort's flat nasal inflection, whether that was meant as praise or sarcastic condemnation. But Valentine hardly cared. He had sufficiently met his social responsibilities, he decided, and fell silent. The Hjort likewise seemed to have no more to say. He finished his breakfast, pushed back his chair with a screech, and in his ungainly Hjortish way lurched toward the door, saying, "Off to the marketplace now. See you around."

Eventually Valentine wandered out into the courtyard, where now an odd game was in progress. Eight figures stood near the far wall, throwing daggers back and forth to one another. Six of them were Skandars, big rough shaggy beings with four arms and coarse gray pelts, and the other two were human. Valentine recognized those two as having been breakfasting when he entered the kitchen—the sleek slim dark-haired woman and a lean, hard-eyed man with eerie white skin and long white hair. The daggers flew with astonishing speed, glittering as they flashed in the morning sun, and there was grim concentration on everyone's face. No one dropped a blade, no one ever seemed to catch one by the sharp side, and Valentine could not even count the number of daggers passing back and forth; everyone appeared constantly to be throwing and catching, all hands full and more weapons traveling through the air. Jugglers, he thought, practicing their trade, getting ready to perform at the festival. The Skandars, four-armed and powerfully built, performed prodigies of coordination, but the man and the woman held their own in the pat-

17

terns, juggling as deftly as the others. Valentine stood at a safe distance, watching in fascination as the daggers flew.

Then one of the Skandars grunted a "Hup!" and the pattern changed: the six aliens began to direct their weapons only at one another, doubling and redoubling the intensity with which they passed, and the two humans moved a short way apart. The girl grinned at Valentine. "Hoy, come join us!"

"What?"

"Play the game with us!" Her eyes sparkled mischievously.

"A very dangerous game, I'd say."

"All the best games are dangerous. Here!" Without warning, she flipped a dagger toward him. "What's your name, fellow?"

"Valentine," he said in a sort of gasp, and desperately nipped the dagger by its haft as it went shooting past his ear.

"Nicely caught," said the white-haired man. "Try this!"

He tossed a blade too. Valentine laughed and caught it, a little less awkwardly, and stood there with one in each hand. The aliens, wholly ignoring the byplay, continued methodically to send cascades of weapons flashing back and forth.

"Return the throw," the girl called.

Valentine frowned. He tossed it too carefully, absurdly fearful of skewering her, and the dagger described a limp arc and landed at her feet.

"You can do better," she said scornfully.

"Sorry," he said.

He threw the other one with more vigor. She plucked it calmly, and took another from the white-haired man, and sent first one, then the other, toward Valentine. There was no time to think. Snap and snap and he caught them both. Sweat broke out on his forehead, but he was getting into the rhythm of it.

"Here," he called. He gave one to her and took another from the white-haired one, and sent a third through the air, and found one coming at him and then another, and he wished that these were play daggers, blunt of blade, but he knew that they were not and he stopped fretting about it. The thing to do was to make oneself into a kind of automaton, keeping the body centered and aware, looking always toward the incoming dagger and letting the outgoing one fly of its own accord. He moved steadily, catching, throwing, catching, throwing, always one blade coming toward him and one departing. Valentine realized that a true juggler would be using both hands at once, but he was no juggler and it was all he could manage to coordinate catching and throwing. Yet he

18

was doing well. He wondered how soon it would be before the inevitable blunder came and he was cut. The jugglers laughed as the tempo increased. He laughed with them, easily, and went on catching and throwing for a good two or three minutes before he felt his reflexes blurring from the strain. This was the moment to stop. He caught and deliberately dropped each of the blades in turn, until all three lay at his feet, and he bent over, chuckling, slapping his thighs, breathing hard.

The two human jugglers applauded. The Skandars had not ceased their formidable whirling of blades, but now one cried another "Hup," and the sextet of aliens reeled in their daggers and moved off without a further word, disappearing in the direction of the sleeping-quarters.

The young woman danced over to Valentine.

"I'm Carabella," she said. She was no taller than Shanamir, and could not have been more than a few years out of girlhood. There was an irrepressible vitality bubbling within her small, muscular frame. She wore a light green doublet of close weave and a triple strand of polished quanna-shells at her throat, and her eyes were as dark as her hair. Her smile was warm and inviting. "Where have you juggled before, fellow?" she asked.

"Never," said Valentine. He dabbed at his sweaty forehead. "A tricky sport. I don't know why I wasn't cut."

"*Never?*" cried the white-haired one. "Never juggled before? That was a show of natural skill and nothing else?"

"I suppose it has to be called that," Valentine said with a shrug.

"Can we believe that?" the white-haired man asked.

"I think so," Carabella said. "He was good, Sleet, but he had no form. Did you see how his hands moved after the daggers, out to here, across to here, a little nervous, a little eager, never waiting for the hafts to come to the proper place? And his throws, how hurried, how wild? No one who has been trained in the art could easily have pretended to such clumsiness, and why should he? This Valentine's eye is good, Sleet, but he tells the truth. He's never thrown."

"His eye is more than good," Sleet muttered. "He has a quickness I envy greatly. He has a gift."

"Where are you from?" Carabella asked.

"The east," said Valentine obliquely.

"I thought so. Your speech is somewhat odd. You come from Velathys? Khyntor, maybe?"

"From that direction, yes."

Valentine's lack of specificity was not lost on Carabella, nor
19

on Sleet: they exchanged quick glances. Valentine wondered if they could be father and daughter. Probably not. Sleet, Valentine saw, was not nearly as old as he had seemed at first. Of middle years, yes, but hardly old; the bleached look of his skin and of his hair exaggerated his age. He was a compact, taut man with thin lips and a short, pointed white beard. A scar, pale now but once no doubt quite vivid, ran across one cheek from ear to chin.

Carabella said, "We are from the south, I from Til-omon, Sleet from Narabal."

"Here to perform at the Coronal's festival?"

"Indeed. Newly hired by the troupe of Zalzan Kavol the Skandar, to help them fulfill the Coronal's recent decree concerning employment of humans. And you? What has brought you to Pidruid?"

"The festival," said Valentine.

"To do business?"

"Merely to see the games and parades."

Sleet laughed knowingly. "No need to be coy with us, friend. Hardly a disgrace to be selling mounts in the market. We saw you come in with the boy last night."

"No," Valentine said. "I met the young herdsman only yesterday, as I was approaching the city. The animals are his. I merely accompanied him to the inn, because I was a stranger here. I have no trade of my own."

One of the Skandars reappeared in a doorway. He was of giant size, half again as tall as Valentine, a formidable hulking creature, heavy-jawed and fierce, with narrow yellow eyes. His four arms hung well below his knees and terminated in hands like great baskets. "Come inside!" he called brusquely.

Sleet saluted and trotted off. Carabella lingered a moment, grinning at Valentine.

"You are very peculiar," she said. "You speak no lies, yet nothing you say sounds right. I think you yourself have little knowledge of your own soul. But I like you. You give off a glow, do you know that, Valentine? A glow of innocence, of simplicity, of warmth, or—of something else. I don't know." Almost shyly she touched two fingers to the side of his arm. "I do like you. Perhaps we'll juggle again."

And she was gone, scampering off after Sleet.

5

He was alone, and there was no sign of Shanamir, and although he found himself wishing mightily he could spend the day with the jugglers, with Carabella, there was no way he could do that. And the morning was still young. He was without plan, and that troubled him, but not excessively. There was all of Pidruid for him to explore.

Out he went, down winding streets heavy with foliage. Lush vines and trees with thick weeping limbs sprouted everywhere, thriving in the moist warm salt air. From far away came band music, a gay if somewhat strident wheezing and pumping melody, maybe a rehearsal for the grand parade. A small river of foaming water rushed along the gutter, and the wildlings of Pidruid frolicked in it, mintuns and mangy dogs and little prickly-nosed droles. Busy, busy, busy, a teeming city where everyone and everything, even the stray animals, had something important to do and were doing it in a hurry. All but Valentine, who strolled aimlessly, following no particular route. He paused now to peer into some dark shop festooned with bolts and swatches of fabric, now into some musty repository of spices, now into some choice and elegant garden of rich-hued blossoms sandwiched between two tall narrow buildings. Occasionally people glanced at him as though marveling that he could allow himself the luxury of sauntering.

In one street he stopped to watch children playing a game, a sort of pantomime, one little boy with a strip of golden cloth tied as a circlet around his forehead making menacing gestures in the center of a ring, and the others dancing around him, pretending to be terrified, singing:

> *The old King of Dreams*
> *Sits on his throne.*
> *He's never asleep,*
> *He's never alone.*
>
> *The old King of Dreams*
> *Comes in the night.*
> *If you've been bad*
> *He'll give you a fright.*
>
> *The old King of Dreams*
> *Has a heart made of stone.*

21

But when the children realized that Valentine was watching, they turned and made grotesque gestures at him, grimacing, crooking their arms, pointing. He laughed and moved on.

By mid-morning he was at the waterfront. Long elbow-angled piers thrust far out into the harbor, and every one seemed a place of mad activity. Longshoremen of four or five races were unloading cargo vessels that bore the arms of twenty ports on all three continents; they used floaters to bring the bales of goods down to dockside and convey them to the warehouses, but there was plenty of shouting and angry maneuvering as the immensely heavy bundles were jockeyed this way and that. As Valentine watched from the shadow of the wharf, he felt a rough thump between his shoulders, and whirled to find a puffy-faced choleric Hjort pointing and waving arms. "Over there," the Hjort said. "We need six more to work the Suvrael ship!"

"But I'm not—"

"Quick! Hurry!"

Very well. Valentine was not disposed to argue; he moved out onto the pier and joined a group of longshoremen who were bellowing and roaring as they guided a cargo of livestock downward. Valentine bellowed and roared with them, until the animals, squealing long-faced yearling blaves, were on their way toward the stockyard or slaughterhouse. Then he quietly slipped away and moved down the quay until he came to an idle pier.

He stood there peacefully for some minutes, staring out across the harbor toward the sea, the bronze-green white-capped sea, squinting as though if he tried hard enough he could see around the bend of the globe to Alhanroel and its Castle Mount, rising heaven-high. But of course there was no seeing Alhanroel from here, across tens of thousands of miles of ocean, across a sea so broad that certain entire planets might conveniently be fitted between the shores of one continent and the other. Valentine looked down, between his feet, and let his imagination plummet into Majipoor's depths, wondering what lay straight through the planet from here. The western half of Alhanroel, he suspected. Geography was vague and puzzling to him. He seemed to have forgotten so much of his schoolboy knowledge, and had to struggle to remember anything. Possibly right now he was diametrically across the world from the lair of the Pontifex, the terrifying

Labyrinth of the old and reclusive high monarch. Or perhaps, more likely, the Isle of Sleep lay downward from here, the blessed Isle where the sweet Lady dwelled, in leafy glades where her priests and priestesses endlessly chanted, sending benevolent messages to the sleepers of the world. Valentine found it hard to believe that such places existed, that there were such personages in the world, such Powers, a Pontifex, a Lady of the Isle, a King of Dreams, even a Coronal, though he had beheld the Coronal with his own eyes only last night. Those potentates seemed unreal. What seemed real was the dockside at Pidruid, the inn where he had slept, the grilled fish, the jugglers, the boy Shanamir and his animals. All else was mere fantasy and mirage.

The day was warm now and growing quite humid, although a pleasant breeze blew toward shore. Valentine was hungry again. At a stand at the edge of the quay he bought, for a couple of coppers, a meal of strips of raw blue-fleshed fish marinated in a hot spicy sauce and served on slivers of wood. He washed it back with a beaker of fireshower wine, startling golden stuff that tasted hotter even than the sauce. Then he thought of returning to the inn. But he realized that he knew neither the name of the inn nor the name of its street, only that it lay a short distance inland from the waterfront district. Small loss if he never found it, for he had no possessions except those he carried on him; but the only people he knew in all of Pidruid were Shanamir and the jugglers, and he did not want to part from them so soon.

Valentine started back and promptly lost himself in a maze of indistinguishable alleyways and streetlets that ran back and forth across Water Road. Three times he found inns that seemed the right one, but each, when he approached it closely, proved to be some other. An hour passed, or more, and it grew to be early afternoon. Valentine understood that it would be impossible for him to find the inn, and there was a pang of sadness at that, for he thought of Carabella and the touch of her fingers to the side of his arm, and the quickness of her hands as she caught the knives, and the brightness of her dark eyes. But what is lost, he thought, is lost, and no use weeping over it. He would find himself a new inn and new friends before dark.

And then he turned a corner and discovered what must surely be Pidruid market.

It was a vast enclosed space nearly as huge as the Golden Plaza, but there were no towering palaces and hotels with golden façades here, only an endless sprawl of tile-roofed

23

sheds and open stockyards and cramped booths. Here was every fragrance and stink in the world, and half the produce of the universe for sale. Valentine plunged in, delighted, fascinated. Sides of meat hung from great hooks in one shed. Barrels of spice, spilling their contents, occupied another. In one stockyard were giddy spinner-birds, standing taller than Skandars on their preposterous bright legs, pecking and kicking at one another while dealers in eggs and wool bargained over them. In another were tanks of shining serpents, coiling and twisting like streaks of angry flame; nearby was a place where small sea-dragons, gutted and pithed, lay stacked for sale in foul-smelling heaps. Here was a place of public scribes, doing letters for the unlettered, and here a moneychanger deftly haggling for currencies of a dozen worlds, and here a row of sausage-stands, fifty of them and identical, with identical-looking Liimen side by side tending their smoky fires and twirling their laden skewers.

And fortunetellers, and sorcerers, and jugglers, though not the jugglers Valentine knew, and in a clear space squatted a storyteller, relating for coppers some involuted and all but incomprehensible adventure of Lord Stiamot, the famed Coronal of eight thousand years ago, whose deeds now were the stuff of myth. Valentine listened for five minutes but could make no sense of the tale, which held fifteen or twenty off-duty porters in rapture. He went on, past a booth where a golden-eyed Vroon with a silver flute played slinky tunes to charm some three-headed creature in a wicker basket, past a grinning boy of about ten who challenged him to a game involving shells and beads, past an aisle of vendors who were selling banners that bore the Coronal's starburst, past a fakir who hovered suspended over a vat of some nasty-looking hot oil, past an avenue of dream-speakers and a passageway thronged with drug-dealers, past the place of the interpreters and the place of the jewel-sellers, and at last, after turning a corner where all manner of cheap garments were for sale, he arrived at the stockyard where mounts were sold.

The sturdy purple beasts were lined up flank to flank by the hundreds, maybe even the thousands, standing impassively and peering without interest at what appeared to be an auction taking place before their noses. Valentine found the auction as difficult to follow as the storyteller's tale of Lord Stiamot: buyers and sellers faced each other in two long rows, and made hacking gestures across their wrists at one another, supplementing those movements with grimaces, the banging together of fists, and the sudden outward thrust of elbows.

Nothing was said, and yet much evidently was communicated, because scribes stationed along the row constantly scribbled deeds of sale that were validated by thumb-chops in green ink, and frantic clerks affixed tags stamped with the labyrinth seal of the Pontifex to the haunches of one beast after another. Moving along the line of the auction, Valentine at last came upon Shanamir, hacking and elbowing and banging fists with consummate ferocity. In minutes it was all over; and the boy came bounding out of the line with a whoop of joy. He caught Valentine by the arm and whirled him gleefully about.

"All sold! All sold! And at a premium price!" He held out a wad of chits that a scribe had given him. "Come with me to the treasury, and then it's nothing left but play for us! How late did you sleep?"

"Late, I suppose. The inn was almost empty."

"I didn't have the heart to wake you. You were snoring like a blave. What have you been doing?"

"Exploring the waterfront, mainly. I stumbled into the marketplace while trying to get back to the inn. It was by luck I came upon you."

"Ten minutes more and you'd have missed me forever," said Shanamir. "Here. This place." He tugged at Valentine's wrist and pulled him into a long, brightly lit arcade where clerks behind wickers were changing chits into coins. "Give me the fifty," Shanamir murmured. "I can have it broken for you here."

Valentine produced the thick gleaming coin and stood aside while the boy joined a line. Minutes later Shanamir returned. "These are yours," he said, dumping into Valentine's outstretched purse a shower of money, some five-royal pieces and a jingle of crowns. "And these are mine," the boy said, grinning wickedly and holding up three big fifty-royal pieces of the kind he had just changed for Valentine. He popped them into a moneyband under his jerkin. "A profitable trip, it was. At festival time everyone's in a fever to spend his money fast. Come, now. Back to the inn, and let's celebrate with a flask of fireshower wine, eh? The treat's mine!"

The inn, it turned out, was no more than fifteen minutes from the market, on a street that suddenly looked familiar as they entered it. Valentine suspected that he had come within a block or two of it in his fruitless quest. No matter: he was here, and with Shanamir. The boy, relieved at being rid of his animals and excited over the price he had had for them, chattered on and on about what he would do in Pidruid before he

25

returned to his countryside home—the dancing, the games, the drinking, the shows.

As they sat in the tavern of the inn at work on Shanamir's wine, Sleet and Carabella appeared. "May we join you?" Sleet asked.

Valentine said to Shanamir, "These are jugglers, members of a Skandar troupe here to play in the parade. I met them this morning." He made introductions. They took seats and Shanamir offered them drinks.

"Have you been to market?" said Sleet.

"Been and done," Shanamir said. "A good price."

"And now?" Carabella asked.

"The festival for a few days," said the boy. "And home to Falkynkip, I suppose." He looked a little crestfallen at the thought.

"And you?" Carabella said, glancing at Valentine. "Do you have plans?"

"To see the festival."

"And then?"

"Whatever seems right."

They were finished with the wine. Sleet gestured sharply and a second flask appeared. It was poured around generously. Valentine felt his tongue tingling with the heat of the liquor, and his head becoming a little light.

Carabella said, "Would you think to be a juggler, and join our troupe, then?"

It startled Valentine. "I have no skill!"

"You have skill aplenty," said Sleet. "What you lack is training. That we could supply, Carabella and I. You would learn the trade quickly. I take an oath on it."

And I would travel with you, and live the life of a wandering player, and go from town to town, is that it?"

"Exactly."

Valentine looked across at Shanamir. The boy's eyes were shining at the prospect. Valentine could amost feel the pressure of his excitement, his envy.

"But what is all this about?" Valentine demanded. "Why invite a stranger, a novice, an ignoramus like me, to become one of your number?"

Carabella signaled to Sleet, who quickly left the table. She said, "Zalzan Kavol will explain. It is a necessity, not a caprice. We are shorthanded, Valentine, and we have need of you." She added, "Besides, have you anything other to do? You seem adrift in this city. We offer you companionship as well as a livelihood."

26

A moment and Sleet returned with the giant Skandar. Zalzan Kavol was an awesome figure, massive, towering. He lowered himself with difficulty into a seat at their table: it creaked alarmingly beneath his bulk. Skandars came from some windswept, icy world far away, and though they had been settled on Majipoor for thousands of years, working in rough trades needing great strength or unusual quickness of eye, they had a way of eternally looking angry and uncomfortable in Majipoor's warm climate. Perhaps it was only a matter of their natural facial features, Valentine thought, but he found Zalzan Kavol and others of his kind an offputtingly bleak tribe.

The Skandar poured himself a stiff drink with his two inner arms and spread the outer pair wide across the table as though he were taking possession of it. In a harsh rumbling voice he said, "I watched you do the knives with Sleet and Carabella this morning. You can serve the purpose."

"Which is?"

"I need a third human juggler, and in a hurry. You know what the new Coronal has lately decreed concerning public entertainers?"

Valentine smiled and shrugged.

Zalzan Kavol said, "It is foolishness and stupidity, but the Coronal is young and I suppose must let fly some wild shafts. It has been decreed that in all troupes of performers made up of more than three individuals, one third of the troupe must be Majipoori citizens of human birth, this to be effective as of this month."

"A decree like that," said Carabella, "can accomplish nothing but to set race against race, on a world where many races have lived in peace for thousands of years."

Zalzan Kavol scowled. "Nevertheless the decree exists. Some jackal in the Castle must have told this Lord Valentine that the other races are growing too numerous, that the humans of Majipoor are going hungry when we work. Foolishness, and dangerous. Ordinarily no one would pay attention to such a decree, but this is the festival of the Coronal, and if we are to be licensed to perform we must obey the rules, however idiotic. My brothers and I have earned our keep as jugglers for years, and done no harm to any human by it, but now we must comply. So I have found Sleet and Carabella in Pidruid, and we are working them into our routines. Today is Twoday. Four days hence we perform in the Coronal's parade, and I must have a third human. Will you apprentice yourself to us, Valentine?"

27

"How could I learn juggling in four days?"

"You will be merely an apprentice," said the Skandar. "We will find something of a juggling nature for you to do in the grand parade that will disgrace neither yourself nor us. The law does not, as I see it, require all members of the troupe to have equal responsibilities or skills. But three of us must be human."

"And after the festival?"

"Come with us from town to town."

"You know nothing about me, and you invite me to share your lives?"

"I know nothing about you and I *want* to know nothing about you. I need a juggler of your race. I'll pay your room and board wherever we go, and ten crowns a week besides. Yes?"

Carabella's eyes had an odd glint, as though she were telling him, *You can ask twice that wage and get it, Valentine.* But the money was unimportant. He would have enough to eat and a place to sleep, and he would be with Carabella and Sleet, who were two of the three human beings he knew in this city, and, he realized with some confusion, in all the world. For there was a vacancy in him where a past should be; he had hazy notions of parents, and cousins and sisters, and a childhood somewhere in eastern Zimroel, and schooling and travels, but none of it seemed real to him, nothing had density and texture and substance. And there was a vacancy in him where a future should be, too. These jugglers promised to fill it. But yet—

"One condition," Valentine said.

Zalzan Kavol looked displeased. "Which is?"

Valentine nodded toward Shanamir. "I think this boy is tired of raising mounts in Falkynkip, and may want to travel more widely. I ask that you offer him a place in your troupe as well—"

"Valentine!" the boy cried.

"—as groom, or valet, or even a juggler if he has the art," Valentine went on, "and that if he is willing to go with us, you accept him along with me. Will you do that?"

Zalzan Kavol was silent a moment, as if in calculation, and there was a barely audible growling sound from somewhere deep within his shaggy form. At length he said, "Have you any interest in joining us, boy?"

"Have I? *Have* I?"

"I feared as much," said the Skandar morosely. "Then it is

28

done. We hire the both of you at thirteen crowns the week with room and board. Done?"

"Done," said Valentine.

"Done!" cried Shanamir.

Zalzan Kavol knocked back the last of the fireshower wine. "Sleet, Carabella, take this stranger to the courtyard and begin making a juggler out of him. You come with me, boy. I want you to have a look at our mounts."

6

They went outside. Carabella darted off to the sleeping-quarters to fetch equipment. Watching her run, Valentine took pleasure in her graceful movements, imagining the play of supple muscles beneath her garments. Sleet plucked blue-white berries from one of the courtyard vines and popped them into his mouth.

"What are they?" Valentine asked.

Sleet tossed him one. "Thokkas. In Narabal, where I was born, a thokka vine will sprout in the morning and be as high as a house by afternoon. Of course the soil bursts with life in Narabal, and the rain falls every dawn. Another?"

"Please."

With a deft quick wrist-flip Sleet chucked a berry over. It was the smallest of gestures, but effective. Sleet was an economical man, bird-light, without an ounce of excess flesh, his gestures precise, his voice dry and controlled. "Chew the seeds," he advised Valentine. "They promote virility." He managed a thin laugh.

Carabella returned, bearing a great many colored rubber balls that she juggled briskly as she crossed the yard. When she reached Valentine and Sleet she flipped one of the balls to Valentine and three to Sleet, without breaking stride. Three she retained.

"Not knives?" Valentine asked.

"Knives are showy things. Today we deal in fundamentals," Sleet said. "We deal in the philosophy of the art. Knives would be a distraction."

"Philosophy?"

"Do you think juggling's a mere trick?" the little man asked, sounding wounded. "An amusement for the gapers? A means of picking up a crown or two at a provincial carnival?

29

It is all those things, yes, but first it is a way of life, a friend, a creed, a species of worship."

"And a kind of poetry," said Carabella.

Sleet nodded. "Yes, that too. And a mathematics. It teaches calmness, control, balance, a sense of the placement of things and the underlying structure of motion. There is silent music to it. Above all there is discipline. Do I sound pretentious?"

"He means to sound pretentious," Carabella said. There was mischief in her eyes. "But everything he says is true. Are you ready to begin?"

Valentine nodded.

Sleet said, "Make yourself calm. Cleanse your mind of all needless thought and calculation. Travel to the center of your being and hold yourself there."

Valentine planted his feet flat on the ground, took three deep breaths, relaxed his shoulders so that he could not feel his dangling arms, and waited.

"I think," said Carabella, "that this man lives most of the time at the center of his being. Or else that he is without a center and so can never be far from it."

"Are you ready?" Sleet asked.

"Ready."

"We will teach you basics, one small thing at a time. Juggling is a series of small discrete motions done in quick sequence, that give the appearance of constant flow and simultaneity. Simultaneity is an illusion, friend, when you are juggling and even when you are not. All events happen one at a time." Sleet smiled coldly. He seemed to be speaking from ten thousand miles away. "Close your eyes, Valentine. Orientation in space and time is essential. Think of where you are and where you stand in relation to the world."

Valentine pictured Majipoor, mighty ball hanging in space, half of it or more than half engulfed by the Great Sea. He saw himself standing rooted at Zimroel's edge with the sea behind him and a continent unrolling before him, and the Inner Sea punctuated by the Isle of Sleep, and Alhanroel beyond, rising on its nether side to the great swollen bulge of Castle Mount, and the sun overhead, yellow with a bronze-green tint, sending blistering rays down on dusty Suvrael and into the tropics, and warming everything else, and the moons somewhere on the far side of things, and the stars farther out, and the other worlds, the worlds from which the Skandars came and the Hjorts and the Liimen and all the rest, even the world from which his own folk had emigrated, Old Earth, fourteen thousand years ago, a small blue world absurdly tiny when compared to Majipoor, far away, half forgotten in some other corner of the universe, and he journeyed back down across the stars to this world, this continent, this city, this inn, this courtyard, this small plot of moist yielding soil in which his boots were rooted, and told Sleet he was ready.

Sleet and Carabella stood with arms hanging straight, elbows at their sides, and brought their forearms up to a level position, cupped hands outstretched, one ball in the right hand. Valentine imitated them. Sleet said, "Pretend that a tray of precious gems rests on your hands. If you move your shoulders or elbows, or raise or lower your hands, the gems will spill. Eh? The secret of juggling is to move your body as little as possible. Things move; you control them; you remain still." The ball that Sleet held traveled suddenly from his right hand to the left, though there had not been a flicker of motion in his body. Carabella's ball did the same. Valentine, imitating, threw the ball from hand to hand, conscious of effort and movement.

Carabella said, "You use too much wrist and much too much elbow. Let the cup of your hand open suddenly. Let the fingers stretch apart. You are releasing a trapped bird—so! The hand opens, the bird flies upward."

"No wrist at all?" Valentine asked.

"Little, and conceal what you use. The thrust comes from the palm of your hand. So."

Valentine tried it. The shortest of upward movements of the forearm, the quickest of snaps with the wrist; propulsion from the center of his hand and from the center of his being. The ball flew to his cupped left hand.

"Yes," said Sleet. "Again."

Again. Again. Again. For fifteen minutes the three of them popped balls from one hand to the other. They made him send the ball up in a neat unvarying arc in front of his face, holding it in a plane with his hands, and they would not permit him to reach upward or outward for a catch; hands waited, ball traveled. After a time he was doing it automatically. Shanamir emerged from the stables and stared, bemused, at the single-minded tossing; then he wandered away. Valentine did not halt. This hardly seemed juggling, this rigid one-ball toss, but it was the event of the moment and he gave himself up to it entirely.

He realized eventually that Sleet and Carabella had stopped throwing, that he alone was proceeding, like a machine. "Here," said Sleet, and flipped him a thokka-berry fresh from the vine. Valentine caught it between ball-tosses and held it as

31

if thinking he might be asked to juggle with it, but no, Sleet pantomimed that he was to eat it. His reward, his incentive.

Carabella now put a second ball in his left hand and a third next to the original one in his right. "Your hands are big," she said. "This will be easy for you. Watch me, then do as I do."

She popped a ball back and forth between her hands, catching it by making a four-pointed basket out of three fingers and the ball she held in the center of each hand. Valentine imitated her. Catching the ball was harder with a full hand than with an empty one, but not greatly so, and soon he was flawless.

"Now," said Sleet, "comes the beginning of art. We make an exchange—so."

One ball traveled in a face-high arc from Sleet's right hand to his left. As it journeyed, he made room for it in his left by popping the ball he held there upward and across, under the incoming ball, into his right. The maneuver seemed simple enough, a quick reciprocal toss, but when Valentine tried it the balls collided and went bounding away. Carabella, smiling, retrieved them. He tried again with the same result, and she showed him how to throw the first ball so it would come down on the far side of his left hand, while the other traveled inside its trajectory when he launched it rightward. He needed several tries to master it, and even after he did he sometimes failed to make the catch, his eyes going in too many directions at once. Meanwhile Sleet, machinelike, completed exchange after exchange. Carabella drilled Valentine in the double throw for what seemed like hours, and perhaps was. He grew bored, at first, once he was perfect at it, and then he passed through boredom into a state of utter harmony, knowing that he could throw the balls like this for a month without wearying or dropping one.

And suddenly he perceived that Sleet was juggling all three at once.

"Go on," Carabella urged. "It only *looks* impossible."

He made the shift with an ease that surprised him, and evidently surprised Sleet and Carabella too, because she clapped her hands and he, without breaking rhythm, released a grunt of approval. Intuitively Valentine threw the third ball as the second was moving from his left hand to the right; he made the catch and returned the toss, and then he was going, a throw, a throw, a throw and a catch, a throw and a catch, a catch, a throw, always a ball on a rising arc and one descending into the waiting hand and one waiting to be thrown, and he kept it up for three, four, five interchanges before he realized the difficulty of what he was doing and broke his timing, sending all three balls spraying across the courtyard as they collided.

"You have a gift," Sleet murmured. "A definite gift."

Valentine was embarrassed by the collision, but the fact that he had dropped the balls did not appear to matter nearly as much as that he had been able to juggle them at all on the first try. He rounded them up and began again, Sleet facing him and continuing the sequence of tosses that he had never interrupted. Mimicking Sleet's stance and timing, Valentine began to throw, dropped two balls on the first try, reddened and muttered apologies, started again, and this time did not stop. Five, six, seven interchanges, ten, and then he lost count, for they no longer seemed like interchanges but all part of one seamless process, infinite and never-ending. Somehow his consciousness was split, one part making precise and accurate catches and tosses, the other monitoring the floating and descending balls, making rapid calculation of speed, angle, and rate of descent. The scanning part of his mind relayed data instantly and constantly to the part of his mind that governed the throwing and catching. Time seemed divided into an infinity of brief strokes, and yet, paradoxically, he had no sense of sequence: the three balls seemed fixed in their places, one perpetually in mid-air, one in each of his hands, and the fact that at each moment a different ball held one of those positions was inconsequential. Each was all. Time was timeless. He did not move, he did not throw, he did not catch: he only observed the flow, and the flow was frozen outside time and space. Now Valentine saw the mystery of the art. He had entered into infinity. By splitting his consciousness he had unified it. He had traveled to the inner nature of movement, and had learned that movement was illusion and sequence an error of perception. His hands functioned in the present, his eyes scanned the future, and nevertheless there was only this moment of now.

And as his soul journeyed toward the heights of exaltation, Valentine perceived, with the barest flicker of his otherwise transcendent consciousness, that he was no longer standing rooted to the place, but somehow had begun to move forward, drawn magically by the orbiting balls, which were drifting subtly away from him. They were receding across the courtyard with each series of throws—and he experienced them now as a series once again, rather than as an infinite seamless continuum—and he was having to move faster and faster to keep pace with them, until he was virtually running, stagger-

33

ing, lurching around the yard, Sleet and Carabella scrambling to avoid him, and finally the balls were out of his reach altogether, beyond even his last desperate lunge. They bounced off in three directions.

Valentine dropped to his knees, gasping. He heard the laughter of his instructors and began to laugh with them.

"What happened?" he asked finally. "I was going so well—and then—and then—"

"Small errors accumulate," Carabella told him. "You get carried away by the wonder of it all, and you throw a ball slightly out of the true plane and you reach forward to catch it, and the reaching causes you to make the next throw out of plane as well, and the next, and so on until everything drifts away from you, and you give chase, and in the end pursuit is impossible. It happens to everyone at the beginning. Think nothing of it."

"Pick up the balls," said Sleet. "In four days you juggle before the Coronal."

7

He drilled for hours, going no further than the three-ball cascade but repeating it until he had penetrated the infinite a dozen times, moving from boredom to ecstasy to boredom so often that boredom itself became ecstasy. His clothing was soaked with sweat, clinging to him like warm wet towels. Even when one of Pidruid's brief light rainshowers began he continued to throw the balls. The rain ended and gave way to a weird twilight glow, the early evening sun masked by light fog. Still Valentine juggled. A crazy intensity overcame him. He was dimly aware of figures moving about the courtyard, Sleet, Carabella, the various Skandars, Shanamir, strangers, coming and going, but he paid no attention. He had been an empty vessel into which this art, this mystery, had been poured, and he dared not stop, for fear he would lose it and be drained and hollow once again.

Then someone came close and he was suddenly empty-handed, and he understood that Sleet had intercepted the balls, one by one, as they arced past his nose. For a moment Valentine's hands went on moving anyway in persistent rhythms. His eyes would not focus on anything but the plane through which he had been throwing the balls.

"Drink this," Carabella said gently, and put a glass to his

34

lips. Fireshower wine: he drank it like water. She gave him another. "You have a miraculous gift," she told him. "Not only coordination but concentration. You frightened us a little, Valentine, when you would not stop."

"By Starday you will be the best of us," said Sleet. "The Coronal himself will single you out for applause. Eh, Zalzan Kavol? What do you say?"

"I say he is soaking wet and needs clean clothes," the Skandar rumbled. He handed Sleet some coins. "Go to the bazaar, buy something that fits him before the booths close. Carabella, take him out back to the cleanser. We eat in half an hour."

"Come with me," Carabella said.

She led Valentine, who still was dazed, through the courtyard to the sleeping-quarters, and behind them. A crude open-air cleanser had been rigged against the side of the building. "The animal!" she said angrily. "He could have given you a word of praise. But praise isn't his way, I suppose. He was impressed, all right."

"Zalzan Kavol?"

"Impressed—yes, astonished. But how could he praise a human? You have only two arms! Well, praise isn't his way. Here. Get out of those."

Quickly she stripped, and he did the same, dropping his soggy garments to the ground. By bright moonlight he saw her nakedness and was delighted. Her body was slim and lithe, almost boyish but for the small round breasts and the sudden flaring of the hips below her narrow waist. Her muscles lay close beneath the skin and were well developed. A flower had been tattooed in green and red on the crest of one flat buttock.

She led him under the cleanser and they stood close together as the vibrations rid them of sweat and grime. Then, still naked, they returned to the sleeping-quarters, where Carabella produced a fresh pair of trousers in soft gray fabric for herself, and a clean jerkin. By then Sleet had come back from the bazaar with new clothes for Valentine: a dark-green doublet with scarlet trim, tight red trousers, and a light cloak of blue that verged on black. It was a costume far more elegant than the one he had shed. Wearing it, he felt like one raised to some high rank, and moved with conscious hauteur as he accompanied Sleet and Carabella to the kitchen.

Dinner was stew—an anonymous meat at its base, and Valentine did not dare ask—washed down with copious drafts of fireshower wine. The six Skandars sat at one end of the table, the four humans at the other, and there was little conversa-

35

tion. At meal's end Zalzan Kavol and his brothers rose without a word and strode out.

"Have we offended them?" Valentine asked.

"It is their normal politeness," said Carabella.

The Hjort who had spoken to him at breakfast, Vinorkis, now crossed the room and hovered by Valentine's shoulder, staring down in that fishy-eyed way of his: evidently it was a habit. Valentine smiled awkwardly.

Vinorkis said, "Saw you juggling in the yard this afternoon. You're pretty good."

"Thank you."

"Hobby of yours?"

"Actually, I've never done it before. But the Skandars seem to have hired me for their troupe."

The Hjort looked impressed. "Really? And will you go on tour with them?"

"So it appears."

"Whereabouts?"

"I have no idea," said Valentine. "Perhaps it hasn't even been decided yet. Wherever they want to go will be good enough for me."

"Ah, the free-floating life," Vinorkis said. "I've meant to try it myself. Perhaps your Skandars would hire me, too."

"Can you juggle?"

"I can keep accounts. I juggle figures." Vinorkis laughed vehemently and gave Valentine a hearty slap on the back. "I juggle figures! Do you like that? Well, good night to you!"

"Who was that?" Carabella asked, when the Hjort was gone.

"I met him at breakfast this morning. A local merchant, I think."

She made a face. "I don't think I like him. But it's so easy not to like Hjorts. Ugly things!" She rose gracefully and stretched. "Shall we go?"

He slept soundly again that night. To dream of juggling might have been expected, after the afternoon's events, but instead he found himself once more on the purple plain—a disturbing sign, for the Majipoori know from childhood that dreams of recurring aspect have extra significance, probably dark. The Lady rarely sends recurring dreams, but the King is given to the practice. Again the dream was a fragment. Mocking faces hovered in the sky. Whirlpools of purple sand churning alongside the path, as if creatures with busy claws and clacking palps were moving beneath. Spikes sprouted from the ground. The trees had eyes. Everything held menace, ugliness,

36

foreboding. But the dream was without characters and without events. It communicated only sinister foreboding.

The world of dreams yielded to the world of daybreak. This time he was the first to waken, when the earliest strands of light entered the hall. Next to him Shanamir slumbered blissfully. Sleet lay coiled like a serpent far down the hall, and near him was Carabella, relaxed, smiling in her dreams. The Skandars evidently slept elsewhere; the only aliens in the room were a couple of lumpish Hjorts and a trio of Vroons tangled in a weave of limbs that defied comprehension. From Carabella's trunk Valentine took three of the juggling balls, and went outside into the misty dawn to sharpen his burgeoning skills.

Sleet, emerging an hour later, found him at it and clapped his hands. "You have the passion, friend. You juggle like one possessed. But don't tire yourself so soon. We have more complicated things to teach you today."

The morning's lesson had to do with variations on the basic position. Now that Valentine had mastered the trick of throwing three balls so that one was always in the air—and he had mastered it, no question of that, attaining in one afternoon a control of technique—that Carabella said had taken her many days of practice—they had him moving about, walking, trotting, turning corners, even skipping, all the while keeping the cascade going. He juggled the three balls up a flight of stairs and down again. He juggled in a squatting position. He juggled standing on one leg like the solemn gihorna-birds of the Zimr Marsh. He juggled while kneeling. By now he was absolutely secure in the harmony of eye and hand, and what the rest of his body might be doing had no effect on that.

In the afternoon Sleet moved him to new intricacies: throwing the ball from behind his back in mid-volley, throwing it up under one leg, juggling with crossed wrists. Carabella taught him how to bounce a ball against a wall and work the return smoothly into the flow, and how to send a ball from one hand to the other by letting it hit the back of his hand, instead of catching and throwing. These things he grasped swiftly. Carabella and Sleet had stopped complimenting him on the quickness of his mastery—it was patronizing to shower him constantly with praise—but he did not fail to observe the little glances of astonishment that often passed between them, and that pleased him.

The Skandars juggled in another part of the courtyard, rehearsing the act they would do in the parade, a miraculous thing involving knives and sickles and blazing torches. Occasionally Valentine glanced over, marveling at what the four-armed ones were achieving. But mainly he concentrated on his own training.

So went Seaday. On Fourday they began teaching him how to juggle with clubs instead of balls. This was a challenge, for although the principles were mainly the same, clubs were bigger and clumsier, and it was necessary for Valentine to throw them higher in order to have time to make the catches. He began with one club, tossing it from hand to hand. This is how you hold it, said Carabella, this is how you throw, this is how you catch, and he did as she said, bending a thumb now and then but soon learning the skills. "Now," she said, "put two balls in your left hand and the club in your right," and he threw, confused for a moment by the differences in mass and spin, but not for long, and after that it was two clubs in his right hand and a ball in his left, and late Fourday afternoon he worked with three clubs, wrists aching and eyes tight with strain, working all the same, unwilling and almost unable to stop.

That evening he asked, "When will I learn how to throw the clubs with another juggler?"

Carabella smiled. "Later. After the parade, as we travel eastward through the villages."

"I could do it now," he said.

"Not in time for the parade. You've performed wonders, but there are limits to what you can master in three days. If we had to juggle with a novice, we'd be forced to come down to your level, and the Coronal won't take much joy in that."

He admitted the justice of what she said. Still, he longed for the time when he would take part in the interplay of the jugglers, and pass clubs or knives or torches with them as a member of a single many-souled entity in perfect coordination.

There was rain Fourday night, unusually heavy rain for subtropical Pidruid in summer, when quick showers were the rule, and Fiveday morning the courtyard was spongy-wet and tricky of footing. But the sky was clear and the sun was bright and hot.

Shanamir, who had been roaming the town during the days of Valentine's training, reported that preparations for the great parade were well advanced. "Ribbons and streamers and flags everywhere," he said, standing at a wary distance as Valentine began a morning warmup with the three clubs. "And the starburst banner—they've lined the route with it, from Falkynkip Gate to Dragon Gate, and out Dragon and all along the waterfront, is what I hear, miles and miles of decoration, even cloth of gold, and green paint in the roadway. They say the cost runs to thousands of royals."

"Who pays?" Valentine asked.

"Why, the people of Pidruid," said Shanamir in surprise. "Who else? Those of Ni-moya? Those of Velathys?"

"Let the Coronal himself pay for his festival, I'd say."

"And whose money would that be, except the taxes of the whole world! Why should cities in Alhanroel pay for festivals in Zimroel? Besides, it's an honor to host the Coronal! Pidruid pays gladly. Tell me: how do you manage to throw a club and catch one at the same time with the same hand, Valentine?"

"The throw comes first, my friend. By only a little. Watch very carefully."

"I *am* watching. I still can't figure it out."

"When we have time, after the parade's done with, I'll show you how it works."

"Where are we going after here?"

"I don't know. Eastward, Carabella told me. We'll go wherever there's a fair or a carnival or a festival that will hire jugglers."

"Will I become a juggler too, Valentine?"

"If you want to. I thought you wanted to go to sea."

"I just want to travel," said Shanamir. "It doesn't have to be by sea. So long as I don't have to go back to Falkynkip. Eighteen hours a day in the stables, currying mounts—oh, no, not for me, not any more! Do you know, the night I left home I dreamed I had learned how to fly. It was a dream from the Lady, Valentine, I knew it at once, and the flying meant I would go where I hoped to go. When you told Zalzan Kavol he had to take me along if he wanted you, I trembled. I thought I was going to—going to—I felt all—" He caught himself. "Valentine, I want to be a juggler as good as you are."

"I'm not very good. I'm only a beginner." But, growing bold, Valentine threw the clubs in lower, faster arcs, showing off.

"I can't believe you just learned how on Twoday."

"Sleet and Carabella are good instructors."

"I never saw anyone learn anything so fast, though," Shanamir said. "You must have an extraordinary mind. I'll bet you were someone important before you became a wanderer, yes. You seem so cheerful, so—simple, and yet—and yet—"

"Hidden depths," Valentine said amiably, trying to throw a club from behind his back and hurling it with an agonizing crack against his left elbow. All three clubs splattered to the wet ground, and he winced and rubbed the bruise. "A master juggler," he said. "You see? Ordinarily it takes weeks of training to learn to hit your elbow like that!"

"You did it to change the subject," Shanamir said, sounding more than half serious.

8

Starday morning, parade day, the Coronal's day, the first day of the grand festival of Pidruid, and Valentine lay curled in sleep, dreaming a quiet dream of lush green hills and limpid pools flecked with blue and yellow pond-anemones, when fingers poking in his ribs awakened him. He sat up, blinking and mumbling. Darkness: long before dawn. Carabella crouching over him: he sensed the catlike grace of her, heard her light laughter, picked up the creamy fragrance of her skin.

"Why so early?" he asked.

"To get a good place when the Coronal goes by. Hurry! Everyone's up already."

He scrambled to his feet. His wrists were a little sore from juggling with the clubs, and he held out his arms, letting his hands loll and flop. Carabella grinned and took them in hers and looked up at him,

"You'll juggle magnificently today," she said softly.

"I hope so."

"There's no doubt of it, Valentine. Whatever you set out to do, you'll do supremely well. That's the sort of person you are."

"You know what sort of person I am?"

"Of course I do. Better than you know, I suspect. Valentine, can you tell the difference between sleeping and waking?"

He frowned. "I don't follow you."

"There are times when I think it's all the same to you, that you're living a dream or dreaming a life. Actually I didn't think that. Sleet did. You fascinate him, and Sleet doesn't fascinate easily. He's been everywhere, he's seen much, he's seen through everything, and yet he talks constantly of you, he tries to comprehend you, to see into your mind."

"I didn't realize I was so interesting. I find myself boring."

"Others don't." Her eyes were sparkling. "Come, now. Dress, eat, off to the parade. In the morning we watch the

40

Coronal go by, in the afternoon we perform, and at night—at night—"

"Yes? At night?"

"At night we hold festival!" she cried, and sprang away from him and out the door.

In the morning mist the troupe of jugglers headed for the place that Zalzan Kavol had secured for them along the grand processional highway. The Coronal's route began in the Golden Plaza, where he was lodged; from there he would move eastward along a curving boulevard that led out one of the city's secondary gates, and around to the great road on which Valentine and Shanamir had entered Pidruid, the one bordered by twin columns of fireshower palms in bloom, and thence via Falkynkip Gate back into the city, and across it down Water Road through the Arch of Dreams and out Dragon Gate to the waterfront, to the edge of the bay, where a reviewing stand had been erected in Pidruid's chief stadium. So the parade was double in nature: first a progress of the Coronal past the people, and then the people past the Coronal. It was an event that would last all through the day and into the night beyond, and probably toward Sunday's dawn.

Because the jugglers were part of the royal entertainment, it was necessary for them to take up a position somewhere near the waterfront end of things; otherwise they would never be able to cross the congested city in time to reach the stadium for their own performance. Zalzan Kavol had obtained a choice location for them close by the Arch of Dreams, but it meant that they would spend the better part of the day waiting for the parade to come to them. No help for it. On foot they cut diagonally through the back streets, emerging at last at the lower end of Water Road. As Shanamir had reported, the city was lavishly decorated, cluttered with ornament, banners and bunting dangling from every building, every lightglobe. The roadbed itself had been freshly painted in the Coronal's colors, gleaming bright green bordered by golden stripes.

At this early hour the route was already lined with viewers, and no open spaces, but a space in the crowd swiftly was made when the Skandar jugglers appeared and Zalzan Kavol produced his sheaf of tickets. People on Majipoor normally tended to courtesy and graceful accommodation. Besides, there were few who cared to argue points of precedence with six surly Skandars.

And then the waiting. The morning was warm and swiftly

41

growing hot, and there was nothing for Valentine to do but stand and wait, staring at the empty highway, at the ornate black polished stonework of the Arch of Dreams, Carabella jammed up against his left side, Shanamir pushed close on the right. Time ticked infinitely slowly that morning. The wells of conversation quickly ran dry. One moment of diversion came when Valentine picked a startling phrase out of the murmur of conversation from the rows behind him:

"—can't see what all this cheering's about. I don't trust him one bit."

Valentine listened more carefully. A pair of spectators— Ghayrogs, by the slippery sound of their voices—were talking about the new Coronal, and not in any complimentary way.

"—issuing too many decrees, if you ask me. Regulating this, regulating that, getting his fingers in here and there. No need for it!"

"He wants to show that he's on the job," the other said mildly.

"No need! No need! Things went along well enough under Lord Voriax, and Lord Malibor before him, without all these fussy rules. Smacks of insecurity, if you ask me."

"Quiet! Today of all days, this is no way to talk."

"If you ask me, the boy's not sure he's really Coronal yet, so he makes sure we all take notice of him. If you ask me."

"I didn't ask you." In worried tones.

"And another thing. These imperial proctors all over the place, suddenly. What's he doing? Setting up his own world-wide police? Spying for the Coronal, are they? What for? What's he up to?"

"If he's up to anything, you'll be the first one pulled in. Will you be quiet?"

"I mean no harm," the first Ghayrog said. "Look, I carry the starburst banner like everyone else! Am I loyal, or am I loyal? But I don't like the way things are going. It's a citizen's right to worry about the state of the realm, isn't it? If matters are not to our liking, we should speak up. That's our tradition, isn't it? If we allow small abuses now, who knows what sort of things he'll be doing five years on!"

Interesting, Valentine thought. For all this frantic cheering and waving, the new Coronal was not universally loved and admired. How many of these others, he wondered, are merely pumping up their enthusiasm out of fear or self-interest?

The Ghayrogs fell silent. Valentine scanned for other conversations, but heard nothing of interest. Again time crawled. He turned his attention to the Arch, and studied it until he

42

had memorized its features, the carved images of ancient Powers of Majipoor, heroes of the murky past, generals in the early Metamorph Wars, Coronals who antedated even legendary Lord Stiamot, Pontifexes of antiquity, Ladies offering benign blessings. The Arch, said Shanamir, was the oldest surviving thing in Pidruid and the holiest, nine thousand years old, carved from blocks of black Velathyntu marble that were immune to the ravages of the weather. To pass beneath it was to ensure the protection of the Lady and a month of useful dreams.

Rumors of the Coronal's progress across Pidruid enlivened the morning. The Coronal, it was said, had left the Golden Plaza; had entered by way of Falkynkip Gate; had paused to bestow double handfuls of five-crown pieces in the sectors of the city inhabited primarily by Vroons and Hjorts; had stopped to comfort a wailing infant; had halted to pray at the shrine of his late brother Lord Voriax; had found the heat too great and was resting for some hours at midday; had done this, had done that, had done something else. The Coronal, the Coronal, the Coronal! All attention was on the Coronal this day. Valentine pondered what sort of life it must be, constantly making grand circuits of this sort, showing oneself in city after city on eternal parade, smiling, waving, throwing coins, taking part in unending gaudy spectacle, demonstrating in one's physical person the embodiment of the power of the government, accepting all this homage, this noisy public excitement, and somehow still managing to hold the reins of the government. Or were there reins to hold? The system was so ancient it probably ran of its own accord. A Pontifex, old and by tradition reclusive, hidden in a mysterious Labyrinth somewhere in central Alhanroel, making the decrees by which the world was ruled, and his heir and adopted son the Coronal reigning as executive officer and prime minister from atop Castle Mount, except when he was engaged in ceremonial progresses such as this—and was either of them needed except as a symbol of majesty? This was a peaceful, sunny, playful world, so Valentine thought, though no doubt it had a dark side hidden somewhere, or else why would a King of Dreams have arisen to challenge the authority of the blessed Lady? These rulers, this constitutional pomp, this expense and tumult—no, Valentine thought, it had no meaning, it was a survival out of some distant era when perhaps it all had had necessity. What had meaning now? To live each day, to breathe sweet air, to eat and drink, to sleep soundly. The rest was foolishness.

"The Coronal comes!" someone cried.

So the cry had arisen, ten times in the past hour, and no Coronal had come. But now, just about noon, it seemed that in fact he was drawing near.

The sound of cheering preceded him: a distant roar, like the crashing of the sea, that spread as a propagating wave along the line of march. As it grew louder, heralds on sprightly mounts appeared in the roadway, moving almost at a gallop, managing occasional trumpet-blasts through lips that must be sore and weary after all this time. And then, mounted on a floater that carried them briskly along, several hundred of the Coronal's personal bodyguard in the green-and-gold starburst uniform, a carefully selected group, both men and women, humans and others, the cream of Majipoor, standing at attention aboard their vehicle, looking, Valentine thought, very dignified and a trifle silly.

And now the Coronal's own chariot was in sight.

It, too, was floater-mounted, hovering several feet above the pavement and moving quickly forward in a ghostly way. Lavishly bedecked with glittering fabric and thick white quarterings sewn from what might well have been the fur of rare beasts, it had an appropriate look of majesty and costliness. On it rode half a dozen of the high officials of the city of Pidruid and the surrounding province, all of them clad in robes of state, mayors and dukes and such, and among them, mounted on a raised platform of some silken scarlet wood, extending his arms benevolently to the onlookers on either side of the road, was Lord Valentine the Coronal, second most luminous of the Powers of Majipoor, and—since his adoptive imperial father the Pontifex was aloof and never to be seen by ordinary mortals—perhaps the truest embodiment of authority that could be beheld in this world.

"Valentine!" the cry arose. "Valentine! Lord Valentine!"

Valentine studied his royal namesake as intently as earlier he had examined the inscriptions on the ancient black Arch of Dreams. This Coronal was an imposing figure, a man of more than middle height, powerful-looking, with strong shoulders and long sturdy arms. His skin was of a rich olive hue, his hair was black and cut to fall just below his ears, his dark beard was a short stiff fringe at his chin.

As the tumult of cheers descended on him, Lord Valentine turned graciously to one side and another, acknowledging, inclining his body slightly, offering his outstretched hands to the air. The floater drifted swiftly past the place where Valentine and the jugglers stood, and in that interval of proximity the

44

Coronal turned toward them, so that for an electric moment Valentine and Lord Valentine had their eyes locked on one another. It seemed that a contact passed between them, a spark leaped the gap. The Coronal's smile was brilliant, his bright dark eyes held a dazzling gleam, his robes of state themselves seemed to have life and power and purpose, and Valentine stood transfixed, caught by the sorcery of imperial might. For an instant he comprehended Shanamir's awe, the awe of all these people at the presence among them of their prince. Lord Valentine was only a man, true, he needed to void his bladder and fill his gut, he slept at night and rose yawning in the morning like ordinary mortals, he had dirtied his diapers when a babe and would drool and doze when he was old, and yet, and yet, he moved in sacred circles, he dwelled on Castle Mount, he was the living son of the Lady of the Isle of Sleep and had been taken as son by the Pontifex Tyeveras, as had his brother, dead Voriax, before him, he had lived most of his life close to the founts of power, he had had given into his charge the government of all this colossal world and its teeming multitudes, and, thought Valentine, such an existence changes one, it sets one apart, it gives one an aura and a strangeness. And as the chariot of the Coronal floated by, Valentine perceived that aura and was humbled by it.

Then the chariot was past the moment was gone, and there was Lord Valentine retreating in the distance, still smiling, still extending his arms, still nodding graciously, still flashing his brilliant gaze at this citizen and that, but Valentine no longer felt himself in the presence of grace and might. Instead he felt vaguely soiled and cheated, and did not know why.

"Come quickly," Zalzan Kavol grunted. "We must get ourselves to the stadium now."

That much was simple. Everyone in Pidruid except the bedridden and the imprisoned stood stationed along the line of parade. The auxiliary streets were empty. In fifteen minutes the jugglers were at the waterfront, in ten more they approached the huge bayside stadium. Here a crowd had already begun to form. Thousands jammed the wharfs just beyond the stadium to have a second glimpse of the Coronal as he arrived.

The Skandars formed themselves into a wedge and cut brutally through this mob, Valentine and Sleet and Carabella and Shanamir following in their wake. Performers were instructed to report to the staging area at the stadium's rear, a great open space fronting the water, and a kind of madness already pre-

45

vailed there, with hundreds of costumed artists jostling for position. Here were giant gladiators of Kwill who made even the Skandars look frail, and teams of acrobats clambering impatiently over each other's shoulders, and an entire nude corps de ballet, and three orchestras of strange outworldly instruments, tuning up in bizarre discord, and animal-trainers tugging strings that controlled floater-borne beasts of improbable size and ferocity, and freaks of every description—a man who weighed a thousand pounds, a woman eleven feet high and slender as a black bamboo rod, a Vroon with two heads, Liimen who were triplets and joined by a rope of ghastly blue-gray flesh from waist to waist to waist, someone whose face was like a hatchet and whose lower body was like a wheel—and so much more that Valentine was dizzied by the sights and sounds and smells of this congregation of the bewildering.

Frantic clerks wearing municipal sashes were trying to arrange these performers into an orderly procession. Some sort of order of march actually existed; Zalzan Kavol barked an identification at a clerk and received in return a number that marked his troupe's place in line. But then it was their task to find their neighbors in the line, and that was not so easy, for everyone in the staging area was in constant motion and finding numbers was like trying to attach name-tags to waves in the sea.

Eventually the jugglers found their place, well back in the crowd, jammed in between a group of acrobats and one of the orchestras. After that there was no moving about, and once more they stood in place for hours. The performers were offered refreshments as they waited: servitors moved among them bearing bits of skewered meat and goblets of green or gold wine, for which no fee was asked. But the air was warm and heavy, and the reek of so many close-packed bodies of so many races and metabolisms made Valentine feel faint. In an hour, he thought, I will be juggling before the Coronal. How odd that sounds! He was aware of Carabella close beside him, jaunty, buoyant, always smiling, unfailingly energetic. "May the Divine spare us from having to do this ever again," she whispered.

At last there was some sense of movement far away near the gate to the stadium, as if some stopcock had been pulled and eddy-currents were drawing the first performers out of the staging area. Valentine stood on tiptoe but had no clear idea of what was happening. The better part of an hour went by before any sort of motion was apparent at their end of the assemblage. Then the line began to go steadily forward.

46

From within the stadium came sounds: music, screeching beasts, laughter, applause. The orchestra that preceded Zalzan Kavol's troupe now was ready to enter—twenty players, of three non-human races, bearing fanciful instruments unknown to Valentine, swirls of shining brass pipe and strange lopsided drums and small five-bodied fifes and the like, everything oddly delicate, but the sound they made was not delicate at all when they struck up and began their march. The last of the musicians disappeared through the great double gates of the stadium and an officious major-domo strutted forward to bar the access of the jugglers.

"Zalzan Kavol and his troupe," the major-domo announced.

"We are here," said Zalzan Kavol.

"You will wait for the signal. Then you enter and follow those musicians in procession from left to right around the stadium. Do not begin to perform until you pass the large green flag that bears the Coronal's emblem. When you reach the pavilion of the Coronal, pause and make obeisance, and hold your place for sixty seconds, performing your act, before moving onward. When you reach the far gate, depart from the area at once. You will be paid your fee as you leave. Is everything clear?"

"Quite," said Zalzan Kavol.

The Skandar turned to his troupe. He had until this moment been nothing other than brusque and rough, but suddenly he displayed another side, for he reached three of his arms toward his brothers, and clasped hands with them, and something that seemed almost like a loving smile appeared on his harsh face. Then the Skandar embraced Sleet, and then Carabella, and then he drew Valentine toward him and said, as gently as a Skandar could, "You have learned quickly and you show signs of mastery. You were only a convenience for us, but I am pleased now that you are among us."

"Thank you," said Valentine solemnly.

"Jugglers!" the major-domo barked.

Zalzan Kavol said, "It's not every day that we juggle for a Power of Majipoor. Let this be our finest performance."

He gestured and the troupe moved through the mighty double gates.

Sleet and Carabella led the way, juggling five knives that they exchanged with one another in staccato patterns constantly varying: then, after a space, Valentine walked alone, juggling his three clubs with a taut intensity likely to conceal the simplicity of his routine, and, behind him, the six Skandar brothers, making utmost use of their twenty-four arms to fill the air with a preposterous miscellany of flying objects. Shanamir, as a kind of esquire, concluded the march, making no performance, merely serving as a human punctuation mark.

Carabella was exuberant, irrepressible: she did high-springs, clicking her heels, clapping her hands, and yet never missing a beat, while beside her Sleet, whiplash-quick, compact, dynamic, made himself a veritable well of energy as he snatched knives from the air and returned them to his partner. Even somber economical Sleet allowed himself a quick implausible somersault while the soft air of Majipoor under the light pull of gravity held the knives aloft for the necessary fraction of a second.

Around the stadium they marched, taking their rhythm from the strident squeaks and tootles and thumps of the orchestra before them. The vast throng, jaded already with novelty after novelty, hardly reacted, but no matter: the jugglers' allegiance was to their art, not to the sweaty faces barely visible in the distant seats.

Valentine had devised yesterday, and privately practiced, a fancy flourish for his routine. The others knew nothing of it, for there were risks in such things for a novice, and a royal performance was perhaps not the right place for a risk—although, he thought, more truthfully a royal performance was the most proper place for extending oneself to the fullest.

So he grasped two of his clubs in his right hand and hurled them high, and as he did so he heard the grunting *"Hoy!"* of surprise from Zalzan Kavol, but there was no time to think on that, for the two clubs were descending and Valentine sent the one in his left hand up between them in a soaring double flip. Deftly he caught one falling club in each hand, sent the one in his right hand aloft, caught the double-flipped one as it dropped, and went serenely and with great relief into his familiar cascade of clubs, looking neither to the right nor to the left as he trailed Carabella and Sleet around the perimeter of the gigantic stadium.

Orchestras, acrobats, dancers, animal-trainers, jugglers, before him and aft, thousands of blank faces in the seats, ribbon-bedecked arcades of grandees—Valentine saw none of it except in the most subliminal way. Throw, throw, throw and catch, throw and catch, throw and catch, on and on, until in the corner of his eye he saw the brilliant green-and-gold draperies flanking the royal pavilion. He turned to face the Coronal. This was a difficult moment, for now he had to divide his attention: keeping the clubs flying, he sought for Lord Valentine himself, and found him, halfway up the sloping pavilion. Valentine prayed for another jolt of interchanged energy, another quick flash of contact with the Coronal's searing eyes. He threw automatically, precisely, each club rising its allotted distance and arcing over to land between his thumb and fingers, and as he did so he searched the Coronal's face, but no, no jolt of energy this time, for the prince was distracted, he did not see the juggler at all, he stared in boredom across the whole width of the stadium, toward some other act, perhaps some fang-and-claw animal number, perhaps the bare-rumped ballet-dancers, perhaps at nothing at all. Valentine persevered, counting out the full sixty seconds of his homage, and toward the end of his minute it seemed to him the Coronal did indeed glance his way a fraction of an instant, but no more than that.

Then Valentine moved on. Carabella and Sleet were already approaching the exit. Valentine turned in a half circle where he stood, and grinned high-heartedly at the Skandars, who marched forward under a dancing canopy of axes and fiery torches and sickles and hammers and pieces of fruit, adding object after object to the multitude of things they whirled aloft. Valentine juggled at them a moment before continuing his solitary orbit of the stadium.

And onward, and outward through the far gate. And caught his clubs and held them as he passed into the outer world. Again, as he left the presence of the Coronal, he felt a letdown, a weariness, an emptiness, as though Lord Valentine did not truly radiate energy but merely drained it from others, giving the illusion of a bright out-flashing aura, and when one moved beyond him one experienced only a sense of loss. Besides, the performance was over; Valentine's moment of glory had come and gone, and no one apparently had noticed.

Except Zalzan Kavol, who looked dour and irritable. "Who taught you that two-club throw?" he demanded, the moment he came through the gate.

"No one," said Valentine. "I invented it myself."

"And if you had dropped your clubs out there?"

"Did I drop them?"

"That was no place for fancy tricks," the Skandar muttered. Then he softened a bit. "But I do admit you carried yourself well." From a second major-domo he received a purse of coins, and dumped them into his two outer hands, counting quickly through them. Most he pocketed, but he tossed one to each of his brothers, and one apiece to Sleet and Carabella, and then, after some thought, smaller coins to Valentine and Shanamir.

49

Valentine saw that he and Shanamir had each received half a crown, and the others a crown apiece. Not important: money was of no real account so long as a few crowns jingled in his pouch. The bonus, however small, was unexpected. He would squander it gleefully tonight on strong wine and spicy fish.

The long afternoon was nearly over. Fog rising off the sea was bringing an early darkness to Pidruid. In the stadium, the sounds of circus still resounded. The poor Coronal, Valentine thought, would be sitting there far into the night.

Carabella tugged at his wrist.

"Come now," she whispered urgently. "Our work is done! Now we make festival!"

9

She sprinted off into the crowd, and Valentine, after a moment's confusion, followed her. His three clubs, fastened by a cord to his waist, clumped awkwardly into his thighs as he ran. He thought he had lost her, but no, she was in sight now, taking high bouncy strides, turning and grinning saucily back at him, waving him on. Valentine caught up with her on the great flat steps that led down to the bay. Barges had been towed into the near harbor, with pyres of slender logs piled on them in intricate patterns, and already, though it was hardly night yet, a few of them had been torched and were burning with a cool green glow, sending up scarcely any smoke.

The entire city had been converted, during the day, into a playground. Carnival booths had sprung up like toadstools after summer rain; revelers in strange costumes swaggered along the quays; there was music on all sides, laughter, a feverish excitement. As the darkness deepened, new fires blazed, and the bay became a sea of colored light; and out of the east erupted some kind of pyrotechnic display, a skyrocket of piercing brilliance that soared to a point high overhead and burst, sending dazzling streamers downward to the tips of Pidruid's highest buildings.

A frenzy was on Carabella, and a frenzy crept into Valentine too. Hand in hand they raced recklessly through the city, from booth to booth, scattering coins like pebbles as they played. Many of the booths were games of skill, knocking down dolls with balls or upsetting some carefully balanced construct. Carabella, with her juggler's eye and juggler's hand,

50

won nearly everything she tried, and Valentine, though less skilled, took his share of prizes too. At some booths the winnings were mugs of wine or morsels of meat; at others they were silly stuffed animals or banners bearing the Coronal's emblem, and these things they abandoned. But they ate the meat, they gulped the wine, and they grew flushed and wild as the night moved on.

"Here!" Carabella cried, and they joined a dance of Vroons and Ghayrogs and drunken Hjorts, a capering circle-dance that seemed to have no rules. For long minutes they pranced with the aliens. When a leathery-faced Hjort embraced Carabella she hugged it back, clasping it so tightly that her small strong fingers sank deep into its puffy hide, and when a female Ghayrog, all snaky locks and myriad swaying breasts, pressed herself against Valentine he accepted her kiss and returned it with more enthusiasm than he would have expected himself to muster.

And then it was onward again, into a open-walled theater where angular puppets were enacting a drama in jerky stylized movements, and on into an arena where, at a cost of a few weights, they watched sea-dragons swim in menacing circles round and round in a glistening tank, and onward from there to a garden of animate plants from Alhanroel's southern shore, ropy tentacular things and tall trembling rubbery columns with surprising eyes near their summits. "Feeding time in half an hour," the keeper called, but Carabella would not stay, and with Valentine in tow she plunged off through the gathering darkness.

Fireworks exploded again, now infinitely more effective against the backdrop of night. There was a triple starburst that gave way to the image of Lord Valentine filling half the sky, and then a dazzle of green and red and blue that took the form of the Labyrinth and yielded to the gloomy visage of old Pontifex Tyeveras, and after a moment, when the colors had cleared, a new explosion threw a sheet of fire across the heavens, out of which coalesced the beloved features of the great royal mother, the Lady of the Isle of Sleep, smiling down on Pidruid with all of love. The sight of her so deeply moved Valentine that he would have fallen to his knees and wept, a mysterious and startling response. But there was no room in the crowd for any of that. He stood trembling an instant. The Lady faded into the darkness. Valentine slipped his hand against Carabella's and held it tightly.

"I need more wine," he whispered.

"Wait. There's one more to come."

51

Indeed. Another skyrocket, another burst of color, this one jagged and uncouth to the eye, yellows and reds, and out of it another face, heavy-jawed and somber-eyed, that of the fourth of the Powers of Majipoor, that darkest and most ambiguous figure of the hierarchy, the King of Dreams, Simonan Barjazid. A hush fell over the crowd, for the King of Dreams was no one's friend, though all acknowledged his power, lest he bring bad fortune and dread punishment.

Now they went for wine. Valentine's hand shook and he downed two mugs quickly, while Carabella looked at him in some concern. Her fingers played with the strong bones of his wrist, but she asked no questions. Her own wine she left barely touched.

The next door that opened before them in the festival was that of a wax museum, in the shape of a miniature Labyrinth, so that when they stumbled inside there was no turning back, and they gave the waxen keeper their three-weight pieces and went forward. Out of the darkness emerged heroes of the realm done in cunning simulation, moving, even speaking in archaic dialects. This tall warrior announced himself to be Lord Stiamot, conqueror of the Metamorphs, and this was the fabled Lady Thiin, his mother, the warrior-Lady who in person led the defense of the Isle of Sleep when it was besieged by aborigines. To them came one claiming to be Dvorn, the first Pontifex, a figure almost as remote in time from the era of Stiamot as Stiamot was from the present, and near him was Dinitak Barjazid, the first King of Dreams, a personage far less ancient. Deeper into the maze went Carabella and Valentine, encountering a host of dead Powers, a cleverly chosen assortment of Pontifexes and Ladies and Coronals, the great rulers Confalume and Prestimion and Dekkeret, and the Pontifex Arioc of curious fame, and last of all, presiding over the exit, the image of a ruddy-faced man in tight black garments, perhaps forty years of age, black-haired and dark-eyed and smiling, and he needed to offer no introductions, for this was Voriax, the late Coronal, brother to Lord Valentine, cut down in the prime of his reign two years past, dead in some absurd hunting accident after holding power only eight years. The image bowed and reached forth its hands, and exclaimed, "Weep for me, brothers and sisters, for I was supreme and perished before my time, and my fall was all the greater since I fell from so lofty a height. I was Lord Voriax, and think long on my fate."

Carabella shuddered. "A gloomy place, and a gloomy finish to it. Away from here!"

Once more she led him breathlessly through the festival grounds, through gaming-halls and arcades and brilliantly lit pavilions, past dining-tables and pleasure-houses, never halting, floating birdlike from place to place, until finally they turned a corner and were in darkness, beyond the zone of revelry altogether. From behind them came the raucous sounds of fading merriment and the dwindling glow of garish light; as they moved forward they encountered the fragrance of heavy blossoms, the silence of trees. They were in a garden, a park.

"Come," Carabella murmured, taking him by the hand.

They entered a moonlit glade where the trees had been pleached overhead to form a tightly woven bower. Valentine's arm slipped easily around her taut, narrow waist. The soft warmth of the day lay trapped under these close-tangled trees, and from the moist soil rose the creamy sweet aroma of huge fleshy flowers, bigger across than a Skandar's head. The festival and all its chaotic excitement seemed ten thousand miles away.

"This is where we'll stay," Carabella announced.

With exaggerated chivalry he spread his cloak, and she drew him to the ground and slid easily and swiftly into his arms. They lay secluded between two high dense bushes of gray-green sticklike branches. A stream ran not far from them and only the most slender gleams of brightness entered overhead.

Fastened to Carabella's hip was a tiny pocket-harp of intricate workmanship. She drew it forth now, strummed a brief melodious prelude, and began to sing in a cool, pure voice:

> *My love is fair as is the spring,*
> *As gentle as the night,*
> *My love is sweet as stolen fruit,*
> *My love is clear and bright.*

> *Not all the richness of the land,*
> *Nor all the gems of sea,*
> *Nor all the wealth of Castle Mount*
> *Is worth my love to me.*

"How lovely that is," Valentine murmured. "And your voice—your voice is so beautiful—"

"Do you sing?" she asked.

"Why—yes, I suppose so."

She handed him the harp. "Sing for me now. One of your favorites."

53

He turned the little instrument over in his hand, puzzled, and said after a moment, "I don't know any songs."

"No songs? No songs? Come, you must know a few!"

"All gone from my mind, so it seems."

Carabella smiled and took back her harp. "I'll teach you a few, then," she said. "But not now, I think."

"No. Not now."

He touched his lips to hers. She purred and chuckled, and her embrace grew tighter. As his eyes became accustomed to the darkness he could see her more clearly, small pointed face, bright sly eyes, glossy tumbling black hair. Her nostrils flared with expectation. He drew back momentarily from what was to occur, obscurely fearing that some sort of contract was about to be sealed, but then he put those fears behind him. It was festival night, and he wanted her, and she him. Valentine's hands slipped down her back, came forward, felt the cage of her ribs lying just below the skin. He remembered her as she had looked standing naked under the cleanser: muscle and bone, bone and muscle, not much meat on her except at thighs and buttocks. A compact bundle of energy. In a moment she was naked again, and so was he. He saw that she was trembling, but not from chill, not on this balmy humid night in this secret bower. A strange, almost frightening intensity seemed to grip her. He stroked her arms, her face, her muscular shoulders, the small hard-tipped spheres of her breasts. His hand found the sleek skin along the inside of her thighs, and she let out her breath sharply and pulled him to her.

Their bodies moved in easy rhythms, as though they had been lovers for months and were well practiced with one another. Her slender powerful legs clasped his waist and they rolled over and over, until they came almost to the edge of the stream and could feel its chilly spray on their sweaty skins. They paused there, laughing, and rolled back the other way. This time they came to rest against one of the gray-green bushes, Carabella pulling him downward, taking the thrust of his weight without difficulty.

"Now!" she cried, and he heard her hiss and moan, and then her fingers dug deep into his flesh and a furious spasm racked her body, and in that same instant he gave himself up fully to the forces that were sweeping through him.

Afterward he lay gasping and half dazed in her embrace, listening to the booming of his own heart.

"We'll sleep here," she whispered. "No one will trouble us on this night." She stroked his forehead, pushing his soft yellow hair back from his eyes, smoothing it into place. Lightly she kissed the tip of his nose. She was casual, playful, kittenish: that dark erotic intensity was gone from her, burned away in the fires of passion. But he felt shaken, stunned, confused. For him there had been sudden sharp ecstasy, yes. But in that moment of ecstasy he had found himself peering through gates of dazzling light into a mysterious realm without color or form or substance, and he had teetered precariously on the brink of that unknown before tumbling back into the world of this reality.

He could not speak. Nothing he might say seemed appropriate. He had not expected such disorientation to come out of the act of love. Carabella evidently sensed the disquiet in him, for she said nothing, only held him, rocked him gently, drew his head against her breast, sang softly to him.

In the warmth of the night he drifted gradually into sleep.

When the dream-images came, they were harsh and terrifying.

He was carried back yet again to that bleak, familiar purple plain. The same mocking faces leered at him from the purple sky, but this time he was not alone. Looming up against him was a figure of dark visage and heavy, oppressive physical presence whom Valentine understood to be his brother, although in the fierce crackling glow of the amber sun he could not clearly see the other man's features. And the dream enacted itself against a background of somber music, the low keening note of mind-music that denoted the peril-dream, the threat-dream, the death-dream.

The two men were locked in a bitter duel, and only one would come forth from the duel alive.

"Brother!" Valentine cried in shock and horror. "No!" He stirred and twisted and came swimming up to the surface of sleep, and hovered there for an instant. But his training lay too deep for that. One did not flee dreams, one did not reject them no matter how appalling. One entered fully into them and accepted their guidance; one came to grips with the unthinkable in dreams, and to avoid it then meant the inevitability of confronting it, and being defeated by it, in waking life.

Deliberately Valentine drove himself downward again, through the borderland between wakefulness and sleep, and felt stealing about him once more the malign presence of his enemy, his brother.

They were armed with swords, but the contest was unequal, for Valentine's weapon was a flimsy rapier, the brother's a massive saber. Through skill and agility Valentine tried des-

55

perately to slip his sword past his brother's guard. Impossible. With slow weighty strokes the other parried steadily, sweeping Valentine's frail blade aside and driving him inexorably backward over the rough gullied terrain.

Vultures circled overhead. Out of the sky came a hissing death-song. There would be blood spilling soon, and a life returning to the Source.

Step by step Valentine yielded, knowing that a ravine lay just behind him and further retreat soon would be forestalled. His arm was aching, his eyes pounded with fatigue, there was the gritty taste of sand in his mouth, his last strength ebbing. Backward—backward—

"Brother!" he cried in anguish. "In the name of the Divine—"

His plea drew harsh laughter and a sharp obscenity. The saber descended in a mighty swing. Valentine thrust out his blade and was shaken by a terrible body-numbing shiver as metal rang against metal and his light sword was snapped to a stump. In the same moment he tripped over a dry sand-scoured snag of wood and tumbled heavily to the ground, landing in a tangle of thorny creeping stems. The huge man with the saber reared above him, blotting out the sun, filling the sky. The death-song took on a murderous screeching intensity of timbre; the vultures fluttered and swooped.

The sleeping Valentine moaned and trembled. He turned again, huddled close against Carabella, took warmth from her as the dread cold of the death-dream enveloped him. It would be so easy to awaken now, to escape the horror and violence of these images, to swim to safety on the shores of consciousness. But no. With fierce discipline he thrust himself again into the nightmare. The giant figure laughed. The saber rose high. The world lurched and crumbled beneath his fallen body. He commended his soul to the Lady and waited for the blow to descend.

And the blow of the saber was awkward and lame, and with a foolish thud his brother's sword buried itself deep in the sand, and the texture and thrust of the dream were altered, for no longer did Valentine hear the wailing hiss of death-songs, and now he found everything reversed, found currents of new and unexpected energy pouring into him. He leaped to his feet. His brother tugged at the saber, cursed, struggled to pull it from the ground, and Valentine snapped it with a contemptuous kick.

He seized the other man barehanded.

Now it was Valentine who commanded the duel, and his

cowering brother who retreated before a shower of blows, sagging now to his knees as Valentine battered him, growling like a wounded bear, shaking his bloody head from side to side, taking the beating and offering no defense, murmuring only, "Brother . . . brother . . ." as Valentine pounded him to the sand.

He lay still and Valentine stood victor over him.

Let it be dawn, Valentine prayed, and released himself from sleep.

It was still dark. He blinked and clasped his arms to his sides and shivered. Violent frenzied images, fragmented but potent, swam in his troubled mind.

Carabella studied him thoughtfully.

"Are you all right?" she asked.

"I dreamed."

"You cried out three times. I thought you would wake. A strong dream?"

"Yes."

"And now?"

"I'm puzzled. Troubled."

"Tell me your dream?"

It was an intimate request. And yet were they not lovers? Had they not gone down into the world of sleep together, partners in the night's quest?

"I dreamed that I fought with my brother," he said hoarsely. "That we dueled with swords in a hot barren desert, that he came close to killing me, that at the last moment I rose from the ground and found new strength and—and—and I beat him to death with my fists."

Her eyes glittered like an animal's in the darkness: she watched him like some wary beady-eyed drole.

"Do you always have such ferocious dreams?" she asked after a time.

"I don't think so. But—"

"Yes?"

"Not only the violence. Carabella, I have no brother!"

She laughed. "Do you expect dreams to correspond exactly to reality? Valentine, Valentine, where were you taught? Dreams have a truth deeper than the reality we know. The brother of your dream could be anyone or no one: Zalzan Kavol, Sleet, your father, Lord Valentine, the Pontifex Tyeveras, Shanamir, even me. You know that unless they be specific sendings, dreams transform all things."

"I know, yes. But what does it mean, Carabella? To duel

57

with a brother—to be killed, almost, by him—to slay him instead—"

"You want me to speak your dream for you?" she said, surprised.

"It speaks nothing to me except fear and mystery."

"You were badly frightened, yes. You were soaked with sweat and you cried out again and again. But painful dreams are the most revealing ones, Valentine. Speak it for yourself."

"My brother—I have no brother—"

"I told you, it doesn't matter."

"Did I make war against myself, then? I don't understand. I have no enemies, Carabella."

"Your father," she suggested.

He considered that. His father? He searched for a face that he could give to the shadowy man with the saber, but he found only more darkness.

"I don't remember him," Valentine said.

"Did he die when you were a boy?"

"I think so." Valentine shook his head, which was beginning to throb. "I don't remember. I see a big man—his beard is dark, his eyes are dark—"

"What was his name? When did he die?"

Valentine shook his head again.

Carabella leaned close. She took his hands in hers and said softly, "Valentine, where were you born?"

"In the east."

"Yes, you've said that. Where? What city, what province?"

"Ni-moya?" he said vaguely.

"Are you asking me or telling me?"

"Ni-moya," he repeated. "A big house, a garden, near the bend of the river. Yes. I see myself there. Swimming in the river. Hunting in the duke's forest. Am I dreaming that?"

"Are you?"

"It feels like—something I've read. Like a story I've been told."

"Your mother's name?"

He began to reply, but when he opened his mouth no name came.

"She died young too?"

"Galiara," Valentine said without conviction. "That was it. Galiara."

"A lovely name. Tell me what she looked like."

"She—she had—" He faltered. "Golden hair, like mine. Sweet smooth skin. Her eyes—her voice sounded like—it's so hard, Carabella!"

58

"You're shaking."

"Yes."

"Come. Here." Once again she drew him close. She was much smaller than he, and yet she seemed very much stronger now, and he took comfort from her closeness. Gently she said, "You don't remember anything, do you, Valentine?"

"No. Not really."

"Not where you were born or where you came from or what your parents looked like or even where you were last Starday, isn't that so? Your dreams can't guide you because you have nothing to speak against them." Her hands roamed his head; her fingers probed delicately but firmly into his scalp.

"What're you doing?" he asked.

"Looking to see if you've been hurt. A blow on the head can take the memory away, you know."

"Is there anything there?"

"No. No, nothing. No marks. No bumps. But that doesn't mean anything. It could have happened a month or two ago. I'll look again when the sun has risen."

"I like the feel of your hands touching me, Carabella."

"I like touching you," she said.

He lay quietly against her. The words that had passed between them just now troubled him intensely. Other people, he realized, had rich memories of their childhood and adolescence, and knew the names of their parents and were sure of the place where they had been born, and he had nothing but his overlay of hazy notions, this mist of thin untrustworthy memories covering a well of blankness, yes, and he had known that the blankness was there but had chosen not to peer into it. Now Carabella had forced that upon him. Why, he wondered, was he unlike others? Why were his memories without substance? Had he taken some blow on the head, as she suggested? Or was it just that his mind was dim, that he lacked the capacity to retain the imprints of experience, that he had wandered for years across the face of Majipoor, erasing each yesterday as each new day dawned?

Neither of them slept again that night. Toward morning, quite suddenly, they began to make love again, in silence, in a kind of driven purposeful way quite different from the earlier playful union; and then they rose, still saying nothing, and bathed in the chilly little brook, and dressed and made their way through town to the inn. There were still some bleary-eyed revelers staggering in the streets as the bright eye of the sun rose high over Pidruid.

10

At Carabella's prompting Valentine took Sleet into his confidence, and told him of his dream and of the conversation that followed it. The little white-haired juggler listened thoughtfully, never interrupting, looking increasingly solemn.

He said when Valentine had done, "You should seek guidance from a dream-speaker. This is too strong a sending to be ignored."

"Do you think it is a sending, then?"

"Possibly it is," said Sleet.

"From the King?"

Sleet spread his hands and contemplated his fingertips. "It could be. You will have to wait and pay close heed. The King never sends simple messages."

"It could be from the Lady just as well," Carabella offered. "The violence of it shouldn't deceive us. The Lady sends violent dreams when the need exists."

"And some dreams," said Sleet with a smile, "come neither from the Lady nor from the King, but up out of the depths of our own foggy minds. Who can tell unaided? Valentine, see a dream-speaker."

"Would a dream-speaker help me find my memories, then?"

"A dream-speaker or a sorcerer, yes. If dreams are no guidance to your past, nothing will be."

"Besides," said Carabella, "a dream so strong should not go unexamined. There is your responsibility to be considered. If a dream commands an action, and you choose not to pursue that action—" She shrugged. "Your soul will answer for it, and swiftly. Find a speaker, Valentine."

"I had hoped," Valentine said to Sleet, "that you would have some wisdom in these things."

"I am a juggler. Find a speaker."

"Can you recommend one in Pidruid?"

"We will be leaving Pidruid shortly. Wait until we are a few days' journey from the city. You will have richer dreams to give the speaker by then."

"I wonder if this is a sending," said Valentine. "And from the King? What business would the King of Dreams have with a wanderer like me? I hardly think it possible. With twenty billion souls on Majipoor, how could the King find time to deal with any but the most important?"

"In Suvrael," said Sleet, "at the palace of the King of Dreams, are great machines that scan this entire world, and send messages into the minds of millions of people every night. Who knows how those millions are chosen? One thing they tell us when we are children, and I know it has truth: at least once before we leave this world, we will feel the touch of the King of Dreams against our spirit, each and all of us. I know that I have."

"You?"

"More than once." Sleet touched his lank, coarse white hair. "Do you think I was born white-haired? One night I lay in a hammock in the jungles outside Narabal, no juggler then, and the King came to me as I slept and placed commands upon my soul, and when I awakened my hair was like this. I was twenty-three years old."

"Commands?" Valentine blurted. "What commands?"

"Commands that turn a man's hair from black to white between darkness and dawn," Sleet said. Obviously he wished to say no more. He got to his feet and glanced at the morning sky as though checking the elevation of the sun. "I think we've had enough talk for now, friend. There still are crowns to earn at the festival. Would you learn a few new tricks before Zalzan Kavol sends us out to work?"

Valentine nodded. Sleet fetched balls and clubs; they went out into the courtyard.

"Watch," said Sleet, and he stood close behind Carabella. She held two balls in her right hand, he one in his left, and they put their other arms around one another. "This is half-juggling," Sleet said. "A simple thing even for beginners, but it looks extremely challenging." Carabella threw; Sleet threw and caught; at once they were in the rhythm of interchange, easily passing the balls back and forth, one entity with four legs and two minds and two juggling arms. Indeed it did look taxing, Valentine thought. Sleet called out, "Feed the clubs to us now!"

As Valentine delivered each club with a quick sharp toss to Carabella's right hand, she worked it into the sequence, one, two, three, until balls and clubs flew from her to Sleet, from Sleet to her, in a dizzying cascade. Valentine knew from his own private trials how difficult it was to deal with that many objects. Five balls would be in his compass in another few weeks, he hoped; four clubs might be feasible soon too; but to handle three of each at the same time, and coordinate this

61

half-juggling as well, was a feat that amazed him with admiration. And some jealousy too, he realized oddly, for here was Sleet with his body tight up against Carabella's, forming a single organism with her, and only a few hours ago she had lain with him by the side of that brook in the Pidruid park.

"Try it," Sleet said.

He stepped aside and Carabella put herself in front of Valentine, arm and arm. They worked with three balls only. At first Valentine had problems judging the height and force of his throws, and sometimes sent the ball popping beyond Carabella's reach, but in ten minutes he had the knack of it and in fifteen they were working together as smoothly as if they had been doing the act for years. Sleet encouraged him with lively applause.

One of the Skandars appeared, not Zalzan Kavol but his brother Erfon, who even as Skandars went was dour and chill. "Are you ready?" he asked gruffly.

The troupe performed that afternoon in the private park of one of the powerful merchants of Pidruid, who was giving an entertainment for a provincial duke. Carabella and Valentine performed their new half-juggling routine, the Skandars did something flamboyant with dishes and crystal goblets and cooking-pans, and, as a climax, Sleet was led forth to juggle blindfolded.

"Is this possible?" Valentine asked, awed.

"Watch!" said Carabella.

Valentine watched, but few others did, for this was Sunday after the great Starday frenzy, and the lordlings who had ordered this performance were a weary, jaded bunch, half asleep, bored with the skills of the musicians and acrobats and jugglers they had hired. Sleet stepped forward carrying three clubs and planted himself in a firm, confident way, standing a moment with his head cocked as though listening to the wind that blows between the worlds, and then, catching his breath sharply, he began to throw.

Zalzan Kavol boomed, "Twenty years of practice, lords and ladies of Pidruid! The keenest sense of hearing is necessary for this! He detects the rustle of the clubs against the atmosphere as they fly from hand to hand!"

Valentine wondered how even the keenest sense of hearing could detect anything against the hum of conversation and the clink of dishes and the loud ostentatious pronouncements of Zalzan Kavol, but Sleet made no errors. That the juggling was difficult even for him was obvious: normally he was smooth as a machine, tireless as a loom, but now his hands were moving in sudden sharp skips and lunges, grasping hastily at a club that was spinning up almost out of reach, snatching with desperate quickness at one that had fallen nearly too far. Still, it was miraculous juggling. It was as if Sleet had some chart in his mind of the location of each of the moving clubs, and put his hand where he expected a club to fall, and found it there, or close enough. He did ten, fifteen, twenty exchanges of the clubs, and then gathered all three to his chest, flipped the blindfold aside, took a deep bow. There was a pattering of applause. Sleet stood rigid. Carabella came to him and embraced him, Valentine clapped him lustily on the shoulder, and the troupe left the stage.

In the dressing room Sleet was quivering from strain and beads of sweat glistened on his forehead. He gulped fireshower wine without restraint, as though it were nothing. "Did they pay attention?" he asked Carabella. "Did they even notice?"

"Some did," she said gently.

Sleet spat. "Pigs! Blaves! They have not enough skill to walk from one side of a room to the other, and they sit there chattering when—when an artist—when—"

Valentine had never seen Sleet show temper before. This blind juggling, he decided, was not good for the nerves. He seized the livid Sleet by both shoulders and leaned close. "What matters," he said earnestly, "is the display of skill, not the manners of the audience. You were perfect."

"Not quite," Sleet said sullenly. "The timing—"

"Perfect," Valentine insisted. "You were in complete command. You were majestic. How could you care what drunken merchants might say or do? Is it for their souls or yours that you mastered the art?"

Sleet managed a weak grin. "The blind juggling cuts deep into the soul."

"I would not see you in such pain, my friend."

"It passes. I feel a little better now."

"Your pain was self-inflicted," Valentine said. "It was unwise to allow yourself such outrage. I say again: you were perfect, and nothing else is important." He turned to Shanamir. "Go to the kitchen and see if we might have some meat and bread. Sleet has worked too hard. He needs new fuel, and fireshower wine isn't enough."

Sleet looked merely tired now, instead of tense and furious. He reached forth a hand. "Your soul is warm and kind, Valentine. Your spirit is a gentle and sunny one."

"Your pain pained me."

"I'll guard my wrath better," Sleet said. "And you're right, Valentine: we juggle for ourselves. *They* are incidental. I should not have forgotten that."

Twice more in Pidruid Valentine saw the blind juggling done; twice more he saw Sleet stalk from a stage, rigid and drained. The attention of the onlookers, Valentine realized, had nothing to do with Sleet's fatigue. It was a demonic hard thing to do, was all, and the price the small man paid for his skill was a high one. When Sleet suffered, Valentine did what he could to beam comfort and strength to him. There was great pleasure for Valentine in serving the other man in that way.

Twice more, too, Valentine had dark dreams. One night the apparition of the Pontifex came to him and summoned him into the Labyrinth, and inward he went, down its many passageways and incomprehensible avenues, and the image of gaunt old Tyeveras floated like a will-o'-the-wisp before him, leading him onward to the core, until at last he attained some inner realm of the great maze and suddenly the Pontifex vanished, and Valentine stood alone in a void of cold green light, all footing gone, falling endlessly toward the center of Majipoor. And another night it was the Coronal, riding in his chariot across Pidruid, who beckoned him and invited him to a game of counters, and they threw the dice and moved the markers, and what they played with was a packet of bleached knucklebones, and when Valentine asked whose bones they were, Lord Valentine laughed and tugged at his stiff black fringe of a beard and fastened his dazzling harsh eyes on him and said, "Look at your hands," and Valentine looked, and his hands were without fingers, mere pink globes at his wrists.

These dreams Valentine shared once more with Carabella and with Sleet. But they offered him no dream-speaking, only repeated their advice that he go to some priestess of the slumber-world once they had left Pidruid.

Departure now was imminent. The festival was breaking up; the Coronal's ships no longer stood in the harbor; the roads were crowded with the outflow, as the people of the province made their way homeward from the capital. Zalzan Kavol instructed his troupe to finish whatever business remained to be done in Pidruid that morning, for on Seaday afternoon they would take to the highway.

The announcement left Shanamir strangely quiet and dejected. Valentine noticed the boy's moodiness. "I thought you'd be eager to move along. Finding the city too exciting to leave?"

Shanamir shook his head. "I could go anytime."

"Then what is it?"

"Last night a dream came to me of my father and brothers."

Valentine smiled. "Homesickness already, and you haven't even left the province?"

"Not homesickness," Shanamir said bleakly. "They were tied and lying in the road, and I was driving a team of mounts, and they cried out to me for help and I drove right on, over their helpless bodies. One doesn't have to go to a dream-speaker for understanding of a dream like that."

"So is it guilt at abandoning your duties at home?"

"Guilt? Yes. The *money!*" Shanamir said. There was an edge on his voice, as though he were a man trying to explain something to a dull child. He tapped his waist. "The money, Valentine. I carry in here some hundred sixty royals from the sale of my animals, have you forgotten? A fortune! Enough to pay my family's way all this year and part of next! They depend on my coming back safely to Falkynkip with it."

"And you were planning not to give it to them?"

"I am hired by Zalzan Kavol. What if his route lies another way? If I bring the money home, I might never find you all again as you wander over Zimroel. If I go off with the jugglers I steal my father's money, that he's expecting, that he needs. You see?"

"Simply enough solved," Valentine said. "Falkynkip is how far from here?"

"Two days fast, three days ordinary."

"Quite close. Zalzan Kavol's route, I'm sure, has not yet been fixed. I'll speak to him right now. One town's as good as the next to him. I'll cajole him into taking the Falkynkip road out of here. When we're close to your father's ranch, you'll slip away by night, give the money quietly to one of your brothers, slip back to us before dawn. And then no guilt will attach, and you'll be free to proceed on your way."

Shanamir's eyes widened. "You think you can win a favor from that Skandar? How?"

"I can try."

"He'll strike you to the ground in anger if you ask for anything. He wants no interference with his plans, any more than you'd allow a flock of blaves to vote on how you should run your affairs."

"Let me talk to him," said Valentine, "and we'll see. I have reason to think Zalzan Kavol's not as rough within as he'd like us to believe. Where is he?"

65

"Seeing after his wagon, readying it for the journey. Do you know where that is?"

"Toward the waterfront," Valentine said. "Yes. I know."

The jugglers traveled between cities in a fine wagon that was parked in a lot several blocks from the inn, for it was too broad of beam to bring down these narrow streets. It was an imposing and costly vehicle, noble and majestic, made with the finest workmanship by artisans of one of the inland provinces. The wagon's main frame was of long pale spars of light, springy wingwood, cunningly laminated into wide arching strips with a colorless fragrant glue and bound with resilient withes found in the southern marshes. Over this elegant armature sheets of tanned stickskin had been stretched and stitched into place with thick yellow fibers drawn from the stick-creatures' own gristly bodies.

Approaching it now, Valentine found Erfon Kavol and another of the Skandars, Gibor Haern, diligently oiling the wagon's traces, while from within came deep booming shouts of rage, so loud and violent that the wagon seemed to sway from side to side.

"Where is your brother?" Valentine asked.

Gibor Haern nodded sourly toward the wagon. "This would not be a wise moment to intrude."

"I have business with him."

"*He* has business," said Erfon Kavol, "with the thieving little sorcerer we pay to guide us through the provinces, and who would resign our service in Pidruid just as we are making ready to leave. Go in, if you will, but you will regret it."

The angry cries from the wagon grew more vociferous. Suddenly the door of the wagon burst open and a tiny figure sprang forth, a wizened old Vroon no bigger than a toy, a doll, a little feather-light creature, with ropy tentacular limbs and skin of a faded greenish tint and huge golden eyes now bright with fear. A smear of something that might be pale yellow blood covered the Vroon's angular cheek close beside its beak of a mouth.

Zalzan Kavol appeared an instant later, a terrifying figure in the doorway, his fur puffed with wrath, his vast basketlike hands impotently churning the air. To his brothers he cried, "Catch him! Don't let him get away!"

Erfon Kavol and Gibor Haern rose ponderously and formed a shaggy wall blocking the Vroon's escape. The little being, trapped, panicky, halted and whirled and threw himself against Valentine's knees.

66

"Lord," the Vroon murmured, clinging hard, "protect me! He is insane and would kill me in his anger!"

Zalzan Kavol said, "Hold him there, Valentine."

The Skandar came forward. Valentine pushed the cowering Vroon out of sight behind him and faced Zalzan Kavol squarely. "Control your temper, if you will. Murder this Vroon and we'll all be stuck in Pidruid forever."

"I mean no murder," Zalzan Kavol rumbled. "I have no appetite for years of loathsome sendings."

The Vroon said tremulously, "He *means* no murder, only to throw me against a wall with all his strength."

Valentine said, "What is the quarrel? Perhaps I can mediate."

Zalzan Kavol scowled. "This dispute does not concern you. Get out of the way, Valentine."

"Better that I don't, until your fury has subsided."

Zalzan Kavol's eyes blazed. He advanced until he was no more than a few feet from Valentine, until Valentine could smell the anger-sharpened scent of the rough-thatched Skandar. Zalzan Kavol still seethed. It may be, Valentine thought, that he will throw both of us against the wall. Erfon Kavol and Gibor Haern stared from the side: possibly they had never seen their brother defied before. There was silence a long moment. Zalzan Kavol's hands twitched convulsively, but he remained where he was.

At length he said, "This Vroon is the wizard Autifon Deliamber, whom I hire to show me the inland roads and to guard me against the deceits of the Shapeshifters. All this week he has enjoyed a holiday at my expense in Pidruid; now it is time to leave and he tells me to find another guide, that he has lost interest in traveling from village to village. Is this your sense of how contracts are kept, wizard?"

The Vroon answered, "I am old and weary and my sorceries grow stale, and sometimes I think I start to forget the road. But if you still wish it, I'll accompany you as before, Zalzan Kavol."

The Skandar looked astounded.

"What?"

"I've changed my mind," said Autifon Deliamber blandly, letting go his fearful clutch of Valentine's legs and stepping out into view. The Vroon coiled and opened his many rubbery boneless arms as if a dread tension were being discharged from them, and peered boldly up at the enormous Skandar. "I will keep to my contract," he declared.

67

Bewilderedly Zalzan Kavol said, "For an hour and a half you've been swearing you'll remain here in Pidruid, ignoring all my entreaties and even ignoring my threats, driving me into such rage that I was ready to smash you to pulp, to my own grievous harm as well as yours, for dead sorcerers give poor service and the King of Dreams would rack me fearfully for such a thing, and still you were stubborn, still you denied the contract and told me to make shift elsewhere for a guide. And now at a moment's notice you retract all that?"

"I do."

"Will you have the grace to tell me why?"

"No reason," said the Vroon, "except perhaps that this young man pleases me, that I admire his courage and his kindness and the warmth of his soul, and because he goes with you I will go with you again, for his sake and no other reason. Does that gratify your curiosity, Zalzan Kavol?"

The Skandar growled and sputtered in exasperation and gestured fiercely with his outer pair of hands, as though trying to pull them free of a tangle of birdnet vines. For an instant it seemed he might burst out in some new uprising of uncontrollable anger, that he was controlling himself only by supreme effort.

He said at last, "Out of my sight, wizard, before I hurl you against a wall anyway. And may the Divine guard your life if you aren't here to depart with us this afternoon."

"At the second hour after midday," Autifon Deliamber said courteously. "I will be punctual, Zalzan Kavol." To Valentine he added, "I thank you for protecting me. I am indebted to you, and will make repayment sooner than you think."

The Vroon slipped quickly away.

Zalzan Kavol said after a moment, "It was a foolishness of you to come between us, Valentine. There could have been violence."

"I know."

"And if I had injured you both?"

"I felt you would have held your anger. I was right, yes?"

Zalzan Kavol offered his sunless Skandar equivalent of a smile. "I held my anger, true, but only because I was so amazed at your insolence that my own surprise halted me. Another moment—or had Deliamber continued to thwart me—"

"But he agreed to honor the contract," Valentine pointed out.

"He did, indeed. And I suppose I too am indebted to you, then. Hiring a new guide might have delayed us for days. I

68

thank you, Valentine," said Zalzan Kavol with clumsy grace.

"Is there truly a debt between us?"

The Skandar suddenly was taut with suspicion. "How do you mean?"

"I need a small favor of you. If I have done you service, may I now ask my return?"

"Go on." Zalzan Kavol's voice was frosty.

Valentine took a deep breath. "The boy Shanamir is from Falkynkip. Before he takes to the road with us, he has an urgent errand to perform there. A matter of family honor."

"Let him go to Falkynkip, then, and rejoin us wherever we may be."

"He fears he won't be able to find us if he parts from us."

"What are you asking, Valentine?"

"That you arrange our route so that we pass within a few hours' journey of the boy's home."

Zalzan Kavol stared balefully at Valentine. Bleakly he said, "I am told by my guide that my contract is worthless, and then I am halted from action by an apprentice juggler, and then I am asked to plan my journey for the sake of a groom's family honor. This is becoming a taxing day, Valentine."

"If you have no urgent engagements elsewhere," said Valentine hopefully, "Falkynkip is only two or three days' journey to the northeast. And the boy——"

"Enough!" cried Zalzan Kavol. "The Falkynkip road it is. And then no more favors. Leave me now. Erfon! Haern! Is the wagon ready for the road?"

11

The wagon of Zalzan Kavol's troupe was as splendid within as without. The floor was of dark shining planks of nightflower wood, buffed to a bright finish and pegged together with consummate artifice. To the rear, in the passenger compartment, graceful strings of dried seeds and tassels dangled from the vaulted ceiling, and the walls were covered with swirl-patterned fur hangings, intricate carved inlays, banners of gossamer-sheer fabrics. There was room for five or six people of Skandar bulk to ride back there, though not in any spacious way. Mid-cabin was a place for the storage of belongings, trunks and parcels and juggling gear, all the paraphernalia of the troupe, and up front, on a raised platform open to the sky, was a driver's seat wide enough for two Skandars or three humans.

Huge and princely though the wagon was, a vehicle fit for a duke or even a Coronal, it was altogether airy and light, light enough to float on a vertical column of warm air generated by magnetic rotors whirling in its belly. So long as Majipoor spun on its axis, so would the rotors, and when the rotors were spinning the wagon would drift a foot or so above the ground, and could readily be drawn along by a harnessed team of mounts.

In late morning they finished loading their goods aboard, and went to the inn for lunch. Valentine was startled to see the Hjort with the orange-daubed whiskers, Vinorkis, appear at this point and take a seat beside Zalzan Kavol. The Skandar hammered on the table for attention and bellowed, "Meet our new road manager! This is Vinorkis, who will assist me in making bookings, look after our properties, and handle all manner of chores that now fall to me!"

"Oh, no," Carabella muttered under her breath. "He's hired a Hjort? That weird one who's been staring at us all week?"

Vinorkis smiled a ghastly Hjort smile, showing triple bands of rubbery chewing-cartilage, and peered about in a goggle-eyed way.

Valentine said, "So you were serious about joining us! I thought that was a joke, about your juggling figures."

"It is well known that Hjorts never makes jokes," said Vinorkis gravely, and broke into vociferous laughter.

"But what becomes of your trade in haigus hides?"

"Sold my stock entirely at market," the Hjort replied. "And I thought of you, not knowing where you'd be tomorrow, and not caring. I admired that. I envied that. I asked myself, Are you going to peddle haigus hides all your days, Vinorkis, or will you try something new? A traveling life, perhaps? So I offered my services to Zalzan Kavol when I happened to overhear he was in need of an assistant. And here I am!"

"Here you are," said Carabella sourly. "Welcome!"

After a hearty meal they began their departure. Shanamir led Zalzan Kavol's quartet of mounts from the stable, talking softly and soothingly to the animals as the Skandars tied them into the traces. Zalzan Kavol took the reins; his brother Heitrag sat beside him, with Autifon Deliamber squeezed in alongside. Shanamir, on his own mount, rode alongside. Valentine clambered into the snug, luxurious passenger compartment along with Carabella, Vinorkis, Sleet, and the other four

Skandars. There was much rearranging of arms and legs to fit everyone in comfortably.

"Hoy!" Zalzan Kavol cried sharply, and it was off and out, through Falkynkip Gate and eastward down the grand highway on which Valentine had entered Pidruid just a week ago Moonday.

Summer's warmth lay heavily on the coastal plain, and the air was thick and moist. Already the spectacular blossoms of the fireshower palms were beginning to fade and decay, and the road was littered with fallen petals, like a crimson snowfall. The wagon had several windows—thin, tough sheets of stickskin, the best quality, carefully matched, perfectly transparent—and in an odd solemn silence Valentine watched Pidruid dwindle and disappear, that great city of eleven million souls where he had juggled before the Coronal and tasted strange wines and spicy foods and spent a festival night in the arms of the dark-haired Carabella.

And now the road lay open before him, and who knew what travels awaited, what adventures would befall?

He was without plan, and open to all plans. He itched to juggle again, to master new skills, to cease being an apprentice and to join with Sleet and Carabella in the most intricate of maneuvers, and perhaps even to juggle with the Skandars themselves. Sleet had warned him about that: that only a master could risk juggling with them, for their double sets of arms gave them an advantage no human could hope to match. But Valentine had seen Sleet and Carabella throwing with the Skandars, and maybe in time he would do so as well. A high ambition! he thought. What more could he ask than to become a master worthy of juggling with Zalzan Kavol and his brothers!

Carabella said, "You look so happy all of a sudden, Valentine."

"Do I?"

"Like the sun. Radiant. Light streams from you."

"Yellow hair," he said amiably. "It gives that illusion."

"No. No. A sudden smile—"

He pressed his hand against hers. "I was thinking of the road ahead. A free and hearty life. Wandering zigzag across Zimroel, and stopping to perform, and learning new routines. I want to become the best human juggler on Majipoor!"

"You stand a good chance," Sleet said. "Your natural skills are enormous. You need only the training."

"For that I count on you and Carabella."

71

Carabella said quietly, "And while you were thinking of juggling, Valentine, I was thinking about you."

"And I about you," he whispered, abashed. "But I was ashamed to say it aloud."

The wagon now had reached the switchbacked ridge road that led upward to the great inland plateau. It climbed slowly. In places the angles of the road were so sharp that the wagon could barely execute the turns, but Zalzan Kavol was as cunning a driver as he was a juggler, and brought the vehicle safely around each tight corner. Soon they were at the top of the ridge. Distant Pidruid now looked like a map of itself, flattened and foreshortened, hugging the coast. The air up here was drier but hardly cooler, and in late afternoon the sun unleashed ghastly blasts, a mummifying heat from which there could be no escape before sundown.

That night they halted in a dusty plateau village along the Falkynkip road. A disturbing dream came to Valentine again as he lay on a scratchy mattress stuffed with straw: once more he moved among the Powers of Majipoor. In a vast echoing stone-floored hall the Pontifex sat enthroned at one end and the Coronal at the other, and set in the ceiling was a terrifying eye of light, like a small sun, that cast a merciless white glare. Valentine bore some message from the Lady of the Isle, but he was unsure whether to deliver it to Pontifex or Coronal, and whichever Power he approached receded to infinity as Valentine neared. All night long he trudged back and forth over that cold slippery floor, reaching hands in supplication toward one Power or the other, and always they floated away.

He dreamed again of Pontifex and Coronal the next night, in a town on the outskirts of Falkynkip. This was a hazy dream, and Valentine remembered nothing of it except impressions of fearsome royal personages, enormous pompous assemblies, and failures of communication. He awoke with a feeling of deep and aching discontent. Plainly he was receiving dreams of high consequence, but he was helpless to interpret them. "The Powers obsess you and will not let you rest," Carabella said in the morning. "You seem tied to them by unbreakable cords. It isn't natural to dream so frequently of such mighty figures. I think surely these are sendings."

Valentine nodded. "In the heat of the day I imagine I feel the hands of the King of Dreams pressing coldly on my temples. And when I close my eyes his fingers enter my soul."

Alarm flashed in Carabella's eyes. "Can you be sure they are his sendings?"

"Not sure, no. But I think——"

"Perhaps the Lady——"

"The Lady sends kinder, softer dreams, so I believe," said Valentine. "These are sendings of the King, I much fear. But what does he want of me? What crime have I done?"

She frowned. "In Falkynkip, Valentine, take yourself to a speaker, as you promised."

"I'll look for one, yes."

Autifon Deliamber, joining the conversation unexpectedly, said, "May I make a recommendation?"

Valentine had not seen the wizened little Vroon approach. He looked down, surprised.

"Pardon," the sorcerer said offhandedly. "I happened to overhear. You are troubled by sendings, you think?"

"They could be nothing else."

"Can you be certain?"

"I'm certain of nothing. Not even of my name, or yours, or the day of the week."

"Sendings are rarely ambiguous. When the King speaks, or the Lady, we know without doubt," Deliamber said.

Valentine shook his head. "My mind is clouded these days. I hold nothing sure. But these dreams vex me, and I need answers, though I hardly know how to frame my questions."

The Vroon reached up to take Valentine's hand with one of his delicate, intricately branched tentacles. "Trust me. Your mind may be clouded, but mine is not, and I see you clearly. My name is Deliamber, and yours is Valentine, and this is Fiveday of the ninth week of summer, and in Falkynkip is the dream-speaker Tisana, who is my friend and ally, and who will help you find your proper path. Go to her and say that I give her greetings and love. Time has come for you to begin to recover from the harm that has befallen you, Valentine."

"Harm? Harm? What harm is that?"

"Go to Tisana," Deliamber said firmly.

Valentine sought Zalzan Kavol, who was speaking with some person of the village. Eventually the Skandar was done, and turned to Valentine, who said, "I ask leave to spend Starday night apart from the troupe, in Falkynkip."

"Also a matter of family honor?" asked Zalzan Kavol sardonically.

"A matter of private business. May I?"

The Skandar shrugged an elaborate four-shouldered shrug. "There is something strange about you, something troublesome to me. But do as you wish. We perform in Falkynkip anyway,

tomorrow, at the market fair. Sleep where you like, but be
ready to leave early Sunday morning, eh?"

12

Falkynkip was nothing in the way of being a city to compare
with huge sprawling Pidruid, but all the same was far from
insignificant, a county seat that served as metropolis for a
ranching district of great size. Perhaps three quarters of a million people lived in and about Falkynkip, and five times as
many in the outlying countryside. But its pace was different
from Pidruid's, Valentine observed. Possibly its location on
this dry, hot plateau rather than along the mild and humid
coast had something to do with that: but people moved deliberately here, with stolid, unhurried manners.

The boy Shanamir made himself scarce on Starday. He had
indeed slipped off secretly the night before to his father's
farm some hours north of the city, where—so he told Valentine the next morning—he had left the money he had earned
in Pidruid and a note declaring that he was going off to seek
adventure and wisdom, and had managed to get away again
without being noticed. But he did not expect his father to take
lightly the loss of so skilled and useful a hand, and fearing
that municipal proctors would be out in search of him, Shanamir proposed to spend the rest of his stay in Falkynkip hidden
in the wagon. Valentine explained this to Zalzan Kavol, who
agreed, with his usual acrid grace.

That afternoon at the fair the jugglers came marching
boldly out, Carabella and Sleet leading the way, he banging a
drum, she tapping a tambourine and singing a lilting jingle:

> Spare a royal, spare a crown,
> Gentlefolk, come sit ye down.
> Astonishment and levity—
> Come and see our jugglery!
>
> Spare an inch and spare a mile,
> Gentlefolk, we'll make you smile.
> Cup and saucer, ball and chair,
> Dancing lightly in the air!
>
> Spare a moment, spare a day,
> And we'll spin your cares away.

74

A moment's time, a coin well spent,
Will bring you joy and wonderment.

But levity and wonderment were far from Valentine's spirit that day, and he juggled poorly. He was tense and uneasy from too many nights of troubled sleep, and also was inflamed with ambitions that went beyond his present skills, which led him to overreach himself. Twice he dropped clubs, but Sleet had shown him ways of pretending that that was part of the routine, and the crowd seemed forgiving. Forgiving himself was a harder matter. He crept off sullenly to a wine-stand while the Skandars took the center of the stage.

From a distance he watched them working, the six huge shaggy beings weaving their twenty-four arms in precise and flawless patterns. Each juggled seven knives while constantly throwing and receiving others, and the effect was spectacular, the tension extreme, as the silent interchange of sharp weapons went on and on. The placid burghers of Falkynkip were spellbound.

Watching the Skandars, Valentine regretted all the more his own faulty performance. Since Pidruid he had yearned to go before an audience again—his hands had twitched for the feel of clubs and balls—and he had finally had his moment and had been clumsy. No matter. There would be other market-places, other fairs. All across Zimroel the troupe would wander, year after year, and he would shine, he would dazzle audiences, they would cry out for Valentine the juggler, they would demand encore after encore, until Zalzan Kavol himself looked black with jealousy. A king of jugglers, yes, a monarch, a Coronal of performers! Why not? He had the gift. Valentine smiled. His dour mood was lifting. Was it the wine, or his natural good spirits reasserting themselves? He had been at the art only a week, after all, and look what he had achieved already! Who could say what wonders of eye and hand he would perform when he had had a year or two of practice?

Autifon Deliamber was at his side. "Tisana is to be found in the Street of Watermongers," the diminutive sorcerer said. "She expects you shortly."

"Have you spoken to her of me, then?"

"No," said Deliamber.

"But she expects me. Hah! Is it by sorcery?"

"Something of that," the Vroon said, giving a Vroonish wriggle of the limbs that amounted to a shrug. "Go to her soon."

75

Valentine nodded. He looked across: the Skandars were done, and Sleet and Carabella were demonstrating one-arm juggling. How elegantly they moved together, he thought. How calm, how confident they were, how crisp of motion. And how beautiful she is. Valentine and Carabella had not been lovers since the night of the festival, though sometimes they had slept side by side; it was a week now, and he had felt aloof and apart from her, though nothing but warmth and support had come from her to him. These dreams were the problem, draining and distracting him. To Tisana, then, for a speaking, and then, perhaps tomorrow, to embrace Carabella again—

"The Street of Watermongers," he said to Deliamber. "Very well. Will there be a sign marking her dwelling?"

"Ask," Deliamber said.

As Valentine set out, the Hjort Vinorkis stepped from behind the wagon and said, "Off for a night on the town, are you?"

"An errand," Valentine said.

"Want some company?" The Hjort laughed his coarse, noisy laugh. "We could hit a few taverns together, hoy? I wouldn't mind getting away from all this jugglery for a few hours."

Uneasily Valentine said, "It's the sort of thing one must do by oneself."

Vinorkis studied him a moment. "Not too friendly, are you?"

"Please. It's exactly as I said: I must do this alone. I'm not going tavern-crawling tonight, believe me."

The Hjort shrugged. "All right. Be like that, see if I care. I just wanted to help you have fun—show you the town, take you to a couple of my favorite places—"

"Another time," said Valentine quickly.

He strode off toward Falkynkip.

The Street of Watermongers was easy enough to find—this was an orderly town, no medieval maze like Pidruid, and there were neat and comprehensible city maps posted at every major intersection—but finding the home of the dreamspeaker Tisana was a slower business, for the street was long and those he asked for directions merely pointed over their shoulders toward the north. He followed along steadfastly and by early evening reached a small gray rough-shingled house in a residential quarter far from the marketplace. It bore on its weatherworn front door two symbols of the Powers, the crossed lightning-bolts that stood for the King of Dreams, and

76

the triangle-within-triangle that was the emblem of the Lady of the Isle of Sleep.

Tisana was a sturdy woman of more than middle years, heavy-bodied and of unusual height, with a broad strong face and cool searching eyes. Her hair, thick and unbound, black streaked with swaths of white, hung far down her shoulders. Her arms, emerging bare from the gray cotton smock that she wore, were solid and powerful, although swinging dewlaps of flesh hung from them. She seemed a person of great strength and wisdom.

She greeted Valentine by name and bade him be comfortable in her house.

"I bring you, as you must already know, the greetings and love of Autifon Deliamber," he said.

The dream-speaker nodded gravely. "He has sent advance word, yes. That rascal! But his love is worth receiving, for all his tricks. Convey the same from me to him." She moved around the small dark room, closing draperies, lighting three thick red candles, igniting some incense. There was little furniture, only a high-piled woven rug in tones of gray and black, a venerable wooden table on which the candles stood, and a tall clothes-cabinet in antique style. She said, as she made her preparations, "I've known Deliamber nearly forty years, would you believe it? It was in the early days of the reign of Tyeveras that we met, at a festival in Piliplok, when the new Coronal came to town, Lord Malibor that drowned on the sea-dragon hunt. The little Vroon was tricky even then. We stood there cheering Lord Malibor in the streets, and Deliamber said, 'He'll die before the Pontifex, you know,' the way someone might predict rain when the south wind blows. It was a terrible thing to say, and I told him so. Deliamber didn't care. A strange business, when the Coronal dies first, when the Pontifex lives on and on. How old d'ye think Tyeveras is by now? A hundred? A hundred twenty?"

"I have no idea," said Valentine.

"Old, very old. He was Coronal a long while before he entered the Labyrinth. And he's been in there for three Coronal-reigns, can you imagine? I wonder if he'll outlive Lord Valentine too." Her eyes came to rest on Valentine's. "I suppose Deliamber knows that too. Will you have wine with me now?"

"Yes," Valentine said, uncomfortable with her blunt, outgoing manner and with the sense she gave him of knowing far more about him than he knew himself.

Tisana produced a carven stone decanter and poured two generous drinks, not the spicy fireshower wine of Pidruid but some darker, thicker vintage, sweet with undertastes of peppermint and ginger and other, more mysterious, things. He took a quick sip, and then another, and after the second she said casually, "It contains the drug, you know."

"Drug?"

"For the speaking."

"Oh. Of course. Yes." His ignorance embarrassed him. Valentine frowned and stared into his goblet. The wine was dark red, almost purple, and its surface gave back his own distorted reflection by candlelight. What was the procedure? he wondered. Was he supposed now to tell his recent dreams to her? Wait and see, wait and see. He drained the drink in quick uneasy gulps and immediately the old woman refilled, topping off her own glass, which she had barely touched.

She said, "A long time since your last speaking?"

"Very long, I'm afraid."

"Evidently. This is the moment when you give me my fee, you know. You'll find the price somewhat higher than you remember."

Valentine reached for his purse. "It's been so long—"

"—that you don't remember. I ask ten crowns now. There are new taxes, and other bothers. In Lord Voriax's time it was five, and when I first took up speaking, in the reign of Lord Malibor, I got two or two and a half. Is ten a burden for you?"

It was a week's pay for him from Zalzan Kavol, above his room and board; but he had arrived in Pidruid with plenty of money in his purse, he knew not how or why, close on sixty royals, and much of that remained. He gave the dream-speaker a royal and she dropped the coin negligently into a green porcelain bowl on the table. He yawned. She was watching him closely. He drank again; she did also, and refilled; his mind was growing cloudy. Though it was still early at night, he would soon be sleepy.

"Come now to the dream-rug," she said, blowing out two of the three candles.

She pulled off her smock and was naked before him.

That was unexpected. Did dream-speaking involve some sort of sexual contact? With this old woman? Not that she seemed so old now: her body looked a good twenty years younger than her face, not a girl's body by any means, but still firm-fleshed, plump but unwrinkled, with heavy breasts and strong smooth thighs. Perhaps these speakers were some sort of holy prostitutes, Valentine thought. She beckoned to him to undress, and he cast his clothes aside. They lay down together on the thick woolen rug in the half-darkness, and she drew

78

him into her arms, but there was nothing at all erotic about the embrace—more maternal, if anything, an all-enfolding engulfment. He relaxed. His head was against her soft warm bosom and it was hard for him to stay awake. The scent of her was strong in his nostrils, a sharp pleasant aroma like that of the gnarled and ageless needle-trees that grew on the high peaks of the north just below the snow-line, an odor that was crisp and pungent and clean. She said softly, "In the kingdom of dreams the only language spoken is that of truth. Be without fear as we embark together."

Valentine closed his eyes.

High peaks, yes, just below the snow-line. A brisk wind blew across the crags, but he was not at all cold, though his feet were bare against the dry stony soil. A trail lay before him, a steeply sloping path in which broad gray flagstones had been laid to form a gigantic staircase leading into a mist-wrapped valley, and without hesitation Valentine started the descent. He understood that these images were not yet those of his dream, only of the prelude, that he had only begun his night's journey and was still merely on the threshold of sleep. But as he went downward he passed others, making the ascent, figures familiar to him from recent nights, the Pontifex Tyeveras with parchment skin and withered face, laboring up the steps in feeble quavering manner, and Lord Valentine the Coronal clambering with bold assertive strides, and dead Lord Voriax floating serenely just above the steps, and the great warrior-Coronal Lord Stiamot out of eight thousand years past, brandishing some mighty staff around the tip of which furious storms swirled, and was this not the Pontifex Arioc who had resigned the Labyrinth six thousand years before to proclaim himself a woman, and become Lady of the Isle of Sleep instead? And this the great ruler Lord Confalume, and the equally great Lord Prestimion who had succeeded him, under whose two long reigns Majipoor had attained its peak of wealth and power? And then came Zalzan Kavol with the wizard Deliamber on his back, and Carabella, naked and nut-brown, sprinting with unfailing vigor, and Vinorkis, goggling and gaping, and Sleet, juggling balls of fire as he climbed, and Shanamir, and a Liiman selling sizzling sausages, and the gentle sweet-eyed Lady of the Isle, and the old Pontifex again, and the Coronal, and a platoon of musicians, and twenty Hjorts bearing the King of Dreams, terrible old Simonan Barjazid, in a golden litter. The mists were thicker down here, the air more dank, and Valentine found his breath coming in short painful bursts, as though instead of descending from the

79

heights he had been climbing all the time, working his way by awful struggle above the line of needle-trees, into the bare granite shields of the high mountains, barefoot on burning strands of snow, swaddled in gray blankets of cloud that concealed all of Majipoor from him.

There was noble austere music in the heavens now, awesome choirs of brass playing solemn and somber melodies suitable for the robing-ceremony of a Coronal. And, indeed, they were robing him, a dozen crouching servants placing on him the cloak of office and the starburst crown, but he shook his head lightly and brushed them away, and with his own hands he removed the crown and handed it to his brother of the menacing saber, and shrugged off his fine robes and distributed them in strips to the poor, who used them to make bindings for their feet, and word went out to all the provinces of Majipoor that he had resigned his high office and given up all power, and once more he found himself on the flagstone steps, descending the mountain trail, seeking that valley of mists that lay in the unattainable beyond.

"But why do you go downward?" asked Carabella, blocking his path, and he had no answer to that, so that when little Deliamber pointed upward he shrugged meekly and began a new ascent, through fields of brilliant red and blue flowers, through a place of golden grass and lofty green cedars. He perceived that this was no ordinary peak he had been climbing and descending and climbing anew, but rather Castle Mount itself, that jutted thirty miles into the heavens, and his goal was that bewildering all-encompassing ever-expanding structure at its summit, the place where the Coronal dwelled, the castle that was called Lord Valentine's Castle but that had, not long before, been Lord Voriax' Castle and before that Lord Malibor's Castle, and other names before that, names of all those mighty princes who had ruled from Castle Mount, each putting his imprint on the growing castle and giving his name to it while he lived there, all the way back to Lord Stiamot the conqueror of the Metamorphs, he who was the first to dwell on Castle Mount and built the modest keep out of which all the rest had sprouted. I will regain the Castle, Valentine told himself, and I will take up residence.

But what was this? Workmen by the thousands, dismantling the enormous edifice! The work of demolition was well under way, and all the outer wings were taken apart, the place of buttresses and arches that Lord Voriax had built, and the grand trophy-room of Lord Malibor, and the great library that Tyeveras had added in his days as Coronal, and much else, all those rooms now mere piles of bricks laid in neat mounds on the slopes of the Mount, and they were working inward toward more ancient wings, to the garden-house of Lord Confalume and the armory of Lord Dekkeret and the archive-vault of Lord Prestimion, removing those places brick by brick by brick like locusts sweeping over the fields at harvest-time. "Wait!" Valentine cried. "No need to do this! I am back, I will take up my robes and crown once again!" But the work of destruction continued, and it was as if the castle were made of sand and the tides were sweeping in, and a gentle voice said, "Too late, too late, much too late," and the watchtower of Lord Arioc was gone and the parapets of Lord Thimin were gone and the observatory of Lord Kinniken was gone with all its star-watching apparatus, and Castle Mount itself was shuddering and swaying as the removal of the castle disrupted its equilibrium, and workmen now were running frantically with bricks in their hands, seeking flat places on which to stack them, and a dread eternal night had come and baleful stars swelled and writhed in the sky, and the machineries that held back the chill of space atop Castle Mount were failing, so that the warm mild air was flowing moonward, and there was sobbing in the depths of the planet and Valentine stood amid the scenes of disruption and gathering chaos, holding forth outstretched fingers to the darkness.

The next thing he knew, morning light was in his eyes, and he blinked and sat up, confused, wondering what inn this was and what he had been doing the night before, for he lay naked on a thick woolly rug in a warm strange room, and there was an old woman moving about, brewing tea, perhaps—

Yes. The dream-speaker Tisana, and this was Falkynkip, in the Street of Watermongers—

His nakedness discomforted him. He rose and dressed quickly.

Tisana said, "Drink this. I'll put some breakfast up, now that you're finally awake."

He looked dubiously at the mug she handed him.

"Tea," she said. "Nothing but tea. The time for dreaming is long past."

Valentine sipped at it while she bustled around the small kitchen. There was a numbness in his spirit, as though he had caroused himself into insensibility and now had a reckoning to pay; and he knew there had been strange dreams, a whole night of them, but yet he felt none of the malaise of the soul that he had known upon awakening these past few mornings, only that numbness, a curious centered calmness, almost an

81

emptiness. Was that the purpose of visiting a dream-speaker? He understood so little. He was like a child loose in this vast and complex world.

They ate in silence. Tisana seemed to be studying Valentine intently across the table. Last night she had chattered much before the drug had had its effect, but now she seemed subdued, reflective, almost withdrawn, as if she needed to be apart from him while preparing to speak his dream.

At length she cleared the dishes and said, "How do you feel?"

"Quiet within."

"Good. Good. That's important. To go away from a dream-speaker in turmoil is a waste of money. I had no doubts, thou-h, Your spirit is strong."

"Is it?"

"Stronger than you know. Reverses that would crush an ordinary person leave you untouched. You shrug off disaster and whistle in the face of danger."

"You speak very generally," Valentine said.

"I am an oracle, and oracles are never terribly specific," she replied lightly.

"Are my dreams sendings? Will you tell me that, at least?"

She was thoughtful a moment. "I am uncertain."

"But you shared them! Aren't you able to know at once if a dream comes from the Lady or the King?"

"Peace, peace, this is not so simple," she said, waving a palm at him. "Your dreams are not sendings of the Lady, this I know."

"Then if they are sendings, they are of the King."

"Here is the uncertainty. They have an aura of the King about them in some way, yes, but not the aura of sendings. I know you find that hard to fathom: so do I. I do believe the King of Dreams watches your doings and is concerned with you, but it doesn't seem to me that he's been entering your sleep. It confounds me."

"Has anything like this been known to you before?"

The dream-speaker shook her head. "Not at all."

"Is this my speaking, then? Only more mysteries and unanswered questions?"

"You haven't had the speaking yet," Tisana answered.

"Forgive my impatience."

"No forgiveness is needed. Come, give me your hands, and I'll make a speaking for you." She reached for him across the table, and grasped and held him, and after a long while said,

"You have fallen from a high place, and now you must begin to climb back to it."

He grinned. "A high place?"

"The highest."

"The highest place on Majipoor," he said lightly, "is the summit of Castle Mount. Is *that* where you would have me climb?"

"There, yes."

"A very steep ascent you lay upon me. I could spend my entire life reaching and climbing that place."

"Nevertheless, Lord Valentine, that ascent awaits you, and it is not I who lays it on you."

He gasped at her use of the royal title to him, and then burst out laughing at the grossness of it, the tastelessness of her joke. "Lord Valentine! Lord Valentine? No, you do me far too much honor, Madame Tisana. Not *Lord* Valentine. Only Valentine, Valentine the juggler, is all, the newest of the troupe of Zalzan Kavol the Skandar."

Her gaze rested steadily on him. Quietly she said, "I beg your pardon. I meant no offense."

"How could it offend me? But put no royal titles on me, please. A juggler's life is royal enough for me, even if my dreams may sometimes be high-flown ones."

Her eyes did not waver. "Will you have more tea?" she asked.

"I promised the Skandar I'd be ready for departure early in the morning, and so I must leave soon. What else does the speaking hold for me?"

"The speaking is over," said Tisana.

Valentine had not expected that. He was awaiting interpretations, analysis, exegesis, counsel. And all he had had from her—

"I have fallen and I must climb back on high. That's all you tell me for a royal?"

"Fees for everything grow larger nowadays," she said without rancor. "Do you feel cheated?"

"Not at all. This has been valuable for me, in its fashion."

"Politely said, but false. Nevertheless you have received value here. Time will make that clear to you." She got to her feet, and Valentine rose with her. There was about her an aura of confidence and strength. "I wish you a good journey," she said, "and a safe ascent."

13

Autifon Deliamber was the first to greet him when he returned from the dream-speaking. In the quiet of dawn the little Vroon was practicing a sort of juggling near the wagon, with shards of some glittering icy-bright crystalline substance: but this was wizard-juggling, for Deliamber only pretended to throw and catch, and appeared actually to be moving the shards by power of mind alone. He stood beneath the brilliant cascade and the shimmering slivers coursed through the air in a circle above him like a wreath of bright light, remaining aloft although Deliamber never touched them.

As Valentine approached, the Vroon gave a twitch of his tentacle-tips and the glassy shards fell instantly inward to form a close-packed bundle that Deliamber snatched deftly from the air. He held them forth to Valentine. "Pieces of a temple building from the Ghayrog city of Dulorn, that lies a few days' journey east of here. A place of magical beauty, it is. Have you been there?"

The enigmas of the dream-speaking night still lay heavy on Valentine, and he had no taste for Deliamber's flamboyant spirit this early in the morning. Shrugging, he said, "I don't remember."

"You'd remember, if you had. A city of light, a city of frozen poetry!" The Vroon's beak clacked: a Vroonish sort of smile. "Or perhaps you wouldn't remember. I suppose not: so much is lost to you. But you'll be there again soon enough."

"Again? I never was there."

"If you were there once, you'll be there again when we get there. If not, not. However it may be for you, Dulorn is our next stop, so says our beloved Skandar." Deliamber's mischievous eyes probed Valentine's. "I see you learned a great deal at Tisana's."

"Let me be, Deliamber."

"She's a marvel, isn't she?"

Valentine attempted to go past. "I learned nothing there," he said tightly. "I wasted an evening."

"Oh, no, no, no! Time is never wasted. Give me your hand, Valentine." The Vroon's dry, rubbery tentacle slipped around Valentine's reluctant fingers. Solemnly Deliamber said, "Know this, and know it well: *time is never wasted*. Wherever we go, whatever we do, everything is an aspect of education. Even when we don't immediately grasp the lesson."

"Tisana told me approximately the same thing as I was leaving," Valentine murmured sullenly. "I think you two are in conspiracy. But what did I learn? I dreamed again of Coronals and Pontifexes. I climbed up and down mountain trails. The dream-speaker made a silly, tiresome joke on my name. I rid myself of a royal better spent on wine and feasting. No, I achieved nothing." He attempted to withdraw his hand from Deliamber's grip, but the Vroon held him with unexpected strength. Valentine felt an odd sensation, as of a chord of somber music rolling through his mind, and somewhere beneath the surface of his consciousness an image glimmered and flashed, like some sea-dragon stirring and sounding in the depths, but he was unable to perceive it clearly: the core of the meaning eluded him. Just as well. He feared to know what was stirring down there. An obscure and incomprehensible anguish flooded his soul. For an instant it seemed to him that the dragon in the depths of his being was rising, was swimming upward through the murk of his clouded memory toward the levels of awareness. That frightened him. Knowledge, terrifying and menacing knowledge, was hidden within him, and now was threatening to break loose. He resisted. He fought. He saw little Deliamber staring at him with terrible intensity, as if trying to lend him the strength he needed to accept that dark knowledge, but Valentine would not have it. He pulled his hand free with sudden violent force and went lurching and stumbling toward the Skandar wagon. His heart was pounding fiercely, his temples throbbed, he felt weak and dizzy. After a few uncertain steps he turned and said angrily, "What did you do to me?"

"I merely touched my hand to yours."

"And gave me great pain!"

"I may have given you access to your own pain," said Deliamber quietly. "Nothing more than that. The pain is carried within you. You have been unable to feel it. But it's struggling to awaken within you, Valentine. There's no preventing it."

"I mean to prevent it."

"You have no choice but to heed the voices from within. The struggle has already begun."

Valentine shook his aching head. "I want no pain and no struggles. I've been a happy man, this last week."

"Are you happy when you dream?"

"These dreams will pass from me soon. They must be sendings intended for someone else."

"Do you believe that, Valentine?"

Valentine was silent. After a moment he said, "I want only to be allowed to be what I want to be."

"And that is?"

"A wandering juggler. A free man. Why do you torment me this way, Deliamber?"

"I would gladly have you be a juggler," the Vroon said gently. "I mean you no sorrow. But what one wants often has little connection with what may be marked out for one on the great scroll."

"I will be a master juggler," said Valentine, "and nothing more than that, and nothing less."

"I wish you well," Deliamber said courteously, and walked away.

Slowly Valentine let his breath escape. His entire body was tense and stiff, and he squatted and put his head down, stretching out first his arms and then his legs, trying to rid himself of these strange knots that had begun to invade him. Gradually he relaxed a little, but some residue of uneasiness remained, and the tension would not leave him. These tortured dreams, these squirming dragons in his soul, these portents and omens—

Carabella emerged from the wagon and stood above him as he stretched and twisted. "Let me help," she said, crouching down beside him. She pushed him forward until he lay sprawled flat, and her powerful fingers dug into the taut muscles of his neck and back. Under her ministrations he grew somewhat less tense, yet his mood remained dark and troubled.

"The speaking didn't help you?" she asked softly.

"No."

"Can you talk about it?"

"I'd rather not," he said.

"Whatever you prefer." But she waited expectantly, her eyes alert, shining with warmth and compassion.

He said, "I barely understood the things the woman was telling me. And what I understood I can't accept. But I don't want to talk about it."

"Whenever you do, Valentine, I'm here. Whenever you feel the need to tell someone—"

"Not right now. Perhaps never." He sensed her reaching toward him, eager to heal the pain in his soul as she had grappled with the tensions in his body. He could feel the love flooding from her to him. Valentine hesitated. He did battle

86

within himself. Haltingly he said, "The things the speaker told me—"

"Yes."

No. To talk of these things was to give them reality, and they had no reality, they were absurdities, they were fantasies, they were foolish vapors.

"—were nonsense," Valentine said. "What she said isn't worth discussing."

Carabella's eyes reproached him. He looked away from her.

"Can you accept that?" he asked roughly. "She was a crazy old woman and she told me a lot of nonsense, and I don't want to discuss it, not with you, not with anyone. It was *my* speaking. I don't have to share it. I—" He saw the shock on her face. In another moment he would be babbling. He said in an entirely different tone of voice, "Get the juggling balls, Carabella."

"Now?"

"Right now."

"But—"

"I want you to teach me the exchange between jugglers, the passing of the balls. Please."

"We're due to leave in half an hour!"

"Please," he said urgently.

She nodded and sprinted up the steps of the wagon, returning a moment later with the balls. They moved apart, to an open place where they would have room, and Carabella flipped three of the balls to him. She was frowning.

"What's wrong?" he asked.

"Learning new techniques when the mind is troubled is never a good idea."

"It might calm me," he said. "Let's try."

"As you wish." She began to juggle the three balls she held, by way of warming up. Valentine imitated her, but his hands were cold, his fingers unresponsive, and he had trouble doing this simplest of all routines, dropping the balls several times. Carabella said nothing. She continued to juggle while he launched one abortive cascade after another. His temper grew edgy. She would not tell him again that this was the wrong moment for attempting such things, but her silence, her look, even her stance, all said it more forcefully than words. Valentine desperately sought to strike a rhythm. *You have fallen from a high place*, he heard the dream-speaker saying, *and now you must begin to climb back to it.* He bit his lip. How could he concentrate, with such things intruding? Hand and eye, he thought, hand and eye, forget all else. Hand and eye. *Nevertheless, Lord Valentine, that ascent awaits you, and it is not I who lays it on you.* No. No. No. No. His hands shook. His fingers were rods of ice. He made a false move and the balls went scattering.

"Please, Valentine," Carabella said mildly.

"Get the clubs."

"It'll be even worse with them. Do you want to break a finger?"

"The clubs," he said.

Shrugging, she gathered up the balls and went into the wagon. Sleet emerged, yawned, nodded a casual greeting to Valentine. The morning was beginning. One of the Skandars appeared and crawled under the wagon to adjust something. Carabella came out bearing six clubs. Behind her was Shanamir, who gave Valentine a quick salute and went to feed the mounts. Valentine took the clubs. Conscious of Sleet's cool eyes on him, he put himself into the juggling position, threw one club high, and botched the catch. No one spoke. Valentine tried again. He managed to get the three clubs into sequence, but for no more than thirty seconds; then they spilled, one landing unpleasantly on his toe. Valentine caught sight of Autifon Deliamber watching the scene from a distance. He picked up the clubs again. Carabella, facing him, patiently juggled her three, studiously ignoring him. Valentine threw the clubs, got them started, dropped one, started again, dropped two, started yet again, made a faulty grab and bent his left thumb badly out of place.

He tried to pretend that nothing had gone wrong. Once more he picked up the clubs, but this time Sleet came over and took Valentine lightly by both wrists.

"Not now," he said. "Give me the clubs."

"I want to practice."

"Juggling isn't therapy. You're upset about something, and it's ruining your timing. If you keep this up you can do damage to your rhythms that will take you weeks to undo."

Valentine tried to pull free, but Sleet held him with surprising strength. Carabella, impassive, went on juggling a few feet away. After an instant Valentine yielded. With a shrug he surrendered the clubs to Sleet, who scooped them up and took them back into the wagon. A moment later Zalzan Kavol stepped outside, elaborately scratched his pelt fore and aft with several of his hands as though searching in it for fleas, and boomed, "Everybody in! Let's move it along!"

88

The road to the Ghayrog city of Dulorn took them eastward
through lush, placid farming country, green and fertile under
the eye of the summer sun. Like much of Majipoor this was
densely populated terrain, but intelligent planning had created wide agricultural zones bordered by busy strip-cities, and
so the day went, through an hour's worth of farms, an hour's
worth of town, an hour of farms, an hour of town. Here in the
Dulorn Rift, the broad sloping lowland east of Falkynkip, the
climate was particularly suited for farming, for the Rift was
open at its northern end to the polar rainstorms that constantly drenched Majipoor's temperate arctic, and the subtropical heat was made moderate by gentle, predictable precipita-
tion. The growing season lasted year round: this was the time
for harvesting the sweet yellow stajja tubers, from which a
bread was made, and for planting such fruits as niyk and
glein.

The beauty of the landscape lightened Valentine's bleak
outlook. By easy stages he ceased to think about things that
did not bear thinking about, and allowed himself to enjoy the
unending procession of wonders that was the planet of Majipoor. The black slender trunks of niyk-trees planted in rigid
and complex geometrical patterns danced against the horizon;
teams of Hjort and human farmers in rural costumes moved
like invading armies across the stajja-fields, plucking the
heavy tubers; now the wagon glided quietly through a district
of lakes and streams, and now through one where curious
blocks of white granite jutted tooth-fashion from the smooth
grassy plains.

At midday they entered a place of particularly strange
beauty, one of the many public forest preserves. At the gateway a sign glowing with green luminosity proclaimed:

BLADDERTREE PRESERVE

Located here is an outstanding virgin tract of Dulorn Bladdertree.
These trees manufacture lighter-than-air gases which keep their upper branches buoyant. As they approach maturity their trunks and
root systems atrophy, and they become epiphytic in nature, depen-
dent almost entirely on the atmosphere for nourishment. Occasionally in extreme old age a tree will sever its contact with the ground
entirely and drift off to found a new colony far away. Bladdertrees

are found both in Zimroel and in Alhanroel but have become rare in recent times. This grove set aside for the people of Majipoor by official decree, 12th. Pont. Confalume Cor. Lord Prestimion.

The jugglers followed the forest trail silently on foot for some minutes without seeing anything unusual. Then Carabella, who led the way, passed through a thicket of dense blueblack bushes and cried out suddenly in surprise.

Valentine ran to her side. She was standing in wonder in the midst of marvels.

Bladdertrees were everywhere, in all stages of their growth. The young ones, no higher than Deliamber or Carabella, were curious ungainly-looking shrublets with thick, swollen branches of a peculiar silvery hue that emerged at awkward angles from squat fleshy trunks. But in trees fifteen or twenty feet tall, the trunks had begun to attenuate and the limbs to inflate, so that now the bulging boughs appeared topheavy and precarious, and in even older trees the trunks had shriveled to become nothing more than rough, scaly guy-ropes by which the trees' buoyant crowns were fastened to the ground. High overhead they floated and bobbed in the gentlest breeze, leafless, turgid, the branches puffed up like balloons. The silvery color of the young branches became, in maturity, a brilliant translucent gleam, so that the trees seemed like glass models of themselves, shining brightly in the shafts of sunlight through which they danced and weaved. Even Zalzan Kavol seemed moved by the strangeness and beauty of the trees. The Skandar approached one of the tallest, its gleaming swollen crown floating far overhead, and carefully, almost reverently, encircled its taut narrow stem with his fingers. Valentine thought Zalzan Kavol might be minded to snap the stem and send the bladdertree floating away like a glittering kite, but no, the Skandar seemed merely to be marking the slenderness of the stem, and after a moment he stepped back, muttering to himself.

For a long while they wandered among the bladdertrees, studying the little ones, observing the stages of growth, the gradual narrowing of the trunks and bloating of the limbs. The trees were leafless and no flowers were apparent: it was difficult to believe that they were vegetable creations at all, so vitreous did they seem. It was a place of magic. The darkness of his earlier mood now seemed a mystery to Valentine. On a planet where such beauty abounded, how could one have any need for brooding or fretting?

"Here," Carabella called. "Catch!"

90

She had gauged the change in his spirits and had gone to the wagon for the juggling balls. Now she threw three of them to him and he went easily into the basic cascade, and she the same, in a clearing surrounded by glistening bladdertrees.

Carabella stood facing him, just a few feet away. They juggled independently for three or four minutes, until a symmetry of phase encompassed them and they were throwing in identical rhythms. Now they juggled together, mirroring one another, Valentine feeling a deeper calmness settling over him with each cycle of throws: he was balanced, centered, tuned. The bladdertrees, stirring lightly in the wind, showered him with dazzles of refracted light. The world was silent and serene.

"When I tell you," Carabella said quietly, "throw the ball from your right hand to my left, at precisely the height you'd throw it if you were giving it to yourself. One . . . two . . . three . . . four . . . five . . *pass!*" And on *pass* he threw to her on a firm straight arc, and she to him. He managed, just barely, to catch the incoming ball and work it into the rhythm, continuing his own cascade, and counting off until it was time to pass again. Back—forth—back—forth—*pass*—

It was hard at first, the hardest juggling he had ever done, but yet he could do it, he was doing it without blundering, and after the first few passes he was doing it without awkwardness, smoothly exchanging throws with Carabella as though he had practiced this routine with her for months. He knew that this was extraordinary, that no one was supposed to master intricate patterns like this on the first try: but as before, he moved swiftly toward the core of the experience, placed himself in a region where nothing existed but hand and eye and the moving balls, and failure became not merely impossible but inconceivable.

"Hoy!" Sleet cried. "Over here now!"

He too was juggling. Momentarily Valentine was baffled by this multiplication of the task, but he forced himself to remain in automatic mode, to throw when it seemed appropriate, to catch what came to him, and constantly to keep the balls that remained to him moving between his hands. So when Sleet and Carabella began to exchange balls he was able to stay in the pattern, and catch from Sleet instead of Carabella. "One—two—one—two—" Sleet called, taking up a position between Valentine and Carabella and making himself the leader of the group, feeding the balls first to one, then to the other, in a rhythm that remained rock-steady for a long while and then accelerated comically to a pace far beyond Valen-

91

tine's abilities. Suddenly there were dozens of balls in the air, or so it seemed, and Valentine grasped wildly at all of them and lost them all and collapsed, laughing, onto the warm springy turf.

"So there are some limits to your skill, eh?" Sleet said gaily. "Good! Good! I was beginning to wonder whether you were mortal."

Valentine chuckled. "Mortal enough, I fear."

"Lunch!" Deliamber called.

He presided over a pot of stew hanging from a tripod above a glowglobe. The Skandars, who had been doing some practice of their own in another part of the grove, appeared as if conjured from the soil and helped themselves with ungracious eagerness. Vinorkis too was quick to fill his plate. Valentine and Carabella were the last to be served, but he hardly cared. He was sweating the good sweat of exertion well exerted, and his blood was pounding and his skin was tingling, and his long night of unsettling dreams seemed far behind him, something he had left in Falkynkip.

All that afternoon the wagon sped eastward. This was definitely Ghayrog country now, inhabited almost exclusively by that glossy-skinned reptilian-looking race. When nightfall came the troupe was still half a day's journey from the provincial seat at Dulorn, where Zalzan Kavol had arranged some sort of theatrical booking. Deliamber announced that a country inn lay not far ahead, and they went on until they came to it.

"Share my bed," Carabella said to Valentine.

In the corridor going to their chamber they passed Deliamber, who paused a moment, touching their hands with tentacle-tips and murmuring, "Dream well."

"Dream well," Carabella repeated automatically.

But Valentine did not offer the customary response with her, for the touch of the Vroon sorcerer's flesh to his had set the dragon stirring within his soul again, and he was disquieted and grave, as he had been before the miracle of the bladdertree grove. It was as though Deliamber had appointed himself the enemy of Valentine's tranquillity, arousing in him inarticulate fears and apprehensions against which he had no defense. "Come," Valentine muttered hoarsely to Carabella.

"In a hurry, are you?" She laughed a light tinkling laugh, but it died away quickly when she saw his expression. "Valentine, what is it? What's the matter?"

"Nothing."

"Nothing?"

"May I be allowed moods, as other human beings some-times have?"

"When your face changes like that, it's like a shadow pass-ing over the sun. And so suddenly—"

"Something about Deliamber," Valentine said, "disturbs and alarms me. When he touched me—"

"Deliamber's harmless. Mischievous, like all wizards, espe-cially Vroonish ones, especially small ones. There's dark mis-chief in very small people. But you have nothing to fear from Deliamber."

"Truly so?" He closed the door, and she was in his arms.

"Truly," she said. "You have nothing to fear from anyone, Valentine. Everyone who sees you loves you. There's no one who would injure you in this world."

"How good to believe that," he said, as she drew him down on the bed.

They embraced, and his lips touched hers gently, and then with more force, and soon their bodies were entwined. He had not made love with her for over a week, and he had looked forward to it with intense longing and delight. But the inci-dent in the hallway had robbed him of desire, had left him numb and isolated, and that mystified and depressed him. Carabella must have sensed the coolness in him, but evidently she chose to ignore it, for her lithe energetic body sought his with fervor and passion. He forced himself to respond, and then after a minute he was no longer forcing, was nearly as enthusiastic as she, but still he stood outside his own sensa-tions, a mere spectator as they made love. It was over quickly, and the light was out, although moonlight entering their win-dow cast a harsh chilly glow over their faces.

"Dream well," Carabella murmured.

"Dream well," he replied.

She was asleep almost at once. He held her, keeping her warm slim body close against him, feeling no sleepiness him-self. After a time he rolled away and drew himself into his favorite sleep position, on his back, arms folded across his chest, but no sleep came, only fitful dreamless dozing. He di-verted himself by counting blaves, by imagining himself jug-gling in patterns of surpassing intricacy with Sleet and Cara-bella, by trying to relax his entire body one muscle at a time. Nothing worked. Wide awake, he propped himself on one arm and lay looking down at Carabella, lovely in the moonlight.

She was dreaming. A muscle flickered in her cheek; her eyes moved beneath their lids; her breasts rose and fell in jag-ged rhythms; she put her knuckles to her lips, murmured something in a thick unintelligible voice, drew her knees tightly to her chest. Her lean bare form looked so beautiful that Valentine wanted to reach out to her, to stroke her cool thighs, to touch his lips lightly to her small rigid nipples, but no, it was uncouth to interrupt a dreamer, it was an unforgivable breach of civility. So he was content to watch her, and to love her from afar, and to savor the reawakened desire that he felt.

Carabella cried out in terror.

Her eyes opened, but she saw nothing—the sign of a sending. A shudder went rippling the length of her body. She trembled and turned to him, still asleep, still dreaming, and he held her while she whimpered and moaned, giving her dream-service, dream-comfort, protecting her against the darkness of the spirit by the strength of his arms, and at last the fury of her dream ran its course and she relaxed, limp, sweat-soaked, against his chest.

She lay still for some moments, until Valentine thought she had fallen peacefully asleep. No. She was awake, but motionless, as if contemplating her dream, confronting it, trying to carry it upward into the realm of wakefulness. Suddenly she sat upright and gasped and covered her mouth with her hand. Her eyes were wild and glassy.

"My lord!" she whispered. She backed away from him, scuttling across the bed in a strange crablike crawl, holding one arm folded above her breasts and the other as a kind of shield across her face. Her lips were quivering. Valentine reached for her, but she pulled away in horror and threw herself to the rough wooden floor, where she crouched in an eerie huddle, folded inward on herself as if trying to conceal her nakedness.

"Carabella?" he said, bewildered.

She looked up at him. "Lord—lord—please—let me be, lord—"

And bowed again, and made the starburst with her fingers, the two-handed gesture of obeisance that one makes only when one comes before the Coronal.

15

Wondering whether it might be he and not she that had been dreaming, and the dream still going on, Valentine rose, found a robe for Carabella to wear, put on one of his own garments.

Still she crouched apart from him, stunned and shattered. When he tried to comfort her she pulled away, huddling still deeper into herself.

"What is it?" he asked. "What happened, Carabella?"

"I dreamed—I dreamed that you were—" She faltered. "So real, so terrible—"

"Tell me. I'll speak your dream for you, if I can."

"It needs no speaking. It speaks of itself." She made the starburst sign at him again. In a cold, low, inflectionless voice she said, "I dreamed that you were the true Coronal Lord Valentine, that had been robbed of your power and all your memory, and set into another's body, and turned loose near Pidruid to roam and live an idle life while someone else ruled in your stead."

Valentine felt himself at the edge of a great abyss, and the ground crumbling beneath his feet.

"Was this a sending?" he asked.

"It was a sending. I know not from whom, Lady or King, but it was no dream of mine, it was something that was placed in my mind from outside. I saw you, lord—"

"Stop calling me that."

"—atop Castle Mount, and your face was the face of the other Lord Valentine, the dark-haired one we juggled for, and then you came down from the Mount to travel on the grand processional in all the lands, and while you were in the south, in my own city of Til-omon it was, they gave you a drug and seized you in your sleep and changed you into this body and cast you out, and no one was the wiser that you had been magicked out of your royal powers. And I have touched you, lord, and shared your bed, and been familiar with you in a thousand ways, and how will I be forgiven, lord?"

"Carabella?"

She cowered and trembled.

"Look up, Carabella. Look at me."

She shook her head. He knelt before her, and touched his hand to her chin. She shuddered as though he had marked her with acid. Her muscles were rigid. He touched her again.

"Raise your head," he said gently. "Look at me."

She looked up, slowly, timidly, the way one might look into the face of the sun, fearing the brightness.

He said, "I am Valentine the juggler and nothing more."

"No, lord."

"The Coronal is a dark-haired man, and my hair is golden."

"I beg you, lord, let me be. You frighten me."

"A wandering juggler frightens you?"

95

"It is not who you are that frightens me. The person you are is a friend I have come to love. It is *who you have been*, lord. You have stood beside the Pontifex and tasted the royal wine. You have walked in the highest rooms of Castle Mount. You have known the fullest power of the world. It was a true dream, lord, it was as clear and real as anything I have ever seen, a sending beyond doubt, not to be questioned. And you are rightful Coronal, and I have touched your body and you have touched mine, and it is sacrilege a thousand times over for an ordinary woman like me to approach a Coronal so closely. And I will die for it."

Valentine smiled. "If I was ever Coronal, love, it was in another body, and there's nothing holy about the one you embraced tonight. But I was never Coronal."

Her gaze rested squarely on him. Her tone was less quavering as she said, "You remember nothing of your life before Pidruid. You were unable to tell me your father's name, and you told me of your childhood in Ni-moya and didn't believe it yourself, and you guessed at a name for your mother. Is this not true?"

Valentine nodded.

"And Shanamir has told me you had much money in your purse, but had no idea what any of it was worth, and tried to pay a sausage-man with a fifty-royal piece. True?"

He nodded again.

"As though you had lived all your life at court, perhaps, and never handled money? You know so little, Valentine! You have to be taught, like a child."

"Something has happened to my memory, yes. But does that make me Coronal?"

"The way you juggle, so naturally, as though all skills are yours if you want them—the way you move, the way you hold yourself, the radiance that comes from you, the sense you give everyone that you were born to hold power—"

"Do I give that?"

"We have talked of little else, since you came among us. That you must be a fallen prince, some exiled duke perhaps. But then my dream—it leaves no doubt, lord—"

Her face was white with strain. For a moment she had overcome her awe, but only for a moment, and now she trembled again. And the awe was contagious, it seemed, for Valentine himself began to feel fear, a coldness of the skin. Was there truth in any of this? Was he an anointed Coronal that had touched hands with Tyeveras in the heart of the Labyrinth and at the summit of Castle Mount?

He heard the voice of the dream-speaker Tisana. *You have fallen from a high place, and now you must begin to climb back to it,* she had said. Impossible. Unthinkable. *Nevertheless, Lord Valentine, that ascent awaits you, and it is not I who lays it on you.* Unreal. Impossible. And yet his dreams, that brother who would have slain him, and whom he had slain instead, and those Coronals and Pontifexes moving through the chambers of his soul, and all the rest. Could it be? Impossible. Impossible.

He said, "You mustn't fear me, Carabella."

She shivered. He reached for her and she shied away, crying, "No! Don't touch me! My lord—"

Tenderly he said, "Even if I was once Coronal—and how strange and foolish that sounds to me—even if, Carabella, I am Coronal no longer, I am not in any anointed body, and what has taken place between us is no sacrilege. I am Valentine the juggler now, whoever I may have been in a former life."

"You don't understand, lord."

"I understand that a Coronal is a man like any other, only he bears more responsibilities than others, but there is nothing magical about him and nothing to fear except his power, and I have none of that. If ever I had."

"No," she said. "A Coronal is touched by the highest grace, and it never goes from him."

"Anyone can be Coronal, given the right training and the right cast of mind. One isn't bred for it. Coronals have come from every district of Majipoor, every level of society."

"Lord, you don't understand. To have been Coronal is to be touched by grace. You have ruled, you have walked on Castle Mount, you have been adopted into the line of Lord Stiamot and Lord Dekkeret and Lord Prestimion, you are brother to Lord Voriax, you are *the son of the Lady of the Isle.* And I am to think of you as an ordinary man? I am to have no fear of you?"

He stared at her in shock.

He remembered what had gone through his own mind when he stood in the streets and beheld Lord Valentine the Coronal in the procession, and had felt himself in the presence of grace and might, and had realized that to be Coronal was to become a being set apart, a personage of aura and strangeness, one who holds power over twenty billions, who carries in himself the energies of thousands of years of famed princes, who is destined to go on to the Labyrinth one day and wear the authority of the Pontifex. Incomprehensible as all this was to

97

him, it was sinking in, and he was dumbfounded and over-whelmed by it. But it was absurd. To fear himself? To sink down in awe at his own imaginary majesty? He was Valentine the juggler, and nothing more!

Carabella was sobbing. In another moment she would be hysterical. The Vroon, surely, would have some sleeping potion that would give her ease.

"Wait," Valentine said. "I'll be back in a moment. I'll ask Deliamber for something to calm you."

He darted from the room, down the hall, wondering which room was the sorcerer's. All doors were closed. He debated knocking at random, hoping not to blunder in on Zalzan Kavol, when a dry voice said out of the darkness from a point somewhere below his elbow, "Do you have trouble sleeping?"

"Deliamber?"

"Here. Close by you."

Valentine peered, narrowing his eyes, and made out the Vroon sitting cross-tentacled in the hallway in some kind of posture of meditation. Deliamber rose.

"I thought you might come in search of me soon," he said.

"Carabella has had a sending. She needs a drug to quiet her spirit. Do you have anything useful?"

"No drugs, no. A touch, though—it can be done. Come." The little Vroon glided along the corridor and into the room that Valentine shared with Carabella. She had not moved, still huddled pitifully beside the bed with her robe wrapped carelessly about her. Deliamber went to her at once; his ropy tendrils delicately enfolded her shoulders, and she loosened her tautly held muscles, and slumped as though rendered boneless. The sound of her heavy breathing was loud in the room. After a moment she looked up, calmer now, but still with a dazed, frozen look in her eyes.

She gestured toward Valentine and said, "I dreamed that he was—that he had been——" She hesitated.

"I know," said Deliamber.

"It is not true," Valentine said thickly. "I am only a juggler."

Mildly Deliamber said, "You are only a juggler *now*."

"You believe this nonsense too?"

"It was obvious from the first. When you stepped between the Skandar and me. This is the act of a king, I told myself, and I read your soul——"

"What?"

"A professional trick. I read your soul, and saw what had been done to you——"

98

"But such a thing is impossible!" Valentine protested. "To take a man's mind from his body, and put it in another's, and put another's mind in his—"

"Impossible? No," Deliamber said. "I think not. There have been tales coming out of Suvrael that studies into this art are being done at the court of the King of Dreams. For several years now the rumors of strange experiments have trickled forth."

Valentine stared sullenly at his fingertips. "It could not be done."

"So I thought too, when first I heard it. But then I considered. There are many wizardries nearly as great whose secrets I myself know, and I am only a minor wizard. The seeds of such an art have long existed. Maybe some Suvraelu sorcerer has found a way to germinate those seeds at last. Valentine, if I were you I would not reject the possibility."

"A change of bodies?" Valentine said, bewildered. "This is not my true body? Whose would it be, then?"

"Who knows? Some unlucky man struck down by accident, drowned perhaps, or choked on a piece of meat, or the victim of some evil toadstool unwisely eaten. Dead, anyway, in some manner that left his body reasonably whole; and taken within the hour of death to some secret place, there to have the Coronal's soul transplanted into the empty shell, and then another man, giving up his own body forever, quickly taking possession of the Coronal's vacated skull, possibly retaining much of the Coronal's own memory and mind in union with his own, so that he can carry on the masquerade of ruling as though he were the true monarch—"

"I accept none of this as remotely real," said Valentine stubbornly.

"Nevertheless," Deliamber said, "when I looked into your soul I saw everything even as I describe it to you now. And felt more than a little fear—in my trade one doesn't often meet Coronals, or stumble on such evidence of gross treason—and I took a moment to compose myself, and asked myself if I would not be wiser to forget what I had seen, and for a time I seriously considered it. But then I knew that I could not, that I would be whipped with monstrous dreams until the end of my days if I ignored what I knew. I told myself that there is much in the world that is in need of repair, and I would, Divine willing, be part of the fixing. And now the fixing has begun."

Valentine said, "There is nothing to it."

"For the sake of argument, say that there is," Deliamber urged. "Pretend that they came upon you in Til-omon and cast you from your body and put a usurper upon the throne. Suppose that is the case. What would you do then?"

"Nothing at all."

"No?"

"Nothing," said Valentine forcefully. "Let him be Coronal who *wants* to be Coronal. I think power is a sickness and governing is a folly for madmen. If I once dwelled on Castle Mount, so be it, but I am not there now, and nothing in my being impels me to go back there. I'm a juggler and a good one getting better, and a happy man. Is the Coronal happy? Is the Pontifex? If I have been cast out of power, I regard it as good fortune. I would not now resume the burden."

"It is what you were destined to carry."

"Destined? Destined?" Valentine laughed. "Just as fair to say that I was destined to be Coronal a little while, and then to be displaced by someone more fitting. One must be crazy to be a ruler, Deliamber, and I'm sane. The government is a burden and a chore. I would not accept it."

"You will," Deliamber said. "You've been tampered with and you are not yourself. But once a Coronal, forever a Coronal. You will be healed and come into your own again, Lord Valentine."

"Don't use that title!"

"It will be yours again," said Deliamber.

Valentine angrily shook the suggestion away. He looked toward Carabella: she was asleep on the floor, head against the bed. Carefully he lifted her and put her under the coverlet. To Deliamber he said, "It grows late, and there's been much foolishness tonight. My head hurts from all this heavy talk. Do to me what you did to her, wizard, and grant me sleep, and say no more to me of responsibilities that have never been mine and are never going to be mine. We must perform tomorrow, and I want to be rested for it."

"Very well. Get into bed."

Valentine settled in beside Carabella. The Vroon touched him lightly, then with more force, and Valentine felt his mind growing cloudy. Sleep came upon him easily, like a thick white mist sweeping up out of the ocean at twilight. Good. Good. Willingly he relinquished consciousness.

And in the night he dreamed, and there was about the dream a bright fierce glow that had the unmistakable aspect of a sending, for it was a dream vivid beyond imagining.

He saw himself crossing the harsh and terrible purple plain

100

that he had visited so often in recent slumber. This time he knew without question where the plain was: no realm of fantasy, but the distant continent of Suvrael, that lay beneath the unshielded glare of the naked sun, and these fissures in the ground were scars of summer, where what little moisture the soil contained had been sucked forth. Ugly twisted plants with swollen grayish leaves lay limp against the ground, and things with thorns and weird angular joints grew tall. Valentine walked swiftly, in the heat and the merciless biting wind and the skin-cracking dryness. He was late, overdue at the palace of the King of Dreams, where he had been hired to perform.

The palace now loomed before him, sinister, blackshadowed, all spidery turrets and jagged porticoes, a building as spiky and forbidding as the plants of the desert. More a jail than a palace it seemed, at least in its outer aspect, but inside everything was different, cool and luxurious, with fountains in the courtyards, and soft plush draperies, and a scent of flowers in the air. Servants bowed and beckoned to him, leading him to inner chambers, stripping away his sand-crusted clothes, bathing him, drying him in feathery towels, giving him fresh clothes, elegant jeweled robes, offering him chilled sherbets, icy wine of a silvery hue, morsels of unknown delicate meats, and at last bringing him to the great high-vaulted throne-room where the King of Dreams sat in state.

At a vast distance Valentine saw him enthroned: Simonan Barjazid, the malign and unpredictable Power who from this wind-swept desert territory sent his messages of terrible import all through Majipoor. He was a heavy-bodied man, his face beardless, fleshy-jowled, eyes deep-set and ringed with dark circles, and around his close-cropped stubby head he wore the golden diadem of his power, the thought-amplifying apparatus that a Barjazid had devised a thousand years ago. To Simonan's left sat his son Cristoph, fleshy like his father, and at his right hand was his son Minax, the heir, a man of lean and forbidding aspect, dark-skinned and sharp-faced, as if honed by the desert winds.

The King of Dreams, with a casual wave of his hand, ordered Valentine to begin.

It was knives he juggled, ten, fifteen of them, thin shining stilettos that would pierce right through his arm if they dropped wrongly, but he handled them with ease, juggling as only Sleet might do, or perhaps Zalzan Kavol, a virtuoso display of skill. Valentine stood still, making only the tiniest flicking motions of his hands and wrists, and the knives soared aloft and flashed with keen brilliance, coursing high

101

through the air and falling perfectly back to his waiting fingers, and as they rose and fell, rose and fell, the arc that they described took on an alteration of form, no longer a mere cascade but becoming the starburst emblem of the Coronal, blades pointing outward as they flew through the air, and abruptly, as Valentine approached the climax of his performance, the knives froze in mid-air, and hovered there just above his questing fingers, and would not descend to them.

And from behind the throne came a scowling fierce-eyed man who was Dominin Barjazid, the third of the sons of the King of Dreams, and he strode toward Valentine and with an easy contemptuous gesture swept the starburst of knives from the air, thrusting them into the sash of his robe.

The King of Dreams smiled mockingly. "You are an excellent juggler, Lord Valentine. At last you find a proper occupation."

"I am Coronal of Majipoor," Valentine replied.

"Were. Were. Were. You are a wanderer now, and fit to be nothing more."

"Lazy," said Minax Barjazid.

"Cowardly," said Cristoph Barjazid. "Idle."

"A shirker of duty," Dominin Barjazid declared.

"Your rank is forfeit," said the King of Dreams. "Your office is vacated. Go. Go and juggle, Valentine the juggler. Go, idler. Go, wanderer."

"I am Coronal of Majipoor," Valentine repeated firmly.

"No longer," said the King of Dreams. He touched his hands to the diadem at his forehead and Valentine rocked and shook as if the ground had opened at his feet, and he stumbled and fell, and when he looked up again he saw that Dominin Barjazid now was clad in the green doublet and ermine robe of a Coronal, and altered in appearance so that his face was the face of Lord Valentine and his body was the body of Lord Valentine, and out of the juggling knives that he had taken from Valentine he had fashioned the starburst crown of a Coronal, which his father Simonan Barjazid now placed upon his brow.

"See?" the King of Dreams cried. "Power passes to the worthy! Go, juggler! Go!"

And Valentine fled into the purple desert, and saw the angry swirls of a sandstorm racing toward him out of the south, and tried to escape, but the storm came at him from all directions. He roared, "I am Lord Valentine the Coronal!" but his voice was lost in the wind and he felt sand in his teeth. He was blown away. He looked toward the palace of the King of

102

Dreams, but it was no longer to be seen, and a great and shattering sense of eternal loss overwhelmed him.

He woke.

Carabella lay peacefully beside him. The first pale light of dawn was entering the room. Although it had been a monstrous dream, a sending of the most portentous sort, he felt utterly calm. For days now he had tried to deny the truth, but there was no rejecting it now, however bizarre, however fantastic it seemed. In another body he had once been Coronal of Majipoor, and body and identity had been stolen somehow from him. Could it be? A dream of such urgency could scarcely be dismissed or ignored. He sorted through the deepest places of his mind, trying to uncover memories of power, ceremonies on the Mount, glimpses of royal pomp, the taste of responsibility. Nothing. Nothing whatever. He was a juggler, and nothing more than a juggler, and he could remember no shred of his life before Pidruid: it was as if he had been born on that hillside, moments before Shanamir the herdsman had encountered him, born there with money in his purse and a flask of good red wine at his hip and a scattering of false memories in his mind.

And if it was true? If he was Coronal?

Why, then, he must go forth, for the sake of the commonwealth of Majipoor, to overthrow the tyrant and reclaim his rightful position. There would be that obligation upon him. But the notion was absurd. It created a dryness in his throat and a pounding in his chest, close to panic. To overthrow that dark-haired man of power, who had ridden in pomp through Pidruid? How could that possibly be done? How even come near to a Coronal, let alone push him from his perch? That it had been done once—maybe—was no argument that it could be done again, and by a wandering juggler, an easy-natured young man who felt no compelling urge to tackle the impossible. Besides, Valentine saw in himself so little aptitude for governing. If he had in fact been Coronal, he must have had years of training on Castle Mount, a lengthy apprenticeship in the ways and uses of power; but not a trace of that was left to him now. How could he pretend to be a monarch, with none of a monarch's skills in his head?

And yet—and yet—

He glanced down at Carabella. She was awake; her eyes were open; she was watching him in silence. The awe was still upon her, but no longer the terror.

She said, "What will you do, lord?"

"Call me Valentine, now and ever."

"If you so command me."

"I do so command you," he said.

"And tell me—Valentine: what will you do?"

"Travel with the Skandars," he replied. "Continue to juggle. Master the art more thoroughly. Keep close watch on my dreams. Bide my time, seek to comprehend. What else can I do, Carabella?" He put his hand lightly to hers, and momentarily she shrank from his touch, and then did not, but pressed her other hand above his. He smiled. "What else can I do, Carabella?"

II

The Book of the Metamorphs

The Ghayrog city of Dulorn was an architectural marvel, a city of frosty brilliance that extended for two hundred miles up and down the heart of the great Dulorn Rift. Though it covered so huge an area, the city's predominant thrust was vertical: great shining towers, fanciful of design but severely restrained in material, that rose like tapered fangs from the soft gypsum-rich ground. The only approved building material in Dulorn was the native stone of the region, a light, airy calcite of high refractive index, that glittered like fine crystal, or perhaps like diamond. Out of this the Dulornese had fashioned their sharp-tipped high-rise structures and embellished them with parapets and balconies, with enormous flamboyant flying buttresses, with soaring cantilevered ribs, with stalactites and stalagmites of sparkling facets, with lacy bridges far above the streets, with colonnades and domes and pendentives and pagodas. The juggling troupe of Zalzan Kavol, approaching the city from the west, came upon it almost exactly at noon, when the sun stood straight overhead and streaks of white flame seemed to dance along the flanks of the titanic towers. Valentine caught his breath in wonder. Such a vast place! Such a wondrous show of light and form!

Fourteen million people dwelled in Dulorn, making it one of the larger cities of Majipoor, although by no means the largest. On the continent of Alhanroel, so Valentine had heard, a city of this size would be nothing remarkable, and even here on the more pastoral continent of Zimroel there were many that matched or surpassed it. But surely no place could equal its beauty, he thought. Dulorn was cold and fiery,

105

both at once. Its gleaming spires insistently claimed one's attention, like chill, irresistible music, like the piercing tones of some mighty organ rolling out across the darkness of space.

"No country inns for us here!" Carabella cried happily. "We'll have a hotel, with fine sheets and soft cushions!"

"Will Zalzan Kavol be so generous?" Valentine asked.

"Generous?" Carabella laughed. "He has no choice. Dulorn offers only luxury accommodations. If we sleep here, we sleep in the street or we sleep like dukes: there's nothing between."

"Like dukes," Valentine said. "To sleep like dukes. Why not?"

He had sworn her, that morning before leaving the inn, to say nothing to anyone about last night's events, not to Sleet, not to any of the Skandars, not even, should she feel the need to seek one, to a dream-speaker. He had demanded the oath of silence from her in the name of the Lady, the Pontifex, and the Coronal. Furthermore he had compelled her to continue to behave toward him as though he had always been, and for the rest of his life would remain, merely Valentine the wandering juggler. In extracting the oath from her Valentine had spoken with force and dignity worthy of a Coronal, so that poor Carabella, kneeling and trembling, was as frightened of him all over again as if he were wearing the starburst crown. He felt more than a little fraudulent about that, for he was far from convinced that the strange dreams of the previous night were to be taken at face value. But still, those dreams could not lightly be dismissed, and so precautions must be taken, secrecy, guile. They came strangely to him, such maneuvers. He swore Autifon Deliamber also to the oath, wondering as he did so how much he could trust a Vroon and a sorcerer, but there seemed to be sincerity in Deliamber's voice as he vowed to keep his confidence.

Deliamber said, "And who else knows of these matters?"

"Only Carabella. And I have her bound by the same pledge."

"You've said nothing to the Hjort?"

"Vinorkis? Not a word. Why do you ask?"

The Vroon replied, "He watches you too carefully. He asks too many questions. I have little liking for him."

Valentine shrugged. "It's not hard to dislike Hjorts. But what do you fear?"

"He guards his mind too well. His aura is a dark one. Keep your distance from him, Valentine, or he'll bring you trouble."

The jugglers entered the city and made their way down broad dazzling avenues to their hotel, guided by Deliamber, who seemed to have a map of every corner of Majipoor engraved in his mind. The wagon halted in front of a tower of splendid height and awesome fantasy of architecture, a place of minarets and arched vaults and shining octagonal windows. Descending from the wagon, Valentine stood blinking and gaping in awe.

"You look as though you've been clubbed on the head," Zalzan Kavol said gruffly. "Never seen Dulorn before?"

Valentine made an evasive gesture. His porous memory said nothing to him of Dulorn: but who, once having seen this city, could forget it?

Some comment seemed called for. He said simply, "Is there anything more glorious on all of Majipoor?"

"Yes," the gigantic Skandar replied. "A tureen of hot soup. A mug of strong wine. A sizzling roast over an open fire. You can't eat beautiful architecture. Castle Mount itself isn't worth a stale turd to a starving man." Zalzan Kavol snorted in high self-approbation and, hefting his luggage, strode into the hotel.

Valentine called bemusedly after him, "But I was speaking only of the beauty of cities!"

Thelkar, usually the most taciturn of the Skandars, said, "Zalzan Kavol admires Dulorn more than you would believe. But he'd never admit it."

"He admits admiration only for Piliplok, where we were born," Gibor Haern put in. "He feels it's disloyal to say a good word for anyplace else."

"Shh!" cried Erfon Kavol. "He comes!"

Their senior brother had reappeared at the hotel door. "Well?" Zalzan Kavol boomed. "Why are you standing about? Rehearsal in thirty minutes!" His yellow eyes blazed like those of some beast of the woods. He growled, clenched his four fists menacingly, and vanished again.

An odd master, Valentine thought. Somewhere far beneath that shaggy hide, he suspected, lay a person of civility and even—who could tell?—of kindness. But Zalzan Kavol worked hard at his bearishness.

The jugglers were booked to perform at the Perpetual Circus of Dulorn, a municipal festivity that was in progress during every hour of the day and on every day of the year. The Ghayrogs, who dominated this city and its surrounding province, slept not nightly but seasonally, for two or three months at a time mainly in winter, and when they were awake were insatiable in their demand for entertainment. According to Deliamber they paid well and there were never enough itinerant performers in this part of Majipoor to satisfy their needs.

When the troupe gathered for the afternoon practice session, Zalzan Kavol announced that tonight's engagement was due to take place between the fourth and sixth hours after midnight.

Valentine was unhappy about that. This night in particular he was eager for the guidance that dreams might bring, after last night's weighty revelations. But what chance could there be for useful dreams if he spent the most fertile hours of the night on stage?

"We can sleep earlier," Carabella observed. "Dreams come at any hour. Or do you have an appointment for a sending?"

It was a sly teasing remark, for one who had trembled in awe of him not so much earlier. He smiled to show he had taken no offense—he could see self-doubt lurking just beneath her mockery of him—and said, "I might not sleep at all, knowing that I must rise so early."

"Have Deliamber touch you as he did last night," she suggested.

"I prefer to find my own path into sleep," he said.

Which he did, after a stiff afternoon of practice and a satisfying dinner of wind-dried beef and cold blue wine at the hotel. He had taken a room by himself here, and before he entered the bed—cool smooth sheets, as Carabella had said, fit for a duke—he commended his spirit to the Lady of the Isle and prayed for a sending from her, which was permissible and frequently done, though not often effective. It was the Lady now whose aid he most dearly needed. If he was in truth a fallen Coronal, then she was his fleshly mother as well as his spiritual one, and might confirm him in his identity and direct him along his quest.

As he moved into sleep, he tried to visualize the Lady and her Isle, to reach out across the thousands of miles to her and create a bridge, some spark of consciousness over that immense gap, by which she could make contact with him. He was hampered by the empty places in his memory. Presumably any adult Majipooran knew the features of the Lady and the geography of the Isle as well as he did the face of his own mother and the outskirts of his city, but Valentine's crippled mind gave him mainly blanks, which had to be filled by imagination and chance. How had she looked that night in the fireworks over Pidruid? A round smiling face, long thick hair. Very well. And the rest? Suppose the hair is black and glossy, black like that of her sons Lord Valentine and dead Lord Voriax. The eyes are brown, warm, alert. The lips full, the cheeks lightly dimpled, a fine network of wrinkles at the corners of

108

the eyes. A stately, robust woman, yes, and she strolls through a garden of lush floriferous bushes, yellow tanigales and camellias and eldirons and purple thwales, everything rich with tropical life; she pauses to pluck a blossom and fasten it in her hair, and moves on, along white marble flagstones that wind sinuously between the shrubs, until she emerges on a broad stone patio set into the side of the hill on which she dwells, looking down on the terraces upon terraces descending in wide sweeping curves toward the sea. And she looks westward to far-off Zimroel, she closes her eyes, she thinks of her lost wandering outcast son in the city of the Ghayrogs, she gathers her force and broadcasts sweet messages of hope and courage to Valentine exiled in Dulorn—

Valentine slipped into deep sleep.

And indeed the Lady came to him as he dreamed. He encountered her not on the hillside below her garden, but in some empty city in a wasteland, a ruined place of weather-beaten sandstone pillars and shattered altars. They approached one another from opposite sides of a tumbledown forum under ghostly moonlight. But her face was veiled and she kept it averted from him: he recognized her by the heavy coils of her dark hair and by the fragrance of the creamy-petaled eldiron flower beside her ear, and knew that he was in the presence of the Lady of the Isle, but he wanted her smile to warm his soul in this bleak place, he wanted the comfort of her gentle eyes, and he saw only the veil, the shoulders, the side of her head. "Mother?" he asked uncertainly. "Mother, it's Valentine! Don't you know me? Look at me, mother!"

Wraithlike she drifted past him, and disappeared between two broken columns inscribed with scenes of the deeds of the great Coronals, and was gone.

"Mother?" he called.

The dream was over. Valentine struggled to make her return, but could not. He awakened and lay peering into the darkness, seeing that veiled figure once more and searching for meaning. She hadn't recognized him. Was he so effectively transformed that not even his own mother could perceive who lay hidden in this body? Or had he never been her son, so that there was no reason for her to know him? He lacked answers. If the soul of dark-haired Lord Valentine was embedded in the body of fair-haired Valentine, the Lady of the Isle in his dream had given no sign of it, and he was as far from understanding as he had been when he closed his eyes.

What follies I pursue, he thought. What implausible speculations, what madnesses!

109

He eased himself back into sleep.

And almost at once, so it seemed, a hand touched his shoulder and someone rocked him until he came reluctantly into wakefulness. Carabella.

"Two hours after midnight," she told him. "Zalzan Kavol wants us down by the wagon in half an hour. Did you dream?"

"Inconclusively. And you?"

"I remained awake," she answered. "It seemed safest. Some nights one prefers not to dream." She said timidly, as he began to dress, "Will I share your room again, Valentine?"

"Would you like to?"

"I have given oath to act with you as I acted before—before I knew— Oh, Valentine, I was so frightened! But yes. Yes, let's be companions again, and even lovers. Tomorrow night!"

"What if I am Coronal?"

"Please. Don't ask such questions."

"What if I am?"

"You've ordered me to call you Valentine and to regard you as Valentine. This I'll do, if you'll let me."

"Do you believe I'm Coronal?"

"Yes," she whispered.

"It no longer frightens you?"

"A little. Just a little. You still seem human to me."

"Good."

"I've had a day to get used to things. And I'm under an oath. I must think of you as Valentine. I swore by the Powers to that." She grinned impishly. "I swore an oath to the Coronal that I would pretend you are not Coronal, and so I must be true to my pledge, and treat you casually, and call you Valentine, and show no fear of you, and behave as though nothing has changed. And so I can share your bed tomorrow night?"

"Yes."

"I love you, Valentine."

He pulled her lightly to him. "I thank you for overcoming your fear. I love you, Carabella."

"Zalzan Kavol will be angry if we're late," she said.

2

The Perpetual Circus was housed in a structure altogether opposite from those most typical of Dulorn: a giant flat unadorned drum of a building, perfectly circular and no more than ninety feet high, that stood by itself on a huge tract of open land on the eastern perimeter of the city. Within, a great central space provided an awesome setting for the stage, and around it ran the seating ring, tier upon tier in concentric circles rising to the roof.

The place could hold thousands, perhaps hundreds of thousands. Valentine was startled to see how nearly full it was, here at what was for him the middle of the night. Looking outward into the audience was difficult, for the stage-lights were in his eyes, but he was able to perceive enormous numbers of people sitting or sprawling in their seats. Nearly all were Ghayrogs, though he caught sight of the occasional Hjort or Vroon or human making a late night of it. There were no places on Majipoor entirely populated by one race—ancient decrees of the government, going back to the earliest days of heavy non-human settlement, forbade such concentrations except on the Metamorph reservation—but the Ghayrogs were a particularly clannish lot, and tended to cluster together in and around Dulorn up to the legal maximum. Though warm-blooded and mammalian, they had certain reptilian traits that made them unlovable to most other races: quick-flicking forked red tongues, grayish scaly skin of a thick, polished consistency, cold green unblinking eyes. Their hair had a medusoid quality, black succulent strands that coiled and writhed unsettlingly, and their odor, both sweet and acrid at once, was not charming to non-Ghayrog nostrils.

Valentine's mood was subdued as he moved out with the troupe onto the stage. The hour was all wrong: his body-cycles were at low ebb, and though he had had enough sleep, he had no enthusiasm for being awake just now. Once again he carried the burden of a difficult dream. That rejection by the Lady, that inability to make contact with her, what did it signify? When he was only Valentine the juggler, significance was insignificant to him: each day had a path of its own, and he had no worries about larger patterns, only to increase the skill of hand and eye from one day to the next. But now that these ambiguous and disturbing revelations had been visited upon him he was forced to consider dreary long-range matters of purpose and destiny and the route on which he was bound. He had no liking for that. Already he tasted a keen nostalgic sorrow for the good old times of the week before last, when he had wandered busy Pidruid in happy aimlessness.

The demands of his art quickly lifted him out of this brood-

111

ing. There was no time, under the glare of the spotlights, to think of anything except the work of performing.

The stage was colossal, and many things were happening on it at once. Vroon magicians were doing a routine involving floating colored lights and bursts of green and red smoke; an animal-trainer just beyond had a dozen fat serpents standing on their tails; a dazzling group of dancers with grotesquely attenuated bodies sprayed in many-faceted silver glowstuff did austere leaps and carries; several small orchestras in widely separated regions played the tinny and tootling wood-wind music beloved of the Ghayrogs; there was a one-finger acrobat, a high-wire woman, a levitator, a trio of glassblowers engaged in fashioning a cage for themselves, an eel-eater, and a platoon of berserk clowns, along with much more beyond Valentine's range of vision. The audience, slouching and lounging out there in the half-darkness, had an easy time watching all this, for, Valentine realized, the giant stage was in gentle motion, turning slowly on hidden bearings, and in the course of an hour or two would make a complete circuit, presenting each group of performers in turn to every part of the auditorium. "It all floats on a pool of quicksilver," Sleet whispered. "You could buy three provinces with the value of the metal."

With so much competition for the eyes of the onlookers, the jugglers had brought forth some of their finest effects, which meant that the novice Valentine was largely excluded, left to toss clubs to himself and occasionally to feed knives or torches to the others. Carabella was dancing atop a silver globe two feet in diameter that rolled in irregular circles as she moved: she juggled five spheres that glowed with brilliant green light. Sleet had mounted stilts, and rose even taller than the Skandars, a tiny figure far above everyone, coolly flipping from hand to hand three huge red-and-black-speckled eggs of the moleeka-hen, that he had bought at market that evening. If he dropped an egg from so great a height, the splash would be conspicuous and the humiliation enormous, but never since Valentine had known him had Sleet dropped anything, and he dropped no eggs tonight. As for the six Skandars, they had arranged themselves in a rigid star-pattern, standing with their backs to one another, and were juggling flaming torches. At carefully coordinated moments each would hurl a torch back-ward over his outer shoulder to his brother at the opposite side of the star. The interchanges were made with wondrous preci-sion, the trajectories of the flying torches were flawlessly timed to create splendid crisscrossing patterns of light, and not

112

a hair on any Skandar's hide was scorched as they casually snatched from the air the firebrands that came hurtling past them from their unseen partners.

Round and round the stage they went, performing in stints of half an hour at a stretch, with five minutes to relax in the central well just below the stage, where hundreds of other off-duty artists gathered. Valentine longed to be doing something more challenging than his own little elementary juggle, but Zalzan Kavol had forbidden it: he was not yet ready, the Skandar said, though he was doing excellently well for a novice.

Morning came before the troupe was allowed to leave the stage. Payment here was by the hour, and hiring was governed by silent response-meters beneath the seats of the audience, monitored by cold-eyed Ghayrogs in a booth in the well. Some performers lasted only a few minutes before universal boredom or disdain banished them, but Zalzan Kavol and his company, who had been guaranteed two hours of work, remained on stage for four. They would have been kept for a fifth if Zalzan Kavol had not been dissuaded by his brothers, who gathered around him for a brief and intense argument.

"His greed," Carabella said quietly, "will lead him to embarrass himself yet. How long does he think people can throw those torches around before someone slips up? Even Skandars get tired eventually."

"Not Zalzan Kavol, from the looks of it," Valentine said.

"*He* may be a juggling machine, yes, but his brothers are mortal. Rovorn's timing is starting to get ragged. I'm glad they had the courage to make a stand." She smiled. "And I was getting pretty tired too."

So successfully were the jugglers received in Dulorn that they were hired for four additional days. Zalzan Kavol was elated—the Ghayrogs gave their entertainers high wages—and declared a five-crown bonus for everyone.

All well and good, Valentine thought. But he had no wish to settle in indefinitely among the Ghayrogs. After the second day, restlessness began to make him chafe.

"You wish to be moving on," Deliamber said—a statement, not a question.

Valentine nodded. "I begin to glimpse the shape of the road ahead of me."

"To the Isle?"

"Why do you bother speaking with people," Valentine said lightly, "if you see everything within their minds?"

"I did no mind-peeking this time. Your next move is obvious enough."

"Go to the Lady, yes. Who else can truly tell me who I am?"

"You still have doubts," Deliamber said.

"I have no evidence other than dreams."

"Which speak powerful truths."

"Yes," Valentine said, "but dreams can be parables, dreams can be metaphors, dreams can be fantasies. It's folly to speak them literally without confirmation. And the Lady can give confirmation, or so I hope. How far is it to the Isle, wizard?"

Deliamber briefly closed his large golden eyes.

"Thousands of miles," he said. "We are now perhaps a fifth of the way across Zimroel. You must make your way eastward through Khyntor or Velathys, and around the territory of the Metamorphs, and then perhaps by riverboat via Ni-moya to Piliplok, where the pilgrim-ships leave for the Isle."

"How long will that take?"

"To reach Piliplok? At our present pace, about fifty years. Wandering with these jugglers, stopping here and there for a week at a time—"

"What if I left the troupe and went on my own?"

"Six months, possibly. The river journey is swift. The overland section takes much longer. If we had airships as they do on other worlds it would be a matter of a day or two to Piliplok, but of course we do without many devices on Majipoor that other people enjoy."

"Six months?" Valentine frowned. "And the cost, if I hired a vehicle and a guide?"

"Perhaps twenty royals. You'll juggle a long time to earn that much."

"When I get to Piliplok," Valentine said, "what then?"

"You book passage to the Isle. The voyage is a matter of weeks. When you reach the Isle you take lodging on the lowest terrace and begin the ascent."

"The ascent?"

"A course of prayer, purification, and initiation. You move upward from terrace to terrace until you reach the Terrace of Adoration, which is the threshold to Inner Temple. You know nothing of any of this?"

"My mind, Deliamber, has been meddled with."

"Of course."

"At Inner Temple, then?"

"You are now an initiate. You serve the Lady as an acolyte,

114

and if you seek an audience with her, you undergo special rites and await the summoning dream."

Uneasily Valentine said, "How long does this entire process take, the terraces, the initiation, the service as acolyte, the summoning dream?"

"It varies. Five years, sometimes. Ten. Forever, conceivably. The Lady has no time for each and every pilgrim."

"And there's no more direct way of gaining audience?"

Deliamber uttered the thick coughing sound that was his laugh. "What? Knock on the temple door, cry out that you are her changeling son, demand entry?"

"Why not?"

"Because," the Vroon said, "the outer terraces of the Isle are designed as filters to keep such things from happening. There are no easy channels of communication to the Lady, and deliberately so. It would take you years."

"I'd find a way." Valentine stared levelly at the little wizard. "I could reach her mind, if I were on the Isle. I could cry out to her, I could persuade her to summon me. Perhaps."

"Perhaps."

"With your assistance it could be done."

"I feared that was coming," said Deliamber dryly.

"You have some skill at making sendings. We could reach, if not the Lady herself, then those close to her. Step by step, drawing ourselves closer to her, cutting short the interminable process on the terraces—"

"It could be done, possibly," Deliamber said. "Do you believe I'm minded to make the pilgrimage with you, though?"

Valentine regarded the Vroon in silence for a long time.

"I'm certain of it," he said finally. "You play at reluctance, but you've engineered my every motive to impel me toward the Isle. With you at my side. Am I right? Eh, Deliamber? You're more eager to have me get there than I am myself."

"Ah," the sorcerer said. "It comes out now!"

"Am I right?"

"If you resolve to go to the Isle, Valentine, I will be at your side. But are you resolved?"

"Sometimes."

"Intermittent resolutions lack potency," said Deliamber.

"Thousands of miles. Years of waiting. Toil and intrigue. Why do I want to do this, Deliamber?"

"Because you are Coronal, and must be again."

"The first may be true, though I have mighty doubts of it. The second is open to question."

Deliamber's look was crafty. "You prefer to live under the rule of a usurper?"

"What's the Coronal and his rule to me? He's half a world away on Castle Mount and I'm a wandering juggler." Valentine extended his fingers and stared at them as though he had never seen his hands before. "I could spare myself much effort if I remained with Zalzan Kavol and let the other, whoever he may be, keep the throne. Suppose he's a wise and just usurper? Where's the benefit for Majipoor, if I do all this work merely to put myself back in his place? Oh, Deliamber, Deliamber, do I sound like a king at all, when I say these things? Where's my lust for power? How can I ever have been a ruler, when I so obviously don't care about what's happened?"

"We've spoken of this before. You have been tampered with, my lord. Your spirit as well as your face has been changed."

"Even so. My royal nature, if ever I had one, is altogether gone from me. That lust for power—"

"Twice you've used the phrase," Deliamber said. "Lust has nothing to do with it. A true king doesn't lust for power: responsibility lusts for him. And takes him, and possesses him. This Coronal is new, he has done little yet but make the grand processional, and already the people grumble at his early decrees. And you ask if he will be wise and just? How can any usurper be just? He is a criminal, Valentine, and he rules already with a criminal's guilty fears eating at his dreams, and as time goes on those fears will poison him and he will be a tyrant. Can you doubt that? He will remove anyone who threatens him—will kill, even, if need be. The poison that courses in his veins will enter the life of the planet itself, will affect every citizen. And you, sitting here looking at your fingers, do you see no responsibility? How can you talk of *sparing yourself much effort?* As if it hardly matters who is the king. It matters very much who is the king, my lord, and you were chosen and trained for it, and not by lottery. Or do you believe anyone can become Coronal?"

"I do. By random stroke of fate."

Deliamber laughed harshly. "Possibly that was true nine thousand years ago. There is a dynasty, my lord."

"An adoptive dynasty?"

"Precisely. Since the time of Lord Arioc, and maybe even earlier, Coronals have been chosen from among a small group of families, no more than a hundred clans, all of them dwellers on Castle Mount and close participants in the government.

116

The next Coronal is already in training, though only he and a few advisers know who he is, and two or three replacements for him must also have been chosen. But now the line is broken, now an intruder has pushed his way in. Nothing but evil can come of that."

"What if the usurper is simply the heir-in-waiting, who grew tired of waiting?"

"No," said Deliamber. "Inconceivable. No one deemed qualified to be Coronal would overthrow a lawfully consecrated prince. Besides, why the mummery of pretending to be Lord Valentine, if he is another?"

"I grant you that."

"Grant me also this: that the person atop Castle Mount now has neither right nor qualification for being there, and must be cast down, and you are the only one who can do it."

Valentine sighed. "You ask a great deal."

"History asks a great deal," said Deliamber. "History has demanded, on a thousand worlds across many thousands of years, that intelligent beings choose between order and anarchy, between creation and destruction, between reason and unreason. And the forces of order and creation and reason have been focused always in a single leader, a king, if you will, or a president, a chairman, a grand minister, a generalissimo, use whatever word you wish, a monarch by some name or other. Here it is the Coronal, or more accurately the Coronal ruling as the voice of the Pontifex who was once Coronal, and it matters, my lord, it matters very much, who is to be Coronal and who is not to be Coronal."

"Yes," Valentine said. "Perhaps."

"You'll go on wavering from *yes* to *perhaps* a long while," said Deliamber. "But *yes* will govern, in the end. And you will make the pilgrimage to the Isle, and with the Lady's blessing you will march on Castle Mount and take your rightful place."

"The things you say fill me with terror. If ever I had the ability to rule, if ever I was given the training for it, these things have been burned from my mind."

"The terror will fade. Your mind will be made whole in the passing of time."

"And time passes, and here we sit in Dulorn, to amuse the Ghayrogs."

Deliamber said, "Not much longer. We'll find our way eastward, my lord. Have faith in that."

There was something contagious about Deliamber's assurance. Valentine's hesitations and uncertainties were gone—for

117

the moment. But when Deliamber had departed, Valentine gave way to uncomfortable contemplation of certain hard realities. Could he simply hire a couple of mounts and set off for Piliplok with Deliamber tomorrow? What about Carabella, who had suddenly become very important to him? Abandon her here in Dulorn? And Shanamir? The boy was attached to Valentine, not to the Skandars: he neither could nor would be left. There was the cost, then, of a journey for four across nearly all of vast Zimroel, food, lodging, transportation, then the pilgrim ship to the Isle, and what then of expenses on the Isle while he schemed to gain access to the Lady? Autifon Deliamber had guessed it might cost twenty royals for him to travel alone to Piliplok. The cost, for the four of them, or for the five if Sleet were added, though Valentine had no idea if Sleet would care to come, might run a hundred royals or more, a hundred fifty perhaps to the lowest terrace of the Isle. He sorted through his purse. Of the money he had had upon him when he found himself outside Pidruid, he had more than sixty royals left, plus a royal or two that he had earned with the troupe. Not enough, not nearly enough. Carabella, he knew, was almost without money; Shanamir had dutifully returned to his family the hundred sixty royals from the sale of his mounts; and Deliamber, if he had any wealth, would not in old age be hauling himself through the countryside under contract to a crowd of ruffian Skandars.

So, then? Nothing to do but wait, and plan, and hope that Zalzan Kavol intended a generally eastward route. And save his crowns and bide his time, until the moment was ripe for going to the Lady.

3

A few days after their departure from Dulorn, purses bulging with the generous Ghayrog pay, Valentine drew Zalzan Kavol aside to ask him about the direction of travel. It was a gentle late-summer day, and here, where they were camped for lunch along the eastern slope of the Rift, a purple mist enfolded everything, a low thick clammy cloud that took its delicate lavender color from pigments in the air, for there were deposits of skuvva-sand just north of here and the winds were constantly stirring the stuff aloft.

Zalzan Kavol looked uncomfortable and irritable in this

118

weather. His gray fur, purpled now by droplets of mist, was clumped in comic bunches, and he rubbed at it, trying to restore it to its proper nap. Probably not the best moment for such a conference, Valentine realized, but it was too late: the issue had been broached.

Zalzan Kavol said hollowly, "Which of us is the leader of this troupe, Valentine?"

"You are, beyond question."

"Then why do you try to govern me?"

"I?"

"In Pidruid," the Skandar said, "you asked me to go next to Falkynkip, for the convenience of your herdsman squire's family honor, and I remind you that you forced me to hire the herdsman boy in the first place, though he is no juggler and never will be. In these things I yielded, I know not why. There was also the matter of your interfering in my quarrel with the Vroon—"

"My interference had benefit," Valentine pointed out, "as you yourself admitted at the time."

"True. But interference of itself is unfamiliar to me. Do you understand that I am absolute master of this troupe?"

Valentine shrugged lightly. "No one disputes that."

"But do you understand it? My brothers do. They are aware that a body can have only one head—unless it's a Su-Suheris body, and we're not talking of those—and here I am the head, it is from my mind that plans and instructions flow, and mine alone." Zalzan Kavol flashed an austere smile. "Is this tyranny? No. This is simple efficiency. Jugglers can never be democrats, Valentine. One mind designs the patterns, one alone, or there is chaos. Now what do you want with me?"

"Only to know the shape of our route."

With barely suppressed anger Zalzan Kavol said, "Why? You are in our employ. You go where we go. Your curiosity is misplaced."

"It doesn't seem that way to me. Some routes are more useful to me than others."

"Useful? To you? You have plans? You told me you had no plans!"

"I do now."

"What do you plan, then?"

Valentine took a deep breath. "Ultimately to make the pilgrimage to the Isle, and become a devotee of the Lady. Since the pilgrim-ships sail from Piliplok, and all of Zimroel lies between us and Piliplok, it would be valuable to me to know

119

whether you plan to go in some other direction, let's say down to Velathys, or maybe back to Til-omon or Narabal, instead of—"

"You are discharged from my service," Zalzan Kavol said icily.

Valentine was astounded. *"What?"*

"Terminated. My brother Erfon will give you ten crowns as your settlement. I want you on your way within an hour."

Valentine felt his cheeks growing hot. "This is totally unexpected! I merely asked—"

"You merely asked. And in Pidruid you merely asked, and in Falkynkip you merely asked, and next week in Mazadone you would merely ask. You annoy my tranquillity, Valentine, and this cancels out your promise as a juggler. Besides, you are disloyal."

"Disloyal? To what? To whom?"

"You hire on with us, but secretly mean to use us as the vehicle to get you to Piliplok. Your commitment to us is insincere. I call that treachery."

"When I hired on with you, I had nothing else in mind but to travel with your troupe wherever you went. But things have changed, and now I see reason to make the pilgrimage."

"Why did you allow things to change? Where's your sense of duty to your employers and teachers?"

"Did I hire on with you for life?" Valentine demanded. "Is it treachery to discover that one has a goal more important than tomorrow's performance?"

"That diversion of energy," said Zalzan Kavol, "is what leads me to be rid of you. I want you thinking about juggling every hour of the day, and not about the departure date of pilgrim-ships from Shkunibor Pier."

"There would be no diversion of energy. When I juggle, I juggle. And I'd resign from the troupe when we approached Piliplok. But until then—"

"Enough," Zalzan Kavol said. "Pack. Go. Take yourself swiftly to Piliplok and sail to the Isle, and may you fare well. I have no further need of you."

The Skandar seemed altogether serious. Scowling in the purple mist, slapping at the soggy patches in his pelt, Zalzan Kavol swung heavily around and began to walk away. Valentine trembled in tension and dismay. The thought of leaving now, of traveling alone to Piliplok, left him aghast; and beyond that he felt part of this troupe, more so than he had ever been aware, a member of a close-knit team, and would not willingly be sundered. At least not now, not yet, while he could remain with Carabella and Sleet and even the Skandars, whom he respected without liking, and continue to increase his skills of eye and hand while moving eastward toward whatever strange destiny Deliamber seemed to have in mind for him.

"Wait!" Valentine called. "What about the law?"

Zalzan Kavol glared over his shoulder. "Which law?"

"The one requiring you to keep three human jugglers in your employ," said Valentine.

"I will hire the herdsman boy in your place," Zalzan Kavol retorted, "and teach him whatever skills he can learn." And he stalked off.

Valentine stood stunned. His conversation with Zalzan Kavol had taken place in a grove of small golden-leafed plants that evidently were psychosensitive: for, he noticed now, the plants had folded their intricate compound leaflets in the course of the quarrel, and looked shriveled and blackened for ten feet on all sides of him. He touched one. It was crisp and lifeless, as though it had been torched. He felt abashed at being a party to such destruction.

"What happened?" Shanamir asked, appearing suddenly and staring in wonder at the withered foliage. "I heard yelling. The Skandar—"

"Has fired me," said Valentine vacantly, "because I asked him which way we were going next, because I admitted to him that I intended eventually to journey on pilgrimage to the Isle and wondered if his route would suit my purpose."

Shanamir gaped. "You are to make the pilgrimage? I never knew!"

"A recent decision."

"Why, then," the boy cried, "we'll make it together, won't we? Come, we'll pack our things, we'll steal a couple of mounts from these Skandars, we'll leave at once!"

"Do you mean that?"

"Of course!"

"It's thousands of miles to Piliplok. You and I, and no one to guide us, and—"

"Why not?" Shanamir asked. "Look, we ride to Khyntor, and there we take a riverboat to Ni-moya, and on from there down the Zimr to the coast, and at Piliplok we buy passage on the pilgrim-ship, and—what's wrong, Valentine?"

"I belong with these people. I'm learning an art from them. I—I—" Valentine broke off in confusion. Was he a juggler-in-training, or a Coronal-in-exile? Was it his purpose to plod along with shaggy Skandars, yes, with Carabella and Sleet

121

also, or was it incumbent on him to move by the fastest means toward the Isle, and then with the Lady's help toward Castle Mount? He was confounded by these uncertainties.

"The cost?" Shanamir said. "Is that what worries you? You had fifty royals and more in Pidruid. You must have some of that left. I have a few crowns myself. If we need more, you can work as a juggler on the riverboat, and I could curry mounts, I suppose, or—"

"Where are you planning to go?" said Carabella, coming abruptly upon them out of the forest. "And what has happened to these sensitivos here? Is there trouble?"

Briefly Valentine told her of his talk with Zalzan Kavol.

She listened in silence, with her hand to her lips; and, when he was done, she darted off abruptly, without a word, in the direction Zalzan Kavol had taken.

"Carabella?" Valentine called. But already she was out of sight.

"Let's go," said Shanamir. "We can be out of here in half an hour, and by nightfall we'll be miles away. Look, you pack our things. I'll take two of the mounts and lead them around through the woods, down the slope toward the little lake we passed when we came in, and you meet me down there by the grove of cabbage trees." Shanamir waved his hands impatiently. "Hurry! I've got to get the mounts while the Skandars aren't around, and they might come back at any minute!"

Shanamir vanished into the forest. Valentine stood frozen. To leave now, so suddenly, with so little time to prepare himself for this upheaval? And what of Carabella? Not even a goodbye? Deliamber? Sleet? He started toward the wagon to gather his few possessions, halted, plucked indecisively at the dead leaves of the poor sensitivo plants, as though by pruning the withered stalks he could instantly induce new growth. Gradually he compelled himself to see the brighter side. This was a disguised blessing. If he stayed with the jugglers, it would delay by months or even years the confrontation with reality that obviously lay in store for him. And Carabella, if any truth lay in the shape of things that began to emerge, could be no part of that reality, anyway. So, then, it behooved him to shrug away his shock and distress, and take to the highway, bound for Piliplok and the pilgrim-ships. Come, he told himself, get moving, collect your things. Shanamir's waiting by the cabbage trees with the mounts. But he could not move.

And then Carabella came bounding toward him, face aglow.

"It's all fixed," she said. "I got Deliamber to work on him. You know, a little trick here and there, a bit of a touch with the tip of a tentacle—the usual wizardry. He's changed his mind. Or we've changed it for him."

Valentine was startled by the intensity of his feeling of relief. "I can stay?"

"If you'll go to him and ask forgiveness."

"Forgiveness for what?"

Carabella grinned. "That doesn't matter. He took offense, the Divine only knows why! His fur was wet. His nose was cold. Who knows? He's a Skandar, Valentine, he has his own weird sense of what's right and wrong, he's not required to think the way humans do. You got him angry and he discharged you. Ask him politely to take you back, and he will. Go on, now. Go."

"But—but—"

"But what? Are *you* going to stand on pride now? Do you want to be rehired or don't you?"

"Of course I do."

"Then go," Carabella said. She seized him by the arm and gave a little tug, to budge him as he stood there faltering and fumbling, and as she did so it must have occurred to her whose arm it was she was tugging, for she sucked in her breath and let go of him and moved away, hovering as if on the verge of kneeling and making the starburst symbol. "Please?" she said softly. "Please go to him, Valentine? Before he changes his mind again? If you leave the troupe, I'll have to leave it too, and I don't want to. Go. Please."

"Yes," said Valentine. She led him over the spongy mist-moistened ground to the wagon. Zalzan Kavol sat sulkily on the steps, huddling in a cloak in the damp, close warmth of the purple mist. Valentine approached him and said straightforwardly, "It was not my intent to anger you. I ask your pardon."

Zalzan Kavol made a low growling sound, almost below the threshold of audibility.

"You are a nuisance," the Skandar said. "Why am I willing to forgive you? From now on you will not speak to me unless I have spoken to you first. Understood?"

"Understood, yes."

"You will make no attempt to influence the route we travel."

"Understood," said Valentine.

"If you irritate me again, you will be terminated without severance pay and you will have ten minutes to get out of my

123

sight, no matter where we are, even if we are camped in the midst of a Metamorph reservation and nightfall is coming, do you understand?"

"I understand," Valentine said.

He waited, wondering if he would be asked to bow, to kiss the Skandar's hairy fingers, to grovel in obeisance. Carabella, standing to one side, seemed to be holding her breath, as though expecting some explosion to come from the spectacle of a Power of Majipoor begging forgiveness from an itinerant Skandar juggler.

Zalzan Kavol regarded Valentine disdainfully, as he might have regarded a cold fish of uncertain vintage presented to him in a congealed sauce for dinner. Acidulously he said, "I am not required to provide my employees with information of no concern to them. But I will tell you, anyway, that Piliplok is my native city, and I return there from time to time, and it is my purpose to arrive there eventually. How soon it will be depends on what engagements I can arrange between here and there; but be informed that our route lies generally eastward, although there may be some departures from that path, for we have a livelihood to earn. I hope this pleases you. When we reach Piliplok, you may resign from the troupe if you still have it in mind to undergo the pilgrimage, but if you induce any members of the troupe other than the herdsman boy to accompany you on that voyage, I will ask an injunction against it in the Coronal's Court, and prosecute you to the fullest. Understood?"

"Understood," said Valentine, though he wondered whether he would deal honorably with the Skandar on this point.

"Lastly," said Zalzan Kavol, "I ask you to remember that you are paid a good many crowns a week, plus expenses and bonuses, to perform in this troupe. If I detect you filling your mind with thoughts of the pilgrimage, or of the Lady and her servants, or of anything else but how to throw things into the air and catch them in a theatrically suitable manner, I'll revoke your employment. In these last few days you've already seemed unacceptably moody, Valentine. Change your ways. I need three humans for this troupe, but not necessarily the ones I have now. Understood?"

"Understood," Valentine said.

"Go, then."

Carabella said, as they walked away, "Was that terribly unpleasant for you?"

"It must have been terribly pleasant for Zalzan Kavol."

"He's just a hairy animal!"

124

"No," said Valentine gravely. "He's a sentient being equal to ourselves in civil rank, and never speak of him as anything else. He only *looks* like an animal." Valentine laughed, and after a moment Carabella laughed with him, a trifle edgily. He said, "In dealing with people who are enormously touchy on matters of honor and pride, I think it's wisest to be accommodating to their needs, especially if they're eight feet tall and provide you with your wages. At this point I need Zalzan Kavol far more than he needs me."

"And the pilgrimage?" she asked. "Are you really planning to undergo it? When did you decide that?"

"In Dulorn. After conversation with Deliamber. There are questions about myself I must answer, and if anyone can help me with those answers, it's the Lady of the Isle. So I'll go to her, or try to. But all that's far in the future, and I've sworn to Zalzan Kavol not to think of such things." He took her hand in his. "I thank you, Carabella, for repairing matters between Zalzan Kavol and me. I wasn't at all ready to be discharged from the troupe. Or to lose you so soon after I had found you."

"Why do you think you would have lost me," she asked, "if the Skandar had insisted on letting you go?"

He smiled. "I thank you for that, too. And now I should go down to the cabbage-tree grove, and tell Shanamir to return the mounts that he's stolen for us."

4

In the next few days the landscape began to grow surpassingly strange, and Valentine had more cause for gladness that he and Shanamir had not tried to proceed by themselves.

The district between Dulorn and the next major city, Mazadone, was relatively thinly populated. Much of it, according to Deliamber, was a royal forest preserve. That bothered Zalzan Kavol, for jugglers would not find employment in forest preserves, nor, for that matter, in low-lying swampy farmland occupied mainly by rice paddies and lusavender-seed plantations; but there was no choice but to follow the main forest highway, since nothing more promising lay to the north or south. On they went, in generally humid and drizzly weather, through a region of villages and farms and occasional thick stands of the fat-trunked comical cabbage trees, short and squat, with massive white fruits sprouting directly from their

125

bark. But as Mazadone Forest Preserve drew closer, the cabbage trees gave way to dense thickets of singing ferns, yellow-fronded and glassy of texture, that emitted piercing discordant sounds whenever they were approached, shrill high-pitched bings and twangs and bleeps, nasty screeches and scrapes. That would not have been so bad—the unmelodious song of the ferns had a certain raucous charm, Valentine thought—but the fern thickets were inhabited by bothersome small creatures far more disagreeable than the plants, little toothy winged rodents known as dhiims, that came flapping up out of hiding every time the proximity of the wagon touched off the fern-song. The dhiims were about the length and breadth of a small finger, and were covered by fine golden fur; they arose in such numbers that they clouded the air, and swarmed about indignantly, sometimes nipping with their tiny but effective incisors. The thickly furred Skandars up front in the driver's seat largely ignored them, merely swatting at them when they clustered too close, but the usually stolid mounts were bothered, and balked in the traces several times. Shanamir, sent out to placate the animals, suffered half a dozen painful bites; and as he scurried back into the wagon a good many dhiims entered with him. Sleet took a frightening nip on his cheek near his left eye, and Valentine, beset by dozens of infuriated creatures at once, was bitten on both arms. Carabella methodically destroyed the dhiims with a stiletto used in the juggling act, skewering them with singleminded determination and great skill, but it was an ugly half hour before the last of them was dead.

Beyond the territory of the dhiims and the singing ferns, the travelers entered into a region of curious appearance, a broad open area of meadows out of which rose hundreds of black granite needles just a few feet wide and perhaps eighty feet high, natural obelisks left behind by some unfathomable geological event. To Valentine it was a region of delicate beauty; to Zalzan Kavol it was merely one more place to pass quickly through, en route to the next festival where jugglers might be hired; but to Autifon Deliamber it seemed something else, a place giving sign of possible menace. The Vroon leaned forward, staring keenly for a long moment through the wagon's window at the obelisks. "Wait," he called finally to Zalzan Kavol.

"What is it?"

"I want to check something. Let me out."

Zalzan Kavol grunted impatiently and tugged on the reins. Deliamber scrambled from the wagon, moving in his supple ropy-limbed Vroonish glide toward the odd rock formations, disappearing among them, coming occasionally into view as he zigzagged from one thin pinnacle to the next.

When he returned, Deliamber looked glum and apprehensive.

"See there," he said, pointing. "Do you make out vines far up, stretched from that rock to that, and from that to that, and on over to there? And some small animals crawling about on the vines?"

Valentine could just barely discern a network of slender glossy red lines high on the pinnacles, forty or fifty feet or more above the ground. And yes, half a dozen slim apelike beasts moving from obelisk to obelisk like acrobats, swinging freely by hands and feet.

"It looks like birdnet vine," said Zalzan Kavol in a puzzled tone.

"It is," Deliamber said.

"But why do they not stick to it? What are those animals, anyway?"

"Forest-brethren," the Vroon answered. "Do you know of them?"

"Tell me."

"They are troublesome. A wild tribe, native to central Zimroel, not usually found this far west. The Metamorphs are known to hunt them for food or perhaps for sport, I'm not sure which. They have intelligence, though of a low order, something greater than dogs or droles, less than civilized folk. Their gods are dwikka-trees; they have some sort of tribal structure; they know how to use poisoned darts, and cause problems for wayfarers. Their sweat contains an enzyme that makes them immune to the stickiness of birdnet vine, which they employ for many purposes."

"If they annoy us," Zalzan Kavol declared, "we will destroy them. Onward!"

Once past the region of the obelisks they saw no further traces of forest-brethren that day. But on the next, Deliamber once again spied ribbons of birdnet vine in the treetops, and a day after that the travelers, now deep in the forest preserve, came upon a grove of trees of truly colossal mass, which, the Vroonish wizard said, were dwikkas, sacred to the forest-brethren. "This explains their presence so far from Metamorph territory," said Deliamber. "These must be a migrating band, come west to pay homage in this forest."

The dwikkas were awesome. There were five of them, set far apart in otherwise empty fields. Their trunks, covered with bright red bark that grew in distinct plates with deep fissures between, were greater in diameter than the long axis of Zalzan Kavol's wagon; and though they were not particularly tall, no higher than a hundred feet or so, their mighty limbs, each as thick as the trunk of an ordinary tree, spread out to such a distance that whole legions might take shelter under the dwikka's gigantic canopy. On stalks as thick as a Skandar's thigh sprouted the leaves, great leathery black things the size of a house, that drooped heavily, casting an impenetrable shade. And from each branch hung suspended two or three elephantine yellowish fruits, bumpy irregular globes a good twelve or fifteen feet in width. One of them had recently fallen, it appeared, from the nearest tree, perhaps on a rainy day when the ground was soft, for its weight had dug a shallow crater in which it lay, split apart, revealing large glistening many-angled black seeds in the mass of scarlet pulp.

Valentine could understand why these trees were gods to the forest-brethren. They were vegetable monarchs, imperious, commanding. He was quite willing to sink to his knees before them himself.

Deliamber said, "The fruit is tasty. Intoxicating, in fact, to the human metabolism and to some others."

"To Skandars?" asked Zalzan Kavol.

"To Skandars, yes."

Zalzan Kavol laughed. "We'll try it. Erfon! Thelkar! Gather pieces of the fruit for us!"

Nervously Deliamber said, "The talismans of the forest-brethren are embedded in the ground before each tree. They've been here recently, and might return, and if they find us desecrating the grove they will attack, and their darts can kill."

"Sleet, Carabella, stand guard to the left. Valentine, Shanamir, Vinorkis, over there. Cry out if you see even one of the little apes." Zalzan Kavol gestured at his brothers. "Collect the fruit for us," he ordered. "Haern, you and I will defend the situation from here. Wizard, remain with us." Zalzan Kavol took two energy-throwers from a rack and gave one to his brother Haern.

Deliamber clucked and muttered in disapproval. "They move like ghosts, they come out of nowhere—"

"Enough," said Zalzan Kavol.

Valentine took up a lookout position fifty yards ahead of the wagon, and peered warily beyond the last of the dwikka-trees into the dark, mysterious forest. He expected to have a fatal dart come winging toward him at any moment. It was an uncomfortable feeling. Erfon Kavol and Thelkar, carrying a big wicker basket between them, made their way toward the fallen fruit, pausing every few steps to look in all directions. When they reached it, they began cautiously to edge around to the far side of it.

"What if a bunch of forest-brethren are sitting behind that thing right now," Shanamir asked, "having a little feast? Suppose Thelkar stumbles over them and—"

A tremendous and terrifying whoop and a roar, such as might come from an outraged bull-bidlak interrupted in its mating, erupted from the vicinity of the dwikka-fruit. Erfon Kavol, looking panic-stricken, came galloping back into view and rushed toward the wagon, followed a moment later by an equally daunted Thelkar.

"Beasts!" cried a ferocious voice. "Pigs and fathers of pigs! Rape a woman enjoying her lunch, will you? I'll teach you to rape! I'll fix you so you'll never rape again! Stand your ground, hairy animals! Stand, I say, stand!"

Out from behind the dwikka-fruit came the largest human woman Valentine had ever seen, a creature so vast she was a proper companion to these trees, and seemed perfectly in scale with them. She stood close to seven feet tall, perhaps more, and her gigantic body was a mountain of flesh rising on legs as sturdy as pillars. A close-fitting shirt and gray leather trousers were her garments, and the shirt was open nearly to the waist, revealing huge jouncing globes of breasts the size of a man's head. Her hair was a mop of wild orange curls; her blazing eyes were pale piercing blue. She carried a vibration-sword of imposing length, which she swung about her with such force that Valentine, a hundred feet away, could feel the breeze it stirred. Her cheeks and breasts were smeared with the scarlet juice of the dwikka-fruit's meat.

In weighty strides she thundered toward the wagon, crying rape and demanding vengeance.

"What is this?" Zalzan Kavol asked, looking as bemused as Valentine had ever seen him. He glared at his brothers. "What did you do to her?"

"We never touched her," said Erfon Kavol. "We were looking for forest-brethren back there, and Thelkar came upon her unexpectedly, and stumbled, and caught her arm to steady himself—"

"You said you never touched her," Zalzan Kavol snapped.

"Not *that* way. It was only an accident, a stumble."

"Do something," Zalzan Kavol said hastily to Deliamber, for the giant woman was almost upon them now.

129

The Vroon, looking pale and cheerless, stepped in front of the wagon and lifted many tentacles toward the apparition that towered, almost Skandar-high, above him.

"Peace," Deliamber said mildly to the onrushing giantess. "We mean you no harm." As he spoke he gestured with manic purposefulness, casting some sort of pacifying spell that manifested itself as a faint bluish glow in the air before him. The huge woman appeared to respond to it, for she slowed her advance and managed to come to a halt a few feet from the wagon.

There she stood, sullenly whipping the vibration-sword back and forth at her side. After a moment she pulled her shirt together in front, fastening it inadequately. Glowering at the Skandars, she indicated Erfon and Thelkar and said in a deep booming voice, "What were those two planning to do to me?"

Deliamber replied, "They had simply gone to collect pieces of the dwikka-fruit. See the basket they were carrying?"

"We had no idea you were there," Thelkar murmured. "We walked around behind the fruit to check for hidden forest-brethren, is all."

"And fell upon me like the oaf you are, and would have violated me if I hadn't been armed, eh?"

"I lost my footing," Thelkar insisted. "There was no intention of molesting you. I was on guard for forest-brethren, and when instead I encountered someone of your size—"

"What? More insults?"

Thelkar took a deep breath. "That is to say—it was unexpected when I—when you—"

Erfon Kavol said, "We had no thought—"

Valentine, who had been observing all of this in gathering amusement, now came over and said, "If they were minded for rape, would they have attempted it in front of so large an audience? We are of your kind here. We wouldn't have tolerated it." He indicated Carabella. "That woman is as fierce in her way as you are in yours, my lady. Be assured that if these Skandars had tried to do you any injury, she alone would have prevented it. It was a simple misunderstanding, nothing more. Put down your weapon and feel no peril among us."

The giantess looked somewhat soothed by the courtliness and charm of Valentine's speech. Slowly she lowered the vibration-sword, allowing it to go inert, and fastened it at her hip.

"Who are you?" she asked querulously. "What is all this procession traveling here?"

130

"My name is Valentine, and we are traveling jugglers, and this Skandar is Zalzan Kavol, the master of our troupe."

"And I am Lisamon Hultin," the giantess responded, "who hires as bodyguard and warrior, though there's been little of that lately."

"And we are wasting time," said Zalzan Kavol, "and should be on our way, if we are properly forgiven for having intruded on your repose."

Lisamon Hultin nodded brusquely. "Yes, be on your way. But are you aware this is dangerous territory?"

"Forest-brethren?" Valentine asked.

"All over the place. The woods are thick with them, just ahead."

"And yet you feel no fear of them?" Deliamber remarked.

"I speak their language," Lisamon Hultin said. "I have negotiated a private treaty with them. Do you think I'd dare be munching on dwikka-fruit otherwise? I may be fat but not between the ears, little sorcerer." She stared at Zalzan Kavol. "Where are you bound?"

"Mazadone," replied the Skandar.

"Mazadone? Is there work for you in Mazadone?"

"We hope to learn that," Zalzan Kavol said.

"There's nothing for you there. I come from Mazadone just now. The duke is lately dead and three weeks of mourning have been decreed in the entire province. Or do you jugglers perform at funerals?"

Zalzan Kavol's face darkened. "No work in Mazadone? No work in the whole province? We have expenses to meet! We have already gone unpaid since Dulorn! What will we do?"

Lisamon Hultin spat out a chunk of dwikka-fruit pulp. "That's no sorrow of mine. Anyway, you can't get to Mazadone."

"What?"

"Forest-brethren. They've blocked the road a few miles ahead. Asking tribute of wayfarers, I think, something absurd like that. They won't let you through. Lucky if they don't fill you with their darts."

"They'll let us through!" Zalzan Kavol exclaimed.

The warrior-woman shrugged. "Not without me, they won't."

"You?"

"I told you, I speak their language. I can buy you a way through, with a little haggling. Are you interested? Five royals ought to do it."

131

"What use do forest-brethren have for money?" the Skandar asked.

"Oh, not for them," she said airily. "Five for me. I'll offer other things to them. Deal?"

"Absurd. Five royals is a fortune!"

"I don't bargain," she said evenly. "There is honor in my profession. Good luck on the road ahead." She favored Thelkar and Erfon Kavol with a frigid stare. "If you wish, you may have some of the dwikka-fruit before you go. But better not be munching on it when you meet the brethren!"

She turned with massive dignity and walked to the great fruit beneath the tree. Drawing her sword, she hacked off three large chunks and shoved them disdainfully toward the two Skandars, who somewhat uneasily nudged them into the wicker basket.

Zalzan Kavol said, "Into the wagon, all of you! We have a long way to Mazadone!"

"You won't travel far today," said Lisamon Hultin, and released a gale of derisive laughter. "You'll be back here soon enough—if you survive!"

5

The poisoned darts of the forest-brethren preoccupied Valentine for the next few miles. Sudden horrible death held no appeal for him, and the woods here were thick and mysterious, with vegetation of a primordial sort, fern-trees with silvery spore-sheaths and glassy-textured horsetails a dozen feet high and thickets of bunch-fungus, pale and pocked with brown craters. In a place of such strangeness anything might happen, and probably would.

But the juice of the dwikka-fruit eased tensions mightily. Vinorkis sliced up one huge chunk and passed cubes of it around: it was piercingly sweet of flavor and granular in texture, dissolving quickly against the tongue, and whatever alkaloids it contained went swiftly through the blood to the brain, faster than the strongest wine. Valentine felt warm and cheerful. He slouched back in the passenger cabin, one arm around Carabella, the other around Shanamir. Up front, Zalzan Kavol evidently was more relaxed as well, for he stepped up the pace of the wagon, pushing it to a rollicking speed not much in keeping with his dour, cautious practices. The usually self-contained Sleet, slicing up more dwikka-fruit, began to sing a rowdy song:

> Lord Barhold came to Belka Strand
> With crown and chain and pail.
> He meant to force old Gornup's hand
> And make him eat his—

The wagon pulled suddenly to a halt, so suddenly that Sleet lurched forward and came close to falling into Valentine's lap, and a slab of soft wet dwikka-fruit smacked into Valentine's face. Laughing and blinking, he wiped himself clean. When he could see again, he found that everyone was gathered at the front of the wagon, peering out between the Skandars on the driver's seat.

"What is it?" he asked.

"Birdnet vine," said Vinorkis, sounding quite sober. "Blocking the road. The giantess told the truth."

Indeed. The sticky, tough red vine had been laced from fern-tree to fern-tree at a dozen angles, forming a sturdy and resilient chain both broad and thick. The forest flanking the road was altogether impenetrable here; the birdnet vine sealed the highway. There was no way the wagon could proceed.

"How hard is it to cut?" Valentine asked.

Zalzan Kavol said, "We could do it in five minutes with energy-throwers. But look there."

"Forest-brethren," Carabella said softly.

They were everywhere, swarming in the woods, hanging from every tree although getting no closer to the wagon than a hundred yards or so. They seemed less like apes at close range, more like savages of an intelligent species. They were small, naked beings with smooth blue-gray skin and thin limbs. Their hairless heads were narrow and long, with sloping flat foreheads, and their elongated necks were flimsy and fragile. Their chests were shallow, their frames meatless and bony. All of them, both men and women, wore dart-blowers of reeds strapped to their hips. They pointed at the wagon, chattered to one another, made little hissing whistling sounds.

"What do we do?" Zalzan Kavol asked Deliamber.

"Hire the warrior-woman, I would think."

"Never!"

"In that case," said the Vroon, "let us prepare to camp in the wagon until the end of our days, or else go back toward Dulorn and find some other road to travel."

"We could parley with them," the Skandar said. "Go out

133

there, wizard. Speak to them in dream-language, monkey-language, Vroon-language, any words that will work. Tell them we have urgent business in Mazadone, that we must perform at the funeral of the duke, and they will be severely punished if they delay us."

Deliamber said calmly to Zalzan Kavol, "*You* tell them."

"I?"

"Whichever of us steps out of the wagon first is apt to be skewered by their darts. I prefer to yield the honor. Perhaps they will be intimidated by your great size and hail you as their king. Or perhaps not."

Zalzan Kavol's eyes blazed. "You refuse?"

"A dead sorcerer," Deliamber said, "will not guide you very far on this planet. I know something of these creatures. They are unpredictable and very dangerous. Pick another messenger, Zalzan Kavol. Our contract doesn't require me to risk my life for you."

Zalzan Kavol made his growling sound of displeasure, but he let the issue drop.

Stymied, they sat tight for long minutes. The forest-brethren began to descend from the trees, remaining at a considerable distance from the wagon. Some of them danced and cavorted now in the roadway, setting up a ragged, tuneless chanting, formless and atonal, like the droning of huge insects.

Erfon Kavol said, "A blast from the energy-thrower would scatter them. It wouldn't take long for us to incinerate the birdnet vine. And then—"

"And then they'd follow us through the forest, pumping darts at us whenever we showed our faces," said Zalzan Kavol. "No. There may be thousands of them all around us. They see us: we can't see them. We can't hope to win by using force against them." Moodily the big Skandar wolfed down the last of the dwikka-fruit. Again he sat in silence for a few moments, scowling, occasionally shaking fists at the tiny folk blocking the path. At length he said in a bitter rumble, "Mazadone is still some days' journey away, and that woman said there was no work to be had there anyway, so we'll have to go on to Borgax or maybe even Thagobar, eh, Deliamber? Weeks more before we earn another crown. And here we sit, trapped in the forest by little apes with poisoned darts. Valentine?"

Startled, Valentine said, "Yes?"

"I want you to slip out of the wagon the back way and

return to that warrior-woman. Offer her three royals to get us out of this."

"Are you serious?" Valentine asked.

Carabella, with a little gasp, said, "No! I'll go instead!"

"What's this?" said Zalzan Kavol in irritation.

"Valentine is—he is—he gets lost easily, he becomes distracted, he—he might not be able to find—"

"Foolishness," the Skandar said, waving his hands impatiently. "The road is straight. Valentine is strong and quick. And this is dangerous work. You have skills too valuable to risk, Carabella. Valentine will have to go."

"Don't do it," Shanamir whispered.

Valentine hesitated. He had not much liking for the idea of leaving the relative safety of the wagon to travel on foot alone in a forest infested with deadly creatures. But someone had to do it, and not one of the slow, ponderous Skandars, nor the splay-footed Hjort. To Zalzan Kavol he was the most expendable member of the troupe; perhaps he was. Perhaps he was expendable even to himself.

He said, "The warrior-woman told us her price was five royals."

"Offer her three."

"And if she refuses? She said it was against her honor to bargain."

"Three," Zalzan Kavol said. "Five royals is an immense fortune. Three is an absurd enough price to pay."

"You want me to run miles through a dangerous forest to offer someone an inadequate price for a job that absolutely must be done?"

"Are you refusing?"

"Pointing out folly," said Valentine. "If I'm to risk my life, there must be the hope of achievement. Give me five royals for her."

"Bring her back here," the Skandar said, "and I'll negotiate with her."

"Bring her back yourself," said Valentine.

Zalzan Kavol considered that. Carabella, tense and pale, sat shaking her head. Sleet warned Valentine with his eyes to hold his position. Shanamir, red-faced, trembling, seemed about ready to burst forth with anger. Valentine wondered if this time he had pushed the Skandar's always volatile temper too far.

Zalzan Kavol's fur stirred as though spasms of rage were contorting his powerful muscles. He seemed to be holding himself in check by furious effort. Doubtless Valentine's latest

135

show of independence had enraged him almost to the boiling point; but there was a glint of calculation in the Skandar's eyes, as though he were weighing the impact of Valentine's open defiance against the need he had for Valentine to do this service. Perhaps he was even asking himself whether his thrift might be foolishness here.

After a long tense pause Zalzan Kavol let out his breath in an explosive hiss and, scowling, reached for his purse. Sourly he counted out the five gleaming one-royal pieces.

"Here," he grunted. "And hurry."

"I'll go as fast as I can."

"If running is too great a burden," said Zalzan Kavol, "go out the front way, and ask the forest-brethren if you may have leave to unhitch one of our mounts, and ride back to her in comfort. But do it quickly, whichever you choose."

"I'll run," Valentine replied, and began to unfasten the wagon's rear window.

His shoulder blades itched in anticipation of the thwock of a dart between them the moment he emerged. But no thwocks came, and soon he was running lightly and easily down the road. The forest that had looked so sinister from the wagon looked much less so now, the vegetation unfamiliar but hardly ominous, not even the pock-marked bunch-fungus, and the fern-trees seemed nothing but elegant as their spore-sheaths glistened in the afternoon sun. His long legs moved in steady rhythm, and his heart pumped uncomplainingly. The running was relaxing, almost hypnotic, as soothing to him as juggling.

He ran a long while, paying no heed to time and distance, until it seemed he surely must have gone far enough. But how could he have run unknowingly past anything so conspicuous as five dwikka-trees? Had he carelessly taken some fork in the road and lost the path? It seemed unlikely. So he simply ran on, and on and on, until eventually the monstrous trees, with the great fallen fruit beneath the closest of them, came into view.

The giantess seemed nowhere around. He called out her name, he peered behind the dwikka-fruit, he made a circuit of the entire grove. No one. In dismay he contemplated running onward, back halfway to Dulorn, maybe, to find her. Now that he had stopped, he felt the effects of his jog: muscles were protesting in his calves and thighs, and his heart was thumping in an unpleasant way. He had no appetite for more running just now.

But then he caught sight of a mount tethered a few hundred yards back of the dwikka-tree grove—an oversize beast, broad-backed and thick-legged, suitable for carrying Lisamon Hultin's bulk. He went to it, and looked beyond, and saw a roughly hacked trail leading toward running water.

The ground sloped off sharply, and gave way to a jagged cliff. Valentine peered over the edge. A stream emerged from the forest here and tumbled down the face of the cliff to land in a rock basin perhaps forty feet below; and alongside that pool, sunning herself after a bath, was Lisamon Hultin. She lay face down, her vibration-sword close beside her. Valentine looked with awe at her wide muscular shoulders, her powerful arms, the massive columns of her legs, the vast dimpled globes of her buttocks.

He called to her.

She rolled over at once, sat up, looked about her.

"Up here," he said. She glanced in his direction and discreetly he turned his head away, but she only laughed at his modesty. Rising, she reached for her clothing in a casual, unhurried way.

"You," she said. "The gentle-spoken one. Valentine. You can come down here. I'm not afraid of you."

"I know you dislike being disturbed at your repose," Valentine said mildly, picking his way down the steep rocky path. By the time he had reached the bottom she had her trousers on and was struggling to pull her shirt over her mighty breasts. He said, "We came to the roadblock."

"Of course."

"We need to get on to Mazadone. The Skandar has sent me to hire you." Valentine produced Zalzan Kavol's five royals. "Will you help us?"

She eyed the shining coins in his hand.

"The price is seven and a half."

Valentine pursed his lips. "You told us five, before."

"That was before."

"The Skandar has given me only five royals to pay you."

She shrugged and began to unfasten her shirt. "In that case, I'll continue to sunbathe. You may stay or not, as you wish, but keep your distance."

Quietly Valentine said, "When the Skandar tried to beat down your price, you refused to bargain, telling him that there is honor in your profession. My notion of honor would require me to abide by a price once I quoted it."

She put her hands to her hips and laughed, a laugh so vociferous he thought it would blow him away. He felt like a plaything beside her: she outweighed him by more than a hundred pounds, and stood at least a head taller. She said,

137

"How brave you are, or how stupid! I could destroy you with a slap of my hand, and you stand here lecturing me about faults of honor!"

"I think you wouldn't harm me."

She studied him with new interest. "Perhaps not. But you take risks, fellow. I offend easily and I do more damage than I intend, sometimes, when I lose my temper."

"Be that as it may. We have to get to Mazadone, and only you can call off the forest-brethren. The Skandar will pay five royals and no more." Valentine knelt and put the five brilliant coins in a row on the rock by the pool. "However, I have a little money of my own. If it'll settle the issue, I'll add that to the fee." He fished in his purse until he found a royal piece, found another, laid a half-royal beside it, and looked up hopefully.

"Five will be enough," Lisamon Hultin said.

She scooped up Zalzan Kavol's coins, left Valentine's, and went scrambling up the path.

"Where's your mount?" she asked, untethering her own.

"I came on foot."

"On foot? On *foot*? You ran all that way?" She peered at him. "What a loyal employee you are! Does he pay you well, to give such service and take such risks?"

"Not particularly."

"No, I suppose not. Well, climb on behind me. This beast would never even notice a little extra weight."

She clambered onto the mount, which, though large for its kind, seemed dwarfed and frail once she was on it. Valentine, after some hesitation, got on behind her and clamped his hands around her waist. For all her bulk there was nothing fat about her: solid muscle girdled her hips.

The mount cantered out of the dwikka-tree grove and down the road. The wagon, when they came to it, was still shut up tight, and forest-brethren still danced and chattered in and around the trees behind the blockade.

They dismounted. Lisamon Hultin walked without sign of fear to the front of the wagon and called something to the forest-brethren in a high, shrill voice. There was a reply of similar pitch from the trees. Again she called; again she was answered; then a long, feverish colloquy ensued, with many brief expostulations and interjections.

She turned to Valentine. "They will open the gate for you," she said. "For a fee."

"How much?"

"Not money. Services."

"What services can we render for forest-brethren?"

She said, "I told them you are jugglers, and I explained what it is that jugglers do. They'll let you proceed if you'll perform for them. Otherwise they intend to kill you and make toys of your bones, but not today, for today is a holy day among the forest-brethren and they kill no one on holy days. My advice to you is to perform for them, but do as you wish." She added, "The poison that they use does not act particularly quickly."

6

Zalzan Kavol was indignant—perform for monkeys? perform without fee?—but Deliamber pointed out that the forest-brethren were somewhat higher on the evolutionary scale than monkeys, and Sleet observed that they had not had their practice today and the workout would do them some good, and Erfon Kavol clinched the matter by arguing that it would not really be a free performance, since it was being traded for passage through this part of the forest, which these creatures effectively controlled. And in any case they had no choice in the matter: so out they came, with clubs and balls and sickles, but not the torches, for Deliamber suggested that the torches might frighten the forest-brethren and cause them to do unpredictable things. In the clearest space they could find they began to juggle.

The forest-brethren watched raptly. Hundreds upon hundreds of them trooped from the forest and squatted alongside the road, staring, nibbling their fingers and their slender prehensile tails, making soft chittering comments to one another. The Skandars interchanged sickles and knives and clubs and hatchets, Valentine whirled clubs aloft, Sleet and Carabella performed with elegance and distinction, and an hour went by, and another, and the sun began to slink off in the direction of Pidruid, and still the forest-brethren watched, and still the jugglers juggled, and nothing was done about unwinding the birdnet vine from the trees.

"Do we play for them all night?" Zalzan Kavol demanded.

"Hush," said Deliamber. "Give no offense. Our lives are in their hands."

They used the opportunity to rehearse new routines. The Skandars polished an interception number, stealing throws from one another in a way that was comical in beings so huge and fierce. Valentine worked with Sleet and Carabella on the interchange of clubs. Then Sleet and Valentine threw clubs rapidly at one another while first Carabella and then Shanamir turned handsprings daringly between them. And so it went, on into a third hour. "These forest-brethren have had five royals' worth of entertainment from us already," Zalzan Kavol grumbled. "When does this end?"

"You juggle very capably," said Lisamon Hultin. "They enjoy your show immensely. I enjoy it myself."

"How pleasant for you," Zalzan Kavol said sourly.

Twilight was approaching. Apparently the coming of darkness signaled some shift in mood for the forest-brethren, for without warning they lost interest in the performance. Five of them, of presence and authority, came forward and set about ripping down the barricade of birdnet vine. Their small sharp-fingered hands dealt easily with the stuff, that would have tangled anyone else hopelessly in snarls of sticky fiber. In a few minutes the way was clear, and the forest-brethren, chattering, faded into the darkness of the woods.

"Have you wine?" Lisamon Hultin asked, as the jugglers gathered their gear and prepared to move along. "All this watching has given me a powerful thirst."

Zalzan Kavol began to say something miserly about supplies running low, but too late: Carabella, with a sharp glare at her employer, produced a flask. The warrior-woman tipped it back, draining it in one long lusty gulp. She wiped her lips with the sleeve of her shirt and belched.

"Not bad," she said. "Dulornese?"

Carabella nodded.

"Those Ghayrogs know how to drink, snakes that they are! You won't find anything like it in Mazadone."

Zalzan Kavol said, "Three weeks of mourning, you say?"

"No less. All public amusements forbidden. Yellow mourning-stripes on every door."

"Of what did the duke die?" Sleet asked.

The giantess shrugged. "Some say it was a sending from the King, that frightened him to death, and others that he choked on a gobbet of half-cooked meat, and still others that he indulged in an excess with three of his concubines. Does it matter? He's dead, that's not to be disputed, and the rest is trifles."

"And no work to be had," said Zalzan Kavol gloomily.

"No, nothing as far as Thagobar and beyond."

"Weeks without earnings," the Skandar muttered.

Lisamon Hultin said, "It must be unfortunate for you. But I

know where you could find good wages just beyond Thago-bar."

"Yes," Zalzan Kavol said. "In Khyntor, I suppose."

"Khyntor? No, times are lean there, I hear. A poor harvest of clennet-puffs this summer, and the merchants have tightened credit, and I think there's little money to be spent on entertainments. No, I speak of Ilirivoyne."

"*What?*" Sleet cried, as though he had been struck by a dart.

Valentine sorted through his knowledge, came up with nothing, and whispered to Carabella, "Where's that?"

"Southeast of Khyntor."

"But southeast of Khyntor is the Metamorph territory."

"Exactly."

Zalzan Kavol's heavy features took on an animated cast for the first time since encountering the roadblock. He swung round and said, "What work is there for us in Ilirivoyne?"

"The Shapeshifters hold festival there next month," Lisamon Hultin replied. "There'll be harvest-dancing and contests of many kinds and merrymaking. I've heard that sometimes troupes from the imperial provinces enter the reservation and earn huge sums at festival time. The Shapeshifters regard imperial money lightly and are quick to dispose of it."

"Indeed," Zalzan Kavol said. The chilly light of greed played across his face. "I had heard the same thing, long ago. But it never occurred to me to test its truth."

"You'll test it without me!" Sleet cried suddenly.

The Skandar glanced at him. "Eh?"

Sleet showed intense strain, as though he had been doing his blind-juggling routine all afternoon. His lips were taut and bloodless, his eyes were fixed and unnaturally bright. "If you go to Ilirivoyne," he said tensely, "I will not accompany you."

"I remind you of our contract," said Zalzan Kavol.

"Nevertheless. Nothing in it obliges me to follow you into Metamorph territory. Imperial law is not valid there, and our contract lapses the moment we enter the reservation. I have no love for the Shapeshifters and refuse to risk my life and soul in their province."

"We'll talk about this later, Sleet."

"My response will be the same later."

Zalzan Kavol looked about the circle. "Enough of this. We've lost hours here. I thank you for your help," he said without warmth to Lisamon Hultin.

"I wish you a profitable journey," she said, and rode off into the forest.

141

Because they had consumed so much time at the roadblock, Zalzan Kavol chose to keep the wagon moving through the night, contrary to his usual practice. Valentine, exhausted by a lengthy run and hours of juggling, and feeling some lingering haziness from the dwikka-fruit he had eaten, fell asleep sitting up in the back of the wagon and knew nothing more until morning. The last he heard was a forceful discussion of the notion of venturing into Metamorph territory: Deliamber suggesting that the perils of Ilirivoyne had been exaggerated by rumor, Carabella noting that Zalzan Kavol would be justified in prosecuting Sleet, and expensively, if he broke his contract, and Sleet insisting with almost hysterical conviction that he dreaded the Metamorphs and would not go within a thousand miles of them. Shanamir and Vinorkis, too, expressed fear of the Shapeshifters, who they said were sullen, tricky, and dangerous.

Valentine woke to find his head nestled cozily in Carabella's lap. Bright sunlight streamed into the wagon. They were camped in some broad and pleasant park, a place of sweeping blue-gray lawns and narrow sharp-angled trees of great height. Low rounded hills surrounded everything.

"Where are we?" he asked.

"Outskirts of Mazadone. The Skandar drove like a madman all night long." Carabella laughed prettily. "And you slept like one who has been dead a long time."

Outside, Zalzan Kavol and Sleet were engaged in heated argument a few yards from the wagon. The small white-haired man seemed half again his normal size with rage. He paced back and forth, pounded fist into palm, shouted, scuffed at the ground, once seemed at the verge of launching a physical attack on the Skandar, who seemed, for Zalzan Kavol, remarkably calm and forbearing. He stood with all his arms folded, looming high over Sleet and making only an occasional quiet cold reply to his outbursts.

Carabella turned to Deliamber. "This has continued long enough. Wizard, can you intervene, before Sleet says something really rash?"

The Vroon looked melancholy. "Sleet has a terror of the Metamorphs that goes beyond all reason. Perhaps it's connected with that sending of the King that he had, long ago in Narabal, that turned his hair white in a single evening. Or perhaps not. In any case, it may be wisest for him to withdraw from the troupe, whatever the consequences."

"But we need him!"

142

"And if he thinks terrible things will befall him in Iliri-voyne? Can we ask him to subject himself to such fears?"

"Perhaps I can calm him," Valentine said.

He rose to go outside, but at that instant Sleet, face dark and set, stormed into the wagon. Without a word the compact little juggler began to stuff his few possessions into a pack; then he swept out, his fury unabated, and striding past the motionless Zalzan Kavol, began to march at a startling clip toward the low hills to the north.

Helplessly they watched him. No one made a move to pursue until Sleet was nearly out of sight. Then Carabella said, "I'll go after him. I can get him to change his mind."

She ran off toward the hills.

Zalzan Kavol called to her as she went past him, but she ignored him. The Skandar, shaking his head, summoned the others from the wagon.

"Where is she going?" he asked.

"To try to bring Sleet back," said Valentine.

"Hopeless. Sleet has chosen to leave the troupe. I'll see to it that he regrets his defection. Valentine, greater responsibilities now will fall upon you, and I'll add five crowns a week to your salary. Is this acceptable?"

Valentine nodded. He thought of Sleet's quiet, steady presence in the troupe, and felt a pang of loss.

The Skandar continued, "Deliamber, I have, as you might suspect, decided to seek work for us among the Metamorphs. Are you familiar with the routes of Ilirivoyne?"

"I have never been there," the Vroon answered. "But I know where it is."

"And which is the quickest way?"

"To Khyntor from here, I think, and then eastward by riverboat some four hundred miles, and at Verf there's a road due south into the reservation. Not a smooth road, but wide enough for the wagon, so I believe. I will study it."

"And how long will it take for us to reach Ilirivoyne, then?"

"Perhaps a month, if there are no delays."

"Just in time for the Metamorph festival," said Zalzan Kavol. "Perfect! What delays do you anticipate?"

Deliamber said, "The usual. Natural disasters, breakdown of the wagon, local disturbances, criminal interferences. Things are not as orderly in mid-continent as they are on the coasts. There are risks involved in traveling in those parts."

"You bet there are!" boomed a familiar voice. "Protection is what you need!"

The formidable presence of Lisamon Hultin suddenly was among them.

She looked rested and relaxed, not at all as though she had ridden all night, nor was her mount particularly spent. In a puzzled voice Zalzan Kavol said, "How did you get here so quickly?"

"Forest trails. I'm big, but not so big as your wagon, and I can take back ways. Going to Ilirivoyne, are you?"

"Yes," said the Skandar.

"Good. I knew you would. And I've come after you to offer my services. I'm out of work, you're going into dangerous parts—it's a logical partnership. I'll escort you safely to Ilirivoyne, that I guarantee!"

"Your wages are too high for us."

She grinned. "You think I always get five royals for a little job like that? I charged so much because you made me angry, tromping in on me while I was trying to have a private feed. I'll get you to Ilirivoyne for another five, no matter how long it takes."

"Three," said Zalzan Kavol sternly.

"You never learn, do you?" The giantess spat almost at the Skandar's feet. "I don't haggle. Get yourselves to Ilirivoyne without me, and good fortune attend you. Though I doubt it will." She winked at Valentine. "Where are the other two?"

"Sleet refused to go to Ilirivoyne. He went roaring out of here ten minutes ago."

"I don't blame him. And the woman?"

"She went after him, to talk him into returning. Up there." Valentine pointed to the path winding up into the hills.

"There?"

"Between that hill and that."

"Into the mouthplant grove?" There was disbelief in Lisamon Hultin's voice.

"What is that?" Valentine asked.

Deliamber, at the same moment, said, "Mouthplants? Here?"

"The park is dedicated to them," the giantess declared. "But there are warning signs at the foot of the hills. They went up that trail? On foot? The Divine protect them!"

Exasperated, Zalzan Kavol said, "They can eat him twice, for all I care. But I need her!"

"As do I," said Valentine. To the warrior-woman he said, "Possibly if we rode up there now, we could find them before they enter the mouthplant grove."

"Your master feels he can't afford my services."

"Five royals?" Zalzan Kavol said. "From here to Iliri-voyne?"

"Six," she said coolly.

"Six, then. But get them back! Get her, at least!"

"Yes," said Lisamon Hultin in disgust. "You people have no sense, but I have no work, so we deserve each other, per-haps. Take one of those mounts," she said to Valentine, "and follow me."

"You want him to go?" Zalzan Kavol wailed. "I'll have no humans at all in my troupe!"

"I'll bring him back," the giantess said. "And, with luck, the other two also." She clambered onto her mount. "Come," she said.

7

The path into the hills was gently sloping, and the blue-gray grass looked soft as velvet. It was hard to believe that any-thing menacing dwelled in this lovely park. But as they reached the place where the path began to rise at a sharper angle, Lisamon Hultin grunted and indicated a bare wooden stake set in the ground. Beside it, half hidden by grass, was a fallen sign. Valentine saw only the words

DANGER
NO FOOT TRAFFIC
BEYOND THIS

in large red letters. Sleet, in his rage, had not noticed; Cara-bella, perhaps in her urgent haste, had failed to see the sign also, or else had ignored it.

Quickly now the path climbed, and just as quickly it leveled off on the far side of the hills, in a place that was no longer grassy but densely wooded. Lisamon Hultin, riding just ahead of Valentine, slowed her mount to a walk as they entered a moist and mysterious copse where trees with slender, strong-ribbed trunks grew at wide intervals, shooting up like bean-stalks to create a thickly interlaced canopy far overhead.

"See, there, the first mouthplants," the giantess said. "Filthy things! If I had the keeping of this planet, I'd put the torch to all of them, but our Coronals tend to be nature-lovers, so it seems, and preserve them in royal parks. Pray that your friends have had the wisdom to stay clear of them!"

On the bare forest floor, in the open spaces between the trees, grew stemless plants of colossal size. Their leaves, four or five inches broad and eight or nine feet in length, sharp-toothed along their sides and metallic of texture, were arranged in loose rosettes. At the center of each gaped a deep cup a foot in diameter, half filled with a noxious-looking greenish fluid, out of which a complex array of stubby organs projected. It seemed to Valentine that there were things like knife-blades in there, and paired grinders that could come together nastily, and still other things that might have been delicate flowers partly submerged.

"These are flesh-eating plants," Lisamon Hultin said. "The forest floor is underlain by their hunting tendrils, which sense the presence of small animals, capture them, and carry them to the mouth. Observe."

She guided her mount toward the closest of the mouth-plants. When the animal was still at least twenty feet from it, something like a live whip suddenly began to writhe in the decaying forest duff. It broke free of the ground to coil itself with a terrifying snapping sound around the animal's pastern just above the hoof. The mount, placid as usual, sniffed in puzzlement as the tendril began to exert pressure, trying to pull it toward the gaping mouth in the plant's central cup.

The warrior-woman, drawing her vibration-sword, leaned down and sliced quickly through the tendril. It snapped back as the tension was released, almost to the cup itself, and at the same time a dozen other tendrils rose from the ground, flailing the air furiously on all sides of the plant.

She said, "The mouthplant lacks the strength to tug anything as big as a mount into its maw. But the mount wouldn't be able to break free. In time it would weaken and die, and then it might be pulled in. One of these plants would live for a year on that much meat."

Valentine shuddered. Carabella, lost in a forest of such things? Her lovely voice stilled forever by some ghastly plant? Her quick hands, her sparkling eyes—no. No. The thought chilled him.

"How can we find them?" he asked. "It might already be too late."

"How are they called?" the giantess asked. "Shout their names. They must be near."

"Carabella!" Valentine roared with desperate urgency. *"Sleet! Carabella!"*

A moment later he heard a faint answering shout; but Lisamon Hultin had heard it first, and was already going forward.

Valentine saw Sleet ahead, down on one knee on the forest floor, and that knee dug in deep to keep him from being dragged into a mouthplant by the tendril that encircled his other ankle. Crouching behind him was Carabella, her arms thrust through his and hooked tight around his chest in a desperate attempt to hold him back. All about them excited tendrils belonging to neighboring plants snapped and coiled in frustration. Sleet held a knife, with which he sawed uselessly at the powerful cable that held him; and there was a trail of skid-marks in the duff, showing that he had already been drawn four or five feet toward the waiting mouth. Inch by inch he was losing the struggle for his life.

"Help us!" Carabella called.

With a stroke of her sword Lisamon Hultin severed the tendril grasping Sleet. He recoiled sharply as he was freed, toppling backward and coming within an eyeblink of being seized around the throat by the tendril of another plant; but with an acrobat's easy grace he rolled over, avoiding the groping filament, and sprang to his feet. The warrior-woman caught him about the chest and lifted him quickly to a place behind her on her mount. Valentine now approached Carabella, who stood shaken and trembling in a safe place between two sets of thrashing tendrils, and did the same for her.

She clung to him so tightly that his ribs ached. He twisted himself around and embraced her, stroking her gently, nuzzling her ear with his lips. His relief was overwhelming and startling: he had not realized how much she had come to mean to him, nor how little he had cared about anything just now except that she was all right. Gradually her terror subsided, but he could feel her still quivering at the horror of the scene. "Another minute," she whispered. "Sleet was starting to lose his foothold—I could feel him slipping toward that plant—" Carabella winced. "Where did she come from?"

"She took some shortcut through the forest. Zalzan Kavol has hired her to protect us on the way to Ilirivoyne."

"She's already earned her fee," Carabella said.

"Follow me," Lisamon Hultin ordered.

She chose a careful route out of the mouthplant grove, but for all her care her mount was seized twice by the leg, and Valentine's once. Each time, the giantess cut the tendril away, and in moments they were out into the clearing and riding back down the path toward the wagon. A cheer went up from the Skandars as they reappeared.

Zalzan Kavol regarded Sleet coldly. "You chose an unwise route for your departure," he observed.

"Not nearly so unwise as the one you've picked," said Sleet. "I beg you excuse me. I will go on toward Mazadone by foot, and seek some sort of employment there."

"Wait," Valentine said.

Sleet looked at him inquiringly.

"Let's talk. Come walk with me." Valentine laid his arm over the smaller man's shoulders and drew him aside, off into a grassy glade, before Zalzan Kavol could provoke some new wrath in him.

Sleet was tense, wary, guarded. "What is it, Valentine?"

"I was instrumental in getting Zalzan Kavol to hire the giantess. But for that, you'd be tidbits for the mouthplant now."

"For that I thank you."

"I want more than thanks from you," said Valentine. "It could be said that you're indebted to me for your life, in a way."

"That may be."

"Then I ask by way of repayment that you withdraw your resignation."

Sleet's eyes flashed. "You don't know what you ask!"

"The Metamorphs are strange and unsympathetic creatures, yes. But Deliamber says they're not as menacing as often reported. Stay with the troupe, Sleet."

"You think I'm being whimsical in quitting?"

"Not at all. But irrational, perhaps."

Sleet shook his head. "I had a sending from the King, once, in which a Metamorph imposed on me a terrible fate. One listens to such sendings. I have no desire to go near the place where those beings dwell."

"Sendings don't always bear the literal truth."

"Agreed. But often they do. Valentine, the King told me I would have a wife that I loved more dearly than my art itself, a wife who juggled with me the way Carabella does, but far more closely, so much in tune with my rhythms that it was as if we were one person." Sweat broke out on Sleet's scarred face, and he faltered, and almost did not go on, but after a moment he said, "I dreamed, Valentine, that the Shapeshifters came one day and stole that wife of mine, and substituted for her one of their own people, disguised so cunningly that I couldn't tell the difference. And that night, I dreamed, we performed before the Coronal, before Lord Malibor that ruled then and drowned soon after, and our juggling was perfection, it was a harmony unequaled in all of my life, and the Coronal feasted us with fine meats and wines, and gave us a bedchamber draped with silks, and I took her in my arms and began to make love, and as I entered her she changed before me and was a Metamorph in my bed, a thing of horror, Valentine, with rubbery gray skin and gristle instead of teeth, and eyes like dirty puddles, who kissed me and pressed close against me. I have not sought the body of a woman," Sleet said, "since that night, out of dread that some such thing might befall me in the embrace. Nor have I told this story to anyone. Nor can I bear the prospect of going to Ilirivoyne and finding myself surrounded by creatures with Shapeshifter faces and Shapeshifter bodies."

Compassion flooded Valentine's spirit. In silence he held the smaller man for a moment, as if with the strength of his arms alone he could eradicate the memory of the horrific nightmare that had maimed his soul. When he released him Valentine said slowly, "Such a dream is truly terrible. But we are taught to use our dreams, not to let ourselves be crushed by them."

"This one is beyond my using, friend. Except to warn me to stay clear of Metamorphs."

"You take it too straightforwardly. What if something more oblique was intended? Did you have the dream spoken, Sleet?"

"It seemed unnecessary."

"It was you who urged me to see a speaker, when I dreamed strangely in Pidruid! I remember your very words. The King never sends simple messages, you said."

Sleet offered an ironic smile. "We are always better doctors for others than for ourselves, Valentine. In any event, it's too late to have a fifteen-year-old dream spoken, and I am its prisoner now."

"Free yourself!"

"How?"

"When a child has a dream that he is falling, and awakens in fright, what does his parent say? That falling dreams are not to be taken seriously, because one doesn't really get hurt in dreams? Or that the child should be thankful for a falling dream, because such a dream is a good dream, that it speaks of power and strength, that the child was not falling but flying, to a place where he would have learned something, if he had not allowed anxiety and fear to shake him loose of the dream-world?"

"That the child should be thankful for the dream," said Sleet.

"Indeed. And so too with all other 'bad' dreams: we must

149

not be frightened, they tell us, but be grateful for the wisdom of dreams, and act on it."

"So children are told, yes. Even so, adults don't always handle such dreams better than children. I recall some cries and whimpers coming from you in your sleep of late, Valentine."

"I try to learn from my dreams, however dark they may be."

"What do you want from me, Valentine?"

"That you come with us to Ilirivoyne."

"Why is that so important to you?"

Valentine said, "You belong to this troupe. We are a whole with you and broken without you."

"The Skandars are masterly jugglers. It hardly matters what the human performers contribute. Carabella and I are with the troupe for the same reason as you, to comply with a stupid law. You'll earn your pay whether I'm with you or not."

"I learn the art from you, though."

"You can learn from Carabella. She's as skilled as I am, and is your lover besides, who knows you better than I ever could. And the Divine spare you," said Sleet in a suddenly terrifying voice, "from losing her to the Shapeshifters in Ilirivoyne!"

"It isn't something I fear," said Valentine. He extended his hands toward Sleet. "I would have you remain with us."

"*Why?*"

"I value you."

"And I value you, Valentine. But it would give me great pain to go where Zalzan Kavol would have us go. Why is it so urgent for you to insist on my enduring that pain?"

"You might be healed of that pain," said Valentine, "if you go to Ilirivoyne and find that the Metamorphs are only harmless primitives."

"I can live with my pain," Sleet replied. "The price of that healing seems too high."

"We can live with the most horrible wounds. But why not attempt to cure them?"

"There is some other thing not being spoken here, Valentine."

Valentine paused and let his breath out slowly. "Yes," he said.

"What is it, then?"

With some hesitation Valentine said, "Sleet, have I figured in your dreams at all, since we met in Pidruid?"

"You have, yes."

"In what way?"

"How does this matter?"

"Have you dreamed," said Valentine, "that I might be somewhat unusual in Majipoor, someone of more distinction and power than I myself comprehend?"

"Your bearing and poise told me that at our first meeting. And the phenomenal skill with which you learned our art. And the content of your own dreams that you've shared with me."

"And who am I, in those dreams, Sleet?"

"A person of might and grace, fallen through deceit from his high position. A duke, maybe. A prince of the realm."

"Or higher?"

Sleet licked his lips. "Higher, yes. Perhaps. What do you want with me, Valentine?"

"To accompany me to Ilirivoyne and beyond."

"Do you tell me that there's truth in what I've dreamed?"

"This I'm yet to learn," said Valentine. "But I think there's truth in it, yes. I feel more and more strongly that there must be truth in it. Sendings tell me there's truth in it."

"My lord——" Sleet whispered.

"Perhaps."

Sleet looked at him in amazement and began to fall to his knees. Valentine caught him hastily and held him upright. "None of that," he said. "The others can see. I want nobody to have an inkling of this. Besides, there remain great areas of doubt. I would not have you kneeling to me, Sleet, or making starbursts with your fingers, or any of that, while I still am uncertain of the truth."

"My lord——"

"I remain Valentine the juggler."

"I am frightened now, my lord. I came within a minute of a foul death today, and this frightens me more, to stand here quietly talking with you about these things."

"Call me Valentine."

"How can I?" Sleet asked.

"You called me Valentine five minutes ago."

"That was before."

"Nothing has changed, Sleet."

Sleet shook the idea away. "Everything has changed, my lord."

Valentine sighed heavily. He felt like an impostor, like a fraud, manipulating Sleet in this way, and yet there seemed purpose to it, and genuine need. "If everything has changed, then will you follow me as I command? Even to Ilirivoyne?"

"If I must," said Sleet, dazed.

"No harm of the kind you fear will come to you among the Metamorphs. You'll emerge from their country healed of the pain that has racked you. You do believe that, don't you, Sleet?"

"It frightens me to go there."

"I need you by me in what lies ahead," said Valentine. "And through no choice of mine, Ilirivoyne has become part of my journey. I ask you to follow me there."

Sleet bowed his head. "If I must, my lord."

"And I ask you, by the same compulsion, to call me Valentine and show me no more respect in front of the others than you would have shown me yesterday."

"As you wish," Sleet said.

"*Valentine.*"

"Valentine," said Sleet reluctantly. "As you wish— Valentine."

"Come, then."

He led Sleet back to the group. Zalzan Kavol was, as usual, pacing impatiently; the others were preparing the wagon for departure. To the Skandar Valentine said, "I've talked Sleet into withdrawing his resignation. He'll accompany us to Ilirivoyne."

Zalzan Kavol looked altogether dumfounded. "How did you manage to do that?"

"Yes," said Vinorkis. "What did you say to him, anyway?"

With a cheerful smile Valentine said, "It would be tedious to explain, I think."

8

The pace of the journey now accelerated. All day long the wagon purred along the highway, and sometimes well into the evening. Lisamon Hultin rode alongside, though her mount, sturdy as it was, needed more rest than those that drew the wagon, and occasionally she fell behind, catching up as opportunity allowed: carrying her heroic bulk was no easy task for any animal.

On they went through a tamed province of city after city, broken only by modest belts of greenery that barely obeyed the letter of the density laws. This province of Mazadone was a place where commercial pursuits kept many millions employed, for Mazadone was the gateway to all the territories of northwestern Zimroel for goods coming from the east, and the chief transshipment point for overland conveyance of merchandise of Pidruid and Til-omon heading eastward. They passed quickly in and out of a host of interchangeable and forgettable cities, Cynthion and Apoortel and Doirectine, Mazadone city itself, Borgax and Thagobar beyond it, all of them subdued and quiescent during the mourning period for the late duke, and strips of yellow dangling everywhere as sign of sorrow. It seemed to Valentine a heavy thing to shut down an entire province for the death of a duke. What would these people do, he wondered, over the death of a Pontifex? How had they responded to the premature passing of the Coronal Lord Voriax two years ago? But perhaps they took the going of their local duke more seriously, he thought, for he was a visible figure, real and present among them, whereas to people of Zimroel, thousands of miles separated from Castle Mount or Labyrinth, the Powers of Majipoor must seem largely abstract figures, mythical, legendary, immaterial. On a planet so large as this no central authority could govern with real efficiency, only symbolic control; Valentine suspected that much of the stability of Majipoor depended on a social contract whereby the local governors—the provincial dukes and the municipal mayors—agreed to enforce and support the edicts of the imperial government, provided that they might do as they pleased within their own territories.

How, he asked himself, can such a contract be upheld when the Coronal is not the anointed and dedicated prince, but some usurper, lacking in the grace of the Divine through which such fragile social constructs are sustained?

He found himself thinking more and more upon such matters during the long, quiet, monotonous hours of the eastward journey. Such thoughts surprised him with their seriousness, for he had grown accustomed to the lightness and simplicity of his mind since the early days of Pidruid, and he could feel a progressive enrichment and growing complexity of mental powers now. It was as if whatever spell had been laid upon him was wearing thin, and his true intellect was beginning to emerge.

If, that is, any such magic had actually befallen him as his gradually forming hypothesis required.

He was still uncertain. But his doubts were weakening from day to day.

In dreams now he often saw himself in positions of authority. One night it was he, not Zalzan Kavol, who led the band of jugglers; on another he presided in princely robes over some high council of the Metamorphs, whom he saw as eerie

153

foglike wraiths that would not hold the same shape more than a minute at a time; a night later he had a vision of himself in the marketplace at Thagobar, dispensing justice to the cloth-sellers and vendors of bangles in their noisy little disputes.

"You see?" Carabella said. "All these dreams speak of power and majesty."

"Power? Majesty? Sitting on a barrel in a market and ex-pounding on equity to dealers in cotton and linen?"

"In dreams many things are translated. These visions are metaphors of high might."

Valentine smiled. But he had to admit the plausibility of the interpretation.

One night as they were nearing the city of Khyntor there came to him a most explicit vision of his supposed former life. He was in a room paneled with the finest and rarest of woods, glistening strips of semotan and bannikop and rich dark swamp mahogany, and he sat before a sharp-angled desk of burnished palisander, signing documents. The starburst crest was at his right hand; obsequious secretaries hovered about; and the enormous curving window before him revealed an open gulf of air, as though it looked out upon the titanic slope of Castle Mount. Was this a fantasy? Or was it some fugitive fragment of the buried past that had broken free and come floating up in his sleep to approach the surface of his con-scious mind? He described the office and desk to Carabella and to Deliamber, hoping they could tell him how the office of the Coronal looked in reality. but they had no more idea of that than they did of what the Pontifex had for breakfast. The Vroon asked him how he had perceived himself when sitting at that palisander desk: was he golden-haired, like the Valen-tine who rode in the jugglers' wagon, or dark, like the Coronal who had made grand processional through Pidruid and the western provinces?

"Dark," said Valentine immediately. Then he frowned. "Or is that so? I was sitting at the desk, not looking at the man who was there because I *was* the man. And yet—and yet—"

Carabella said, "In the world of dreams we often see our-selves with our own eyes."

"I could have been both fair and dark. Now one, now the other—the point escaped me. Now one, now the other, eh?"

"Yes," Deliamber said.

They were almost into Khyntor now, after too many days of steady, wearying overland travel. This, the major city of north-central Zimroel, lay in rugged, irregular terrain, broken by lakes and highlands and dark, virtually impassable forests.

The route chosen by Deliamber took the wagon through the city's southwestern suburbs, known as Hot Khyntor because of the geothermal marvels there—great hissing geysers, and a broad steaming pink lake that bubbled and gurgled ominously, and a mile or two of gray rubbery-looking fumaroles from which, every few minutes, came clouds of greenish gases accompanied by comic belching sounds and deeper, stranger subterranean groans. Here the sky was heavy with big-bellied clouds the color of dull pearls, and although the last of summer still held the land, there was a cool autumnal quality to the thin, sharp wind that blew from the north.

The River Zimr, largest in Zimroel, divided Hot Khyntor from the city proper. When the travelers came upon it, the wagon emerging suddenly from an ancient district of narrow streets to enter a broad esplanade leading to Khyntor Bridge, Valentine gasped with amazement.

"What is it?" Carabella asked.

"The river—I never expected it to be as big as this!"

"Are rivers unfamiliar to you?"

"There are none of any consequence between Pidruid and here," he pointed out. "I remember nothing clearly before Pidruid."

"Compared with the Zimr," said Sleet, "there are no rivers of any consequence anywhere. Let him be amazed."

To the right and left, so far as Valentine could see, the dark waters of the Zimr stretched to the horizon. The river was so broad here that it looked more like a bay. He could barely make out the square-topped towers of Khyntor on the far shore. Eight or ten mighty bridges spanned the waters here, so vast that Valentine wondered how it had been possible to build them at all. The one that lay directly ahead, Khyntor Bridge, was four highways wide, a structure of looping arches that rose and descended and rose and descended in great leaps from bank to bank; a short way downstream was a bridge of entirely different design, a heavy brick roadbed resting on astounding lofty piers, and just upstream was another that seemed made of glass, and gleamed with a dazzling brightness. Deliamber said, "That is Coronal Bridge, and to our right the Bridge of the Pontifex, and farther downstream is the one known as the Bridge of Dreams. All of them are ancient and famous."

"But why try to bridge the river at a place where it's so wide?" Valentine asked in bewilderment.

Deliamber said, "This is one of the narrowest points."

The Zimr's course, declared the Vroon, was some seven

thousand miles, rising northwest of Dulorn at the mouth of the Rift and flowing in a southeasterly direction across all of upper Zimroel toward the coastal city of Piliplok on the Inner Sea. This happy river, navigable for its entire length, was a swift and phenomenally broad stream that flowed in grand sweeping curves like some amiable serpent. Its shores were occupied by hundreds of wealthy cities, major inland ports, of which Khyntor was the most westerly. On the far side of Khyntor, running off to the northeast and only dimly visible in the cloudy sky, were the jagged peaks of the Khyntor Marches, nine great mountains on whose chilly flanks lived tribes of rough, high-spirited hunters. These people could be found in Khyntor much of the year, exchanging hides and meat for manufactured goods.

That night in Khyntor, Valentine dreamed he was entering the Labyrinth to confer with the Pontifex.

This was no vague and misty dream, but one with sharp, painful clarity. He stood under harsh winter sunlight on a barren plain, and saw before him a roofless temple with flat white walls, which Deliamber told him was the gateway to the Labyrinth. The Vroon and Lisamon Hultin were with him, and Carabella too, walking in a protective phalanx, but when Valentine stepped out onto the bare slate platform between those white walls he was alone. A being of sinister and forbidding aspect confronted him. This creature was of alien shape, but belonged to none of the non-human forms long settled on Majipoor—neither Liiman nor Ghayrog nor Vroon nor Skandar nor Hjort nor Su-Suheris, but something mysterious and disturbing, a muscular thick-armed creature with cratered red skin and a blunt dome of a head out of which blazed yellow eyes bright with almost intolerable rage. This being demanded Valentine's business with the Pontifex in a low, resonant voice.

"Khyntor Bridge is in need of repair," Valentine replied. "It is the ancient duty of the Pontifex to deal with such matters."

The yellow-eyed creature laughed. "Do you think the Pontifex will care?"

"It is my responsibility to summon his aid."

"Go, then." The guardian of the portal beckoned with sardonic politeness and stepped aside. As Valentine went past, the being uttered a chilling snarl, and slammed shut a gateway behind Valentine. Retreat was impossible. Before him lay a narrow winding corridor, sourcelessly lit by some cruel white light that numbed the eyes. For hours Valentine descended on a spiral path. Then the walls of the corridor widened, and he found himself in another roofless temple of white stone, or perhaps the same one as before, for the pockmarked red-skinned being again blocked his way, growling with that unfathomable anger.

"Behold the Pontifex," the creature said.

And Valentine looked beyond it into a darkened chamber and saw the imperial sovereign of Majipoor seated upon a throne, clad in robes of black and scarlet, and wearing the royal tiara. And the Pontifex of Majipoor was a monster with many arms and many legs, and the face of a man but wings of a dragon, and he sat shrieking and roaring upon the throne like a madman. A terrible whistling sound came from his lips, and the smell of the Pontifex was a frightful stink, and the black leathery wings flailed the air with fierce intensity, buffeting Valentine with cold gales. "Your majesty," Valentine said, and bowed, and said, again, "Your majesty."

"Your lordship," replied the Pontifex. And laughed, and reached for Valentine and tugged him forward, and then Valentine was on the throne and the Pontifex, laughing insanely, was fleeing up the brightly lit corridors, running and flapping wings and raving and shrieking, until he was lost from sight.

Valentine woke, wet with perspiration, in Carabella's arms. She showed a look of concern bordering on fear, as if the terrors of his dream had been only too obvious to her, and she held him a moment, saying nothing, until he had had a chance to comprehend the fact that he was awake. Tenderly she stroked his cheeks. "You cried out three times," she told him.

"There are occasions," he said after gulping a little wine from a flask beside the bed, "when it seems more wearying to sleep than to remain awake. My dreams are hard work, Carabella."

"There's much in your soul that seeks to express itself, my lord."

"It expresses itself in a very strenuous way," Valentine said, and nestled down against her breasts. "If dreams are the source of wisdom, I pray to grow no wiser before dawn."

9

In Khyntor, Zalzan Kavol booked passage for the troupe aboard a riverboat bound toward Ni-moya and Piliplok. They

157

would be journeying only a short way down the river, though, to the minor city of Verf, gateway to the Metamorph territory.

Valentine regretted having to leave the riverboat at Verf, when he could easily, for another ten or fifteen royals, sail all the way to Piliplok and take ship for the Isle of Sleep. That, after all, and not the Shapeshifter reservation, was his most urgent immediate destination: the Isle of the Lady, where perhaps he might find confirmation of the visions that tormented him. But that was not to be, just yet.

Destiny, Valentine thought, could not be rushed. Thus far things had moved with deliberate speed but toward some definite, if not always understandable, goal. He was no longer the cheerful and simple idler of Pidruid, and, although he had no sure knowledge of what it was he was becoming, he had a definite sense of inner transition, of boundaries passed and not to be recrossed. He saw himself as an actor in some vast and bewildering drama the climactic scenes of which were still far away in space and time.

The riverboat was a grotesque and fanciful structure, but not without a beauty of sorts. Oceangoing ships such as had been in port at Pidruid were designed for grace and sturdiness, since they would face journeys of thousands of miles between harbors; but the riverboat, a short-haul vessel, was squat and broad-beamed, more of a floating platform than a ship, and as if to compensate for the inelegance of its design its builders had festooned it with ornament—a great soaring bridge topped with triple figureheads painted in brilliant reds and yellows, an enormous central courtyard almost like a village plaza, with statuary and pavilions and game-parlors, and, at the stern, an upswept superstructure of many levels in which passengers were housed. Belowdecks were cargo holds, steerage quarters, dining halls, and cabins for the crew, as well as the engine room, from which two gigantic smokestacks sprouted that came curving up the sides of the hull and rose skyward like the horns of a demon. The entire frame of the ship was of wood, metal being too scarce on Majipoor for such large-scale enterprises and stone being generally deemed undesirable for maritime use; and the carpenters had exerted their imaginations over nearly every square foot of the surface, decorating it with scrollwork, bizarre dadoes, outjutting joists, and similar flourishes of a hundred kinds.

The riverboat seemed a vast and teeming microcosm. As they waited for sailing, Valentine and Deliamber and Carabella strolled the deck, thronged with citizens of many districts and of all the races of Majipoor. Valentine saw frontiersmen from the mountains beyond Khyntor, Ghayrogs in the finery affected in Dulorn, people of the humid southlands in cool white linens, travelers in sumptuous robes of crimson and green which Carabella said were typical of western Alhanroel, and many others. The ubiquitous Liimen sold their ubiquitous grilled sausages; officious Hjorts strutted about in uniforms of the riverboat line, giving information and instructions to those who asked and to many who did not; a Su-Suheris family in diaphanous green robes, conspicuous because of their unlikely doubleheaded bodies and aloof, imperious mien, drifted like emissaries from the world of dreams through the crowds, who gave way in automatic deference. And there was one small group of Metamorphs on deck that afternoon.

Deliamber saw them first. The little Vroon made a clucking sound and touched Valentine's hand. "See them? Let's hope Sleet doesn't."

"Which ones?" Valentine asked.

"By the railing. Standing alone, looking uneasy. They wear their natural form."

Valentine stared. There were five of them, perhaps a male and a female adult and three younger ones. They were slender, angular, long-legged beings, the older ones taller than he, with a frail, insubstantial look to them. Their skins were sallow, almost green in hue. Their faces approached the human pattern in construction, except that their cheekbones were sharp as blades, their lips were almost nonexistent and their noses were reduced to mere bumps, and their eyes, set on angles that sloped inward toward the center, were tapered and without pupils. Valentine was unable to decide whether these Metamorphs bore themselves with arrogance or with timidity: certainly they must regard themselves as in hostile territory aboard this riverboat, these natives of the ancient race, these descendants of those who had possessed Majipoor before the coming of the first Earthborn settlers fourteen thousand years ago. He could not take his eyes from them.

"How is the changing of shape accomplished?" he asked.

"Their bones are not joined like those of most races," answered Deliamber. "Under muscular pressure they will move and take up new patterns. Also they have mimicry cells in their skins, that allow them to alter color and texture, and there are other adaptations. An adult can transform itself almost instantaneously."

"And what purpose does this serve?"

"Who can say? Most likely the Metamorphs ask what pur-

159

pose there was in creating races in this universe that are unable to shift shape. It must have some value to them."

"Very little," said Carabella acidly, "if they could have such powers and still have their world snatched away from them."

"Shifting shape is not enough of a defense," Deliamber replied, "when people travel from one star to another to steal your home."

The Metamorphs fascinated Valentine. To him they represented artifacts of Majipoor's long history, archaeological relicts, survivors from the era when there were no humans here, nor Skandars nor Vroons nor Ghayrogs, only these fragile green people spread out across a colossal planet. Before the settlers came—the intruders, ultimately the conquerors. How long ago it had been! He wished they would perform a transformation as he watched, perhaps turn into Skandars or Liimen before his eyes. But they remained unwavering in their identities.

Shanamir, looking agitated, appeared suddenly out of the crowd. He seized Valentine's arm and blurted, "Do you know what's on board with us? I heard the cargo-handlers talking. There's a whole family of Shape—"

"Not so loud," Valentine said. "Look yonder."

The boy looked and shivered. "Scary things, they are."

"Where's Sleet?"

"On the bridge, with Zalzan Kavol. They're trying to get a permit to perform tonight. If he sees them—"

"He'll have to confront Metamorphs sooner or later," Valentine murmured. To Deliamber he said, "Is it uncommon for them to be seen outside their reservation?"

"They are found everywhere, but never in great numbers, and rarely in their own form. There might be eleven of them living in Pidruid, say, and six in Falkynkip, nine in Dulorn—"

"Disguised?"

"Yes, as Ghayrogs or Hjorts or humans, whatever seems best in a certain place."

The Metamorphs began to leave the deck. They moved with great dignity, but, unlike the little Su-Suheris group, there was nothing imperious about them; they seemed rather to give an impression of wishing they were invisible.

Valentine said, "Do they live in their territory by choice or compulsion?"

"Some of each, I think. When Lord Stiamot completed the conquest, he forced them to leave Alhanroel entirely. But Zimroel was barely settled then, just the coastal outposts, and they were allowed most of the interior. They chose only the territory between the Zimr and the southern mountains, though, where access could easily be controlled, and withdrew into that. By now there's a tradition that the Metamorphs dwell only in that territory, except for the unofficial few living out in the cities. But I have no idea whether that tradition has force of law. Certainly they pay little attention to the decrees that emerge from the Labyrinth or Castle Mount."

"If imperial law matters so little to them, are we not taking great risks in going to Ilirivoyne?"

Deliamber laughed. "The days when Metamorphs attacked outsiders for the sheer love of vengeance are long over, so I am assured. They are a shy and sullen people, but they will do us no harm, and we'll probably leave their country intact and well laden with the money that Zalzan Kavol loves so much. Look, here he comes now."

The Skandar, with Sleet beside him, approached, looking self-satisfied.

"We have arranged the right to perform," he announced. "Fifty crowns for an hour's work, right after dinner! We'll give them our simplest tricks, though. Why exert ourselves before we get to Ilirivoyne?"

"No," Valentine said. "We should do our best." He looked hard at Sleet. "There's a party of Metamorphs aboard this boat. Perhaps they'll carry the word of our excellence ahead of us to Ilirivoyne."

"Wisely argued," said Zalzan Kavol.

Sleet was taut and fearful. His nostrils flickered, his lips compressed, he made holy signs with his left hand at his side. Valentine turned to him and said in a low voice, "Now the process of healing begins. Juggle for them tonight as you would for the court of the Pontifex."

Hoarsely Sleet said, "They are my enemies!"

"Not these. They are not the ones of your dream. Those have done you all the damage that lay in their power, and it was long ago."

"It sickens me to be on the same boat."

"There's no leaving it now," Valentine said. "There are only five of them. A small dose—good practice for meeting what awaits us in Ilirivoyne."

"Ilirivoyne—"

"There is no avoiding Ilirivoyne," said Valentine. "Your pledge to me, Sleet—"

Sleet regarded Valentine in silence a moment.

"Yes, my lord," he whispered.

161

"Come, then. Juggle with me: we both need practice. And remember to call me Valentine!"

They found a quiet place belowdecks and worked out with the clubs; there was an odd reversal in their roles at first, for Valentine juggled flawlessly, while Sleet was as clumsy as a tyro, dropping the clubs constantly and in several instances bruising his fingers. But in a few minutes his disciplines asserted themselves. He filled the air with clubs, interchanging them with Valentine in patterns of such complexity that it left Valentine laughing and gasping, and finally he had to beg a halt and ask Sleet to return to more manageable cascades.

That night at the deckside performance—their first since the impromptu event staged for the amusement of the forest-brethren—Zalzan Kavol ordered a program that they had never done before an audience. The jugglers divided into three groups of three—Sleet, Carabella, and Valentine; Zalzan Kavol, Thelkar, and Gibor Haern; Heitrag Kavol, Rovorn, and Erfon Kavol—and engaged in simultaneous triple exchanges in the same rhythm, one group of Skandars juggling knives, the other flaming torches, and the humans silver clubs. It was one of the most severe tests of his skills that Valentine had yet experienced. The symmetry of the routine depended on perfection. One dropped implement by any of the nine would ruin the total effect. He was the weakest link; on him the entire impact of the performance depended, therefore.

But he dropped no clubs, and the applause, when the jugglers had ended their act in a flurry of high throws and jaunty catches, was overwhelming. As he took his bows Valentine noticed the family of Metamorphs seated only a few rows away. He glanced at Sleet, who bowed and bowed again, ever more deeply.

As they skipped from the stage Sleet said, "I saw them when we started, and then I forgot about them. I forgot about them, Valentine!" He laughed. "They were nothing at all like the creature I remember from my dream."

10

The troupe slept that night in a dank, crowded hold in the bowels of the riverboat. Valentine found himself jammed between Shanamir and Lisamon Hultin on the thinly cushioned floor, and the proximity of the warrior-woman seemed to guarantee that he would have no sleep, for her snoring was a fierce insistent buzz, and more distracting even than the snore was the fear that as her vast body rolled and thrashed about beside him he would be crushed beneath it. Several times indeed she fetched up against him and he was hard put to extricate himself. But soon she lay more quietly, and he felt sleep stealing over him.

A dream came in which he was Coronal, Lord Valentine of the olive skin and black beard, and sat once more in Castle Mount wielding the seals of power, and then somehow he was in a southern city, a moist steaming tropical place of giant vines and gaudy red blossoms, a city that he knew to be Tilomon at the far side of Zimroel, and he attended there a grand feast in his honor. There was another high guest at the table, a somber-eyed man with coarse skin, who was Dominin Barjazid, second son of the King of Dreams, and Dominin Barjazid poured wine in honor of the Coronal, and offered toasts, crying out long life and predicting a glorious reign, a reign to rank with those of Lord Stiamot and Lord Prestimion and Lord Confalume. And Lord Valentine drank, and drank again, and grew flushed and merry, and offered toasts of his own, to his guest and to the mayor of Til-omon and to the duke of the province, and to Simonan Barjazid the King of Dreams, and to the Pontifex Tyeveras, and to the Lady of the Isle, his own beloved mother, and the goblet was filled and filled once again, amber wine and red wine and the blue wine of the south, until finally he could drink no more, and went to his bedchamber and dropped instantly into sleep. As he slept figures moved about him, the men of Dominin Barjazid's entourage, lifting him and carrying him wrapped in silken sheets, taking him somewhere, and he could give no resistance, for it seemed to him that his arms and legs would not obey him, as if this were a dream, this scene within a dream. And Valentine beheld himself on a table in a secret room, and now his hair was yellow and his skin was fair, and it was Dominin Barjazid who wore the face of the Coronal.

"Take him to some city in the far north," said the false Lord Valentine, "and turn him loose, and let him make his own way upon the world."

The dream would have continued, but Valentine found himself smothering in his sleep, and came up into consciousness to discover Lisamon Hultin sprawled against him with one of her beefy arms over his face. With some effort he freed himself, but then there was no returning to sleep.

In the morning he said nothing to anyone of his dream: it was becoming time, he suspected, to keep the informations of the night to himself, for they were starting to border on affairs of state. This was the second time he had dreamed of having been supplanted as Coronal by Dominin Barjazid, and Carabella, weeks ago, had dreamed that enemies unknown had drugged him and stolen his identity. All these dreams might yet prove to be nothing but fantasy or parable, but Valentine inclined now to doubt that. There was too strong a consistency to them, too frequent a repetition of underlying structures.

And if a Barjazid now wore the starburst crown? What then, what then?

The Valentine of Pidruid would have shrugged and said, No matter, one overlord is the same as another; but the Valentine now sailing from Khyntor to Verf took a more thoughtful view of things. There was a balance of power in this world, a balance carefully designed over a span of thousands of years, a system that had been evolving since Lord Stiamot's time, or perhaps earlier, out of whatever forgotten polities had ruled Majipoor in the first centuries of the settlement. And in that system an inaccessible Pontifex ruled through the vehicle of a vigorous and dynamic Coronal of his own choosing, with the official known as the King of Dreams functioning to execute the commands of the government and chastise lawbreakers by virtue of his entry into the minds of sleepers, and the Lady of the Isle, mother of the Coronal, contributing a tempering of love and wisdom. There was strength to the system, or else it could not have endured so many thousands of years; under it, Majipoor was a happy and prosperous world, subject, true, to the frailties of flesh and the vagaries of nature, but mainly free of conflict and suffering. What now, Valentine wondered, if a Barjazid of the King's blood were to put aside a lawfully constituted Coronal and interpose himself in that divinely ordained balance? What harm to the commonwealth, what disruption of public tranquillity?

And what might be said of a fallen Coronal who chooses to accept his altered destiny and leaves the usurper unchallenged? Was that not an abdication, and had there ever been an abdication of a Coronal in Majipoor's history? Would he not thereby become a co-conspirator in Dominin Barjazid's overthrow of order?

The last of his hesitations were going from him. It had seemed a comical thing, or a bizarre one, to Valentine the juggler when the first hints had come to him that he might be truly Lord Valentine the Coronal. That had been an absurdity, a lunacy, a farce. No longer. The texture of his dreams carried the weight of plausibility. A monstrous thing had happened, indeed. The full import of it was only now coming clear to him. And it was his task, that he must accept without further question, to set things right.

But how? Challenge an incumbent Coronal? Rise up in juggler's costume to claim Castle Mount?

He spent the morning quietly, giving no hint of his thoughts. Mostly he remained at the rail, staring at the far-off shore. The river's immensity was beyond his understanding: at some points here it was so wide that no land could be seen, and in other places what Valentine took to be the shore turned out to be islands, themselves of great size, with miles of water between their farther sides and the riverbank. The flow of the river was strong, and the huge riverboat was being swept rapidly along eastward.

The day was bright, and the river rippled and glinted in the sparkling sunlight. In the afternoon a light rain began to fall, out of clouds so compact that the sunlight remained bright around them. The rain increased in intensity and the jugglers were forced to cancel their second performance, to Zalzan Kavol's great annoyance. They huddled under cover.

That night Valentine took care to sleep beside Carabella, and left the snores of Lisamon Hultin for the Skandars to cope with. He waited almost eagerly for revealing new dreams. But what came to him was useless, the ordinary formless hodgepodge of fantasy and chaos, of nameless streets and unfamiliar faces, of bright lights and garish colors, of absurd disputes, disjointed conversations, and unfocused images, and in the morning the riverboat arrived at the port of Verf on the river's southern bank.

11

"The province of the Metamorphs," said Autifon Deliamber, "is named Piurifayne, after the name by which the Metamorphs call themselves in their own language, which is Piurivar. It is bounded on the north by the outlying suburb of Verf, on the west by the Velathys Scarp, on the south by the substantial range of mountains known as the Gonghars, and on the east by the River Steiche, an important tributary of the Zimr. I have beheld each of those boundary zones with my own eyes, though I have never entered Piurifayne itself. To enter is difficult, for the Velathys Scarp is a sheer wall a mile

165

high and three hundred miles long; the Gonghars are storm-swept and disagreeable; and the Steiche is a wild unruly river full of rapids and turbulence. The only rational way in is through Verf and down through Piurifayne Gate."

The jugglers now were only a few miles north of that entrance, having left the drab mercantile city of Verf as quickly as possible. The rain, light but insistent, had continued all morning. The countryside here was unexciting, a place of light sandy soil and dense stands of dwarf trees with pale green bark and narrow, twittering leaves. There was little conversation in the wagon. Sleet seemed lost in meditation, Carabella juggled three red balls obsessively in the mid-cabin space, the Skandars who were not driving engaged in some intricate game played with slivers of ivory and packets of black drole-whiskers, Shanamir dozed, Vinorkis made entries in a journal he carried, Deliamber entertained himself with minor incantations, the lighting of tiny necromantic candles, and other wizardly amusements, and Lisamon Hultin, who had hitched her mount to the team drawing the wagon so that she could come in from the rain, snored like a beached sea-dragon, awakening now and then to gulp a globelet of the cheap gray wine she had bought in Verf.

Valentine sat in a corner, up against a window, thinking of Castle Mount. What could it be like, a mountain thirty miles high? A single stone shaft rising like a colossal tower into the dark night of space? If Velathys Scarp, a mile high, was as Deliamber said an impassable wall, what sort of barrier was a thing thirty times as tall? What shadow did Castle Mount cast when the sun was in the east? A dark stripe running the length of Alhanroel? And how were the cities on its lofty slope provided with warmth, and air to breathe? Some machines of the ancients, Valentine had heard, that manufactured heat and light, and dispensed sweet air, miraculous machines of that forgotten technological era of thousands of years ago, when the old arts brought from Earth still were widely practiced here; but he could no more comprehend how such machines might work than he understood what forces operated the engines of memory in his own mind to tell him that this dark-haired woman was Carabella, this white-haired man Sleet. He thought too of Castle Mount's highest reaches, and that building of forty thousand rooms at its summit, Lord Valentine's Castle now, Lord Voriax' not so long ago, Lord Malibor's when he was a boy in that childhood he no longer remembered. Lord Valentine's Castle! Was there really such a place, or was the Castle and its Mount only a fable, a vision, a

166

fantasy such as comes in dreams? Lord Valentine's Castle! He imagined it clinging to the mountaintop like a coat of paint, a bright splash of color just a few molecules thick, or so it would seem against the titanic scale of that impossible mountain, a splash that coursed irregularly down the flank of the summit in a tentacular way, hundreds of rooms extending on this face, hundreds more on that, a cluster of great chambers extending themselves pseudopod-fashion here, a nest of courtyards and galleries over there. And in its innermost place the Coronal in all grandeur, dark-bearded Lord Valentine, except that the Coronal would not be there now, he would still be making his grand processional through the realm, in Ni-moya by now or some other eastern city. And I, thought Valentine, I once lived on that Mount? Dwelled in that Castle? What did I do, when I was Coronal—what decrees, what appointments, what duties? The whole thing was inconceivable, and yet, and yet, he felt the conviction growing in him, there was fullness and density and substance to the phantom bits of memory that drifted through his mind. He knew now that he had been born not in Ni-moya by the river's bend, as the false recollections planted in his mind had it, but rather in one of the Fifty Cities high up on the Mount, almost at the verge of the Castle itself, and that he had been reared among the royal caste, among that cadre from which princes were chosen, that his childhood and boyhood had been one of privilege and comfort. He still had no memory of his father, who must have been some high prince of the realm, nor could he recall anything of his mother except that her hair was dark and her skin was swarthy, as his once had been, and—a memory rushed into his awareness out of nowhere—and that she had embraced him a long while one day, weeping a little, before she told him that Voriax had been chosen as Coronal in the place of the drowned Lord Malibor, and she would go thenceforth to live as Lady on the Isle of Sleep. Was there truth to that, or had he imagined it just now? He would have been—Valentine paused, calculating—twenty-two years old, very likely, when Voriax came to power. Would his mother have embraced him at all? Would she have wept, on becoming Lady? Or rather rejoice, that she and her eldest son were chosen Powers of Majipoor? To weep and to rejoice at once, maybe. Valentine shook his head. These mighty scenes, these moments of potent history: would he ever regain access to them, or was he always to labor under the handicap placed upon him by those who had stolen his past?

There was a tremendous explosion in the distance, a long

low groundshaking boom that brought everyone in the wagon to attention. It continued for several minutes and gradually subsided to a quiet throb, then to silence.

"What was that?" Sleet cried, groping in the rack for an energy-thrower.

"Peace, peace," Deliamber said. "It is the sound of Piurifayne Fountain. We are approaching the boundary."

"Piurifayne Fountain?" Valentine asked.

"Wait and see," Deliamber told him.

The wagon came to a halt a few minutes later. Zalzan Kavol turned round from the driver's seat and yelled, "Where's that Vroon? Wizard, there's a roadblock up ahead!"

"We are at Piurifayne Gate," said Deliamber.

A barricade made of stout glossy yellow logs lashed with a bright emerald twine spanned the narrow roadway, and to the left of it was a guardhouse occupied by two Hjorts in customs-official uniform of gray and green. They ordered everyone out of the wagon and into the rain, though they themselves were under a protective canopy.

"Where bound?" asked the fatter Hjort.

"Ilirivoyne, to play at the Shapeshifter festival. We are jugglers," said Zalzan Kavol.

"Permit to enter Piurifayne Province?" the other Hjort demanded.

"No such permits are required," Deliamber said.

"You speak too confidently, Vroon. By decree of Lord Valentine the Coronal more than a month past, no citizens of Majipoor enter the Metamorph territory except on legitimate business."

"Ours is legitimate business," growled Zalzan Kavol.

"Then you would have a permit."

"But we knew nothing of the need for one!" the Skandar protested.

The Hjorts looked indifferent to that. They seemed ready to turn their attention to other matters.

Zalzan Kavol glanced toward Vinorkis as though expecting him to have some sort of influence with his compatriots. But the Hjort merely shrugged. Zalzan Kavol glared at Deliamber next and said, "It falls within your responsibilities, wizard, to advise me of such matters."

The Vroon shrugged. "Not even wizards can learn of changes in the law that happen while they travel in forest preserves and other remote places."

"But what do we do now? Turn back to Verf?"

The idea seemed to bring a glow of delight to Sleet's eyes.

Reprieved from this Metamorph adventure after all! But Zalzan Kavol was fuming. Lisamon Hultin's hand strayed to the hilt of her vibration-sword. Valentine stiffened at that.

He said quietly to Zalzan Kavol, "Hjorts are not always incorruptible."

"A good thought," the Skandar murmured.

Zalzan Kavol drew forth his money-pouch. Instantly the attention of the Hjorts sharpened. This was indeed the right tactic, Valentine decided.

"Perhaps I have found the necessary document," said Zalzan Kavol. Ostentatiously removing two one-crown pieces from the pouch, he caught a Hjort's rough-skinned puffy hand in one of his, and with the others pressed a coin into each palm, smiling his most self-satisfied smile. The Hjorts exchanged glances, and they were not glances of bliss. Contemptuously they allowed the coins to fall to the muddy ground.

"A crown?" Carabella muttered in disbelief. "He expected to buy them with a *crown?*"

"Bribing an officer of the imperial government is a serious offense," the fatter Hjort declared ominously. "You are under arrest and remanded for trial to Verf. Remain in your vehicle until appropriate escort can be found for you."

Zalzan Kavol looked outraged. He whirled, began to say something to Valentine, choked it off, gestured angrily at Deliamber, made a growling noise, and spoke in a low voice and in the Skandar language to the three nearest of his brothers. Lisamon Hultin again began to finger her sword-hilt. Valentine felt despair. There would be two dead Hjorts here in another moment, and the jugglers would all be criminal fugitives at the edge of Piurifayne. That was not likely to speed his journey to the Lady of the Isle.

"Do something quickly," Valentine said under his breath to Autifon Deliamber.

But the Vroonish sorcerer was already in motion. Stepping forward, he snatched up the money and offered it again to the Hjorts, saying, "Your pardon, but you must have dropped these small coins." He dropped them into the Hjorts' hands, and at the same time allowed the tips of his tentacles to coil lightly about their wrists for an instant.

When he released them, the thinner Hjort said, "Your visa is good for three weeks only, and you must leave Piurifayne by way of this gate. Other exit points are illegal for you."

"Not to mention very dangerous," added the other. He gestured and unseen figures pulled the barricade sideways fifteen feet along a buried track, so that there was room for the wagon to proceed.

As they entered the wagon Zalzan Kavol said furiously to Valentine. "In the future, give me no illegal advice! And you, Deliamber: make yourself aware of the regulations that apply to us. This could have caused us great delay, and much loss of income."

"Perhaps if you had tried bribing with royals instead of crowns," Carabella said beyond the Skandar's range of hearing, "we would have had a simpler time of it."

"No matter, no matter," Deliamber said. "We were admitted, were we not? It was only a small sorcery, and cheaper than a heavy bribe."

"These new laws," Sleet began. "So many decrees!"

"A new Coronal," said Lisamon Hultin. "He wants to show his power. They always do. They decree this, they decree that, and the old Pontifex goes along with everything. This one decreed me right out of a job, do you know that?"

"How so?" Valentine asked.

"I was bodyguard to a merchant in Mazadone, much afraid of jealous rivals. This Lord Valentine placed a new tax on personal bodyguards for anyone below noble rank, amounting to my whole year's salary; and my employer, damn his ears, let me go on a week's notice! Two years, and it was goodbye, Lisamon, thank you very much, take a bottle of my best brandy as your going-away gift." She belched resonantly. "One day I was the defender of his miserable life, the next I was a superfluous luxury, and all thanks to Lord Valentine! Oh, poor Voriax! D'ye think his brother had him murdered?"

"Guard your tongue!" Sleet snapped. "Such things aren't done on Majipoor."

But she persisted. "A hunting accident, was it? And the last one, old Malibor, drowned while out fishing? Why are our Coronals suddenly dying so strangely? It never happened before like this, did it? They went on to become Pontifex, they did, and hid themselves away in the Labyrinth and lived next to forever, and now here we have Malibor feeding the sea-dragons and Voriax taking a careless bolt in the forest." She belched again. "I wonder. Up there on Castle Mount, maybe they're getting too hungry for the taste of power."

"Enough," Sleet said, looking uncomfortable with such talk.

"Once a new Coronal's picked, all the rest of the princes are finished, you know, no hope of advancement. Unless, unless, unless, unless the Coronal should die, and back they go

170

into the hopper to be picked again. When Voriax died and this Valentine came to rule, I said—"

"Stop it!" Sleet cried.

He rose to his full height, which was hardly chest-high to the warrior-woman, and his eyes blazed as if he planned to chop her off at the thighs to equalize matters between them. She remained at her ease, but her hand again was wandering toward her sword. Smoothly Valentine interposed himself.

"She means no offense to the Coronal," he said gently. "She is fond of wine, and it loosens her tongue." And to Lisamon Hultin he said, "Forgive him, will you? My friend is under strain in this part of the world, as you know."

A second enormous explosion, five times as loud and fifty times as frightening as the one that had occurred half an hour earlier, interrupted the discussion. The mounts reared and squealed; the wagon lurched; Zalzan Kavol shouted ferocious curses from the driver's seat.

"Piurifayne Fountain," Deliamber announced. "One of the great sights of Majipoor, well worth getting wet to see."

Valentine and Carabella rushed from the wagon, the others close behind. They had come to an open place in the road, where the forest of little green-boled trees fell away to create a kind of natural amphitheater, completely without vegetation, running perhaps half a mile back from the highway. At its farther end a geyser was in eruption, but a geyser that was to the ones Valentine had seen at Hot Khyntor as a sea-dragon is to a minnow. This was a column of frothing water that seemed taller than the tallest tower in Dulorn, a white shaft rising five hundred feet, six hundred, possibly even more, roaring out of the ground with incalculable force. At its upper end, where its unity broke and gave way to streamers and spouts and ropes of water that darted off in many directions, a mysterious light appeared to glow, kindling a whole spectrum of hues at the fringes of the column, pinks and pearls and crimsons and pale lavenders and opals. A warm spray filled the air.

The eruption went on and on—an incredible volume of water driven by incredible might into the sky. Valentine felt his entire body massaged by the subterranean forces that were at work. He stared in awe and wonder, and it was almost with shock that he realized that the event was ending, the column now was shrinking, no more than four hundred feet, three hundred, now just a pathetic strand of white sinking toward the ground, now only forty feet, thirty, and then gone, gone, vacant air where that stunning shaft had been, droplets of warm moisture as its only revenant.

"Every thirty minutes," Autifon Deliamber informed them. "As long as the Metamorphs have lived on Majipoor, so it is said, that geyser has never been a minute late. It is a sacred place to them. See? There are pilgrims now."

Sleet caught his breath and began making holy signs. Valentine put a steadying hand to his shoulder. Indeed Metamorphs, Shapeshifters, Piurivars, a dozen or more of them, gathered at a kind of wayside shrine not far ahead. They were looking at the travelers, and, Valentine thought, not in a particularly friendly way. Several of the aborigines in the front of the group stepped briefly behind others, and when they reappeared they looked strangely blurred and indistinct, but that was not all, for they had undergone transformations. One had sprouted great cannonballs of breasts, in caricature of Lisamon Hultin, and another had grown four shaggy Skandararms, and another was mimicking Sleet's white hair. They made a curious thin sound which might have been the Metamorph version of laughter, and then the entire group slipped away into the forest.

Valentine did not release his grip on Sleet's shoulder until he felt some of the tension ebb from the little juggler's rigid body. Lightly he said, "A good trick that is! If we could do that—perhaps grow some extra arms in the middle of our act—what do you say, Sleet, would you like that?"

"I would like to be in Narabal," Sleet said, "or Piliplok, or someplace else very far from here."

"And I in Falkynkip, feeding slops to my mounts," said Shanamir, who looked pale and shaken.

"They mean us no harm," Valentine said. "This will be an interesting experience, one that we will never forget."

He smiled broadly. But there were no smiles about him, not even on Carabella, Carabella the inextinguishably buoyant. Zalzan Kavol himself looked oddly discomforted, as if perhaps he might now be having second thoughts about the wisdom of pursuing his love of royals into the Metamorph province. Valentine could not, by sheer force of optimistic energy alone, give his companions much cheer. He looked toward Deliamber.

"How far is it to Ilirivoyne?" he asked.

"It lies somewhere ahead," the Vroon replied. "How far, I have no idea. We will come to it when we come to it."

It was not an encouraging reply.

12

This was primordial country, timeless, unspoiled, an outpost of time's early dawn on civilized and housebroken Majipoor. The Shapeshifters lived in rain-forest land, where daily downpours cleansed the air and let vegetation run riot. Out of the north came the frequent storms, down into that natural funnel formed by Velathys Scarp and the Gonghars; and as the moist air rose in the ascent of the Gonghar foothills, gentle rains were released, that soaked the light spongy soil. Trees grew tall and slender-trunked, sprouting high and forming thick canopies far overhead; networks of creepers and lianas tied the treetops together; cascades of dark leaves, tapering, drip-tipped, glistened as if polished by the rain. Where there were breaks in the forest, Valentine could see distant green-cloaked mist-wrapped mountains, heavy-shouldered, forbidding, great mysterious bulks crouching on the land. Of wildlife there was little, at least not much that let itself be seen: an occasional red-and-yellow serpent slithering along a bough, an infrequent green-and-scarlet bird or toothy web-winged brown aeorlizard fluttering overhead, and once a frightened bilantoon that scampered delicately in front of the wagon and vanished into the woods with a flurry of its sharp little hooves and panicky wigwagging of its upturned tufted tail. Probably forest-brethren lurked here, since several groves of dwikka-trees came into view. And no doubt the streams were thick with fish and reptiles, the forest floor teemed with burrowing insects and rodents of fantastic hue and shape, and for all Valentine knew, each of the innumerable dark little lakes held its own monstrous submerged amorfibot, that arose by night to prowl, all neck and teeth and beady eyes, for whatever prey came within reach of its massive body. But none of these things made themselves apparent as the wagon sped southward over the rough, narrow wilderness road.

Nor were the Piurivars themselves much in evidence—now and then a well-worn trail leading into the jungle, or a few flimsy wickerwork huts visible just off the road, or a party of half a dozen pilgrims heading on foot up toward the shrine at the Fountain. They were, said Deliamber, a folk that lived by hunting and fishing, and collecting wild fruits and nuts, and a certain amount of agriculture. Possibly their civilization had once been more advanced, for ruins had been discovered, especially on Alhanroel, of large stone cities thousands of years old, that might have dated from early Piurivar times before the starships arrived—although, Deliamber said, there were some historians who maintained that the ruins were those of ancient human settlements, founded and destroyed in the turbulent pre-Pontifical period twelve to thirteen thousand years ago. At any rate the Metamorphs, if they had ever had a more complex way of life, now preferred to be forest-dwellers. Whether that was retrogression or progress Valentine could not say.

By mid-afternoon the sound of Piurifayne Fountain could no longer be heard behind them, and the forest was more open, more thickly settled. The road was unmarked, and, unexpectedly, it forked in a place where no clues were to be had to anything beyond. Zalzan Kavol looked for guidance to Deliamber, who looked to Lisamon Hultin.

"Damn my gut if I could say," the giantess boomed. "Pick one at random. We've got a fifty-fifty chance of getting to Ilirivoyne on it."

But Deliamber had a better idea, and knelt down in the mud to cast an inquiry-spell. He took from his pack a couple of cubes of a wizardy incense. Shielding them from the rain with his cloak, he ignited them to create a pale brown smoke. This he inhaled, while waving his tentacles in intricate curlicues.

The warrior-woman snorted and said, "It's only a fraud. He'll wiggle his arms for a while and then he'll make a guess. Fifty-fifty for Ilirivoyne."

"The left fork," Deliamber announced eventually.

It was good sorcery or else lucky guessing, for shortly signs of Metamorph occupation increased. There were no more isolated scatterings of lonely huts, but now little clumps of wickerwork dwellings, eight or ten or more close together every hundred yards, and then even closer. There was much foot traffic too, mainly aboriginal children carrying light burdens in slings dangling from their heads. Many stopped as the wagon went by, and stared and pointed and made little chittering sounds between their teeth.

Definitely they were approaching a large settlement. The road was crowded with children and older Metamorphs, and dwellings were numerous. The children were an unsettling crew. They seemed to be practicing their immature skills at transformation as they walked along, and took many forms, most of them bizarre: one had sprouted legs like stilts, another had tentacular Vroonish arms that dangled almost to the ground, a third had swollen its body to a globular mass supported by tiny props. "Are we the circus entertainers," Sleet asked, "or are they? These people sicken me!"

"Peace," Valentine said softly.

In a grim voice Carabella said, "I think some of the entertainments here are dark ones. Look."

Just ahead were a dozen large wicker cages by the side of the road. Teams of bearers, having apparently just put them down, were resting beside them. Through the bars of the cages small long-fingered hands were thrust, and some prehensile tails coiling in anguish. As the wagon drew alongside, Valentine saw that the cages were full of forest-brethren, jammed three and four together, on their way to Ilirivoyne for—what? To be slaughtered for food? To be tormented at the festival? Valentine shivered.

"Wait!" Shanamir blurted, as they rode past the final cage. "What's that in there?"

The last cage was bigger than the others, and what it held was no forest-brother, but rather some other sort of captive, a being of obvious intelligence, tall and strange, with dark blue skin, fierce and desolate purple eyes of extraordinary intensity and luminosity, and a wide, thin-lipped slash of a mouth. Its clothing—a fine green fabric—was ripped and tattered, and splotched with dark stains, possibly blood. It gripped the bars of its cage with terrible force, shaking and tugging at them, and cried out hoarsely at the jugglers for help in an odd, totally unfamiliar accent. The wagon went on.

Chilled, Valentine said to Deliamber, "That is no being of Majipoor!"

"No," Deliamber said. "None that I've seen before."

"I saw one once," Lisamon Hultin put in. "An offworlder, native to some star close by here, though I forget the name of it."

"But what would offworlders be doing here?" Carabella asked. "There's little traffic between the stars these days, and few ships come to Majipoor."

"Still, some do," Deliamber said. "We're not yet totally cut off from the starlanes, though certainly we're considered a backwater in the commerce of the worlds. And—"

"Are you all mad?" Sleet burst out in exasperation. "Sitting here like scholars, discussing the commerce between the worlds, and in that cage is a civilized being crying for help, who probably will be stewed and eaten at the Metamorph festival? And we pay no attention to its cries, but ride blithely onward into their city?" He made a tormented sound of anger and went rushing forward to the Skandars on the driver's seat. Valentine, fearing trouble, went after him. Sleet tugged at Zalzan Kavol's cloak. "Did you see it?" he demanded. "Did you hear? The offworlder in the cage?"

Without turning, Zalzan Kavol said, "So?"

"You'll ignore its cries?"

"This is no affair of ours," the Skandar replied evenly. "Shall we liberate the prisoners of an independent people? They must have some reason for arresting that being."

"Reason? Yes, to cook him for dinner! And we'll be in the next pot. I ask you to go back and release—"

"Impossible."

"At least let's ask of it why it's caged! Zalzan Kavol, we may be riding blithely to our deaths! Are you in such a hurry to reach Ilirivoyne that you'll ride right past someone who may know something about conditions here, and who is in such a plight?"

"What Sleet says has wisdom in it," Valentine remarked.

"Very well!" Zalzan Koval snorted. He pulled the wagon to a halt. "Go and investigate, Valentine. But be quick about it."

"I'll go with him," Sleet said.

"Stay here. If he feels he needs a bodyguard, let him take the giantess."

That seemed sensible. Valentine beckoned to Lisamon Hultin, and they got down from the wagon and strode back toward the place of the cages. Instantly the forest-brethren set up a frantic screeching and banging on their bars. The Metamorph bearers—armed, Valentine noticed now, with effective-looking short dirks of polished horn or wood—unhurriedly formed themselves into a phalanx in the road, keeping Valentine and Lisamon Hultin from a closer approach to the large cage. One Metamorph, plainly the leader, stepped forward and waited with menacing calmness for inquiries.

Valentine said quietly to the giantess, "Will he speak our language?"

"Probably. Try it."

"We are a troupe of roving jugglers," Valentine said in a loud, clear voice, "come to perform at the festival we hear you hold at Ilirivoyne. Are we near Ilirivoyne now?"

The Metamorph, half a head taller than Valentine, though much flimsier of build, seemed amused.

"You are in Ilirivoyne," was the cool, remote reply.

Valentine moistened his lips. These Metamorphs gave off a thin, sharp odor, acrid but not disagreeable. Their strangely sloped eyes were frighteningly expressionless. He said, "To

176

whom would we go to make arrangements for performing in Ilirivoyne?"

"The Danipiur interviews all strangers who come to Ilirivoyne. You will find her at the House of Offices."

The Metamorph's frosty self-contained manner was disconcerting. After a moment Valentine said, "One thing more. We see that in that large cage you keep a being of an unfamiliar sort. May I ask, for what purpose?"

"Punishment."

"A criminal?"

"So it is said," the Metamorph replied distantly. "Why does this concern you?"

"We are strangers in your land. If strangers are placed in cages here, we might prefer to find employment somewhere else."

There was a flicker of some emotion—amusement? contempt?—around the Metamorph's mouth and nostrils. "Why should you fear such a thing? Are you criminals?"

"Hardly."

"Then you will not be caged. Pay your respects to the Danipiur and address further questions to her. I have important tasks to complete."

Valentine looked toward Lisamon Hultin, who shrugged. The Metamorph walked away. There was nothing more to do but return to the wagon.

The bearers were lifting the cages and fastening them to poles laid across their backs. From the large cage came a roar of anger and despair.

13

Ilirivoyne was neither a city nor a village, but something intermediate, a forlorn concentration of many low, impermanent-looking structures of withes and light woods, arranged along irregular unpaved streets that seemed to stretch for considerable distances into the forest. The place had a makeshift look, as though Ilirivoyne might have been located elsewhere a few years ago and might be in an altogether other district a few years hence. That it was festival-time in Ilirivoyne was signaled, apparently, by fetish-sticks of some sort planted in front of almost every house, thick shaven stakes to which bright ribbons and bits of fur had been attached; also on many streets scaffolding had been erected, as for performances, or, thought Valentine uneasily, for tribal rites of some darker kind.

Finding the House of Offices and the Danipiur was simple. The main street opened into a broad plaza bordered on three sides by small domed buildings with ornately woven roofs, and on the fourth by a larger structure, the first three-story building they had seen in Ilirivoyne, with an elaborate garden of globular thick-stemmed gray-and-white shrubs in front of it. Zalzan Kavol drew the wagon into a clearing just outside the plaza.

"Come with me," the Skandar said to Deliamber. "We'll see what we can arrange."

They were inside the House of Offices a long while. When they emerged, a female Metamorph of great presence and authority was with them, doubtless the Danipiur, and the three stood together by the garden in elaborate conversation. The Danipiur pointed; Zalzan Kavol alternately nodded and shook his head; Autifon Deliamber, dwarfed between the two tall beings, made frequent graceful gestures of diplomatic conciliation. Finally Zalzan Kavol and the Vroon returned to the wagon. The Skandar's mood seemed brighter.

"We've come just in time," he announced. "The festival has already begun. Tomorrow night is one of the major holidays."

"Will they pay us?" Sleet asked.

"So it would seem," said Zalzan Kavol. "But they will supply us with no food, and no lodging either, for Ilirivoyne is without hostelries. And there are certain specified zones of the city that we may not enter. I have had friendlier welcomes in other places. But also less friendly ones now and then, I suppose."

Crowds of solemn, silent Metamorph children trailed after them as they moved the wagon from the plaza to an area just back of it where they could park. In late afternoon they held a practice session, and though Lisamon Hultin did her formidable best to clear the young Metamorphs from the scene and keep them away, it was impossible to prevent them from slipping back, emerging between trees and out of bushes to stare at the jugglers. Valentine found it unnerving to work in front of them, and he was plainly not the only one, for Sleet was tense and uncharacteristically awkward, and even Zalzan Kavol, the master of masters, dropped a club for the first time in Valentine's memory. The silence of the children was disturbing—they stood like blank-eyed statues, a remote audience that drained energy and gave none in return—but even more troublesome was their trick of metamorphosis, their way of slipping from one shape to another as casually as a human child might suck its thumb. Mimicry was their apparent purpose, for the forms they took were crude, half-recognizable versions of the jugglers, such as the older Metamorphs had attempted earlier at Piurifayne Fountain. The children held the forms only briefly—their skills seemed feeble—but in the pauses between routines Valentine saw them now sprouting golden hair for him, white for Sleet, black for Carabella, or making themselves bearish and many-armed like the Skandars, or trying to imitate faces, individual features, expressions, everything done in a distorted and unflattering way.

The travelers slept crammed aboard the wagon that night, one packed close upon the other, and all night, so it seemed, a steady rain fell. Valentine only occasionally was able to sleep; he dropped into light dozes, but mainly he lay awake listening to Lisamon Hultin's lusty snoring or the even more grotesque sounds coming from the Skandars. Somewhere in the night he must have had some real sleep, for a dream came to him, hazy and incoherent, in which he saw the Metamorphs leading a procession of prisoners, forest-brethren and the blue-skinned alien, up the road toward Piurifayne Fountain, which erupted and rose above the world like a colossal white mountain. And again toward morning he slept soundly for a time, until Sleet woke him by shaking his shoulder a little before dawn.

Valentine sat up, rubbing his eyes. "What is it?"

"Come outside. I have to talk."

"It's still dark!"

"Even so. Come!"

Valentine yawned, stretched, got creakily to his feet. He and Sleet picked their way carefully over the slumbering forms of Carabella and Shanamir, went warily around one of the Skandars, and down the steps of the wagon. The rain had stopped, but the morning was dark and chilly, and a nasty fog rose from the ground.

"I have had a sending," Sleet said. "From the Lady, I think."

"Of what sort?"

"About the blue-skinned one, in the cage, that they said was a criminal going to be punished. In my dream he came to me and said he was no criminal at all, but only a traveler who had made the error of entering Shapeshifter territory, and had been captured because it's their custom to sacrifice a stranger in Piurifayne Fountain at festival-time. And I saw how it is done, the victim bound hand and foot and left in the basin of

179

the Fountain, and when the explosion comes he is hurled far into the sky."

Valentine felt a chill that did not come from the morning mist. "I dreamed something similar," he said.

"In my dream I heard more," Sleet went on. "That we are in danger too, not perhaps from sacrifice but in danger all the same. And if we rescue the alien, he will help us to safety, but if we leave him to die, we will not leave Piurivar country alive. You know I fear these Shapeshifters, Valentine, but this dream is something new. It came to me with the clarity of a sending. It ought not be dismissed as more fears of foolish Sleet."

"What do you want to do?"

"Rescue the alien."

Valentine said uneasily, "And if he really was a criminal? By what right do we meddle in Piurivar justice?"

"By right of sending," said Sleet. "Are those forest-brethren criminals too? I saw them also go into the Fountain. We are among savages, Valentine."

"Not savages, no. But strange folk, whose way is not like the ways of Majipoor."

"I'm determined to set the blue-skinned one free. If not with your help, then by myself."

"Now?"

"What better time?" Sleet asked. "It's still dark. Quiet. I'll open the cage; he'll slip off into the jungle."

"You think the cage is unguarded? No, Sleet. Wait. This makes no sense. You'll jeopardize us all if you act now. Let me try to find out more about this prisoner and why he's caged, and what's intended for him. If they do mean to sacrifice him, they'd do it at some high point of the festival. There's time."

"The sending is on me now," Sleet said.

"I dreamed a dream something like yours."

"But not a sending."

"Not a sending, no. Still, enough to let me think your dream holds truth. I'll help you, Sleet. But not now. This isn't the moment for it."

Sleet looked restless. Clearly in his mind he was already on the way to the place of the cages, and Valentine's opposition was thwarting him.

"Sleet?"

"Yes?"

"Hear me. This is not the moment. There is time."

Valentine looked steadily at the juggler. Sleet returned his gaze with equal steadfastness for a moment; then, abruptly, his resolve broke and he lowered his eyes.

"Yes, my lord," he said quietly.

During the day Valentine tried to gain information about the prisoner, but with little success. The cages, eleven holding forest-brethren and the twelfth holding the alien, now had been installed in the plaza opposite the House of Offices, stacked in four tiers with the alien's cage alone on high, far above the ground. Piurivars armed with dirks guarded them.

Valentine approached, but he was only halfway across the plaza when he was stopped. A Metamorph told him, "This is forbidden for you to enter."

The forest-brethren began frantically to rattle their bars. The blue-skinned one called out, thickly accented words that Valentine could barely understand. Was the alien saying, "Flee, fool, before they kill you too!" or was that only Valentine's heightened imagination at work? The guards held a tight cordon around the place. Valentine turned away. He attempted to ask some children nearby if they could explain the cages to him; but they looked at him in obstinate silence, giving him cool blank-eyed stares and murmuring to one another and making little partial metamorphoses that mimicked his fair hair, and then they scattered and ran as though he were some sort of demon.

All morning long Metamorphs entered Ilirivoyne, swarming in from the outlying forest settlements. They brought with them decorations of many sorts, wreaths and buntings and draperies and mirror-bedecked posts and tall poles carved with mysterious runes; everyone seemed to know what to do, and everyone was intensely busy. No rain fell after sunrise. Was it by witchcraft, Valentine wondered, that the Piurivars provided a rare dry day for their high holiday, or only coincidence?

By mid-afternoon the festivities were under way. Small bands of musicians played heavy, pulsating, jangling music of eccentric rhythm, and throngs of Metamorphs danced a slow and stately pattern of interweavings, moving almost like sleepwalkers. On certain streets races were run, and judges stationed at points along the course engaged in intricate arguments as the racers went past them. Booths apparently constructed during the night dispensed soups, stews, beverages, and grilled meats.

Valentine felt like an intruder in this place. He wanted to apologize to the Metamorphs for having come among them at their holiest time. Yet no one but the children seemed to be paying the slightest attention to them, and the children evidently regarded them as curiosities brought here for their amusement. Young shy Metamorphs lurked everywhere, flashing jumbled imitations of Deliamber and Sleet and Zalzan Kavol and the rest, but never allowing anyone to get close to them.

Zalzan Kavol had called a rehearsal for late afternoon, back of the wagon. Valentine was one of the first to arrive, glad of an excuse to remove himself from the crowded streets. He found only Sleet and two of the Skandars.

It seemed to him that Zalzan Kavol was eyeing him in an odd way. There was something new and disturbing about the quality of the Skandar's attentiveness. After a few minutes Valentine was so troubled by it that he said, "Is something wrong?"

"What would be wrong?"

"You seem out of countenance."

"I? I? Nothing's the matter. A dream, is all. I was thinking on a dream I had last night."

"You dreamed of the blue-skinned prisoner?"

Zalzan Kavol looked baffled. "Why do you think that?"

"I did, and Sleet."

"My dream had nothing at all to do with the blue-skinned one," the Skandar replied. "Nor do I wish to discuss it. It was foolishness, mere foolishness." And Zalzan Kavol, moving away, picked up a double brace of knives and began to juggle them in an edgy, absent-minded way.

Valentine shrugged. It had not even occurred to him that Skandars had dreams, let alone that they might have troublesome ones. But of course: they were citizens of Majipoor, they shared in all the attributes of people here, and so they must live full and rich dream-lives like everyone else, with sendings from King and Lady, and stray intrusions from the minds of lesser beings, and upwellings of self from their own deeper reaches, even as humans did, or, Valentine supposed, Hjorts and Vroons and Liimen. Still, it was curious. Zalzan Kavol was so guarded of emotion, so unwilling to let anything of himself be seen by others save greed and impatience and irritation, that Valentine found it strange that he would admit something so personal as that he was pondering a dream.

He wondered if Metamorphs had meaningful dreams, and sendings, and all of that.

The rehearsal went well. Afterward the jugglers made a light and not very satisfying dinner of fruits and berries that Lisamon Hultin had gathered in the forest, and washed it down with the last of the wine they had brought from Khyntor. Bonfires now were blazing in many streets of Ilirivoyne, and the discordant music of the various bands set up weird clashing near-harmonies. Valentine had assumed the performance would take place in the plaza, but no, Metamorphs in what perhaps were priestly costumes came at darkness to escort them to some entirely other part of town, a much larger oval clearing that already was ringed by hundreds or even thousands of expectant onlookers. Zalzan Kavol and his brothers went over the ground carefully, checking for pitfalls and irregularities that might disrupt their movements. Sleet usually took part in that, but, Valentine noticed abruptly, Sleet had vanished somewhere between the rehearsal place and this clearing. Had his patience run out, had he gone off to do something rash? Valentine was just about to set out in search when Sleet appeared, breathing lightly as though he had just been jogging.

"I went to the plaza," he said in a low voice. "The cages are still piled up. But most of the guards must be off at the dancing. I was able to exchange a few words with the prisoner before I was chased."

"And?"

"He said he's to be sacrificed at midnight in the Fountain, exactly as in my sending. And tomorrow night the same will happen to us."

"What?"

"I swear it by the Lady," said Sleet. His eyes were like augers. "It was under pledge to you, my lord, that I came into this place. You assured me no harm would befall me."

"Your fears seemed irrational."

"And now?"

"I begin to revise my opinion," Valentine said. "But we'll get out of Ilirivoyne in good health. I pledge you that. I'll speak with Zalzan Kavol after the performance, and after I've had a chance to confer with Deliamber."

"It would please me more to get on the road sooner."

"The Metamorphs are feasting and drinking this evening. They'll be less likely to notice our departure later," said Valentine, "and less apt to pursue us, if pursuit is their aim. Besides, do you think Zalzan Kavol would agree to cancel a performance merely on the rumor of danger? We'll do our act, and then we'll begin to extricate ourselves. What do you say?"

"I am yours, my lord," Sleet replied.

14

It was a splendid performance, and no one was in better form
than Sleet, who did his blind-juggling routine and carried it
off flawlessly. The Skandars flung torches at one another
with giddy abandon, Carabella cavorted on the rolling globe,
Valentine juggled while dancing, skipping, kneeling, and running. The Metamorphs sat in concentric circles around them,
saying little, never applauding, peering in at them out of the
foggy darkness with unfathomable intensity of concentration.

Working to such an audience was hard. It was worse than
working in rehearsal, for no one expects an audience then, but
now there were thousands of spectators and they were giving
nothing to the performers; they were statue-still, as the children had been, an austere audience that offered neither approval nor disapproval but only something that had to be interpreted as indifference. In the face of that, the jugglers
presented ever more taxing and marvelous numbers, but for
more than an hour they could get no response.

And then, astoundingly, the Metamorphs began a juggling
act of their own, an eerie dreamlike counterfeit of what the
troupe had been doing.

By twos and threes they came forward from the darkness,
taking up positions in the center of the ring only a few yards
from the jugglers. As they did so they swiftly shifted forms, so
that six of them now wore the look of bulky shaggy Skandars,
and one was small and lithe and much like Carabella, and one
had Sleet's compact form, and one, yellow-haired and tall,
wore the image of Valentine. There was nothing playful about
this donning of the jugglers' bodies: to Valentine it seemed
ominous, mocking, distinctly threatening, and when he looked
to the side at the non-performing members of the troupe he
saw Autifon Deliamber making worried gestures with his tentacles, Vinorkis scowling, and Lisamon Hultin rocking evenly
back and forth on the balls of her feet as if readying herself
for combat.

Zalzan Kavol looked disconcerted also by this development.

"Continue," he said in a ragged tone. "We are here to perform for them."

"I think," said Valentine, "we are here to amuse them, but
not necessarily as performers."

"Nevertheless, we are performers, and we will perform."

He gave a signal and launched, with his brothers, into a dazzling interchange of multitudinous sharp and dangerous objects. Sleet, after a moment's hesitation, scooped up a handful of clubs and began to throw them in cascades, as did Carabella. Valentine's hands were chilled; he felt no willingness in them to juggle.

The nine Metamorphs alongside them were beginning to juggle now too.

It was only counterfeit juggling, dream-juggling, with no true art or skill to it. It was mockery and nothing more. They held in their hands rough-skinned black fruits, and bits of wood, and other ordinary things, and threw them from hand to hand in a child's parody of juggling, now and again failing to make even those simple catches and bending quickly to retrieve what they had dropped. Their performance aroused the audience as nothing that the true jugglers had done had managed to do. The Metamorphs now were humming—was this their form of applause?—and rocking rhythmically, and clapping hands to knees, and, Valentine saw, some of them were transforming themselves almost at random, taking on odd alternate forms, human or Hjort or Su-Suheris as the whim struck, or modeling themselves after the Skandars or Carabella or Deliamber. At one point he saw six or seven Valentines in the rows nearest him.

Performing was all but impossible in such a circus of distractions, but the jugglers clung grimly to their routines for some minutes more, doing poorly now, dropping clubs, missing beats, breaking up long-familiar combinations. The humming of the Metamorphs grew in intensity.

"Oh, look, look!" Carabella cried suddenly.

She gestured toward the nine mock jugglers, and pointed at the one who represented Valentine.

Valentine gasped.

What the Metamorph was doing defied all comprehension, and struck him rigid with terror and astonishment. For it had begun to oscillate between two forms. One was the Valentine-image, the tall, wide-shouldered, big-handed, golden-haired young man.

And the other was the image of Lord Valentine the Coronal.

The metamorphosis was almost instantaneous, like the flashing of a light. One moment Valentine saw his twin before him, and the next instant there was, in his place, the black-bearded fierce-eyed Coronal, a figure of might and presence, and then he was gone and the simple juggler was back. The humming

185

of the crowd became louder: they approved of the show. Valentine . . . Lord Valentine . . . Valentine . . . Lord Valentine . . .

As he watched, Valentine felt a trail of icy chill go down his back, felt his scalp prickle, his knees quiver. There was no mistaking the import of this bizarre pantomime. If ever he had hoped for confirmation of all that had swept through him these weeks since Pidruid, he was getting it now. But here? In this forest town, among these aboriginal folk?

He looked into his own mimicked face.

He looked into the face of the Coronal.

The other eight jugglers leaped and pranced in a nightmarish dance, their legs rising high and stamping down, the false Skandar-arms waving and thumping against their sides, the false Sleet-hair and Carabella-hair wild in the night wind, and the Valentine-figure remained still, alternating one face and the other, and then it was over; nine Metamorphs stood in the center of the circle, holding out their hands to the audience, and the rest of the Piurivars were on their feet and dancing in the same wild way.

The performance was ended. Still dancing, the Metamorphs streamed out into the night, toward the booths and games of their festival.

Valentine, stunned, turned slowly and saw the frozen, astonished faces of his companions. Zalzan Kavol's jaw sagged, his arms dangled limply. His brothers clustered close behind him, their eyes wide in awe and shock. Sleet looked frighteningly pale; Carabella the opposite, her cheeks flushed, almost feverish. Valentine held out a hand toward them. Zalzan Kavol came stumbling forward, dazed, all but tripping over his own feet. The giant Skandar paused a few feet from Valentine. He blinked, he ran his tongue over his lips, he seemed to be working hard to make his voice function at all.

Finally he said, in a tiny, preposterous voice: "My lord . . . ?"

First Zalzan Kavol and then his five brothers dropped hesitantly and awkwardly to their knees. With trembling hands Zalzan Kavol made the starburst symbol; his brothers did the same. Sleet, Carabella, Vinorkis, Deliamber, all knelt as well. The boy Shanamir, looking frightened and baffled, stared open-mouthed at Valentine. He seemed paralyzed with wonder and surprise. Slowly he bent to the ground also.

Lisamon Hultin cried out, "Have you all gone crazy?"

"Down and pay homage!" Sleet ordered her hoarsely. "You saw it, woman! He is the Coronal! Down and pay homage!"

186

"The Coronal?" she repeated in confusion.

Valentine stretched his arms out over them all in a gesture that was as much one of comfort as blessing. They were frightened of him and of what had just befallen; so too was he, but his fear was passing quickly, and in its place came strength, conviction, sureness. The sky itself seemed to cry at him: You are Lord Valentine who was Coronal on Castle Mount, and you shall have the Castle again one day, if you fight for it. Through him now flowed the power of his former imperial office. Even here, in this rainswept remote hinterland, in this ramshackle aboriginal town, here with the sweat of juggling still on his body, here in these coarse common clothes, Valentine felt himself to be what he once had been, and although he did not understand what metamorphosis had been worked on him to make him what he now was, he no longer questioned the reality of the messages that had come in dreams. And he felt no guilt, no shame, no deceitfulness, at receiving this homage from his stupefied companions.

"Up," he said gently. "All of you. On your feet. We must get out of this place. Shanamir, round up the mounts. Zalzan Kavol, get the wagon ready." To Sleet he said, "Everyone should be armed. Energy-throwers for those who know how to use them, juggling knives for the rest. See to it."

Zalzan Kavol said heavily, "My lord, there is in all this the flavor of a dream. To think that all these weeks I traveled with—to think I spoke roughly to—that I quarreled with—"

"Later," Valentine said. "We have no time for discussing these things now."

He turned to Lisamon Hultin, who seemed busy in some conversation with herself, moving her lips, gesturing, explaining things to herself, debating these bewildering events. In a quiet, forceful voice Valentine said, "You were hired only to bring us as far as Ilirivoyne. I need you to give us your strength as we escape. Will you stay with us to Ni-moya and beyond?"

"They made the starburst at you," she said puzzledly. "They all kneeled. And the Metamorphs—they—"

"I was once Lord Valentine of Castle Mount. Accept it. Believe it. The realm has fallen into dangerous hands. Remain at my side, Lisamon, as I journey east to set things right."

She put her huge meaty hand over her mouth and looked at him in amazement.

Then she began to sag into an homage, but he shook his head, caught her by the elbow, would not let her kneel. "Come," he said. "That doesn't matter now. Out of here!"

They gathered up their juggling gear and sprinted through the darkness toward the wagon, far across town. Shanamir and Carabella had already taken off, and were running well ahead. The Skandars moved in a single ponderous phalanx, shaking the ground beneath them; Valentine had never seen them move so quickly before. He ran just behind them, alongside Sleet. Vinorkis, splay-footed and slow, struggled to keep pace with them. To the rear was Lisamon Hultin. She had scooped up Deliamber and was carrying the little wizard perched in the crook of her left arm; in her right she bore her unsheathed vibration-sword.

As they neared the wagon Sleet said to Valentine, "Shall we free the prisoner?"

"Yes."

He beckoned to Lisamon Hultin. She put Deliamber down and followed him.

With Sleet in the lead, they ran toward the plaza. To Valentine's relief it was all but empty, no more than a handful of Piurivar guards on duty. The twelve cages still were stacked in tiers at the far end, four on the bottom, then rows of four and three, and the one containing the blue-skinned alien perched on top. Before the guards could react Lisamon Hultin was among them, seizing them two at a time and hurling them far across the plaza.

"Take no lives," Valentine warned.

Sleet, monkey-swift, was scrambling up the stack of cages. He reached the top and began to cut through the thick withes that held the cage door shut. With brisk sawing motions of the knife he slashed while Valentine held the withes taut. In a moment the last of the fibers was severed and Valentine hoisted the door. The alien clambered out, stretching his cramped limbs and looking questioningly at his rescuers.

"Come with us," Valentine said. "Our wagon is over there, beyond the plaza. Do you understand?"

"I understand," said the alien. His voice was deep, harsh, resonant, with a sharp clipped edge to each syllable. Without another word he swung himself down past the cages of the forest-brethren to the ground, where Lisamon Hultin had finished dealing with the Metamorph guards and was piling them tidily in a heap.

Impulsively Valentine sliced through the lashings on the cage of forest-brethren nearest to him. The busy little hands of the creatures reached through the bars and pulled the latch, and out they came. Valentine went on to the next cage. Sleet had already descended.

"One moment," Valentine called. "The job's not quite done."

Sleet drew his knife and set to work. In moments all the cages were open, and the forest-brethren, dozens of them, were disappearing into the night.

As they ran to the wagon Sleet said, "Why did you do that?"

"Why not?" Valentine asked. "They want to live too."

Shanamir and the Skandars had the wagon ready to go, the mounts hitched, the rotors turning. Lisamon Hultin was the last one in; she slammed the door behind her and yelled to Zalzan Kavol, who took off immediately.

And just in time, for half a dozen Metamorphs appeared and began running frantically after them, shouting and gesticulating. Zalzan Kavol stepped up the wagon's speed. Gradually the pursuers fell behind and were lost to sight as the wagon entered the utter darkness of the jungle.

Sleet peered worriedly back. "Do you think they're still following us?"

"They can't keep up with us," said Lisamon Hultin. "And they travel only by foot. We're safely out of there."

"Are you sure?" Sleet asked. "What if they have some side route to take in catching up with us?"

"Worry about that when we must," said Carabella. "We're moving quickly." She shuddered. "And let it be a long while before we see Ilirivoyne again!"

They fell silent. The wagon glided swiftly onward.

Valentine sat slightly apart from the others. It was inevitable, yet it distressed him, for he was still more Valentine than Lord Valentine, and it was strange and disagreeable to set himself up above his friends. But there was no helping it. Carabella and Sleet, learning privately of his identity, had come to terms with it privately in their own ways; Deliamber, who had known the truth before Valentine himself, had never been overly awed by it; but the others, whatever suspicions they may have had that Valentine was something more than a happy-go-lucky wanderer, were dumfounded by the open acknowledgment of his rank that had come out of the grotesque Metamorph performance. They stared; they were speechless; they sat in stiff, unnatural postures, as if afraid to slouch in the presence of a Coronal. But how should one behave in the presence of a Power of Majipoor? They could not sit here constantly making starbursts at him. The gesture seemed absurd to Valentine anyway, a comical outpoking of the fingers and nothing more: his growing sense of his own importance did not seem to include much spirit of self-importance yet.

The alien introduced himself as Khun of Kianimot, a world of a star relatively close by Majipoor. He seemed a dark and brooding sort, with a crystalline anger and despair at his core, something integral to his being, that expressed itself, Valentine thought, in the set of his lips and the tone of his voice and particularly in the intense gaze of his strange, haunted purple eyes. Of course it was possible, Valentine conceded, that he was projecting his own human notions of expression onto this alien being, and that perhaps Khun was, as Kianimot folk went, a person of total jollity and amiability. But he doubted that.

Khun had come to Majipoor two years before, on business that he chose not to explain. It was, he said bitterly, the greatest mistake of his life, for among the merry Majipoorans he had been parted from all his money, he had unwisely embarked on a journey to Zimroel unaware that there was no starport on that continent from which he could depart for his home world, and he had even more foolishly ventured into Piurivar territory, thinking he could recoup his losses in some sort of trade with the Metamorphs. But they had seized him instead and thrust him in the cage, and held him prisoner for weeks, meaning to give him to the Fountain on the high night of their festival.

"Which would perhaps have been best," he said. "One quick blast of water and all this wandering would be at an end. Majipoor makes me weary. If I am destined to die on this world of yours, I think I would prefer it to be soon."

"Pardon us for rescuing you," Carabella said sharply.

"No. No. I mean no ingratitude. But only—" Khun paused. "This place has been grief for me. So too was Kianimot. Is there any place in the universe where life does not mean suffering?"

"Has it been that bad?" asked Carabella. "We find it tolerable here. Even the worst is tolerable enough, considering the alternative." She laughed. "Are you always this gloomy?"

The alien shrugged. "If you are happy, I admire and envy you. I find existence painful and life meaningless. But these are dark thoughts for one who has just been rescued. I thank you for your aid. Who are you, and what rashness brought you to Piurifayne, and where do you go now?"

"We are jugglers," said Valentine, with a sharp glance at the others. "We came to this province because we thought there was work for us here. And if we succeed in getting away from this place, we'll head for Ni-moya, and down the river to Piliplok."

"And from there?"

Valentine gestured vaguely. "Some of us will make the pilgrimage to the Isle. Do you know what that is? And the others—I can't say where they'll go."

"I must reach Alhanroel," Khun said. "My only hope lies in going home, which is impossible from this continent. In Piliplok perhaps I can arrange passage across the sea. May I travel with you?"

"Of course."

"I have no money."

"We see that," said Valentine. "It makes no difference."

The wagon moved on swiftly through the night. No one slept, except in occasional quick naps. A light rain was falling now. In the darkness of the forest, dangers might lie on any side, but there was a paradoxical comfort in not being able to see anything, and the wagon sped on unmolested.

After an hour or so Valentine looked up and saw Vinorkis standing before him, gaping like a gaffed fish and quivering with what must be unbearable tension.

"My lord?" he said in a tiny voice.

Valentine nodded to the Hjort. "You're trembling, Vinorkis."

"My lord—how do I say this?—I have a terrible confession to make—"

Sleet opened his eyes and glared bleakly. Valentine signaled him to be calm.

Vinorkis said, "My lord—" and faltered. He began again. "My lord, in Pidruid a man came to me and said, 'There is a tall fair-haired stranger at a certain inn and we believe he has committed monstrous crimes.' And this man offered me a bag of crowns if I would keep close by the fair-haired stranger, and go wherever he went, and give news of his doings to the imperial proctors every few days."

"A spy?" Sleet blurted. His hand flew to the dagger at his hip.

"Who was this man who hired you?" Valentine asked quietly.

The Hjort shook his head. "Someone in the service of the Coronal, by the way he dressed. I never knew his name."

"And you gave these reports?" Valentine said.

"Yes, my lord," Vinorkis murmured, staring at his feet. "In every city. After a time I hardly believed that you could be the criminal they said you were, for you seemed kind and

191

gentle and sweet of soul, but I had taken their money, and there was more money for me every time I reported—"

"Let me kill him now," Sleet muttered harshly.

"There'll be no killing," Valentine said. "Neither now nor later."

"He's dangerous, my lord!"

"Not any longer."

"I never trusted him," Sleet said. "Nor did Carabella, nor Deliamber. It wasn't just that he was Hjort. There was always something shifty about him, sly, insinuating. All those questions, all that sucking around for information—"

Vinorkis said, "I ask pardon. I had no idea whom I was betraying, my lord."

"You believe that?" Sleet cried.

"Yes," Valentine said. "Why not? He had no more idea who I was than—than I did. He was told to trail a fair-haired man and give information to the government. Is that so evil a thing? He was serving his Coronal, or so he thought. His loyalty must not be repaid by your dagger, Sleet."

"My lord, sometimes you are too innocent," Sleet said.

"Perhaps true. But not this time. We have much to gain by forgiving this man, and nothing at all by slaying him." To the Hjort Valentine said, "You have my pardon, Vinorkis. I ask only that you be as loyal to the true Coronal as you've been to the false."

"You have my pledge, my lord."

"Good. Get yourself some sleep, now, and put away your fear."

Vinorkis made the starburst and backed away, settling down in mid-cabin beside two of the Skandars.

Sleet said, "That was unwise, my lord. What if he continues to spy on us?"

"In these jungles? Messages to whom?"

"And when we leave the jungles?"

"I think he can be trusted," said Valentine. "I know, this confession may have been only a double ruse, to lull us into casting aside our suspicions. I'm not as naïve as you think, Sleet. I charge you to keep private watch over him when we reach civilization again—just in case. But I think you'll find his repentance is genuine. And I have uses for him that will make him valuable to me."

"Uses, my lord?"

"A spy can lead us to other spies. And there'll be other spies, Sleet. We may want Vinorkis to maintain his contacts with the imperial agents, eh?"

192

Sleet winked. "I see your meaning, my lord!"

Valentine smiled, and they fell silent.

Yes, he told himself, Vinorkis' horror and remorse were genuine. And provided much that Valentine needed to know; for if the Coronal had been willing to pay good sums to have an insignificant wanderer followed from Pidruid to Ilirivoyne, how insignificant could that wanderer actually be? Valentine felt a weird prickling along his skin. More than anything else, Vinorkis' confession was a confirmation of all that Valentine had discovered about himself. Surely, if the technique that had been used to cast him from his body was new and relatively untried, the conspirators would be uncertain about how permanent the mind-wiping would be, and would hardly dare to allow the outcast Coronal to roam about the land free and unobserved. A spy, then, and probably others close by; and the threat of quick preventive action if word got back to the usurper that Valentine was beginning to recover his memory. He wondered how carefully the imperial forces were tracking him, and at what point they would choose to intercept him on his journey toward Alhanroel.

Onward the wagon moved in the blackness of night. Deliamber and Lisamon Hultin conferred endlessly with Zalzan Kavol about the route; the other main Metamorph settlement, Avendroyne, lay somewhere to the southeast of Ilirivoyne, in a gap between two great mountains, and it seemed likely that the road they were on would take them there. To ride blithely into another Metamorph town hardly seemed wise, of course. Word must have gone on ahead of the freeing of the prisoner and the escape of the wagon. Still, there was even greater peril in trying to go back toward Piurifayne Fountain.

Valentine, not at all sleepy, re-enacted the Metamorph pantomime a hundred times in his mind. It had the quality of a dream, yes, but no dream was so immediate: he had been close enough to touch his Metamorph counterpart; he had seen, beyond all doubt, those shifts of features from fair to dark, dark to fair. The Metamorphs knew the truth, more clearly than he himself. Could they read souls, as Deliamber sometimes did? What had they felt, knowing they had a fallen Coronal in their midst? No awe, certainly: Coronals were nothing to them, mere symbols of their own defeat thousands of years ago. It must have seemed terribly funny to them to have a successor to Lord Stiamot tossing clubs at their festival, amusing them with silly tricks and dances, far from the splendors of Castle Mount, a Coronal in their own muddy wooden village. How strange, he thought. How much like a dream.

193

Toward dawn huge rounded mountains became visible, with a broad notch between them. Avendroyne could not be far. Zalzan Kavol, with a deference he had never shown before, came aft to consult Valentine on strategy. Lie low in the woods all day, and wait until nightfall to try to get past Avendroyne? Or attempt a bold daylight passage?

Leadership was unfamiliar to Valentine. He pondered a moment, trying to look far-seeing and thoughtful.

At length he said, "If we go forward by day, we are too conspicuous. On the other hand, if we waste all day hiding here, we give them more time to prepare plans against us."

"Tonight," Sleet pointed out, "is the high festival again in Ilirivoyne, and probably here also. We might slip by them while they're merrymaking, but in daylight we have no chance."

"I agree," said Lisamon Hultin.

Valentine looked around. "Carabella?"

"If we wait, we give the Ilirivoyne people time to overtake us. I say go onward."

"Deliamber?"

The Vroon delicately touched tentacle-tips together. "Onward. Bypass Avendroyne, double back toward Verf. There'll be a second road to the Fountain from Avendroyne, surely."

"Yes," Valentine said. He looked to Zalzan Kavol. "My thoughts run with Deliamber and Carabella. What of yours?"

Zalzan Kavol scowled. "Mine say, let the wizard make this wagon fly, and take us tonight to Ni-moya. Otherwise, continue on without waiting."

"So be it," said Valentine, as if he had made the decision single-handedly. "And when we approach Avendroyne, we'll send scouts out to find a road that bypasses the town."

On they went, moving more cautiously as daybreak arrived. The rain was intermittent, but when it came now it was no gentle spatter, more an almost tropical downpour, a heavy cannonade of drops that rattled with malign force against the wagon's roof. To Valentine the rain was welcome: perhaps it would keep the Metamorphs indoors as they went through.

There were signs of outskirts now, scattered wicker huts. The road forked and forked again, Deliamber offering a guess at each point of division, until finally they knew they must be close to Avendroyne. Lisamon Hultin and Sleet rode out as scouts, and returned in an hour with good news: one of the two roads just ahead ran right into the heart of Avendroyne, where festival preparations were under way, and the other curved toward the northeast, bypassing the city entirely and going through what looked like a farming district on the farther slopes of the mountains.

They took the northeast road. Uneventfully they passed the Avendroyne region.

Now, in late afternoon, they journeyed down the mountain pass and into a broad, thickly forested plain, rainswept and dark, that marked the eastern perimeter of Metamorph territory. Zalzan Kavol drove the wagon furiously onward, pausing only when Shanamir insisted that the mounts absolutely had to rest and forage; virtually tireless they might be, and of synthetic origin, but living things were what they were, and now and then they needed to halt. The Skandar yielded reluctantly; he seemed possessed by desperate need to put Piurifayne far behind him.

Toward twilight, as they went in heavy rain through rough, irregular country, trouble came suddenly upon them.

Valentine was riding in mid-cabin, with Deliamber and Carabella; most of the others were sleeping, and Heitrag Kavol and Gibor Haern were driving. There came a crashing, crackling, smashing sound from ahead, and a moment later the wagon jolted to a stop.

"Tree down in the storm!" Heitrag Kavol called. "Road blocked in front of us!"

Zalzan Kavol muttered curses and tugged Lisamon Hultin awake. Valentine saw nothing but green ahead, the entire crown of some forest giant blocking the road. It might take hours or even days to clear that. The Skandars, hoisting energy-throwers to their shoulders, went out to investigate. Valentine followed. Darkness was falling rapidly. The wind was gusty, and shafts of rain swept almost horizontally into their faces.

"Let's get to work," Zalzan Kavol growled, shaking his head in annoyance. "Thelkar! You start cutting from down there! Rovorn! The big side branches! Erfon—"

"It might be swifter," Valentine suggested, "to back up and look for another fork in the road."

The idea startled Zalzan Kavol, as if the Skandar would never in a century have conceived such a notion. He mulled it for a moment. "Yes," he said finally. "That does make some sense. If we—"

And a second tree, larger even than the first, toppled to the ground a hundred yards behind them. The wagon was trapped.

Valentine was the first to comprehend what must be happening. "Into the wagon, everyone! It's an ambush!" He rushed toward the open door.

Too late. Out of the darkening forest came a stream of Metamorphs, fifteen or twenty of them, perhaps even more, bursting silently into their midst. Zalzan Kavol let out a terrible cry of rage and opened fire with his energy-thrower; the blaze of light cast a strange lavender glow over the roadside and two Metamorphs fell, charred hideously. But in the same instant Heitrag Kavol uttered a strangled gurgle and dropped, a weapon-shaft through his neck, and Thelkar fell, clutching at another in his chest.

Suddenly the rear end of the wagon was ablaze. Those within came scrambling out, Lisamon Hultin leading the way with her vibration-sword high. Valentine found himself attacked by a Metamorph wearing his own face; he kicked the creature away, pivoted, slashed a second one with the knife that was his only weapon. That was strange, to inflict a wound. In weird fascination, he watched the bronze-hued fluid begin to flow.

The Valentine Metamorph came at him again. Claws went for his eyes. Valentine dodged, twisted, stabbed. The blade sank deep and the Metamorph reeled back, clutching at its chest. Valentine trembled in shock, but only for an instant. He turned to confront the next.

This was a new experience for him, this fighting and killing, and it made his soul ache. But to be gentle now was to invite a quick death. He thrust and cut, thrust and cut. From behind him he heard Carabella call, "How are you doing?"

"Holding—my—own—" he grunted.

Zalzan Kavol, seeing his magnificent wagon on fire, howled and caught a Metamorph by the waist and hurled it into the pyre; two more rushed at him, but another Skandar seized them and snapped them like sticks with each pair of hands. In the frantic melee Valentine caught sight of Carabella wrestling with a Metamorph, forcing it to the ground with the powerful forearm muscles years of juggling had developed; and there was Sleet, ferociously vindictive, pounding another with his boots in savage joy. But the wagon was burning. The wagon was burning. The woods were full of Metamorphs, night was swiftly coming on, the rain was a torrent, and the wagon was burning.

As the heat of the fire increased, the center of the battle shifted from the roadside to the forest, and matters became even more confused, for in the darkness it was hard to tell friend from foe. The Metamorph trick of shapeshifting added another complication, although in the frenzy of the fight they were unable to hold their transformations for long, and what seemed to be Sleet, or Shanamir, or Zalzan Kavol, reverted quickly to its native form.

Valentine fought savagely. He was slippery with his own sweat and the blood of Metamorphs, and his heart hammered mightily with the furious exertion. Panting, gasping, never still an instant, he waded through the tangle of enemies with a zeal that astonished him, never pausing for an instant's rest. Thrust and cut, thrust and cut—

The Metamorphs were armed with only the simplest of weapons, and, though there seemed to be dozens of them, their numbers soon were dwindling rapidly. Lisamon Hultin was doing awful destruction with her vibration-sword, swinging it two-handed and lopping off the boughs of trees as well as the limbs of Metamorphs. The surviving Skandars, spraying energy-bolts wildly around the scene, had ignited half a dozen trees and had littered the ground with fallen Metamorphs. Sleet was maiming and slaughtering as if he could in one wild minute avenge himself for all the pain he fancied the Metamorphs had brought upon him. Khun and Vinorkis too were fighting with passionate energy.

As suddenly as the ambush had begun, it was over.

By the light of the fires Valentine could see dead Metamorphs everywhere. Two dead Skandars lay among them. Lisamon Hultin bore a bloody but shallow wound on one thigh; Sleet had lost half his jerkin and had taken several minor cuts; Shanamir had clawmarks across his cheek. Valentine too felt some trifling scratches and nicks, and his arms had a leaden ache of fatigue. But he had not been seriously harmed. Deliamber, though—where was Deliamber? The Vroon wizard was nowhere to be seen. In anguish Valentine turned to Carabella and said, "Did the Vroon stay in the wagon?"

"I thought we all came out when it burst afire."

Valentine frowned. In the silence of the forest the only sounds were the terrible hissing and crackling of fire and the quiet mocking patter of the rain. "Deliamber?" Valentine called. "Deliamber, where are you?"

"Here," answered a high-pitched voice from above. Valentine looked up and saw the sorcerer clinging to a sturdy bough, fifteen feet off the ground. "Warfare is not one of my skills," Deliamber explained blandly, swinging outward and letting himself drop into Lisamon Hultin's arms.

Carabella said, "What do we do now?"

Valentine realized that she was asking him. He was in command. Zalzan Kavol, kneeling by his brothers' bodies, seemed stunned by their deaths and by the loss of his precious wagon.

He said, "We have no choice but to cut through the forest. If we try to take the main road we'll meet more Metamorphs. Shanamir, what of the mounts?"

"Dead," the boy sobbed. "Every one. The Metamorphs—"

"On foot, then. A long wet journey it will be, too. Deliamber, how far do you think we are from the River Steiche?"

"A few days' journey, I suspect. But we have no sure notion of the direction."

"Follow the slope of the land," Sleet said. "Rivers won't lie uphill from here. If we keep going east we're bound to hit it."

"Unless a mountain stands in our way," Deliamber remarked.

"We'll find the river," Valentine said firmly. "The Steiche flows into the Zimr at Ni-moya, is that right?"

"Yes," said Deliamber, "but its flow is turbulent."

"We'll have to chance it. A raft, I suppose, will be quickest to build. Come. If we stay here much longer we'll be set upon again."

They could salvage nothing from the wagon, neither clothing nor foor nor belongings nor their juggling gear—all lost, every scrap, everything but what had been on them when they came forth to meet the ambushers. To Valentine that was no great loss; but to some of the others, particularly the Skandars, it was overwhelming. The wagon had been their home a long while.

It was difficult to get Zalzan Kavol to move from the spot. He seemed frozen, unable to abandon the bodies of his brothers and the ruin of his wagon. Gently Valentine urged him to his feet. Some of the Metamorphs, he said, might well have escaped in the skirmish; they could soon return with reinforcements; it was perilous to remain here. Quickly they dug shallow graves in the soft forest floor and laid Thelkar and Heitrag Kavol to rest. Then, in steady rain and gathering darkness, they set out in what they hoped was an easterly direction.

For over an hour they walked, until it became too dark to see; then they camped miserably in a little soggy huddle, clinging to one another until dawn. At first light they rose, cold and stiff, and picked their way onward through the tangled forest. The rain, at least, had stopped. The forest here was less of a jungle, and gave them little challenge, except for an occasional swift stream that had to be forded with care. At one of those, Carabella lost her footing and was fished out by Lisamon Hultin; at another it was Shanamir who was swept downstream, and Khun who plucked him to safety. They walked until midday, and rested an hour or two, making a scrappy meal of raw roots and berries. Then they went on until darkness.

And passed two more days in the same fashion.

And on the third came to a grove of dwikka-trees, eight fat squat giants in the forest, with monstrous swollen fruits hanging from them.

"Food!" Zalzan Kavol bellowed.

"Food sacred to the forest-brethren," Lisamon Hultin said. "Be careful!"

The famished Skandar, nevertheless, was on the verge of cutting down one of the enormous fruits with his energy-thrower when Valentine said sharply, "No! I forbid it!"

Zalzan Kavol stared incredulously. For an instant his old habits of command asserted themselves, and he glared at Valentine as if about to strike him. But he kept his temper in check.

"Look," Valentine said.

Forest-brethren were emerging from behind every tree. They were armed with their dart-blowers; and seeing the slender apelike creatures encircling them, Valentine in his weariness felt almost willing to be slain. But only for a moment. He recovered his spirits and said to Lisamon Hultin, "Ask them if we may have food and guides to the Steiche. If they ask a price, we can juggle for them with stones, or pieces of fruit, I suppose."

The warrior-woman, twice as tall as the forest-brethren, went into their midst and talked with them a long time. She was smiling when she returned.

"They are aware," she said, "that we are the ones who freed their brothers in Ilirivoyne!"

"Then we are saved!" cried Shanamir.

"News travels swiftly in this forest," Valentine said.

Lisamon Hultin went on, "We are their guests. They will feed us. They will guide us."

That night the wanderers ate richly on dwikka-fruit and other forest delicacies, and there was actually laughter among them for the first time since the ambush. Afterward the forest-brethren performed a sort of dance for them, a monkey-

199

ish prancing thing, and Sleet and Carabella and Valentine responded with impromptu juggling using objects collected in the forest. Afterward Valentine slept a deep, satisfying sleep. In his dreams he had the gift of flight, and saw himself soaring to the summit of Castle Mount.

And in the morning a party of chattering forest-brethren led them to the River Steiche, three hours' journey from the dwikka-tree grove, and bade them farewell with little twittering cries.

The river was a sobering sight. It was broad, though nothing remotely like the mighty Zimr, and it sped northward with startling haste, flowing so energetically that it had carved out a deep bed bordered in many places by high rocky walls. Here and there ugly stone snags rose above the water, and downstream Valentine could see white eddies of rapids.

The building of rafts took a day and a half. They cut down the young slim trees that grew by the riverbank, trimmed and trued them with knives and sharp stones, lashed them together with vines. The results were hardly elegant, but the rafts, though crude, did look reasonably riverworthy. There were three altogether—one for the four Skandars, one for Khun, Vinorkis, Lisamon Hultin, and Sleet, and one occupied by Valentine, Carabella, Shanamir, and Deliamber.

"We will probably become separated as we go downriver," Sleet said. "We should choose a meeting-place in Ni-moya."

Deliamber said, "The Steiche and the Zimr flow together at a place called Nissimorn. There is a broad, sandy beach there. Let us meet at Nissimorn Beach."

"At Nissimorn Beach, yes," Valentine said.

He cut loose the cord that bound his raft to the shore, and was carried off into the river.

The first day's journey was uneventful. There were rapids, but not difficult ones, and they poled safely past them. Carabella showed skill at handling the raft, and deftly steered them around the occasional rocky patches.

After a time the rafts became separated, Valentine's taking some subcurrent and moving rapidly ahead of the other two. In the morning he waited, hoping the others would catch up. But there was no sign of them and eventually he decided to depart.

On, on, on, for the most part swept easily along, with occasional moments of anxiety in the white-water stretches. By afternoon of the second day the course was becoming rougher. The land seemed to dip here, sloping downward as the Zimr drew near, and the river, following the line of descent, plunged and bucked. Valentine began to worry about water-falls ahead. They had no charts, no notion of dangers: they took everything as it came. He could only trust to luck that this swift water would deliver them safely to Ni-moya.

And then? By boat to Piliplok, and by pilgrim-ship to the Isle of Sleep, and somehow procure an interview with the Lady his mother, and then? And then? How did one claim the Coronal's throne, when one's face was not the face of Lord Valentine the rightful ruler? By what claim, by what authority? It seemed to Valentine an impossible quest. He might be better remaining here in the forest, ruling over his little band. They, readily enough, accepted him for what he thought himself to be; but in that world of billions of strangers, in that vast empire of giant cities that lay beyond the edge of the horizon, how, how, how would he ever manage to convince the unbelievers that he, Valentine the juggler, was—

No. These thoughts were foolish. He had never, not since he had appeared, shorn of memory and past, on the verge overlooking Pidruid, felt the need to rule over others; and if he had come to command this little group, it was more by natural gift and by Zalzan Kavol's default than out of any overt desire on his part. And yet he was in command, however tentatively and delicately. So it would be as he traveled onward through Majipoor. He would take one step at a time, and do that which seemed right and proper, and perhaps the Lady would guide him, and if the Divine so willed it he would one day stand again on Castle Mount, and if that was not part of the great plan, why, that would be acceptable also. There was nothing to fear. The future would unroll serenely in its own true course, as it had done since Pidruid. And—

"*Valentine!*" Carabella shouted.

The river seemed to sprout giant stony teeth. There were boulders everywhere, and monstrous white whirlpools, and, just ahead, an ominous tumbling descent, a place where the Steiche leaped out into space and went roaring down a series of steps to a valley far below. Valentine gripped his pole, but no pole could help him now. It lodged between two snags and was ripped from his grasp; a moment later there was a ghastly grinding sound as the flimsy raft, battered by submerged rocks, swung around at right angles to its course and split apart. He was hurled into the chilly stream and swept forward like a cork. For a moment he grasped Carabella by the wrist; but then the current pulled her free, and as he clutched desperately for her he was engulfed by the swift water and driven under.

Gasping and choking, Valentine struggled to get his head above water. When he did, he was already far downstream. The wreckage of the raft was nowhere in sight.

"Carabella?" he yelled. "Shanamir? Deliamber? Hoy! Hoy!"

He roared until his voice was ragged, but the booming of the rapids so thoroughly covered his cries that he could scarcely hear them himself. A terrible sense of pain and loss numbed his spirit. All gone, then? His friends, his beloved Carabella, the wily little Vroon, the clever, cocky boy Shanamir, all swept to death in an instant? No. No. Unthinkable. That was an agony far worse than this business, still unreal to him, of being a Coronal thrust from the Castle. What did that mean? These were beings of flesh and blood, dear to him; that was only a title and power. He would not stop calling their names as the river threw him about. *"Carabella!"* he shouted. *"Shanamir!"*

Valentine clawed at rocks, trying to halt his willy-nilly descent, but he was in the heart of the rapids now, buffeted and battered by the current and by the stones of the riverbed. Dazed and exhausted, half paralyzed by grief, Valentine gave up struggling and let himself be carried, down the giant staircase of the river, a tiny plaything spinning and bouncing along. He drew his knees to his chest and wrapped his arms over his head, attempting to minimize the surface he presented to the rocks. The power of the river was awesome. So here is how it ends, he thought, the grand adventure of Valentine of Majipoor, once Coronal, later wandering juggler, now about to be broken to bits by the impersonal and uncaring forces of nature. He commended himself to the Lady whom he thought to be his mother, and gulped air, and went heels over head, head over heels, down and down and down, and struck something with frightening force and thought this must be the end, only it was not the end, and struck something again that gave him an agonizing blow in the ribs, knocking the air from him, and he must have lost consciousness for a time, for he felt no further pain.

And then he found himself lying on a pebble-strewn strand, in a quiet sidestream of the river. It seemed to him that he had been shaken in a giant dice-box for hours, and cast up at random, discarded and useless. His body ached in a thousand places. His lungs felt soggy when he breathed. He was shivering and his skin was covered with goosebumps. And he was alone, under a vast cloudless sky, at the edge of some unknown wilderness, with civilization some unknown distance ahead and his friends perhaps dashed to death on the boulders.

But he was alive. That much was sure. Alone, battered, helpless, grief-stricken, lost . . . but alive. The adventure, then, was not ended. Slowly, with infinite effort, Valentine hauled himself out of the surf and tottered to the riverbank, and let himself carefully down on a wide flat rock, and with numb fingers undid his clothing and stretched out to dry himself under the warm friendly sun. He looked toward the river, hoping to see Carabella come swimming along, or Shanamir with the wizard perched on his shoulder. No one. But that doesn't mean they're dead, he told himself. They may have been cast up on farther shores. I'll rest here for a time, Valentine resolved, and then I'll go searching for the others, and then, with them or without, I'll set out onward, toward Nimoya, toward Piliplok, toward the Isle of the Lady, onward, onward, onward toward Castle Mount or whatever else lies ahead for me. Onward. Onward. Onward.

III

The Book of the Isle of Sleep

For what felt like months or perhaps years Valentine lay sprawled naked on his warm flat rock on the pebbly beach where the unruly River Steiche had deposited him. The roar of the river was a constant drone in his ears, oddly soothing. The sunlight enfolded him in a hazy golden nimbus, and he told himself that its touch would heal his bruises and abrasions and contusions, if only he lay still long enough. Vaguely he knew he ought to rise and see about shelter, and begin to search for his companions, but he barely could find the strength to turn from one side to the other.

This was no way, he knew, for a Coronal of Majipoor to conduct himself. Such self-indulgence might be acceptable for merchants or tavernkeepers or even jugglers, but a higher discipline rested upon one who had pretensions to govern. Therefore get to your feet, he told himself, and clothe your body, and start walking northward along the riverbank until you reach those who can help you regain your lofty place. Yes. Up, Valentine! But he remained where he was. He had expended every scrap of energy in him, Coronal or not, during the helter-skelter plunge down the rapids. Lying here like this, he had a powerful sense of the immensity of Majipoor, its many thousands of miles of circumference stretching out beneath his limbs, a planet large enough comfortably to house twenty billion people without crowding, a planet of enormous cities and wondrous parks and forest preserves and sacred districts and agricultural territories, and it seemed to him that if he took the trouble to rise it would be necessary for him to cover all that colossal domain on foot, step by step by step. It seemed simpler to stay where he was.

Something tickled the small of his back, something rubbery and insistent. He ignored it.

"Valentine?"

He ignored that too, for a moment.

The tickling occurred again. But by then it had filtered through his fatigue-dulled brain that someone had spoken his name, and therefore that one of his companions must have survived after all. Joy flooded his soul. With what little energy he could muster, Valentine raised his head and saw the small many-limbed figure of Autifon Deliamber standing beside him. The Vroonish wizard was about to prod him a third time.

"You're alive!" Valentine cried.

"Evidently I am. And so are you, more or less."

"And Carabella? Shanamir?"

"I have not seen them."

"As I feared," Valentine murmured dully. He closed his eyes and lowered his head, and in leaden despair lay once more like jetsam.

"Come," Deliamber said. "There is a vast journey ahead of us."

"I know. That's why I don't want to get up."

"Are you hurt?"

"I don't think so. But I want to rest, Deliamber. I want to rest a hundred years."

The sorcerer's tentacles probed and poked Valentine in a dozen places. "No serious damage," the Vroon murmured. "Much of you is still healthy."

"Much of me isn't," said Valentine indistinctly. "What about you?"

"Vroons are good swimmers, even old ones like me. I am unhurt. We should go on, Valentine."

"Later."

"Is this how a Coronal of Majip—"

"No," Valentine said. "But a Coronal of Majipoor would not have had to shoot the Steiche rapids on a slapped-together log raft. A Coronal would not have been wandering in this wilderness for days and days, sleeping in the rain and eating nothing but nuts and berries. A Coronal—"

"A Coronal would not allow his lieutenants to see him in a condition of indolence and spiritlessness," Deliamber said sharply. "And one of them is approaching right now."

Valentine blinked and sat up. Lisamon Hultin was striding

205

along the beach toward them. She looked a trifle disarranged, her clothing in shreds, her gigantic fleshy body purpled with bruises here and there, but her pace was jaunty and her voice, when she called out to them, was as booming as ever.

"Hoy! Are you intact?"

"I think so," Valentine answered. "Have you seen any others?"

"Carabella and the boy, half a mile or so back that way."

He felt his spirits soar. "Are they all right?"

"She is, at any rate."

"And Shanamir?"

"Doesn't want to wake up. She sent me out to look for the sorcerer. Found him sooner than I thought. Phaugh, what a river! That raft came apart so fast it was almost funny!"

Valentine reached for his clothing, found it still wet, and, with a shrug, dropped it to the rocks. "We must get to Shanamir at once. Have you news of Khun and Sleet and Vinorkis?"

"Didn't see them. I went into the river and when I came up I was alone."

"And the Skandars?"

"No sign of them at all." To Deliamber she said, "Where do you think we are, wizard?"

"Far from anywhere," the Vroon replied. "Safely out of the Metamorph lands, at any rate. Come, take me to the boy."

Lisamon Hultin scooped Deliamber to her shoulder and strode back along the beach, while Valentine limped along behind them, carrying his damp clothing over his arm. After a time they came upon Carabella and Shanamir camped in an inlet of bright white sand surrounded by thick river-reeds with scarlet stems. Carabella, battered and weary-looking, wore only a brief leather skirt. But she seemed in reasonably good shape. Shanamir lay unconscious, breathing slowly, his skin an odd dark hue.

"Oh, Valentine!" Carabella cried, springing up and running to him. "I saw you swept away—and then—and then— Oh, I thought I'd never see you again!"

He held her close against him. "And I thought the same. I thought you were lost to me forever, love."

"Were you hurt?"

"Not permanently," he said. "And you?"

"I was tossed and tossed and tossed until I couldn't remember my own name. But then I found a calm place and I swam to shore, and Shanamir was already there. But he wouldn't wake up. And Lisamon came out of the underbrush and said she'd try to find Deliamber, and— Will he be all right, wizard?"

"In a moment," said Deliamber, arranging his tentacle-tips over the boy's chest and forehead, as if making some transfer of energy. Shanamir grunted and stirred. His eyes opened tentatively, closed, opened again. In a thick voice he began to say something, but Deliamber told him to be silent, to lie still, to let the strength flow back into him.

There was no question of attempting to move on that afternoon. Valentine and Carabella constructed a crude shelter out of reeds; Lisamon Hultin assembled a meager dinner of raw fruit and young pininna-sprouts; and they sat in silence beside the river, watching a spectacular sunset, bands of violet and gold streaking the great dome of the sky, reflections in luminous tones of orange and purple in the water, undertones of pale green, satiny red, silken crimson, and then the first puffs of gray and black, the swift descent of night.

In the morning they all felt able to proceed, though stiff from a night in the open. Shanamir showed no ill effects: Deliamber's care and the natural resilience of youth had restored his vitality.

Patching together their clothing as best they could, they set out to the north, following the beach until it gave out, then continuing through the forest of gawky androdragma-trees and flowering alabandina that flanked the river. The air was soft and mild here, and the sun, descending in dappled splotches through the treetops, gave a welcome warmth to the weary stragglers.

In the third hour of the march Valentine caught the scent of fire just ahead, and what smelled very much like the aroma of grilled fish. He jogged forward, salivating, prepared to buy, beg, if necessary steal, some of that fish, for it had been more days than he cared to count since he had last tasted cooked food. Down a rough talus slope he skidded, into sunlight on white pebbles, so bright he could barely see. In the glare he made out three figures crouched over a fire by the river's edge, and when he shaded his eyes he discovered that one was a compact human with pale skin and a startling shock of white hair, and another was a long-legged blue-skinned being of alien birth, and the third a Hjort.

"Sleet!" Valentine cried. "Khun! Vinorkis!"

He ran toward them, slipping and sliding over the rocks.

They watched his wild approach calmly, and when he was

207

close by them Sleet, in a casual manner, handed him a stake on which was spitted a fillet of some pink-fleshed river fish.

"Have some lunch," Sleet said amiably.

Valentine gaped. "How did you get so far ahead of us? What did you build this fire with? How did you catch the fish? What have you—"

"Your fish will get cold," Khun said. "Eat first, questions after."

Valentine took a hasty bite—he had never tasted anything so delicious, a tender moist meat splendidly seared, surely as elegant a morsel as had ever been served in the feasts on Castle Mount—and, turning, called to his companions to come down the slope. But they were already on their way, Shanamir whooping and cavorting as he ran, Carabella gracefully darting over the rocks, Lisamon Hultin, bearing Deliamber, pounding thunderously toward him.

"There's fish for all!" Sleet proclaimed.

They had caught at least a dozen, which circled sadly in a shallow rock-rimmed pool near the fire. Efficiently Khun plucked them forth and split and gutted them. Sleet held them briefly over the flame and passed them to the others, who ate ravenously.

Sleet explained that when their raft had broken up they had found themselves clinging to a fragment some three logs wide, and had managed to hang on all the way through the rapids and far downstream. They vaguely remembered having seen the beach where Valentine was cast ashore, but they had not noticed him on it as they passed by, and they had drifted another few miles before they had recovered enough from their rapids-running to want to let go of their logs and swim to the bank. Khun had caught the fish bare-handed: he had, said Sleet, the quickest hands he had ever seen, and would probably make a magnificent juggler. Khun grinned—the first time Valentine had seen anything but a grim expression on his face.

"And the fire?" Carabella asked. "You started it by snapping your fingers, I suppose?"

"We attempted it," Sleet answered smoothly. "But it proved to be strenuous work. So we walked over to the village of fisherfolk just beyond the bend and asked to borrow a light."

"Fisherfolk?" Valentine said, startled.

"An outpost of Liimen," said Sleet, "who evidently don't know that it's their racial destiny to sell sausages in the western cities. They gave us shelter last night, and have agreed to

208

ferry us up to Ni-moya this afternoon, so that we can wait for our friends at Nissimorn Beach." He smiled. "I suppose we'll need to hire a second boat now."

Deliamber said, "Are we that close to Ni-moya?"

"Two hours by boat, so I'm told, to the place where the rivers flow together."

Suddenly the world seemed less huge to Valentine, and the chores that awaited him less overwhelming. To have eaten a real meal once again, and to know that a friendly settlement lay nearby, and that he would soon be leaving the wilderness behind, was tremendously cheering. Only one thing troubled him now: the fate of Zalzan Kavol and his three surviving brothers.

The Liiman village was indeed close at hand—perhaps five hundred souls, short flat-headed dark-skinned people whose triple sets of bright fiery eyes regarded the wanderers with little curiosity. They lived in modest thatched huts close beside the river, and raised an assortment of crops in small gardens to supplement the catch that their fleet of crude fishing-boats brought in. Their dialect was a difficult one, but Sleet seemed able to communicate with them and managed to arrange not only another boat but also the purchase, for a couple of crowns, of fresh clothing for Carabella and Lisamon Hultin.

In early afternoon they set out, with four taciturn Liimen as their crew, on the journey to Ni-moya.

The river ran as swift as ever here, but there were few rapids of any consequence, and the two boats sped nicely along through countryside increasingly populous and tame. The steep riverbanks of the uplands gave way, down here, to broad alluvial plains of heavy black silt, and shortly an almost continuous strip of farming villages appeared.

Now the river widened and grew calm, becoming a broad, even waterway with a deep blue glint. The land here was flat and open, and though the settlements on both sides were doubtless goodly cities with populations of many thousands, they seemed mere hamlets, so dwarfed were they by the gigantic surroundings. Ahead lay a dark, immense headwater that seemed to span the entire horizon as though it were the open sea.

"River Zimr," announced the Liiman at the helm of Valentine's boat. "Steiche ends here. Nissimorn Beach on left."

Valentine beheld a huge crescent strand, bordered by a dense grove of palm trees of a peculiarly lopsided shape, purplish fronds jutting up like ruffled feathers. As they drew near, Valentine was startled to see a raft of crudely trimmed logs on the beach, and, sitting beside it, four giant shaggy four-armed figures. The Skandars were waiting for them.

2

Zalzan Kavol saw nothing extraordinary about his voyage. His raft had come to the rapids; he and his brothers had poled their way through, getting jounced about a little, but not seriously; they had continued on downstream to Nissimorn Beach, where they had camped in growing impatience, wondering what was delaying the rest of the party. It had not occurred to the Skandar that the other rafts might have been wrecked in the passage, nor had he seen any of the castaways along the riverbank en route. "Did you have trouble?" he asked in what seemed to be genuine innocence.

"Of a minor sort," Valentine replied dryly. "But we seem to be reunited, and it will be good to sleep in proper lodgings again tonight."

They resumed the journey, and presently they passed into the great confluence of the Steiche and the Zimr, a water so wide that it was impossible for Valentine to conceive it as the mere meeting-place of two rivers. At the town of Nissimorn on the southwestern shore they parted from the Liimen and boarded the ferry that would take them on across to Ni-moya, largest of the cities of the continent of Zimroel.

Thirty million citizens dwelled here. At Ni-moya the River Zimr made a great bend, changing its course sharply from easterly to southeasterly. There a prodigious megalopolis had taken form. It spread for hundreds of miles along both banks of the river and up several tributaries that flowed in from the north. Valentine and his companions saw first the southern suburbs, residential districts that gave way, in the extreme south, to the agricultural territory stretching down into the Steiche Valley. The main urban zone lay on the north bank, and could only dimly be seen at first, tier upon tier of flat-topped white towers descending toward the river. Ferries by the dozens plied the water here, linking the myriad riverside towns. The crossing took several hours, and twilight was beginning before Ni-moya proper was clearly in view.

The city looked magical. Its lights, just coming on, sparkled invitingly against the backdrop of heavily forested green hills and impeccable white buildings. Giant fingers of piers thrust into the river, and an astounding bustle of vessels great and small lined the waterfront. Pidruid, which had seemed so mighty to Valentine in his early days of wandering, was a minor city indeed compared with this.

Only the Skandars, Khun, and Deliamber had seen Ni-moya before. Deliamber spoke of the city's marvels: its Gossamer Galleria, a mercantile arcade a mile long, raised above the ground on nearly invisible cables; its Park of Fabulous Beasts, where the rarest of Majipoor's fauna, those creatures brought closest to extinction by the spread of civilization, roved in surroundings approximating their natural habitats; its Crystal Boulevard, a glittering street of revolving reflectors that awed the eye; its Grand Bazaar, fifteen square miles of mazelike passageways housing uncountable thousands of tiny shops under continuous roofs of dazzling yellow sparklecloth; its Museum of Worlds, its Chamber of Sorcery, its Ducal Palace, built on a heroic scale said to be surpassed only by Lord Valentine's Castle, and many other things that sounded, to Valentine, more like the stuff of myth and fantasy than anything one might encounter in a real city. But they would see none of these things. The thousand-instrument municipal orchestra, the floating restaurants, the artificial birds with jeweled eyes, and all the rest would have to wait until, if ever the day came, he returned to Ni-moya in a Coronal's robes.

As the ferry neared the slip Valentine called everyone together and said, "Now we must determine our individual courses. I mean to take passage here for Piliplok, and make my way from there to the Isle. I've prized your companionship this far, and I would have it even longer, but I can offer you nothing except endless journeying and the possibility of an early death. My hope of success is slight and the obstacles are formidable. Will any of you continue with me?"

"To the other side of the world!" Shanamir cried.

"And I," said Sleet, and Vinorkis the same.

"Would you have doubted me?" Carabella asked.

Valentine smiled. He looked to Deliamber, who said, "The sanctity of the realm is at stake. How could I not follow the rightful Coronal wherever he asks?"

"This mystifies me," Lisamon Hultin said. "I understand none of this business of a Coronal roaming out of his proper body. But I have no other employment, Valentine. I am with you."

"I thank you all," Valentine said. "I will thank you again, and more grandly, in the feasting-hall on Castle Mount."

Zalzan Kavol said, "And have you no use for Skandars, my lord?"

Valentine had not expected that. "Will you come?"

"Our wagon is lost. Our brotherhood is broken by death. We are without our juggling gear. I feel no calling to be a pilgrim, but I will follow you to the Isle and beyond, and so also will my brothers, if you want us."

"I want you, Zalzan Kavol. Is there such a post as juggler to the royal court? You will have it, I promise!"

"Thank you, my lord," said the Skandar gravely.

"There is one more volunteer," said Khun.

"You too?" Valentine said in surprise.

The dour alien replied, "It matters little to me who is king of this planet where I am stranded. But it matters much to me to behave honorably. I would be dead now in Piurifayne but for you. I owe you my life and I will give you such aid as I can."

Valentine shook his head. "We did for you only what any civilized being would do for any other. No debt exists."

"I see it otherwise. Besides," said Khun, "my life until now has been trivial and shallow. I left my native Kianimot for no good reason to come here, and I lived foolishly here and nearly paid with my life, and why go on as I have been doing? I will join your cause and make it mine, and perhaps I will come to believe in it, or feel that I do, and if I die to make you king, it will only even the debt between us. With a death well accomplished I can repay the universe for a life poorly spent. Can you use me?"

"With all my heart I welcome you," Valentine said.

The ferry released a grand blast of its horn and glided smoothly into its slip.

They stayed the night at the cheapest waterfront hotel they could find, a clean but stark place of whitewashed stone walls and communal tubs, and treated themselves to a modestly lavish dinner at an inn nearby. Valentine called for a pooling of funds and appointed Shanamir and Zalzan Kavol joint treasurers, since they seemed to have the finest appreciation of the value and uses of money. Valentine himself had much remaining of the funds he had had in Pidruid, and Zalzan Kavol produced from a hidden pouch a surprising stack of ten-royal pieces. Together they had enough to get them all to the Isle of Sleep.

In the morning they bought passage aboard a riverboat similar to the one that had carried them from Khyntor to Verf, and began their voyage to Piliplok, the great port at the mouth of the Zimr.

For all they had traveled across the face of Zimroel, some thousands of miles still separated them from the east coast. But on the broad breast of the Zimr vessels moved swiftly and serenely. Of course, the riverboat stopped again and again at the innumerable towns and cities of the river, Larnimisculus and Belka and Clarischanz, Flegit, Hiskuret, Centriun, Obliorn Vale, Salvamot, Gourkaine, Semirod and Cerinor and Haunfort Major, Impemond, Orgeliuse, Dambemuir, and many more, an unending flow of nearly indistinguishable places, each with its piers, its waterfront promenades, its planting of palms and alabandinas, its gaily painted warehouses and sprawling bazaars, its ticket-clutching passengers eager to come on board and impatient for departure once they had ascended the ramp. Sleet whittled juggling clubs out of some scraps of wood he begged from the crew, and Carabella found balls somewhere to juggle, and at meals the Skandars quietly palmed dishware and slipped it out of sight, so that the troupe gradually accumulated implements to work with, and from the third day on they earned some extra crowns by performing on the plaza-deck. Zalzan Kavol gradually regained some of his old gruff self-assurance now that he was performing again, although he still was oddly subdued, his soul moving on tiptoe through situations that once would have called forth angry storms.

This was the native territory of the four Skandars, who had been born in Piliplok and began their careers on circuit through the inland towns of the huge province, ranging as far upriver as Stenwamp and Port Saikforge, a thousand miles from the coast. This familiar countryside brightened them, these rolling tawny hills and bustling little cities of wooden buildings, and Zalzan Kavol spoke lengthily of his early career here, his successes and failures—very few of those—and of a dispute with an impresario that led him to seek fortune at the other end of Zimroel. Valentine suspected that there was some violence involved, perhaps some embroilment with the law, but he asked no questions.

One night after much wine the Skandars even broke into song, for the first time in Valentine's time with them—a Skandar song, mournful and lugubrious, sung in a minor key as the singers shuffled about and about in a slump-shouldered circling march:

Dark my heart
Dark my fears
Dim my eyes
And full of tears.

> *Death and woe,*
> *Death and woe,*
> *Follow us*
> *Where'er we go.*

Far the lands
I used to roam.
Far the hills
And streams of home.

> *Death and woe,*
> *Death and woe,*
> *Follow us*
> *Where'er we go.*

Seas of dragons,
Lands of pain,
I shall not see
My home again.

> *Death and woe,*
> *Death and woe,*
> *Follow us*
> *Where'er we go.*

The song was so unrelievedly gloomy, and the enormous Skandars looked so absurd as they lurched about chanting it, that it was all that Valentine and Carabella could do to hold back laughter at first. But by the second chorus Valentine actually found himself moved by it, for there seemed real emotion in the song: the Skandars *had* met death and woe, and though they were close to home now, they had spent much of their lives far from Piliplok; and perhaps, Valentine thought, it was a harsh and painful thing to be a Skandar on Majipoor, a shaggy-pelted creature moving ponderously in the warm air among smaller and sleeker beings.

The summer now was over, and in eastern Zimroel it was the dry season, when warm winds blew from the south, vegetation went dormant until the spring rains, and, so said Zalzan Kavol, tempers became short and crimes of passion common. Valentine found this region less interesting than the jungles of the mid-continent or the subtropic floribundance of the far west, though he decided after a few days of close observation

214

that it did have a certain austere beauty of its own, restrained and severe, quite unlike the riotous lushness of the west. All the same, he was pleased and relieved when, after day upon day on this changeless and seemingly unending river, Zalzan Kavol announced that the outskirts of Piliplok were in view.

3

Piliplok was about as old and about as large as its counterpart port on the farther shore of the continent, Pidruid; but the resemblance went no deeper. For Pidruid had been built without a plan, a random tangle of streets and avenues and boulevards winding around one another according to whim, whereas Piliplok had been laid out, untold thousands of years ago, with rigid, almost maniacal, precision.

It occupied a promontory of great magnitude on the southern shore of the mouth of the Zimr. The river here was of inconceivable width, sixty or seventy miles across at the point where it flowed into the Inner Sea, and carrying the burden of silt and debris accumulated in all its swift seven-thousand-mile flow out of the far northwest, it stained the blue-green waters of the ocean with a dark tinge that, it was said, could be seen hundreds of miles out. The north headland at the rivermouth was a chalk cliff a mile high and many miles wide, which even from Piliplok was visible on a clear day, a shining white wall dazzling in the morning light. There was nothing over there that could in any way be used as a harbor, and so it had never been settled, but was set aside as a holy preserve. Devotees of the Lady lived there in a withdrawal from the world so total that no one had intruded on them in a hundred years. But Piliplok was another matter: eleven million people occupying a city that radiated in stern spokes from its magnificent natural harbor. A series of curving bands crossed the axis of these spokes, the inner ones mercantile, then zones of industry and recreation, and in the outer reaches the residential neighborhoods, fairly sharply delimited by levels of wealth and to a lesser degree by race. There was a heavy concentration of Skandars in Piliplok—it seemed to Valentine that every third person on the waterfront belonged to Zalzan Kavol's people—and it was a little intimidating to see so many giant hairy four-armers swaggering about. Here, too, lived many of the aloof and aristocratic two-headed Su-Suheris folk, dealers in luxury commodities, fine fabrics and jewelry and the rarest handicrafts of every province. The air here was crisp and dry, and, feeling the unyielding southerly wind hot against his cheeks, Valentine began to understand what Zalzan Kavol had meant about the short tempers kindled by that wind.

"Does it ever stop blowing?" he asked.

"On the first day of spring," said Zalzan Kavol.

Valentine hoped to be elsewhere by then. But a problem immediately appeared. With Zalzan Kavol and Deliamber he went to Shkunibor Pier at the eastern end of Piliplok harbor to arrange transport to the Isle. For months now Valentine had imagined himself in this city and at that pier, and it had taken on an almost legendary glamour in his mind, a place of vast perspectives and sweeping architecture; and so it disappointed him more than a little to get there and find that the chief place of embarkation for the pilgrim-ships was a ramshackle, dilapidated structure, peeling green paint on its sides, tattered banners flapping in the wind.

Worse was in store. The pier seemed deserted. After some prowling Zalzan Kavol found a departure schedule posted in a dark corner of the ticket house. Pilgrim-ships sailed for the Isle the first of every month—except in autumn, when sailings were spaced more widely because of prevailing unfavorable winds. The last ship of the season had departed a week ago Starday. The next left in three months.

"Three months!" Valentine cried. "What will we do in Piliplok for three months? Juggle in the streets? Beg? Steal? Read the schedule again, Zalzan Kavol!"

"It will say the same," the Skandar declared. He grimaced. "I am fond of Piliplok beyond any place, but I have no love for it at wind-time. What foul luck!"

"Do no ships at all sail in this season?" Valentine asked.

"Only the dragon-ships," said Zalzan Kavol.

"And what are they?"

"Fishing vessels, that prey on the sea-dragons, which come together in herds to mate at this time of year, and are easily taken. Plenty of dragon-ships set forth now. But what use are they to us?"

"How far out to sea do they go?" Valentine asked.

"As far as they must to make their catch. Sometimes as far as the Rodamaunt Archipelago, if the dragons are swarming easterly."

"Where is that?"

Deliamber said, "It is a long chain of islands far out in the Inner Sea, perhaps midway from here to the Isle of Sleep."

"Inhabited?"

216

"Quite heavily."

"Good. Surely there's commerce between islands, then. What if we hire one of these dragon-ships to take us on as passengers, and carry us as far as the Archipelago, and there we commission some local captain to transport us to the Isle?"

"Possibly," Deliamber said.

"There's no rule requiring all pilgrims to arrive by pilgrim-ship?"

"None that I know of," said the Vroon.

"The dragon-ships will not care to bother with passengers," Zalzan Kavol objected. "They never carry any such trade."

"Would a few royals arouse their interest in doing so?"

The Skandar looked doubtful. "I have no idea. Their trade's a lucrative one as it is. They might consider passengers a nuisance, or even bad luck. Nor would they necessarily agree to haul us out to the Archipelago, if it happens to lie beyond this year's hunting track. Nor can we be sure, even if we do reach the Archipelago, that anyone there would be willing to carry us farther."

"On the other hand," Valentine said, "it might all be quite easy to arrange. We have money, and I'd rather use it persuading sea-captains to give us passage than spend it on lodgings and food for the next three months in Piliplok. Where can we find the dragon-hunters?"

An entire section of the waterfront spanning three or four miles was set apart for their use, pier after pier after pier, and there were dozens of the huge wooden vessels in harbor, being outfitted for the new hunting season just beginning. The dragon-ships were of one design, and an ominous and morbid one it was, Valentine thought, for they were great bloated things with flaring outbellying hulls and enormous fanciful three-pronged masts, and terrifying toothy figureheads at their prows and long spiky tails at their sterns. Most were decorated along their flanks with bold scarlet-and-yellow eye-patterns or rapacious-looking rows of white teeth; and high abovedecks were bristling cupolas for the harpooners and mammoth winches for the nets, and bloodstained platforms where the butchering took place. To Valentine it was incongruous to make use of such a killer-vessel in reaching the peaceful and holy Isle of Sleep. But he had no other way.

And even this way soon began to seem doubtful. From ship to ship they went, from wharf to wharf, from drydock to drydock, and the dragon-captains listened without interest to their proposal and made swift refusals. Zalzan Kavol did most of the speaking, for the captains were mainly Skandars and

217

might give sympathetic ear to one of their own kind. But no persuasion would sway them.

"You would be a distraction to the crew," said the first captain. "Forever stumbling over gear, getting seasick, making special requests for service—"

"We are not chartered to carry passengers," said the second. "The rules are strict."

"The Archipelago lies south of our preferred waters," the third declared.

"I have long believed," said the fourth, "that a dragon-ship that goes to sea with strangers to the guild on board is a ship that will never return to Piliplok. I choose not to test that superstition this year."

"Pilgrims are no concern of mine," the fifth told them. "Let the Lady waft you to the Isle, if she will. You won't get there aboard my ship."

The sixth also refused, adding that no captain was likely to aid them. The seventh said the same. The eighth, having heard that a party of drylanders was wandering the decks looking for passage, refused even to speak with them.

The ninth captain, a grizzled old Skandar with gaps in her teeth and faded fur, was more friendly than the others, though just as unwilling to make room for them on her vessel. She did, at least, have a suggestion. "On Prestimion Pier," she said, "you will find Captain Gorzval of the *Brangalyn*. Gorzval has made several unlucky voyages and is known to be short of funds; I heard him in a tavern just the other night trying to arrange a loan to pay for repairs to his hull. It may be that some extra revenue from passengers would be useful to him now."

"And where is Prestimion Pier?" Zalzan Kavol asked.

"The farthest in this line, beyond Dekkeret and Kinniken, just west of the salvage-yard."

A berth close by the salvage-yard seemed appropriate for the *Brangalyn*, Valentine thought bleakly an hour later, upon having his first view of Captain Gorzval's vessel. It looked about ready to be broken up for scrap. It was a smaller and older ship than the others he had seen, and at some point in its long history it must have suffered a staved hull, for in its rebuilding it had become malproportioned, with mismatched timbers and an oddly sloping look to starboard. The painted eyes and teeth along the waterline had lost their luster; the figurehead was awry; the tailspikes had been snapped off eight or ten feet from their mountings, perhaps in a petulant swipe by an angry dragon; the masts had lost some of their

218

yards also. Crewmen with a sluggish and dispirited look to them were at work, but not in any very effective way, caulking and coiling ropes and mending sail.

Captain Gorzval himself seemed as weary and worn as his vessel. He was a Skandar not quite as tall as Lisamon Hultin—virtually a dwarf among his race—with a cast in one eye and a stump where his outer left arm should be. His fur was matted and coarse; his shoulders were slumped; his entire look was one of fatigue and defeat. But he brightened immediately at Zalzan Kavol's query about taking passengers to the Rodamaunt Archipelago.

"How many?"

"Twelve. Four Skandars, a Hjort, a Vroon, five humans, and one—other."

"All pilgrims, you say?"

"All pilgrims."

Gorzval made the sign of the Lady in a perfunctory way and said, "You know it's irregular for passengers to travel on a dragon-ship. But I owe the Lady recompense for past favors received. I'm willing to make an exception. Cash in advance?"

"Of course," said Zalzan Kavol.

Valentine quickly released his breath. This was a miserable dilapidated ship, and Gorzval probably a third-rate navigator dogged by bad fortune or even downright incompetence; nevertheless, he was willing to take them, and no one else would even entertain the idea.

Gorzval named his price and waited, with obvious tension, to be haggled with. What he asked was less than half what they had unsuccessfully offered the other captains. Zalzan Kavol, bargaining out of habit and pride, no doubt, attempted to cut three royals from that. Gorzval, plainly dismayed, offered a reduction of a royal and a half; Zalzan Kavol appeared ready to shave another few crowns, but Valentine, pitying the hapless captain, cut in quickly to say, "Done. When do we sail?"

"In three days," Gorzval said.

It turned out to be four, actually—Gorzval spoke vaguely of some need for additional refitting, by which he meant, Valentine discovered, patching of some fairly serious leaks. He had not been able to afford it until his passengers had hired on. According to the gossip in the dockside taverns, Lisamon Hultin reported, Gorzval had been trying to mortgage part of his catch to raise the money for carpenters, but found no takers. He had, she said, a doubtful reputation: his judgment was inferior, his luck poor, his crew ill-paid and shiftless. Once he

219

had missed the sea-dragon swarm entirely and returned empty to Piliplok; on another voyage he had lost his arm to a lively little dragon not quite as dead as he thought; and on this last one the *Brangalyn* had been struck amidships by an irritated beast and nearly sent to the bottom. "We might do better," Lisamon Hultin suggested, "by trying to swim to the Isle."

"Possibly we'll bring our captain better luck than he's had," said Valentine.

Sleet laughed. "If optimism alone could carry one to the throne, my lord, you'd be on Castle Mount by Winterday."

Valentine laughed with him. But after the disaster in Piurifayne he hoped he was not leading these folk into new catastrophe aboard this ill-favored vessel. They were following him, after all, on faith alone, on the evidence of dreams and wizardry and an enigmatic Metamorph prank: it would be shame and pain for him if, in his haste to reach the Isle, he caused them more grief. Yet Valentine felt powerful sympathy for the bedraggled stump-armed Gorzval. An unlucky mariner he might be—but a fitting helmsman, perhaps, for a Coronal so frowned upon by fortune that he had managed to lose throne and memory and identity all in a single night!

On the eve of the *Brangalyn*'s departure Vinorkis drew Valentine aside and said in a troubled tone, "My lord, we are being watched."

"How do you know?"

The Hjort smiled and preened his orange mustachios. "When one has done a little spying, one recognizes the traits in others. I've noticed a grayish Skandar lounging around the docks these past few days, asking questions of Gorzval's people. One of the ship's carpenters told me he was curious about the passengers Gorzval had taken on, and about our destination."

Valentine scowled. "I hoped we had shaken them off our track in the jungles!"

"They must have discovered us again in Ni-moya, my lord."

"Then we must lose them again in the Archipelago," said Valentine. "And be wary until then of other spies along our way. I thank you, Vinorkis."

"No thanks are needed, my lord. It is my duty."

A strong wind blew from the south in the morning when the ship set forth. Vinorkis kept close look for the inquisitive Skandar at the pier during the embarkation, but he was nowhere in view; his work was done, Valentine supposed, and some other informant farther on would continue the surveillance on the usurper's behalf.

The route lay to the east and south; these dragon-ships were accustomed to tack against that constant hostile wind all the way to the hunting grounds. It was a wearying business, but there was no avoiding it, for the sea-dragons were within the reach of hunters only at this season. The *Brangalyn* had supplementary engine power, but not any great deal of it, fuels of all kinds being so scarce on Majipoor. With a certain majestic clumsiness the *Brangalyn* picked up the side wind and moved out of Piliplok harbor into the open sea.

This was the smaller sea of Majipoor, the Inner Sea, which separated eastern Zimroel from western Alhanroel. It was no trifle—some five thousand miles from shore to shore—yet it was a mere puddle compared with the Great Sea that occupied most of the other hemisphere, an ocean beyond the possibility of navigation, untold thousands of miles of open water. The Inner Sea was more human in scale, and was broken midway between the continents by the Isle of Sleep—itself big enough so that on another world, of less extraordinary size, it would be considered a continent—and by several major island chains.

The sea-dragons spent their lives in unending migration between the two oceans. Round and round the globe they went, taking years or even decades, so far as anyone knew, to make the circumnavigation. Perhaps a dozen great herds of them inhabited the ocean, traveling constantly from west to east. Every summer one of those herds would complete its journey across the Great Sea, passing south of Narabal and up the southern coast of Zimroel toward Piliplok. It was forbidden to hunt them then, for the herd abounded at that time with pregnant cows. By autumn the young were born, the herd now having reached the windswept waters between Piliplok and the Isle of Sleep, and the annual hunt began. Out from Piliplok came the dragon-ships in great numbers. The herds were thinned of both young and old, and the survivors made their way back into the tropics, passing south of the Isle of Sleep, rounding the hump of Alhanroel's lengthy Stoienzar Peninsula, and heading on eastward below Alhanroel to the Great Sea, where they would swim unmolested until their time brought them round to Piliplok again.

Of all the beasts of Majipoor, the sea-dragons were by far the largest. Newborn, they were tiny, no more than five or six feet in length, but through all their lives they continued to grow, and their lifespans were long, although no one knew just how long. Gorzval, who let his passengers share his table and proved to be a talkative man now that his anxieties were behind him, was fond of telling tales of the immensity of certain sea-dragons. One that had been taken in the reign of Lord Malibor was a hundred and ninety feet in length, and another, of Confalume's time, two hundred forty, and in the era when Prestimion was Pontifex and Lord Dekkeret the Coronal they had caught one thirty feet longer than that. But the champion, said Gorzval, was one that had boldly appeared almost in the mouth of Piliplok harbor in the reign of Thimin and Lord Kinniken, and had reliably been measured at three hundred fifteen feet. That monster, known as Lord Kinniken's dragon, had escaped unharmed because the entire fleet of dragonships was then far out to sea. Allegedly it had been sighted again several times by hunters in succeeding centuries, most recently in the year Lord Voriax became Coronal, but no one had ever laid a harpoon on it, and among hunters it had a baleful reputation. "It must be five hundred feet long by now," said Gorzval, "and I pray that some other captain is given the honor of encountering it when it returns to our waters."

Valentine had seen small sea-dragons, pithed, gutted, salted, and dried, sold in marketplaces all over Zimroel, and on occasion he had tasted their meat, which was dark, tangy, and tough. Dragons less than ten feet long were the ones prepared in this way. The meat of larger ones, up to fifty feet or so, was butchered and sold fresh along the eastern coast of Zimroel, but difficulties of transportation kept it from finding markets far from the sea. Beyond that length the dragons were too old to be edible, but their flesh was rendered into oil that had many purposes, petroleum and other fossil hydrocarbons being scarce on Majipoor. The bones of sea-dragons of all sizes had their uses in architecture, for they were nearly as strong as steel and far more readily obtained, and there was medicinal value in the unborn dragon-eggs, found in quantities of many hundreds of pounds in the abdomens of mature females. Dragon-skin, dragon-wings, dragon this and dragon that, everything was put to some benefit and nothing wasted. "This, for example, is dragon-milk," said Gorzval, offering his guests a flask of a pale bluish liquid. "In Ni-moya or Khyntor they'd pay ten crowns for a flask like this. Here, taste it."

Lisamon Hultin took a hesitant sip and spat it on the floor. "Dragon-milk or dragon-piss?" she demanded.

The captain smiled frostily. "In Dulorn," he said, "what

you spat out would cost you at least a crown, and you'd count yourself lucky to find some." He pushed the flask toward Sleet, who shook his head, and then to Valentine. After a moment's pause Valentine put it to his lips.

"Bitter," he said, "and a musty taste, but not entirely terrible. What's the secret of its appeal?"

The Skandar patted his thighs. "Aphrodisiac!" he boomed. "Stirs the juices! Heats the blood! Prolongs the life!" He pointed jovially at Zalzan Kavol, who, unasked, had taken a robust swig of the stuff. "See? The Skandar knows! The man of Piliplok doesn't need to be begged to drink it!"

Carabella said, "Dragon-*milk?* These are mammals?"

"Mammals, yes. The eggs are hatched within, so, and the young born alive, ten or twenty in a litter, rows of nipples all up and down the belly. You think it's odd, milk from dragons?"

"I think of dragons as reptiles," said Carabella, "and reptiles give no milk."

"Think of dragons as dragons, better. You want to taste?"

"Thank you, no," she replied. "My juices need no stirring."

The meals in the captain's cabin were the best part of the voyage, Valentine decided. Gorzval was good-natured and outgoing, as Skandars went, and he set a decent table, with wine and meats and fish of various sorts, including a good deal of dragon-flesh. But the ship itself was creaky and cramped, poorly designed and even more poorly maintained, and the crew, a dozen Skandars and an assortment of Hjorts and humans, was uncommunicative and often downright hostile. Obviously these dragon-hunters were a proud and insular lot, even the crew of a bedraggled vessel like the *Brangalyn,* and resented the presence of outsiders among them as they practiced their mysteries. Only Gorzval seemed at all hospitable; but he clearly felt grateful to them, for their fare was all that had allowed him to get his ship seaworthy.

They were far from land now, in a featureless realm where pale blue ocean met pale blue sky to obliterate all sense of place and direction. The course was south-southeasterly, and the farther they got from Piliplok the warmer grew the wind, hot now and dry as ever. "We call the wind our sending," said Gorzval, "because it comes straight from Suvrael. The little gift of the King of Dreams, it is, as delightful as all his others." The sea was empty: no islands, no drifting logs, no sign of anything, not even dragons. The dragons had gone far past the coast this year, as they sometimes did, and were basking in the tropical waters close by the fringes of the Archipelago.

Occasionally a gihorna-bird passed far overhead, making its autumn migration from the islands to the Zimr Marsh, which was not near the Zimr at all but on the coast five hundred miles south of Piliplok; these long-legged creatures must have made tempting targets, but no one took aim at them. Another tradition of the sea, it seemed.

The first dragons manifested themselves the second week out from Piliplok. Gorzval predicted their arrival a day in advance, having dreamed that they were near. "Every captain dreams dragons," he explained. "Our minds are attuned to them; we feel their souls approaching us. There's a captain, a woman with some teeth out, Guidrag's her name, who can dream them a week away, sometimes more. Heads right to them and they're always there. Me, I'm not that good, can't do better than a day's distance. But nobody's as good as Guidrag, anyway. I do my best. We'll have dragons off the bow in another ten, twelve hours, that's a guarantee."

Valentine had little confidence in the Skandar captain's guarantees. But in mid-morning the lookout high in the mast sang out, "Hoy! Dragons ho!"

A great many of them, forty, fifty, maybe more, swarmed just off the *Brangalyn*'s bow. They were big-bellied ungraceful beasts, broad in cross-section like the *Brangalyn* itself, with long thick necks, heavy triangular heads, short tails terminating in flat flaring flukes, and prominent ridges of bony projections running the length of their high-vaulted backs. Their wings were the strangest feature of all—fins, really, for it was inconceivable that these huge creatures should ever take to the air, but they looked far more like wings than fins, batwings, dark and leathery, sprouting from massive stumpy bases below the sea-dragons' necks and sweeping down half the length of their bodies. Most of the dragons kept their wings folded like cloaks, but some had them fully outspread, fanning them out along the axes provided by long fragile-looking finger-bones, and with them they covered the water about them for astonishing spreads, unfurling them like black tarpaulins.

Most of the dragons were young, twenty to fifty feet in length, but there were many newborn ones, six-footers or thereabouts, swimming and splashing freely or else gripping the nipples of their mothers, who tended to be of mid-size range. But among the school drifted a few monsters, half submerged and somnolent, their spine-ridges rising high above the water like the central hills of some floating island. They were unimaginably bulky. It was hard to judge their full magnitude,

224

for their hindquarters tended to droop out of sight, but two or three of them looked at least as large as the ship. As Gorzval passed him on the deck Valentine said, "We don't have Lord Kinniken's dragon out there, do we?"

The Skandar captain chuckled indulgently. "Nay, the Kinniken's three times the size of those, at least. Three? More than three! Those are hardly hundred-fifty-footers. I've seen dozens bigger. So will you, friend, before long."

Valentine tried to imagine dragons three times the size of the biggest out there. His mind rebelled. It was like trying to visualize the full scope of Castle Mount: one simply could not do it.

The ship moved in for the kill. It was a smoothly coordinated operation. Boats were lowered, with a lance-wielding Skandar strapped upright in the bow of each. Among the nursing dragons the boats quietly moved, the lancer spearing one here, one there, apportioning the kill among the mothers so that none was aroused by total loss of her young. These young dragons were lashed by their tails to the boats; and as the boats returned to the ship, nets were lowered to hoist the catch. Only when some dozen young dragons had been taken did the hunters go for bigger game. The boats were retracted and the harpooner, a giant Skandar with a naked dull-blue swath across his chest where the fur had long ago been ripped away, took his place in the cupola. Unhurriedly he selected his weapon and nocked it into its catapult while Gorzval maneuvered the ship to give him a good shot at the chosen victim. The harpooner took aim; the dragons grazed on, heedless; Valentine discovered that he was holding his breath and intently squeezing Carabella's hand. Then the gleaming somber shaft of the harpoon was released.

It buried itself to its haft in the blubbery shoulder of a dragon some ninety feet long and instantly the sea came alive.

The wounded dragon lashed the surface with its tail and unfurled its wings, which beat against the water in titanic fury, as though the animal meant to burst into the air and soar off, dragging the dangling *Brangalyn* behind it. At that first frantic outburst of pain the mother-dragons opened their wings as well, gathering their nurslings into a protective shield, and with powerful strokes of their tails began to move away, while the largest of the herd, the utter monsters, simply sank from view, letting themselves glide into the depths with scarcely a ripple of energy. This left a dozen or so adolescent dragons, who knew that something disturbing was happening but were not sure how to react; they swam in wide circles around their wounded comrade, holding their wings tentatively half-spread and slapping lightly at the water with them. Meanwhile the harpooner, still choosing his weapons in absolute tranquillity, put a second and a third into his prey, close by the first.

"Boats!" cried Gorzval. "Nets!"

Now began a strange proceeding. Once more the boats were lowered, and the hunters rowed forth. Toward the ring of excited dragons they headed, and hurled into the water grenades of some sort that exploded with dull booming sounds, spreading a slick coating of bright yellow dye. The explosions and, it seemed, the dye sent the remaining dragons into a frenzy of terror. With wild thrashings of wings and tails they swam swiftly out of sight. Only the victim remained, very much alive but held fast. It too was swimming, in a northerly direction, but it towed the entire mass of the *Brangalyn* along behind it, and it was visibly weakened moment by moment by the effort. The boatmen, with their dye-grenades, attempted to force the dragon closer to the ship; at the same time the netmen lowered a colossal webwork of fabric which by some interior mechanism opened and spread out over the water, and closed again when the dragon had entangled itself in its meshes.

"Winches!" Gorzval roared, and the net rose from the water.

The dragon dangled in mid-air. Its enormous weight caused the huge ship to list alarmingly. Far above, the harpooner rose in his cupola for the coup de grace. He gripped the catapult with all four hands and let fly. A ferocious grunt came from him as he released the weapon and an instant later came an answering sound, hollow, agonized, from the dragon. The harpoon penetrated the dragon's skull at a point just behind the great saucerlike green eyes. The mighty wings raked the air in one last terrible convulsion.

The rest was mere butchery. The winches did their work, the dragon was hoisted to the slaughter-block, the stripping of the carcass began. Valentine watched awhile, until the gory spectacle palled: the flensing of the blubber, the securing of the valuable internal organs, the severing of the wings, and all the rest. When he had had enough he went below, and when he returned a few hours later the skeleton of the dragon rose like a museum exhibit over the deck, a great white arch topped by that bizarre spiny ridge, and the hunters were at work disassembling even that.

"You look grim," Carabella said to him.

"I lack appreciation of this art," he answered.

It seemed to Valentine that Gorzval could entirely have filled the hold of his vessel, large as it was, with the proceeds of this one school of dragons. But he had chosen a handful of young and only one adult, not by any means the largest, and had deliberately driven the others away. Zalzan Kavol explained that there were quotas, decreed by Coronals in centuries past, to prevent overfishing: herds were to be thinned, not exterminated, and a ship that returned too soon from its voyage would be called to account and subjected to severe penalties. Besides, it was essential to get the dragons quickly on board, before predators arrived, and to process the flesh swiftly; a crew that hunted too greedily would be unable to handle its own catch in an effective and profitable way.

The season's first kill seemed to make Gorzval's crew more mellow. They nodded occasionally at the passengers, even smiled now and then, and went about their own tasks in a relaxed and almost cheerful way. Their sullen silence melted; they laughed, joked, sang on deck:

> Lord Malibor was fine and bold
> And loved the heaving sea,
> Lord Malibor came off the Mount,
> A hunter for to be.

> Lord Malibor prepared his ship,
> A gallant sight was she,
> With sails all of beaten gold,
> And masts of ivory.

Valentine and Carabella heard the singers—it was the squad barreling the blubber—and went aft to listen more closely. Carabella, quickly picking up the simple robust melody, quietly began to finger it on her pocket-harp, adding little fanciful cadenzas between the verses.

> Lord Malibor stood at the helm
> And faced the heaving wave,
> And sailed in quest of the dragon free,
> The dragon fierce and brave.

> Lord Malibor a challenge called,
> His voice did boom and ring.
> "I wish to meet, I wish to fight,"
> Quoth he, "the dragon-king."

> *"I hear, my lord," the dragon cried,*
> *And came across the sea.*
> *Twelve miles long and three miles wide*
> *And two miles deep was he.*

"Look," Carabella said. "There's Zalzan Kavol."

Valentine glanced across the way. Yes, there was the Skandar, listening at the far side near the rail, all his arms folded, a deepening scowl on his face. He did not seem to be enjoying the song. What was the matter with him?

> *Lord Malibor stood on the deck*
> *And fought both hard and well.*
> *Thick was the blood that flowed that day*
> *And great the blows that fell.*

> *But dragon-kings are old and sly,*
> *And rarely are they beaten.*
> *Lord Malibor, for all his strength,*
> *Eventually was eaten.*

> *All sailors bold, who dragons hunt,*
> *Of this grim tale take heed!*
> *Despite all luck and skill, you may*
> *End up as dragon-feed.*

Valentine laughed and clapped his hands. That brought an immediate fierce glare from Zalzan Kavol, who strode toward them looking huffy with indignation.

"My lord!" he cried. "Will you tolerate such irreverent—"

"Not so loud on the *my lord*," Valentine said crisply. "Irreverent, you say? What are you talking about?"

"No respect for a terrible tragedy! No respect for a fallen Coronal! No respect for—"

"Zalzan Kavol!" Valentine said slyly. "Are you such a lover of respectability, then?"

"I know what is right and what is wrong, my lord. To mock the death of Lord Malibor is—"

"Be more easy, my friend," Valentine said gently, putting his hand on one of the Skandar's gigantic forearms. "Where Lord Malibor has gone, he is far beyond matters of respect or disrespect. And I thought the song was a delight. If *I* take no offense, Zalzan Kavol, why should you?"

But Zalzan Kavol continued to grumble and bluster. "If I may say it, my lord, you may not yet be returned to a full sense of the rightness of things. If I were you, I would go to

228

those sailors now and order them never to sing such a thing again in your presence."

"In my presence?" Valentine said, with a broad grin. "Why should they care dragon-spittle for my presence? Who am I but a passenger, barely tolerated at all? If I said any such thing, I'd be over the rail in a minute, and dragon-feed myself the next. Eh? Think about it, Zalzan Kavol! And calm yourself, fellow. It's only a silly sailor-song."

"Nevertheless," the Skandar muttered, walking stiffly away.

Carabella giggled. "He takes himself so seriously."

Valentine began to hum, then to sing:

> *All sailors bold, who dragons hunt,*
> *Of this—*
> *Of this sad tale?—*
> *Of this sad tale take heed!*

"Yes, that's it," he said. "Love, will you do me a service? When those men are through with their work, draw one of them aside—the red-bearded one, I think, with the deep bass voice—and have him teach you the words. And then teach them to me. And I can sing it to Zalzan Kavol to make him smile, eh? How does it go? Let's see—"

> *"I hear, my lord," the dragon cried,*
> *And came across the sea.*
> *Twelve miles long and three miles wide*
> *And two miles deep was he—*

A week or thereabouts passed before they sighted dragons again, and in that time not only Carabella and Valentine learned the ditty, but Lisamon Hultin as well, who took pleasure in bellowing it across the decks in her raucous baritone. But Zalzan Kavol continued to growl and snort whenever he heard it.

The second school of dragons was much larger than the first, and Gorzval allowed the taking of some two dozen small ones, one mid-sized one, and one titan at least a hundred thirty feet long. That kept all hands busy for the next few days. The deck ran purple with dragons' blood, and bones and wings were stacked all over the ship as the crew labored to get everything down to storable size. At the captain's table delicacies were offered, from the most mysterious inner parts of the creature, and Gorzval, ever more expansive, brought forth casks of fine wines, quite unsuspected from someone who had been at the edge of bankruptcy. "Piliplok golden," he said, pouring with a lavish hand. "I have saved this wine for some special occasion, and doubtless this is it. You have brought us excellent luck."

"Your fellow captains will not be joyed to hear that," Valentine said. "We might easily have sailed with them, if they had only known how charmed we were."

"Their loss, our gain. To your pilgrimage, my friends!" cried the Skandar captain.

They were moving now through ever more balmy waters. The hot wind out of Suvrael relented here at the edge of the tropics, and a kinder, moister breeze came to them out of the southwest, from the distant Stoienzar Peninsula of Alhanroel. The water was a deep green hue, sea-birds were numerous, algae grew so thick in places that navigation was sometimes impeded, and brightly colored fish could be seen darting just below the surface—the prey of the dragons, who were flesh-eaters and swam open-mouthed through swarms of lesser sea-creatures. The Rodamaunt Archipelago now lay not far away. Gorzval proposed to complete his haul here: the *Brangalyn* had room for another few large dragons, two more of mid-size, and perhaps forty of the small, and then he would drop his passengers and head for Piliplok to market his catch.

"Dragons ho!" came the lookout's cry.

This was the greatest school yet, hundreds of them, spiny humps rising above the water everywhere. For two days the *Brangalyn* moved among them, slaughtering at will. On the horizon other ships could be seen, but they were far off, for strict rules governed impinging on hunting territory.

Gorzval seemed to glow with the success of his voyage. He himself took frequent turns in the boat-crews, which Valentine gathered was unusual, and once he even made his way to the cupola to wield a harpoon. The ship now was settling low to the waterline with the weight of dragon-flesh.

On the third day dragons were still close about them, undismayed by the carnage and unwilling to scatter. "One more big one," Gorzval vowed, "and then we make for the islands."

He selected an eighty-footer for the final target.

Valentine had grown bored, and more than bored, with the butchery, and as the harpooner sent his third shaft into the prey he turned away, and walked to the far side of the deck. There he found Sleet, and they stood by the rail, peering off to the east.

"Do you think we can see the Archipelago from here?" Val-

230

entine asked. "I long for solid land again, and an end to the stink of dragon-blood in my nostrils."

"My eyes are keen, my lord, but the islands are two days' sailing from here, and I think even my vision has limits. But—" Sleet gasped. "My lord—"

"What is it?"

"An island comes swimming toward us, my lord!"

Valentine stared, but with difficulty at first: it was morning and a brilliant fiery glare lit the surface of the sea. But Sleet took Valentine's hand and pointed with it, and then Valentine saw. A ridged dragon-spine broke the water, a spine that went on and on and on, and below it a vast and implausible bulk was dimly visible.

"Lord Kinniken's dragon!" Valentine said in a choked voice. "And it comes straight at us!"

4

Kinniken's it might be, or more likely some other not nearly so great, but it was great enough, larger than the *Brangalyn*, and it was bearing down on them steadily and unhesitatingly—either an avenging angel or else an unthinking force, there was no knowing that, but its mass was unarguable.

"Where is Gorzval?" Sleet blurted. "Weapons—guns—"

Valentine laughed. "As easily stop a rock-slide with a harpoon, Sleet. Are you a good swimmer?"

Most of the hunters were preoccupied with their catch. But some had looked the other way now, and there was frantic activity on deck. The harpooner had whirled round and stood outlined against the sky, weapons in every hand. Others had mounted the adjoining cupolas. Valentine, searching for Carabella and Deliamber and the others, caught sight of Gorzval rushing madly toward the helm; the Skandar's face was livid and his eyes were bugging, and he looked like one who stood in the presence of the ministers of death.

"Lower the boats!" someone screamed. Winches turned. Figures ran about wildly. One, a Hjort black-cheeked with fear, shook a fist at Valentine and caught him roughly by the arm, muttering, "You brought this on us! You should never have been allowed on board, any of you!"

Lisamon Hultin appeared from somewhere and swept the Hjort aside like so much chaff. Then she flung her powerful

231

arms around Valentine as if to protect him from any harm that might come.

"The Hjort was right, you know," said Valentine calmly. "We *are* an ill-omened bunch. First Zalzan Kavol loses his wagon, and now poor Gorzval loses——"

There was a ghastly impact as the onrushing dragon crashed broadside into the *Brangalyn*.

The ship heeled over as though it had been pushed by a giant's hand, then rolled dizzyingly back the other way. An awful shudder shook its timbers. A secondary impact came—the wings hitting the hull, the thrashing flukes?—and then another, and the *Brangalyn* bobbed like a cork. "We're stove in!" a desperate voice cried. Things rolled free on the deck, a giant rendering cauldron breaking its moorings and tumbling over three hapless crewmen, a case of boning-axes ripping loose and skidding over the side. As the ship continued to sway and lurch, Valentine caught a glimpse of the great dragon on the far side, where the recent catch still hung, unbalancing everything; and the monster swung around and headed in for another attack. There could be no doubt now of the purposefulness of its onslaught.

The dragon struck, shoulder-side on; the *Brangalyn* rocked wildly; Valentine grunted as Lisamon Hultin's grip became an almost crushing embrace. He had no idea where any of the others might be, nor whether they would survive. Clearly the ship was doomed. Already it was listing badly as water poured into the hold. The tail of the dragon rose nearly to deck-level and struck again. Everything dissolved into chaos. Valentine felt himself flying; he soared gracefully, he dipped and bobbed, he plunged with elegance and skill toward the water.

He landed in something much like a whirlpool and was drawn down into the terrible turbulent spin.

As he went under Valentine could not help but hear the ballad of Lord Malibor ringing in his mind. In truth that Coronal had taken a fancy for dragon-hunting some ten years back, and had gone out in what was said to be the finest dragon-ship in Piliplok, and the ship had been lost with all hands. No one knew what had happened, but—so it came out of Valentine's spotty recollections—the government had spoken of a sudden storm. More likely, he thought, it had been this killer-beast, this avenger of dragonkind.

> *Twelve miles long and three miles wide*
> *And two miles deep was he—*

232

And now a second Coronal, successor but one to Malibor, would meet the same fate. Valentine was oddly unmoved by that. He had thought himself dying in the rapids of the Steiche, and had survived that; here, with a hundred miles of sea between him and any sort of safety, and a rampaging monster lashing about close at hand, he was even more surely doomed, but there was no use bemoaning it. The Divine had clearly withdrawn its favor from him. What grieved him was that others whom he loved would die with him, merely because they had been loyal, because they had pledged themselves to follow him on his journey to the Isle, because they had tied themselves to a luckless Coronal and a luckless dragon-captain and now must share their evil destinies.

He was sucked deep into the heart of the ocean and ceased to ponder the tides of luck. He struggled for breath, coughed, choked, spat out water and swallowed more. His head pounded mercilessly. *Carabella*, he thought, and darkness engulfed him.

Valentine had never, since awakening out of his broken past to find himself near Pidruid, given much thought to a philosophy of death. Life held challenges enough for him. He recalled vaguely what he had been taught in boyhood, that all souls return to the Divine Source at their last moment when the release of life-energy comes, and travel over the Bridge of Farewells, the bridge that is the prime responsibility of the Pontifex. But whether there might be truth in that, whether there was a world beyond, and if so of what sort, Valentine had never paused to consider. Now, though, he returned to consciousness in a place so strange that it surpassed the imaginings of even the most fertile of thinkers.

Was this the afterlife? It was a giant chamber, a great silent room with thick moist pink walls and a roof that was in places high and domed, supported by mighty pillars, and in other places drooped until it nearly touched the floor. In that roof were mounted huge glowing hemispheres that emitted a faint blue light, as if by phosphorescence. The air in here was rank and steamy, and had a sharp, bitter flavor, unpleasant and stifling. Valentine lay on his side against a wet slippery surface, rough to the touch, deeply corrugated, quivering with constant deep palpitations and tremors. He put the flat of his hand to it and felt a kind of convulsion deep within. The texture of the ground was like nothing he had known before, and those tiny but perceptible motions within it made him wonder if what he had entered was not the world after death but merely some grotesque hallucination.

Valentine got unsteadily to his feet. His clothing was soaked, he had lost one boot somewhere, his lips burned with the taste of salt, his lungs seemed full of water, and he felt shaky and dazed; furthermore it was hard to keep upright on this unendingly trembling surface. Looking about, he saw by the dim pale luminosity a kind of vegetation, pliant whip-shaped growths, thick and fleshy and leafless, sprouting from the ground. They too writhed with inner animation. Making his way between two lofty pillars and through an area where ceiling and floor almost met, he caught sight of what seemed to be a pond of some greenish fluid. Beyond that he was unable to see in the dimness.

He walked toward the pond and perceived something exceedingly odd in it: hundreds of brightly colored fish, of the kind that he had seen flitting about in the water before the day's hunt had begun. They were not swimming now. They were dead and decaying, flesh stripping away from bones, and below them in the pool was a carpet of similar bones, many feet thick.

Suddenly there was a sound as of the roaring of the wind behind him. Valentine turned. The walls of the chamber were in motion, pulling back, the drooping places in the ceiling retracting to create a vast open space; and a torrent of water came rushing toward him, as high as his hips. He barely had time to reach one of the ceiling-pillars and fling his arms tight about it; then the inrushing of water sluiced about him with tremendous force. He held on. It seemed that half the Inner Sea was pouring past him, and for a moment he thought he would lose his grip, but then the flow subsided and the water drained away through slits that materialized abruptly in the floor—leaving in its wake scores of stranded fish. The floor convulsed; the fleshy whips swept the desperate flopping fish across the floor to the greenish pool; and once they entered it they quickly ceased to move.

Suddenly Valentine understood.

I am not dead, he knew, nor is this any place of afterlife. I am within the belly of the dragon.

He began to laugh.

Valentine threw back his head and let giant guffaws pour from him. What other response was fitting? To cry? To curse? The vast beast had gobbled him whole at a gulp, had sucked in the Coronal of Majipoor as heedlessly as it might a minnow. But he was too big to be propelled into that digestive pond down there, so here he was, camped on the floor of the dragon's maw, in this cathedral of an alimentary canal. What now? Hold court for the fishes? Dispense justice among them as they came sweeping in? Settle down here and spend the rest of his days dining on raw fish stolen from the monster's catch?

It was high comedy, Valentine thought.

But dark tragedy as well, for Sleet and Carabella and young Shanamir and all the others, drawn down to death in the wreck of the *Brangalyn*, victims of their own sympathies and of his awesomely bad luck. For them he felt only anguish. Carabella's lilting voice silenced forever, and Sleet's miraculous skills of hand and eye forever lost, and the rough-souled Skandars no longer to fill the air with whirling multitudes of knives and sickles and torches, and Shanamir cut off before he had fairly begun his life—

Valentine could not bear thinking about them.

For himself, though, there was only cosmic amusement at this absurd plight. To take his mind from grief and pain and loss he laughed again, and stretched his arms wide to the distant walls of the strange room. "Lord Valentine's Castle, this is!" he cried. "The throne-room! I invite you all to dine with me in the grand feasting-hall!"

Out of the murky distance a booming voice called, "By my gut, I accept that invitation!"

Valentine was astounded beyond all measure.

"Lisamon?"

"No, it's the Pontifex Tyeveras and his cross-eyed uncle! Is that you, Valentine?"

"Yes! Where are you?"

"In the gizzard of this stinking dragon! Where are you?"

"Not far from you! But I can't see you!"

"Sing," she called. "Stay where you are and sing, and keep singing! I'll try to reach you!"

Valentine began, in the loudest voice he could muster:

> *Lord Malibor was fine and bold*
> *And loved the heaving sea—*

Again the roaring sound came; again the great creature's gullet opened to admit a cascade of sea-water and a horde of fish; again Valentine clung to a pillar as the influx hit him.

"Oh—by the Divine's toes," Lisamon cried. "Hang on, Valentine, hang on!"

He hung on until the force was spent, and slumped against the pillar, soaked, panting. Somewhere in the distance the giantess called to him, and he called back. Her voice grew nearer. She urged him to keep singing, and he did:

> *Lord Malibor stood at the helm*
> *And faced the heaving wave,*
> *And sailed in quest of the dragon free—*

He heard her occasionally bawling a snatch of the ballad herself, with amiably bawdy embellishments, as she approached through the intricacies of the dragon's interior, and then he looked up and saw by the faint luminous light her enormous form looming above him. He smiled at her. She smiled, and laughed, and he laughed with her, and they clasped one another in a wet, slippery embrace.

But the sight of one who had survived put him in mind again of those who surely had not, and plunged him once more into grief and shame. He turned away, biting at his lip.

"My lord?" she said puzzledly.

"Only we two remain, Lisamon."

"Yes, and praises be for that!"

"But the others—they'd live now, if they hadn't been so stupid as to go chasing across the world with me—"

She caught him by the arm. "My lord, will mourning them bring them back to life, if dead they be?"

"I know all that. But—"

"We are safe. If we have lost our friends, my lord, that's cause for sorrow indeed, but not for guilt. They followed you of their own free choice, eh, my lord? And if their time has come, well, it is because their time has come, and how could that have been otherwise? Will you give up this grief, my lord, and rejoice that we are safe?"

He shrugged. "Safe, yes. And yes, grief brings no one back to life. But how safe are we? How long can we survive in here, Lisamon?"

"Long enough for me to cut us free." She pulled her vibration-sword out of its sheath.

Amazed, he said, "You think you can hack a path to the outside?"

"Why not? I've cut through worse."

"At the first touch of that thing to the dragon's flesh it'll dive to the bottom of the sea. We're safer in here than trying to swim up from five miles underneath."

"It was said of you that you are an optimist at the darkest time," the warrior-woman declared. "Where's that optimism now? The dragon lives at the surface. It might thrash a bit, but it won't dive. And if we do emerge five miles down? At least it's a quick death. Can you breathe this foul muck forever? Can you wander for long inside a single giant fish?"

Gingerly Lisamon Hultin touched the tip of the vibration-sword to the side wall. The thick moist flesh quivered a bit but did not recoil. "You see? It's got no nerves in here," she said, driving the weapon a little deeper and turning it to excavate a cavity. There were tremors and twitches. She kept digging. "Do you think anyone else was swallowed with us?" she asked.

"Yours was the only voice I've heard."

"And I only yours. Phaugh, what a monster! I tried to hold you as we went overboard, but when we were struck the last time I lost my grip on you. We came to the same place, anyway." She had by now opened a hole a foot deep and two feet wide in the side of the dragon's stomach. It seemed hardly to feel the surgery at all. We are like maggots gnawing within it, Valentine thought. Lisamon Hultin said, "While I cut, you see if you can find anyone else. But don't stray too far, hear?"

"I'll be careful."

He chose a route along the stomach wall, groping in the half-darkness, pausing twice to hang on through inrushes of water, and calling out constantly in the hope that someone might reply. No replies came. Her excavation was enormous now; he saw her deep within the dragon's flesh, still hacking away. Gobbets of severed meat were piled on all sides and thick purplish blood stained her entire body. She was singing cheerfully as she cut.

> Lord Malibor stood on the deck
> And fought both hard and well.
> Thick was the blood that flowed that day
> And great the blows that fell.

"How far do you think it is to the outside?" he asked.

"Half a mile or so."

"Really?"

She laughed. "I suppose ten or fifteen feet. Here, clear the opening behind me. This meat's piling up faster than I can sweep it away."

Feeling like a butcher, and not enjoying the sensation much, Valentine seized the chunks of severed flesh and hauled them back out of the cavity, tossing them as far as he could. He shivered in horror as he saw the fleshy whips of the stomach floor seize the meat and sweep it blithely on toward

237

the digestive pond. Any protein was welcome here, so it seemed.

Deeper, deeper they traveled into the dragon's abdominal wall. Valentine tried to calculate the probable width of it, taking the length of the creature at no less than three hundred feet; but the arithmetic became a muddle. They were working in close quarters and in a foul, hot atmosphere. The blood, the raw meat, the sweat, the narrowness of the cavity—it was hard to imagine a more repellent place.

Valentine looked back. "The hole's closing behind us!"

"Beast that lives forever must have tricks of healing," the giantess muttered. She thrust and gouged and hacked. Uneasily Valentine watched new flesh sprouting as if by magic, the wound healing with phenomenal speed. What if they became encapsulated in this opening? Smothered by joining flesh? Lisamon Hultin pretended to be unworried, but he saw her working harder, faster, grunting and moaning, standing with colossal legs planted far apart and shoulders braced. The gash was sealed to their rear, pink new meat covering the hole, and now it was closing at the sides. Lisamon Hultin slashed and cut with furious intensity, and Valentine continued his humbler task of clearing the debris, but she was plainly wearying now, her giant strength visibly diminished, and the hole seemed to be closing almost as fast as she could cut.

"Don't know if I—can keep—it up—" she muttered.

"Give me the sword, then!"

She laughed. "Watch out! You can't do it!" In wild rage she returned to the struggle, bellowing curses at the dragon's flesh as it sprouted around her. It was impossible now to tell where they were; they were burrowing through a realm without landmarks. Her grunts grew sharper and shorter.

"Maybe we should try to go back to the stomach area," he suggested. "Before we're trapped so—"

"No!" she roared. "I think we're getting there! Not so meaty here—tougher, more like muscle—maybe the sheath just under the hide—"

Suddenly sea-water poured in on them.

"We're through!" Lisamon Hultin cried. She turned, seizing Valentine as though he were a doll, and pushed him forward, headfirst into the opening in the monster's flank. Her arms were locked in a fierce grip around his hips. She gave one tremendous thrust and he barely had time to fill his lungs with air before he was projected out through the slippery walls into the cool green embrace of the ocean. Lisamon Hultin emerged just after him, still gripping him tightly, now by his

238

ankle and then by his wrist, and they rocketed upward, upward, rising like corks.

For what seemed like hours they flew toward the surface. Valentine's forehead ached. His ribs soon would burst. His chest was on fire. We are climbing from the very bottom of the sea, he thought bleakly, and we will drown before we reach the air, or our blood will boil the way it does in divers who go too deep in search of the eyestones off Til-omon, or we will be squeezed flat by the pressure, or—

He erupted into clear sweet air, popping nearly the full length of his body out of the water and falling back with a splash. Limply he floated, a straw on the waters, weak, trembling, struggling for breath. Lisamon Hultin floated alongside. The warm beautiful sun blazed wonderfully, straight overhead.

He was alive, and he was unharmed, and he was free of the dragon.

And he bobbed somewhere on the breast of the Inner Sea, a hundred miles from anywhere.

5

When the first moments of exhaustion had passed, he raised his head and peered about. The dragon was still visible, hump and ridge above the surface, only a few hundred yards away. But it seemed placid and appeared to be swimming slowly in the opposite direction. Of the *Brangalyn* there was no trace—only scattered timbers over a broad span of ocean. Nor were other survivors in view.

They swam to the nearest timber, a good-sized strip of the hull, and flung themselves across it. For a long while neither of them spoke. At length Valentine said, "And now do we swim to the Archipelago? Or should we simply go straight on to the Isle of Sleep?"

"Swimming is hard work, my lord. We could ride on the dragon's back."

"But how guide him?"

"Tug on the wings," she suggested.

"I have my doubts of that."

They were silent again.

Valentine said, "At least in the belly of the dragon we had a fresh catch of fish delivered every few minutes."

239

"And the inn was large," Lisamon Hultin added. "But poorly ventilated. I think I prefer it here."

"But how long can we drift like this?"

She looked at him strangely. "Do you doubt that we'll be rescued, my lord?"

"It seems reasonably in doubt, yes."

"It was prophesied to me in a dream from the Lady," said the giantess, "that my death would come in a dry place when I was very old. I am still young and this place is the least dry on all of Majipoor, except perhaps the middle of the Great Sea. Therefore there is nothing to fear. I will not perish here, and neither will you."

"A comforting revelation," Valentine said. "But what will we do?"

"Can you accomplish sendings, my lord?"

"I was Coronal, not King of Dreams."

"But any mind can reach any other, with true intent! Do you think only the King and Lady have such skills? The little wizard Deliamber talked into minds at night, I know that, and Gorzval said he spoke with dragons in his sleep, and you—"

"I am barely myself, Lisamon. Such of my mind as is left to me will send no sendings."

"Try. Reach out across the waters. To the Lady your mother, my lord, or to her people on the Isle, or to the folk of the Archipelago. You have the power. I am only a stupid swinger of swords, but you, lord, have a mind that was deemed worthy of the Castle, and now, in the hour of our need—" The giantess seemed transfigured with passion. "Do it, Lord Valentine! Call for help, and help will come!"

Valentine was skeptical. He knew little of the network of dream-communication that seemed to bind this planet together; it did appear that mind often called to mind, and of course there were the Powers of the Isle and of Suvrael supposedly sending directed messages forth by some means of mechanical amplification, but yet, drifting here on a slab of wood in the ocean, body and clothes filthied with the flesh and blood of the giant beast that lately had swallowed him, spirit so drained by unending adversity that even his legendary sunny faith in luck and miracles was put to rout—how could he hope to summon aid across such a gulf?

He closed his eyes. He sought to concentrate the energies of his mind in a single point deep within his skull. He imagined a glowing spark of light there, a hidden radiance that he could tap and beam forth. But it was useless. He found himself wondering what toothy creature might soon be nibbling at his dangling feet. He distracted himself with fears that any messages he might send would reach only as far as the hazy mind of the dragon nearby, that had destroyed the *Brangalyn* and almost all its people, and now might wish to turn back and finish the job. Still, he tried. For all his doubts, he owed it to Lisamon Hultin to make the attempt. He held himself still, barely breathing, seeking intently to do whatever it might be that could transmit such a message.

On and off during the afternoon and early evening he attempted it. Darkness came on quickly, and the water grew strangely luminescent, flickering with a ghostly greenish light. They did not dare sleep at the same time, for fear they might slip from the timber and be lost; so they took turns, and when it was Valentine's turn he fought hard for wakefulness, thinking more than once that he was losing consciousness. Creatures swam near them in the night, making tracks of cold fire through the luminous wavelets.

From time to time Valentine tried the sending-forth of messages again. But he saw no avail in it.

We are lost, he thought.

Toward morning he gave himself up to sleep, and had perplexing dreams of dancing eels atop the water. Vaguely, while sleeping, he strived to reach far-off minds with his mind, and then he slipped into a slumber too deep for that.

And woke to the touch of Lisamon Hultin's hand on his shoulder.

"My lord?"

He opened his eyes and looked at her in bewilderment.

"My lord, you may stop making sendings now. We are saved!"

"What?"

"A boat, my lord! See? From the east?"

Wearily he raised his head and followed her gesture. A boat, yes, a small one, coming toward them. Oars flashing in the sunlight. Hallucination, he thought. Delusion. Mirage.

But the boat grew larger against the horizon, and then it was there, and hands were groping for him, hauling him up, and he was sprawled feebly against someone and someone else was putting a flask to his lips, a cool drink, wine, water, he had no way of telling, and they were peeling off his soggy befouled garments and wrapping him in something clean and dry. Strangers, two men and a woman, with great manes of tawny hair and clothing of an unfamiliar sort. He heard Lisamon Hultin talking with them, but the words were blurred and indistinct, and he made no attempt to discern their mean-

ing. Had he conjured up these rescuers with his mental broad-
cast, then? Angels, were they? Spirits? Valentine settled back,
hardly caring, totally spent. He thought hazily of drawing Lisamon Hultin aside and telling her to make no mention of his
true identity, but he lacked even the energy for that, and
hoped she would have sense enough not to compound absurdity with absurdity by saying any such thing. "He is Coronal of
Majipoor in disguise, yes, and the dragon swallowed us both
but we were able to cut ourselves free, and—" Yes. Certainly
that would have the ring of unanswerable truth to these people. Valentine smiled faintly and drifted into a dreamless
sleep.

When he woke he was in a pleasant sunlit room, facing out
on a broad golden beach, and Carabella was looking down at
him with an expression of grave concern.

"My lord?" she said softly. "Do you hear me?"

"Is this a dream?"

"This is the island of Mardigile in the Archipelago," she
told him. "You were picked up yesterday, drifting in the
ocean, along with the giantess. These islanders are fisherfolk,
who have been scouting the sea for survivors since the ship
went down."

"Who else lives?" Valentine asked quickly.

"Deliamber and Zalzan Kavol are here with me. The Mardigile folk say that Khun, Shanamir, Vinorkis, and some
Skandars—I don't know if they're ours—were picked up by
boats from a neighboring island. Some of the dragon-hunters
escaped in their own boats and have reached the islands too."

"And Sleet? What of Sleet?"

Carabella showed, for a flashing moment, a look of fear. "I
have no news of Sleet," she said. "But the rescue is continuing. He may be safe on one of these islands. There are dozens
hereabouts. The Divine has preserved us so far: we will not be
cast aside now." She laughed lightly. "Lisamon Hultin has told
a wonderful story of how you both were swallowed by the
great dragon, and hacked your way out with the vibration-
sword. The islanders love it. They think it's the most splendid
fable since the tale of Lord Stiamot and the—"

"It happened," Valentine said.

"My lord?"

"The dragon. Swallowing us. She tells the truth."

Carabella giggled. "When I first learned in dreams of your
real self, I believed that. But when you tell me—"

"Within the dragon," Valentine said earnestly, "there were
great pillars holding up the vault of the stomach, and an open-

ing at one end through which sea-water came rushing every few minutes, and with it came fish that were pushed by little whips toward a greenish pond where they were digested, and where the giantess and I would have been digested too, if we were less lucky. Did she tell you that? And do you think we spent our time out there inventing a fable to amuse you all?"

Eyes wide, Carabella said, "She told the same story, yes. But we thought—"

"It's true, Carabella."

"Then it is a miracle of the Divine, and you will be famous in all time to come!"

"I'm already going to be famous," said Valentine acidly, "as the Coronal who lost his throne, and took up juggling for lack of a royal occupation. That will win me a place in the ballads alongside the Pontifex Arioc, who made himself Lady of the Isle. The dragon, now, that only embellishes the legend I'm creating around myself." His expression changed suddenly. "You've told none of these people who I am, I hope?"

"Not a word, my lord."

"Good. Keep it that way. They have enough difficult things to believe about us, as it is."

An islander, slim and tanned and with the great sweep of fair hair that seemed the universal style here, brought Valentine a tray of food: some clear soup, a tender piece of baked fish, triangular wedges of a fruit with dark indigo flesh dotted with tiny scarlet seeds. Valentine found himself ravenously hungry.

Afterward he strolled with Carabella on the beach outside his cottage. "Once again I thought you were lost to me forever," he said softly. "I thought I would never hear your voice again."

"Do I matter that much to you, my lord?"

"More than I could ever tell you."

She smiled sadly. "Such pretty words, eh, Valentine? For so I call you, *Valentine*, but you are *Lord* Valentine, and how many fancy women do you have, Lord Valentine, waiting for you on Castle Mount?"

He had now and then been thinking the same thing himself. Had he a lover there? Many of them? An intended bride, even? So much of his past was still shrouded. And if he reached the Castle, and if a woman who had waited for him came forth to him—

"No," he said. "You are mine, Carabella, and I am yours, and whatever may have been in the past—if ever anything was—lies in the past now. I have a different face these days. I have a different soul."

She looked skeptical, but did not challenge what he had said, and he lightly kissed her frown away.

"Sing to me," he said. "The song you sang under the bush in Pidruid, the festival-night. *Not all the wealth of Castle Mount*, it went, *Is worth my love to me.* Eh?"

"I know another much like it," she said, and took up the pocket-harp from her hip:

> My love has donned a pilgrim's robe
> Afar across the sea
> My love has gone to the Isle of Sleep
> Across the dreaming sea.
>
> Sweet my love, and fair as dawn
> Afar across the sea
> Lost my love to an island tall
> Across the dreaming sea.
>
> Lady kind of the distant Isle
> Afar across the sea
> Fill my dreams with my lover's smile
> Across the dreaming sea.

"A different sort of song, that one," Valentine said. "A sadder one. Sing me that other, love."

"Another time."

"Please. This is a time of joy, of reuniting, Carabella. Please."

She smiled and sighed and took up the harp again.

> My love is fair as is the spring,
> As gentle as the night,
> My love is sweet as stolen fruit—

Yes, he thought. Yes, that one was better. He let his hand rest tenderly on the nape of her neck, and stroked it as they walked along the beach. It was astonishingly beautiful here, warm and peaceful. Birds of fifty hues perched in the tortuous-limbed little trees of the shore, and a crystalline sea, surfless, transparent, lapped at the fine sand. The air was soft and mild, fragrant with the perfumes of unknown blossoms. From far away came the sound of laughter and of a gay, bright, tinkling music. How tempting it was, Valentine thought, to abandon all fantasies of Castle Mount and settle forever on Mardigile, and go out at dawn on a fishing-boat for

244

the catch, and spend the rest of each day frolicking in the hot sunshine.

But there would be no such abdications for him. In the afternoon Zalzan Kavol and Autifon Deliamber, both healthy and well rested after their ordeals at sea, came to call on him, and soon they were talking of ways and means to continue the journey.

Zalzan Kavol, parsimonious as always, had had the money-pouch on him when the *Brangalyn* went down, and so at least half their treasury had survived, even if Shanamir had lost the rest. The Skandar laid out the glittering coins. "With this," he said, "we can hire these fisherfolk to convey us to the Isle. I have spoken with our hosts. This Archipelago is nine hundred miles in length, and numbers three thousand islands, more than eight hundred of them inhabited. No one here wishes to journey all the way to the Isle, but for a few royals we can hire a large trimaran that will carry us to Rodamaunt Graun, near the mid-point of the chain, and there we can probably find transport the rest of the way."

"When can we leave?" Valentine asked.

"As soon," said Deliamber, "as we are reunited once more. I am told that several of our people are on their way across from the nearby isle of Burbont at this moment."

"Which ones?"

"Khun, Vinorkis, and Shanamir," Zalzan Kavol answered, "and my brothers Erfon and Rovorn. With them is Captain Gorzval. Gibor Haern is lost at sea—I saw him perish, struck by a timber and sent under—and of Sleet there is no news."

Valentine touched the Skandar's shaggy forearm. "I grieve for your latest loss."

Zalzan Kavol's feelings seemed well under control. "Let us rather rejoice that some of us still live, my lord," he said quietly.

In early afternoon a boat from Burbont brought the other survivors. There were embraces all around; and then Valentine turned to Gorzal, who stood apart, looking numb and bewildered, rubbing at the stump of his severed arm. The dragon-captain seemed in shock. Valentine would have put his arms around the hapless man, but the instant he approached, Gorzval sank to his knees in the sand and touched his forehead to the ground and stayed there, trembling, arms outspread in the starburst gesture. "My lord—" he whispered harshly. "My lord—"

Valentine, displeased, looked around. "Who has been talking?"

Silence a moment. Then Shanamir, a bit frightened, said, "I, my lord. I meant no harm. The Skandar seemed so injured by the loss of his ship—I thought to console him by telling him who his passenger had been, that he had become part of the history of Majipoor by giving you voyage. This was before we knew that you had survived the wreck." The boy's lip quivered. "My lord, I meant no harm by it!"

Valentine nodded. "And no harm was done. I forgive you. Gorzval?"

The cowering dragon-captain remained huddled at Valentine's feet.

"Look up, Gorzval. I can't talk to you this way."

"My lord?"

"Get to your feet."

"My lord—"

"Please, Gorzval. Get up!"

The Skandar, amazed, peered at Valentine and said, *"Please,* you say? *Please?"*

Valentine laughed. "I've forgotten the habits of power, I suppose. All right: Up! I command it!"

Shakily Gorzval rose. He was a miserable sight, this little three-armed Skandar, his fur matted, sandy, his eyes bloodshot, his expression downcast.

Valentine said, "I brought foul luck upon you, and you had no need of more of that. Accept my apologies; and if fortune begins to smile more kindly on me, I will repair the harm you have suffered, someday. I promise you that. What will you do now? Gather your crew and return to Piliplok?"

Gorzval shook his head pathetically. "I could never go there again. I have no ship, I have no reputation, I have no money. I have lost everything and it can never be regained. My people were released of their indentures when the *Brangalyn* sank. I am alone now. I am ruined."

"Come with us to the Isle of the Lady, then, Gorzval."

"My lord?"

"You can't stay here. I think these islanders prefer not to take in settlers, and this is no climate for a Skandar, anyway. Nor can a dragon-hunter become a fisherman, I think, without knowing pain every time he casts his nets. Come with us. If we get no farther than the Isle, you may find peace there in the service of the Lady; and if we continue on our quest, there will be honor for you as we make the ascent of Castle Mount. What do you say, Gorzval?"

"It frightens me to be near you, my lord."

"Am I so terrifying? Do I have a dragon's mouth? Do you

246

see these people green-faced with fear?" Valentine clapped the Skandar on his shoulder. To Zalzan Kavol he said, "No one can replace the brothers you have lost. But at least I give you another companion of your own kind. And now let's make arrangements for departure, eh? The Isle is still many days' journey away."

Within an hour Zalzan Kavol had secured an island craft to carry them eastward in the morning. That evening the hospitable islanders provided them with a splendid feast, cool green wines and sleek sweet fruits and fine fresh sea-dragon flesh. That last made Valentine queasy, and he would have pushed it away, but he saw Lisamon Hultin shoveling it in as though it were the last meal she would eat. As an exercise in self-discipline he decided to force a morsel into his own throat, and found the flavor so irresistible that he renounced on the spot any discomfort that sea-dragons might arouse in his mind. As they ate, sunset came, at an early hour here in the tropics, and an extraordinary one it was, streaking the sky with rich throbbing tones of amber and violet and magenta and gold. Surely these were blessed islands, Valentine thought, extraordinarily joyous places even on a world where most places were happy ones and most lives fulfilled. The population seemed generally homogeneous, handsome long-legged folk of human blood with thick unshorn golden hair and smooth honey-colored skin, though there was a scattering of Vroons and even Ghayrogs among them, and Deliamber said that other islands in the chain had people of different stocks. According to Deliamber, who had been mingling freely since his rescue, the islands were largely out of touch with the mainland continents, and went their way in a world of their own, ignorant of matters of high destiny in the greater world. When Valentine asked one of his hosts if Lord Valentine the Coronal had happened to pass this way on his recent journey to Zimroel, the woman gave him a blank look and said ingenuously, "Is the Coronal not Lord Voriax?"

"Dead two years or more, I hear," one of the other islanders declared, and it seemed to come as news to most of the people at the table.

Valentine shared his cottage with Carabella that night. They stood together a long while on the veranda, eyes fixed on the brilliant white track of moonlight gleaming out across the sea toward distant Piliplok. He thought of the sea-dragons grazing in that sea, and of the monster in whose belly he had made that dreamlike sojourn, and, with pain, of his two lost comrades, Gibor Haern and Sleet, one of whom was deep in the sea now, the other perhaps. So great a journey, he thought, remembering Pidruid, Dulorn, Mazadone, Ilirivoyne, Nimoya, remembering the flight through the forest, the turbulence of the Steiche, the coldness of the Piliplok dragon-captains, the look of the dragon as it bore down on poor Gorzval's doomed vessel. So great a journey, so many thousands of miles, and so many miles yet to cover before he could begin to answer the questions that flooded his soul.

Carabella nestled close beside him, silent. Her attitude toward him was constantly evolving, and now had become a mixture of awe and love, of deference and irreverence, for she accepted and respected him as true Coronal, and yet remembered his innocence, his ignorance, his naïveté, qualities which had not yet left him even now. And clearly she feared she would lose him when he had again come into his own. Simply on the level of dealing daily with the world, she was far more competent than he, far more experienced, and that colored her view of him, making her see him as terrifying and childlike both at once. He understood that and took no issue with it, for, although fragments of his earlier self and princely education returned to him almost daily, and he grew daily more accustomed to the postures of command, most of his former identity still was inaccessible to him and he was, in large part, still Valentine the easy-going wanderer, Valentine the innocent, Valentine the juggler. That darker figure, the Lord Valentine he once had been, that he might someday be again, was a hidden substratum in his spirit, rarely operative but never to be ignored. He thought Carabella was making the best of a difficult position.

She said at last, "What are you thinking of, Valentine?"

"Sleet. I miss that tough little man."

"He'll turn up. We'll find him four islands from here."

"I hope so." Valentine cupped his arm about her shoulders. "I think also of all that has happened, and all that will happen. I move as though through a world of dreams, Carabella."

"Who can tell, really, what is the dream and what is not? We move as the Divine instructs us, and we ask no questions, because there are no answers. Do you know what I mean? There are questions and there are answers, of course. I can tell you what day this is, and what we had for dinner, and how this island is called, if you ask me, but there are no *questions*, there are no *answers*."

"So I believe also," Valentine said.

6

Zalzan Kavol had hired one of the grandest fishing-boats on the island, a marvelous turquoise trimaran named *Pride of Mardigile*. It was a splendid fifty-footer rising nobly on its three sleek hulls, and its sails, spotless and dazzling in the morning sunlight, bore bright vermilion edging that gave the craft a festive, jubilant air. Their captain was a man past middle years, one of the most prosperous fishermen of the island, Grigitor by name, tall and sturdy, with hair down to his waist and skin so vigorous it looked to have been oiled; he was one of those who had rescued Deliamber and Zalzan Kavol, when the first alarms of a sinking ship had reached the island. He had a crew of five, his sons and daughters, all strapping and handsome after his image.

The route of the voyage lay first toward Burbont, less than half an hour's sail away, and then into an open channel of shallow greenish water that linked the two outermost islands to the rest. The sea-bottom here was of clean white sand, and sunlight penetrated easily to it, setting off patterns of sparkling coruscations that revealed the undersea dwellers, the rip-toads and the twitch-crabs and the big-leg lobsters, and the gaudy-hued multitudes of fish, and the sinister, lurking sand-eels. Once even a small sea-dragon flitted by, far too close to land for its own good and obviously confused; one of Grigitor's daughters urged that they go after it, but he shook the notion off, saying that their responsibility was to get their passengers swiftly to Rodamaunt Graun.

All morning they sailed, passing three more islands—Richelure, Grialon, Voniaire, said their captain—and at noon they dropped anchor for lunch. Two of Grigitor's children went over the side to hunt, moving like magnificent animals, naked in the brilliant water, quickly spearing crustaceans and fish with rarely a missed thrust. Grigitor himself prepared the meal, cubes of raw white flesh marinated in a spicy sauce and washed down with cheering pungent green wine. Deliamber withdrew after eating only a little, and perched himself on the tip of one of the outer hulls, staring intently to the north. After a while Valentine noticed, and would have gone to him, but Carabella caught him by the wrist.

"He is in trance," she said. "Let him be."

They delayed their departure after lunch by some minutes,

until the little Vroon descended from his place and rejoined them. The wizard looked pleased.

"I have cast my mind forth," he announced, "and I bring you good news. Sleet lives!"

"Good news indeed!" Valentine cried. "Where is he?"

"An island in that group," said Deliamber, gesturing vaguely with a cluster of tentacles. "He is with several of Gorzval's people who escaped by boat from the disaster."

Grigitor said, "Tell me which island, and we'll make for it."

"It has the shape of a circle, with an opening at one side, and a body of water at its center. The people are dark-skinned and wear their hair in long ringlets, with jewels in their earlobes."

"Kangrisorn," said one of Grigitor's daughters instantly.

Her father nodded. "Kangrisorn it is," he said. "Pull up anchor!"

Kangrisorn lay an hour to the windward, somewhat off the route Grigitor had chartered. It was one of half a dozen small sandy atolls, mere rings of upraised reef surrounding little lagoons, and it must have been uncommon for people of Mardigile to visit it, for long before the trimaran had entered the harbor children of Kangrisorn were flocking out in boats to view the strangers. They were as dark as the Mardigilese were golden, and just as beautiful in their solemn way, with shining white teeth and hair so black it seemed almost blue. With much laughter and waving of arms they guided the trimaran through the entrance to the lagoon, and there, squatting at the edge of the water, was Sleet indeed, looking sunburned and a bit ragged but mainly intact. He was juggling five or six globes of bleached white coral for an audience that consisted of a few dozen islanders and five members of Gorzval's crew, four humans and a Hjort.

Gorzval seemed apprehensive at encountering his erstwhile employees. He had begun to recover his spirits during the morning's voyage, but now he grew tense and withdrawn as the trimaran entered the lagoon. Carabella was the first off, splashing through the shallow water to embrace Sleet; Valentine followed close behind. Gorzval lurked to the rear, eyes lowered.

"How did you find us?" Sleet asked.

Valentine indicated Deliamber. "Sorcery. How else? Are you well?"

"I thought I'd die of seasickness getting here, but I've had a day or two to recover." With a shudder he said, "And you? I saw you sucked under, and believed all was over."

250

"So it seemed," said Valentine. "A strange story, which I'll tell you another time. We are all together again, eh, Sleet? All but Gibor Haern," he added mournfully, "who perished in the wreck. But we've taken on Gorzval as one of our companions. Come forward, Gorzval! Aren't you pleased to see your men again?"

Gorzval muttered something indistinct and looked between Valentine and the others, meeting no one's eyes. Valentine comprehended the situation and turned to the crew people, meaning to ask them to hold no ill will toward the former captain for a disaster far beyond mortal control. He was taken aback to discover the five of them groveling at his feet.

Sleet said, abashed, "I thought you were dead, my lord. I couldn't resist telling them my tale."

"I see," said Valentine, "that the news is apt to spread more rapidly than I wish, no matter how solemnly I swear you all to silence. Well, it's pardonable, Sleet." To the others he said, "Up. Up. This crawling in the sand does none of us any good."

They rose. Their contempt for Gorzval was impossible for them to hide; but it was overshadowed by the astonishment they felt at being in the presence of the Coronal. Of the five, Valentine quickly learned, two—the Hjort and one of the humans—chose to remain on Kangrisorn in the hope of finding, eventually, some way to return to Piliplok and resume their trade. The other three begged to accompany him on his pilgrimage.

The new members of the rapidly expanding band were two women—Pandelon and Cordeine, a carpenter and a sailmender—and a man, Thesme, one of the winchwinders. Valentine bade them be welcome, and accepted pledges of allegiance from them, a ceremony that stirred vague discomfort in him. Yet he was growing accustomed to taking on these trappings of rank.

Grigitor and his children had paid no attention to the kneelings and hand-kissings among the passengers. Just as well: until he had conferred with the Lady, Valentine wished not to spread news across the world of his return to self-awareness. He was still uncertain of his strategy and unsure of his powers. Besides, if he advertised his existence he might draw the attention of the present Coronal, who was not likely to stay his hand if he discovered that a pretender was journeying toward Castle Mount.

The trimaran resumed its voyage. From isle to golden isle it went, staying well within the coastal channels and only occasionally venturing into deeper, bluer waters. Past Lormanar and Climidole they sailed, and Secundail, Blayhar Strand, Garhuven, and Wiswis Keep; past Quile and Fruil; past Dawnbreak, Nissemhold, and Thiaquil; past Roazen and Piplinat; and past the great crescent sand-spit known as Damozal. They stopped at the island of Sungyve for fresh water, at Musorn for fruit and leafy vegetables, at Cadibyre for casks of the young pink wine of that island. And after many days of traveling through these small sun-blessed places they pulled into the spacious harbor of Rodamaunt Graun.

This was a large lush island of mountainous origin, surrounded by black volcanic beaches and equipped along its southern shore with a splendid natural breakwater. Rodamaunt Graun was dominant in the Archipelago, by far the largest in the chain, with a population, so Grigitor asserted, of five and a half million. Twin cities spread out like wings from both sides of the harbor, but the flanks of the island's looming central peak were also well populated, with dwellings of rattan and skupik-wood rising in neat ranks almost to mid-point. About the last line of houses the slopes were thickly covered with jungle, and at the highest level rose a plume of thin white smoke, for Rodamaunt Graun was an active volcano. The last eruption, said Grigitor, had occurred less than fifty years before. But that was hard to believe, when one looked at the impeccable houses and the unbroken forest growth above them.

Here the *Pride of Mardigile* would turn back for home, but Grigitor arranged for the voyagers to shift to a trimaran even more noble, the *Rodamaunt Queen*, which would carry them to the Isle of Sleep. Her skipper was one Namurinta, a woman of regal poise and bearing, with long straight hair as white as Sleet's and a youthful, unlined face. Her manner was fastidious and quizzical: she studied her assortment of passengers closely, as if trying to determine what pull had drawn such a mixture into an off-season pilgrimage, but she said only, "If you are refused at the Isle, I will return you to Rodamaunt Graun, but there will be extra costs for your upkeep in that event."

"Does the Isle often refuse pilgrims?" Valentine asked.

"Not when they come at the proper time. But the pilgrimships, as I suppose you know, don't sail in autumn. There may not be facilities ready for receiving you."

"We've come this far with only minor difficulties," said Valentine jauntily. He heard Carabella snicker and Sleet make stagy coughing sounds. "I feel confident," he went on, "that we'll meet no obstacles greater than those we've already encountered."

"I admire your determination," Namurinta said, and signaled to her crew to prepare for departure.

The Archipelago in its eastern half hooked somewhat to the north, and the islands here were generally unlike Mardigile and its neighbors, being mainly the tops of a submerged mountain chain, not flat coral-based platforms. Studying Namurinta's charts, Valentine concluded that this part of the Archipelago had once been a long tail of a peninsula jutting out of the southwest corner of the Isle of Sleep, but had been swallowed by some rising of the Inner Sea in ancient times. Only the tallest peaks had remained above water; and between the easternmost island of the Archipelago and the coast of the Isle there now lay some hundreds of miles of open sea—a formidable journey for a trimaran, even so well equipped a trimaran as Namurinta's.

But the voyage was uneventful. They stopped at four ports—Hellirache, Sempifiore, Dimmid, and Guadeloom—for water and victuals, sailed on serenely past Rodamaunt Ounze, the last island of the Archipelago, and entered Ungehoyer Channel, which separated the Archipelago from the Isle of Sleep. This was a broad but shallow seaway, richly endowed with marine life and heavily fished by the island folk, all but the easternmost hundred miles, which formed part of the holy perimeter of the Isle. In these waters were monsters of a harmless kind, great balloon-shaped creatures known as volevants that anchored themselves to deep rocks and lived by filtering plankton through their gills; these creatures excreted a constant stream of nutrient matter, which sustained the enormous population of life-forms about them. Valentine saw dozens of volevants in the next few days: swollen globular sacks of a deep carmine hue, fifty to eighty feet across at their upper ends, plainly visible just a few feet below the calm surface. They bore dark semicircular markings on their skins, which Valentine imagined were eyes and noses and lips, so that he saw faces peering gravely up from the water, and it seemed to him that the volevants were beings of the deepest melancholy, philosophers of weight and wisdom reflecting eternally on the ebb and flow of the tides. "They sadden me," he told Carabella. "Forever hovering there, tied by their tails to hidden boulders, swaying slowly as the currents move them. How thoughtful they are!"

"Thoughtful! Primitive gasbags, no cleverer than a sponge!"

"But look carefully at them, Carabella. They want to fly, to soar—they look up at the sky, at the whole world of the air, and long to encounter it, but all they can do is hang below the waves, and sway, and fill themselves with invisible organisms. Just in front of their faces lies another world, and it would be death to them to enter it. Are you untouched by that?"

"Silly," Carabella said.

On the second day in the channel the *Rodamaunt Queen* came upon five fishing-boats that had uprooted a volevant, brought it to the surface, and slit it into gores; they clustered about the huge outspread skin of it, cutting it into smaller sections and stacking them like hides on their decks. Valentine was appalled. When I am Coronal again, he thought, I will prohibit the killing of these creatures, and then he looked at the thought in amazement, asking himself if it was his inten-.tion to promulgate laws on the basis of sympathies alone, without study of the facts. He asked Namurinta what use was made of volevant-skin.

"Medicinal," she replied. "For the comfort of the very old, when their blood flows sluggishly. One of them provides enough of the drug for all the islands for a year or more: what you see is a rare event."

When I am Coronal again, Valentine resolved, I will re-serve judgment until I am in full possession of the truth, if such a thing is ever possible.

Nevertheless, the imagined solemn profundity of the vole-vants haunted him with strange emotions, and he was relieved to pass beyond their zone, and into the cool waters that bor-dered the Isle of Sleep.

7

The Isle now lay clearly in view to the east, growing percepti-bly larger every hour. Valentine had seen it only in dreams and fantasies, and those based on nothing but his own imagin-ings and whatever residue of remembered reality still en-crusted his mind; and he was not at all prepared for the ac-tuality of the place.

It was immense. That should not have been surprising on a planet itself gigantic, and where so many things were in a scale with the planetary dimensions. But Valentine had misled himself into thinking an island necessarily was something of convenient and accessible scope. He had expected something perhaps two or three times as big as Rodamaunt Graun, which was foolishness: the Isle of Sleep, he saw now, spanned the entire horizon and looked as large from this distance as had the coast of Zimroel when they were a day or two out of Piliplok. An island it was, but by that token so too were Zimroel and Alhanroel and Suvrael; and the only reason the Isle was not called a continent, as were they, was that they were colossal, and the Isle merely very big.

And the Isle was dazzling. Like the promontory across the mouth of the river from Piliplok, it was ramparted by cliffs of pure white chalk that blazed brilliantly in the afternoon sunlight. They formed a wall hundreds of feet high and perhaps hundreds of miles in length across the western face of the Isle. Atop that wall spread a dark-green crown of forest, and, so it seemed, there was a second wall of chalk inland at a higher elevation, topped also by forest, and then a third yet farther from the sea, so that the Isle from this side gave an appearance of tier upon tier of brightness, rising to some unknown and perhaps inaccessible central fastness. He had heard of the terraces of the Isle, which he gathered were artificial constructs of great age, symbolic markers of the ascent toward initiation. But the island itself seemed a place of terraces, natural ones, that enhanced its mystery. Small wonder that this place had become the abode of the sacred on Majipoor.

Namurinta said, pointing, "That notch in the cliff is Taleis, where the pilgrim-ships land. It's one of the Isle's two harbors; the other's Numinor, over around Alhanroel side. But you must know all this, being pilgrims."

"We have had little time to study," said Valentine. "This pilgrimage came on us suddenly."

"Will you pass the rest of your lives here in the service of the Lady?" she asked.

"In the service of the Lady, yes," Valentine said. "But I think not here. The Isle is only a way-station for some of us, on a much greater journey."

Namurinta looked puzzled at that, but she asked no further questions.

The wind blew briskly from the southwest here, and carried the *Rodamaunt Queen* easily and swiftly toward Taleis. Soon the great chalk wall altogether filled the view, and the opening in it was revealed as no mere notch, but a harbor of heroic size, a huge gouge in the whiteness. With sails full, the trimaran entered. Valentine, in the bow, hair streaming in the breeze, was awestruck by the scope of the place, for within the sharp-angled V that was Taleis the cliffs descended almost vertically toward the water from a height of a mile or more,

255

and at their base was a flat strip of land bordered by a broad white beach. At one side were wharfs and piers and docks, everything dwarfed by the scale of this gigantic amphitheater. It was hard to imagine how one could get from this port at the foot of the cliffs to the interior of the island: the place was a natural fortress.

And it was silent. There were no vessels in the harbor and an eerie echoing quietness prevailed, against which the sound of the wind or the screeching of an occasional gull took on magnified significance.

"Is there anyone here?" Sleet asked. "Who will greet us?"

Carabella closed her eyes. "To have to go around to the Numinor side now—worse, to return to the Archipelago—"

"No," Deliamber said. "We will be met. Fear nothing."

The trimaran glided toward the shore and came to rest at a vacant pier. The grandeur of the surroundings was overwhelming here, deep in the V of the harbor, with the cliffs rising so high they seemed to be on the verge of toppling. A crewman made the boat fast and they stepped forth.

Deliamber's confidence seemed misplaced. There was no one here. Everything remained still, a silence so mighty that Valentine wanted to put his hands to his ears to shut it out. They waited. They exchanged uncertain glances.

"Let's explore," he said finally. "Lisamon, Khun, Zalzan Kavol—examine the buildings to our left. Sleet, Deliamber, Vinorkis, Shanamir—down that way. You, Pandelon, Thesme, Rovorn—to that curve of the beach, and look beyond it. Gorzval, Erfon—"

Valentine, with Carabella and the sailmender Cordeine, went straight ahead, to the foot of the titanic chalk cliff. Some sort of pathway began there, and angled upward at an impossible slope, close to vertical, toward the upper reaches of the cliff, where it vanished between two white spires. Climbing that path would require the agility of a forest-brother and the gall of a tandy-prancer, Valentine decided. Yet no other place of exit from the beach was apparent. He peered into the small wooden shack at the base of the path and found nothing but a few floater-sleds, presumably used in riding the path. He hauled one out, set it on the thrusting-pad at ground level, and mounted it; but he saw no way of activating it.

Baffled, he returned to the pier. Most of the others had come back already. "The place is deserted," said Sleet.

Valentine looked toward Namurinta. "How long would it take you to carry us around to the Alhanroel side?"

"To Numinor? Weeks. But I would not go there."

"We have money," said Zalzan Kavol.

She looked indifferent. "My trade is fishing. The time of harvest for the thorn-fish is at hand. If I take you to Numinor, I will miss it, and half the gissoon season as well. You could not recompense me for that."

The Skandar produced a five-royal piece, as though by its glitter alone he could change the captain's mind. But she shook it away.

"For half of what you paid me to bring you from Rodamaunt Graun to here, I'll return you to Rodamaunt Graun, but that's the best I can do for you. In a few months the pilgrim-ships will be sailing again and this harbor will come to life, and then, if you wish, I'll bring you here again for the same half fee. However you decide, I am at your service. But I will sail from this place before it grows dark, and not for Numinor."

Valentine considered the situation. This was a greater nuisance than being swallowed by the sea-dragon; for he had quickly enough been set free from that, but this unexpected obstacle threatened to delay him well into winter, or even beyond, and all this while Dominin Barjazid ruled at Castle Mount, new laws went forth, history was altered, the usurper consolidated his position. But what, then? He glanced at Deliamber, but the wizard, though he looked bland and untroubled, offered no suggestions. They could not climb this wall. They could not fly it. They could not leap in mighty bounds to the unreachable, infinitely desirable forest groves that cloaked its shoulders. Back to Rodamaunt Graun, then?

"Will you wait with us here a day?" Valentine asked. "For an additional fee, that is? Possibly in the morning we'll find someone who——"

"I am far from Rodamaunt Graun," Namurinta replied. "I yearn to see its shores again. Waiting here another hour, even, would gain you nothing and me even less. The season is wrong; the people of the Lady expect no one to arrive at Taleis, and will not be here."

Shanamir tugged tightly at Valentine's sleeves. "You are Coronal of Majipoor," the boy whispered, "*Command* her to wait! Reveal yourself and force her to her knees!"

Smiling, Valentine said softly, "I think the trick might not work. I've left my crown elsewhere."

"Then have Deliamber witch her into yielding!"

That was a possibility. But Valentine disliked it: Namurinta had taken them on in good faith, and by rights was free to leave, and probably was correct that waiting here another day or two or three was pointless. Compelling her to yield by Deliamber's powers was distasteful to him. On the other hand—

"Lord Valentine!" a woman's voice called, far away. "Here! Come!"

He looked toward the far end of the harbor. It was Pandelon, Gorzval's carpenter, who had gone with Thesme and Rovorn to inspect what lay around the curve. She was waving, beckoning. He sprinted down toward her, the others following after a moment.

When he reached her she led him through the shallow water around a jutting fold of rock that concealed a much smaller beach. There he saw a single-story structure of pink sandstone that bore the triangle-within-triangle emblem of the Lady and was perhaps some sort of shrine. In front of it was a garden of flowering shrubs arranged in symmetrical patterns of red, blue, orange, and yellow blossoms. Two gardeners, a man and a woman, were tending it. They looked up without interest as Valentine approached. Awkwardly he made the sign of the Lady at them, and they returned it more adeptly.

He said, "We are pilgrims, and need to be told the way to the terraces."

"You come out of season," the woman said. Her face was wide and pale, with a sprinkling of pale freckles on it. There was nothing friendly in her voice.

"Because of our eagerness to enter into the Lady's service."

The woman shrugged and returned to her weeding. The man, a thick-muscled, short-statured person with thinning gray hair, said, "You should have gone to Numinor at this time of year."

"We came from Zimroel."

That produced a minor flicker of attention. "Through the dragon-winds? You must have had a difficult crossing."

"There were some troublesome moments," Valentine said, "but they lie behind us now. We feel only joy at having reached this Isle at last."

"The Lady will comfort you," said the man indifferently, and he began to work with a pruning-shears.

After a moment of silence that grew swiftly dismaying, Valentine said, "And the way to the terraces?"

The freckled woman said, "You won't be able to operate it."

"But will you help us?"

Silence again.

Valentine said, "It would be only a moment, and then we'd disturb you no more. Show us the way."

"We have our duties here," said the balding man.

Valentine moistened his lips. This was leading nowhere; and for all he knew, Namurinta had left the other beach five minutes ago and was on her way back to Rodamaunt Graun, marooning them. He looked to Deliamber. Some wizardly compulsion might be in order. Deliamber ignored the hint. Valentine moved toward him and murmured, "Touch your tentacles to them and inspire them to cooperate."

"I think my sorceries are of little value on this holy Isle," said Deliamber. "Try wizardries of your own."

"I have none!"

"Try," said the Vroon.

Valentine confronted the gardeners once again. I am Coronal of Majipoor, he told himself, and I am the son of the Lady whom these two worship and serve. It was impossible to say any of that to the gardeners, but he could transmit it, perhaps, through sheer force of soul. He stood tall and moved toward the center of his being, as he would have done if he were preparing to juggle before the most critical of audiences, and he smiled a smile so warm it might have opened buds on the branches of the flowering shrubs, and after a moment the gardeners, looking up from their work, saw it and showed an unmistakable response, a reaction of surprise, bewilderment, and—submission. He bathed them in glowing love. "We have come thousands of miles," he said gently, "to give ourselves up to the peace of the Lady, and we beg you, in the name of the Divine that we both serve, to assist us on our pathway; for our need is great and we are weary of wandering."

They blinked, as if the sun had emerged from behind a gray cloud.

"We have our tasks," said the woman lamely.

"We are not supposed to ascend until the garden is cared for," the man said, almost in a mumble.

"The garden thrives," said Valentine, "and will thrive without your aid for a few hours today. Help us, before the darkness comes. We ask only that you point us on our way, and I tell you that the Lady will reward you for it."

The gardeners looked troubled. They glanced at one another, and then toward the sky, as though to see how late it was. Frowning, they rose and brushed the sandy soil from their knees, and, like sleepwalkers, moved to the water's edge, and out into the light surf, and around the point to the greater

259

beach, and down toward the foot of the cliff where that vertical path began its skyward climb.

Namurinta was still there, but she was nearly ready for departure. Valentine went to her.

"For your aid we thank you deeply," he said.

"You are staying?"

"We have found a way to the terraces."

She smiled in unfeigned pleasure. "I was not eager to abandon you, but Rodamaunt Graun was calling me. I wish you well as you make your pilgrimage."

"And I wish you a safe voyage home."

He turned away.

"One thing," the captain said.

"Yes?"

"When the woman called to you from down there," she said, "she hailed you as *Lord* Valentine. What was the meaning of that?"

"A joke," said Valentine. "Only a joke."

"Lord Valentine is how the new Coronal is named, so I have been told, the one that rules since a year or two past."

"Yes," Valentine said. "But he is a dark-haired man. It was only a joke, a play on names, for I am Valentine too. A safe journey, Namurinta."

"A fruitful pilgrimage, Valentine."

He walked toward the cliff. The gardeners had taken several of the floater-sleds from the shack, and had placed them in riding sequence on the thrusting-pad. Silently they gestured the travelers aboard. Valentine mounted the first sled, with Carabella, Deliamber, Shanamir, and Khun. The female gardener went into the shack, where, it seemed, the controls of the floaters must be located, for an instant afterward the sled drifted free of the pad and began the dizzying, terrifying ascent of the towering white cliff.

8

"You have come," said the acolyte Talinot Esulde, "to the Terrace of Assessment. Here you will be weighed in the balance. When it is time to move onward, your path takes you to the Terrace of Inception, and then to the Terrace of Mirrors, where you will confront yourself. If what you see is satisfactory to you and to your guides, you move inward to Second Cliff, where another group of terraces awaits you. And so you proceed until the Terrace of Adoration. There, if the favor of the Lady is upon you, you will receive your summons to Inner Temple. But I would not expect that to happen quickly. I would not expect that to happen at all. Those who *expect* to attain the Lady are the least likely to reach her."

Valentine's mood darkened at that, for not only did he expect to attain the Lady, it was absolutely vital that he do so; and yet he understood what the acolyte was saying. In this holy place one made no demands on the fabric of existence. One surrendered; one gave up demands and needs and desires; one yielded, if one hoped to find peace. This was no place for a Coronal. The essence of a Coronal's being was the wielding of power, wisely if he was capable of wisdom, but in any event steadfastly; the essence of a pilgrim was surrender. In that contradiction he might easily be lost. Yet he had no choice but to go to the Lady.

He had, at least, reached the outer fringes of the Lady's domain. At the top of the cliff they had been greeted by unsurprised acolytes, plainly aware that out-of-season pilgrims were floating toward them. And now, looking pious and faintly absurd in the soft pale robes of pilgrims, they were gathered in a low long building of smooth pink stone near the crest of the cliff. Flags of the same pink stone formed a massive semicircular promenade that stretched for what appeared to be a great distance along the edge of the forest that topped the cliff: this was the Terrace of Assessment. Beyond it lay more forest; the other terraces were farther beyond; and deeper in, not visible from where they were now, rose the second chalk cliff atop the plateau that the outer one formed. A third cliff yet, Valentine knew, rose above the second somewhere hundreds of miles inland, and this was the holiest precinct, where Inner Temple was, where the Lady dwelled. For all that he had traveled so far, it seemed impossible that he would ever complete those last hundreds of miles.

Night was falling swiftly. He could look back through the circular window behind him and see the darkening sky and the broad dark bosom of the sea, lit only by the purpling light of the vanishing sun as it fled toward Piliplok. There was a speck out there, a scratch on the smooth surface of the water, that he thought and hoped was the trimaran *Rodamaunt Queen*, heading homeward, and out there too were the volevants dreaming their endless dream, and the sea-dragons making their way toward a greater sea, and beyond all that was Zimroel, its teeming cities, its forest preserves and parklands, its festivals, its billions of souls. There was much for him to

261

look back on; but now he must look forward. He stared intently at Talinot Esulde, their first guide in this place, a tall slender person with milk-white skin and a shaven skull, who might be of either sex. Male was Valentine's guess—the height and something about the breadth of shoulders argued that, though not absolutely—but the delicacy of Talinot Esulde's facial bones, notably the fragile curve of the light ridges above the strange blue eyes, argued otherwise.

Talinot Esulde was explaining things: the daily routine of prayer and work and meditation, the system of dream-speaking, the arrangement of living-quarters, the dietary restrictions, which excluded all wines and certain spices, and much else. Valentine tried to master it all, but there were so many regulations and requirements and obligations and customs that they tangled in his mind, and he ceased making the effort after a time, hoping that daily practice would instill the rules in him.

As darkness came Talinot Esulde led them from the indoctrination hall, past the sparkling spring-fed rock pool where they had been bathed before being given their robes and where they would bathe twice each day until they left this terrace, and to the dining-hall, farther from the cliff's rim. Here they were served a simple meal of soup and fish, flavorless and unappealing even though they were furiously hungry. Their servitors were novices like themselves, in robes of light green. The hall, a large one, was only partly full—the hour for dining was almost past, Talinot Esulde pointed out. Valentine looked at his fellow pilgrims. They were of all sorts, perhaps half of human stock, but also a great many Vroons and Ghayrogs, a sprinkling of Skandars, some Liimen, some Hjorts though not very many, and, far across the way, a little insular Su-Suheris group. The net of the Lady caught all the races of Majipoor, it would seem. All but one. "Do Metamorphs ever seek the Lady?" Valentine asked.

Talinot Esulde smiled seraphically. "If a Piurivar came to us, we would accept it. But they take no part in our rites. They live to themselves as though they were alone on all of Majipoor."

"Perhaps some have come here disguised in other forms," Sleet suggested.

"We would know that," said Talinot Esulde calmly.

After dinner they were taken to their rooms—individual chambers, hardly bigger than closets, in a hivelike lodge. A couch, a sink, a place for clothes, and nothing more. Lisamon Hultin glowered at hers. "No wine," she said, "and I give up

262

my sword, and now I sleep in this box? I think I'm going to be a failure as a pilgrim, Valentine."

"Peace, and make the effort. We'll travel through the Isle as swiftly as we can."

He entered his room, which was between the warrior-woman's and Carabella's. Immediately the lightglobe dimmed, and when he settled in on his couch he found himself disappearing instantly into slumber, though the hour was still early. As consciousness left him a new light glowed softly in his mind, and he beheld the Lady, the unmistakable, unquestionable Lady of the Isle.

Valentine had seen her in dreams many times before since Pidruid, the gentle eyes, the dark hair, the flower at her ear, the olive-hued skin, but now the image was sharper, the vision more detailed, and he noticed the small lines in the corners of her eyes and the tiny green jewels set in her earlobes and the thin silver band that encircled her brow. In his dream he held his hands to her and said, "Mother, here I am. Call me to you, mother."

She smiled at him, but she made no answer.

They were in a garden, with alabandinas in bloom all about them. She nipped at the plants with a small golden implement, clipping away flowerbuds so the remaining ones would yield larger blossoms. He stood beside her, waiting for her to turn to him, but the work of nipping went on and on, and finally she said, still not looking his way, "One must give constant attention to one's task if it is to be done properly."

"Mother, I am Valentine your son!"

"See, each branch has five buds? Let them be and they all will open, but I take two away here, one here, one here, and the blooms are glorious." And as she spoke the buds unfurled, and the alabandinas filled the air with a fragrance so keen it stunned him, while the great yellow petals stretched forth like platters, revealing the black stamens and pistils within. She touched them lightly, sending a scattering of purple pollen into the air. And said, "You are who you are, and always will be." The dream changed then, with nothing of the Lady remaining in it, but only a bower of thorny bushes waving rigid arms at him, and moleeka-birds of colossal size strutting about, and other images, confused and ever-altering and telling him nothing that had coherent pattern.

When he woke he was expected to report at once to his dream-speaker, not Talinot Esulde but another acolyte of the guide level, this a person named Stauminaup, shaven also and also of ambiguous sex, but more likely than not a woman.

These acolytes were of a medium level of initiation, Valentine had learned yesterday. They returned from Second Cliff to serve the needs of novices here.

Dream-speaking on the Isle was nothing like that which he had experienced in Falkynkip with Tisana. There were no drugs, there was no lying-together of bodies. He merely came into the presence of the speaker and described his dream. Stauminaup listened impassively. Valentine suspected that the speaker had had access to his dream as he was experiencing it, and merely wanted to contrast Valentine's account of it with her own perceptions, to see what gulfs and contradictions might lie between. Therefore he presented the dream exactly as he recalled it, saying, as he had in sleep, "Mother, I am Valentine your son!" and studying Stauminaup for a reaction to that. But he might as well have been studying the chalk face of the cliff.

When he was done the speaker said, "And what color were the alabandina blooms?"

"Why, yellow, with black centers!"

"A lovely flower. In Zimroel the alabandinas are scarlet, and yellow at the center. Do you like the colors of yours better?"

"I have no preference," said Valentine.

Stauminaup smiled. "The alabandinas of Alhanroel are yellow, with black centers. You may go now."

The speakings were much the same every day: a cryptic comment, or one that was perhaps not so cryptic, but lay open to varying interpretations, only no interpretations ever were offered. Stauminaup was like a repository for his dreams, absorbing them without providing counsel. Valentine became accustomed to that.

He became accustomed, too, to the daily routines of labor. He worked in the garden two hours each morning, doing minor trimming and weeding and much turning of soil, and in the afternoons he was a mason, taking instruction in the art of pointing the flagstones of the terrace. There were long sessions of meditation in which he was given no guidance whatever, only sent off to his room to stare at the walls. He saw hardly anything of his companions of the journey, except when they bathed together, at mid-morning and again just before dinner, in the sparkling pool; and they had little to say. It was easy to get into the rhythm of this place and cast aside all urgencies. The tropic air, the perfume of millions of blossoms, the gentle tone of everything that went on here, lulled and soothed like a warm bath.

264

But Alhanroel lay thousands of miles to the east, and he was moving not an inch toward his goal so long as he remained at the Terrace of Assessment. Already a week had gone by. During his meditation sessions Valentine entertained fantasies of collecting his people and slipping away by night, passing illicitly through terrace after terrace, scaling Second Cliff and Third, presenting himself ultimately to the Lady at the threshold of her temple; but he suspected they would not get far, in a place where dreams were open books.

So he fretted. He knew that fretting would win him no advancement here, and he taught himself instead to relax, to give himself up utterly to his tasks, to clear his mind of all needs and compulsions and attachments, and thus to open the way toward the dream of summoning by which the Lady would beckon him inward. That had no effect either. He plucked weeds, he cultivated the warm rich soil, he carried buckets of mortar and grout to the farthest reaches of the terrace, he sat crosslegged in his meditation hours with his mind entirely empty, and night after night he went to bed praying that the Lady would appear and tell him, "It is time for you to come to me," but nothing happened.

"How long will this continue?" he asked Deliamber at the pool one day. "It's the fifth week! Or maybe the sixth—I'm losing count. Do I stay here a year? Two? Five?"

"Some of the pilgrims among us have done just that," said the Vroon. "I spoke with one, a Hjort who served in patrols under Lord Voriax. She has spent four years here and seems quite resigned to staying at the outermost terrace forever."

"She has no need to go elsewhere. This is a pleasant enough inn, Deliamber. But I—"

"—have urgent appointments to the east," Deliamber said. "And therefore you are condemned to remain here. There's a paradox in your dilemma, Valentine. You strive to renounce purpose; but your renunciation itself has a purpose. Do you see? Your speaker surely does."

"Of course I see. But what do I do? How do I pretend not to care whether I stay here forever?"

"Pretense is impossible. The moment you genuinely don't care, you'll move onward. Not until then."

Valentine shook his head. "That's like telling me that my salvation depends on never thinking of gihorna-birds. The harder I'd try not to think of them, the more flocks of gihornas would fly through my mind. What am I to do, Deliamber?"

But Deliamber had no other suggestions. The next day,

Valentine learned that Shanamir and Vinorkis had received advancement to the Terrace of Inception.

Two more days passed before Valentine saw Deliamber again. The wizard remarked that Valentine did not look well; and Valentine replied, with an impatience he could not control, "How do you expect me to look? Do you know how many weeds I've pulled, how much masonry I've pointed, while in Alhanroel a Barjazid sits on Castle Mount and—"

"Peace," Deliamber said softly. "This is not like you."

"Peace? Peace? How long can I be peaceful?"

"Perhaps your patience is being tested. In which case, my lord, you are failing the test."

Valentine considered that. After a moment he said, "I admit your logic. But perhaps it's my ingenuity that's being tested. Deliamber, put a summoning-dream into my head tonight."

"My sorceries, you know, seem of little value on this island."

"Do it. Try it. Concoct a message from the Lady and plant it in my mind, and then we'll see."

Deliamber, shrugging, touched his tentacles to Valentine's hands for the moment of thought-transference. Valentine felt the faint distant tingle of contact.

"Your sorceries still work," he said.

And that night there came to him a dream in which he drifted like a volevant in the bathing-pool, attached to the rocks by some membrane that had sprouted from his feet, and as he sought to free himself the face of the Lady appeared, smiling, in the night sky, and whispered to him, "Come, Valentine, come to me, come," and the membrane dissolved, and he floated upward and soared on the breeze, borne by the wind toward Inner Temple.

Valentine relayed the dream to Stauminaup in his dream-speaking session. She listened as though he were telling her of a dream of plucking weeds in the garden. The next night Valentine pretended he had had the same dream, and again she made no comment. He offered the dream on the next, and asked for a speaking of it.

Stauminaup said, "The speaking of your dream is that no bird flies with another's wings."

His cheeks reddened. He went slinking away from her chamber.

Five days later, he was told by Talinot Esulde that he had been granted admission to the Terrace of Inception.

"But *why?*" he asked Deliamber.

The Vroon replied, *"Why?* is a useless question in matters of spiritual progress. Obviously something has altered in you."

"But I've had no legitimate summoning dream!"

"Perhaps you have," said the sorcerer.

One of the acolytes took him, by foot, through the forest paths to the next terrace. The road was a maze, zigzagging, bewilderingly, several times requiring them to turn in what seemed like precisely the wrong direction. Valentine was altogether lost by the time they emerged, some hours later, into a cleared area of immense size. Pyramids of dark-blue stone ten feet high rose there at regular intervals from the pink flagstone of the terrace.

Life was much the same here—menial tasks, meditation, daily dream-speaking, stark ascetic quarters, drab food. But there was also the beginning of holy instruction, an hour each afternoon in which the principles of the grace of the Lady were explained by means of elliptical parables and circuitous dialogues.

Valentine listened restlessly to all that at first. It seemed vague and abstract to him, and it was hard to concentrate on such cloudy matters when what possessed him was a direct political passion—to reach Castle Mount and settle the questioning of the governing of Majipoor. But by the third day it struck him that what the acolyte was saying about the role of the Lady was entirely political. She was a tempering force, Valentine realized, a mortar of love and faith binding together the centers of power on this world. However she worked her magic of dream-sending—and it was impossible to believe the popular myth, that she was in touch with the minds of millions of people every night—it was clear that her calm spirit soothed and eased the planet. The apparatus of the King of Dreams, Valentine knew, sent direct and specific dreams that lashed the guilty and admonished the uncertain, and the sendings of the King could be fierce. But as the warmth of the ocean moderates the climate of the land, so did the Lady make gentle the harsh forces of control on Majipoor, and the theology that had arisen around the person of the Lady as Divine Mother Incarnate was, Valentine now understood, only a metaphor for the division of power that the early rulers of Majipoor had devised.

So he listened with keener interest. He put aside his eagerness to move to loftier terraces for a time, in order to learn more here.

Valentine was entirely alone at this terrace. That was new. Shanamir and Vinorkis were nowhere to be seen—had they been sent on already to the Terrace of Mirrors?—and the rest, so far as he knew, remained behind. Most of all he missed Carabella's sparkling energies and Deliamber's sardonic wisdom, but the others too had become part of his soul in the long difficult journey across Zimroel, and not to have them about him here was discomforting. His days as a juggler seemed long gone and never to be recaptured. Occasionally now he would, in leisure moments, take fruits from the trees and toss them in the old familiar patterns, to the amusement of passing novices and acolytes. One in particular, a thick-shouldered black-bearded man named Farssal, made a point of watching closely whenever Valentine juggled.

"Where did you learn those arts?" Farssal asked.

"In Pidruid," Valentine said. "I was with a juggling troupe."

"It must have been a fine life."

"It was," said Valentine, remembering the excitement of standing before the dark-visaged Lord Valentine in the arena at Pidruid, and of stepping out onto the vast stage of Dulorn's Perpetual Circus, and all the rest, unforgettable scenes of his past.

Farssal said, "Can those skills be taught, or is it an inborn knack?"

"Anyone can learn, anyone with a quick eye and the willingness to concentrate. I learned myself in just a week or two, last year in Pidruid."

"No! Surely you've juggled all your life!"

"Not before last year."

"What led you to take it up, then?"

Valentine smiled. "I needed a livelihood, and there were traveling jugglers in Pidruid for the Coronal's festival, who had need of an extra pair of hands. They taught me quickly, as I could teach you."

"You could, do you think?"

"Here," Valentine said, and tossed the black-bearded man one of the fruits he was juggling, a firm green bishawar. "Throw that back and forth between your hands awhile, to loosen your fingers. You must master a few basic positions, and certain habits of perception, which will take practice, and then—"

"What did you do before you were a juggler?" asked Farssal as he tossed the fruit.

"I wandered about," said Valentine. "Here: hold your hands in this fashion—"

He drilled Farssal half an hour, trying to train him as Carabella and Sleet had done for him at the inn in Pidruid. It was a welcome diversion in this placid and monotonous life. Farssal had quick hands and good eyes, and learned rapidly, though not nearly so rapidly as Valentine had. Within a few days he had developed most of the elementary skills and could juggle after a fashion, though not gracefully. He was an outgoing and talkative man, who kept up a steady flow of conversation as he flipped the bishawars from hand to hand. Born in Ni-moya, he said; for many years a merchant in Piliplok; recently overtaken by a spiritual crisis that had thrust him into confusion and then sent him on the Isle pilgrimage. He talked of his marriage, his unreliable sons, his winning and losing huge fortunes at the gaming-tables; and he wanted to know all about Valentine as well, his family, his ambitions, the motives that had brought him to the Lady. Valentine dealt with these queries as plausibly as he could, and turned aside the most awkward ones with quickly contrived dissertations on the art of juggling.

At the end of the second week—toil, study, meditation, periods of free time spent juggling with Farssal, a stable and static round—Valentine felt restlessness coming over him again, the yearning to be moving onward.

He had no idea how many terraces there were—nine? ninety?—but if he spent this much time at each, he might be years in reaching the Lady. Some means of abbreviating the process of ascent was needed.

Counterfeit summoning-dreams did not seem to work. He trotted forth his drifting-in-the-pool dream for Silimein, his dream-speaker here, but she was no more impressed by it than Stauminaup had been. He tried, during his meditation periods and when he was falling asleep at night, to reach forth to the mind of the Lady and implore her to summon him. This produced nothing useful either.

He asked those who sat near him in the dining-hall how long they had been at the Terrace of Inception. "Two years," said one. "Eight months," said another. They looked untroubled.

"And you?" he asked Farssal.

Farssal said he had arrived only a few days before Valentine. But he felt no impatience about moving on. "There's no hurry, is there? We serve the Lady wherever we may be, don't you think? So one terrace is as good as another."

Valentine nodded. He hardly dared disagree.

Late in the third week he thought he caught sight of Vinorkis far across the field of stajja where he was working. But he was not sure—was that a flash of orange on that Hjort's whiskers?—and the distance was too great for shouting. The next day, though, as Valentine stood casually juggling with Farssal near the bathing-pool, he saw Vinorkis, unquestionably Vinorkis, watching from the other side of the plaza. Valentine excused himself and jogged over. After so many weeks sundered from his old companions here, even the Hjort was a welcome sight.

"Then it *was* you in the stajja-fields," Valentine said.

Vinorkis nodded. "These past few days I've had several glimpses of you, my lord. But the terrace is so huge—I've never been able to come close. When did you arrive?"

"About a week after you. Are there others of us here?"

"Not so far as I know," the Hjort replied, "Shanamir was, but he's moved on. I see you've lost none of your juggling skill, my lord. Who's your partner?"

"A man of Piliplok. Quick with his hands."

"And with his tongue as well?"

Valentine frowned. "What do you mean?"

"Have you said much to this man of your past, my lord, or of your future?"

"Of course not." Valentine stared. "No, Vinorkis! Surely no spies of the Coronal right here on the Lady's own Isle!"

"Why not? Is it so hard to infiltrate this place?"

"But why do you suspect—"

"Last night, after I glimpsed you in the fields, I came here to make inquiry about you. One of those I spoke to was your new friend, my lord. Asked him if he knew you and he started questioning *me*. Was I your friend, had I known you in Pidruid, why had we come to the Isle, and so on and so on. My lord, I am uneasy when strangers ask questions. Especially in this place, where one is taught to remain apart from others."

"You may be too suspicious, Vinorkis."

"Maybe so. But guard yourself anyway, my lord."

"That I will," said Valentine. "He'll learn nothing from me but what he's already had. Which is merely some juggling."

"He may already know too much about you," said the Hjort gloomily. "But let us watch him, even as he watches you."

The notion that he might be under surveillance even here dismayed him. Was there no sanctuary? Valentine wished he had Sleet beside him, or Deliamber. A spy now might well become an assassin later, as Valentine drew closer to the Lady and became that much more of a peril to the usurper.

But Valentine seemed to be drawing no closer to the Lady.

270

Another week went by in the same fashion as before. Then, just as he was coming to believe he would spend the rest of his days at the Terrace of Inception, and when he was reaching a point where it mattered little to him if he did, he was called from the fields and told to make ready to go on to the Terrace of Mirrors.

9

This third terrace was a place of dazzling beauty, with a glitter that reminded Valentine of Dulorn. It nestled against the base of Second Cliff, a forbidding vertical wall of white chalk that seemed an absolute barrier to further inward progress, and when the sun was in the west the face of the cliff was such a wonder of reflected brilliance that it stunned the eye and wrung gasps of awe from the soul.

Then, too, there were the mirrors—great rough-hewn slabs of polished black stone set edgewise in the ground everywhere about this terrace, so that wherever one looked one encountered one's own image, glowing against a shining inner light. Valentine at first studied himself critically, searching for the changes that his journey had brought upon him, some dimming of the warm radiance that had flowed from him since the Pidruid days, or perhaps marks of weariness or stress. But he saw none of that, only the familiar golden-haired smiling man, and he waved to himself and winked amiably and saluted, and then, after a week or so, ceased to notice his reflection at all. If he had been ordered to ignore the mirrors he would probably have lived in guilty tension, flicking his gaze involuntarily toward them and wrenching it away; but no one here told him what purpose the mirrors served or what attitude he should take toward them, and in time he simply forgot them. This, he realized much later, was the key to forward movement on the Isle: evolution of the spirit from within, a growing ability to discern and discard the irrelevant.

He was entirely alone here. No Shanamir, no Vinorkis, and no Farssal. Valentine kept close watch for the black-bearded man: if indeed he was some sort of spy, he would doubtless find a way to follow Valentine from terrace to terrace. But Farssal did not arrive.

Valentine stayed at the Terrace of Mirrors eleven days and went onward, in the company of five other novices, via a floater-sled to the rim of Second Cliff and the Terrace of Consecration.

From here there was a magnificent view back over the first three terraces, far below, to the distant sea. Valentine could barely see the Terrace of Assessment—only a thin line of pink against the dark green of the forest—but the great Terrace of Inception spread out awesomely at the mid-point of the lower plateau, and the Terrace of Mirrors, just below, blazed like a million bright pyres in noonday light.

It was becoming unimportant to him, now, how swift his pace might be. Time was losing its meaning. He had slipped entirely into the rhythm of the place. He worked in the fields; he attended lengthy sessions of spiritual instruction; he spent much of his time in the darkened stone-roofed building that was the shrine of the Lady, asking, in a way that was not really asking at all, that illumination be granted him. Occasionally he remembered that he had intended to go quickly to the heart of the Isle and to the woman who dwelled there. But there seemed little urgency to any of that now. He had become a true pilgrim.

Beyond the Terrace of Consecration lay the Terrace of Flowers, and beyond that the Terrace of Devotion, and then the Terrace of Surrender. All these were of Second Cliff, as was the Terrace of Ascent, which was the final stage before one went up onto the plateau where the Lady lived. Each of the terraces, Valentine came to understand, completely encircled the island, so that there might be a million votaries in each at any time, or even more, and each pilgrim saw only a tiny segment of the whole as he pursued his course toward the center. How much effort had gone into constructing all this! How many lives had been given over entirely to the Lady's service! And each pilgrim moved within a sphere of silence: no friendships were begun here, no confidences were exchanged, no lovers embraced. Farssal had been a mysterious exception to that custom. It was as though this place existed outside of time and apart from the ordinary rituals of life.

In this middle zone of the Isle there was less emphasis on teaching, more on toil. When he reached Third Cliff, he knew, he would join those who actually carried out the Lady's work in the world at large; for it was not the Lady herself, he now understood, who emanated most sendings to the world, but rather the millions of advanced acolytes of Third Cliff, whose minds and spirits became amplifiers for the Lady's benevolence. Not that everyone reached Third Cliff: many of the older acolytes, he gathered, had spent decades on Second

Cliff, performing administrative tasks, with neither the hope nor the desire of moving toward the more taxing responsibilities of the inner zone.

In his third week at the Terrace of Devotion, Valentine was granted what he knew to be an unmistakable summoning-dream.

He saw himself crossing that parched purple plain that had darkened his sleep in Pidruid. The sun was low at the horizon and the sky was harsh and bleak, and ahead of him lay two broad mountain ranges that rose like giant swollen fists. In the jagged boulder-strewn valley between them the last ruddy glimmer of sunlight was visible, a peculiar oily light, ominous, more a stain than a radiance. A cool dry wind blew out of that strangely illuminated valley, and on it came sighing, singing sounds, soft melancholy melodies riding the breeze. Valentine walked for hours but made no progress: the mountains grew no nearer, the desert sands extended themselves infinitely as he trekked, that last shard of light did not depart. His strength was ebbing. Menacing mirages danced before him. He saw Simonan Barjazid, the King of Dreams, and his three sons. He saw the ghastly senile Pontifex roaring on his subterranean throne. He saw monstrous amorfibots crawling sluggishly in the dunes, and the snouts of massive dhumkars rising like augers out of the sands, probing the air for prey. Things hissed and twanged and whispered; insects swarmed in nasty little clouds; a rain of dry sand began to fall, lightly, clogging his eyes and nostrils. He was weary and ready at any moment to yield and halt, to lie down in the sand and let the shifting dunes cover him, but one thing drew him on, for in the valley a glowing figure moved to and fro, a smiling woman, the Lady his mother, and so long as she could be seen there he would not cease pressing forward. He felt the warmth of her presence, the pull of her love. "Come," she murmured. "Come to me, Valentine!" Her arms reached toward him across that terrible desert of monstrosities. His shoulders sagged. His knees weakened. He could not continue, though he knew he must. "Lady," he whispered, "I am at my end, I must rest, I must sleep!" At that the glow between the mountains grew warmer and brighter. "Valentine," she called. "Valentine, my son!" He could scarcely keep his eyes open. It was so tempting to lie down in the warm sand. "You are my son," came the voice of the Lady across that impossible distance, "and I have need of you," and as she said these words he found new strength, and walked more rapidly, and then began to run lightly over the hard, crusted desert floor, his heart lifting, his

273

stride widening. Now the distances quickly dwindled, and Valentine could see her clearly, awaiting him on a terrace of violet-hued stone, smiling, reaching to him with outstretched arms, calling his name in a voice that rang like the bells of Ni-moya.

He awoke with the sound of her voice still ringing in his mind.

It was dawn. Wondrous energy flooded his spirit. He rose and went down to the great amethystine basin that was the bathing-pool at the Terrace of Devotion, and plunged boldly into the chilly spring-water. Afterward he trotted to the chamber of Menesipta, his dream-speaker here, a compact, fine-honed person with flashing dark eyes and a taut, spare face, and poured forth the dream to her in one long rush of words.

Menesipta sat silently.

The coolness of her response dampened Valentine's exuberance. He remembered going to Stauminaup at the Terrace of Assessment with the fraudulent summoning-dream of the volevant, and how swiftly Stauminaup had dismissed that dream. But this was no fraud. He had no Deliamber here to do witcheries on his mind.

Valentine said at length, "May I ask an evaluation?"

"The dream has familiar overtones," Menesipta replied calmly.

"Is that your whole speaking of it?"

She seemed amused. "What more would you have me say?"

Valentine clenched his fists in frustration. "If someone came to me for a speaking of such a dream, I would call it a dream of summoning."

"Very well."

"Do you agree? Would *you* call it a dream of summoning?"

"If it would please you."

"Pleasing me isn't the point," said Valentine, irritated. "Either the dream was a dream of summoning or it wasn't. What is your view of it?"

Smiling obliquely, the dream-speaker said, "I call your dream a dream of summoning."

"And now?"

"Now? Now you have your morning duties to observe."

"A dream of summoning, as I understand it," said Valentine tightly, "is required in order to attain the presence of the Lady."

"Indeed."

"Should I not advance now to Inner Temple?"

Menesipta shook her head. "No one goes from Second Cliff

274

to Inner Temple. Only when you reach the Terrace of Adoration does a summoning-dream suffice of itself to call you inward. Your dream is interesting and important, but it changes nothing. Go to your duties, Valentine."

Anger throbbed in him as he left her chamber. He knew he was being foolish, that a mere dream could not be enough to sweep him past the remaining hurdles that separated him from the Lady, and yet he had expected so much from it—he had hoped Menesipta would clap her hands and cry out in joy and ship him at once to Inner Temple, and none of that had happened, and the letdown was painful and infuriating.

More pain ensued. As he came from the fields two hours later an acolyte intercepted him and said bluntly, "You are ordered immediately to the harbor at Taleis, where new pilgrims await your guidance."

Valentine was stunned. The last thing he wanted now was to be sent back to the starting point.

He was to set out at once, on foot and alone, making his way outward from terrace to terrace and getting himself to the Terrace of Assessment in the shortest possible time. They provided him at the terrace commissary with enough food to see him as far as the Terrace of Flowers. They gave him also a direction-finding device, an amulet to be fastened to his arm, that would scan for buried roadmarkers and emit a soft high pinging sound.

At midday he left the Terrace of Devotion. But the path he chose was the one inward toward the Terrace of Surrender, not the one that would take him back toward the coast.

The decision came suddenly and with unarguable force. He simply *could not* allow himself to be turned away from the Lady. Slipping off on an unauthorized trek, on this highly disciplined island, held serious risks, but he had no choice.

Valentine circled past the rim of the terrace and found the grassy path that cut diagonally across the recreation field to the main road. There he was supposed to turn left toward the outer terraces. But—feeling extraordinarily conspicuous—he turned right instead and set out briskly toward the interior. Soon he was beyond the settled part of the terrace and the road had narrowed from wide paved highway to earthen track, with forest pressing close on all sides.

Within half an hour he was at a fork in the road. When he started at random down the left-hand branch, the quiet pinging tone of the direction-finding amulet vanished, returning when he had made his way back to the other fork. A useful device, he thought.

He walked steadily until nightfall. Then he camped in a pleasant grove beside a gentle stream, and allowed himself a sparing meal of cheese and sliced meat. He slept fitfully, stretched out on the cool moist ground between two slender trees.

The first pink glimmer of dawn woke him. He stirred, stretched, opened his eyes. A quick splash in the stream, yes, and then a bit of breakfast, and then—

Valentine heard sounds in the forest behind him—twigs snapping, something moving through the bushes. Quietly he slipped behind a thick-trunked tree by the edge of the stream and peered warily around it. And saw a powerfully built black-bearded man emerge from the underbrush, pause by his campsite, look cautiously about.

Farssal.

In a pilgrim's robe. But with a dagger strapped to his left forearm.

Some twenty-five feet separated the two men. Valentine frowned, considered his options, calculated tactics. Where had Farssal found a dagger on this peaceful island? Why was he tracking Valentine through the forest, if not to slay him?

Violence was alien to Valentine. But to take Farssal by surprise seemed the only course that made sense. He rocked back and forth a moment on the balls of his feet, centered his mind as though he were about to juggle, and sprang from his hiding place.

Farssal whirled and managed to get the dagger from its scabbard just as Valentine crashed into him. With a sudden desperate hacking motion Valentine slammed the side of his hand into the underside of Farssal's arm, numbing it, and the dagger dropped to the ground; but an instant later Farssal's meaty arms wrapped Valentine in a crushing grip.

They stood locked, face to face. Farssal was a head shorter than Valentine, but deeper of chest, broader of shoulder, a bull-bodied man. He strained to throw Valentine to the ground; Valentine struggled to break free; neither was able to sway the other, though veins bulged on their foreheads and their faces went red and swollen with strain.

"This is madness," Valentine murmured. "Let go, back off. I mean you no harm."

Farssal only tightened his grip.

"Who sent you?" Valentine asked. "What do you want with me?"

Silence. The mighty arms, Skandar-strong, continued inexorably pressing inward. Valentine fought for breath. Pain dazed him. He tried to force his elbows outward and snap the hold. No. Farssal's face was ugly and distorted with effort, his eyes fierce, his lips tightly set. And slowly but measurably he was pushing Valentine to the ground.

Resisting that terrible grip was impossible. Valentine abruptly ceased trying, and let himself go limp as a bundle of rags. Farssal, surprised, twisted him to one side; Valentine allowed his knees to buckle, and offered no resistance as Farssal hurled him down. But he landed lightly, on his back with his legs coiled above him, and as Farssal lunged furiously for him Valentine brought his feet up with all his force into the other man's gut. Farssal gasped and grunted and staggered back, stunned. Valentine, springing to his feet, seized Farssal with arms made greatly muscular by months of juggling, and pushed him down roughly to the ground, and held him pinned there, knees against Farssal's outspread arms, hands gripping his shoulders.

How strange this is, Valentine thought, to be fighting hand-to-hand with another being, as though we were unruly children! It had the quality of a dream.

Farssal glared at him in rage, slammed his feet angrily against the ground, tried in vain to push Valentine off.

"Talk to me now," Valentine said. "Tell me what this means. Did you come here to kill me?"

"I will say nothing."

"You who talked so much when we were juggling?"

"That was before."

"What am I to do with you?" Valentine asked. "If I let you up, you'll be at me again. But if I hold you here, I hold myself as well!"

"You can't hold me long this way."

Once more Farssal heaved. His strength was enormous. But Valentine's grip on him was firm. Farssal's face was scarlet; thick cords stood out on his throat; his eyes blazed with fury and frustration. For a long moment he lay still. Then he appeared to gather all his strength, going tense and thrusting upward. Valentine could not withstand that awesome push. There was a wild moment when neither man was in control of the situation, Valentine half flung aside, Farssal writhing and flexing as he tried to roll over. Valentine grabbed Farssal's thick shoulders and attempted to force him back to the ground. Farssal shook him away and his fingers clawed for Valentine's eyes. Valentine ducked below the clutching fingers. Then, without pausing to think about it, he seized Farssal by his coarse black beard and pulled him to one side, slamming his head into a rock that jutted from the moist soil close beside him.

Farssal made a heavy grunting sound and lay still.

Springing to his feet, Valentine seized the fallen dagger and stood above the other. He was trembling, not out of fear but from the release of tension, like a bowstring after the arrow has been let go. His ribs ached from that awful hug, and the muscles of his arms and shoulders were twitching and throbbing in fifty different rhythms.

"Farssal?" he said nudging him with one foot.

No response. Dead? No. The great barrel of a chest was slowly rising and falling, and Valentine heard the sound of hoarse, ragged breathing.

Valentine hefted the knife. What now? Sleet might say, finish the fallen man off before he came to. Impossible. One did not kill, except in self-defense. One certainly did not kill an unconscious man, would-be assassin though he might be. To kill another intelligent being meant a lifetime of punishing dreams, the vengeance of the murdered. But he could scarcely just walk away, leaving Farssal to recover and come after him. Some birdnet-vine would be a useful thing to have just now. Valentine did see another sort of vine, a sturdy-looking liana with green-and-yellow stems as thick as his fingers, scrambling far up the side of a tree; and with some fierce tugging he pulled down five huge strands of it. These he wound tightly around Farssal, who stirred and moaned but did not regain consciousness. In ten minutes Valentine had him securely trussed, bound like a mummy from chest to ankles. He tested the vines and they held tight at his pull.

Valentine gathered his few possessions and hurried away.

The savage encounter in the forest had shaken him badly. Not only the fighting, though that was barbaric enough, and would disturb him a long while; but also the idea that his enemy no longer was content merely to spy on him, but was sending murderers to him. And if that is so, he thought, can I doubt any longer the truth of the visions that tell me I am Lord Valentine?

Valentine barely comprehended the concept of deliberate murder. One absolutely did not take the lives of others. In the world he knew, that was basic. Not even the usurper, overthrowing him, had dared to kill him, for fear of the dark dreams that would come; but evidently now he was willing to accept that dread risk. Unless, Valentine thought, Farssal had resolved on the assassination attempt by himself, as a ghastly way of winning the favor of his employers, when he discov-

278

ered Valentine slipping away toward the inner zone of the Isle.

A somber business. Valentine shuddered. More than once, as he strode along the forest trails, he looked tensely behind him, half expecting to see the black-bearded man pursuing him again.

But no pursuers came. By mid-afternoon Valentine saw the Terrace of Surrender in the distance, and the flat white face of Third Cliff far beyond it.

No one was likely to notice an unauthorized pilgrim quietly moving about among all these millions. He entered the Terrace of Surrender with what he hoped was an innocent expression, as if he had every right to be there. It was an opulent, spacious place, with a row of lofty buildings of dark blue stone at its eastern end and a grove of bassa-trees in fruit closer at hand. Valentine added half a dozen of the tender, succulent bassa-fruits to his pack and continued to the terrace baths, where he rid himself of the grime of his first day's trek. Growing even bolder, he found the dining-hall and helped himself to soup and stewed meat. And as casually as he had come, he slipped out the far end of the terrace just as night was descending.

Again he slept in an improvised forest bed, dozing and waking often to thoughts of Farssal, and when there was light enough he rose and went onward. The stupefying white wall of Third Cliff loomed high above the forest before him.

All day he walked, and all the next, and still he seemed no closer to the cliff. Traveling on foot through these woods, he was covering, he guessed, no more than fifteen or eighteen miles a day; might it be fifty or eighty to Third Cliff? And then, how far from there to Inner Temple? This journey might take weeks. He walked on. His stride grew ever more springy; this forest life was agreeing with him.

On the fourth day Valentine reached the Terrace of Ascent. He paused briefly to refresh himself, slept in a quiet grove, and in the morning went onward until he arrived at the base of Third Cliff.

He knew nothing of the mechanism that transported the floater-sleds up the cliff walls. From here he could see the small settlement at the floater station, a few cottages, some acolytes working in a field, sleds stacked by the foot of the cliff. He considered waiting until darkness and then trying to run the sleds, but decided against it: climbing that giddy height unaided, using equipment he did not understand, seemed too risky. Forcing the acolytes to aid him was even less to his liking.

One option remained. He tidied his travel-stained robes, donned an air of supreme authority, and advanced at a dignified pace toward the floater station.

The acolytes—there were three of them—regarded him coolly.

He said, "Are the floaters ready for operation?"

"Have you business on Third Cliff?"

"I do." Valentine turned on them his most dazzling smile, letting them see, also, an underlying aspect of confidence, strength, total self-assurance. He said crisply, "I am Valentine of Alhanroel, under special summons to the Lady. They wait for me above to escort me to Inner Temple."

"Why were we not told of this?"

Valentine shrugged. "How would I know? Someone's error, obviously. Shall I wait here until the papers arrive for you? Shall the Lady wait for me? Come, get your floaters floating!"

"Valentine of Alhanroel—special summons to the Lady—" The acolytes frowned, shook their heads, peered uncomfortably at one another. "This is all very irregular. Who did you say is to be your escort up there?"

Valentine took a deep breath. "The High Speaker Tisana of Falkynkip herself has been sent to fetch me!" he announced resonantly. "She, too, will be kept waiting while you fidget and fumble! Will you answer to her for this delay? You know what sort of temper the High Speaker has!"

"True, true," the acolytes agreed nervously, nodding to one another as though such a person actually existed and her wrath were something greatly to be dreaded.

Valentine saw that he had won. With brisk impatient gestures he mobilized them to their tasks, and in a moment he was aboard a sled and floating serenely toward the highest and most sacred of the three cliffs of the Isle of Sleep.

10

The air atop Third Cliff was clear and pure and cool, for this level of the Isle lay thousands of feet above sea level, and up here in the eyrie of the Lady the environment was quite different from that of the two lower steps. The trees were tall and slim, with needlelike leaves and open, symmetrical boughs, and the shrubs and plants about them had a subtropical hardiness to them, thick glossy leaves and sturdy rubbery stems. Looking back, Valentine could not see the ocean from here, only the forested sprawl of Second Cliff and a hint of First Cliff far beyond.

A pathway of elegantly joined stone blocks led from the rim of Third Cliff toward the forest. Unhesitatingly Valentine set out upon it. He had no idea of the topography of this level, only that there were many terraces, and the last of them was the Terrace of Adoration, where one awaited the call to the Lady. He did not expect to get all the way to the threshold of Inner Temple unintercepted; but he would go as far as he could, and when they seized him as a trespasser he would give them his name and ask that it be conveyed to the Lady, and the rest would be subject to her mercy, her grace.

He was halted before he reached the outermost of Third Cliff's terraces.

Five acolytes in the robes of the inner hierarchy, gold with red trim, emerged from the forest and arrayed themselves coolly across his path. There were three men, two women, all of considerable age, and they showed no fear of him at all.

One of the women, white-haired, with thin lips and dark, intense eyes, said, "I am Lorivade of the Terrace of Shadows and I ask you in the Lady's name how you come to be here."

"I am Valentine of Alhanroel," he replied evenly, "and I am of the Lady's own flesh and would have you take me to her."

The brazen statement produced no smiles among the hierarchs.

Lorivade said, "You claim kinship with the Lady?"

"I am her son."

"Her son's name is Valentine, and he is Coronal on Castle Mount. What madness is this?"

"Bring to the Lady the news that her son Valentine has come to her across the Inner Sea and all of Zimroel, and that he is a fair-haired man, and I ask no more than that."

One of the men at Lorivade's side said, "You wear the robes of Second Cliff. It is forbidden for you to have made this ascent."

With a sigh Valentine said, "I understand that. My ascent was unauthorized, illegal, and presumptuous. But I claim the highest reasons of state. If my message is delayed in reaching the Lady, you will answer for it."

"We are not accustomed to threats here," Lorivade declared.

"I make no threat. I speak only of inevitable consequences."

A woman to the right of Lorivade said, "He's a lunatic. We'll have to confine him and treat him."

"And censure the crew below," said another man.

"And discover which terrace he's from, and how he was allowed to wander away from it," said a third.

"I ask only that you send my message to the Lady," Valentine said quietly.

They surrounded him and, moving in formation, walked him briskly along the forest path to a place where three floaters were parked and a number of younger acolytes waited. Evidently they had been prepared for serious trouble. Lorivade gestured to one of the acolytes and issued brief orders; then the five hierarchs boarded one of the floaters and were borne away.

Acolytes moved toward Valentine. None too gently they caught him and propelled him toward a floater. He smiled and indicated he would make no resistance, but they held him firmly and pushed him roughly into a seat. The floater rose to full hover and, at a signal, the mounts tethered to it began to trot toward the nearby terrace.

It was a place of wide, low buildings and great stone plazas, this Terrace of Shadows, and the shadows that gave it its name were black as the darkest ink, mysterious all-engulfing pools of night that stretched in strangely significant patterns over the abstract stone statuary. But Valentine's tour of the terrace was brief. His captors halted outside a squat stark building without windows; a cunningly fashioned door slid open on silent hinges at the lightest of touches; he was ushered inside.

The door closed and left no trace in the wall.

He was a prisoner.

The room was square, low-ceilinged, and bleak. A single dim glow-float cast a mellow greenish light. There was a cleanser, a sink, a commode, a mattress. Beyond that, nothing.

Would they send his message to the Lady?

Or would they leave him here to grow dusty, while they investigated the irregularities of his advent on Third Cliff, rummaging for weeks in the island bureaucracy?

An hour passed, two, three. Let them send an interrogator, he prayed, an inquisitor, anyone, only not this silence, this boredom, this solitude. He counted paces. The room was not precisely square: one pair of walls was a pace and a half longer than the other pair. He searched for the outlines of the doorway, and could not find them. The fit was seamless, a marvel of design that gave him little cheer. He invented dialogues and silently embellished them: Valentine and Deliamber, Valentine and the Lady, Valentine and Carabella, Valentine and Lord Valentine. But it was an amusement that soon palled.

He heard a faint whining sound and whirled to see a slot open in the wall and a tray come sliding into his cell. They had given him baked fish, a cluster of ivory-colored grapes, a beaker of cool red juice. "For this repast I thank you kindly," he said out loud. His fingers probed the wall, seeking the place where the tray had entered: no trace.

He ate. He invented more dialogues, conversing in his mind with Sleet, with the old dream-speaker Tisana, with Zalzan Kavol, with Captain Gorzval. He asked them about their childhoods, their hopes and dreams, their political opinions, their tastes in food and drink and clothing. Again the game wore thin after a while, and he stretched out to sleep.

Sleep was thin too, a shallow doze, broken half a dozen times by white dreary spells of wakefulness. His dreams were patchy ones; through them drifted the Lady, Farssal, the King of Dreams, the Metamorph chieftain, and the hierarch Lorivade, but they offered only muddled and murky words. When he woke, finally, a tray of breakfast had appeared in the room.

A long day passed.

He had never known a day so interminable. There was nothing at all to do, nothing, nothing whatever, an endless stretch of gray nothingness. He would have juggled his dishes, but they were light and flimsy things and it would have been like juggling feathers. He tried to juggle his boots, but he had only two of those and juggling things in twos was a fool's sport. He juggled memories instead, reliving all that had befallen him since Pidruid, but the prospect of an infinity of hours doing that dismayed him. He meditated until there was a dull buzz of fatigue between his ears. He crouched in the center of the room, trying to anticipate the moment when the next meal would arrive, but the tension he generated out of that yielded only feeble entertainment.

On the second night Valentine made an attempt to communicate with the Lady. He prepared himself for sleep, but as his mind began to release itself from consciousness he endeavored to slip into an intermediate place between waking and sleeping, a trance-state of sorts. It was a ticklish business, for if he concentrated too intently he would tip himself back into full

283

wakefulness, and if he relaxed too thoroughly he would fall asleep; he balanced there a long time, at the floating-point, wishing he had taken the opportunity in some quiet part of his Zimroel journey to have Deliamber train him in these matters.

At last he sent forth his spirit.

—*Mother?*

He imagined his soul coursing high over the Terrace of Shadows and drifting inward, inward, past terrace after terrace, to the core of Third Cliff, to Inner Temple, to the chamber where the Lady of the Isle rested.

—*Mother, it's Valentine. It's your son Valentine. I have so much to tell you, mother, and so much to ask! But you have to help me reach you.*

Valentine lay still. He was wholly calm. A pure white radiance seemed to glow in his mind.

—*Mother, I'm on Third Cliff, in a prison cell in the Terrace of Shadows. I've come so far, mother. But now I'm stopped. Send for me, mother!*

—*Mother—*

—*Lady—*

—*Mother—*

He slept.

The radiance still glowed. He perceived the first tingling music of the dream-state, the overture, the initial sensations of contact. Visions came. No longer was he imprisoned. He lay beneath the cool white stars on a great circular platform of finely polished stone, as though an altar, and to him came a white-robed woman with lustrous dark hair, who knelt beside him and touched him lightly, saying in a tender voice, "You are my son Valentine, and I do acknowledge you before all Majipoor to be my son, and I summon you now to my side."

That was all. When he woke he could recall nothing of the dream but that.

There was no breakfast tray for him that morning. Was it truly morning, then, or had he awakened in the middle of the night? Hours passed. No tray. Had they forgotten him? Did they plan to starve him to death? He felt a twinge of terror: was that an improvement over boredom? He thought he preferred boredom to terror, but not by much. He called out, but he knew it was useless. This place was sealed like a tomb. Like a tomb. Glumly Valentine looked at the accumulation of old trays, stacked against the far wall. He remembered the wonders and joys of food, the sausages of the Liiimen, the fish that Khun and Sleet had grilled on the banks of the Steiche, the flavor of dwikka-fruit, the potent tang of fireshower wine in Pidruid. His hunger was growing intense. And he was frightened. Not bored at all now, but frightened. They had held a meeting, perhaps, and condemned him to death for overwhelming folly.

Minutes. Hours. Half a day gone now.

Folly to think he could touch the Lady's mind in sleep. Folly to think he could float effortlessly into Inner Temple and win her aid. Folly to think he could regain Castle Mount, or that he had ever had it at all. He had propelled himself halfway around the world on no force other than folly, and now, he thought bitterly, he would have the reward of his presumption and his foolishness.

Then at last he heard the familiar faint whine. But it was not the food-slot opening: it was the door.

Two white-haired hierarchs entered the cell. They favored him with a look of bleak and sour bafflement.

"Have you come to deliver my breakfast?" Valentine asked.

"We have come," said the taller one, "to conduct you to Inner Temple."

11

He insisted that they feed him first—a wise move, for the trip proved to be a lengthy one, all the rest of the day by swift mount-drawn floater-wagon. The hierarchs sat flanking him in chilly silence throughout. When he asked a question—the name of some terrace through which they were passing, for example—they would reply in the fewest possible words; otherwise they offered no chatter.

Third Cliff had many terraces—Valentine lost count after about seven—and they were much closer together than those of the outer cliffs, with only token strips of forest separating them. This central zone of the Isle seemed a busy and populous place.

At twilight they came to the Terrace of Adoration, a domain of serene gardens and rambling low buildings of white-washed stone. Like all the other terraces it was circular in outline, but it was much smaller than the others, here at the innermost part of the island, a mere ringlet that probably could be walked in all its circumference in an hour or two, whereas it might take months to complete the circuit of a First Cliff terrace. Ancient gnarled trees with close-set oval leaves rose at regular intervals along its rampart. Bowers of richly blossoming vines coiled between the buildings; small court-yards were everywhere, decorated with slender pillars of polished black stone and bedecked with flowering shrubs. In twos and threes the servants of the Lady moved quietly through these peaceful precincts. Valentine was conducted to a chamber far more gracious than his last, with a broad sunken bath, an inviting bed, windows facing into a garden, baskets of fruit on the table. The hierarchs left him here. He bathed, nibbled fruit, waited for the next event. That was some time in arriving, an hour or more: a knock on the door, a soft voice asking if he wished dinner, a cart rolled into the room bearing more substantial fare than he had had since coming to the Isle—grilled meats, blue gourds artfully stuffed with minced fish, a beaker of something cold that might almost have been wine. Valentine ate eagerly. Afterward he stood by his windows a long time, studying the darkness. He saw nothing; he heard no one. He tested his door: locked. So he was still a prisoner, although in far more pleasing surroundings than before.

He slept a dreamless sleep. A flood of golden sunlight cascading into his room awakened him. He bathed; the same discreet servitor appeared outside, with a breakfast of sausages and stewed pink fruit; and a short while after he was done the two somber hierarchs came to him, saying, "The Lady has summoned you this morning."

They led him through a garden of marvelous beauty and across a slender bridge of pure white stone that rose in a gentle arch above a dark pond in which golden fish swam in sparkling patterns. Ahead lay a wondrously manicured greensward. At the center of it was a one-story building of great size, extraordinarily delicate in form, with long narrow wings radiating in the form of starbeams from the circular center.

This could only be Inner Temple, Valentine thought.

Now he trembled. He had journeyed, for more months than he could remember, toward this very spot, toward the threshold of the mysterious woman whose realm this was, whom he fancied to be his mother. At last he was here; and what if it proved all to be foolishness, or fantasy, or terrible error, what if he was no one in particular, a yellow-haired idler from Zimroel, bereft of his memory through some stupidity and filled by trifling companions with nonsensical ambitions? The thought was unbearable. If the Lady repudiated him now, if she denied him—

He entered the temple.

The hierarchs still close at his sides, Valentine marched

endlessly down an impossibly elongated entrance hall that was guarded every twenty feet by a grim-faced rigid warrior, and into an interior room, octagonal in shape, with walls of the finest white stone and a pool, octagonal also, at its center. Morning light entered through an open eight-sided skylight. At each corner of the room stood a stern figure in hierarchical robes. Valentine, a little dazed, looked from one to the next and saw no welcome on their faces, only a sort of pursed-lip disapproval.

There was a single note of music, softly swelling, then dying away, and when it was gone the Lady of the Isle was in the room.

She seemed much like the figure Valentine had seen so often in dreams: a woman of middle years and ordinary height, dusky of skin, with glossy black hair, warm soft eyes, a full mouth that hovered always at the edge of a smile, a silver band at her brow, and, yes, a flower behind one ear, with many thick green petals. It seemed, though, that there was an aura about her, a nimbus, a radiance of force and authority and majesty, such as befitted the Power of Majipoor that she was, and he had not been prepared for that, expecting as he had been only the warm motherly woman, and forgetting that she was a queen, a priestess, almost a goddess, as well. He stood speechless before her, and for a long moment she studied him from the far side of the pool, her gaze resting lightly but penetratingly on his face. Then she waved one hand sharply in an unmistakable gesture of dismissal. Not of him: of the hierarchs. Their glacial calm was broken by that. They looked to one another, obviously confused. The Lady repeated the gesture, a mere shallow snap of the wrist, and something imperious flashed in her eyes, a look of almost terrifying strength. Three or four of the hierarchs left the room; the others dawdled, as if not believing that the Lady proposed to be left alone with the prisoner. For an instant it seemed that a third wave of her hand might be necessary, as one of the oldest and most imposing of the hierarchs extended a quivering arm toward her in a motion of obvious protest. But at a glance from the Lady the Hierarch's arm dropped back to his side. Slowly the last of them went out of the room.

Valentine fought the impulse to fall to his knees.

He said in a barely audible voice, "I have no idea of the proper obeisance to make. Nor do I know, Lady, how I should address you, without giving offense."

Calmly she replied, "It will be enough, Valentine, if you call me mother."

The quiet words stunned him. He took a faltering few steps toward her, halted, stared.

"Is it so?" he asked in a whisper.

"There can be no doubt of it."

He felt his cheeks ablaze. He stood helpless, numbed by her grace. She beckoned to him, the tiniest movement of her fingertips, and he shook as though he were caught in an ocean gale.

"Come close," she said. "Are you afraid? Come to me, Valentine!"

He crossed the room, went round the pool, drew near her. She put her hands into his. Instantly he felt a jolt of energy, a tangible, palpable throbbing, somewhat akin to what he had felt when Deliamber touched him to do wizardry-work, but enormously more powerful, enormously more awesome. He would have withdrawn his hands at that first throb of force, but she held him, and he could not, and her eyes close by his seemed to be seeing through him, entering all his mysteries.

"Yes," she said finally. "By the Divine, yes, Valentine, your body is strange but your soul is of my own making! Oh, Valentine, Valentine, what have they done to you? What have they done to Majipoor?" She tugged at his hands, and pulled him close to her, and then he was in her arms, the Lady straining upward to embrace him, and he felt her trembling now, no goddess but only a woman, a mother holding her troubled son. In her grasp he felt such peace as he had not known since his awakening in Pidruid, and he clung to her, praying she would never release him.

Then she stood back and surveyed him, smiling. "You were given a handsome body, at least. Nothing like what you once were, but pleasing to the eye, and strong as well, and healthy. They could have done much worse. They could have made you something weak and sickly and deformed, but I suppose they lacked the courage, knowing that eventually they would be repaid tenfold for all their crimes."

"Who, mother?"

She seemed surprised at his question. "Why, Barjazid and his brood!"

Valentine said, "I know nothing, mother, except what has come to me in dreams, and even that has been befogged and muddled."

"And what is it that you know?"

"That my body has been taken from me, that in some witchery of the King of Dreams I was left outside Pidruid as you see me, that someone else, I think it may be Dominin

Barjazid, rules now from Castle Mount. But I know all this only in the most untrustworthy of ways."

"It is all true," the Lady replied.

"When was it that this happened?"

"In early summer," she said. "When you made the grand processional in Zimroel. I have no knowledge of how it was done; but one night as I lay sleeping I felt a wrenching, a tearing, as of the heart of the planet being ripped loose, and I awakened knowing that something evil and monstrous had occurred, and I sent out my soul toward you and was unable to reach you. There was only a silence where you had been, a void. Yet it was different from the silence that struck me when Voriax was slain, for I still felt your presence, but beyond my reach, as if behind a thick sheet of glass. I asked at once for news of the Coronal. He is in Til-omon, my people told me. And is he well? I asked. Yes, they said, he is well, he sails today toward Pidruid. But I could make no contact, Valentine. I sent forth my soul as I had not done in years, to every part of the world, and you were nowhere and somewhere, both at once. I was frightened and confused, Valentine, but I could do nothing but seek and wait, and news came to me that Lord Valentine had reached Pidruid, that he was guest in the mayor's grand house, and I had a vision of him across all this distance and his face was the face of my son. But his mind was other, and it was closed to me. I attempted a sending, and I could not send to him. And at last I began to understand."

"Did you know where I was?"

"Not at first. They had witched your mind so well it was altogether changed. Night after night I cast my soul forth into Zimroel in search of you—neglecting everything else here, but this was no trifling matter, this substitution of Coronals—and I thought I felt glimmers, a shard of your true self, a fragment—and after a time I was able to determine that you were alive, that you were in northwestern Zimroel, but there was still no reaching you. I had to wait until you had awakened more to yourself, until their witcheries had faded a bit and your true mind was restored at least in part."

"It is still far from whole, mother."

"I know that. But that can be remedied, I believe."

"When did you finally reach me?"

She paused a moment in thought. "It was near the Ghayrog city, I think, Dulorn, and I saw you first through the minds of others who were dreaming the truth about you. And I touched their minds, I refined and clarified what was in them, and I saw that your soul had imprinted its stamp on them and that they knew better than you did yourself what had befallen you. I circled about you in this way, and then I was able to enter you. And from that moment on you have gained in knowledge of your former self, as I have labored across so many thousands of miles to heal you and to draw you to me. But none of it was easy. The world of dreams, Valentine, is a difficult and shifting place, even for me, and to attempt to control it is like writing a book in the sand beside an ocean: the tide returns and obliterates nearly everything, and you must write it again, and again and again. But at last you are here."

"Did you know it when I reached the Isle?"

"I knew it, yes. I could feel your closeness."

"And yet you let me drift for months from terrace to terrace!"

She laughed. "There are millions of pilgrims in the outer terraces. Sensing you was one thing, actually locating you another, far more difficult. Besides, you were not ready to come to me, nor I to receive you. I was testing you, Valentine. Watching you from afar, studying to see how much of your soul had survived, whether there still was any of the Coronal remaining in you. Before I acknowledged you I had to know these things."

"And does much of Lord Valentine remain in me, then?"

"A great deal. Far more than your enemies could ever suspect. Their scheme was faulty: they thought they had expunged you, when they only fuddled and disordered you."

"Would it not have been wiser for them to have killed me outright, than to have put my soul in some other body?"

"Wiser, yes," the Lady replied. "But they did not dare. Yours is an anointed spirit, Valentine. These Barjazids are superstitious beasts; they will risk overthrowing a Coronal, it seems, but not destroying him altogether, for fear of your spirit's vengeance. And their cowardly hesitation now will bring about the ruin of their scheme."

Valentine said softly, "Do you think I can ever regain my place?"

"Do you doubt it?"

"Barjazid wears the face of Lord Valentine. The people accept him as Coronal. He controls the power of Castle Mount. I have perhaps a dozen followers and am unknown. If I proclaim myself rightful Coronal, who will believe me? And how long then before Dominin Barjazid deals with me the way he should have dealt with me in Til-omon?"

290

"You have the support of the Lady your mother."

"And have you an army, mother?"

The Lady smiled gently. "I have no army, no. But I am a Power of Majipoor, which is not a small thing. I have the strength of righteousness and love, Valentine. I also have this."

She touched the silver circlet at her brow.

"Through which you make your sendings?" Valentine asked.

"Yes. Through which I can reach the minds of all Majipoor. I lack the ability of the Barjazids to control and direct, which their devices are capable of doing. But I can communicate, I can guide, I can influence. You will have one of these circlets before you leave the Isle."

"And I'll go quietly through Alhanroel, beaming messages of love to the citizens, until Dominin Barjazid descends from the Mount and gives me back the throne?"

The Lady's eyes flashed with the kind of anger Valentine had seen in them when she was sending the hierarchs from the room.

"What sort of talk is that?" she snapped.

"Mother—"

"Oh, they *have* changed you! The Valentine I bore and reared accepted no thought of defeat."

"Nor do I, mother. But it all seems so immense, and I'm so weary. And to make war against citizens of Majipoor—even against a usurper— Mother, there's been no war on Majipoor since earliest times. Am I the one to break the peace?"

Her eyes were merciless. "The peace is already broken, Valentine. It falls to you to restore the order of the realm. A false Coronal has reigned nearly a year now. Cruel and foolish laws are proclaimed daily. The innocent are punished, the guilty flourish. Balances constructed thousands of years ago are being destroyed. When our people came here from Old Earth, fourteen thousand years past, many mistakes were made, much suffering was endured, before we found our way of government, but since the time of the first Pontifex we have lived without major upheaval, and since the time of Lord Stiamot there has been peace on this world. Now there has been a rupture of that peace, and it falls to you to put things to rights."

"And if I accept what Dominin Barjazid has done? If I decline to embroil Majipoor in civil war? Would the consequences be so evil?"

"You know the answers to those questions already."

"I would hear them from you, because my resolve wavers."

"It shames me to hear you speak those words."

"Mother, I have undergone strange things on this journey and they have taken much of my strength. Am I not allowed a moment of fatigue?"

"You are a king, Valentine."

"I was, perhaps, and perhaps will be again. But much of my kingliness was stolen from me in Til-omon. I am an ordinary man now. And not even kings are immune to weariness and discouragement, mother."

In a tone more gentle than the one she had been using, the Lady said, "The Barjazid does not yet rule as an absolute tyrant, for that might turn the people against him, and he is still insecure in his power—while you live. But he rules for himself and for his family, not for Majipoor. He lacks a sense of right, and does only what seems useful and expedient. As his confidence grows, so too will his crimes, until Majipoor groans under the whip of a monster."

Valentine nodded. "When I am not so weary, I see that, yes."

"Think, too, of what will happen when the Pontifex Tyeveras dies, which must sooner or later happen, and more probably sooner than later."

"Barjazid goes to the Labyrinth then, and becomes a powerless recluse. Is that what you mean?"

"The Pontifex is not powerless, and he does not need to be a recluse. In your lifetime there has been only Tyeveras, growing older and older and steadily more strange. But a Pontifex in full vigor is a very different entity. What if Barjazid is Pontifex five years from now? Do you think he'll be content to sit in that underground hole the way Tyeveras now does? He'll rule with force, Valentine." She looked at him intently. "And who do you think will become Coronal?"

Valentine shook his head.

She said, "The King of Dreams has three sons. Minax is the oldest, who will have the throne in Suvrael one of these days. Dominin is now Coronal and will be Pontifex, if you choose to let him. Whom will he select as new Coronal but his younger brother, Cristoph?"

"But it goes against all nature for a Pontifex to give Castle Mount to his own brother!"

"It goes against all nature for a son of the King of Dreams to overthrow a rightful Coronal, too," said the Lady. Once more her eyes flashed. "Consider this, also: when there is a

292

change in Coronals, there is a change in the Lady of the Isle! I go to live out my days in the palace for retired Ladies in the Terrace of Shadows, and who comes to Inner Temple? The mother of the Barjazids! Do you see, Valentine, they will have everything, they will control all of Majipoor!"

"This must not be," Valentine said.

"This will not be."

"What shall I do?"

"You will take ship from my port of Numinor to Alhanroel, with all your people and others I will provide for you. You will land in the Stoienzar, and journey to the Labyrinth for the blessing of Tyeveras."

"But if Tyeveras is a madman—"

"Not entirely mad. He lives in a perpetual dream, and a strange one, but I have touched his spirit lately, and the old Tyeveras still exists somewhere within. He has been Pontifex forty years, Valentine, and was Coronal a long while before that, and he knows the way our realm was meant to be governed. If you can reach him, if you can demonstrate to him that you are the true Lord Valentine, he will give you aid. Then you must march on Castle Mount. Do you shrink from that task?"

"I shrink only from bringing chaos upon Majipoor."

"The chaos is already at hand. What you bring is order and justice." She moved close to him, so that all the frightening power of her personality was exposed to him, and touched his hand, and said in a low, vehement tone, "I bore two sons, and from the moment one looked at them in their cradles, one knew they were meant to be kings. The first was Voriax—do you remember him? I suppose not, not yet—and he was magnificent, a splendid man, a hero, a demigod, and even in his childhood they said of him on Castle Mount, This is the one, this will be Coronal when Lord Malibor becomes Pontifex. Voriax was a marvel, but there was a second son, Valentine, as strong and as splendid as Voriax, not so much given to sport and exploits as he, but a warmer soul, and a wiser one, one who understood without being told what was right and what was wrong, one who had no cruelty in his spirit whatever, one who was of even and balanced and sunny temperament, so that everyone loved him and respected him, and it was said of Valentine that he would be an even finer king than Voriax, but of course Voriax was older and would be chosen, with Valentine fated to be nothing more than a high minister. And Malibor did not become Pontifex, but died before his time hunting dragons, and emissaries of Tyeveras came to Voriax and said, You are Coronal of Majipoor, and the first to fall before him and make the starburst was his brother Valentine. And so Lord Voriax ruled on Castle Mount, and ruled well, and I came to the Isle of Sleep as I had always known I would, and for eight years all was well on Majipoor. And then what happened was something no one could have foretold, that Lord Voriax would perish before his time as Lord Malibor had, hunting in the forest and struck down by a stray bolt. Yet there still was Valentine, and though it was rare for the brother of a Coronal to become Coronal after him, there was little debate, for everyone recognized his high qualifications. Thus Lord Valentine came to the Castle and I who was mother to two kings remained at Inner Temple, satisfied with the sons I had given to Majipoor and confident that the reign of Lord Valentine would be one of Majipoor's glories. Do you think I can allow Barjazids to sit for long where my sons once sat? Do you think I can endure the sight of Lord Valentine's face masking the Barjazid's shabby soul? Oh, Valentine, Valentine, you are only half what you once were, less than half, but you will be yourself again, and Castle Mount will be yours and the destinies of Majipoor will not be altered to something evil, and talk no more of shrinking from bringing chaos into the world. The chaos is upon us. You are the deliverer. Do you understand?"

"I understand, mother."

"Then come with me, and I will make you whole."

12

She led him from the octagonal chamber, down one of the spokes of Inner Temple, past rigid guards and a group of frowning, bewildered hierarchs, into a small bright room bedecked with brilliant flowers of a dozen colors. Here was a desk fashioned of a single slab of gleaming darbelion, and a low couch, and a few small pieces of furniture; this was the Lady's study, it seemed. She beckoned Valentine to a seat and took from the desk two small ornate flasks. "Drink this wine in a single draught," she told him, handing him one flask.

"Wine, mother? On the Isle?"

"You and I are not pilgrims here. Drink it."

He uncorked the flask and put it to his lips. The flavor was familiar to him, dark and spicy and sweet, but it was a moment before he could identify it: the wine dream-speakers used, that contained the drug that made minds open to minds. The Lady downed the contents of the second flask.

Valentine said, "Are we then to do a speaking?"

"No. This must be done while awake. I have thought long about how to manage this." From her desk she withdrew a shimmering silver circlet, identical to her own, and gave it to him. "Let it rest on your brow," she said. "From this time until you ascend Castle Mount, wear it constantly, for it will be the center of your power."

Cautiously he slipped the circlet over his head. It fit snugly at his temples, a strange close sensation, not entirely to his liking, although the metal band was so fine he was surprised to notice it at all. The Lady drew near him and smoothed his thick long hair over it.

"Golden hair," she said lightly. "I never thought to have a son with golden hair! What do you feel, with the circlet on you?"

"The tightness of it."

"Nothing else?"

"Nothing else, mother."

"The tightness will soon cease to matter, as you get used to it. Do you feel the drug yet?"

"A slight cloudiness in my mind, only. I think I could sleep, if I were allowed."

"Sleep will soon be the last thing you crave," said the Lady. She extended both her hands to him. "Are you a good juggler, my son?" she asked unexpectedly.

He grinned. "So they tell me."

"Good. Tomorrow you must show me some of your skills. I would find that amusing. But now give me your hands. Both. Here."

She held her fine-boned strong-looking hands over his for an instant. Then she interlaced her fingers with his in a quick, decisive gesture.

It was as though a switch had been thrown, a circuit had been closed. Valentine staggered with shock. He stumbled, almost fell, and felt the Lady grasping him tightly, steadying him as he lurched about the room. There was a sensation in his mind as of a spike being driven through the base of his skull. The universe reeled about him; he was unable to control his eyes or to focus them, and he saw only fragmentary blurred images: the face of his mother, the shining surface of the desk, the blazing hues of the flowers, everything pulsing and throbbing and whirling.

His heart pounded. His throat was dry. His lungs felt

empty. This was more terrifying than being drawn into the vortex of the sea-dragon and disappearing into the deep waters. Now his legs betrayed him entirely, and, unable any longer to stand, he sagged to the floor, kneeling there, somehow aware of the Lady kneeling before him, her face close to him, her fingers still locked between his, the terrible searing contact of their souls unbroken.

Memories flooded him.

He saw the vast gigantic splendor that was Castle Mount and the sprawling unthinkable enormity of the Coronal's Castle at its impossible summit. His mind roved with lightning speed through rooms of state with gilded walls and soaring arched ceilings, through banquet halls and council-chambers, through corridors wide as plazas. Brilliant lights flashed and sparkled and dazed him. He sensed a male presence beside him, tall, powerful, confident, strong, holding one of his hands, and a woman equally strong and self-assured holding the other, and knew them to be his father and mother, and saw a boy just ahead who was his brother Voriax.

—What is this room, father?

—The Confalume throne-room, it is called.

—And that man with the long red hair? Sitting on the big chair?

—He is the Coronal Lord Malibor.

—What does that mean?

—Silly Valentine! He doesn't know what the Coronal is!

—Quiet, Voriax. The Coronal is the king, Valentine, one of the two kings, the younger one. The other is the Pontifex, who once was Coronal himself.

—Which one is he?

—The tall thin one, with the very dark beard.

—His name is Pontifex?

—His name is Tyeveras. Pontifex is what he is called as our king. He lives near the Stoienzar, but he is here today because Lord Malibor the Coronal is going to be married.

—And will Lord Malibor's children be Coronals too, mother?

—No, Valentine.

—Who will be Coronal next?

—No one knows that yet, son.

—Will I? Will Voriax?

—It could happen, if you grow up wise and strong.

—Oh, I will, father, I will, I will!

The room dissolved. Valentine saw himself in another room, similarly magnificent but not quite as large, and he was older now, not a boy but a young man, and there was Voriax with the starburst crown on his head, looking somewhat befuddled by it.

—Voriax! Lord Voriax!

Valentine dropped to his knees and raised his hands, spreading his fingers wide. And Voriax smiled and gestured at him.

—Get up, brother, get up. It is not fitting that you crawl like this in front of me.

—You will be the most splendid Coronal in the history of Majipoor, Lord Voriax.

—Call me brother, Valentine. I am Coronal, but I am still your brother.

—Long life to you, brother! Long life to the Coronal!

And others were shouting it about him:

—Long life to the Coronal! Long life to the Coronal!

But something had changed, though the room was the same, for Lord Voriax was nowhere in view, and it was Valentine who wore the strange crown now, and the others who were shouting to him, and kneeling before him, and waving their fingers in the air, crying his name. He looked at them in wonder.

—Long life to Lord Valentine!

—I thank you, my friends. I will try to be worthy of my brother's memory.

—Long life to Lord Valentine!

"Long life to Lord Valentine," said the Lady softly.

Valentine blinked and gaped. For a moment he was entirely disoriented, wondering why he was kneeling like this, and what room he was in, and who this woman was with her face so close to his. Then the shadows cleared from his mind.

He rose to his feet.

He felt altogether transformed. Through his mind coursed turbulent memories: the years on Castle Mount, the studies, all that dry history, the roster of the Coronals, the list of the Pontifexes, the volumes of constitutional lore, the economic surveys of the provinces of Majipoor, the long sessions with his tutors, with his constantly probing father, with his mother—and the other, less dedicated moments: the games, the river-journeys, the tournaments, his friends, Elidath and Stasilaine and Tunigorn, the free-flowing wine, the hunts, the good times with Voriax, the two of them the center of all eyes, the princes of princes. And the terrible moment of the death of Lord Malibor at sea, and Voriax' look of fright and joy at being named Coronal, and then the time eight years later when the delegation of high princes came to Valentine to offer him his brother's crown—

He remembered.

He remembered everything, up to a night in Til-omon, when all recollection ceased. And after that he knew only the sunshine of Pidruid, pebbles tumbling past him from a ridge, the boy Shanamir standing above him with his mounts. He looked at himself in his mind and it seemed to him that he cast a double shadow, one bright and one dark; and he looked through the insubstantial haze of false memories that they had given him in Til-omon, looked back over an impenetrable gap of darkness to the time when he was Coronal. He knew that his mind now was as whole as it was ever likely to be.

Again the Lady said, "Long life to Lord Valentine."

"Yes," he said in wonder. "Yes, I am Lord Valentine, and will be again. Mother, give me ships. The Barjazid has already had too much time on the throne."

"Ships are waiting in Numinor, and people loyal to me who will enter your service."

"Good. There are people here who must be gathered, I don't know from which terraces, but they'll have to be found swiftly. A little Vroon, some Skandars, a Hjort, a blue-skinned stranger from another world, and several humans. I'll give you the names."

"We will find them," said the Lady.

Valentine said, "And I thank you, mother, for returning me to myself."

"Thanks? Why thanks? I gave you to yourself originally. No thanks were required for that. Now you are brought forth again, Valentine, and if needs be I'll do it a third time. But let needs not be. Your fortunes now resume their upward path." Her eyes were bright with merriment. "Will I see you juggle this evening, Valentine? How many balls can you keep in the air at once?"

"Twelve," he said.

"And blaves can dance. Speak the truth!"

"Less than twelve," he admitted. "But more than two. I'll stage a performance after we dine. And—mother?"

"Yes?"

"When I regain Castle Mount I'll hold a grand festival, and you'll come from the Isle, and you'll see me juggle again, from the steps of the Confalume Throne. I promise you that, mother. From the steps of the throne."

IV

The Book of the Labyrinth

From Numinor port the ships of the Lady departed, seven of them, with broad sails and high splendid prows, under the command of the Hjort Asenhart, chief of the Lady's admirals, and bearing as passengers Lord Valentine the Coronal, his chief minister Autifon Deliamber the Vroon, his aides-de-camp Carabella of Til-omon and Sleet of Narabal, his military adjutant Lisamon Hultin, his ministers-at-large Zalzan Kavol the Skandar and Shanamir of Falkynkip, and various others. The fleet's destination was Stoien at the tip of Alhanroel's Stoienzar Peninsula, at the far side of the Inner Sea. Already the ships had been at sea for weeks, scudding ahead of the brisk westerlies that blew in late spring in these waters, but there was no sign yet of land, nor would there be for many days.

Valentine found the long journey comforting. He was not at all fearful of the tasks ahead, but neither was he impatient to begin them; rather, he needed a time to sort through his newly regained mind, and discover who he had been and what he had hoped to become. Where better than on the great bosom of the ocean, where nothing altered from day to day except the patterns of the clouds, and time seemed to stand still? And so he stood for hours at a time at the rail of his flagship, the *Lady Thiin*, apart from his friends, visiting with himself.

The person who he had been pleased him: stronger and more forceful of character than Valentine the juggler, but with no uglinesses of soul as sometimes are found among persons of power. To Valentine his former self seemed reasonable, judicious, calm, and moderate, a man of serious demeanor

299

but not without playfulness, one who understood the nature of responsibility and obligation. He was well educated, as might be supposed of one whose entire life had been spent in training for high office, with a thorough grounding in history, the law, government, and economics, somewhat less thorough in literature and philosophy, and, so far as Valentine could tell, only the merest smattering of mathematics and the physical sciences, which were much in eclipse on Majipoor.

The gift of his former self was like the finding of a treasure trove. Valentine was still not fully united to that other self, and tended to think of "him" and "me," or of "us," instead of viewing himself as a single integrated personality; but the split grew less apparent every day. There had been enough damage to the Coronal's mind in the overthrow at Til-omon that a cleavage now marked the discontinuity between Lord Valentine the Coronal and Valentine the juggler, and perhaps there would always be scar tissue along that cleft, the Lady's ministrations notwithstanding. But Valentine could cross the place of discontinuity at will, could travel to any point along his previous time-line, into his childhood or young manhood or his brief period of rule, and wherever he looked was such a wealth of knowledge, of experience, of maturity, as in his simple wandering days he had never hoped to master. If at the moment he must enter those memories as one might enter an encyclopedia, or a library, so be it; he was sure that a fuller joining of self and self would occur in time.

In the ninth week of the voyage a thin green line of land appeared at the horizon.

"Stoienzar," said Admiral Asenhart. "See, there, to the side, that darker place? Stoien harbor."

Through his double vision Valentine studied the shore of the approaching continent. As Valentine he knew next to nothing of Alhanroel, only that it was the largest of Majipoor's continents and the first to be settled by humans, a place of enormous population and tremendous natural wonders, and the seat of the planetary government, home to Coronal and Pontifex both. But out of Lord Valentine's memory came much more. To him Alhanroel meant Castle Mount, almost a world in itself, on whose vast slopes one could spend one's entire life among the Fifty Cities and not exhaust their marvels. Alhanroel was Lord Malibor's Castle crowning the Mount—for so he had called it through all his boyhood, and the habit had persisted even into his own reign. He saw the Castle now in the eye of his mind, enfolding the summit of the Mount like some many-armed creature spreading over

300

crags and peaks and alpine meadows, and down into the great terminal valleys and folds, a single structure of so many thousands of rooms that it was impossible to count them, a building that seemingly had a life of its own, and added annexes and outbuildings at the far perimeters of itself by authority of itself alone. And Alhanroel was, also, the great hump mounded up over the Labyrinth of the Pontifex, and the subterranean Labyrinth itself, reverse counterpart of the Lady's Isle, for where the Lady dwelled at Inner Temple on a sunsplashed wind-washed height surrounded by ring upon ring of open terraces, the Pontifex laired like a mole deep underground, at the lowest place of his realm, surrounded by the coils of his Labyrinth. Valentine had been to the Labyrinth only once, on a mission from Lord Voriax, years ago, but the memory of those winding caverns still glowed darkly in him.

Alhanroel, too, meant the Six Rivers that spilled down from the slopes of Castle Mount, and the creature-plants of the Stoienzar that he soon would see again, and the tree-houses of Treymone, and the stone ruins of Velalisier Plain, said to be older than the advent of humankind on Majipoor. Looking eastward at that faint line, growing larger but still barely perceptible, Valentine sensed all the vastness of Alhanroel unrolling like a titanic scroll before him, and the tranquillity that had governed his frame of mind during the voyage melted at once. He was eager to be ashore, to commence his march to the Labyrinth.

To Asenhart he said, "When will we reach land?"

"Tomorrow evening, my lord."

"We'll have feasting and games tonight, then. The best wines broken out, all hands to share. And afterward a performance deckside, a small jubilee."

Asenhart regarded him gravely. The admiral was an aristocrat among Hjorts, more slender than most of his kind, though with the coarse and pebbled skin that was their mark, and he had an odd sobriety of manner that Valentine found a bit offputting. The Lady held him in the highest regard.

"A performance, my lord?"

"A little jugglery," said Valentine. "My friends feel a nostalgic need to practice their art again, and what better moment than to celebrate the safe conclusion of our long voyage?"

"Of course," said Asenhart with a formal nod. But obviously the admiral disapproved of such goings-on aboard his flagship.

Zalzan Kavol had suggested it. The Skandar was plainly

301

restless aboard ship; he could often be seen moving his four arms rhythmically in the gestures of juggling, though no objects were in his hands. More than anyone he had had to adapt to circumstances in this trek across the face of Majipoor. A year ago Zalzan Kavol had been a prince of his profession, master among masters of the juggling art, traveling in splendor from city to city in his wondrous wagon. Now all that was gone from him. The wagon was ashes somewhere in the forests of Piurifayne; two of his five brothers lay dead there too, and a third at the bottom of the sea; no longer did he growl orders to his employees and have them leap to obey; and instead of performing nightly before wonder-struck audiences that filled his pouch with crowns, he wandered now from place to place in Valentine's wake, a mere subsidiary. Unused strengths and drives were accumulating in Zalzan Kavol. His face and demeanor showed it, for in the old days his temper had been churlish and he vented it freely, but now he seemed repressed, almost meek, and Valentine knew that must be a sign of severe inner distress. The agents of the Lady had found Zalzan Kavol still at the Terrace of Assessment at the outer rim of the Isle, at work at his menial pilgrim-tasks in a shambling, sleepwalking way, as if he had resigned himself to spending the rest of his life pulling weeds and pointing masonry.

"Can you do the routine with torches and knives?" Valentine asked him.

Zalzan Kavol brightened instantly. "Of course. And do you see those pins there?" He pointed to some huge wooden clubs, nearly four feet long, stowed in a rack near the mast. "Last night Erfon and I practiced with those, when everyone slept. If your admiral has no objections, we'll use them tonight."

"Those? How can you juggle anything so long?"

"Get me the admiral's permission, my lord, and tonight I'll show you!"

All afternoon the troupe rehearsed in a large vacant chamber down in the hold. It was the first time they had done such a thing since Ilirivoyne, what seemed like half a lifetime ago. But, using the improvised array of objects that the Skandars had quietly gathered, they fell swiftly into the rhythm of it.

Valentine, watching, felt a warm glow at the sight of them—Sleet and Carabella furiously passing clubs back and forth, Zalzan Kavol and Rovorn and Erfon devising intricate new patterns of interchange to replace those that had been destroyed with the death of their three brothers. For a moment it was like the innocent old times in Falkynkip or Du-

302

lorn, when nothing mattered except getting hired on at the festival or the circus, and the only challenge life offered was the one of keeping hand and eye coordinated. There was no going back to those days. Now that they had been swept up into high intrigue, the making and unmaking of Powers, none of them would ever be as they had been before. These five had dined with the Lady, had shared lodgings with the Coronal, were sailing onward toward a rendezvous with the Pontifex; they were already a part of history, even if Valentine's campaign came to nothing. Yet here they were juggling again as though juggling were all there was in life.

It had taken many days to bring his people together at Inner Temple. Valentine had imagined that the Lady or her hierarchs had merely to close their eyes and they could reach any mind on Majipoor, but it was not that simple; communication was imprecise and limited. They had located the Skandars first, in the outermost terrace. Shanamir had reached Second Cliff and in his youthful guileless way was advancing swiftly inward; Sleet, neither youthful nor guileless, had likewise wangled advancement to Second Cliff, and so had Vinorkis; Carabella was just behind them, at the Terrace of Mirrors, but through an error she was sought elsewhere at first; finding Khun and Lisamon Hultin had been no great task, since they were so much unlike all other pilgrims in appearance, but Gorzval's three former crewmen, Pandelon, Cordeine, and Thesme, had vanished into the population of the island as though they were invisible, so that Valentine would have had to abandon them had they not turned up at the last moment. Hardest of all to track down was Autifon Deliamber. The Isle had many Vroons, some of them as diminutive as the little wizard, and all efforts at tracing him led to mistakes of identity. With the fleet ready to sail, Deliamber had still been unfound, but on the eve of departure, Valentine desperately torn between the need to move onward and the unwillingness to part from his most useful counselor, the Vroon appeared at Numinor, offering no explanations of where he had been or how he had crossed the Isle undetected. So all were united, those who had survived the long trek from Pidruid.

On Castle Mount, Valentine knew, Lord Valentine had had his own ring of intimates, whose faces and names now had been restored to his knowledge, princes and courtiers and officials close to him since childhood, Elidath, Stasilaine, Tunigorn, the dearest comrades he had; and yet, though he still felt loyalty to those people, they had become terribly distant from his soul, and this random assortment of companions acquired

303

during his time of wanderings now stood nearest to him. He wondered how it would be when he returned to Castle Mount and had to reconcile one group with the other.

On one score, at least, he had reassured himself out of his newly regained memories. No wife awaited him at the Castle, nor intended bride, nor even an important lover to contest Carabella's place at his side. As prince and as young Coronal he had lived a carefree and unattached life, the Divine be thanked. It would be difficult enough, imposing on the court the notion that the Coronal's beloved was a commoner, a woman of the lowland cities, a wandering juggler; but it would be altogether impossible if his heart had already been given, and now he were to claim to have given it again.

"Valentine!" Carabella called.

Her voice broke him free of reverie. He looked toward her and she giggled and tossed him a club. He caught it as they had taught him so long ago, between thumb and fingers with the club's head pointing at an angle. An instant later came a second one from Sleet, and then a third from Carabella. He laughed and sent the clubs whirling above his head in the old familiar pattern, throw and throw and catch, and Carabella clapped her hands and sent another one his way. It was good to be juggling again. Lord Valentine—a superb athlete, quick of eye and skilled at many games, though hampered somewhat by a slight limp from an old riding injury—had not known juggling. Juggling was the art of the simpler Valentine. Aboard this ship, wearing now the aura of authority that had come upon him by his mother's healing of his mind, Valentine had felt his companions holding him at arm's length, try as they might to regard him as the old Valentine of the Zimroel days. So it gave him special pleasure to have Carabella so irreverently fling a club his way.

And it gave him pleasure, too, to be handling the clubs— even when he dropped one, and, stooping for it, was hit on the head by another, provoking a snort of contempt out of Zalzan Kavol.

"Do that tonight," the Skandar called, "and you'll forfeit your wine for a week!"

"Have no fear," Valentine retorted. "I drop the clubs now only for practice in recovering them. You'll see no such blunders this evening."

Nor were there any. The ship's entire company gathered at sundown on the deck for the entertainment. To one side, Asenhart and his officers occupied a platform where they would have the best view; but when the admiral beckoned to

Valentine, offering him the chair of honor, he declined with a smile. Asenhart looked puzzled at that, but his expression was not nearly so strained as it became a few moments later, when Shanamir and Vinorkis and Lisamon Hultin began to pound on drums and tootle on coilpipes, and the jugglers emerged from a hatch in a gleeful sprint, and as they began to perform their wonders the figure of Lord Valentine the Coronal appeared among them, blithely hurling clubs and dishes and pieces of fruit like any vulgar entertainer.

2

If Admiral Asenhart had had his way, there would have been a grand celebration in Stoien to mark Valentine's arrival, something at least as splendid as the festival held in Pidruid at the time of the visit of the false Coronal. But Valentine, as soon as he got word of Asenhart's plan, put a stop to it. He was not yet ready to claim the throne, to make public accusations against the individual who called himself Lord Valentine, or to ask for any sort of homage from the citizenry at large. "Until I have the support of the Pontifex," Valentine told Asenhart sternly, "I mean to move quietly and gather strength without attracting attention. There will be no festivals for me in Stoien."

So it was that the *Lady Thiin* made a relatively inconspicuous landfall at that great port at the southwestern tip of Alhanroel. Even though there were seven ships in the fleet—and ships of the Lady, though common enough in the harbor at Stoien, did not generally arrive in such numbers—they came in quietly, flying no fancy banners. The port officials asked few questions: obviously they traveled on the business of the Lady of the Isle, and her doings were beyond the purview of customs-clerks.

To reinforce this, Asenhart sent purchasing agents through the wharfside district the first day, buying quantities of glue and sailcloth and spices and tools and the like. Meanwhile Valentine and his company covertly took lodgings in an unassuming commercial hotel.

Stoien was predominantly a maritime city—export-import, warehousing, shipbuilding, all the occupations and enterprises that go with a prime coastal location and a superb harbor. The city, of some fourteen million souls, spread for hundreds of miles along the rim of the great promontory that divided the

Gulf of Stoien from the main body of the Inner Sea. It was not the mainland port closest to the Isle—that was Alaisor, far up Alhanroel's coast, thousands of miles to the north—but at this season, prevailing winds and currents being what they were, it was quicker to make the long journey down to Stoien than to brave the shorter but rougher crossing due east to Alaisor.

After pausing here to restock the ships, they would sail the placid Gulf, going along the north shore of the huge Stoienzar Peninsula in tropic ease to Kircidane and then up to Treymone, the coastal city nearest the Labryinth. It would be a relatively short overland trek from there to the abode of the Pontifex.

Valentine found Stoien strikingly beautiful. The entire peninsula was altogether flat, hardly twenty feet above sea level at its highest point, but the city-dwellers had devised a wondrous arrangement of platforms of brick faced with white stone to provide the illusion of hills. No two of these platforms were of identical height, some providing an elevation of no more than a dozen feet, others looming hundreds of feet in the air. Whole neighborhoods rose atop giant pedestals several dozen feet high and more than a square mile in area; certain significant buildings had platforms of their own, standing as if on stilts above their surroundings; alternations of high platforms and low ones created eye-jiggling vistas of startling contour.

What might have been an effect of sheerly mechanical whimsy, rapidly coming to seem brutal or arbitrary or fatiguing to behold, was softened and mellowed by tropical plantings unrivaled in Valentine's experience. At the base of every platform grew dense beds of broad-crowned trees, interlaced branch by branch to form impenetrable cloaks. Leafy vines cascaded over the platform walls. The wide ramps that led from street level to the higher platforms were bordered by generous concrete tubs housing clusters of bushes whose narrow tapered leaves were marked with astonishing splashes of color, claret and cobalt and vermilion and scarlet and indigo and topaz and sapphire and amber and jade hues all mixed together in irregular patterns. And in the great public places of the city were the most startling displays of all, gardens of the famous animate plants that grew wild a few hundred miles to the south, on the torrid coast that looked toward the distant desert continent of Suvrael. These plants—and plants they were, for they manufactured their food by photosynthesis and lived their lives rooted to a single place—had a fleshy look to

306

them, with arms that moved and coiled and grasped, eyes that stared, tubular bodies that undulated and swayed, and though they derived nourishment enough from sunlight and water they were quite willing and able to devour and digest any small creature rash enough to come within their reach. Elegantly arranged groups of them, bordered by low stone walls that served as warnings as well as decorations, were planted everywhere in Stoien. Some were as tall as small trees, others short and globular, still others bushy and angular. All were in constant motion, reacting to breezes, odors, sudden shouts, the voices of their keepers, and other stimuli. Valentine found them sinister but fascinating. He wondered if a collection of them might not be brought to Castle Mount.

"Why not?" Carabella said. "They can be kept alive as sideshow displays in Pidruid. There ought to be a way to keep them in good health at Lord Valentine's Castle."

Valentine nodded. "We'll hire a staff of keepers out of Stoien. We'll find out what they eat and have it shipped up to the Mount regularly."

Sleet shuddered. "These creatures give me a creepy feeling, my lord. Do you find them so lovely?"

"Not exactly lovely," said Valentine. "Interesting."

"As I suppose you found the mouthplants, eh?"

"The mouthplants, yes!" Valentine cried. "We'll bring some of them to the Castle too!"

Sleet groaned.

Valentine paid little notice. His face glowed with sudden enthusiasm. Taking Sleet and Carabella by the hands, he said, "Each Coronal has added something to the Castle: an observatory, a library, a parapet, a battlement of prisms and shields, an armory, a feasting-hall, a trophy-room, reign by reign the Castle growing, changing, becoming richer and more complex. In my short time I had no chance even to think about what I would contribute. But listen: what Coronal has seen Majipoor the way I have? Who has traveled so far, in so turbulent a fashion? To commemorate my adventures I'll collect the weirdities I've seen, the mouthplants and these animate plants and the bladder-trees and a good-sized dwikka or two and a grove of fireshower palms and sensitivos and those singing ferns, all the wonders of our journey. There's nothing like that at the Castle now, only the little glassed-in plant-houses that Lord Confalume built. I'll do it grandly! Lord Valentine's garden! How do you like the sound of that?"

"It will be a marvel, my lord," said Carabella.

Sleet said sourly, "I would not care to stroll among the

mouthplants of Lord Valentine's garden, not for three dukedoms and the revenues of Ni-moya and Piliplok."

"We excuse you from garden tours," said Valentine, laughing.

But there would be no garden tours, nor any garden, until Valentine dwelled again in Lord Valentine's Castle. For an interminable week he idled in Stoien, waiting for Asenhart to complete his provisioning. Three of the ships were going to return to the Isle, bearing the goods bought here for island use; the other four would continue on as Valentine's surreptitious escort. The Lady had provided him with more than a hundred of her sturdiest bodyguards, under the command of the formidable hierarch Lorivade: not warriors, exactly, for there had not been violence on the Isle of Sleep since the Metamorphs last invaded it thousands of years ago, but these were competent and fearless men and women, loyal to the Lady and ready to give their lives if need be to restore the harmony of the realm. They were the nucleus of a private army—the first such military force, so far as Valentine knew, organized on Majipoor since ancient times.

At last the fleet was ready to depart. The Isle-bound ships left first, early on a warm Twoday morning, heading northnorthwest. The others waited until Seaday afternoon, when they sailed on the same course, but swung about after dark to head due east into the Gulf of Stoien.

The Stoienzar Peninsula, long and narrow, jutted like a colossal thumb out of the central mass of Alhanroel. On its southern, or ocean, side it was intolerably hot. There were few settlements on that jungled insect-ridden coast. Most of the peninsula's considerable population was clustered along the Gulf coast, which had a major city every hundred miles or so and a virtually unbroken line of fishing villages and farming districts and resort towns between. It was early summer now, and a heavy haze of heat lay over the tepid, virtually motionless waters of the Gulf. The fleet paused a day for further provisioning at Kircidane, where the coast began its sweeping northward curve, and then began the crossing to Treymone.

Valentine spent many of the quiet seaward hours alone in his cabin, practicing the use of the circlet the Lady had given him. In a week he mastered the art of entering a light dozing trance—he could slide his mind instantly below the threshold of sleep now, and just as readily emerge from it, all the while staying aware of ongoing events. In the trance-state he was able, although spottily and without much force, to make contact with other minds, to wander out aboard ship and locate the aura of a sleeping soul, sleepers being far more vulnerable to such intrusions than those who were awake. He could lightly touch Carabella's mind, or Sleet's, or Shanamir's, and transmit his own image, or some genial message of good will. Reaching a less familiar mind—that of Pandelon the carpenter, say, or the hierarch Lorivade—was still too hard for him except in the briefest, most fragmentary bursts, and he had no success at all entering minds of nonhuman origin, even ones so well known to him as those of Zalzan Kavol or Khun or Deliamber. But he was still learning. He felt his skills growing day by day, as they had when he first had taken up juggling; and this was juggling of a sort, for to use the circlet he had to occupy a position at the very center of his soul, undistracted by irrelevant thought, and coordinate all aspects of his being toward the single thrust of making contact. By the time the *Lady Thiin* was in view of Treymone, Valentine had advanced to the level where he could plant the beginnings of dreams, with events and incidents and images, in the minds of his subjects. To Shanamir he sent a dream of Falkynkip, and mounts grazing in a field, and a great gihorna-bird circilng overhead, descending in a foolish flapping of mighty wings. At table the next morning the boy described the dream in all details, except only that the bird was a milufta, a carrion-feeder, with bright orange beak and ugly blue claws. "What does it mean, that I would dream of miluftas swooping down?" Shanamir asked, and Valentine said, "Could it be that you misremember the dream, and it was another bird you saw, a gihorna, perhaps, a bird of good omen?" But Shanamir, in that straightforward and innocent way of his, merely shook his head and said, "If I can't tell a gihorna from a milufta, my lord, even in my sleep, I ought to be back in Falkynkip cleaning out the stables." Valentine looked away, hiding a smile, and resolved to work more diligently on his image-sending technique.

To Carabella he sent a dream of juggling crystal goblets filled with golden wine, and she reported it accurately, down to the tapered shape of the goblets. To Sleet he sent a dream of Lord Valentine's garden, a wonderland of glistening feathery-leaved white bushes and solemn spherical prickly things on long stems and little three-forked plants with winking playful eyes at their tips, all of them imaginary and not a mouthplant among them, and Sleet described that imaginary garden in delight, saying that if only the Coronal would plant a garden like that on Castle Mount he would be well pleased to stroll in it.

Dreams came to him as well. Almost nightly the Lady his

mother touched his soul from afar. Her serene presence passed through his sleeping spirit like a cool shaft of moonlight, calming and reassuring him. He dreamed, too, of old times on Castle Mount, memories of his early days upwelling, tournaments and races and games, his friends Tunigorn and Elidath and Stasilaine by his side, and his brother Voriax teaching him to use sword and bow, and Lord Malibor the Coronal traveling from city to city on the Mount like some grand and shining demigod, and much more of the same, a flood of images released from the depths of his mind.

Not all the dreams were agreeable. The night before the *Lady Thin* reached the mainland he saw himself going ashore, landing on some forlorn, windswept beach of low and twisted scrub that had a dull, weary look in the late afternoon light. And he began to walk inland toward Castle Mount, rising in the distance, a jagged and sharp-tipped spire. But there was a wall in his way, a wall higher than the white cliffs of the Isle of Sleep, and that wall was a band of iron, more metal than existed on all of Majipoor, a dark and terrible iron girdle that seemed to span the world from pole to pole, and he was on one side of it and Castle Mount on the other. As he drew near he perceived that the wall crackled as if with electricity, and a low humming sound came from it, and when he looked closely at it he saw his reflection in the shining metal, and the face that peered back at him out of that frightful iron band was the face of the son of the King of Dreams.

3

Treymone was the city of the celebrated tree-houses, famed throughout Majipoor. His second day ashore, Valentine went to visit them, in the coastal district just south of the mouth of the River Trey.

Nowhere else but in the Trey's alluvial plain did the tree-houses live. They had short stout trunks a little like those of dwikkas, though not nearly so thick, and their bark was a handsome pale green, with a high gloss to it. From these barrel-like boles rose sturdy flattened branches that curved upward and outward like the fingers of two hands pressed together at the heels, and viny twigs wandered from branch to branch, adhering in many places, creating a snug cup-shaped enclosure.

The tree-folk of Treymone shaped their dwellings to suit

their whims by pulling the pliant branches into the forms of rooms and corridors and fastening them into place until the natural adhesion of bark to bark made the join permanent. From the trees came leaves tender and sweet for salads, fragrant cream-colored flowers whose pollen was a mild euphoric, tart bluish fruits that had many uses, and a sweet pale sap, easily tapped, that served in place of wine. Each tree lived a thousand years or more; families maintained jealous control over them; ten thousand trees filled the plain, all mature and inhabited. Valentine saw a few skinny saplings at the edge of the district. "These," he was told, "are newly planted, to replace some that died in recent years."

"Where does a family go when its tree dies?"

"Into town," said the guide, "to what we call houses of mourning, until the new tree is grown. That may be twenty years. We dread such a thing, but it happens only one generation out of ten."

"And there's no way to grow the trees elsewhere?"

"Not an inch beyond where you see them. Only in our climate will they thrive, and only in the soil on which you stand can they grow to fullness. Elsewhere they live a year or two, small stunted things."

Quietly to Carabella Valentine said, "We can make the experiment anyway. I wonder if they can spare some of their precious soil for Lord Valentine's garden."

She smiled. "Even a small tree-house—a place where you can go when the cares of government grow too heavy, and sit hidden in the leaves, and breathe the perfume of the flowers, and pluck the fruits—oh, if you could have such a thing!"

"Someday I will," said Valentine. "And you'll sit beside me in it."

Carabella gave him a startled look. "I, my lord?"

"If not you, then who? Dominin Barjazid?" Lightly he touched her hand. "Do you think our travels together end when we reach Castle Mount?"

"We should not talk of such things now," she told him severely. To the guide she said in a louder tone, "And these young trees—how do you care for them? Are they watered often?"

From Treymone it was several weeks' journey by fast floater-car to the Labyrinth, which lay in south-central Alhanroel. The countryside here was mainly a lowland, with rich red soil in the river valley and thin, gray sandy stuff beyond it, and settlements grew more sparse as Valentine and his party moved inland. There was occasional rain, but it seemed to sink immediately into the porous soil. The weather was warm and sometimes there was an oppressive weight to the heat. Day after day slipped by in bland, monotonous driving. To Valentine this sort of travel wholly lacked the magic and mystery—now enhanced by nostalgia—of the months he had spent crossing Zimroel in Zalzan Kavol's elegant wagon. Then, every day had seemed a venture into the unknown, with fresh challenges at each turn, and always the excitement of performing, of stopping in strange towns to put on shows. Now? Everything was done for him by adjutants and aides-de-camp. He was becoming a prince again—though a prince of very modest puissance indeed, with hardly more than a hundred followers—and he was not at all certain he cared for it.

Late in the second week the landscape abruptly changed, turning rough and broken, with black flat-topped hills rising now from a dry, deeply ridged tableland. The only plants that grew here were small scraggly bushes, dark twisted things with tiny waxen leaves, and, on the higher slopes, thorny candelabra-like growths of moon-cactus, ghostly white, twice as tall as a man. Little long-legged animals with red fur and puffy yellow tails skittered about nervously, vanishing into holes whenever a floater came too close.

Deliamber said, "This is the beginning of the Desert of the Labyrinth. Soon we will see the stone cities of the ancients."

Valentine had approached the Labyrinth from the other side, the northwest, the time he had been to it in his former life. There was desert there too, and the great haunted ruined city of Velalisier; but he had come down from Castle Mount by riverboat, bypassing all the unlucky dead lands that surrounded the Labyrinth, and the texture of this bleak and forbidding zone was new to him. He found it absorbingly strange at first, especially at sunset, when the vast cloudless sky was streaked with grotesque bands of violent color and the parched soil took on an eerie metallic look. But after a few days the starkness and austerity ceased to give him pleasure, and became disturbing, unsettling, menacing. Something about this sharp desert air, perhaps, was working unfavorably on his sensibilities. He had never experienced desert before, for there was none in Zimroel and none except this interior pocket of dryness in well-watered Alhanroel. Desert conditions were something he associated with Suvrael, which he had visited often enough in dreams, all of them troublesome ones; and he could not escape the notion, irrational and bizarre, that he was riding toward a rendezvous with the King of Dreams.

After a time Deliamber said, "There are the ruins."

It was difficult at first to distinguish them from the rocks of the desert. All Valentine saw were tumbled dark monoliths, scattered as though by a giant's contemptuous hand, in little patches every mile or two. But gradually he discerned form: this was a bit of wall, this the foundation of some cyclopean palace, this perhaps an altar. Everything was built to titanic scale, although the individual groups of ruins, half covered by drifting sand, were unimpressive isolated outposts.

Valentine called the caravan to a halt at one particularly broad strew of ruins and led an inspection party to the site. He touched the rocks cautiously, fearing he might be committing some sort of sacrilege. The stone was cool, smooth to the touch, faintly encrusted by leathery growths of yellow lichen.

"And are these the work of the Metamorphs?" he asked.

Deliamber shrugged. "So we think, but no one knows."

"I have heard it said," remarked Admiral Asenhart, "that the first human settlers built these cities soon after the Landing-time, and that they were overthrown in the civil wars before the Pontifex Dvorn established government."

"Of course, few records survive of those days," said Deliamber.

Asenhart squinted at the Vroon. "Are you of a contrary opinion, then?"

"I? I? I hold no opinion at all of events of fourteen thousand years ago. I am not as old as you suspect, admiral."

The hierarch Lorivade said in a dry deep tone, "It seems unlikely to me that the early settlers would build so far from the sea. Or that they would trouble themselves to haul such huge blocks of stone about."

"Then you too think these were Metamorph cities?" said Valentine.

"The Metamorphs are wild savages who live in the jungles and dance to bring rain," Asenhart said.

Lorivade, looking bothered at the admiral's interruption, said with testy precision, "I think it altogether likely." To Asenhart she added, "Not savages, admiral, but refugees. They may well have fallen from a higher estate."

"Pushed, rather," said Carabella.

Valentine said, "The government should organize studies of these ruins, if it hasn't already been done. We need to know more about pre-human civilizations on Majipoor, and if these are Metamorph places, we might consider giving them a kind of custodianship of them. We—"

"The ruins need no custodians other than the ones they already have," said a new voice suddenly.

Valentine turned, startled. A bizarre figure had emerged from behind a monolith—a gaunt, almost fleshless man of sixty or seventy, with fierce blazing eyes set in jutting bony rims and a thin, wide, virtually toothless mouth now curved in a mocking grin. He was armed with a long narrow sword and was clad in a strange garment made entirely from the red fur of the desert-animals. Atop his head was a cap of thick yellow tail-fur, which he swept off in a grand gesture as he made a deep, sweeping bow. When he straightened, his hand rested on the pommel of his sword.

Valentine said courteously, "And are we in the presence of one of those custodians?"

"More than one," the other replied. And from the rocks there quietly came eight or ten similar fantasticos, as angular and bony as the first, and like the first all clad in scruffy fur leggings and jackets and wearing absurd furry caps. All carried swords, and all seemed ready to use them. A second group appeared behind them, materializing as though out of the air, and then a third, a good-sized troop, thirty or forty in all.

There were eleven in Valentine's party, mostly unarmed. The others were back in the floater-cars, two hundred yards away on the main highway. While they had stood here debating nice points of ancient history, they had allowed themselves to be surrounded.

The leader said, "By what right do you trespass here?"

Valentine heard a faint clearing of the throat from Lisamon Hultin. He saw a stiffening also of Asenhart's posture. But Valentine signaled them to be calm.

He said, "May I know who it is that addresses me?"

"I am Duke Nascimonte of Vornek Crag, Overlord of the Western Marches. About me you see the chief nobles of my realm, who serve me loyally in all things."

Valentine had no recollection of a province known as the Western Marches, nor of any such duke. Possibly he had forgotten some of his geography when his mind was meddled with; but not, he suspected, quite so much. Yet he did not choose to trifle with Duke Nascimonte.

Solemnly he said, "We meant no trespass, your grace, in passing through your domain. We are travelers bound for the Labyrinth on business with the Pontifex, and this seemed the most direct route between Treymone and there."

"So it is. You would have done better to approach the Pontifex by a less direct route."

314

Liasmon Hultin roared suddenly, "Give us no trouble! Have you any idea who this man is?"

Annoyed, Valentine snapped his fingers at the giantess to silence her.

Nascimonte said blandly, "Not in the least. But he could be Lord Valentine himself and he would not pass here lightly. Lord Valentine less than any other, in fact."

"Have you some special quarrel with Lord Valentine, then?" Valentine asked.

The bandit laughed harshly. "The Coronal is my most hated enemy."

"Why, then, your hand must be set against all of civilization, for everyone owes allegiance to the Coronal and must for order's sake oppose his enemies. Can you truly be a duke, and not accept the Coronal's authority?"

"Not *this* Coronal's," Nascimonte replied. He sauntered coolly across the open space that separated him from Valentine, hand still resting on his sword, and peered closely at him. "You wear fine clothes. You smell of city comforts. You must be rich, and live in a great house somewhere high up on the Mount, and have servants to meet your every need. What would you say, if one day all that were stripped from you, eh? If by the whim of another you were cast down into poverty?"

"I have had that experience," said Valentine evenly.

"Have you, now? You, traveling in that cavalcade of floater-cars, with your retinue about you? Who are you, anyway?"

"Lord Valentine the Coronal," Valentine answered without hesitation.

Nascimonte's fiery eyes flared with rage. For an instant it appeared as if he would draw his sword; then, as if seeing a jest much to his own ferocious humor, he relaxed and said, "Yes, you are Coronal the way I am a duke. Well, Lord Valentine, your kindness will repay me for my earlier losses. The fee for crossing the zone of ruins today is one thousand royals."

"We have no such sum," Valentine said mildly.

"Then you'll make camp with us until your lackeys fetch it." He gestured to his men. "Seize them and bind them. Turn one loose—this one, the Vroon—to be the messenger." To Deliamber he said, "Vroon, carry word to those in the floaters that we hold these folk here for payment of a thousand royals, to be delivered within a month. And if you return with militia instead of money, why, bear in mind that we know these hills, and the officers of the law do not. You'll never see any of your people alive again."

315

"Wait," Valentine said, as Nascimonte's men stepped forward. "Tell me your quarrel with the Coronal."

Nascimonte scowled. "He came through this part of Alhanroel last year, returning from Zimroel where he made the grand processional. I lived then in the foothills of Mount Ebersinul, looking out on Lake Ivory, and I raised ricca and thuyol and milaile, and my plantation was the finest in the province, for my family has spent sixteen generations cultivating it. The Coronal and his party were billeted on me, as best able to meet the needs of hospitality for him, and at the height of thuyol-harvest he came to me with all his hundreds of hangers-on and lackeys, his myriad courtiers, enough mounts to graze half a continent bare, and between one Starday and the next they drank my cellars dry, they made festival in the fields and spoiled the crops, they torched the manor-house in drunken play, they shattered the dam and drowned my fields, they ruined me entirely for their own sport, and then they marched away, not even knowing what they had done to me, or caring. The moneylenders have it all now, and I live in the rocks of Vornek Crag courtesy of Lord Valentine and his friends, and where is justice? It will cost you a thousand royals to leave these ancient ruins, stranger, and though I hold you no malice I will slit your throat as coolly as Lord Valentine's men opened my dam, and with as little concern, if the money fails to come." He turned away and said again, "Bind them."

Valentine drew breath deep into his lungs and closed his eyes, and, as the Lady had taught him, let himself slip into waking sleep, into the trance that brought his circlet to life. And sent his mind out toward the dark and bitter soul of the Overlord of the Western Marches, and flooded it with love.

The effort called forth all the strength that was in him. He swayed and braced his legs, and leaned against Carabella, one hand on her shoulder, drawing further energy and vitality from her and pumping it toward Nascimonte. He understood now what price Sleet paid for his blind juggling, for this was draining him of all the stuff of life. Yet he sustained the outpouring of spirit for moment after long moment.

Nascimonte stood frozen, facing half away from him with his body twisted around, his eyes locked on Valentine's. Valentine held his grip unrelentingly on the other's soul, and bathed it with compassion until Nascimonte's iron resentments softened and loosened and dropped from him like a shell, and then into the suddenly vulnerable man Valentine poured a vision of all that had befallen him since his overthrow in Til-

316

omon so long ago, everything compressed into a single dazzling point of illumination.

He broke the contact and, staggering, lurched hard against
Carabella, who supported him unflinchingly.

Nascimonte stared at Valentine like one who has been
touched by the Divine.

Then he dropped to his knees and made the starburst sign.

"My lord—" he said thickly, deep in his throat, a barely
audible sound. "My lord—forgive me—forgive—"

4

That there should be bandits at large in this desert surprised
and dismayed Valentine, for there was little history of such
anarchy on well-mannered Majipoor. That the bandits should
be well-to-do farming folk made paupers by the callousness of
the present Coronal dismayed him also. It was not the custom
on Majipoor for the ruling class so carelessly to exploit its
position. Dominin Barjazid, if he thought he could conduct
himself that way and hold his throne for long, was not merely
a villain but a fool.

"Will you put down the usurper?" Nascimonte asked.

"In time," replied Valentine. "But there is much to do before that day arrives."

"I am yours to command, if I can be of service."

"Are there other bandits between here and the mouth of the
Labyrinth?"

Nascimonte nodded. "Many. It becomes the fashion in this
province to run wild in the hills."

"And have you influence over them, or is your title of duke
only irony?"

"They obey me."

"Good," said Valentine. "I ask you then to conduct us
through these lands to the Labyrinth, and to keep your ma-
rauding friends from delaying us in our journey."

"I will, my lord."

"But not a word to anyone of what I've shown you. Regard
me simply as an official of the Lady, on embassy to the Pontifex."

The faintest glint of suspicion flickered momentarily in
Nascimonte's eyes. Uneasily he said, "I may not proclaim you
as true Coronal? Why is that?"

Valentine smiled. "This is my entire army you see here in

317

these few floater-cars. I would not announce war against the usurper until my forces are larger. Hence this secrecy; and hence my visit to the Labyrinth. The sooner I win the support of the Pontifex the sooner the true campaign begins. How quickly can you be ready to depart?"

"Within the hour, my lord."

Nascimonte and a few of his men rode with Valentine in the lead floater. The landscape grew steadily more barren: now it was a brown and almost lifeless wasteland, where swirls of dust rose under the harsh hot wind. Occasionally men in rough clothes could be seen riding in bands of three or four, far from the main highway, pausing to peer at the travelers, but there were no incidents. On the third day Nascimonte proposed a shortcut that would save several days in reaching the Labyrinth. Unhesitatingly Valentine agreed, and the caravan plunged off to the northeast over an enormous dry lakebed and then down a tortured land of steep gullies and flat-topped eroded hills, past a range of blunt mountains of a red sandy rock, and finally out into a vast windy tableland that seemed altogether featureless, a mere expanse of grit and pebbles filling the entire horizon. Valentine saw Sleet and Zalzan Kavol exchanging troubled glances as the floaters entered this bleak useless place, and he supposed they were muttering privately about treachery and betrayal, but his own faith in Nascimonte was unshaken. He had touched the bandit chieftain's mind with his own, through the circlet of the Lady, and what he had sensed in it was not the soul of a traitor.

Another day, and another, and another, on this track through the midst of nowhere, and now Carabella was frowning, and the hierarch Lorivade looked more grim than usual, and Lisamon Hultin at last drew Valentine aside and said, as quietly as she could say anything, "What if this man Nascimonte is a hireling of the false Coronal, who has been paid to lose you in a place where no one will ever find you?"

"Then we are lost and our bones will lie here forever," said Valentine. "But I give no weight to such fears."

All the same, a certain edginess grew in him. He remained confident of Nascimonte's good faith—it seemed unlikely that any agent of Dominin Barjazid would choose so dreary and drawn-out a method of getting rid of him, when a single sword-stroke back at the Metamorph ruins would have accomplished it—but he had no real assurance that Nascimonte knew where he was going. There was no water out here, and even the mounts, able to transform any sort of organic matter into fuel, were—so said Shanamir—growing thin and slack-muscled on the scattered scrawny weeds that now were their entire fare. If anything went wrong in this place there would be no hope of rescue. But Valentine's touchstone was Autifon Deliamber: the wizard had a hearty and expert skill at self-preservation, and Deliamber looked unworried, altogether tranquil, as the drab days passed.

And at length Nascimonte halted the caravan at a place where two lines of steep bare hills converged to confine them in a high-walled narrow canyon. He said to Valentine, "Do you think we have lost our way, my lord? Come, let me show you something."

Valentine and some of the others followed him to the head of the canyon, a distance of some fifty paces. Nascimonte stretched his arms toward the immense valley that began where the canyon opened.

"Look," he said.

The valley was more desert, a giant fan-shaped expanse of pale tawny sand, spreading outward and extending northward and southward for at least a hundred miles. And precisely in the middle of that valley Valentine saw a darker circle, itself of colossal size, that rose a short way above the flat valley floor. He recognized it from an earlier time, when he had seen it from the far side: it was the giant mound of brown earth that covered the Labyrinth of the Pontifex.

"We will be at the Mouth of Blades the day after tomorrow," said Nascimonte.

There were seven mouths all told, Valentine remembered, arranged equidistantly around the enormous structure. When he had come as emissary from Voriax he had entered by way of the Mouth of Waters, on the opposite side, where the River Glayge descended through the fertile northeastern provinces from Castle Mount. That was the genteel way to reach the Labyrinth, used by high officials when they had dealings with the ministers of the Pontifex; on all other sides the Labyrinth was surrounded by far less agreeable country, the least agreeable of all being the desert through which Valentine now advanced. But there was comfort in knowing that even if he must approach through this land of deadness he would leave the Labyrinth by its happier side.

The area covered by the Labyrinth was huge, and since it was constructed on many levels, spiraling down and down and piling tier upon tier in the bowels of the planet, its actual population was incalculable. The Pontifex himself occupied only the innermost sector, to which scarcely anyone ever gained admission. In the zone surrounding that was the domain of the governmental ministers, a multitude of mysterious dedicated souls who spent all their lives toiling underground at tasks that defied Valentine's understanding, record-keeping and tax-decreeing and census-taking and such. And around the governmental zone there had developed, over thousands of years, the protective outer skin of the Labyrinth, a maze of circular passageways inhabited by millions of shadowy figures, bureaucrats and merchants and beggars and clerks and cutpurses and who knew what else, a world unto itself, where the kindly warmth of the sun was never felt, where the cool clean shafts of the moon could not penetrate, where all the beauty and wonder and joy of giant Majipoor had been exchanged for the pallid pleasures of a life underground.

The floater-cars followed the line of the outer mound for an hour or so, and came at last to the Mouth of Blades.

This was no more than a timber-roofed opening giving access to a tunnel disappearing into the earth. A line of ancient rusty swords was set in concrete across its front, forming a barrier more symbolic than actual, since they were spaced far apart. How long, Valentine wondered, does it take to turn swords rusty in this dry desert climate?

The guardians of the Labyrinth waited just within the entrance.

There were seven of them—two Hjorts, a Ghayrog, a Skandar, a Liiman, and two humans—and all were masked after the universal manner of the officials of the Pontifex. The mask too was mainly symbolic, a mere strip of some glossy yellow stuff angled across the eyes and bridge of the nose of the humans and in equivalent places on the others; but it created an effect of great strangeness about these people, as it was meant to do.

The guardians stolidly confronted Valentine and his party in silence. Deliamber said quietly to him, "They will ask a price for admission. All this is traditional. Go up to them and state your business."

To the guardians Valentine said, "I am Valentine, brother to the late Voriax, son of the Lady of the Isle, and I have come to seek audience with the Pontifex."

Not even so bizarre and provocative an announcement as that stirred much reaction from the masked ones. The Ghayrog said only, "The Pontifex admits no one to his presence."

"Then I would have audience with his high ministers, who can bear my message to the Pontifex."

"They will not see you either," replied one of the Hjorts.

Valentine said, "In that case I will make application to the

320

ministers of the ministers. Or to the ministers of the ministers of the ministers, if I must. All I ask of you is that you grant admission to the Labyrinth for my companions and me."

The guardians conferred solemnly among themselves, in low droning tones, evidently going through some ritual of a purely mechanical sort, since they barely seemed to be listening to one another. When their mutterings died away the Ghayrog spokesman swung about to face Valentine and said, "What is your offering?"

"Offering?"

"The entry-price."

"Name it and I'll pay it." Valentine signaled to Shanamir, who carried a purse of coins. But the guardians looked displeased, shaking their heads, several of them actually turning away as Shanamir produced some half-royal pieces.

"Not money," the Ghayrog said disdainfully. "An *offering*."

Valentile was baffled. In confusion he looked toward Deliamber, who moved his tentacles, waving several of them up and down in a rhythmic tossing gesture. Valentine frowned. Then he understood. Juggling!

"Sleet—Zalzan Kavol—"

From one of the cars they brought clubs and balls. Sleet, Carabella, and Zalzan Kavol stationed themselves before the guardians and, at a signal from the Skandar, began to juggle. Motionless as statues, the seven masked ones watched. The entire proceeding seemed so preposterous to Valentine that he was hard put to keep a straight face, and several times had to choke back giggles; but the three jugglers performed their routines austerely and with the utmost dignity, as though this were some crucial religious rite. They went through three complete patterns of interchange and stopped with one accord, bowing stiffly to the guardians. The Ghayrog nodded almost imperceptibly—the only acknowledgment of the performance.

"You may enter," he said.

5

They drove the floaters between the blades and into a sort of vestibule, dark and musty, that opened into a wide sloping roadway. A short distance down that and they intersected a curving tunnel, the first of the rings of the Labyrinth.

It was high-roofed and brightly lit, and could well have

been a market street in any busy city, with stalls and shops and pedestrian traffic and vehicles of all shapes and sizes floating along. But a moment's careful inspection made it clear that this was no Pidruid, no Piliplok, no Ni-moya. The people in the streets were eerily pale, with a ghostly look that told of lifetimes spent away from the rays of the sun. Their clothing was curiously archaic in style, and of dull, dark colors. There were many masked individuals, servants of the pontifical bureaucracy, unremarkable in the context of the Labyrinth and moving in the crowds without attracting the slightest attention for their maskedness. And, thought Valentine, everyone, masked and maskless alike, had a tense and drawn expression, a strange haunted look about the eyes and mouth. Out in the world of fresh air, under the warm and cheerful sun, people on Majipoor smiled freely and easily, not only with their mouths but with their eyes, their cheeks, their entire faces, their whole souls. Down in this catacomb souls were of a different sort.

Valentine turned to Deliamber. "Do you know your way around in this place?"

"Not at all. But guides should be easily come by."

"How?"

"Halt the cars, get out, stand around, look befuddled," the Vroon said. "You'll have guides aplenty in a minute."

It took less than that. Valentine, Sleet, and Carabella left their car, and instantly a boy no more than ten, who had been running along the street with some younger children, whirled about and called, "Show you the Labyrinth? One crown, all day!"

"Do you have an older brother?" Sleet asked.

The boy glared at him. "You think I'm too young? Go on, then! Find your own way around! You'll be lost in five minutes!"

Valentine laughed. "What's your name?"

"Hissune."

"How many levels must we go, Hissune, before we reach the government sector?"

"You want to go *there*?"

"Why not?"

"They're all crazy there," the boy said, grinning. "Work, work, shuffle papers all day long, mumble and mutter, work hard and hope you'll get promoted even deeper down. Talk to them and they don't even answer you. Minds all mumbly from too much work. It's seven levels under. Court of Columns first, Hall of Winds, Place of Masks, Court of Pyramids,

Court of Globes, the Arena, and then you get to the House of Records. I'll take you there. Not for one crown, though."

"How much?"

"Half a royal."

Valentine whistled. "What would you do with so much money?"

"Buy my mother a cloak, and light five candles to the Lady, and get my sister the medicine she needs." The boy winked. "And maybe a treat or two for myself."

During this exchange a goodly crowd had gathered—at least fifteen or twenty children no older than Hissune, some younger ones, and some adults, all clustered together in a tight semicircle and watching tensely to see if Hissune got the job. None of them called out, but out of the corner of his eye Valentine saw them straining for his attention, standing on tiptoes, trying to look knowledgeable and responsible. If he refused the boy's offer, he would have fifty more the next moment, a wild clamor of voices and a forest of waving hands. But Hissune seemed to know his business, and his blunt, coolly cynical approach had charm.

"All right," Valentine said. "Take us to the House of Records."

"All these cars yours?"

"That one, that, that—yes, all."

Hissune whistled. "Are you important? Where are you from?"

"Castle Mount."

"I guess you're important," the boy conceded. "But if you come from Castle Mount, what are you doing on the Blades side of the Labyrinth?"

The boy was clever. Valentine said, "We've been traveling. We've just come from the Isle."

"Ah." Hissune's eyes widened just for an instant, the first breach in his jaunty street-wise coolness. Doubtless the Isle was a virtually mythical place to him, as far off as the farthest stars, and despite himself he showed awe at finding himself in the presence of someone who had actually been there. He moistened his lips. "And how shall I call you?" he asked after a moment.

"Valentine."

"Valentine," the boy repeated. "Valentine from Castle Mount. Very nice name." He clambered into the first floater-car. As Valentine got in beside him Hissune said, "Really? *Valentine?*"

"Really."

"Very nice name," he said again. "Pay me half a royal, Valentine, and I'll show you the Labyrinth."

Half a royal, Valentine knew, was outrageous, several days' pay for a skilled artisan, and yet he made no objection: it seemed improper for someone of his station to be haggling with a child over money. Hissune, perhaps, had calculated the same thing. In any event the fee turned out to be a worthwhile investment, for the boy proved expert in the twists and turns of the Labyrinth, guiding them with surprising swiftness toward the lower and inner coils of the place. Down they went, down and around, making unexpected turns and shortcuts through narrow, barely manageable alleyways, descending on hidden ramps that seemed to make transit across implausible gulfs of space.

The Labyrinth grew darker and more intricate as they went downward. Only the outermost level was well lit. The circles within it were shadowy and sinister, with dim corridors radiating in unlikely directions from the main ones, and hints of strange statuary and architectural ornamentation vaguely visible in the musty, dismal corners. Valentine found the place disturbing. It reeked of mildew and history; it had the chill clamminess of unimaginable antiquity; it was sunless and airless and joyless, a giant cavern of forlorn dreary gloom, through which scowling harsh-eyed figures moved on errands as mysterious as their own somber selves.

Down—down—down—

The boy maintained a constant flow of chatter. He was marvelously articulate, lively and funny, somehow not at all a proper product of this morbid place. He told of tourists from Ni-moya who had been lost between the Hall of Winds and Place of Masks for a month, living on scraps provided by lower-level dwellers, but too proud to admit they were unable to find their way out. He told of the architect of the Court of Globes who had aligned every spheroid in that elaborate chamber with regard to some monumentally complex numerological system, only to find that the workmen, having lost the key to his charts, had installed everything according to an improvised system of their own: he had bankrupted himself to rebuild the whole thing in the right deployment at his own expense, discovering in the end that his computations were wrong and the pattern was impossible. "They buried him right where he fell," said Hissune. And the boy told the tale of the Pontifex Arioc, he who had, when a vacancy developed in the Ladyship, proclaimed himself female, appointed himself to the Isle, and abdicated his throne: barefoot and clad in loose flowing robes, the boy said, Arioc marched publicly out of the depths of the Labyrinth, followed by a cluster of his highest ministers, who frantically tried to dissuade him from his course. "On this spot," said Hissune, "he called the people together and told them he was now their Lady, and ordered up a chariot to take him to Stoien. And the ministers could do nothing. Nothing! I wish I had seen their faces."

Down—

All day the caravan descended. They passed through the Court of Columns, where thousands of huge gray pillars sprouted like titanic toadstools, and sluggish pools of oily black water covered the stone floor to a depth of three or four feet. They crossed the Hall of Winds, a terrifying place where cold gusts of air streamed inexplicably from finely carved stone grids in the walls. They saw the Place of Masks, a twisting corridor in which giant bodiless faces, with blind empty slits for eyes, stood mounted on marble plinths. They viewed the Court of Pyramids, a forest of stark white polyhedral figures set so close together that it was impossible to move between them, a spiky-tipped maze of monoliths, some perfectly tetrahedral but most weirdly elongated, spindly, ominous. A level below it they wandered in the celebrated Court of Globes, an even more complex structure a mile and a half long, where spherical objects, some no larger than a fist and others as big as great sea-dragons, hung eerily and invisibly suspended, illuminated from below. Hissune took care to point out the architect's grave—unmarked, a slab of black stone beneath the greatest of the globes.

Down—down—

Valentine had seen nothing of this on his earlier visit. From the Mouth of Waters one descended swiftly, through passageways used only by the Coronal and Pontifex, to the imperial lair at the heart of the Labyrinth.

Someday, thought Valentine, if I am Coronal again, it will happen that I must succeed Tyeveras as Pontifex. And when that day comes I will let the people know that I do not choose to live in the Labyrinth, but will build a palace for myself in some more cheering place.

He smiled. He wondered how many Coronals before him, seeing the hideous enormity of the Labyrinth, had vowed the same vow. And yet somehow they all, sooner or later, withdrew from the world and took up residence down here. It was easy enough now, when he was young and full of vitality, to make such resolutions—easy enough to think of taking the Pontificate out of Alhanroel altogether, off to some congenial spot on the younger continent, Ni-moya, perhaps, or Dulorn, and live among beauty and delight. He found it hard to imagine himself voluntarily walling himself up in this fantastic and repellent Labyrinth. But yet, but yet, they had all done it before him, Dekkeret and Confalume and Prestimion and Stiamot and Kinniken and the others of times gone by, they had moved from Castle Mount to this dark hole when their moment came. Perhaps it was not as bad as it seemed. Perhaps when one is Coronal long enough one is glad to retire from the heights of Castle Mount. I will think more of these matters, Valentine told himself, when the appropriate time is at hand.

The caravan of floater-cars executed a hairpin turn and entered yet a lower level.

"The Arena," Hissune announced grandly.

Valentine stared into a huge hollow chamber, so great in length and width that he was unable to see its walls, only the twinkling of distant lights in the shadowed corners. There were no visible supports to its ceiling. It was astonishing to think of the massive weight of the upper levels, those millions of people, those endless winding streets and alleyways, those buildings and statues and vehicles and all, pressing down on the roof of the Arena, and this vast nothingness resisting the colossal pressure.

"Listen," said Hissune. He scrambled out of the car, put his hands to his mouth, and unleashed a piercing cry. And echoes returned, sharp stabbing sounds bouncing from this wall and that, the first few magnified in sound, the rest diminished until they were no more than the twittering chirping sounds of droles. He sent forth another cry, and another on its heels, so that sounds crashed and reverberated all about them for more than a minute. Then, with a self-satisfied smirk, the boy returned to the car.

"What purpose does this place serve?" Valentine asked.

"None."

"None? None at all?"

"It's just an emptiness. The Pontifex Dizimaule wanted a large empty space here. Nothing ever happens in it. No one's allowed to build in it, not that anyone would want to. It just sits. It makes good echoes, don't you think? That's the only use it has. Go on, Valentine, make an echo."

Valentine smiled and shook his head. "Another time," he said.

Crossing the Arena seemed to take all day. On and on they went, never once seeing a wall or a column; it was like traversing an open plain, except for the vaguely visible ceiling far above. Nor was Valentine able to discern the moment when they began to leave the Arena. He realized after a time that the floor of the place had turned somehow into a ramp, and that they had made an imperceptible transition to a lower level that returned to the familiar claustrophobic closeness of the Labyrinth's coils. As they proceeded down this new semi-circular corridor it grew gradually more brightly lit, until soon it was nearly as well illuminated as that level close to the mouth where the shops and markets were. Ahead, rising to an extraordinary height directly before them, was a screen of some sort on which inscriptions in brilliant luminous colors could be seen.

Hissune said, "We are coming to the House of Records. I can go with you no farther."

Indeed the road terminated in a five-sided plaza in front of the great screen—which, Valentine now saw, was a kind of chronicle of Majipoor. Down its left-hand side were the names of the Coronals, a list so long that he could scarcely read its upper reaches. Down the right was the corresponding list of Pontifexes. Beside each name was the date of reign.

His eyes searched the lists. Hundreds, hundreds of names, some the familiar ones, the great resonant names of the planet's history, Stiamot, Thimin, Confalume, Dekkeret, Prestimion, and some that were only meaningless arrangements of letters, names that Valentine had seen when as a boy he had whiled away rainy afternoons reading the lists of the Powers, but that had no significance other than that they were on the list—Prankipin and Hunzimar and Meyk and Struin and Scaul and Spurifon, men who had held power on Castle Mount and then in the Labyrinth a thousand years ago, three thousand, five, had been the center of all conversation, the object of all homage, had danced across the imperial stage and done their little show and vanished into history. Lord Spurifon, he thought. Lord Scaul. Who were they? What color was their hair, what games did they enjoy, what laws had they decreed, how calmly and bravely had they met their deaths? What impact had they had on the lives of the billions of Majipoor, or had they none? Some, Valentine saw, had ruled only a few years as Coronal, carried off quickly to the Labyrinth by the death of a Pontifex. And some had occupied the summit of Castle Mount for a generation. This Lord Meyk, Coronal for thirty years, and Pontifex for—Valentine scanned the dizzying lists—Pontifex for twenty more. Fifty years of supreme power, and who knew anything of Lord Meyk and Meyk the Pontifex today?

He looked toward the bottom of the lists, where they trailed off into blankness. Lord Tyeveras—Lord Malibor—Lord Voriax—Lord Valentine—

That was where the left-hand list ended, of course. Lord Valentine, reign three years old and unfinished—

Lord Valentine, at least, would be remembered. Not for him the oblivion of the Spurifons and Scauls; for they would tell the tale on Majipoor, for generations to come, of the dark-haired young Coronal who was cast by treachery into a fair-haired body, and lost his throne to the son of the King of Dreams. But what would they say of him? That he was a guileless fool, as comic a figure as Arioc who made himself Lady of the Isle? That he was a weakling who had failed to guard himself against evil? That he had suffered an astounding fall, and had valiantly regained his place? How would the history of Lord Valentine be told, a thousand years hence? One thing he prayed, as he stood before the great list of the House of Records: let it not be said of Lord Valentine that he regained his throne with magnificent heroism, and then ruled feebly and aimlessly for fifty years. Better to abandon the Castle to the Barjazid than to be known for that.

Hissune tugged at his hand.

"Valentine?"

He looked down, startled.

The boy said, "I leave you here. The people of the Pontifex will come for you soon."

"Thank you, Hissune, for all you've done. But how will you get back by yourself?"

Hissune winked. "It won't be by walking, I promise you that." He peered solemnly up and said, after a pause, "Valentine?"

"Yes?"

"Aren't you supposed to have dark hair and a beard?"

Valentine laughed. "You think I'm the Coronal?"

"Oh, I know you are! It's written all over your face. Only—only your face is wrong."

"It's not a bad face," said Valentine lightly. "A little more kindly than my old one, and maybe more handsome. I think I'm going to keep it. I suppose whoever had it first has no more need for it now."

The boy's eyes were wide. "Are you in disguise, then?"

"You might say that."

"I thought so." He put his small hand in Valentine's. "Well, good luck, Valentine. If you ever come back to the Labyrinth, ask for me and I'll be your guide again, and the next time for free. Remember my name: Hissune."

"Goodbye, Hissune."

The boy winked again, and was gone.

Valentine looked toward the great screen of history.

Lord Tyeveras—Lord Malibor—Lord Voriax—Lord Valentine—

And perhaps someday Lord Hissune, he thought. Why not? The boy seemed at least as qualified as many who had ruled, and probably would have had sense enough not to drink Dominin Barjazid's. drugged wine. I must remember him, he told himself. I must remember him.

6

From a gateway at the far side of the plaza of the House of Records now came three figures, a Hjort and two humans, in the masks of Labyrinthine officialdom. Unhurriedly they advanced toward the place where Valentine stood with Deliamber, Sleet, and a few others.

The Hjort gave Valentine careful scrutiny and did not seem awed.

"Your business here?" she asked.

"To apply for an audience with the Pontifex."

"An audience with the Pontifex," the Hjort repeated in wonder, as if Valentine had said, To apply for a pair of wings, To apply for permission to drink the ocean dry. "An audience with the Pontifex!" She laughed. "The Pontifex grants no audiences."

"Are you his chief ministers?"

The laughter was louder. "This is the House of Records, not the Court of Thrones. There are no ministers of state here."

The three officials turned and started back toward the gateway.

"Wait!" Valentine called.

He slipped into the dream-state and sent an urgent vision toward them. There was no specific content to it, only a broad and general sense that the stability of things was in peril, that the bureaucracy itself was sorely threatened, and that only they could stave off the forces of chaos. They walked on, and Valentine redoubled the intensity of his sending, until he began to sweat and tremble with the effort of it. They halted. The Hjort looked around.

"What do you want here?" she asked.

"Admit us to the ministers of the Pontifex."

There was a whispered conference.

"What do we do?" Valentine asked Deliamber. "Juggle for them?"

"Try to be patient," the Vroon murmured.

Valentine found that difficult; but he held his tongue, and after some moments the officials returned to say that he could enter, and five of his companions. The others must take lodgings on an upper level. Valentine scowled. But there seemed no arguing with these masked ones. He chose Deliamber, Carabella, Sleet, Asenhart, and Zalzan Kavol to continue on with him.

"How will the rest find lodgings?" he asked.

The Hjort shrugged. That was none of her affair.

From the shadows to Valentine's left came a high clear voice. "Does someone need a guide to the upper levels?"

Valentine chuckled. "Hissune? Still here?"

"I thought I might be needed."

"You are. Find a decent place for my people to stay, in the outer ring near the Mouth of Waters, where they can wait for me until I've finished down here."

Hissune nodded. "I ask only three crowns."

"What? You need a ride up to the top anyway! And five minutes ago you said that the next time you were my guide, you wouldn't charge anything!"

"That's next time," replied Hissune gravely. "This is still this time. Would you deprive a poor boy of his livelihood?"

Sighing, Valentine said to Zalzan Kavol, "Give him three crowns."

The boy hopped into the first car. Shortly the entire caravan swung around and departed. Valentine and his five companions passed through the gateway of the House of Records.

Corridors went in all directions. In poorly lit cubicles clerks bent low over mounds of documents. The air was musty and dry here; the general feel of the place was even more repellent than that of the earlier levels. This, Valentine realized, was the administrative core of Majipoor, the place where the real business of governing twenty billion beings was carried on. The awareness that these scurrying gnomes, these burrowers in the earth, held the actual power of the world chilled him.

He had tended to think it was the Coronal who was the true king, and the Pontifex a mere figurehead, since it was the Coronal who was seen actively commanding the forces of order whenever chaos threatened, the vigorous and dynamic Coronal, whereas the Pontifex remained immured down below, emerging from the Labyrinth only on the highest occasions of state.

But now he was not so certain.

The Pontifex himself might be merely a crazy old man, but the minions of the Pontifex, these hundreds of thousands of drab bureaucrats in their odd little masks, might collectively wield more authority on Majipoor than the dashing Coronal and all his princely aides. Down here the tax rolls were determined, here the balances of trade between province and province were adjusted, here the maintenance of highways and parks and educational establishments and all the other functions under provincial control were coordinated. Valentine was not at all convinced that true central government was possible on a world as big as Majipoor, but at least the basic forms of it existed, the structural outlines, and he saw, as he moved through the inner maze of the Labyrinth, that government on Majipoor was not altogether a matter of grand processionals and dream-sendings. The mighty hidden bureaucracy down here did most of the work.

And he was caught in its toils. There were lodgings several levels down from the House of Records for provincial officials who were visiting the Labyrinth on government business; there he was given a suite of modest rooms, and there he stayed, ignored, for the next few days. There seemed to be no way to move beyond this point. As Coronal he would have the right of immediate access to the Pontifex, of course; but he was not Coronal, not in any effective sense, and to claim that he was would probably make it impossible for him to proceed at all.

He recalled, after some rooting about in his memory, the names of the chief ministers of the Pontifex. Unless things had changed lately, Tyeveras kept five plenipotentiary officials close by him—Hornkast, his high spokesman; Dilifon, his private secretary; Shinaam, a Ghayrog, his minister of external affairs; Sepulthrove, his minister of scientific matters and personal physician; and Narrameer, his dream-speaker, who was rumored to be the most powerful of all, the adviser who had chosen Voriax and then Valentine to be Coronal.

But to reach any of these five seemed as hard as to reach the Pontifex himself. Like Tyeveras they were buried in the depths, remote, inaccessible. Valentine's skill with the circlet his mother had given him did not extend to making contact with the mind of someone unknown to him, at an unknown distance.

331

He learned shortly that two lesser, but still significant, officials served as the guardians of the central levels of the Labyrinth. These were the imperial major-domos, Dondak-Sajamir of the Su-Suheris stock and Gitamorn Suul, a human. "But," said Sleet, who had been talking with the keepers of the hostelry, "these two have been feuding for a year or more. They cooperate with one another as little as possible. And you must have the approval of both in order to see the higher ministers."

Carabella snorted in annoyance. "We'll spend the rest of our lives gathering dust down here! Valentine, why are we bothering with the Labyrinth at all? Why not clear out of here and march straight for Castle Mount?"

"My idea exactly," said Sleet.

Valentine shook his head. "The support of the Pontifex is essential. So the Lady told me, and I agree."

"Essential for what?" Sleet demanded. "The Pontifex sleeps far below the ground. He knows nothing of anything. Does the Pontifex have any army to lend you? Does the Pontifex even exist?"

"The Pontifex has an army of petty clerks and officials," Deliamber pointed out mildly. "We will find them extremely useful. They, not warriors, control the balance of power in our world."

Sleet was unconvinced. "I say hoist the starburst banner and sound the trumpets and bang the drums and set out across Alhanroel, proclaiming you as Coronal and letting the whole world know of Dominin Barjazid's little trick. In each city along the way, you meet with the key people and win their support with your warmth and sincerity, and maybe a little help from the Lady's circlet. By the time you're at Castle Mount, ten million people are marching behind you, and the Barjazid will surrender without a fight!"

"A pretty vision," said Valentine. "But I think we still must have the instrumentalities of the Pontifex working for us before we try to make any open challenge. I will pay calls on these two major-domos."

In the afternoon he was conducted to the headquarters of Dondak-Sajamir—a surprisingly bleak little office deep in a tangle of tiny clerkish cubicles. For more than an hour Valentine was kept waiting in a cramped and cluttered vestibule, before at last being admitted to the major-domo's presence.

Valentine was not entirely sure how to manage things with a Su-Suheris. Was one head Dondak and the other Sajamir? Did you address both at once, or speak only to the head that spoke to you? Was it proper to keep your attention moving from one head to the other while talking?

Dondak-Sajamir regarded Valentine as though from a great height. There was tense silence in the office as the four cool green eyes of the alien dispassionately surveyed the visitor. The Su-Suheris was a slender, elongated creature, hairless and smooth-skinned, tubular and shoulderless in form, with a rod-shaped neck that rose like a pedestal to a height of ten or twelve inches and forked to provide support for the two narrow spindle-shaped heads. He bore himself with such an air of superiority that one could easily think that the office of major-domo to the Pontifex was far more important than that of the Pontifex himself. But some of that frosty hauteur, Valentine knew, was simply a function of the major-domo's race: a Su-Suheris could not help looking naturally imperious and disdainful.

Eventually Dondak-Sajamir's left-hand head said, "Why have you come here?"

"To apply for an audience with the chief ministers of the Pontifex."

"So it says in your letter. But what business do you have with them?"

"A matter of the greatest urgency, an affair of state."

"Yes?"

"You hardly expect me to discuss it with anyone below the highest levels of authority, surely."

Dondak-Sajamir considered that point interminably. When he spoke again, it was from the right-hand head. The second voice was much deeper than the first. "If I waste the time of the chief ministers, it will go hard for me."

"If you place obstacles between me and my seeing them, it will also go hard for you, ultimately."

"A threat?"

"Not at all. I can tell you only that the consequences of their not receiving the information I bear will be very serious for all of us—and no doubt they will be distressed to learn that it was you who kept that information from reaching them."

"Not I alone," said the Su-Suheris. "There is a second major-domo, and we must act jointly in approving applications of this sort. You have not spoken to my colleague yet."

"No."

"She is insane. She has deliberately and malevolently withheld her cooperation from me for many months." Now Dondak-Sajamir spoke from both heads simultaneously, in

333

tones not quite an octave apart. The effect was weirdly disconcerting. "Even if I gave you approval, she would refuse. You will never get to see the chief ministers."

"But this is impossible! Can't we go around her somehow?"

"It would be illegal."

"If she blocks all legitimate business, though——"

The Su-Suheris looked indifferent. "The responsibility is hers."

"No," Valentine said. "You both share it! You can't simply say that because she won't cooperate, I can't go forward, when the survival of the government itself is at stake!"

"Do you think so?" asked Dondak-Sajamir.

The question left Valentine baffled. Was it the idea of a threat to the realm that he was challenging, or merely the notion that he bore equal responsibility for blocking Valentine?

Valentine said, after a moment, "What do you suggest I do?"

"Return to your home," said the major-domo, "and live a fruitful and happy life, and leave the problems of government to those of us whose fate it is to wrestle with them."

7

He had no better satisfaction from Gitamorn Suul. The other major-domo was less supercilious than the Su-Suheris, but hardly more cooperative.

She was a woman ten or twelve years older than Valentine, tall and dark-haired, with a businesslike, competent air about her. She did not appear at all insane. On her desk, in an office notably more cheerful and attractive, though no larger, than Dondak-Sajamir's, was a file containing Valentine's application. She tapped it several times and said, "You can't see them, you know."

"May I ask why not?"

"Because no one sees them."

"No one?"

"No one from outside. It is no longer done."

"Is that because of the friction between you and Dondak-Sajamir?"

Gitamorn Suul's lips quirked testily. "That idiot! But no—even if he were performing his duties properly, it still wouldn't be possible for you to reach the ministers. They don't want to be bothered. They have heavy responsibilities. The Pontifex is old, you know. He gives little time to matters of government, and therefore the burdens on those about him have increased. Do you understand?"

"I *must* see them," said Valentine.

"I can't help that. Not even for the most urgent reason can they be disturbed."

"Suppose," Valentine said slowly, "the Coronal had been overthrown, and a false ruler held possession of the Castle?"

She pushed up her mask and looked at him in astonishment. "Is that what you want to tell them? Here. Application dismissed." Rising, she made brisk shooing gestures at him. "We have madmen enough in the Labyrinth already, without new ones coming down out of—"

"Wait," said Valentine.

He let the trance-state possess him, and summoned the power of the circlet. Desperately he reached toward her soul with his, touched it, enfolded it. It had not been part of his plan to reveal much to these minor officials, but there seemed no alternative but to take her into his confidence. He sustained the contact until he felt himself growing dizzy and weak; then he broke it off and returned hurriedly to full wakefulness. She was staring at him, dazed; her cheeks were flushed, her eyes were wild, her breasts heaved in agitation. It was a moment before she could speak.

Finally she said, "What kind of trick is that?"

"No trick. I am the Lady's son, and she herself taught me the art of sendings."

"Lord Valentine is a dark-haired man."

"So he was. Not any longer."

"You ask me to believe—"

"Please," he said. He threw all the intensity of his spirit into the word. "Please. Believe me. Everything depends on my telling the Pontifex what has happened."

But her suspicions ran deep. From Gitamorn Suul came no kneelings, no homages, no starburst gesticulations, only a kind of sullen bewilderment, as if she might be inclined to think his bizarre story was true, but wished he had inflicted it on some other functionary.

She said, "The Su-Suheris would veto anything I proposed."

"Even if I showed him what I've shown you?"

She shrugged. "His obstinacy is legendary. Not even to save the life of the Pontifex would he approve one of my recommendations."

"But this is madness!"

"Exactly so. You've talked to him?"

"Yes," Valentine said. "He seemed unfriendly and puffed up with pride. But not mad."

"Deal with him a little longer," Gitamorn Suul advised, "before you form your final judgment of him."

"What if we were to forge his approval, so that I could go in without his knowing?"

She looked shocked. "You want me to commit a crime?"

Valentine struggled to maintain his even temper. "A crime has already been committed, and not a trifling one," he said in a low, steady voice. "I am Coronal of Majipoor, deposed through treachery. Your help is vital to my restoration. Doesn't that override all these petty regulations? Can't you see that I have the power to pardon you for breaking those regulations?" He leaned toward her. "Time is wasting. Castle Mount houses a usurper. I run back and forth between subordinates of the Pontifex, when I should be leading an army of liberation across Alhanroel. Give me your approval, and let me be on my way, and there'll be rewards for you when everything's again as it should be on Majipoor."

Her eyes were cold and suddenly bleak. "Your story makes great demands on my powers of belief. What if it is all false? What if you are in the pay of Dondak-Sajamir?"

Valentine groaned. "I beg you—".

"No. It's entirely likely. This is a trap, perhaps. You, your fantastic story, some sort of hypnosis, all designed to destroy me, to leave the Su-Suheris unchallenged here, to give him the supreme power he has so long desired—"

"I swear by the Lady my mother I have not lied to you."

"A true criminal would swear by anybody's mother, but what is that?"

Valentine hesitated, then boldly reached forth and took Gitamorn Suul's hands in his. Intently he stared into her eyes. What he was about to do was disagreeable to him, but so was all that these petty bureaucrats had been doing to him. The time had come for a little shamelessness, or he would be forever entangled down here.

He said, peering close, "Even if I were in Dondak-Sajamir's pay, I could never betray a woman as beautiful as you."

She looked scornful. But color flared again in her cheeks.

He went on, "Trust me. Believe in me. I am Lord Valentine, and you will be one of the heroes of my return. I know the thing you want most in the world, and it will be yours when I have regained the Castle."

"You know it?"

"Yes," he whispered, gently stroking the hands that now lay limply in his. "To have sole authority over the inner Labyrinth, is that not it? To be the only major-domo?"

She nodded as though in a dream.

"It will be done," he said. "Ally yourself with me, and Dondak-Sajamir will be stripped of his rank, for making himself an obstacle to me. Will you do that? Will you help me reach the chief ministers, Gitamorn Suul?"

"It will be—difficult—"

"But it can be done! Anything can be done! And when I am Coronal again, the Su-Suheris loses his post! I promise you that."

"Swear it!"

"I swear it," Valentine said passionately, feeling foul and depraved. "I swear it on my mother's name. I swear it by all that's holy. Is it agreed?"

"Agreed," she said in a small faltering voice. "But how is it to be done? You need both signatures on the pass, and if mine is on it, he'll refuse to add his."

Valentine said, "Write me out a pass and sign it. I'll go back to him and talk him into countersigning it."

"He will never do it."

"Let me work on him. I can be persuasive. Once I have his signature, I can enter the inner Labyrinth and achieve what I must achieve. When I emerge, it will be with the full authority of the Coronal—and I will have Dondak-Sajamir removed from office, that I promise you."

"But how will you get his signature? He's refused all countersignatures for months!"

"Leave that to me," said Valentine.

She drew from her desk a dark green cube of some sleek glistening material and placed it briefly in a machine that cast an incandescent yellow glow over it. When she removed it, the surface of the cube was infused with a new brightness. "Here. This is your pass. But I warn you that without his countersignature it is worthless."

"I'll get it," Valentine said.

He returned to Dondak-Sajamir. The Su-Suheris was reluctant to see him, but Valentine persevered.

"I understand now your loathing of Gitamorn Suul," he said.

Dondak-Sajamir smiled coolly. "Is she not hateful? I suppose she refused your application."

"Oh, no," said Valentine, taking the cube from his cloak and placing it before the major-domo. "She granted that will-

337

ingly enough, knowing that you had refused me and her permission would be worthless. It was her other rejection that wounded me so deeply."

"And which was that?"

Serenely Valentine said, "This may sound foolish to you, or even repellent, but I was powerfully overcome by her beauty. To human eyes, I must tell you, that woman has extraordinary physical presence, a nobility of bearing, a luminous erotic force, that—well, no matter. I threw myself before her in an embarrassingly naïve way. I made myself open and vulnerable. And she mocked me cruelly. She scorned me in a way that was like a blade twisting in my vitals. Can you understand that, that she would be so merciless, so contemptuous, toward a stranger who had only the warmest and most profoundly passionate feelings for her?"

"Her beauty escapes me," said Dondak-Sajamir. "But I know her coldness and arrogance quite well."

"Now I share your enmity for her," Valentine said. "If you will have me, I offer myself to your service, so that we can work together to destroy her."

Dondak-Sajamir said thoughtfully, "Yes, this would be a fine moment to bring about her downfall. But how?"

Valentine tapped the cube that rested on the major-domo's desk. "Add your countersignature to this pass. I'll then be free to enter the inner Labyrinth. While I'm there, you launch an official inquiry into the circumstances under which I was admitted, claiming that you gave no such permission. When I've returned from my business with the Pontifex, summon me to testify. I'll say you rejected my application, and that I got the pass, already fully countersigned, from Gitamorn Suul, never suspecting it might be forged by someone meaning to spite you by admitting me. Your accusation of forgery, coupled with my testimony that you had declined to approve my application, will be her ruination. What do you say?"

"A magnificent plan," replied Dondak-Sajamir. "I could have devised nothing better!"

The Su-Suheris slipped the cube into a machine that gave it a brilliant pink glow superimposed over Gitamorn Suul's yellow one. The pass now was valid. All this intrigue, Valentine thought, was nearly as much of a strain on the mind as the intricacies of the Labyrinth itself; but it was done, and done successfully. Now let these two plot and scheme against each other as they wished, while he made his way unimpeded toward the ministers of the Pontifex. They were apt to be disappointed with the way he fulfilled his promises to them, for he

338

intended, if he could, to sweep both the bickering rivals from power. But he did not ask pure and total saintliness of himself in his dealings with those whose chief role in the government appeared to be to impede and obstruct.

He took the cube from Dondak-Sajamir and inclined his head in gratitude.

"May you come to have all the power and prestige you deserve," said Valentine unctuously, and departed.

8

The guardians of the innermost Labyrinth seemed astounded that anyone from outside had contrived to gain entry to their realm. But though they subjected the pass-cube to a thorough scanning, they grudgingly conceded that it was legitimate and sent Valentine and his companions inward.

A narrow, snub-snouted car carried them silently and swiftly down the passages of this interior universe. The masked officials who accompanied them did not seem to be guiding it themselves, nor would that have been an easy task, for in these levels the Labyrinth branched and rebranched, curved and recurved. Any intruder would quickly become hopelessly bewildered amid these thousand twistings, twinings, sinuosities, and tangles. The car, though, appeared to be floating over a concealed guidance track that controlled its journey, along a swift if not particularly straightforward route, deeper and deeper into the coils of sequestered alleys.

At checkpoint after checkpoint Valentine was interrogated by disbelieving functionaries almost unable to comprehend the notion that an outlander had come calling on the ministers of the Pontifex. Their endless thrusts were wearying but futile. He waved his pass-cube at them as though it were a magic wand. "I am on a mission of the highest urgency," he said again and again, "and will speak only with the supreme members of the Pontifical court." Arming himself with all the dignity and presence at his command, Valentine brushed aside every objection, every quibble. "It will not go well for you," he warned, "if you delay me further."

And finally—it felt as though a hundred years had passed since Valentine had juggled his way into the Labyrinth at the Mouth of Blades—he found himself standing before Shinaam, Dilifon, and Narramee, three of the five great ministers of the Pontifex.

They received him in a somber and clammy chamber made of huge blocks of black stone, with a lofty ceiling and ornamentation of pointed arches. It was a heavy, oppressive place more suitable as a dungeon than a council-chamber. Entering it, Valentine felt all the weight of the Labyrinth bearing down on him, level upon level, Arena and House of Records and Court of Globes and Hall of Winds and all the rest, the dark corridors, the cluttered cubicles, the multitudes of toiling clerks. Somewhere far above, the sun was shining, the air was fresh and crisp, a breeze blew out of the south, bearing the perfume of alabandinas and eldirons and tanigales. And he was here pinned beneath a giant mound of earth and miles of tortuous passageways, in a kingdom of eternal night. His journey downward and inward in the Labyrinth had left him feverish and drawn, as though he had not slept for weeks.

He touched his hand to Deliamber and the Vroon gave him a tingling jolt of energy, shoring up his ebbing strength. He looked to Carabella, who smiled and blew him a kiss. He looked to Sleet, who nodded and grinned grimly. He looked to Zalzan Kavol, and the fierce grizzled Skandar made a quick juggling motion with all his hands by way of encouragement. His companions, his friends, his bulwarks throughout all this long and strange travail.

He looked toward the ministers.

Maskless, they sat side by side on chairs majestic enough to be thrones. Shinaam was in the center, the minister of external affairs, of Ghayrog birth, reptilian-looking, with chilly lidless eyes and busily flicking forked red tongue and hair of a coarse snaky appearance that moved in slow wriggles. To his right was Dilifon, private secretary to Tyeveras, a frail and spectral figure, hair as white as Sleet's, skin parched and withered, eyes blazing like jets of fire out of the ancient face. And on the other side of the Ghayrog was Narrameer, the imperial dream-speaker, a slender and elegant woman who must surely be of great age, for her association with Tyeveras went back as far as the long-ago era when he was Coronal. Yet she seemed to be barely of middle years. Her skin was smooth and unlined, her auburn hair was lustrous and full. Only by the remote and enigmatic expression of her eyes could Valentine detect any hint of the wisdom, the experience, the accumulated power of many decades, that was hers. Some sorcery at work, he decided.

"We have read your petition," said Shinaam. His voice was deep and crisp, with the merest trace of a hiss in it. "The story you bring strains our credulity."

340

"Have you spoken with the Lady my mother?"

"We have spoken with the Lady, yes," the Ghayrog replied coolly. "She accepts you as her son."

"She urges us to cooperate with you," said Dilifon in a cracked and scratchy voice.

"In sendings she appeared to us," said Narrameer, softly, musically, "and commended you to us, asking that we give you such aid as you require."

"Well, then?" Valentine demanded.

Shinaam said, "The possibility exists that the Lady is capable of being deceived."

"You think I'm an impostor?"

"You ask us to believe," said the Ghayrog, "that the Coronal of Majipoor was taken unawares by a younger son of the King of Dreams and evicted from his own body, that he was stripped of his memory and placed—such fragment of him as remained—in quite another body that conveniently happened to be available, and that the usurper successfully entered the empty husk of the Coronal and imposed his own consciousness on it. We find it strenuous to believe such things."

"The skills exist to move bodies from mind to mind," said Valentine. "There is precedent."

"No precedent," Dilifon said, "for the displacement of a Coronal in that fashion."

"Nevertheless it happened," Valentine replied. "I am Lord Valentine, restored to my memory by the kindness of the Lady, and I ask the backing of the Pontifex in regaining the responsibilities to which he called me upon my brother's death."

"Yes," said Shinaam. "If you are who you claim to be, it would be fitting for you to return to Castle Mount. But how are we to know that? These are serious matters. They portend civil war. Shall we advise the Pontifex to plunge the world into agony on the mere assertion of some young stranger who—"

"I've already convinced my mother of my authenticity," Valentine pointed out. "My mind lay open to her at the Isle, and she saw me to be who I am." He touched the silver circlet at his brow. "How do you think I came by this device? It was her gift, by her own hands, as we stood together in Inner Temple."

Quietly Shinaam said, "That the Lady accepts and supports you is not in doubt."

"But you question her judgment?"

"We require deeper proof of your claims," said Narrameer.

341

"Then allow me to cast forth a sending here and now, so that I can convince you that I speak the truth."

"As you wish," said Dilifon.

Valentine closed his eyes and let the trance-state come upon him.

From him, with passion and conviction, came the radiant stream of his being, flooding forth as it had when he had needed to gain the trust of Nascimonte in that bleak ruin-strewn wilderness beyond Treymone, and when he had swayed the minds of the three officials at the gateway to the House of Records, and when he had revealed himself to the major-domo Gitamorn Suul. With varying degrees of success he had accomplished what had to be accomplished with all of those.

But now he felt himself unable to surmount the impenetrable skepticism of the ministers of the Pontifex.

The mind of the Ghayrog was altogether opaque to him, a wall as blank and inaccessible as the towering white cliffs of the Isle of Sleep. Valentine sensed only the most cloudy flickerings of a consciousness behind Shinaam's mental shield, and could not break through, though he poured against it everything at his command. The mind of shriveled old Dilifon was an equally remote thing, not because it was shielded but because it seemed porous, open, a honeycomb that offered no resistance: he went through it, air passing through air, encountering nothing tangible. Only with the mind of the dream-speaker Narrameer did Valentine sense contact, but that too was unsatisfactory. She seemed to be drinking in his soul, absorbing all that he was giving and letting it drain into some fathomless cavern of her being, so that he could send and send and send and never reach the center of her spirit.

Yet he refused to give up. With furious intensity he hurled forth the fullness of his soul, proclaiming himself to be Lord Valentine of Castle Mount and urging them to give proof that he was anything else. He reached deep for memories—of his mother, his royal brother, his princely education, his overthrow in Til-omon, his wanderings in Zimroel, everything that had gone into the shaping of the man who had battled his way to the bowels of the Labyrinth to gain their aid. He offered himself totally, recklessly, ferociously, until he could send no more, until he was reeling and numb with exhaustion, hanging between Sleet and Carabella like some limp and useless garment that its owner had discarded.

He brought himself up from the trance-state, fearing that he had failed.

He was trembling and weak. Sweat bathed his body. His vision was blurred and there was a savage pain in his temples.

He fought to recover his strength, closing his eyes, sucking air deep into his lungs. Then he looked up at the trio of ministers.

Their faces were harsh and somber. Their eyes were cold and unmoved. Their expressions were aloof, disdainful, even hostile. Valentine was suddenly terrified. Could these three be in league with Dominin Barjazid himself? Was he pleading before his own enemies?

But that was unthinkable and impossible, a phantom of his exhausted mind, he told himself desperately. He could not let himself believe that the plot against him had reached as far as the Labyrinth.

In a hoarse, ragged voice he said, "Well? What do you say now?"

"I experienced nothing," said Shinaam.

"I am unconvinced," said Dilifon. "Any wizard can make sendings of this sort. Your sincerity and passion can be feigned."

Narrameer said, "I agree. Through sendings can come lies as well as truth."

"No!" Valentine cried. "You had me wide open before you. You can't possibly have failed to see—"

"Not wide open enough," said Narrameer.

"What do you mean?"

She said, "Let us do a dream-speaking, you and I. Here, now, in this chamber, before these people. Let our minds truly become one. And then I can evaluate the plausibility of your story. Are you willing? Will you drink the drug with me?"

In alarm Valentine looked to his companions—and saw alarm reflected on their faces, all but that of Deliamber, whose expression was as bland and neutral as though he were someplace entirely else. Risk a speaking? Did he dare? The drug would render him unconscious, utterly transparent, wholly vulnerable. If these three were allied with the Barjazid and sought to render him helpless, there would be no easier way. Nor was this any ordinary village speaker who proposed to enter his mind; this was the speaker of the Pontifex, a woman of at least a hundred years, wily and powerful, reputed to be the true master of the Labyrinth, controlling all others, including old Tyeveras himself. Deliamber studiously was giving him no clue. This was entirely his decision to make.

"Yes," he said, his eyes directly on hers. "If nothing else avails, let it be a speaking. Here. Now."

9

They seemed to be prepared for it. At a signal, aides brought in the paraphernalia of a speaking: a thick rug of rich glowing colors, dark gold edged with scarlet and green; a slim tall decanter of polished white stone; two delicate porcelain cups. Narrameer stepped down from her lofty chair and poured the dream-wine with her own hands, offering Valentine the first cup.

He held it a moment without drinking it. He had had wine from the hands of Dominin Barjazid in Til-omon, and all had changed for him in a single draught. Was he to drink this, now, without fear of consequences? Who knew what fresh enchantment was being prepared for him? Where would he awaken, in what altered guise?

Narrameer watched him in silence. The dream-speaker's eyes were unreadable, mysterious, penetrating. She was smiling, an altogether ambiguous smile, whether one of encouragement or of triumph Valentine could not tell. He raised the cup in brief salute and put it to his lips.

The effect of the wine was instantaneous and unexpectedly powerful. Valentine swayed dizzily. Fogs and cobwebs assailed his mind. Was this stuff stronger than what the dream-speaker Tisana had given him in Falkynkip so long ago—some special demon-brew of Narrameer's? Or was it simply that he was more susceptible at this moment, weakened and drained as he was by his using of the circlet? Through eyes that were becoming unwilling to focus he saw Narrameer down her own wine, toss the empty cup to an aide, and slide swiftly out of her robe. Her naked body was supple, smooth, youthful—flat belly, slender thighs, high round breasts. A sorcery, he thought. A sorcery, yes. Her skin was a deep shade of brown. Her nipples, almost black, stared at him like blind eyes.

He was already too deeply drugged to manage his own disrobing. The hands of his friends plucked at the catches and hasps of his clothing. He felt cold air about him and knew he was naked.

Narrameer beckoned him to the dream-rug.

On wobbly legs Valentine went to her, and she drew him

down. He closed his eyes, imagining he was with Carabella, but Narrameer was nothing at all like Carabella. Her embrace was dry and cold, her flesh hard, unresilient. She had no warmth, no vibrance. That youthfulness of hers was only a cunning projection. Lying in her arms was like lying on a bed of smooth chilly stone.

An all-engulfing pool of darkness was rising about him, a thick warm oily fluid growing deeper and deeper, and Valentine let himself slip easily into it, feeling it slide up comfortingly about his legs, his waist, his chest.

It was much like the time the great sea-dragon had smashed Gorzval's ship, and he had found himself being sucked down by the whirlpool. Not resisting was so easy, so much easier than fighting. To yield all will, to relax, to accept whatever might befall, to allow himself to be swept under—so tempting, so very appealing. He was tired. He had struggled a long time. Now he could rest and allow the black tide to cover him. Let others battle valiantly for honor and power and acclaim. Let others—

No.

That was what they wanted: to ensnare him in his own weaknesses. He was too trusting, too guileless; he had supped with an enemy, unknowingly, and had been undone; he would be undone once more if he abandoned the effort now. This was not the moment for slipping into warm dark pools.

He began to swim. At first the going was difficult, for the pool was deep and the black fluid, viscous and heavy, tugged at his arms. But after a few strokes Valentine found a way to make his body more angular, a blade slicing deep. He moved rapidly and more rapidly yet, arms and legs pistoning in smooth coordination. The pool that had tempted him with oblivion now offered him support: Buoyant, firm, it bore him up as he swam swiftly toward the distant shore. The sun, bright, immense, a great purple-yellow globe, cast dazzling rays, a track of fire over the sea.

"Valentine."

The voice was deep, rolling, a sound like thunder. He did not recognize it.

"Valentine, why are you swimming so hard?"

"To reach the shore."

"But why do that?"

Valentine shrugged and kept swimming. He saw an island, a broad white beach, a jungle of tall slender trees growing one up against the next, with tangled vines binding their crowns into a dense canopy. But though he swam and swam and swam he came no closer to it.

"You see?" the great voice said. "There's no sense in bothering!"

"Who are you?" Valentine asked.

"I am Lord Spurifon," came the majestic resonant reply.

"Who?"

"Lord Spurifon the Coronal, successor to Lord Scaul now Pontifex, and I tell you to give up this folly. Where can you hope to get?"

"Castle Mount," answered Valentine, swimming harder.

"But I am Coronal!"

"Never—heard of—you—"

Lord Spurifon made a shrill shrieking sound. The smooth oily surface of the sea rippled and then grew puckered, as though a million needles were piercing it from below. Valentine forced himself onward, no longer trying to be angular, but rather now transforming himself into something blunt and obstinate, a log with arms, battering through the turbulence.

Now the shore was within reach. He lowered his feet and felt sand below, hot, squirming, writhing sand that ran in trickles away from him wherever he touched it, making walking a chore, but not so grave a chore that he was unable to push himself to land. He scrambled up on the beach and knelt a moment. When he looked up, a pale, thin man with worried blue eyes was studying him.

"I am Lord Hunzimar," he said mildly. "Coronal of Coronals, never to be forgotten. And these are my immortal companions." He gestured, and the beach was filled with men much like himself, insignificant, diffident, trifling. "This is Lord Struin," declared Lord Hunzimar, "and this Lord Prankipin, and Lord Meyk, and Lord Scaul, and Lord Spurifon. Coronals of grandeur and puissance. Bow down before us!"

Valentine laughed. "You're all completely forgotten!"

"No! No!"

"Such a squeaking!" He pointed at the last in the row. "You—Spurifon! No one remembers you."

"*Lord* Spurifon, if you please."

"And you—Lord Scaul. Three thousand years have entirely evaporated your fame."

"You are mistaken in this. My name is inscribed on the roster of the Powers."

Valentine shrugged. "So it is. But what does that matter? Lord Prankipin, Lord Meyk, Lord Hunzimar, Lord Struin—nothing but names, now—nothing—but—names—"

346

"Nothing—but—names—" they echoed, in high thin wailing tones, and began to dwindle and shrink, until they were drole-high on the beach, small scurrying things that ran about pitifully, crying out their names in sharp little squeaks. Then they were gone, and in their place were small white spheres, no bigger than juggling-balls, which, Valentine realized, as he bent down to inspect them, were skulls. He scooped them up and tossed them blithely in the air, and caught them as they descended and threw them again, arraying them in a gleaming cascade. Their jaws clicked and chattered as they soared and fell. Valentine grinned. How many could he juggle at once? Spurifon, Struin, Hunzimar, Meyk, Prankipin, Scaul—that was only six. There had been hundreds of Coronals, one every ten or twenty or thirty years for the past eleven thousand years or thereabouts. He would juggle them all. From the air he plucked more of them, greater ones, Confalume, Prestimion, Stiamot, Dekkeret, Pinitor, a dozen, a hundred, filling the air with them, hurling and catching, hurling and catching. Never since the days of the first settlement had there been such a display of juggling skill on Majipoor! No longer was he throwing skulls; they had become glittering many-faceted diadems, orbs, indeed a thousand imperial orbs that cast sparkling light in every direction. He juggled them flawlessly, knowing each for the Power that it represented, now Lord Confalume, now Lord Spurifon, now Lord Dekkeret, now Lord Scaul, keeping them all aloft, spreading them out through the air so that they formed a great inverted pyramid of light, all the royal persons of Majipoor dancing above him, all converging toward the fair-haired smiling man who stood with legs planted firmly in the warm sand of that golden beach. He supported them all. The entire history of the world was in his hands, and he sustained it in its flight.

The dazzling diadems formed a great starburst of radiance overhead.

Without missing a beat, Valentine began to walk inland, over the smoothly rising dunes toward the dense jungle wall. The trees parted as he approached, bowing to left and right, clearing a track for him, a scarlet-paved way leading to the unknown interior of the island. He looked ahead and saw foothills before him, low gray hills that rose in slow ascent to become steeply rising granite flanks, beyond which lay jagged peaks, a formidable sharp-tipped cordillera stretching on and on and on to the heart of a continent. And on the highest peak of all, on a summit so lofty that the air about it shimmered with a pale luminous glow seen only in dreams, sprawled the buttressed walls of the Castle. Valentine marched toward it, juggling as he went. Figures passed him along the path, coming the other way, waving, smiling, bowing. Lord Voriax was one, and his mother the Lady another, and the tall solemn figure of the Pontifex Tyeveras, all greeting him cordially, and Valentine waved back to them without dropping a diadem, without breaking the smooth serene flow of his juggling. He was on the foothill trail now, and effortlessly moving upward, with a crowd growing about him, Carabella and Sleet close at hand, Zalzan Kavol and the whole juggling band of Skandars, Lisamon Hultin the giantess and Khun of Kianimot, Shanamir, Vinorkis, Gorzval, Lorivade, Asenhart, hundreds of others, Hjorts and Ghayrogs and Liimen and Vroons, merchants, farmers, fishers, acrobats, musicians, Duke Nascimonte the bandit chieftain, Tisana the dreamspeaker, Gitamorn Suul and Dondak-Sajamir arm in arm, a horde of dancing Metamorphs, a phalanx of dragon-captains merrily brandishing harpoons, a skittering cavorting troop of forest-brethren swinging hand over hand through the trees alongside the path, everyone singing, laughing, prancing, following him toward the Castle, Lord Malibor's Castle, Lord Spurifon's Castle, Lord Confalume's Castle, Lord Stiamot's Castle, Lord Valentine's Castle—

—Lord Valentine's Castle—

He was nearly there. Though the mountain road led virtually straight upward, though mists thick as wool hung low over the trail, he went onward, faster now, skipping and running, gloriously juggling his hundreds of gleaming baubles. Just ahead he saw three great pillars of fire, which as he drew closer resolved themselves into faces—Shinaam, Dilifon, Narrameer, side by side in his path.

They spoke in a single voice: "Where are you going?"

"To the Castle."

"Whose Castle?"

"Lord Valentine's Castle."

"And who are you?"

"Ask them," said Valentine, gesturing to those who danced behind him. "Let them tell you my name!"

"Lord Valentine!" cried Shanamir, first to hail him.

"He is Lord Valentine!" cried Sleet and Carabella and Zalzan Kavol.

"Lord Valentine the Coronal!" cried the Metamorphs and the dragon-captains and the forest-brethren.

"Is this so?" asked the ministers of the Pontifex.

"I am Lord Valentine," said Valentine gently, and threw

348

the thousand diadems high overhead, and they rose until they were lost to sight in the darkness that dwells between the worlds, and out of that darkness they came floating silently down, twinkling, sparkling like snowflakes falling on the slopes of the mountains of the north, and when they touched the figures of Shinaam and Dilifon and Narrameer the three ministers vanished instantly, leaving only a silver gleam behind, and the gates of the Castle lay open.

10

Valentine woke.

He felt the wool of the rug against his bare skin, and saw the pointed arches of the gloomy stone ceiling far above. For a moment the world of the dream remained so vivid in his mind that he sought to return to it, not wanting at all to be in this place of musty air and dark corners. Then he sat up and looked about, shaking the fog from his mind.

He saw his companions Sleet and Carabella and Deliamber and Zalzan Kavol and Asenhart huddled together strangely against the far wall, tense, apprehensive.

He turned the other way, expecting to see the three ministers of the Pontifex once more enthroned. As indeed they were, but two more of the magnificent chairs had been brought to the room, and now five seated figures confronted him. Narrameer, robed again, sat at the left. Beside her was Dilifon. At the center of the group was a round-faced man with a blunt broad nose and dark solemn eyes, whom Valentine recognized, after a moment's thought, as Hornkast, high spokesman of the Pontificate. Next to him sat Shinaam, and in the rightmost chair was a person Valentine did not know, a sharp-featured man, thin-lipped, gray-skinned, strange. The five were watching him sternly, in a distant, preoccupied way, as though they were judges of a secret court, gathered to pass a verdict that was long overdue in rendering.

Valentine stood. He made no attempt to retrieve his clothing. That he was naked before this tribunal seemed somehow appropriate.

Narrameer said, "Is your mind clear?"

"I believe it is."

"You have slept more than an hour past the end of your dream. We have waited for you." She indicated the gray-

349

skinned man at the far side of the group and said, "This is Sepulthrove, physician to the Pontifex."

"So I suspected," Valentine said.

"And this man"—she indicated the one in the center—"I think you already know."

Valentine nodded. "Hornkast, yes. We have met." And then the import of Narrameer's choice of words reached him. He smiled broadly and said, "We have met, but I was in another body then. You accept my claim?"

"We accept your claim, Lord Valentine," said Hornkast in a rich, melodious voice. "A great strangeness has been perpetrated upon this world, but it will be set to rights. Come: clothe yourself. It is hardly fit that you go before the Pontifex naked like this."

Hornkast led the procession to the imperial throne-room. Narrameer and Dilifon walked behind him, with Valentine between; Sepulthrove and Shinaam brought up the rear. Valentine's companions were not permitted to come.

The passageway was a narrow high-vaulted tunnel of a glimmering greenish glassy stuff, in the depths of which strange reflections, elusive and distorted, sparkled and swam. It coiled round and round, spiraling inward on a slight downward grade. Every fifty paces there was a bronze door that entirely sealed the tunnel: at each, Hornkast touched his fingers to a hidden panel, and the door slid noiselessly aside to admit them to the next segment of the passage, until at last they came to a door more ornate than the others, richly embellished with the symbol of the Labyrinth in chasings of gold, and the imperial monogram of Tyeveras superimposed on it. This was the very heart of the Labyrinth, Valentine knew, its deepest and most central point. And when this final door slipped aside at Hornkast's touch it revealed a huge bright chamber of spherical form, a great glassy-walled globe of a room, in which the Pontifex of Majipoor sat enthroned in splendor.

Valentine had beheld the Pontifex Tyeveras on five occasions. The first had been when Valentine was a child, and the Pontifex had come to Castle Mount to attend Lord Malibor's wedding; then again years later, at the coronation of Lord Voriax, and again a year afterward at the marriage of Voriax, and a fourth time when Valentine had visited the Labyrinth as emissary from his brother, and one last meeting just three years ago—though it felt now more like thirty—when Tyeveras had attended Valentine's own coronation. The Pontifex had already been old at the first of these events, an enormously tall, gaunt, forbidding-looking man with harsh angular features, a beard of midnight black, deep-set mournful eyes; and as he grew even older those characteristics became greatly accentuated, so that there came to be something cadaverous about him, a stiff, slow-moving, wintry old dry stalk of a man, but nevertheless alert, aware, still vigorous in his fashion, still projecting an aura of immense power and majesty. But now—

But now—

The throne on which Tyeveras sat was the one he had occupied on Valentine's earlier visit to the Labyrinth, a splendid high-backed golden seat atop three wide low steps; but now it was wholly enclosed in a sphere of lightly tinted blue glass, into which ran a vast and intricate network of life-support conduits that formed a complex, almost unfathomable cocoon. Those clear pipes bubbling with colored fluids, those meters and dials, those measuring plaques mounted on the Pontifex' cheeks and forehead, those wires and nodes and connectors and clamps, had a weird and frightening aspect, for plainly they said that the life of the Pontifex resided not in the Pontifex but in the machinery surrounding him.

"How long has he been like this?" Valentine murmured.

"The system has been developing for twenty years," said the physician Sepulthrove with obvious pride. "But only in the last two have we kept him constantly in it."

"Is he conscious?"

"Oh, yes, yes, definitely conscious!" Sepulthrove replied. "Go closer. Look at him."

Uneasily Valentine advanced until he stood at the foot of the throne, peering up at the eerie old man within the glass bubble. Yes, he saw the light still aglow in the eyes of Tyeveras, saw the fleshless lips still clamped in a look of resolve. Now the skin of the Pontifex was like parchment over his skull, and his long beard, though still strangely black, was sparse and wispy.

Valentine glanced at Hornkast. "Does he recognize people? Does he speak?"

"Of course. Give him a moment."

Valentine's eyes met those of Tyeveras. There was a terrible silence. The old man frowned, stirred vaguely, let his tongue flicker briefly over his lips.

From the Pontifex came an unintelligible quavering sound, a kind of whining moan, soft and strange.

Hornkast said, "The Pontifex gives greeting to his beloved son Lord Valentine the Coronal."

Valentine repressed a shudder. "Tell his majesty—tell him—tell him that his son Lord Valentine the Coronal comes to him in love and respect, as always."

That was the convention: that one did not ever speak directly to the Pontifex, that one phrased one's sentences as though the high spokesman would repeat everything, although in fact the spokesman did not do so.

The Pontifex spoke again, as indistinctly as before.

Hornkast said, "The Pontifex expresses his concern for the disturbance that has occurred in the realm. He asks what plans Lord Valentine the Coronal has for restoring the proper system of things."

"Tell the Pontifex," said Valentine, "that I plan to march toward Castle Mount, calling upon all citizens to give me their allegiance. I ask from him a general directive branding Dominin Barjazid a usurper and denouncing all those who support him."

From the Pontifex now came more animated sounds, sharp and high of pitch, with weird compelling energy behind them.

Hornkast said, "The Pontifex wishes to be assured that you will avoid battle and the destruction of lives, if at all possible."

"Tell him that I would prefer to regain Castle Mount without the loss of a single life on either side. But I have no idea whether that can be achieved."

Odd gurgling sounds. Hornkast looked puzzled. He stood with his head cocked, listening intently.

"What does he say?" Valentine whispered.

The high spokesman shook his head. "Not everything his majesty says can be interpreted. Sometimes he moves in realms too remote from our experience."

Valentine nodded. He looked with pity and even with love on the grotesque old man, caged within the globe that sustained his life, able to communicate only in this dreamlike moaning. More than a century old, for decade after decade supreme monarch of the world, now drooling and babbling like a child—and yet somewhere within that decaying softening brain still ticked the mind of the Tyeveras that had been, trapped in the breakdown of the flesh. To behold him now was to understand the ultimate meaninglessness of supreme rank: a Coronal lived in the world of deeds and moral responsibility, only to succeed to the Pontificate and finally to vanish into the Labyrinth and crazy senility. Valentine wondered how often a Pontifex had become the captive of his spokesman and his doctor and his dream-speaker, and finally had had to be eased from the world so that the grand rotation of the Powers could bring a more vital man to the throne. Valentine comprehended now why the system separated the doer and the ruler, why the Pontifex eventually hid himself away from the world in this Labyrinth. His own time would come, down here: but, the Divine willing, it would not be soon.

He said, "Tell the Pontifex that Lord Valentine the Coronal, his worshipful son, will do his utmost to repair the rift in the fabric of society. Tell the Pontifex that Lord Valentine counts on his majesty's support, without which there can be no swift restoration." ·

There was silence from the throne, and then a long painful outwelling of incomprehensibility, a jumble of fluting gargling sounds that wandered up and down the scale like the eerie melodies of the Ghayrog mode. Hornkast appeared to be straining to catch even a syllable of sense here and there. The Pontifex ceased speaking, and Hornkast, troubled, tugged at his jowls, chewed at his lip.

"What was all that?" Valentine asked.

"He thinks you are Lord Malibor," said Hornkast dejectedly. "He cautions you against the risks of going to sea to hunt dragons."

"Wise counsel," said Valentine. "But it comes too late."

"He says the Coronal is too precious to gamble his life in such amusements."

"Tell him that I agree, that if I regain Castle Mount I'll cling closely to my tasks, and avoid any such diversions."

The physician Sepulthrove came forward and said quietly, "We are tiring him. This audience must end, I fear."

"One moment more," Valentine said.

Sepulthrove frowned. But Valentine, with a smile, advanced again to the foot of the throne, and knelt there, and held his outspread hands up toward the ancient creature within the glass bubble, and, slipping into the trance-state, sent forth his spirit toward Tyeveras, bearing impulses of reverence and affection. Had anyone ever shown affection toward the formidable Tyeveras before? Very likely not. But for decades this man had been the center and soul of Majipoor, and now, sitting here lost in a timeless dream of governance, aware only intermittently of the responsibilities that once had been his, he deserved such love as his adoptive son and someday successor could bestow, and Valentine gave as fully as the powers of the circlet would permit.

And Tyeveras seemed to grow stronger, his eyes to brighten, his cheeks to take on a ruddy tint. Was that a smile on those shriveled lips? Did the left hand of the Pontifex lift, ever so slightly, in a gesture of blessing? Yes. Yes. Yes. Beyond doubt the Pontifex felt the flow of warmth from Valentine, and welcomed it, and was responding.

Tyeveras spoke briefly and almost coherently.

Hornkast said, "He says he grants you his full support, Lord Valentine."

Live long, old man, Valentine thought, getting to his feet and bowing. Probably you would rather sleep forever, but I must wish upon you a longer life even than you have already had, for there is work for me to do on Castle Mount.

He turned away.

"Let's go," he told the five ministers. "I have what I need."

They marched soberly from the throne-room. As the door swung shut behind them Valentine glanced at Sepulthrove and said, "How long can he survive like that?"

The physician shrugged. "Almost indefinitely. The system sustains him perfectly. We could keep him going, with some repairs every now and then, another hundred years."

"That won't be necessary. But he may have to stay with us another twelve or fifteen. Can you do that?"

"Count on it," said Sepulthrove.

"Good. Good." Valentine stared at the shining winding passageway that sloped upward before him. He had been in the Labyrinth long enough. The time had come to return to the world of sun and wind and living things, and to settle matters with Dominin Barjazid. To Hornkast he said, "Return me to my people and prepare transportation for us to the outer world. And before my departure I'll want a detailed study of the military forces and supporting personnel you'll be able to place at my disposal."

"Of course, my lord," the high spokesman said.

My lord. It was the first indication of submission that he had had from the ministers of the Pontifex. The main battle was yet to come; but Valentine felt, hearing those two small words, almost as though he had already regained Castle Mount.

V

The Book of the Castle

The ascent from the depths of the Labyrinth was far more swiftly accomplished than the descent had been; for on the interminable downward spiral Valentine had been an unknown adventurer, clawing his way past a stolidly uncaring bureaucracy, and on the upward journey he was a Power of the realm.

Not for him, now, the tortuous climb through level after level, ring after ring, back up through all the intricacies of the Pontifical lair, House of Records and Arena and Place of Masks and Hall of Winds and all the rest. Now he and his followers rose, quickly and without hindrance, using the passage reserved for Powers alone.

In just a few hours he attained the outer ring, that brightly lit and populous halfway house on the rim of the underground city. For all the speed of his climb, the news of his identity had traveled even faster. Word somehow had spread through the Labyrinth that the Coronal was here, a Coronal mysteriously transformed but Coronal none the less, and as he emerged from the imperial passageway a great crowd stood assembled, staring as if some creature with nine heads and thirty legs had come forth.

It was a silent crowd. Some made the sign of the starburst, a few called out his name. But most were content simply to gape. The Labyrinth was the domain of the Pontifex, after all, and Valentine knew that the adulation a Coronal would receive elsewhere in Majipoor was not likely here. Awe, yes. Respect, yes. Curiosity, above all. But none of the cheering and waving that Valentine had seen bestowed on the counter-

355

feit Lord Valentine when he rode in grand processional through the streets of Pidruid. Just as well, thought Valentine. He was out of practice at being the object of adulation, and he had never cared much for it, anyway. It was enough—more than enough—that they accepted him, now, as the personage he claimed to be.

"Will it all be that easy?" he asked Deliamber. "Simply ride across Alhanroel proclaiming myself the real Lord Valentine, and have everything fall into my hands?"

"I doubt it mightily. Barjazid still wears the Coronal's countenance. He still holds the seals of power. Down here, if the ministers of the Pontifex say you are the Coronal, the citizens will hail you as Coronal. If they had said you were Lady of the Isle, they probably would hail you as Lady of the Isle. I think it will be different outside."

"I want no bloodshed, Deliamber."

"No one does. But blood will flow before you mount the Confalume Throne once more. There's no avoiding it, Valentine."

Gloomily Valentine said, "I would almost rather abandon power to the Barjazid than plunge this land into some convulsion of violence. Peace is what I love, Deliamber."

"And peace is what there will be," said the little wizard. "But the road to peace is not always peaceful. See, there— your army is gathering already, Valentine!"

Valentine saw, not far ahead, a knot of people, some familiar, some unknown to him. All those who had gone into the Labyrinth with him were there, the band he had accumulated in his journey across the world, Skandars, Lisamon Hultin, Vinorkis, Khun, Shanamir, Lorivade and the bodyguard of the Lady, and the rest. But also there were several hundred in the colors of the Pontifex, already assembled, the first detachment of—what? Not troops; the Pontifex had no troops. A civilian militia, then? Lord Valentine's army, at any rate.

"My army," Valentine said. The word had a bitter taste. "Armies are something out of Lord Stiamot's time, Deliamber. How many thousands of years has it been since there has been war on Majipoor?"

"Things have been quiet a long while," the Vroon said. "But nevertheless there are small armies in existence. The bodyguards of the Lady, the servitors of the Pontifex—and what about the knights of the Coronal, eh? What do you call them, if not an army? Carrying weapons, drilling on the fields of Castle Mount—what are they, Valentine? Lords and ladies amusing themselves in games?"

356

"So I thought, Deliamber, when I was one of them."

"Time to think otherwise, my lord. The knights of the Coronal form the nucleus of a military force, and only an innocent would believe anything else. As you will discover quite inescapably, Valentine, when you come closer to Castle Mount."

"Can Dominin Barjazid bring my own knights out in battle against me?" Valentine asked in horror.

The Vroon gave him a long cool stare. "The man you call Dominin Barjazid is, at the moment, Lord Valentine the Coronal, to whom the knights of Castle Mount are bound by oath. Or have you forgotten that? With luck and craft you may be able to convince them that their oath is to the soul and spirit of Lord Valentine, and not to his face and beard. But some will remain loyal to the man they think is you, and they will lift swords against you in his name."

The thought was sickening. Since the restoration of his memory Valentine had thought more than once of the companions of his earlier life, those noble men and women with whom he had grown up, with whom he had learned the princely arts in happier days, whose love and friendship had been central to his life until the day the usurper had shattered that life. That bold huntsman Elidath of Morvole, and the fair-haired and agile Stasilaine, and Tunigorn, who was so quick with the bow, and so many more—only names to him now, shadowy figures out of a distant past, and yet in a moment those shadows could be given life and color and vigor. Would they now come forth against him in war? His friends, his beloved companions of long ago—if he had to do battle with them for Majipoor's sake, so be it, but the prospect was dismaying.

He shook his head. "Perhaps we can avoid that. Come," he said. "The time for leaving this place is at hand."

Near the gateway known as the Mouth of Waters Valentine held a jubilant reunion with his followers and met the officers that had been provided for him by the ministers of the Pontifex. They seemed a capable crew, perceptibly quickened in spirit by this chance to leave the dreary depths of the Labyrinth. Their leader was a short, tight-coiled man named Ermanar, with close-cropped reddish hair and a short sharp-pointed beard, who in his size and movements and straightforwardness might well have been brother to Sleet. Valentine liked him at once. Ermanar made the starburst at Valentine in a quick, perfunctory way, smiled warmly, and said, "I will be at your side, my lord, until the Castle is yours again."

"May the journey north be an easy one," Valentine said.

"Have you chosen a route?"

"By riverboat up the Glayge would be swiftest, would it not?"

Ermanar nodded. "At any other time of year, yes. But the autumn rains have come, and they have been unusually heavy." He drew forth a small map of central Alhanroel, showing the districts from the Labyrinth to Castle Mount in glowing red on some bit of dark fabric. "See, my lord, the Glayge descending from the Mount, and pouring into Lake Roghoiz, and its remnant emerging here to continue on to the Mouth of Waters before us? Just now the river is swollen and dangerous from Pendiwane to the lake—that is, for hundreds of miles. I propose a land route at least as far as Pendiwane. There we can arrange shipping for ourselves nearly to the source of the Glayge."

"It sounds wise. Do you know the roads?"

"Fairly well, my lord." He poked his finger at the map. "Much depends on whether the plain of the Glayge is flooded as badly as reports have it. I would prefer to move through the Glayge Valley, in this fashion, simply skirting the northern side of Lake Roghoiz, never getting too far from the river as we proceed."

"And if the valley's flooded?"

"Then there are roads farther north we can use. But the land there is dry, unpleasant, almost a desert. We would have trouble finding provisions. And we would swing much too close to this place for my comfort."

He tapped the map at a point just northwest of Lake Roghoiz.

"Velalisier?" Valentine said. "The ruins? Why do you look so troubled, Ermanar?"

"An unhealthy place, my lord, a place of foul luck. Spirits wander there. Unavenged crimes stain the air. The stories told of Velalisier are not to my liking."

"Floods to one side of us, haunted ruins to the other, eh?" Valentine smiled. "Why not go south of the river entirely, then?"

"South? No, my lord. You recall the desert through which you came on your journey from Treymone? It's worse down there, much worse; not a drop of water, nothing to eat but stones and sand. I'd rather march straight through the middle of Velalisier than attempt the southern desert."

"Then we have no choice, do we? The Glayge Valley route

it is, then, and let's hope the flooding isn't too bad. When do we leave?"

"When do you wish to leave?" Ermanar asked.

"Two hours ago," said Valentine.

2

In early afternoon the forces of Lord Valentine came forth from the Labyrinth through the Mouth of Waters. This gateway was broad and splendidly ornamented, as was fitting for the chief entrance to the Pontifical city, through which Powers traditionally passed. A horde of Labyrinth-dwellers assembled to watch Valentine and his companions ride out.

It was good to see the sun again. It was good to breathe fresh true air once more—and not dry cruel desert air, but the mild sweet soft air of the lower Glayge Valley. Valentine rode in the first of a long procession of floater-cars. He ordered the windows swung open wide. "Like young wine!" he cried, breathing deep. "Ermanar, how can you bear living in the Labyrinth, knowing there's this just outside?"

"I was born in the Labyrinth," said the officer quietly. "My people have served the Pontifex for fifty generations. We are accustomed to the conditions."

"Do you find the fresh air offensive, then?"

"Offensive?" Ermanar looked startled. "No, no, hardly offensive! I appreciate its qualities, my lord. It seems merely— how shall I say it?—it seems *unnecessary* to me."

"Not to me," Valentine said, laughing. "And look how green everything looks, how fresh, how new!"

"The autumn rains," said Ermanar. "They bring life to this valley."

"Rather too much life this year, I understand," Carabella said. "Do you know yet how bad the flooding is?"

"I have sent scouts forward," Ermanar replied. "We'll soon have word."

Onward the caravan rolled, through a placid and gentle countryside just north of the river. The Glayge did not look particularly unruly here, Valentine thought—a quiet meandering stream, silvery in the late sunlight. But of course this was not the true river, only a sort of canal, built thousands of years ago to link Lake Roghoiz and the Labyrinth. The Glayge itself, he remembered, was far more impressive, swift and wide, a noble river, though hardly more than a rivulet by comparison with the titanic Zimr of the other continent. His other time at the Labyrinth, Valentine had ridden the Glayge by summer, and a dry summer at that, and it had seemed calm enough; but this was a different season, and Valentine wanted no more taste of rivers in flood, for his memories of the roaring Steiche were still keen. If they had to go north a bit, that was all right; even if they had to go through the Velalisier ruins, it would not be so bad, though the superstitious Ermanar might need comforting.

That night Valentine felt the first direct counterthrust of the usurper. As he lay sleeping there came upon him a sending of the King, baleful and stark.

He felt first a warmth in his brain, a quickly gathering heat that became a raging conflagration and pressed with furious intensity against the throbbing walls of his skull. He felt a needle of brilliant light probing his soul. He felt the pounding of agonizing pulsations behind his forehead. And with these sensations came something even more painful, a spreading sense of guilt and shame pervading his spirit, an awareness of failure, of defeat, accusations of having betrayed and cheated the people he had been chosen to govern.

Valentine accepted the sending until he could take no more. At last he cried out and woke, bathed in sweat, shivering, shaken, as bruised by a dream as he had ever been.

"My lord?" Carabella whispered.

He sat up, covered his face with his hands. For a moment he was unable to speak. Carabella cradled him against her, stroking his head.

"Sending," he managed to say at last. "Of the King."

"It's gone, love, it's over, it's all over." She rocked back and forth, embracing him, and gradually the terror and panic ebbed from him. He looked up.

"The worst," he said. "Worse than that one in Pidruid, our first night."

"Can I do anything for you?"

"No. I don't think so." Valentine shook his head. "They've found me," he whispered. "The King has a reading on me, and he'll never leave me alone now."

"It was only a nightmare, Valentine—"

"No. No. A sending of the King. The first of many."

"I'll get Deliamber," she said. "He'll know what to do."

"Stay here, Carabella. Don't leave me."

"It's all right now. You can't have a sending while you're awake."

"Don't leave me," he murmured.

But she soothed him and coaxed him into lying down again; and then she went for the wizard, who looked grave and troubled, and touched Valentine to put him into a sleep without dreams.

The next night he feared to sleep at all. But sleep finally came, and with it a sending again, more terrifying than the last. Images danced in his mind—bubbles of light with hideous faces, and blobs of color that mocked and jeered and accused, and darting slivers of hot radiance that held a stabbing impact. And then Metamorphs, fluid, eerie, circling around him, waving long thin fingers at him, laughing in shrill hollow tones, calling him coward, weakling, fool, babe. And loathsome oily voices singing in distorted echoes the little children's song:

> The old King of Dreams
> Has a heart made of stone.
> He's never asleep
> He's never alone.

Laughter, discordant music, whispers just beyond the threshold of his hearing—skeletons in long rows, dancing—the dead Skandar brothers, ghastly and mutilated, calling his name—

Valentine forced himself to wake, and paced, haggard and drained, for hours in the cramped floater.

And a night later came a third sending, worse than the other two.

"Am I never to sleep again?" he demanded.

Deliamber visited him with the hierarch Lorivade as he sat slumped, white-faced, exhausted. "I have heard of your troubles," Lorivade said. "Has the Lady not shown you how to defend yourself with your circlet?"

Valentine looked at her blankly. "What do you mean?"

"One Power may not assail another, my lord." She touched the silver band at his forehead. "This will ward off attack, if you use it properly."

"And how is that?"

"As you prepare yourself for sleep," she said, "weave about yourself a wall of force. Project your identity; fill the air around you with your spirit. No sending can harm you then."

"Will you train me?"

"I will try, my lord."

In his sapped and wearied condition it was all he could do

361

to project a shadow of strength, let alone the full potency of a Coronal; and even though Lorivade drilled him for an hour in the exercise of using the circlet, a fourth sending came to him that night. But it was weaker than the others, and he was able to escape its worst effects, and sleep of a restful kind finally embraced him. By day he felt nearly restored to himself; and he drilled with the circlet for hours.

Other sendings came to him on the nights that followed—faint, probing ones, testing for some opening in his armor. With growing confidence Valentine warded them off. He felt the strain of constant vigilance, and it weakened him; and there were few nights when he did not sense the tendrils of the King of Dreams attempting to steal into his sleeping soul; but he maintained his guard and went unharmed.

For five days more they made their way north along the lower Glayge, and on the sixth Ermanar's scouts returned with news of the territories ahead.

"The flooding is not as severe as we had heard," Ermanar said.

Valentine nodded. "Excellent. We'll continue on to the lake, then, and take ship there?"

"There are hostile forces between us and the lake."

"The Coronal's?"

"One would assume so, my lord. The scouts said only that they ascended Lumanzar Ridge, which gives a view of the lake and the surrounding plain, and saw troops camped there, and a considerable force of mollitors."

"War at last!" Lisamon Hultin cried. She sounded far from displeased.

"No," Valentine said somberly. "This is too early. We are thousands of miles from Castle Mount. We can hardly begin battling so far south. Besides, it's still my hope to avoid warfare altogether—or at least to delay it until the last."

"What will you do, my lord?"

"Proceed north through the Glayge Valley, as we've been doing, but begin moving northwest if there's any movement toward us by that army. I mean to go around them, if we can, and sail up the river behind them, leaving them sitting down at Roghoiz still waiting for us to appear."

Elmanar blinked. "Go *around?*"

"Unless I miss my guess, the Barjazid has put them there to guard the approach to the lake. They won't follow us very far inland."

"But inland—"

"Yes, I know." Valentine let his hand rest lightly on Er-

362

manar's shoulder and said softly, with all the warmth and sympathy at his command, "Forgive me, friend, but I think we may have to detour as far from the river as Velalisier."

"Those ruins frighten me, my lord, and I am not the only one."

"Indeed. But we have a powerful wizard in our company, and many brave folk. What can a ghost or two do against the likes of Lisamon Hultin, of Khun or Kianimot, or Sleet, or Carabella? Or Zalzan Kavol? We'll just let the Skandar roar at them a bit, and they'll run all the way to Stoien!"

"My lord, your word is law. But since I was a boy I have heard dark tales of Velalisier."

"Have you ever been there?"

"Naturally not."

"Do you know anyone who has?"

"No, my lord."

"Can you say, then, that you have knowledge, certain knowledge, of the perils of the place?"

Ermanar toyed with the coils of his beard. "No, my lord."

"But ahead of us lies an army of our enemy, and a horde of ugly mollitors of war, eh? We have no idea what ghosts can do to us, but we're quite sure of the troubles warfare can bring. I say sidestep the fighting, and take our chances with the ghosts."

"I would prefer it the other way round," said Ermanar, managing a smile. "But I will be at your side, my lord, even if you ask me to go on foot through Velalisier on a night of no moon. You may rely on that."

"I will," said Valentine. "And we will come forth from Velalisier unharmed by its phantoms, Ermanar. You may rely on that."

For the time being they continued on the road they had been traveling, keeping the Glayge to their right. The land gradually rose as they moved north—not yet the great surge that marked the foothills of Castle Mount, Valentine knew, but only a minor step-stage, an outer ripple of that vast up-thrusting of the planet's skin. Soon the river lay a hundred feet below them in the valley, a narrow bright thread bordered by thick wild brush. And now the road wound by switchbacks up the side of a long tilted block of terrain that Ermanar said was Lumanzar Ridge, from the summit of which one could see for an extraordinary distance.

With Deliamber, Sleet, and Ermanar, Valentine went to the rim of the ridge to take stock of the situation. Below, the land swept away in natural terraced contours, level after level descending the ridge to the broad huge plain in which Lake Roghoiz was the centerpiece.

The lake looked enormous, almost an ocean. Valentine remembered it as large, as well it should be, for the Glayge drained the entire southwestern slope of Castle Mount and fed virtually all its waters into this lake; but the size he remembered was nothing like this. Now he knew why the towns at the lake's margin all were built high on pilings: those towns now were no longer at the lake's margin, but deep within its bounds, and the water must be lapping at the lower stories of the stilt-bottomed buildings. "It is much swollen," he said to Ermanar.

"Yes, almost twice its usual area, I think. Still, the tales we heard made it even worse."

"As is often the case," Valentine said. "And where is the army your scouts saw?"

Ermanar scanned the horizon a long moment with his seeing-tube. Perhaps, Valentine thought eagerly, they have packed up and gone back to the Mount, or maybe it was an error of the scouts, no army here at all, or possibly—

"There, my lord," Ermanar said finally.

Valentine took the tube and peered down the ridge. At first he saw only trees and meadows and stray outfloodings of the lake; but Ermanar directed the tube, and suddenly Valentine saw. To the naked eye the soldiers had seemed like a congregation of ants near the edge of the lake.

But these were no ants.

Camped by the lake were perhaps a thousand troops, perhaps fifteen hundred—not a gigantic army, but large enough on a world where the concept of war was all but forgotten. They outnumbered Valentine's forces several times over. Grazing nearby were eighty or a hundred mollitors—massive armor-plated creatures, of synthetic origins from the ancient days. In the knightly games on Castle Mount mollitors often were used as instruments of combat. They moved with surprising swiftness on their short thick legs, and were capable of great feats of destruction, poking their heavy black-jawed heads out of their impervious carapaces to snap and crush and rend. Valentine had seen them rip up an entire field with their fierce curved claws as they lumbered back and forth, crashing up against one another and butting heads in dull-witted rage. A dozen of them, blocking a road, would be as effective a barrier as a wall.

Sleet said, "We could take them by surprise, send one squad

down to drive the mollitors into confusion, and swing around on them from the other side when——"

"No," Valentine said. "It would be a mistake to fight."

"If you think," Sleet persisted, "that you're going to regain Castle Mount without anybody's suffering so much as a cut finger, my lord, you——"

"I expect there to be bloodshed," said Valentine crisply. "But I intend to minimize it. Those troops down there are the troops of the Coronal; remember that, and remember who is truly Coronal. They are not the enemy. Dominin Barjazid is the only enemy. We will fight only when we must, Sleet."

"Change routes as planned, then?" Ermanar asked glumly.

"Yes. We go northwest, out toward Velalisier. Then swing around the far side of the lake, and up the valley toward Pendiwane, if there are no more armies waiting for us between here and there. Do you have maps?"

"Just of the valley and the road to Velalisier, perhaps halfway. The rest's only wasteland, my lord, and the maps show very little."

"Then we'll manage without maps," said Valentine.

As the caravan moved back down Lumanzar Ridge to the crossroads that would take them away from the lake, Valentine summoned the brigand Duke Nascimonte to his car. "We are heading toward Velalisier," he said, "and may need to go right through it. Are you familiar with that area?"

"I was there once, my lord, when I was much younger."

"Looking for ghosts?"

"Looking for treasures of the ancients, to decorate my mansion-house. I found very little. The place must have been well plundered when it fell."

"You had no fears, then, of looting a haunted city?"

Nascimonte shrugged. "I knew the legends. I was younger, and not very timid."

"Speak with Ermanar," Valentine said, "and introduce yourself as one who has been to Velalisier and lived to tell the tale. Can you guide us through it?"

"My memories of the place are forty years old, my lord. But I'll do my best."

Studying the patchy, incomplete maps Ermanar provided, Valentine concluded that the only road that would not take them perilously near the army waiting by the lake would in fact bring them almost to the edge of the ruined city, if not actually into it. He would not regret that. The Velalisier ruins, however much they terrified the credulous, were by all reports a noble sight; and besides, Dominin Barjazid was unlikely to have troops waiting for him out there. The detour could be turned to advantage, if the false Coronal expected Valentine to take the predictable route up the Glayge: perhaps, if desert travel did not prove too taxing, they might be able to keep away from the river much of the way north, and gain the benefit of some surprise as they turned at last toward Castle Mount.

Let Velalisier produce what ghosts it may, Valentine thought. Better to dine with phantoms than to march down Lumanzar Ridge into the jaws of Barjazid's mollitors.

3

The road away from the lake led through increasingly more arid terrain. The thick dark alluvial soil of the flood-plain gave way to light, gritty, brick-red stuff that supported a skimpy population of gnarled and thorny plants. The road grew rougher here, no longer paved, just an irregular gravel-strewn track winding gradually upward into the low hills that divided the Roghoiz district from the desert of Velalisier Plain.

Ermanar sent out scouts, hoping to find a passable road on the lakeward side of the hills and thus avoid having to approach the ruined city. There was none, nothing but a few hunters' trails crossing country too rugged for their vehicles. Over the hills it was, then, and down into the haunted regions beyond.

In late afternoon they began the descent of the far side. Heavy clouds were gathering—the trailing edge, perhaps, of some storm system now buffeting the upper Glayge Valley—and sunset, when it came, spread over the western sky like a great bloody stain. Just before darkness a rift appeared in the overcast and a triple beam of dark red light burst through, illuminating the plain, bathing in strange dreamlike radiance the sprawling immensity of the Velalisier ruins.

Great blocks of blue stone littered the landscape. A mighty wall of shaped monoliths, two and in some places three courses high, ran for more than a mile at the western edge of the city, ending abruptly in a heap of tumbled stone cubes. Closer at hand the outlines of vast shattered buildings still were visible, a whole forum of palaces and courtyards and basilicas and temples, half buried in the drifting sands of the plain. To the east rose a row of six colossal narrow-based sharp-topped pyramids set close together in a straight line, and the stump of a seventh, which had been dismantled apparently with furious energy, for its fragments lay strewn across a wide arc around it. Just ahead, where the mountain road made its entry into the city, were two broad stone platforms, eight or ten feet above the surface of the plain and wide enough for the maneuvers of a substantial army. In the distance Valentine saw the huge oval form of what might have been an arena, high-walled, many-windowed, breached at one end by a rough ragged gap. The scale of everything was astonishing, that and the enormous area. This place made the nameless ruins on the other side of the Labyrinth, where Duke Nascimonte had first found them, seem trivial indeed.

The rift in the clouds suddenly closed. The last daylight disappeared; the destroyed city became a place of mere formless confusion, chaotic humps against the desert skyline, as night descended.

Nascimonte said, "The road, my lord, runs between those platforms, through the group of buildings just behind them, and around the six pyramids, going out by the northeast side. It will be difficult to follow in the dark, even by moonlight."

"We won't try to follow it in the dark. We'll camp here and go through in the morning. I plan to explore the ruins tonight, as long as we're here." That brought a grunt and a muffled cough from Ermanar. Valentine glanced at the little officer, whose face was drawn and bleak. "Courage," he murmured. "I think the ghosts will let us be, this evening."

"My lord, this is not a joking matter for me."

"I mean no mockery, Ermanar."

"You will go into the ruins alone?"

"Alone? No, I don't think so. Deliamber, will you accompany me? Sleet? Carabella? Zalzan Kavol? And you, Nascimonte—you've survived them once; you have less to fear in there than any of us. What do you say?"

The bandit chieftain smiled. "I am yours to command, Lord Valentine."

"Good. And you, Lisamon?"

"Of course, my lord."

"Then we have a party of seven explorers. We'll set out after dinner."

"Eight explorers, my lord," said Ermanar quietly.

Valentine frowned. "There's scarcely any need for—"

"My lord, I swore to remain at your side until the Castle is yours again. If you go into the dead city, I go into the dead city with you. If the dangers are unreal, there is nothing to fear, and if they are real, my place is with you. Please, my lord."

Ermanar seemed entirely sincere. His face was tense, his expression strained, but more, Valentine thought, out of concern that he might be excluded from the expedition than out of fear of what might lurk in the ruins.

"Very well," said Valentine. "A party of eight."

The moon was nearly full that evening, and its cold brilliant light illuminated the city in fine detail, mercilessly revealing the effects of thousands of years of abandonment in a way that the softer, more fantastical red glow of twilight had not. At the entrance, a worn and nearly illegible marker proclaimed Velalisier to be a royal historic preserve, by order of Lord Siminave the Coronal and the Pontifex Calintane. But they had ruled some five thousand years ago, and it did not seem as though much maintenance had been practiced here since their day. The stones of the two great platforms that flanked the road were cracked and uneven. In the furrows between them grew small ropy-stemmed weeds that with irresistible patience were prying the huge blocks apart: already in some places canyons were opening between block and block, wide enough for sizable shrubs to have taken root. Conceivably in another century or two a forest of twisted woody vegetation would hold possession of these platforms and the mighty square blocks would be wholly lost to view.

Valentine said, "All this must be cleared away. I'll have the ruins restored to the way they were before this overgrowth began to sprout. How could such neglect have been permitted?"

"No one cares about this place," said Ermanar. "No one will lift a finger for this place."

"Because of the ghosts?" Valentine asked.

"Because it's Metamorph," Nascimonte said. "That makes it doubly accursed."

"Doubly?"

"You don't know the story, my lord?"

"Tell me."

Nascimonte said, "This is the legend I was raised on, at any rate. When the Metamorphs ruled Majipoor, Velalisier was their capital, oh, twenty, twenty-five thousand years ago. It was the greatest city on the planet. Two or three million of them lived here, and from all over Alhanroel came people of the outlying tribes, bringing tribute. They held Shapeshifter festivals on top of these platforms, and every thousand years they held a special festival, a superfestival, and to mark each of those they built a pyramid, so the city was at least seven thousand years old. But evil took hold here. I don't know what sort of things a Metamorph would regard as evil, but whatever they were, they were practiced here. This was the capital city of all abominations. And the Metamorphs of the provinces grew disgusted, and then they grew outraged, and one day they marched in here and smashed the temples and pulled down most of the city walls and destroyed the places where the evils were practiced and drove the citizens into exile and slavery. We know they weren't massacred, because there's been plenty of treasure-digging here—I've done a little of it myself, as you know—and if there were a few million skeletons buried here, they'd have been found. So the place was torn apart and abandoned, long before the first humans came here, and a curse was put on it. The rivers that fed the city were dammed and diverted. The entire plain became a desert. And for fifteen thousand years no one has lived here except the ghosts of those who died when the city was destroyed."

"Tell the rest of it," said Ermanar.

Nascimonte shrugged. "That's all I know, mate."

"The ghosts," Ermanar said. "Those who haunt here. Do you know how long they're fated to wander the ruins? Until Metamorphs rule Majipoor again. Until the planet is returned to them, and the last of us are made into slaves. And then Velalisier will be rebuilt on the old site, grander ever than it was before, and it'll be reconsecrated as the Shapeshifter capital, and the spirits of the dead finally will be released from the stones that hold them trapped here."

"They'll cling to the stones a long time, then," said Sleet. "Twenty billion of us and just a handful of them, living in the jungles—what kind of a threat is that?"

Ermanar said, "They've waited eight thousand years already, since Lord Stiamot broke their power. They'll wait eight thousand more, if they have to. But they dream of Velalisier reborn, and they won't give up that dream. Sometimes in sleep I've listened to them, planning for the day when the towers of Velalisier rise again, and it frightens me. That's why I don't like to be here. I feel them watching over the place—I can feel their hatred all around us, like something in the air, something invisible but real—"

"So this city is accursed by them and holy to them both at once," Carabella said. "Small wonder we have trouble comprehending how their minds work!"

Valentine wandered off down the path. The city awed him. He tried to imagine it as it had been, a kind of prehistoric

369

Ni-moya, a place of majesty and opulence. And now? Lizards with beady clicking eyes scuttered from rock to rock. Weeds grew thick in the grand ceremonial boulevards. Twenty thousand years! What would Ni-moya look like in twenty thousand years? Or Pidruid, or Piliplok, or the fifty great cities on the slopes of Castle Mount? Were they building here on Majipoor a civilization that would endure forever, as the civilization of the old mother-world Earth was said to endure? Or, he wondered, would wide-eyed tourists someday prowl the shattered ruins of the Castle and the Labyrinth and the Isle, trying to guess what significance they had had to the ancients? We have done well enough so far, Valentine told himself, thinking back over the thousands of years of peace and stability. But now dissonances were breaking through; the ordered pattern of things had been disrupted; there was no telling what might befall. The Metamorphs, the defeated and evicted Metamorphs whose misfortune it had been to possess a world desired by other and stronger folk, might yet have the last laugh.

Suddenly he halted. What was that sound ahead? A footfall? And a flicker of shadow against the rocks? Valentine peered tensely into the darkness before him. An animal, he thought. Something nocturnal slithering around in search of a meal. Ghosts don't have shadows, do they? Do they? There are no ghosts here, Valentine thought. There are no ghosts anywhere.

But all the same—

Cautiously he edged forward a few steps. Too dark here, too many avenues of tumbledown structures leading off to every side. He had laughed at Ermanar; but Ermanar's fears had somehow insinuated themselves into his imagination. He had fantasies of austere mysterious Metamorphs gliding between the fallen buildings just beyond his vision—phantoms half as old as time—forms without bodies, shapes without substance—

And then footsteps, unmistakable footsteps, behind him—

Valentine whirled. Ermanar was trotting after him, that was all.

"Wait, my lord!"

Valentine allowed him to catch up. He forced himself to relax, though his fingers, strangely, were trembling. He put his hands behind his back.

"You ought not go off by yourself," Ermanar said. "I know you make light of the dangers I imagine here, but those dangers might yet exist. You owe it to us all to take more care of your safety, my lord."

The others rejoined him, and they continued on, slowly and in silence, through the moonlit ruins. Valentine said nothing of what he had thought he had seen and heard. Surely it had been only some animal. And shortly animals appeared: some sort of small apes, perhaps akin to forest-brethren, that nested in the fallen buildings and several times caused startlement as they went scrambling over the stones. And nocturnal mammals of a lower kind, mintuns or droles, darted swiftly through the shadows. But did apes and droles, Valentine wondered, make sounds like footfalls?

For more than an hour the eight moved deeper into the ruins. Valentine stared warily into the recesses and caverns, studying the pools of blackness with care.

As they passed through the fragments of a collapsed basilica, Sleet, who had gone off a short way by himself, jogged back in distress to tell Valentine, "I heard something strange to one side, in there."

"A ghost, Sleet?"

"It might be, for all I know. Or simply a bandit."

"Or a rock-monkey," Valentine said lightly. "I've heard all kinds of noises."

"My lord—"

"Are you catching Ermanar's terrors now?"

"I think we have wandered here long enough, my lord," said Sleet in a low, taut voice.

Valentine shook his head. "We'll keep close watch on dark corners. But there's more to see here."

"I wish we would turn back now, my lord."

"Courage, Sleet."

The juggler shrugged and turned away. Valentine peered into the darkness. He did not underestimate the acuteness of Sleet's hearing, he who juggled blindfolded by sheer sound alone. But to flee this place of marvels because they heard odd rustlings and footsteps in the distance—no, not so soon, not so hastily.

Yet, without communicating his uneasiness to the others, he moved still more cautiously. Ermanar's ghosts might not exist, yet it was folly to be too rash in this strange city.

And as they were exploring one of the most ornate of the buildings in the central area of palaces and temples, Zalzan Kavol, who was leading the way, stopped short abruptly when a slab of rock, dislodged from above, came clattering down practically at his feet. He cursed and growled, "Those stinking apes—"

"No, not apes, I think," said Deliamber quietly. "There's something bigger up there."

Ermanar flashed a light toward the overhanging ledge of an adjoining structure. For an instant a silhouette that might have been human was in view; then it vanished. Without hesitating, Lisamon Hultin began to run to the far side of the building, followed by Zalzan Kavol, who brandished his energy-thrower. Sleet and Carabella went the other way. Valentine would have gone with them, but Ermanar caught him by the arm and held him with surprising strength, saying apologetically, "I may not permit you to place yourself in risk, my lord, when we have no idea—"

"Halt!" came the mighty booming voice of Lisamon Hultin.

There was the sound of a scuffle in the distance, and then that of someone clambering over the mounds of fallen masonry in no very ghostlike way. Valentine longed to know what was happening, but Ermanar was right: to go darting off after an unknown enemy in the darkness of an unfamiliar place was a privilege denied to the Coronal of Majipoor.

He heard grunts and cries, and a high-pitched sound of pain. Moments later Lisamon Hultin reappeared, dragging a figure who wore the starburst emblem of the Coronal on his shoulder. She had her arm locked about his chest and his feet were dangling six inches off the ground.

"Spies," she said. "Skulking around up there, keeping watch on us. There were two of them, I think."

"Where's the other?" Valentine asked.

"Might have gotten away," said the giantess. "Zalzan Kavol went after him." She dumped her prisoner down before Valentine, and held him to the ground with a foot pressed against his middle.

"Let him up," Valentine said.

The man rose. He looked terrified. Brusquely Ermanar and Nascimonte checked him for weapons and found none.

"Who are you?" Valentine asked. "What are you doing here?"

No reply.

"You can speak. We won't harm you. You have the starburst on your arm. Are you part of the Coronal's forces?"

A nod.

"Sent out here to trail us?"

Again a nod.

"Do you know who I am?"

The man stared silently at Valentine.

"Are you able to speak?" Valentine asked. "Do you have a voice? Say something. Anything."

"I—if I—"

"Good. You can talk. Again: do you know who I am?"

In a thin whisper the captive replied, "They say you would steal the throne from the Coronal."

"No," Valentine said. "You have it wrong, fellow. The thief is he who sits now on Castle Mount. I am Lord Valentine, and I demand your allegiance."

The man stared, bewildered, uncomprehending.

"How many of you were up there?" Valentine asked.

"Please, sir—"

"How many?"

Sullen silence.

"Let me twist his arm a little," Lisamon Hultin begged.

"That won't be necessary." Valentine moved closer to the cowering man and said gently, "You understand nothing of this, but all will be made clear in time. I am the true Coronal, and by the oath you swore to serve me, I ask you now to answer. How many of you were up there?"

Conflicts raged in the man's face. Slowly, reluctantly, bewilderedly, he replied, "Just two of us, sir."

"Can I believe that?"

"By the Lady, sir!"

"Two of you. All right. How long were you following us?"

"Since—since Lumanzar."

"Under what orders?"

Hesitation again. "To—to observe your movements and report to camp in the morning."

Ermanar scowled. "Which means that other one is probably halfway to the lake by now."

"You think so?"

It was the rough, harsh voice of Zalzan Kavol. The Skandar strode into their midst and dumped down before Valentine, as though it were a sack of vegetables, the body of a second figure wearing the starburst emblem. Zalzan Kavol's energy-thrower had seared a hole through him from back to front. "I chased him about half a mile, my lord. A quick devil he was, too! He was moving more easily than I over the heaps of stones, and starting to pull away from me. I ordered him to stop, but he kept going, and so—"

"Bury him somewhere off the path," Valentine said curtly.

"My lord? Did I do wrong to kill him?"

"You had no choice," Valentine said in a softer tone. "I

373

wish you had managed to catch him. But you couldn't, so you had no choice. Very well, Zalzan Kavol."

Valentine turned away. The slaying had shaken him, and he could hardly pretend otherwise. This man had died only because he was loyal to the Coronal, or to the person he believed to be the Coronal.

The civil war had had its first casualty. The bloodshed had begun, here in this city of the dead.

4

There was no thought of continuing the tour now. They returned with the prisoner to their camp. And in the morning Valentine gave orders to move on through Velalisier and begin the northeastward swing.

By day the ruined city seemed not as magical, although no less impressive. It was hard to understand how so frail and unmechanical a folk as the Metamorphs had ever moved these giant blocks of stone about; but perhaps twenty thousand years ago they had not been quite so unmechanical. The glowering Shapeshifters of the Piurifayne forests, those people of wicker huts and muddy streets, were only the broken remnant of the race that once had ruled Majipoor.

Valentine vowed to return here, once this business with Dominin Barjazid was settled, and explore the ancient capital in detail, clearing underbrush and excavating and reconstructing. If possible, he thought, he would invite Metamorph leaders to take part in that work—though he doubted they would care to cooperate. Something was needed to reopen lines of communication between the two populations of the planet.

"If I am Coronal again," he said to Carabella as the cavalcade rode past the pyramids and headed out of Velalisier, "I intend—"

"*When* you are Coronal again," she said.

Valentine smiled. "When I am Coronal again, yes. I intend to examine the entire problem of the Metamorphs. Bring them back into the mainstream of Majipooran life, if that can be done. Give them a place in the government, even."

"If they'll have it."

"I mean to overcome that anger of theirs," said Valentine. "I'll dedicate my reign to it. Our entire society, our wonderful and harmonious and loving realm, was founded on an act of

374

theft and injustice, Carabella, and we've succeeded in teaching ourselves to overlook that."

Sleet glanced up. "The Shapeshifters weren't making full use of this planet. There weren't twenty million of them on the entire enormous place when our ancestors came here."

"But it was *theirs!*" Carabella cried. "By what right—"

"Easily, easily," Valentine said. "There's no use fighting over the deeds of the first settlers. What's done is done, and we must live with it. But it's within our power to change the way we've been living with it, and if I'm Coronal again, I—"

"*When,*" said Carabella.

"When," Valentine echoed.

Deliamber said mildly, in that far-off way of his that gained the immediate attention of all listeners, "It may be that the present troubles of the realm are the beginning of the retribution for the suppression of the Metamorphs."

Valentine stared at him. "What do you mean by that?"

"Only that we have gone a long way, here on Majipoor, without paying any sort of price for the original sin of the conquerors. The account accumulates interest, you know. And now this usurpation, the evils of the new Coronal, the prospect facing us of war, death and destruction, chaos—perhaps the past is starting to send us its reckoning at last."

"But Valentine had nothing to do with the oppression of the Metamorphs," Carabella protested. "Why should he be the one to suffer? Why was he chosen to be cast down from power, and not some high-handed Coronal of long ago?"

Deliamber shrugged. "Such things are never fairly distributed. What makes you think that only the guilty are punished?"

"The Divine—"

"Why do you think the Divine is fair? In the long run, all wrongs are righted, every minus is balanced with a plus, the columns are totaled and the totals are found correct. But that's in the long run. We must live in the short run, and matters are often unjust there. The compensating forces of the universe make all the accounts come out even, but they grind down the good as well as the wicked in the process."

"More than that," said Valentine suddenly. "It may be that I was chosen to be an instrument of Deliamber's compensating forces, and it was necessary for me to suffer in order to be effective."

"How so?"

"If nothing unusual had ever happened to me, I might have

ruled like all the others before me on Castle Mount, self-satisfied, amiable, accepting things as they were because from where I sat I saw no wrong in them. But these adventures of mine have given me a view of the world I'd never have had if I had remained snug in the Castle. And perhaps now I'm ready to play the role that needs to be played, whereas otherwise—" Valentine let his voice trail away. After a moment he said, "All this talk is mere vapor. The first thing to do is regain the Castle. Then we can debate the nature of the compensating forces of the universe and the tactics of the Divine."

He looked back at fallen Velalisier, the accursed city of the ancients, chaotic but yet magnificent on the forlorn desert plain. And then he turned away to sit in silence and contemplate the changing countryside ahead.

The road now curved about sharply toward the northeast, passing up and over the range of hills they had crossed to the south, and descending into the fertile flood-plain of the Glayge near the northernmost limb of Lake Roghoiz. They were emerging hundreds of miles north of the field where the Coronal's army had been camped.

Ermanar, bothered by the presence of the two spies in Velalisier, had sent out scouts to ascertain that the army had not moved north to meet them. Valentine judged that a sensible move; but he did scouting of his own, by way of Deliamber.

"Cast me a spell," he ordered the wizard, "that will tell me where enemy armies lie in wait. Can you do that?"

The Vroon's great shining golden eyes flickered in amusement. "Can I do that? Can a mount eat grass? Can a seadragon swim?"

"Then do it," said Valentine.

Deliamber withdrew and muttered words and waved his tentacles about, coiling and intertwining them in the most intricate of patterns. Valentine suspected that much of Deliamber's sorcery was staged for the benefit of onlookers, that the real transactions did not involve the waving of tentacles or the muttering of formulas at all, but only the casting forth of Deliamber's shrewd and sensitive consciousness to pick up the vibrations of outlying realities. But that was all right. Let the Vroon stage his little show. A certain amount of show business, Valentine recognized, was an essential lubricant in many civilized activities, not only those of wizards and jugglers, but those also of the Coronal, the Pontifex, the Lady, the King of Dreams, the speakers of dreams, the teachers of holy mysteries, perhaps even the customs-officials at the provincial boundaries and the sellers of sausages in streetside booths. In plying one's trade one could not be too bald and blunt; one had to cloak one's doings in magic, in theater.

Deliamber said, "The troops of the Coronal appear to remain where they were camped."

Valentine nodded. "Good. May they camp there a long while, waiting for us to return from our Velalisier excursion. Can you locate other armies north of here?"

"Not for a great distance," said Deliamber. "I feel the presence of knightly forces gathered on Castle Mount. But there always are. I detect minor detachments here and there in the Fifty Cities. But nothing unusual about that either. The Coronal has plenty of time. He'll simply sit at the Castle and wait for you to approach. And then will come the grand mobilization. What will you do, Valentine, when a million warriors march down Castle Mount toward you?"

"Do you think I've given that no thought?"

"I know you've thought of little else. But it needs some heavy thinking about—our hundreds against their millions."

"A million is a clumsy size for an army," said Valentine easily. "Far simpler to do one's juggling with clubs than with the trunks of dwikka-trees. Are you frightened of what lies ahead, Deliamber?"

"Not at all."

"Neither am I," Valentine said.

But of course there was show-business bravado, Valentine knew, in talk of that sort. Was he frightened? No, not really: death comes to all, sooner or later, and to fear it is folly. Valentine knew he had little fear of death, for he had faced it in the forest near Avendroyne, and in the turbulent rapids of the Steiche, and in the belly of the sea-dragon and when wrestling with Farssal on the Isle, and on none of those occasions had he felt anything he could identify as fear. If the army that waited for him on Castle Mount overwhelmed his little force and cut him down, it would be regrettable—as being tumbled to pieces on the rocks of the Steiche would have been regrettable—but the prospect caused him no dread. What he did feel, and it was a more significant thing than fear for his own life, was a degree of fear for Majipoor. If he failed, through hesitation or foolishness or mere inadequacy of strength, the Castle would remain in the hands of the Barjazids, and the course of history would forever change, and ultimately billions of innocent beings would suffer. Preventing that was a high responsibility, and he felt the weight of it. If he died valiantly trying to scale Castle Mount, his hardships at least would be over; but the agonies of Majipoor would only just be beginning.

Now they traveled through placid rural districts, the perimeter of the great agricultural belt that flanked Castle Mount and supplied the Fifty Cities with produce. Valentine chose main highways at all times. The moment for secrecy was past; so conspicuous a caravan as this could hardly be concealed, and the time was at hand when the world had to learn that a struggle for possession of Lord Valentine's Castle was about to commence.

The world was starting to learn it, in any case. Ermanar's scouts, returning from the city of Pendiwane farther up the Glayge, brought news of the usurper's first countermeasures.

"No armies lie between us and Pendiwane," Ermanar reported. "But posters are up in the city, branding you a rebel and a subversive, an enemy of society. The proclamations of the Pontifex in your favor have not yet been announced, it seems. Citizens of Pendiwane are being urged to band together in militias to defend their rightful Coronal and the true order of things against your uprising. And sendings are widespread."

Valentine frowned. "Sendings? What sort of sendings?"

"Of the King. Apparently you can scarcely fall asleep at night but the King is in your dreams, buzzing to you about loyalty and warning of terrible consequences if the Coronal is overthrown."

"Naturally," Valentine muttered. "He'd have the King working for him with all the energy at his command. They must be sending night and day in Suvrael. But we'll turn that against him, eh?" He looked to Deliamber. "The King of Dreams is telling the people how dreadful it is to overthrow a Coronal. Good. I want them to believe exactly that. I want them to realize that a terrifying thing *has already happened* to Majipoor, and that it's up to the people to put things to rights."

"Nor is the King of Dreams precisely a disinterested party in this war," Deliamber said. "We should make them aware of that too—that he stands to gain from his son's treachery."

"We will," said the hierarch Lorivade vehemently. "Out of the Isle now are coming the sendings of the Lady with redoubled force. They'll counteract the King's poisonous dreams. Last night as I slept she came to me and showed me what kind of message will go forth. It is the vision of the drugging at Til-omon, the changing of the Coronal. She will show them your new face, Lord Valentine, and will surround you with the radiance of the Coronal, the starburst of authority. And will portray the false Coronal as a traitor, mean and dark of spirit."

"When will this begin?" Valentine asked.

"She waits for your approval."

"Then open your mind to the Lady today," he told the hierarch, "and tell her that the sendings must start."

Khun of Kianimot said quietly, "How strange this seems to me! A war of dreams! If ever I doubted I was on an alien world, these strategies would make it certain to me."

Valentine said, with a smile, "Better to fight with dreams than with swords and energy-throwers, friend. What we seek is best won by persuasion, not by killing."

"A war of dreams," Khun repeated, bemused. "We do things differently on Kianimot. Who's to say which way makes more sense? But I think there'll be fighting as well as sendings before this is done, Lord Valentine."

Valentine looked somberly at the blue-skinned being. "I fear you are right," he said.

Five days more and they were in the outlying suburbs of Pendiwane. By now news of their advance had spread throughout the countryside; farmers stopped in their fields to stare as the cavalcade of vehicles floated by, and crowds thronged the highway in the more thickly populated sectors.

Valentine found this all to the good. Thus far no hands were being lifted against them. They were regarded as curiosities, not as menaces. More than that he could not ask.

But when they were a day's journey outside of Pendiwane, the advance party returned with news that a force was gathered to meet them near the city's western gate.

"Soldiers?" Valentine asked.

"Citizen-militia," said Ermanar. "Hastily organized, from the looks of them. They wear no uniforms, only ribbons round their arms, with the starburst emblem on it."

"Excellent. The starburst is consecrated to my favor. I'll go to them and ask their allegiance."

Vinorkis said, "What will you wear, my lord?"

Puzzled, Valentine indicated the simple clothes in which he had been traveling since the Isle of Sleep, a white belted tunic and a light overblouse.

"Why, these, I suppose," he said.

The Hjort shook his head. "You should wear finery, and a crown, I think. I think it very strongly."

"My thought was not to appear overly ostentatious. If they see a man in a crown, whose face is not the face they know as Lord Valentine's, *usurper* will be the first thought to come to their minds, will it not?"

"I think otherwise," Vinorkis replied. "You come to them and say, I am your rightful king. But you don't *look* like a king. A simple costume and easy manners may win you friends in quiet conversation, but not when large forces are assembled. You would do well to dress more awesomely."

Valentine said, "My hope was to rely on simplicity and sincerity, as I have done ever since Pidruid."

"Simplicity and sincerity, by all means," said Vinorkis. "But also a crown."

"Carabella? Deliamber? Advise me!"

"A little ostentation might not be harmful," said the Vroon.

"And this will be your first public appearance as claimant to the Castle," Carabella said. "Some look of regal splendor, I think, may serve you well."

Valentine laughed. "I've grown away from such costumes in these many months of wandering, I fear. The idea of a crown now seems only comic to me. A thing of twisted metal, poking up from my scalp, a bit of jewelry—"

He stopped. He saw them all gaping at him.

"A crown," he said in a less lighthearted tone, "is only an outward thing, a trinket, an ornament. Children might be impressed by such toys, but adult citizens who—"

He stopped again.

Deliamber said, "My lord, can you remember how you felt, the first time they came to you at the Castle and put the starburst upon your brow?"

"There was a chill down my back, I do confess."

"Yes. A crown may be a child's ornament, a silly trinket, true. But it is also a symbol of power, that sets the Coronal apart from all others, and transforms mere Valentine into *Lord* Valentine the heir of Lord Prestimion and Lord Confalume and Lord Stiamot and Lord Dekkeret. We live by such symbols. My lord, your mother the Lady did much to restore you to the person you were before Til-omon, but there is still a good deal of Valentine the juggler about you, even now. And that is not a bad thing. Still, more impressiveness and less simplicity is called for here, I suspect."

Valentine was silent, thinking of Deliamber mumbling and waving his tentacles, and his own realization that sometimes one had to indulge in theatrics to achieve one's proper effects. They were right and he was wrong.

He said, "Very well. I will wear a crown, if one can be fashioned for me in time."

One of Ermanar's men quickly assembled one for him out of scraps of a defective floater-engine, the only spare metal that was at hand. Considering its hastily improvised nature, it was a decent job of crown-making, Valentine thought, the joinings not too rough, the spokes of the starburst reasonably equally spaced, the inner orbits of the armature smoothly coiled. Of course it was nothing to compare with the authentic crown, with its inlays and chasings of seven different precious metals, its finials of rare gems, its three gleaming diniaba-stones mounted on the browband. But that crown—made in the great reign of Lord Confalume, who must have taken a hearty joy in all the trappings of imperial pomp—was else-where at the moment, and this one, once it took its place upon his consecrated brow, would most likely magically invest itself with the proper grandeur. Valentine held it in his hands a long moment. Despite the scorn for such things he had ex-pressed the day before, he felt a little awed by it himself.

Deliamber said mildly, "The militia of Pendiwane are wait-ing, my lord."

Valentine nodded. He was garbed in borrowed finery, a green doublet that belonged to one of Ermanar's comrades, a yellow cloak that Asenhart had produced, a heavy golden chain belonging to the hierarch Lorivade, high glossy boots lined with the white fur of the northern steetmoy, that were contributed by Nascimonte. Not since the ill-fated banquet in Til-omon, when he had worn another body entirely, had he dressed with such gaudiness. It was a strange feeling to be clad so pretentiously. He lacked only the crown.

He started to put it on, and stopped abruptly, realizing that there was history in this moment, whether he liked the idea or not: the first time he donned the starburst in this his second incarnation. Suddenly this event began to seem less like a masquerade and more like a coronation. Valentine looked around uneasily.

"I should not put this on my head myself," he said. "De-liamber, you're my chief minister. You do it."

"My lord, I am not tall enough."

"I could kneel."

"That would not be fitting," said the Vroon, a little sharply.

Plainly Deliamber did not want to do it. Valentine looked next toward Carabella. But she recoiled, horrified, whisper-ing, "I am a commoner, my lord!"

"What does that have to do with—" Valentine shook his

head. This was becoming an annoyance. They were making too much of an occasion out of it. He glanced around the group and saw the hierarch Lorivade, that cool-eyed and stately woman, and said, "You are the representative of the Lady my mother in this group, and you are a woman of rank. May I ask you—"

But Lorivade said gravely, "The crown, my lord, descends to the Coronal by authority of the Pontifex. It seems more fitting that Ermanar place it on you, as the highest official of the Pontifex among us today."

Valentine sighed and turned to Ermanar. "I suppose that's right. Will you do it?"

"It will be a great honor, my lord."

Valentine handed the crown to Ermanar and moved the silver circlet of his mother as far down his scalp as it would go. Ermanar, who was not a man of great height, took the crown in both hands, trembling a little, and reached up, straining to extend his arms. With great care he lowered the crown over Valentine's head and slipped it into place. It fit perfectly.

"There," Valentine said. "I'm glad that's—"

"Valentine! Lord Valentine! Hail, Lord Valentine! Long life to Lord Valentine!"

They were kneeling to him, making the starburst to him, shouting out his name, all of them, Sleet, Carabella, Vinorkis, Lorivade, Zalzan Kavol, Shanamir, everyone, Nascimonte, Asenhart, Ermanar, even—surprisingly—the offworlder Khun of Kianimot.

Valentine gestured in protest, embarrassed at all this, wanting to tell them that this was no true ceremony, that it was done only for the sake of impressing the citizens of Pendiwane. But the words did not leave his throat, for he knew that they were untrue, that this improvised affair was in fact his second crowning. And he felt the chill down his spine, the shiver of wonder.

He stood with arms outspread, accepting their homage.

Then he said, "Come. On your feet, all of you. Pendiwane is waiting for us."

The scouts' report had it that the militia and the high personages of the city had been camped outside Pendiwane's western gate for some days, awaiting his arrival. Valentine wondered what the condition of the townspeople's nerves might be, after so long and uncertain a vigil, and what sort of reception they planned to give him.

It was only an hour's ride to Pendiwane now. They moved quickly through a region of pleasant forests and broad, rolling, rain-sleekened meadows that soon gave way to agreeable residential districts, small stone houses with conical red-tiled roofs the predominant style. The city ahead was a major one, capital of its province, with a population of twelve or thirteen million; it was chiefly a trade depot, Valentine recalled, through which the agricultural produce of the lower Glayge Valley was funneled on its way upriver to the Fifty Cities.

At least ten thousand militia waited at the gate.

They filled the road, and spilled over into the lanes of the marketplace that nestled against the outer wall of Pendiwane. They were armed with energy-throwers, though not a great many, and with simpler weapons, and those in the front line were standing in a tense, stiff manner, holding themselves self-consciously in soldierlike poses that surely were altogether unfamiliar to them. Valentine ordered the floater-cars to halt a few hundred yards from the nearest of them, so that the roadway between formed a wide clear space, a kind of buffer zone.

He stepped forth, crowned and robed and cloaked. The hierarch Lorivade walked just to his right, clad in the glowing vestments of the Lady's high ministry, and Ermanar was to his left, wearing on his breast the glittering Labyrinth emblem of the Pontifex. At Valentine's rear were Zalzan Kavol and his formidable brothers, glowering and massive, followed by Lisamon Hultin in full battle regalia, with Sleet and Carabella flanking her. Autifon Deliamber rode on the arm of the giantess.

In a slow, easy, unmistakably majestic way, Valentine advanced into the open space before him. He saw the citizens of Pendiwane stirring, exchanging troubled glances, moistening their lips, shifting their feet, rubbing their hands over their chests or arms. A terrible silence had fallen.

He paused twenty yards from the front line and said, "Good people of Pendiwane, I am the rightful Coronal of Majipoor, and I ask your aid in regaining that which was granted to me by the will of the Divine and the decree of the Pontifex Tyeveras."

Thousands of wide eyes stared rigidly at him. He felt wholly calm.

Valentine said, "I call forth from among you Duke Holmstorg of Glayge. I call forth from among you Redvard Haligorn, Mayor of Pendiwane."

There were movements in the crowd. Then came a parting, and out from the midst emerged a rotund man in a blue tunic trimmed with orange, whose heavy-fleshed face seemed gray

383

with fear or tension. The black sash of mayoralty lay across his broad chest. He took a few steps toward Valentine, hesitated, signaled furiously behind his back in what was meant to be a gesture unseen by those facing him; and after a moment five or six lesser municipal officials, looking as abashed and reluctant as children commanded to sing at a school assembly, came warily out behind the mayor.

The plump man said, "I am Redvard Haligorn. Duke Holmstorg has been summoned to Lord Valentine's Castle."

"We have met before, Mayor Haligorn," said Valentine amiably. "Do you recall? It was some years ago, when my brother Lord Voriax was Coronal, and I journeyed to the Labyrinth as emissary to the Pontifex. I stopped in Pendiwane and you gave me a banquet, in the high palace at river's edge. Do you recall, Mayor Haligorn? It was summer, a year of drought, the river was very much shrunken, nothing at all like it is today."

Haligorn's tongue traversed his lips. He tugged at a jowl.

Hoarsely he said, "Indeed he who became Lord Valentine was here in the dry year. But he was a dark man, and bearded."

"True. There has been a witchery of fearful nature, Mayor Haligorn. A traitor now holds Castle Mount and I have been transformed and cast out. But I am Lord Valentine and by the power of the starburst you wear on your sleeve I call upon you to accept me as Coronal."

Haligorn looked bewildered. Clearly he would prefer to be almost anywhere else at this moment, even in the trackless corridors of the Labyrinth, or the burning wastes of Suvrael.

Valentine continued, "Beside me is the hierarch Lorivade of the Isle of Sleep, closest of the companions of my mother your Lady. Do you think she deceives you?"

The hierarch said icily, "This is the true Coronal, and the Lady will withdraw her sublime love from those who oppose him."

Valentine said, "And here stands Ermanar, high servitor of the Pontifex Tyeveras."

In his blunt straightforward way Ermanar said, "You have all heard the decree of the Pontifex that the fair-haired man must be hailed as Lord Valentine the Coronal. Who among you will stand up against the decree of the Pontifex?"

Haligorn's face showed terror. Dealing with Duke Holmstorg might have been harder for Valentine, for he was of high blood and great haughtiness, and might not have been so easily intimidated by one who came before him wearing a home-made crown and leading a little band of such oddly assorted followers. But Redvard Haligorn, a mere elected official, who for years had dealt with nothing more challenging than state banquets and debates over flood-control taxes, was far beyond his depth.

He said, almost mumbling it, "The command has come down from Lord Valentine's Castle that you are to be apprehended and bound over for trial."

"Many commands lately have come down from Lord Valentine's Castle," said Valentine, "and not a few have been unwise, unjust, or ill-timed, eh, Mayor Haligorn? They are the commands of the usurper, and worthless. You have heard the voices of the Lady and the Pontifex. You have had sendings urging you to give allegiance to me."

"And sendings of the other kind," said Haligorn feebly.

"From the King of Dreams, yes!" Valentine laughed. "And who is the usurper? Who is it that has stolen the throne of the Coronal? Dominin Barjazid is the one! The son of the King of Dreams! Now do you comprehend those sendings out of Suvrael? Now do you see what has been done to Majipoor?"

Valentine let the trance-state come over him, and flooded the hapless Redvard Haligorn with the full force of his soul, the full impact of a waking sending from the Coronal.

Haligorn tottered. His face reddened and grew blotchy. He reeled and clutched at his comrades for support, but they had received the outflow from Valentine as well, and were barely able to sustain themselves.

Valentine said, "Give me your support, friends. Open your city to me. From here I will launch the reconquest of Castle Mount, and great will be the fame of Pendiwane, as the first city of Majipoor to turn against the usurper!"

6

So Pendiwane fell, without a blow being struck. Redvard Haligorn, wearing the expression of a man who has just swallowed a Stoienzar oyster and feels it squirming in his gullet, dropped down and offered Valentine the starburst gesture, and then two of his vice-mayors did the same, and suddenly there was a contagion of it, thousands of people giving homage, and crying out, first without much conviction, then more lustily as they decided to commit themselves to the idea: "Valentine! Lord

Valentine! Long life to the Coronal!" And the gates of Pendiwane were opened.

"Too easy," Valentine muttered to Carabella. "Can it continue this way right up Castle Mount? Browbeat a fat mayor
or two and win back the throne by acclamation?"

"If only you could," she said. "But the Barjazid waits up
there with his bodyguards, and browbeating him will take
more than words and fine dramatic effects. There will be bat-
tles, Valentine."

"Let there be no more than one, then."

She touched his arm lightly. "For your sake I hope no more
than one, and that one just a small one."

"Not for my sake," he said. "For the sake of all the world. I
want none of my people to perish in repairing what Dominin
Barjazid has brought upon us."

"I had not thought kings would be so gentle, my love," Carabella said.

"Carabella—"

"You look so sad just now!"

"I fear what comes."

"What comes," she said, "is a necessary struggle, and joyous triumph, and the restoration of order. And if you would
be a proper king, my lord, wave to your people, and smile,
and put that tragic look from your face. Yes?"

Valentine nodded. "You speak the truth," he said, and
catching up her hand, brushed his lips quickly but tenderly
across her small sharp knuckles. And turned to stare at the
multitudes who shouted his name, and lifted his arms to them
and acknowledged their greeting.

It seemed wondrously familiar to be riding into a great city
down boulevards lined with cheering throngs. Valentine remembered, though it seemed like the memory of a dream, the
beginnings of his abortive grand processional, when in the
springtime of his reign he had gone by river to Alaisor on the
western coast, and across to the Isle to kneel beside his mother
at Inner Temple, and then on the great sea-journey westward
to Zimroel, and crowds hailing him in Piliplok and Velathys
and Narabal, down there in the lush leafy tropics. Those parades, those banquets, the excitement, the splendor, and then
on to Til-omon, once more the crowds, once more the cries,
"Valentine! Lord Valentine!" He remembered too in Til-omon
a surprise, that Dominin Barjazid the son of the King of
Dreams had come up from Suvrael to greet him and honor
him in a feast, for the Barjazids customarily stayed down
there in their sunswept kingdom, dwelling apart from human-

ity, tending their dream-machines, sending forth their nightly messages to instruct and command and chastise. And the banquet at Til-omon, and the flask of wine from the hand of Barjazid, and the next thing Valentine knew he was staring down at the city of Pidruid from a limestone ridge, with muddled memories in his mind of having grown up in eastern Zimroel and somehow having wandered across the entire continent to its western shore. Now, so many months later, they were shouting his name again in the streets of a mighty city, after the long and strange interruption.

In the royal suite at the mayoral palace Valentine summoned Mayor Haligorn, who still had a stunned and dazed look about him, and said, "I'll need from you a flotilla of riverboats to take me up the Glayge to its rising. The costs will be met by the imperial treasury after the restoration."

"Yes, my lord."

"And how many troops can you supply me?"

"Troops?"

"Troops, militia, warriors, bearers of arms. Do you follow my meaning, Mayor Haligorn?"

The mayor showed dismay. "We of Pendiwane are not known for our skills in warfare, my lord."

Valentine smiled. "We are not known for our skills in warfare anywhere on Majipoor, the Divine be thanked. Nevertheless, peaceful though we are, we fight when we are threatened. The usurper threatens us all. Haven't you felt the sting of strange new taxes and unfamiliar decrees in this year just past?"

"Of course, but—"

"But what?" Valentine asked sharply.

"We assumed it was only a new Coronal, feeling his power."

"And you would blandly let yourselves be oppressed by the one whose role it is to serve you?"

"My lord—"

"Never mind. You have as much to gain as I in putting things to rights, do you see? Give me an army, Mayor Haligorn, and for thousands of years the bravery of the people of Pendiwane will be sung in our ballads."

"I am responsible for the lives of my people, my lord. I would not have them slain or—"

"*I* am responsible for the lives of your people, and twenty billion others besides," said Valentine briskly. "And if five drops of anyone's blood are shed as I move toward Castle Mount, that will be six drops too many to suit me. But without an army I'm too vulnerable. With an army I become a royal presence, an imperial force moving toward a reckoning with the enemy. Do you understand, Haligorn? Call your people together, tell them what must be done, call for volunteers."

"Yes, my lord," said Haligorn, trembling.

"And see to it that the volunteers are willing to volunteer!"

"It will be done, my lord," the mayor murmured.

Assembling the army went faster than Valentine expected—a matter of days for choosing, equipping, and provisioning. Haligorn was cooperative indeed—as though he were eager to see Valentine rapidly on his way to some other region.

The citizen-militia that had been scraped together to defend Pendiwane against an invading pretender now became the nucleus of the hastily constructed loyalist army—some twenty thousand men and women. A city of thirteen million might well have produced a larger force; but Valentine had no wish to disrupt Pendiwane to any greater extent. Nor had he forgotten his own axiom about juggling with clubs rather than with dwikka-trunks. Twenty thousand troops provided him with something that looked decently military, and it was his strategy, as it had been for a long while, to gain his purpose by gradual accumulation of support. Even the colossal Zimr, he reasoned, begins as mere trickles and rivulets somewhere in the northern mountains.

They set forth on the Glayge on a day that was rainy before dawn, gloriously bright and sunny afterward. Every riverboat for fifty miles on either side of Pendiwane had been commandeered for army transport. Serenely the great flotilla moved northward, the green-and-gold banners of the Coronal waving in the breeze.

Valentine stood near the prow of his flagship. Carabella was beside him, and Deliamber, and Admiral Asenhart of the Isle. The rain-washed air smelled sweet and clean: the good fresh air of Alhanroel, blowing toward him from Castle Mount. It was a fine feeling to be on his way home at last.

These riverboats of eastern Alhanroel were more streamlined, less fancifully baroque, than the ones Valentine had known on the Zimr. They were big, simple vessels, high of draft and narrow of beam, with powerful engines designed to drive them against the strong flow of the Glayge.

"The river is swift against us," said Asenhart.

"As well it should be," Valentine said. He pointed toward some invisible summit far to the north and high in the sky. "It rises on the lower slopes of the Mount. In its few thousand miles it drops almost ten, and all the weight of that water comes rushing against us as we go toward the source."

The Hjort seaman smiled. "It makes ocean sailing seem like child's play, to think of coping with such a force. Rivers always were strange to me—so narrow, so quick. Give me the open sea, dragons and all, and I'm happy!"

But the Glayge, though swift, was tame. Long ago it had been a thing of rapids and waterfalls, ferocious and all but innavigable for hundreds of miles. Fourteen thousand years of human settlement on Majipoor had changed all that. By dams, locks, bypass canals, and other devices, the Glayge, like all the Six Rivers that descended from the Mount, had been made to serve the needs of its masters through nearly all its course. Only in the lower stretches, where the flatness of the surrounding valley made flood-control an ongoing challenge, was there any difficulty, and that merely during seasons of heavy rain.

And the provinces along the Glayge were tame as well: lush green farming country, interrupted by great urban centers. Valentine stared into the distance, narrowing his eyes against the brightness of the morning light and searching for the gray bulk of Castle Mount somewhere ahead; but, immense as it was, not even the Mount could be seen from two thousand miles away.

The first important city upriver from Pendiwane was Makroprosopos, famed for its weavers and artists. As Valentine's ship approached, he saw that the waterfront of Makroprosopos was bedecked with mammoth Coronal-ensigns, probably hastily woven, and even more were still being hung.

Sleet said thoughtfully, "Do those flags mean defiant expression of loyalty to the dark Coronal, I wonder, or capitulation to your claim?"

"Surely they pay homage to you, my lord," Carabella said. "They know you're advancing up the river—therefore they put out flags to welcome you!"

Valentine shook his head. "I think these folk are merely being cautious. If things go badly for me on Castle Mount, they can always claim that those were ensigns of loyalty to the other. And if he is the one who falls, they can say they were second only to Pendiwane in recognizing me. I think we ought not to allow them the luxury of such ambiguities. Asenhart?"

"My lord?"

"Take us to harbor at Makroprosopos."

For Valentine it was something of a gamble. There was no

real need to land here, and the last thing he wanted was a battle at some irrelevant city far from the Mount. But to test the effectiveness of his strategy was important.

That test was passed almost at once. He heard the cheering when he was still far from shore: "Long life to Lord Valentine! Long life to the Coronal!"

The Mayor of Makroprosopos came scurrying to the pier to greet him, bearing gifts, great generous bales of his city's finest fabrics. He fell all over himself bowing and scraping, and was pleased to arrange a levy of eight thousand of his citizens to join the army of restoration.

"What is happening?" Carabella asked quietly. "Will they accept anyone as Coronal who claims the throne loudly enough and waves a few energy-throwers around?"

Valentine shrugged. "These are peaceful folk, comfortable, luxury-loving, timid. They've known only prosperity for thousands of years, and they want nothing but thousands more of it. The idea of armed resistance is foreign to them, so they yield quickly when we come sailing in."

"Aye," said Sleet, "and if the Barjazid comes here next week, they'll bow down just as willingly to him."

"Perhaps. Perhaps. But I'm gaining momentum. As these cities join me, others farther up will fear to hold back their allegiance. Let it come to be a stampede, eh?"

Sleet scowled. "All the same, what you're doing now, someone else can do another time, and I don't like it. What if a red-haired Lord Valentine appears next year, and says *he's* the true Coronal? What if some Liiman shows up, insisting that everyone kneel to him, that the rivals are mere sorcerers? This world will dissolve into madness."

"There is only one anointed Coronal," said Valentine calmly, "and the people of these cities, whatever their motives, are simply bowing to the will of the Divine. Once I've returned to Castle Mount there'll be no further usurpers and no further pretenders, I promise you that!"

Yet privately he recognized the wisdom of what Sleet had said. How frail, he thought, is the compact that holds our government together! Good will alone is all that sustains it. Now Dominin Barjazid had shown that treachery could undo good will, and Valentine was discovering—thus far—that intimidation could counter treachery. But would Majipoor ever be the same again, Valentine wondered, when all this conflict was ended?

7

After Makroprosopos was Apocrune, and then Stangard Falls, and Nimivan, Threiz, South Gayles, and Mitripond. All of these cities, with some fifty million people among them, lost no time in accepting the sovereignty of the fair-haired Lord Valentine.

It was as Valentine had expected. These river-dwellers lacked the taste for warfare, and no one city cared to make a stand in battle for the sake of determining which of the rivals might be the true Coronal. Now that Pendiwane and Makroprosopos had yielded, the rest were eagerly falling into line; but these victories were trivial, he knew, for the river-cities would change allegiance again just as readily if they saw the tides of fortune swinging toward the darker overlord. Legitimacy, anointedness, the will of the Divine, all these things meant far less in the real world than one raised in the courts of Castle Mount might believe.

Still, better to have the nominal support of the river-cities than to have them scoff at his claim. At each, he decreed a new troop-levy—but a minor one, only a thousand per city, for his army was growing too large too soon, and he feared unwieldiness. He wished he knew what Dominin Barjazid thought of the events along the Glayge. Did he cower in the Castle, fearing that all the billions of Majipoor were marching angrily toward him? Or was he only biding his time, preparing his inner line of defense, ready to bring the entire realm down in chaos before he yielded possession of the Mount?

The river-journey continued.

Now the land was rising steeply. They were on the fringes of the great plateau, where the planet swelled and puckered into its mighty upjutting limb, and there were days when the Glayge seemed to rise before them like a vertical wall of water.

This now was familiar territory to Valentine, for in his youth on the Mount he had gone often to the headwaters of each of the Six Rivers, hunting and fishing with Voriax or Elidath or merely escaping a bit from the complexities of his education. His memory was nearly totally restored to him, the healing process having continued steadily ever since his stay on the Isle, and the sight of these well-known places sharpened and brightened his images of that past which Dominin

Barjazid had tried to snatch from him. In the city of Jerrik, here in the narrower reaches of the upper Glayge, Valentine had gambled all night with an old Vroon not much unlike Autifon Deliamber, though he remembered him as less dwarfish, and in that endless rolling of the dice he had lost his purse, his sword, his mount, his title of nobility, and all his lands except one small bit of swamp, and then had won it all back before dawn—though he always suspected his companion had prudently chosen to reverse his flow of success rather than try to make good his winnings. It had been a useful lesson, at any rate. And at Ghiseldorn, where people dwelled in tents of black felt, he and Voriax had enjoyed a night of pleasure with a dark-haired witch at least thirty years old, who had awed them in the morning by casting their futures with pingla-seeds and proclaiming that they both were destined to be kings. Voriax had been greatly troubled by that prophecy, Valentine recalled, for it seemed to say that they would rule jointly as Coronal, in the way that they had jointly embraced the witch, and that was unheard of in the history of Majipoor. It had not occurred to either of them that she was saying that Valentine would be the successor of Voriax. And in Amblemorn, the most southwesterly of the Fifty Cities, an even younger Valentine had fallen heavily while racing through the forest of pygmy trees with Elidath of Morvole, and had cracked the big bone in his left leg with frightful pain, so that the jagged end stuck through the skin, and Elidath, though half sick with shock himself, had to adjust the fracture before they could go for help. Even after there had been a slight limp in that leg—but leg and limp as well, Valentine thought with some strange delight, now belonged to Dominin Barjazid, and this body they had given him was whole and flawless.

All those cities, and a good many more, surrendered to him as he arrived at them. Some fifty thousand troops now followed his banner, here at the edge of Castle Mount.

Amblemorn was as far as the army could travel by water. The river here became a maze of tributaries, shallow of channel and impossibly steep of grade. Valentine had sent Ermanar and ten thousand warriors ahead to arrange for landvehicles. So potent now was the gathering force of Valentine's name that Ermanar, without opposition, had been able to requisition virtually every floater-car in three provinces, and an ocean of vehicles waited in Amblemorn by the time the main body of troops arrived.

Commanding an army so large was no longer a task Valentine alone could handle. His orders descended through Ermanar, his field marshal, to five high officers, each of whom was given charge of a division: Carabella, Sleet, Zalzan Kavol, Lisamon Hultin, and Asenhart. Deliamber was ever at Valentine's side with advice; and Shanamir, now not at all boyish, but much toughened and grown since his days herding mounts in Falkynkip, served as chief liaison officer, keeping communications channels open.

Three days were needed to complete the mobilization. "We are ready to begin moving, my lord," Shanamir reported. "Shall I give the order?"

Valentine nodded. "Tell the first column to get going. We'll be past Bimbak by noon, if we start now."

"Yes, sir."

"And—Shanamir?"

"Sir?"

"I know this is war, but you don't have to look so serious all the time. Eh?"

"Do I look too serious, my lord?" Shanamir reddened. "But this is a serious matter! This is the soil of Castle Mount beneath our feet!" Simply saying that seemed to awe him, this farmboy from far-off Falkynkip.

Valentine understood how he must feel. Zimroel seemed a million miles away.

He smiled and said, "Tell me, Shanamir, do I have it right? A hundred weights make a crown, ten crowns make a royal, and the price of these sausages is—"

Shanamir looked puzzled; then he smirked and fought to hold back laughter, and finally let the laughter come. "My lord!" he cried, tears at the edge of his eyes.

"Remember, there in Pidruid? When I would have bought sausages with a fifty-royal piece? Remember when you thought I was a simpleton? 'Easy of mind,' that's the phrase you used. Easy of mind. I suppose I *was* a simpleton, those first days in Pidruid."

"A long time ago, my lord."

"Indeed. And perhaps I'm a simpleton still, clambering up Castle Mount like this to try to snatch back that grinding, wearying job of governing. But perhaps not. I hope not, Shanamir. Remember to smile more often, that's all. Tell the first column to start moving out."

The boy ran off. Valentine watched him go. So far away, Pidruid, so remote in time and space, a million miles, a million years. So it seemed. And yet it was only a year and some months ago that he had perched on that ledge of white stone on that hot sticky day, looking down into Pidruid and wondering what to do next. Shanamir, Sleet, Carabella, Zalzan Kavol! All those months of juggling in provincial arenas, and sleeping on straw mattresses in flea-infested country inns! What a wonderful time that had been, Valentine thought—how free, how light a life. Nothing more important to do than get hired in the next town down the road, and make sure that you didn't drop your clubs on your foot. He had never been happier. How good it had been of Zalzan Kavol to take him into the troupe, how kind of Sleet and Carabella to train him in their art. A Coronal of Majipoor among them, and they never knew! Who among them could have imagined then that before they were much older they would be jugglers no longer, but rather generals, leading an army of liberation against Castle Mount?

The first column was moving now. The floater-cars were getting under way, forward up the endless vast slopes that lay between Amblemorn and the Castle.

The Fifty Cities of Castle Mount were distributed like raisins in a pudding, in roughly concentric circles radiating outward from the peak of the Castle. There were a dozen in the outermost ring—Amblemorn, Perimor, Morvole, Canzilaine, Bimbak East, Bimbak West, Furible, Deepenhow Vale, Normork, Kazkas, Stipool, and Dundilmir. These, the so-called Slope Cities, were centers of manufacturing and commerce, and the smallest of them, Deepenhow Vale, had a population of seven million. The Slope Cities, founded ten to twelve thousand years ago, tended to be archaic in design, with street plans that might once have been rational but had long since become congested and confused by random modification. Each had its special beauties, famed throughout the world. Valentine had not visited them all—in a lifetime on Castle Mount, there was not time enough to get to know all of the Fifty Cities—but he had seen a good many, Bimbak East and Bimbak West with their twin mile-high towers of lustrous crystalline brick, Furible and its fabled garden of stone birds, Canzilaine where statues talked, Dundilmir of the Fiery Valley. Between these cities were royal parks, preserves for flora and fauna, hunting zones, and sacred groves, everything broad and spacious, for there were thousands of square miles, room enough for an uncrowded and unhurried civilization to develop.

A hundred miles higher on the Mount lay the ring of nine Free Cities—Sikkal, Huyn, Bibiroon, Stee, Upper Sunbreak, Lower Sunbreak, Castlethorn, Gimkandale, and Vugel. There was debate among scholars as to the origin of the term Free

Cities, for no city on Majipoor was more free, or less, than any other; but the most widely accepted notion was that somewhere around the reign of Lord Stiamot these nine had been exempted from a tax levied on the others, in recompense for special favors rendered the Coronal. To this day the Free Cities were known to claim such exemptions, often with success. Of the Free Cities the largest was Stee on the river of the same name, with thirty million people—that is, a city the size of Ni-moya, and, according to rumor, even more grand. Valentine found it hard to conceive a place that so much as equaled Ni-moya in splendor; but he had never managed to visit Stee in his years on Castle Mount, and would pass nowhere near it now, for it lay on the far side entirely.

Higher yet were the eleven Guardian Cities—Sterinmor, Kowani, Greel, Minimool, Strave, Hoikmar, Ertsud Grand, Rennosk, Fa, Sigla Lower, and Sigla Higher. All of these were large, seven to thirteen million people. Because the circumference of the Mount was not as great at their altitude, the Guardian Cities were closer together than those below, and it was thought that in another few centuries they might form a continuous band of urban occupation encircling the Mount's middle reaches.

Within that band lay the nine Inner Cities—Gabell, Chi, Haplior, Khresm, Banglecode, Bombifale, Guand, Peritole, and Tentag—and the nine High Cities—Muldemar, Huine, Gossif, Tidias, Low Morpin, High Morpin, Sipermit, Frangior, and Halanx. These were the metropolises best known to Valentine from his youth. Halanx, a city of noble estates, was the place of his birth; Sipermit was where he had lived during the reign of Voriax, for it was close by the Castle; High Morpin was his favorite holiday resort, where he had often gone to play on the mirror-slides and to ride the juggernauts. So long ago, so long ago! Often now, as his invading force floated up the roadways of the Mount, he looked into the sun-dappled distance, into the cloud-shrouded heights, hoping for a glimpse of the high country, a quick view of Sipermit, of Halanx, of High Morpin somewhere far ahead.

But it was still too soon to expect such things. From Amblemorn the road took them between Bimbak East and Bimbak West, and then on a dogleg detour around the impossibly steep and jagged Normork Crest to Normork itself, of the celebrated stone outer wall built—so legend had it—in imitation of the great wall of Velalisier. Bimbak East welcomed Valentine as legitimate monarch and liberator. The reception at Bimbak West was distinctly less cordial, although there was no show of resistance: its people plainly had not made up their minds where their advantage lay in the strange struggle now unfolding. And at Normork the great Dekkeret Gate was closed and sealed, perhaps for the first time since it had been erected. That seemed unfriendly, but Valentine chose to interpret it as a declaration of neutrality, and passed Normork by without making any attempt to enter. The last thing he cared to do now was divert his energies by laying siege to an impregnable city. Easier by far, he thought, simply not to regard it as his enemy.

Beyond Normork the route crossed Tolingar Barrier, which was no barrier at all, but only an immense park, forty miles of manicured elegance for the amusement of the citizens of Kazkas, Stipool, and Dundilmir. Here it was as if every tree, every bush, had been clipped and wired and pruned into the most shapely of shapes. There was not a branch askew, not a limb out of proportion. If all the billion people who dwelled on Castle Mount had served as gardeners in Tolingar Barrier, they could not have achieved such perfection with round-the-clock toil. It had been accomplished, Valentine knew, by a program of controlled breeding, four thousand years and more in the past, beginning in the reign of Lord Havilbove and continuing through the reigns of three of his successors: these plants were self-shaping, self-pruning, unendingly monitoring themselves for symmetry of form. The secret of such horticultural wizardry had been lost.

And now the army of restoration was entering the level of the Free Cities.

It was possible here, at Bibiroon Sweep atop Tolingar Barrier, to look back down the slopes for a view that was still comprehensible, though already unimaginably mighty. Lord Havilbove's wondrous park coiled like a tongue of green just below, curving off toward the east, and beyond it, mere gray dots, lay Dundilmir and Stipool, with just the finest suggestion of the secretive bulk of walled Normork visible at the side. Then there was the stupefying downward glide of the land toward Amblemorn and the sources of the Glayge. And, hazy as dream-fog on the horizon, the outlines, more likely than not painted by the imagination alone, of the river and its teeming cities, Nimivan, Mitripond, Threiz, South Gayles. Of Makroprosopos and Pendiwane there was not even a hint, though Valentine saw the natives of those cities staring long and hard, and pointing with vehemence, telling one another that that hummock or this nub was their home.

Shanamir said, standing beside Valentine, "I imagined that

you could see all the way to Pidruid from Castle Mount! But we can't even see the Labyrinth. Is there a longer view from higher up?"

"No," Valentine said. "Clouds conceal everything below the Guardian Cities. Sometimes, up there, one can forget that the rest of Majipoor exists."

"Is it very cold up there?" the boy asked.

"Cold? No, not cold at all. As mild as it is here. Milder, even. A perpetual springtime. The air is soft and easy, and flowers always bloom."

"But it reaches so far into the sky! The mountains of the Khyntor Marches are not nearly so high as this—they're not even a patch on Castle Mount—and yet I've been told that snow falls on the March peaks, and sometimes remains all summer long. It should be black as night at the Castle, Valentine, and cold, cold as death!"

"No," Valentine said. "The machines of the ancients create an unending springtime. They have roots deep in the Mount, and suck out energy—I have no idea how—and transform it into warmth, light, good sweet air. I've seen the machines, in the depths of the Castle, huge things of metal, enough metal to build a city with, and giant pumps, and enormous brass tubes and pipes—"

"When will we be there, Valentine? Are we close?"

Valentine shook his head. "Not even halfway."

8

The most direct route upward through the Free Cities lay between Bibiroon and Upper Sunbreak. That was a wide, gently rising shoulder of the Mount, where the slope was so easy that little time would be wasted on switchbacks. As they neared Bibiroon, Valentine learned from Gorzval the Skandar, who was serving as quartermaster, that the army was running low on fresh fruit and meat. It seemed wisest to reprovision at this level, before tackling the ascent to the Guardian Cities.

Bibiroon was a city of twelve million, arrayed in spectacular fashion along a hundred-mile ridge that seemed to hang suspended over the face of the Mount. There was only one approach to it—from the Upper Sunbreak side, through a gorge so steep and narrow that a hundred warriors could defend it against a million. Not at all to Valentine's surprise, the gorge was occupied when he came to it, and by somewhat more than a hundred warriors.

Ermanar and Deliamber went forward to parley. A short while later they returned with the news that Duke Heitluig of Chorg, of whose province Bibiroon was the capital, was in command of the troops in the gorge and was willing to speak with Lord Valentine.

Carabella said, "Who is this Heitluig? Do you know him?"

Valentine nodded. "Distantly. He belongs to the family of Tyeveras. I hope he holds no grudges against me."

"He could win much grace with Dominin Barjazid," said Sleet darkly, "by striking you down in this pass."

"And suffer for it in all his sleeping hours?" Valentine asked, laughing. "A drunkard he may be, but not a murderer, Sleet. He is a noble of the realm."

"As is Dominin Barjazid, my lord."

"Barjazid himself did not dare to slay me when he had the chance. Am I to expect assassins wherever I parley? Come: we waste time in this."

On foot Valentine went to the mouth of the gorge, accompanied by Ermanar, Asenhart, and Deliamber. The duke and three of his followers were waiting.

Heitluig was a broad-shouldered, powerful-looking man with thick, coarsely curling white hair and a florid, fleshy face. He stared intently at Valentine, as though searching the features of this fair-haired stranger for some hint of the presence of the soul of the true Coronal. Valentine saluted him as was fitting for a Coronal greeting a provincial duke, bland stare and outturned palm, and immediately Heitluig was in difficulties, obviously unsure of the proper form of response. He said after a moment, "The report is that you are Lord Valentine, changed by witchery. If that is so, I bid you welcome, my lord."

"Believe me, Heitluig, it is so."

"There have been sendings to that effect. And also contrary ones."

Valentine smiled. "The sending of the Lady are the trustworthy ones. Those of the King are worth about as much as you might expect, considering what his son has done. Have you had instructions from the Labyrinth?"

"That we are to recognize you, yes. But these are strange times. If I am to mistrust what I hear from the Castle, why should I give faith to orders out of the Labyrinth? They might be forgeries or deceptions."

"Here we have Ermanar, high servitor to your great-uncle

the Pontifex. He is not here as my captive," said Valentine. "He can show you the Pontifical seals that give him authority."

The duke shrugged. His eyes continued to probe Valentine's. "This is a mysterious thing, that a Coronal should be changed this way. If such a thing can be true, anything can be true. What is it you want in Bibiroon—my lord?"

"We need fruit and meat. We have hundreds of miles yet to go, and hungry soldiers are not the best kind."

With a twitch of his cheek, Heitluig said, "Surely you know you are at a Free City."

"I know that. But what of that?"

"The tradition is ancient, and perhaps forgotten by others. But we of the Free Cities hold that we are not required to provide goods for the government, beyond the legally specified taxes. The cost of provisions for an army the size of yours—"

"—will be borne entirely by the imperial treasury," said Valentine crisply. "We are asking nothing from Bibiroon that will cost Bibiroon as much as a five-weight piece."

"And the imperial treasury marches with you?"

Valentine let a flicker of anger show. "The imperial treasury resides at Castle Mount, as it has since Lord Stiamot's day, and when I have reached it and have hurled down the usurper I'll make full payment for what we purchase here. Or is the credit of the Coronal no longer acceptable in Bibiroon?"

"The credit of the *Coronal* still is, yes," said Heitluig carefully. "But there are doubts, my lord. We are thrifty people here, and great shame would come upon us if it developed that we had extended credit to—to one who made false claim upon us."

Valentine struggled for patience.

"You call me 'my lord,' and yet you talk of doubts."

"I am uncertain, yes. I admit that."

"Heitluig, come off and talk alone with me a moment."

"Eh?"

"Come off ten steps! Do you think I'll slit your throat the moment you leave your bodyguard? I want to whisper something to you that you might not want me to say in front of others."

The duke, looking baffled and uneasy, nodded grudgingly and let Valentine lead him away. In a low voice Valentine said, "When you came to Castle Mount for my coronation, Heitluig, you sat at the table of the kin of the Pontifex, and you drank four or five flasks of Muldemar wine, do you remember? And when you were properly sozzled you stood up to dance, and tripped over the leg of your cousin Elzandir, and went sprawling on your face, and would have fought Elzandir on the spot if I had not put my arm around you and drawn you aside. Eh? Does any of that strike an echo in you? And would I know any of that if I were some upstart out of Zimroel trying to seize Lord Valentine's Castle?"

Heitluig's face was scarlet. "My lord—"

"Now you say it with some conviction!" Valentine clasped the duke warmly by the shoulder. "All right, Heitluig. Give me your aid, and when you come to the Castle to celebrate my restoration, you'll have five flasks more of good Muldemar. And I hope you'll be more temperate than the last time."

"My lord, how can I serve you?"

"I told you. We need fruit and fresh meat, and we'll settle the bill when I'm Coronal again."

"So be it. But will you be Coronal?"

"What do you mean?"

"The army that waits above is not a small one, my lord. Lord Valentine—I mean, he who claims to be Lord Valentine—is summoning citizens by the hundreds of thousands to the defense of the Castle."

Valentine frowned. "And where is this army assembling?"

"Between Ertsud Grand and Bombifale. He's drawing on all the Guardian Cities and every city above them. Rivers of blood will run down the Mount, my lord."

Valentine turned away and closed his eyes a moment. Pain and dismay lashed his spirit. It was inevitable, it was not in the least surprising, it was entirely as he had expected from the start. Dominin Barjazid would allow him to march freely through the lower slopes, then would make a fierce defense in the upper reaches, using against him his own royal bodyguard, the knights of high birth with whom he had been reared. In the front lines against him—Stasilaine, Tunigorn, Mirigant his cousin, Elidath, Divvis his brother's son—

For an instant Valentine's resolve wavered once more. Was it worth the turmoil, the bloodshed, the agony of his people, to make himself Coronal a second time? Perhaps it had been the will of the Divine that he be cast down. If he thwarted that will, perhaps, he would accomplish only some terrible cataclysm on the plains above Ertsud Grand, and leave scars on the souls of all people, that would fill his nights with dark accusing dreams of lacerating guilt and make his name accursed forever.

He could turn back now, he could resign from the confrontation with the forces of the Barjazid, he could accept the verdict of destiny, he could——

No.

This was a struggle he had fought and won within himself before, and he would not fight it again. A false Coronal, mean and petty and dangerous, held the highest seat of the land, and ruled rashly and illegitimately. This must not be allowed to remain the case. Nothing else mattered.

"My lord?" Heitluig said.

Valentine looked back at the duke. "The idea of war makes me ache, Heitluig."

"There is no one who relishes it, my lord."

"Yet a time comes when war must happen, lest even worse things befall. I think we are at such a time now."

"So it seems."

"Do you accept me as Coronal, Heitluig?"

"No pretender would have known of my drunkenness at the coronation, I think."

"And will you fight beside me above Ertsud Grand?"

Heitluig regarded him steadily. "Of course, my lord. How many troops of Bibiroon will you require?"

"Say, five thousand. I want no enormous army up there—merely a loyal and brave one."

"Five thousand warriors are yours, my lord. More if you ask for them."

"Five thousand will do, Heitluig, and I thank you for your faith in me. Now let's see about the fresh fruit and meat!"

9

The stay at Bibiroon was brief, just long enough for Heitluig to gather his forces and supply Valentine with the necessary provisions, and then it was on upward, upward, upward. Valentine rode in the vanguard, with his dear friends of Pidruid close at his side. It delighted him to see the look of awe and wonder in their eyes, to see Shanamir's face aglow with excitement, to hear Carabella's little indrawn gasp of ecstasy, to notice even gruff Zalzan Kavol muttering and rumbling in astonishment, as the splendors of Castle Mount unrolled before them.

And he—how radiant he felt at the thought of coming home!

The higher they went, the sweeter and more pure became the air, for they were drawing ever closer to the great engines that sustained the eternal springtime of the Mount. Soon the outlying districts belonging to the Guardian Cities were in view.

"So much—" Shanamir murmured in a thickened voice. "So grand a sight—"

Here the Mount was a great gray shield of granite that rolled heavenward in a gentle but inexorable sweep, disappearing into the white billow of clouds that cloaked the upper slopes. The sky was a dazzling electric blue, deeper in tone than in Majipoor's lowlands. Valentine remembered that sky, how he had loved it, how he had loathed going down into the ordinary world of ordinary colors beyond the Mount. His breast tightened at the sight of it now. Every hill and ridge seemed outlined with a sparkling halo of mysterious brightness. The dust itself, blowing along the edge of the highway, appeared to glitter and shine. Satellite towns and lesser cities could be seen dotting the distant landscape, shimmering like places of awesome magic, and, high above, several of the major urban centers now came in view. Ertsud Grand lay straight ahead, its huge black towers just visible on the horizon, and to the east was a darkness that probably was the city of Minimool; Hoikmar, famed for its quiet canals and byways, could barely be perceived at the extreme westernmost edge of the landscape.

Valentine blinked away the unexpected and troublesome moistness that suddenly was welling in his eyes. He tapped Carabella's pocket-harp and said, "Sing to me."

She smiled and took up the little harp. "We sang this in Til-omon, where Castle Mount was only a storybook place, a romantic dream—"

> There is a land in the far-off east
> That we shall never see,
> Where marvels sprout on mighty peaks,
> Bright cities three by three.
>
> On Castle Mount where Powers dwell,
> And heroes sport all day—

She halted, strummed a quick fretful discord, put down the harp. She turned her face from him.

"What is it, love?" Valentine asked.

Carabella shook her head. "Nothing. I forget the words."

402

"Carabella?"

"It's nothing, I said!"

"Please—"

She looked toward him, biting at her lip, her eyes tear-flooded. "It's so wondrous here, Valentine," she whispered. "And so strange—so frightening—"

"Wondrous, yes. Frightening, no."

"It's beautiful, I know. And bigger than I ever imagined, all these cities, these mountains that are part of the big mountain, everything marvelous. But—but—"

"Tell me."

"You're coming home, Valentine! All your friends, your family, your—your lovers, I suppose— Once we've won the war, you'll have them around you, they'll sweep you away for banquets and celebrations, and—" She paused. "I promised myself I would not say any of this."

"Say it."

"My lord—"

"Not so formal, Carabella." He took her hands. Shanamir and Zalzan Kavol, he noticed, had moved to another part of the floater-car and sat with their backs to them.

She said in a rush of words, "My lord, what happens to the little juggler-girl from Til-omon when you are back among the princes and ladies of Castle Mount?"

"Have I given you reason to think I'll abandon you?"

"No, my lord. But—"

"Call me Valentine, if you will. But what?"

Her cheeks colored. She drew her hand from him and ran it tensely through her dark glossy hair. "Your Duke Heitluig, yesterday, saw us together, saw your arm around me— Valentine, you didn't notice his smile! As though I were some pretty toy of yours, some pet, some little trinket to be discarded when the time comes."

"You read too much into Heitluig's smile, I think," said Valentine slowly, although he had noticed it too, and had been troubled by it. To Heitluig, he knew, and to others of his rank, Carabella would seem only an upstart concubine of unimaginable lower-class origins, to be treated at best with scorn. In his former life on Castle Mount such distinctions of class had been an unchallengeable assumption of the nature of things; but he had been down from the Mount a long time, and saw things differently these days. Carabella's fears were real. Yet it was a problem that could be conquered only in its proper moment. There were other conquests to deal with first. He said gently, "Heitluig is too fond of wine, and his soul is a coarse one. Ignore him. You will find a place among the high ones of the Castle, and no one will dare slight you when I am Coronal again. Come now, finish the song."

"You love me, Valentine?"

"I love you, yes. But I love you less when your eyes are red and puffy, Carabella."

She snorted. "That's the sort of thing one would say to a child! Do you see me as a child, then?"

With a shrug Valentine replied, "I see you as a woman, and a shrewd and lovely one. But what am I supposed to answer, when you ask me if I love you?"

"That you love me. And nothing more by way of decoration."

"I'm sorry, then. I must rehearse these things more carefully. Will you sing again?"

"If you wish," she said, and took up her pocket-harp.

All morning they rode higher, into the open spaces beyond the Free Cities. Valentine chose the Pinitor Highway, that wound between Ertsud Grand and Hoikmar through an empty countryside of rocky plateaus broken only by sparse copses of ghazan-trees, with stout ashen-colored trunks and gnarled convoluted arms—trees that lived ten thousand years and made a soft sighing sound when their time was come. This was stark and silent land, where Valentine and his forces could gather their souls for the effort that lay before them.

All this while their climb went unopposed. "They will not try to stop you," Heitluig said, "until you are above the Guardian Cities. The world is narrower up there. The land is folded and wrinkled. There will be places to trap you."

"There will be room enough," said Valentine.

In a barren valley rimmed with jagged spires, beyond which the city of Ertsud Grand could be seen only some twenty miles to the east, he drew his army to a halt and conferred with his commanders. Scouts had already gone forward to inspect the enemy force, bringing back news that weighed on Valentine like a leaden cloak: an immense army, they reported, a sea of warriors filling the broad flat plain that occupied hundreds of square miles below the Inner City of Bombifale. Most were foot-soldiers, but there were floater-cars gathered as well, and a regiment of mounted troops, and a corps of great thundering mollitors, at least ten times as many of the massive tanklike war-beasts as had been camped in wait for them by the banks of the Glayge. But he let no hint of disheartenment show. "We are outnumbered twenty to one," Valentine said. "I find that encouraging. Too bad there aren't even more of them—but an army that size ought to be unwieldy enough to make life easy for us." He tapped the chart before him. "They camp here, on Bombifale Plain, and surely they can see that we are marching straight toward that plain. They'll expect us to attempt to make our ascent via the Peritole Pass, west of the plain, and that will have the heaviest guard. We will indeed go toward Peritole Pass." Valentine heard a gasp of dismay from Heitluig, and Ermanar looked at him with sudden pained surprise. Untroubled, Valentine went on, "And as we do, they'll send reinforcements in that direction. Once they've begun to move into the pass it should be difficult for them to regroup and redirect themselves. As they start into motion, we'll swing back toward the plain, ride straight into the heart of their camp, and go through them and on to Bombifale itself. Above Bombifale is the High Morpin road that will take us unhindered to the Castle. Are there questions?"

Ermanar said, "What if they have a second army waiting for us between Bombifale and High Morpin?"

"Ask me that again," Valentine replied, "when we get beyond Bombifale. Any other questions?"

He glanced around. No one spoke.

"Good. Onward, then!"

Another day and the terrain grew more fertile, as they entered the great green apron that encircled the Inner Cities. They were in the cloud zone now, cool and moist, where the sun could be seen, but only indistinctly, through the coiling strands of mist that never lifted. In this humid region plants that, below, were merely knee-high grew to giant size, with leaves like platters and stems like tree-trunks, and everything glittered with a coating of shining droplets of water.

The landscape here was a broken one, with steep-sided mountain ranges rising abruptly out of deep-cut valleys, and roads that wound precariously around fierce conical peaks. Choices of route became fewer: to the west were the Banglecode Pinnacles, a region of impassable fanglike mountains that had scarcely ever been explored, to the east was the wide and easy slope of Bombifale Plain, and straight ahead, bordered on both sides by sheer rock walls, was the series of gigantic natural steps known as Peritole Pass, where—unless Valentine entirely missed his guess—the usurper's finest troops lay in wait.

In an unhurried way Valentine led his forces toward the pass. Four hours forward, camp for two, travel five hours more, make camp for the night, late start in the morning. In the exhilarating air of Castle Mount it would have been easy enough to travel much faster. But beyond doubt the enemy was watching his progress from on high, and he wanted to give them plenty of time to observe his route and take the necessary countermeasures.

The next day he stepped up the pace, for now the first of the huge deep steps of the pass was in sight. Deliamber, sending forth his spirit through wizardry, returned with word that the defending army was indeed in possession of the pass, and that secondary troops were streaming westward out of Bombifale Plain to give support.

Valentine smiled. "It won't be long now. They're falling into our hands."

Two hours before twilight he gave the order to make camp, at a pleasant meadow beside a cold, plunging stream. The wagons were drawn up in defensive formation, foragers went out to collect timber for fires, the quartermasters began distributing dinner—and, as night came on, word suddenly circulated through camp that they were to pull up and take to the road again, leaving all fires burning and many of the wagons still in formation.

Valentine felt excitement rising thunderously within him. He saw a renewed gleam in Carabella's eyes, and Sleet's old scar stood out angrily against his cheek as his heart pumped faster. And there was Shanamir, going this way and that but never foolishly, handling many small responsibilities and large ones with sober-faced expertness, at once comic and admirable. These were unforgettable hours, taut with the potential of great events about to be born.

Carabella said, "In the old days on the Mount, you must have studied the art of war deeply, to have devised a maneuver such as this."

With a laugh Valentine said, "Art of war? Whatever art of war was once known on Majipoor was forgotten before Lord Stiamot was a hundred years dead. I don't know a thing about war, Carabella."

"But how—"

"Guesswork. Luck. A gigantic kind of juggle. I'm making it up as I go along." He winked. "But don't tell the others that. Let them think their general's a genius, and they may make him into one!"

In the cloud-shrouded sky no stars could be seen and the light of the moon was only the faintest of reddish glows. Valentine's army moved along the road to Bombifale Plain by the

406

illumination of light-globes at their dimmest intensity, and Deliamber sat beside Valentine and Ermanar in deep trance, roving forward to search for barriers and obstacles ahead. Valentine was silent, still, feeling strangely calm. This was indeed a sort of gigantic juggle, he thought. And now, as he had done so many times with the troupe, he was moving toward that quiet place at the center of his consciousness, where he could process the information of a constantly changing pattern of events without being in any overt way aware of processing, or of information, or even of events: everything done in its proper time, with serene awareness of the only effective sequence of things.

It was an hour before dawn when they reached the place where the road swung uphill toward the entrance to the plain. Again Valentine summoned his commanders.

"Three things only," he told them. "Stay in tight formation. Take no lives needlessly. Keep pressing forward." He went to each of them in turn with a word, a handclasp, a smile. "We'll have lunch today in Bombifale," he said. "And dinner tomorrow night in Lord Valentine's Castle, I promise you!"

10

This was the moment Valentine had dreaded for months, when he must lead citizens of Majipoor into war against citizens of Majipoor, when he must stake the blood of the companions of his boyhood. Yet now that the moment was at hand he felt firm and quiet of spirit.

By the gray light of dawn the invading army rolled out across the rim of the plain, and in the mists of morning Valentine had his first glimpse of the legions that confronted him. The plain seemed to be filled with black tents. Soldiers were everywhere, vehicles, mounts, mollitors—a confused and chaotic tide of humanity.

Valentine's forces were arrayed in the form of a wedge, with his bravest and most dedicated followers in the lead wagons of the phalanx, Duke Heitluig's troops forming the middle body of the army, and the thousands of unwarlike militia from Pendiwane, Makroprosopos, and the other cities of the Glayge forming a rear guard more significant for its mass than for its prowess. All the races of Majipoor were represented in the forces of liberation—a platoon of Skandars, a detachment of

Vroons, a whole horde of burning-eyed Liimen, a great many Hjorts and Ghayrogs, even a small elite corps of Su-Suheris. Valentine himself rode at one of the triple points of the wedge's front face, but not the central point: Ermanar was there, prepared to bear the brunt of the usurper's counteroffensive. Valentine's car was on the right wing, Asenhart's on the left, and the columns led by Sleet, Carabella, Zalzan Kavol, and Lisamon Hultin just to their rear.

"Now!" Valentine cried, and the battle was begun.

Ermanar's car plunged forward, horns blowing, lights flashing. A moment later Valentine followed, and, looking across to the far side of the battlefield, he saw Asenhart keeping pace. In tight formation they charged into the plain, and at once the huge mass of defenders was thrown into disarray. The front line of the usurper's forces collapsed with startling abruptness, almost as though it were a deliberate strategy. Panicky troops ran this way and that, colliding, entangling, scrambling for weapons or merely heading for safety. The great open space of the plain became an ocean of desperate surging figures, without leadership, without plan. Onward through them the invading phalanx rode. There was little exchange of fire; an occasional energy-bolt cast its lurid glare over the landscape, but chiefly the enemy seemed too bewildered for any coherent pattern of defense, and the attacking wedge, cutting forward at will, had no need to take lives.

Deliamber, at Valentine's side, said quietly, "They are strung out across an enormous front, a hundred miles or more. It will take them time to concentrate their strength. But after the first panic they will regroup, and things will become less easy for us."

Indeed that was happening already.

The inexperienced citizen-militia that Dominin Barjazid had levied out of the Guardian Cities might be in disarray, but the nucleus of the defending army consisted of knights of Castle Mount, trained in warlike games if not in the techniques of war itself, and they were rallying now, closing in on all sides around the small wedge of invaders that had thrust deep among them. A platoon of mollitors had somehow been rounded up and was advancing on Asenhart's flank, jaws snapping, huge clawed limbs seeking to do harm. On the other side a cavalry detachment had found its mounts and was striving to get into some kind of formation; and Ermanar had run into a steady barrage of fire from energy-throwers.

"Hold your formation!" Valentine cried. "Keep moving forward!"

They were still making progress, but the pace was slowing perceptibly. If at the outset Valentine's forces had cut through the enemy like a hot blade through butter, now it was more like trying to push through a wall of thick mud. Many of the vehicles were surrounded and some were altogether stopped. Valentine had a glimpse of Lisamon Hultin on foot, striding through a mob of defenders and hurling them like twigs to left and right. Three gigantic Skandars were out on the field also—they could only be Zalzan Kavol and his brothers—doing terrible carnage with their many arms, each wielding a weapon of some sort.

Then Valentine's own vehicle was engulfed, but his driver pulled it into reverse and swung it sharply around, knocking the enemy soldiers aside.

Onward—onward—

There were bodies everywhere. It had been folly for Valentine to hope that the reconquest of the Mount could be achieved bloodlessly. Already it seemed hundreds must be dead, thousands injured. He scowled and aimed his own energy-thrower at a tall hard-faced man who was bearing down on his car, and sent him sprawling. Valentine blinked as the air crackled about him in the wake of his own energy discharge, and fired again, again, again.

"Valentine! Lord Valentine!"

The cry was universal. But it was coming from the throats of warriors on both sides of the fray, and each side had its own Lord Valentine in mind.

Now the advance seemed altogether blocked. The tide had definitely shifted; the defenders were launching a counter-attack. It was as though they had not quite been ready for the first onslaught, and had merely allowed Valentine's army to come crashing through; but now they were regrouping, gathering strength, adopting a semblance of strategy.

"They appear to have new leadership, my lord," Ermanar reported. "The general who guides them now holds powerful control, and spurs them fiercely toward us."

A line of mollitors had formed, leading the counterthrust with the usurper's troops coming in great numbers behind them. But the dull-witted unruly beasts were causing more difficulty from sheer bulk than with their claws and jaws: simply getting past their mammoth humpbacked forms was a challenge. Many of Valentine's officers were out of their vehicles now—he caught sight again of Lisamon Hultin, and of Sleet, and Carabella fighting furiously, all with knots of their own troops doing their best to protect them. Valentine himself would have left the wagon, but Deliamber ordered him to stay off the field. "Your person is sacred and indispensable," the Vroon said brusquely. "The hand-to-hand warriors will have to make do without you."

"But—"

"It is essential."

Valentine scowled. He saw the logic of what Deliamber said, but he despised it. Nevertheless he yielded.

"Forward!" he roared in frustration into the dark ivory horn of his field communicator.

But they could not go forward. Clouds of defending warriors were coming now from all sides, driving Valentine's forces back. The new strength of the usurper's army appeared to be centered not far from Valentine, just beyond a rise in the plain, and radiated outward from there in bands of virtually visible power. Yes, some new general, Valentine thought, some powerful field commander providing inspiration and strength, rallying the troops that had been so dispirited. As I should be doing, he thought, down on the field among them. As I should be doing.

Ermanar's voice came to him. "My lord, do you see that low knoll to your right? Beyond it is the enemy command post—their general is there, in the midst of the battle."

"I want to look at him," Valentine said, signaling his driver to move to higher ground.

"My lord," Ermanar went on, "we must concentrate our attack there, and remove him before he gains greater advantage."

"Certainly," Valentine murmured remotely. He stared, narrowing his eyes. The scene seemed all confusion down there. But gradually he discerned a form to the flow. Yes, that must be he. A tall man, taller than Valentine, with a strong wide-mouthed face, piercing dark eyes, a heavy shock of glossy black hair braided in back. He looked oddly familiar—so very familiar, beyond question familiar, one whom Valentine had known, and known well, in his days on Castle Mount, but his mind was so muddled by the chaos of the battle that for a moment he found it hard to reach into his store of renewed memory and identify—

Yes. Of course.

Elidath of Morvole.

How could he have forgotten, even for an instant, even amidst all this madness, the companion of his youth, Elidath, at times closer even to him than his brother Voriax, Elidath the dearest of all his friends, the sharer of so many of his boldest early exploits, the nearest to him in abilities and temperament, Elidath whom all considered, even Valentine himself, to be next in line to be Coronal—

Elidath leading the enemy army. Elidath the dangerous general who must be removed.

"My lord?" Ermanar said. "We await your instructions, my lord."

Valentine faltered. "Surround him," he replied. "Neutralize him. Take him prisoner, if you can."

"We could center our fire on—"

"He is to be unharmed," Valentine ordered bluntly.

"My lord—"

"*Unharmed*, I said."

"Yes, my lord." But there was not much conviction in Ermanar's reply. To Ermanar, Valentine knew, an enemy was merely an enemy, and this general would do least damage if he were quickly slain. But Elidath—!

In tension and distress Valentine watched as Ermanar swung his forces about and guided them toward Elidath's camp. Simple enough to order that Elidath not be harmed; but how could that be controlled, in the heat of battle? This was what Valentine had feared most of all, that some beloved companion of his would lead the opposing troops—but to know that it was Elidath, that Elidath was in jeopardy on the field, that Elidath must fall if the army of liberation was to go forward—what agony that was!

Valentine stood up. Deliamber said, "You must not—"

"I must," he said, and rushed from the wagon before the Vroon could place some wizardry on him.

Out here in the midst of things all was incomprehensible: figures rushing to and fro, enemies indistinguishable from friends, all noise, tumult, shouting, alarms, dust, and insanity. The patterns of battle that Valentine had been able to discern from his floater-car were not visible here. He thought he perceived Ermanar's troops closing in on one side, and a muddled and chaotic struggle going on somewhere in the direction of Elidath's camp.

"My lord," Shanamir called to him, "you should not be in plain view! You—"

Valentine waved him off and moved toward the thickest part of the battle.

The tide had shifted again, so it seemed, with Ermanar's concerted attack on Elidath's camp. The invaders were breaking through and once more casting the enemy into disorder. They were falling back, knights and citizens alike, running in

411

random circles, trying to flee the merciless oncoming attackers, while somewhere far ahead a knot of defenders held firm round Elidath, a single sturdy rock in the raging torrent.

Let Elidath not be harmed, Valentine prayed. Let him be taken, and taken swiftly, but let him not be harmed.

He pressed forward, all but unnoticed on the battlefield. Once again victory seemed to be within his grasp: but at too high a cost, much too high, if bought with the death of Elidath.

Valentine saw Lisamon Hultin and Khun of Kianimot just ahead, side by side, hacking a path through which the others could follow, and they were driving all before them. Khun was laughing, as if he had waited all his life for this moment of fierce commitment.

Then an enemy bolt struck the blue-skinned alien in the chest. Khun staggered and swung around. Lisamon Hultin, seeing him beginning to fall, caught him and steadied him, and lowered him gently to the ground.

"Khun!" Valentine cried, and rushed toward him.

Even from twenty yards away he could see that the alien had been terribly wounded. Khun was gasping; his lean, sharp-featured face looked mottled, almost gray; his eyes were dull. At the sight of Valentine he brightened a little and tried to sit up.

"My lord," the giantess said, "this is no place for you."

He ignored her and bent to the alien. "Khun? Khun?" he whispered urgently.

"It's all right, my lord. I knew—there was a reason—why I had come to your world—"

"Khun!"

"Too bad—I'll miss the victory banquet—"

Helpless, Valentine grasped the alien's sharp-boned shoulders and held him, but Khun's life slipped swiftly and quietly away. His long strange journey was at its end. He had found purpose at last, and peace.

Valentine rose and looked about, perceiving the madness of the battlefield as though in a dream. A cordon of his people surrounded him, and someone—Sleet, he realized—was pulling at him, trying to get him to a safer place.

"No," Valentine muttered. "Let me fight—"

"Not out here, my lord. Would you share Khun's fate? What of all of us, if you perish? The enemy troops are streaming toward us from Peritole Pass. Soon the fighting will grow even more furious. You should not be on the field."

Valentine understood that. Dominin Barjazid was nowhere

on the scene, after all, and probably neither should he be. But how could he sit snug in a floater-car, when others were dying for him, when Khun, who was not even a creature of this world, had already given his life for him, when his beloved Elidath, just beyond that rise in the plain, was perhaps in grave peril from Valentine's own troops? He swayed in indecision. Sleet, bleak-faced, released him, but only to summon Zalzan Kavol: the giant Skandar, swinging swords in three arms and wielding an energy-thrower with the fourth, was not far away. Valentine saw Sleet conferring sternly with him, and Zalzan Kavol, holding defenders at bay almost disdainfully, began to fight his way toward Valentine. In a moment, Valentine suspected, the Skandar might haul him forcibly, crowned Power or not, from the field.

"Wait," Valentine said. "The heir presumptive is in danger. I command you to follow me!"

Sleet and Zalzan Kavol looked baffled by the unfamiliar title.

"The heir presumptive?" Sleet repeated. "Who's—"

"Come with me," Valentine said. "An order."

Zalzan Kavol rumbled, "Your safety, my lord, is—"

"—not the only important thing. Sleet, at my left! Zalzan Kavol, at my right!"

They were too bewildered to disobey. Valentine summoned Lisamon Hultin also; and, guarded by his friends, he moved rapidly over the rise toward the front line of the enemy.

"Elidath!" Valentine cried, bellowing it with all his strength.

His voice carried across half a league, so it seemed, and the sound of that mighty roar caused all action about him to cease for an instant. Past an avenue of motionless warriors Valentine looked toward Elidath, and as their eyes met he saw the dark-haired man pause, return to look, frown, shrug.

To Sleet and Zalzan Kavol Valentine shouted, "Capture that man! Bring him to me—unharmed!"

The instant of stasis ended; with redoubled intensity the tumult of battle resumed. Valentine's forces swarmed once more toward the hard-pressed and yielding enemy, and for a second he caught sight of Elidath, surrounded by a shield of his own people, fiercely holding his ground. Then he could see no more, for everything became chaotic again. Someone was tugging at him—Sleet, perhaps? Carabella?—urging him again to return to the safety of his car, but he grunted and pulled himself free.

"Elidath of Morvole!" Valentine called. "Elidath, come to parley!"

"Who calls my name?" was the reply.

Again the surging mob opened between him and Elidath. Valentine stretched his arms toward the frowning figure and began to make answer. But words would be too slow, too clumsy, Valentine knew. Abruptly he dropped into the trance-state, putting all his strength of will into his mother's silver circlet, and casting forth across the space that separated him from Elidath of Morvole the full intensity of his soul in a single compressed fraction of an instant of dream-images, dream-force—

—two young men, boys really, riding sleek fast mounts through a forest of stunted dwarfish trees—

—a thick twisted root rising like a serpent out of the ground across the path, a mount stumbling, a boy flung head-long—

—a terrible cracking sound, a white shaft of jagged bone jutting horridly through torn skin—

—the other boy reining in, riding back, whistling in astonishment and fright as he saw the extent of the injury—

Valentine could sustain the dream-pictures no longer. The moment of contact ended. Drained, exhausted, he slipped back into waking reality.

Elidath stared at him, bewildered. It was as though the two of them alone were on the battlefield, and all that was going on about them was mere noise and vapor.

"Yes," Valentine said. "You know me, Elidath. But not by this face I wear today."

"Valentine?"

"No other."

They moved toward each other. A ring of troops of both armies surrounded them, silent, mystified. When they were a few feet apart they halted and squared off uncertainly, as if they were about to launch into a duel. Elidath studied Valentine's features in a stunned, astounded way.

"Can it be?" he asked finally. "Such a witchery, is it possible?"

"We rode together in the pygmy forest under Amblemorn," said Valentine. "I never felt such pain as on that day. Remember, when you moved the bone with your hands, putting it in its place, and you cried out as if the leg were your own?"

"How could you know such things?"

"And then the months I spent sitting and fuming, while you

414

and Tunigorn and Stasilaine roamed the Mount without me? And the limp I had, that stayed with me even after I was healed?" Valentine laughed. "Dominin Barjazid stole that limp when he took my body from me! Who would have expected such a favor from the likes of him?"

Elidath seemed like one who walked in dreams. He shook his head, as though to rid it of cobwebs.

"This is witchery," he said.

"Yes. And I am Valentine!"

"Valentine is in the Castle. I saw him but yesterday, and he wished me well, and spoke of the old times, the pleasures we shared—"

"Stolen memories, Elidath. He fishes in my brain, and finds the old scenes embedded there. Have you noticed nothing strange about him, this past year?" Valentine's eyes looked deep into Elidath's and the other man flinched, as if fearing sorcery. "Have you not thought your Valentine oddly withdrawn and brooding and mysterious lately, Elidath?"

"Yes, but I thought—it was the cares of the throne that made him so."

"You noticed a difference, then! A change!"

"A slight one, yes. A certain coldness—a distance, a chill about him—"

"And still you deny me?"

Elidath stared. "Valentine?" he murmured, not yet believing. "You, really you, in that strange guise?"

"None other. And he up there in the Castle has deceived you, you and all the world."

"This is so strange."

"Come, give me your embrace, and cease your mumbling, Elidath!" Smiling broadly, Valentine seized the other man and pulled him close, and held him as friend holds friend. Elidath stiffened. His body was as rigid as wood. After a moment he pushed Valentine away and stepped back a pace, shivering.

"You need not fear me, Elidath."

"You ask too much of me. To believe such—"

"Believe it."

"I do, at least by half. The warmth of your eyes—the smile—the things you remember—"

"Believe the other half," Valentine urged passionately. "The Lady my mother sends you her love, Elidath. You will see her again, at the Castle, the day we hold festival to mark my restoration. Turn your troops around, dear friend, and join us as we march up the Mount."

There was warfare on Elidath's face. His lips moved, a muscle in his cheek twitched violently. In silence he confronted Valentine.

Then at last he said, "This may be madness, but I accept you as what you claim."

"Elidath!"

"And I will join you, and may the Divine help you if I am misled."

"I promise you there will be no regretting this."

Elidath nodded. "I'll send messengers to Tunigorn—"

"Where is he?"

"He holds Peritole Pass against the thrust we expected from you. Stasilaine is there too. I was bitter, being left in command here in the plain, for I thought I'd miss all the action. Oh, Valentine, is it really you? With golden hair, and that sweet innocent look to your face?"

"The true Valentine, yes. I who slipped off with you to High Morpin when we were ten, borrowing the chariot of Voriax, and rode the juggernaut all day and half the night, and afterward had the same punishment as you—"

"—crusts of old stajja-bread for three days, indeed—"

"—and Stasilaine brought us a platter of meat secretly, and was caught, and he ate crusts with us too the next day—"

"—I had forgotten that part. And do you remember Voriax making us polish every part of the chariot where we had muddied it—"

"Elidath!"

"Valentine!"

They laughed and pounded each other joyously with their fists.

Then Elidath grew somber and said, "But where have you been? What has befallen you all this year? Have you suffered, Valentine? Have you—"

"It is a very long story," Valentine said gravely, "and this is not the place to tell it. We must halt this battle, Elidath. Innocent citizens are dying for Dominin Barjazid's sake, and we cannot allow that. Rally your troops, turn them around."

"In this madhouse it won't be easy."

"Give the orders. Get the word to the other commanders. The killing has to stop. And then ride with us, Elidath, onward to Bombifale, and then past High Morpin to the Castle."

11

Valentine returned to his car, and Elidath vanished into the confused and ragged line of the defenders. During the parley, Valentine discovered now from Ermanar, his people had made strong advances, keeping their wedge tight and pushing deep into the plain, throwing the vast but formless army of the false Coronal into nearly complete disarray. Now that relentless wedge continued to roll on, through helpless troops that had neither the will nor the desire to hold them back. With Elidath's leadership and formidable battlefield presence negated, the defenders were spiritless and disorganized.

But it was that very pandemonium and tumult among the defenders that made halting the wasteful battle almost impossible. With hundreds of thousands of warriors moving in patternless streams over Bombifale Plain, and thousands more rushing in from the pass as news spread of Valentine's attack, there was no way of exercising command over the entire mass. Valentine saw Elidath's starburst banner flying in the midst of the madness, halfway across the field, and knew that he was striving to make contact with his fellow officers and tell them of the switch in loyalties; but the army was out of control, and soldiers were dying needlessly. Every casualty brought a stab of pain to Valentine.

He could do nothing about that. He signaled Ermanar to keep pressing onward.

Over the next hour a bizarre transformation of the battle began. Valentine's wedge sliced forward almost without opposition, and a second phalanx now moved parallel to his, off to the east, led by Elidath, advancing with equal ease. The rest of the gigantic army that had occupied the plain was divided and confounded, and in a muddled way was fighting against itself, breaking into small groups that clung vociferously to tiny sectors of the plain and beat off anyone who approached.

Soon these feckless hordes lay far to Valentine's rear, and the double column of invaders was entering the upper half of the plain, where the land began to curve bowl-fashion toward the crest on which Bombifale, oldest and most beautiful of the Inner Cities, stood. It was early afternoon, and as they ascended the slope the sky grew ever more clear and bright and the air warmer, for they were beginning to leave the Mount-girdling cloud-belt behind and emerge into the lower flanks of the summit zone, that lay bathed forever in shimmering sunlight.

And now Bombifale came into view, rising above them like a vision of antique splendor: great scalloped walls of burnt-orange sandstone set with huge diamond-shaped slabs of blue seaspar fetched from the shores of the Great Sea in Lord Pinitor's time, and lofty needle-sharp towers sprouting on the battlements at meticulously regular intervals, slender and graceful, casting long shadows into the plain.

Valentine's spirit throbbed with gathering joy and delight. Hundreds of miles of Castle Mount lay behind him, ring after ring of grand bustling cities, Slope Cities and Free Cities and Guardian Cities far below. The Castle itself was less than a day's journey above, and the army that would have thwarted his climb had crumbled into pathetic turmoil behind him. And though he still felt the distant threatening twinges of the King of Dreams' sendings at night, they were becoming only the merest tickle at the edges of his soul, and his beloved friend Elidath was ascending the Mount by his side, with Stasilaine and Tunigorn riding now to join them.

How good it was to behold the spires of Bombifale, and know what lay beyond! These hills, that towered city ahead, the dark thick grass of the meadows, the red stones of the mountain road from Bombifale to High Morpin, the dazzling flower-strewn fields that linked the Grand Calintane Highway from High Morpin to the southern wing of the Castle—he knew these places better than the sturdy but still somewhat unfamiliar body he now wore. He was almost home.

And then?

Deal with the usurper, yes, and set things to order—but the task was so awesome he scarcely knew where he would begin. He had been absent from Castle Mount almost two years, and deprived of power most of that time. The laws promulgated by Dominin Barjazid would have to be examined, and very likely repealed by blanket ordinance. And there was also the problem, which he had barely considered before this moment, of integrating the companions of his long wanderings into the former imperial officialdom, for surely he must find posts of power for Deliamber and Sleet and Zalzan Kavol and the rest, but there was Elidath to think of, and the others who had been central in his court. He could hardly discard them merely because he was coming home from his exile with new favorites. That was perplexing, but he hoped he would find some way of handling it that would breed no resentments and would cause no—

Deliamber said abruptly, "I fear new troubles heading in our direction, and not small ones."

"What do you mean?"

"Do you see any changes in the sky?"

"Yes," Valentine said. "It grows brighter and a deeper blue as we escape from the cloud-belt."

"Look more closely," said Deliamber.

Valentine peered upslope. Indeed he had spoken carelessly and too soon, for the brightening of the sky that he had noticed a short while ago was altered now, in a strange manner: there was a faint tinge of darkness overhead, as though a storm were coming on. No clouds were in sight, but an odd and sinister gray tint was moving in behind the blue. And the banners mounted on the floater-cars, which had been fluttering in a mild western breeze, had shifted and stood out stiffly to the south, blown by winds of sudden strength coming down from the summit.

"A change in the weather," Valentine said. "Rain, perhaps? But why are you concerned?"

"Have you ever known sudden changes in the weather to occur this high on Castle Mount?"

Valentine frowned. "Not commonly, no."

"Not ever," said Deliamber. "My lord, why is the climate of this region so benign?"

"Why, because it's controlled from the Castle, artificially generated and governed by the great machines that—"

He broke off, staring in horror.

"Exactly," Deliamber said.

"No! It's unthinkable!"

"Think it, my lord," said the Vroon. "The Mount pierces high into the cold night of space. Above us in the Castle hides a terrified man who holds his throne by treachery, and who has just seen his most trusted generals desert to the side of his enemy. Now an invincible army climbs the summit of the Mount unhindered. How can he keep them from reaching him? Why, shut down the weather-machines and let this sweet air freeze in our lungs, let night fall in an afternoon and the darkness of the void come sweeping over us, turn this Mount back into the lifeless tooth of rock it was ten thousand years ago. Look at the sky, Valentine! Look at the banners in the wind!"

"But a billion people live on the Mount!" Valentine cried. "If he shuts down the weather-machines he destroys them along with us! And himself as well—unless he's found some way to seal the Castle against the cold."

"Do you think he cares about his own survival now? He's doomed in any event. But this way he can bring you down with him—you and everyone else on Castle Mount. Look at the sky, Valentine! Look at it darkening!"

Valentine found himself trembling, not out of fear but in anger that Dominin Barjazid should be willing to destroy all the cities of the Mount in this monstrous final cataclysm, to murder children and babes and mothers with child, and farmers in the fields and merchants in their shops, millions upon millions of the innocent who had no part in this struggle for the Castle. And why this slaughter? Why, merely to vent his rage at having lost what was never rightfully his! Valentine looked toward the sky, hoping to find some sign that this was only some natural phenomenon after all. But that was foolishness. Deliamber was right: on Castle Mount the weather was *never* a natural phenomenon.

In anguish Valentine said, "We are still far from the Castle. How long will it be before the freezing begins?"

Deliamber shrugged. "When the weather-machines first were constructed, my lord, it took many months before there was air dense enough to support life at these altitudes. Night and day the machines labored, yet it took months. Undoing that work will probably be faster than the doing of it was; but it will need more than an instant, I think."

"Can we reach the Castle in time to halt it?"

"It will be a close business, my lord," said the Vroon.

Grim-faced, scowling, Valentine ordered the car to halt and summoned his officers. Elidath's vehicle, he saw, was already making its way laterally across the plain toward him in advance of the summons: plainly Elidath too had noticed that something was awry. As Valentine stepped from his car he shivered at the first touch of the air—though it was a shiver more of apprehension than of chill, for there was only the lightest hint of cooling thus far. Yet that was sufficiently ominous.

Elidath came running to his side. His expression was bleak. He pointed toward the darkening sky and said, "My lord, the madman is doing the worst!"

"I know. We also see the change beginning."

"Tunigorn is close below us now, and Stasilaine coming across by the Banglecode side. We must go on toward the Castle as fast as possible."

"Do you think we'll have time?" Valentine asked.

Elidath managed a frosty grin. "Little enough to spare. But it'll be the quickest homeward journey I'll ever have made."

Sleet, Carabella, Lisamon Hultin, Asenhart, Ermanar, all were gathered close now, looking wholly mystified. These strangers to Castle Mount perhaps had noted the change in the weather, but had not drawn from it Elidath's conclusions. They glanced from Valentine to Elidath and back again, troubled, dismayed, knowing that something was amiss but unable to comprehend the nature of it.

Crisply Valentine explained. Their looks of confusion gave way to disbelief, shock, rage, consternation.

"There will be no halt in Bombifale," Valentine said. "We go straight on to the Castle, via the High Morpin road, and no stopping of any kind between here and there." He looked toward Ermanar. "There is, I suppose, the possibility of panic among our forces. This must not happen. Assure your troops that we will be safe if only we reach the Castle in time, that panic is fatal and swift action the only hope. Understood? A billion lives depend on how fast we travel now—a billion lives and our own."

12

This was not the joyous ascent of the Mount that Valentine had imagined. With the victory of Bombifale Plain he had felt a great burden lift from him, for he saw no further barriers standing between him and what he sought. He had envisioned a serene journey to the Inner Cities, a triumphant banquet in Bombifale while the Barjazid cowered in fearful anticipation above, then the climactic entry into the Castle, the seizure of the usurper, the proclamation of restoration, everything unfolding with grand inevitability. But that pleasant fantasy was blasted now. Upward they sped in desperate haste, and the sky grew darker moment by moment, and the wind down from the summit gained in force, and the air became raw and biting. What did they make of these changes, in Bombifale and Peritole and Banglecode, and higher yet in Halanx and the Morpins, and in the Castle itself? Certainly they must realize something hideous was in the making, as all the fair land of Castle Mount suffered under unfamiliar frigid blasts and the balmy afternoon turned into mysterious night. Did they understand the doom that was rushing upon them? What of the Castle folk—were they frantically trying to reach the

421

weather-machines that their mad Coronal had shut down, or did the usurper have them barricaded and guarded, so that death might strike everyone impartially?

Bombifale now was close at hand. Valentine regretted passing it by, for his people had fought hard and were weary; but if they rested now in Bombifale they would rest there forever.

So it was upward and upward through the gathering night. However fast they moved, it was too slow for Valentine, who imagined the terrified crowds gathering in the grand plazas of the cities—vast chaotic hordes of the frightened, weeping, turning to one another, staring at the sky, crying out, "Lord Valentine, save us!" and not even knowing that the dark man to whom they sent their prayers was the instrument of their destruction. In his mind's eye he saw the people of Castle Mount streaming out by the millions into the roads, beginning a dreadful panicky migration to the lower levels, hopeless, doomed, a frantic useless effort to outrace death. Valentine imagined, too, tongues of piercing wintry air sliding down the slopes, licking at the flawless plants of Tolingar Barrier, chilling the stone birds of Furible, blackening the elegant gardens of Stee and Minimool, turning the canals of Hoikmar to sheets of ice. Eight thousand years in the making, this miracle that was Castle Mount, and it might be destroyed in the twinkling of an eye by the folly of one cold and treacherous soul.

Valentine could reach out and touch Bombifale, so it seemed. Its walls and towers, perfect and heartachingly beautiful even in this strange failing light, beckoned to him. But he went on, and on and on, hastening now on the steep mountain road paved with ancient blocks of red stone. That was Elidath's car close beside his on the left, and Carabella's on the right, and not far away rode Sleet, Zalzan Kavol, Ermanar, Lisamon Hultin, and all the hordes of troops he had accumulated on his long journey. All hurried after their lord, not understanding the doom that was coming upon the world but aware that this was a moment of apocalypse when monumental evil stood near to triumph, and only courage, courage and haste, could block its victory.

Onward. Valentine clenched his fists and through sheer power of will tried to force the car higher. Deliamber, beside him, urged him to be calm, to be patient. But how? How, when the very air of Castle Mount was being stripped away molecule by molecule, and the darkest of nights was taking hold?

"Look," Valentine said. "Those trees that flank the road— the ones that bear the crimson-and-gold flowers? Those are halatingas, planted four hundred years ago. A festival is held at High Morpin when they come into bloom, and thousands of people dance down the road beneath them. And see, see? The leaves are shriveling already, turning black at the edges. They have never known temperatures so low, and the cold has only begun. What will happen to them in eight more hours? And what will happen to the people who loved to dance beneath them? If a mere chill withers the leaves, Deliamber, what will true frost do, and snow? Snow, on Castle Mount! Snow, and worse than snow, when the air is gone, when everything stands naked to the stars, Deliamber—"

"We are not yet lost, my lord. What city is that, now, above us?"

Valentine peered through the deepening shadows. "High Morpin—the pleasure-city, where the games are held."

"Think of the games that will be held there next month, my lord, to celebrate your restoration."

Valentine nodded. "Yes," he said, without irony. "Yes. I will think of the games next month, the laughter, the wine, the flowers on the trees, the songs of the birds. Is there no way to make this thing go faster, Deliamber?"

"It floats," said the Vroon, "but it will not fly. Be patient. The Castle is near."

"Hours, yet," Valentine said sullenly.

He struggled to regain his balance of soul. He reminded himself of Valentine the juggler, that innocent young man buried somewhere within him, standing in the stadium at Pidruid and reducing himself to nothing more than hand and eye, hand and eye, to perform the tricks he had only just learned. Steady, steady, steady, keep to the center of your soul, remember that life is merely a game, a voyage, a brief amusement, that Coronals can be gobbled by sea-dragons and tumbled about in rivers and mocked by pantomiming Metamorphs in a drizzly forest, and what of it? But those were poor consolations now. This was not a matter of one man's misfortunes, which under the eye of the Divine were trivial enough, though that man had been a king. A billion innocent lives were threatened here, and a work of splendid art, this Mount, that might be unique in all the cosmos. Valentine stared at the deep reaches of the darkening sky, where, he feared, the stars would soon be shining through in afternoon. Stars out there, multitudes of worlds, and in all those worlds was there anything to compare with Castle Mount and the Fifty Cities? And would it all perish in an afternoon?

"High Morpin," said Valentine. "I had hoped my return to it would be happier."

"Peace," Deliamber whispered. "Today we pass it by. Another day you'll come to it in joy."

Yes. The shining airy webwork that was High Morpin rose to view on the right, that fantasy-city, that city of play, all wonder and dream, a city spun from wires of gold, or so Valentine had often thought as a boy, looking at its marvelous buildings. He glanced at it now and quickly away. It was ten miles from High Morpin to the perimeter of the Castle—a moment, an eye-blink.

"Does this road have a name?" asked Deliamber.

"The Grand Calintane Highway," Valentine replied. "A thousand times I traveled it, Deliamber, back and forth to the pleasure-city. The fields beside it are so arranged that something is in bloom on every day of the year, and always in pleasing patterns of color, the yellows beside the blues, the reds far from the oranges, the whites and pinks in the borders, and look now, look at the flowers turning away from us, drooping on their stems—"

"They can be planted again, if the cold destroys them," said Deliamber. "But there's time yet. These plants may not be as tender as you think."

"I feel the cold on them as though it were on my own skin."

Now they were in the highest reaches of Castle Mount, so far above the plains of Alhanroel that it was almost as though they had attained some other world, or some moon that hovered motionless in the sky of Majipoor.

Everything came to an end here in a fantastic upsweep of sharp-tipped peaks and crags. The summit aimed itself at the stars like a hundred spears, and in the midst of those strangely delicate stony spikes rose the odd rounded hump of the highest place of all, where Lord Stiamot had boldly planted his imperial residence eight thousand years ago in celebration of his conquest of the Metamorphs, and where, ever since, Coronal after Coronal had commemorated his own reign by adding rooms and outbuildings and spires and battlements and parapets. The Castle sprawled incomprehensibly over thousands of acres, a city in itself, a labyrinth more bewildering even than the lair of the Pontifex. And the Castle lay just ahead.

It was dark now. The cold pitiless splendor of the stars blazed overhead.

"The air must be gone," Valentine murmured. "The death will come soon, will it not?"

"This is true night, not the calamity," Deliamber answered. "We have journeyed all day without rest, and you've had no sense of the passing of time. The hour is late, Valentine."

"And the air?"

"Growing colder. Growing thinner. But not yet gone."

"And there is time?"

"There is time."

They came around the last stupefying turn in the Calintane Highway. Valentine remembered it well: the turn that whipped at a sharp curve around the neck of the mountain and presented stunned travelers with their first view of the Castle.

Valentine had never seen Deliamber amazed before.

In a hushed voice the wizard said, "What are those buildings, Valentine?"

"The Castle," he replied.

The Castle, yes. Lord Malibor's Castle, Lord Voriax' Castle, Lord Valentine's Castle. Nowhere could one see the whole structure, or even any significant part of it, but from here, at least, one beheld an awesome segment of it, a great pile of masonry and brick rising in level upon level, in maze upon maze, spiraling round and round upon itself, dancing up the peak in eye-dazzling fashion, sparkling with the glow of a million lights.

Valentine's fears dissolved, his morbid gloom lifted. At Lord Valentine's Castle, Lord Valentine could feel no sorrow. He was coming home, and whatever wound had been inflicted upon the world would soon be healed.

The Calintane Highway reached its end at the Dizimaule Plaza, which lay before the Castle's southern wing, a huge open space paved with cobblestones of green porcelain, with a golden starburst at its center. Here Valentine halted and descended from his car to assemble his officers.

A cold bleak wind was blowing, biting and brisk.

Carabella said, "Are there gates? Will we have to lay siege?"

Valentine smiled and shook his head. "No gates. Who would ever invade the Castle of the Coronal? We simply ride in, through the Dizimaule Arch yonder. But once we're inside, we may face enemy troops again."

"The guards of the Castle are in my command," said Elidath. "I'll deal with them."

"Good. Keep moving, keep in touch, trust in the Divine. By morning we'll gather to celebrate our victory, I swear you that."

425

"Long life to Lord Valentine!" Sleet called out.

"Long life! Long life!"

Valentine lifted his arms, both as an acknowledgement and to silence their uproar.

"We celebrate tomorrow," he said. "Tonight we give battle, and may it be the last!"

13

How strange it felt, finally to be passing under the Dizimaule Arch, and to see the baffling myriad splendors of the Castle before him!

As a boy he had played in these boulevards and avenues, had lost himself in the wonders of the endlessly intertangling passageways and corridors, had stared in awe at the mighty walls and towers and enclosures and vaults. As a young man in the service of Lord Voriax his brother he had dwelled within the Castle, over yonder in the Pinitor Court, where high officials had their residences, and many a time he had strolled on the parapet of Lord Ossier, with its stupendous view of the Morpin Plunge and the High Cities. And as Coronal, that brief time he had occupied the innermost zones of the Castle, he had with delight touched the ancient weather-beaten stones of Stiamot Keep, and walked alone through the vast echoing chamber of the Confalume throne-room, and studied the patterns of the stars from Lord Kinniken's Observatory, and pondered what additions he would make to the Castle himself in years to come. Now that he was back, he realized how much he loved this place, and not merely because it was a symbol of power and imperial grandeur that had been his, but mainly because it was such a fabric of the ages, such a living, breathing weave of history.

"The Castle is ours!" cried Elidath jubilantly as Valentine's army burst through the unguarded gate.

But what good was that, Valentine thought, if death for all the Mount and its squabbling mortals lay just a few hours away? Already too much time had elapsed since the thinning of the atmosphere had begun. Valentine wanted to reach out, to claw the fleeing air and hold in back.

The deepening chill that now lay like a terrible weight on Castle Mount was nowhere more manifest than in the Castle itself, and those within it, already dazed and bewildered by the events of the civil war, stood like waxen figures, unblinking and numb, shivering and immobile while the invading parties rushed inward. Some, shrewder or quicker of wit than the others, managed to croak, "Long live Lord Valentine!" as the unfamiliar golden-haired figure rode by; but most behaved as though their minds had already begun to freeze.

The hordes of attackers, flowing inward, moved swiftly and precisely toward the tasks Valentine had assigned. Duke Heitluig and his Bibiroon warriors had charge of seizing control of the Castle perimeter, flushing out and neutralizing any hostile forces. Asenhart and six detachments of valley people had the work of sealing all of the Castle's many gates, so none of the usurper's followers might escape. Sleet and Carabella and their troops went upward, toward the imperial halls of the inner sector to take possession of the seat of government. Valentine himself, with Elidath and Ermanar and their combined forces, set out on the spiraling lower causeway to the vaults where the weather-machines were housed. The rest, under command of Nascimonte, Zalzan Kavol, Shanamir, Lisamon Hultin, and Gorzval, went forth in random streams, spreading out over the Castle in search of Dominin Barjazid, who might be hiding in any of the thousands of rooms, even the meanest.

Down the causeway Valentine raced, until, in the murky depths of the cobbled passage, the floater-car could go no farther; and then on foot he sped toward the vaults. The cold was numbing against his nose and lips and ears. His heart pounded, his lungs worked fiercely in the thin air. These vaults were all but unknown to him. He had been down here only once or twice, long ago. Elidath, though, seemed to know the way.

Through corridors, down endless flights of wide stone stairs, into a high-roofed arcade lit by twinkling points far overhead—and all the time the air grew perceptibly more chilly, the unnatural night gripped the Mount more tightly—

A great arched wooden door, banded with thick metal inlays, loomed up before them.

"Force it," Valentine ordered. "Burn through it, if we must!"

"Wait, my lord," a mild quavering voice said.

Valentine whirled. An ancient Ghayrog, ashen-skinned, his serpent hair limp in the cold, had stepped from a doorway in the wall and came shambling uncertainly toward them.

"The keeper of the weather-machines," Elidath muttered.

The Ghayrog looked half dead. Bewilderedly he glanced from Elidath to Ermanar, from Ermanar to Valentine; and

427

then he threw himself to the ground before Valentine, plucking at the Coronal's boots.

"My lord—Lord Valentine—" He stared up in torment. "Save us, Lord Valentine! The machines—they have turned off the machines—"

"Can you open the gate?"

"Yes, my lord. The control-house is in this alley. But they have seized the vaults—his troops are in command, they forced me out—what damage are they doing in there, my lord? What will become of us all?"

Valentine pulled the quivering old Ghayrog to his feet. "Open the gate," he said.

"Yes, my lord. It will be only a moment—"

An eternity, rather, Valentine thought. But there came the sound of awesome subterranean machinery and gradually the sturdy wooden barrier, creaking and groaning, began to move aside.

Valentine would have been the first to dart through the opening, but Elidath caught him ungently by the arm and pulled him back. Valentine slapped at the hand that held him as though it were some bothersome vermin, some dhiim of the jungles. Elidath held firm.

"No, my lord," he said crisply.

"Let go, Elidath."

"If it costs me my head, Valentine, I will not let you go in there. Stand aside."

"Elidath!"

Valentine glanced toward Ermanar. But he found no support there. "The Mount freezes, my lord, while you delay us," Ermanar said.

"I will not allow—"

"Stand aside!" Elidath commanded.

"I am Coronal, Elidath."

"And I am responsible for your safety. You may direct the offensive from the outside, my lord. But there are enemy soldiers in there, desperate men, defending the last place of power the usurper controls. Let one sharp-eyed sniper see you, and all our struggle has been in vain. Will you stand aside, Valentine, or must I commit treason on your body to push you out of the way?"

Fuming, Valentine yielded, and watched in anger and frustration as Elidath and a band of picked warriors slipped past him into the inner vault. There was the sound of fighting almost at once within; Valentine heard shouts, energy-bolts, cries, moans. Though guarded by Ermanar's watchful men, he was a dozen times at the brink of pulling away from them and entering the vault himself, but held back. Then a messenger came from Elidath to say that the immediate resistance was wiped out, that they were penetrating deeper, that there were barricades, traps, pockets of enemy soldiers every few hundred yards. Valentine clenched his fists. It was an impossible business, this thing of being too sacred to risk his skin, of standing about in an antechamber while the war of restoration raged all about him. He resolved to go in, and let Elidath bluster all he liked.

"My lord?" A messenger from the other direction, breathless, came running up.

Valentine hovered at the entrance to the vault. "What is it?" he snapped.

"My lord, I am sent by Duke Nascimonte. We have found Dominin Barjazid barricaded in the Kinniken Observatory, and he asks you to come quickly to direct the capture."

Valentine nodded. Better that than standing about idly here. To an aide-de-camp he said, "Tell Elidath I'm going back up. He has full authority to reach the weather-machines any way he can."

But Valentine was only a short distance up the passageways when Gorzval's aide arrived, to say that the usurper was rumored to be in the Pinitor Court. And a few minutes later came word from Lisamon Hultin, that she was pursuing him swiftly down a spiraling passageway leading to Lord Siminave's reflecting-pool.

In the main concourse Valentine found Deliamber, watching the action with a look of bemused fascination. Telling the Vroon of the conflicting reports, he asked, "Can he be in all three places?"

"None, more likely," the wizard replied. "Unless there are three of him. Which I doubt, though I feel his presence in this place, dark and strong."

"In any particular area?"

"Hard to tell. Your enemy's vitality is such that he radiates himself from every stone of the Castle, and the echoes confuse me. But I will not be confused much longer, I think."

"Lord Valentine?"

A new messenger—and a familiar face, deep coarse brows meeting in the center, a jutting chin, an easy confident smile. Another unit of the vanished past fitting itself back into place, for this man was Tunigorn, second closest of all Valentine's boyhood friends, now one of the high ministers of the realm, and now looking at the stranger before him with bright pene-

429

trating eyes, as if trying to find the Valentine behind the strangeness. Shanamir was with him.

"Tunigorn!" Valentine cried.

"My lord! Elidath said you were altered, but I had no idea—"

"Am I too strange to you with this face?"

Tunigorn smiled. "It will take some getting used to, my lord. But that can come in time. I bring you good news."

"Seeing you again is good news enough."

"But I bring you better. The traitor has been found."

"I have been told already three times in half an hour that he is in three different places."

"I know nothing of those reports. We have him."

"Where?"

"Barricaded in the inner chambers. The last to see him was his valet, old Kanzimar, loyal to the end, who finally saw him gibbering with terror and understood at last that this was no Coronal before him. He has locked off the entire suite, from the throne-room to the robing-halls, and is alone in there."

"Good news indeed!" To Deliamber Valentine said, "Do your wizardries confirm any of this?"

Deliamber's tentacles stirred. "I feel a sour, malign presence in that lofty building."

"The imperial chambers," said Valentine. "Good." He turned to Shanamir and said, "Send out the word to Sleet, Carabella, Zalzan Kavol, Lisamon Hultin. I want them with me as we close in."

"Yes, my lord!" The boy's eyes gleamed with excitement. Tunigorn said, "Who are those people you named?"

"Companions of my wanderings, old friend. In my time of exile they became very dear to me."

"Then they will be dear to me as well, my lord. Whoever they may be, those who love you are those I love." Tunigorn drew his cloak close about him. "But what of this chill? When will it begin to lift? I heard from Elidath that the weather-machines—"

"Yes."

"And can they be repaired?"

"Elidath has gone to them. Who knows what damage the Barjazid has done? But have faith in Elidath." Valentine looked toward the inner palace high above him, narrowing his eyes as though he could in that manner see through the noble stone walls to the frightened shameless creature hiding behind them. "This coldness gives me great grief, Tunigorn," he said somberly. "But curing it now is in the hands of the Divine—

and Elidath. Come. Let's see if we can pluck that insect from its nest."

14

The moment of final reckoning with Dominin Barjazid was close at hand now. Valentine moved swiftly, onward and inward and upward through all the familiar wonderful places.

This vaulted building was the archive of Lord Prestimion, where that great Coronal had assembled a museum of the history of Majipoor. Valentine smiled at the thought of installing his juggling clubs alongside the sword of Lord Stiamot and the jewel-studded cape of Lord Confalume. There, rising in amazing swoops, was the slender, fragile-looking watchtower built by Lord Arioc, a strange construction indeed, giving indication perhaps of the greater strangeness that Arioc would perpetrate when he moved on to the Pontificate. That, a double atrium with an elevated pool in its center, was the chapel of Lord Kinniken, adjoining the lovely white-tiled hall that was the residence of the Lady whenever she came to visit her son. And there, sloping glass roofs gleaming in the starlight, was Lord Confalume's garden-house, the cherished private indulgence of that grandeur-loving pompous monarch, a place where tender plants from every part of Majipoor had been collected. Valentine prayed they would survive this night of wintry blasts, for he longed to go among them soon, with eyes made wiser by his travels, and revisit the wonders he had seen in the forests of Zimroel and on the Stoienzar shores.

Upward—

Through a seemingly endless maze of hallways and staircases and galleries and tunnels and outbuildings, onward, onward. "We will die of old age, not cold, before we reach the Barjazid!" Valentine muttered.

"It will not be long now, my lord," Shanamir said.

"Not soon enough to please me."

"How will you punish him, my lord?"

Valentine glanced at the boy. "Punish? Punish? What punishment can there be for what he's done? A whipping? Three days on stajja-crusts? Might as well punish the Steiche for having jostled us on the rocks."

Shanamir looked puzzled. "No punishment at all?"

"Not as you understand punishment, no."

"Turn him loose to do more mischief?"

"Not that either," said Valentine. "But first we must catch him, and then we can talk about what to do with him."

Half an hour more—it seemed forever—and Valentine stood before the core of the Castle, the walled imperial chambers, not nearly the oldest but by far the most sacrosanct of all its precincts. Early Coronals had had their governing-halls here, but they had long since been replaced by the finer and more awesome rooms of the great rulers of the past thousand years, and now constituted a glittering palatial seat of power, apart from all the other tangled intricacies of the Castle. The highest ceremonies of state took place in those high-vaulted splendid chambers; but now one single miserable being lurked in there, behind the ancient massive doors, protected by heavy ornate bolts of enormous size and weighty symbolic significance.

"Poison gas," Lisamon Hultin said. "Pump one canister of gas through the walls and drop him wherever he is."

Zalzan Kavol nodded vehemently. "Yes! Yes! See, a thin pipe slipped through these cracks—there is a gas they use in Piliplok for killing fish, that would do the job in—"

"No," Valentine said. "He will be brought out alive."

"Can it be done, my lord?" Carabella asked.

"We could smash the doors," rumbled Zalzan Kavol.

"Ruin Lord Prestimion's doors, that were thirty years making, to fetch one rascal out of hiding?" Tunigorn asked. "My lord, this talk of a poison gas does not seem so foolish to me. We should not waste time—"

Valentine said, "We must take care not to act like barbarians. There will be no poisonings here." He caught Carabella's hand, and Sleet's, and raised them. "You are jugglers, with quick fingers. And you, Zalzan Kavol. Have you no experience at using those fingers for other things?"

"Picking locks, my lord?" Sleet asked.

"And things of that order, yes. There are many entrances to these chambers, and perhaps not all are secured by bolts. Go, try to find a way past the barriers. And while you do that I'll seek another way."

He stepped forward to the giant gilded door, twice the height of the tallest of Skandars, carved over every square inch with images in high relief of the reign of Lord Prestimion and his celebrated predecessor Lord Confalume. He put his hands to the heavy bronze handles as though he meant to open the door with a single hearty heave.

For a long moment Valentine stood that way, casting from his mind all awareness of the tension that swirled about him.

He attempted to move to the quiet place at the center of his soul. But a powerful obstacle blocked him:

His mind was filled suddenly with overwhelming hatred for Dominin Barjazid.

Behind that great door was the man who had thrust him from his throne, who had sent him forth as a hapless wanderer, who had ruled rashly and unjustly in his name, and—worst of all, wholly monstrous and unforgivable—who had chosen to destroy a billion blameless and unsuspecting people when his own schemes began to falter.

Valentine loathed him for that. For that, Valentine ached to destroy Dominin Barjazid.

As he stood clinging to the handles of the door, fierce violent images assailed his mind. He saw Dominin Barjazid flayed alive, cloaked in his own blood, screaming screams that could be heard from there to Pidruid. He saw Dominin Barjazid nailed to a tree with barbed arrows. He saw Dominin Barjazid crushed beneath a hail of stones. He saw—

Valentine trembled with the force of his own terrible rage.

But one did not flay one's enemies alive in a civilized society, and one did not freely vent one's anger in violence—not even upon a Dominin Barjazid. How, Valentine wondered, can I claim the right to rule a world, when I can't even rule my own emotions? So long as this rage roiled his soul he was as unfit to govern, he knew, as Dominin Barjazid himself. He must do battle with it. That pounding in the temples, that rush of blood, that savage hunger for vengeance—all must be purged before he made any move toward Dominin Barjazid.

Valentine struggled. He let the clenched muscles of his back and shoulders relax, and filled his lungs with the sharp chill air, and moment by moment allowed the tension to drain from his body. He searched his soul where the hot fiery vengeance-lust had so suddenly flared in it, and swept it clean. And then he was able to move at last to the quiet place at the center of his soul and hold himself there, so that he felt himself alone in the Castle but for Dominin Barjazid somewhere on the far side of the door, only the two of them and a single barrier between. Conquest over self was the finest of victories: all else must follow, Valentine knew.

He yielded himself up to the power of the silver circlet of the Lady his mother, and entered into the dream-state, and sent forth the strength of his mind toward his enemy.

It was no dream of vengeance and punishment that Valentine sent. That would be too obvious, too cheap, too easy. He sent a gentle dream, a dream of love and friendship, of sadness for what had befallen. Dominin Barjazid could only be astounded by such a message. Valentine showed Dominin Barjazid the dazzling glittering pleasure-city of High Morpin, and the two of them walking side by side down the Avenue of Clouds, talking amiably, smiling, discussing the differences that separated them, trying to resolve frictions and apprehensions. It was a risky way to begin these dealings, for it exposed him to derision and contempt, if Dominin Barjazid chose to misunderstand Valentine's motives. Yet there was no hope of defeating him through threats and rage; perhaps a softer way might win. It was a dream that took vast reserves of spirit, for it was naïve to expect Barjazid to be seduced by guile, and unless the love that radiated from Valentine was genuine, and made itself felt to be genuine, the dream was a foolishness. Valentine had not known he could find love in him for this man who had worked so much harm. But he found it; he spun it forth; he sent it through the great door.

When he had done, he clung to the door-handles, recouping his strength, and waited for some sign from within.

Unexpectedly what came was a sending: a powerful blast of mental energy, startling and overwhelming, that roared out of the imperial chambers like the fury of a hot Suvrael wind. Valentine felt the searing blast of Dominin Barjazid's mocking rejection. Barjazid wanted no love, no friendship. He sent defiance, hatred, anger, contempt, belligerence: a declaration of perpetual war.

The impact was intense. How did it come to pass, Valentine wondered, that the Barjazid was capable of sendings? Some machine of his father, no doubt, some witchery of the King of Dreams. He realized that he should have anticipated something like that. But no matter. Valentine stood fast in the withering force of the dream-energy Dominin Barjazid hurled at him.

And afterward sent back another dream, as easy and trusting as Dominin Barjazid's had been harsh and hostile. He sent a dream of pardon, of total forgiveness. He showed Dominin Barjazid a harbor, a fleet of Suvraelu ships waiting to return him to his father's land, and even a grand parade, Valentine and Barjazid side by side in a chariot, riding down to the waterfront for the ceremonies of departure, standing together on the quay, laughing as they exchanged their farewells, two good enemies who had had at each other with all the power at their command and now were parting pleasantly.

From Dominin Barjazid came an answering dream of death and destruction, of loathing, of abomination, of scorn.

Valentine shook his head slowly, heavily, trying to clear it of the muck of poison coming toward him. A third time he gathered his strength and readied a sending for his foe. Still he would not descend to Barjazid's level; still he hoped to overwhelm him with warmth and kindness, though another might say it was folly even to make the attempt. Valentine shut his eyes and centered his consciousness in the silver circlet.

"My lord?"

A woman's voice, cutting through his concentration just as he was slipping into trance.

The interruption was jarring and painful. Valentine spun around, ablaze with unaccustomed fury, so shaken by surprise that it was a moment before he could recognize the woman as Carabella, and she drew back from him, gasping, momentarily afraid.

"My lord—" she said in a tiny voice. "I didn't know—"

He struggled to control himself. "What is it?"

"We—we have found a way to open a door."

Valentine closed his eyes and felt his rigid body going slack with relief. He smiled and drew her to him, and held her a moment, trembling as tension discharged itself in him. Then he said, "Take me there!"

Carabella led him down corridors rich with antique draperies and thick well-worn carpets. She moved with a sureness of direction surprising in one who had never walked these halls before. They came to a part of the imperial chambers that Valentine did not remember, a service access somewhere beyond the throne-room, a simple and humble place. Sleet, riding on Zalzan Kavol's shoulders, had the upper half of his body poked deep within some transom, and was reaching down to perform delicate manipulations on the inner side of a plain door. Carabella said, "We've opened three doors this way and now Sleet's infiltrating the fourth. In another moment—"

Sleet pulled his head out and looked around, dusty, grimy, wondrously pleased with himself.

"It's open, my lord."

"Well done!"

"We'll go in and get him," Zalzan Kavol growled. "Do you want him in three pieces or five, my lord?"

"No," Valentine said. "I'll go in. Alone."

"You, my lord?" Zalzan Kavol asked in an incredulous tone.

"Alone?" said Carabella.

435

Sleet, looking outraged, cried, "My lord, I forbid you—" and stopped, bewildered by the sacrilege of his own words.

Mildly Valentine said, "Have no fears for me. This is something I must do without help. Sleet, step aside. Zalzan Kavol—Carabella—stand back. I order you not to enter until you're summoned."

They stared at one another in confusion. Carabella began to say something, faltered, closed her mouth. Sleet's scar throbbed and blazed. Zalzan Kavol made odd rumbling sounds and swung his four arms impotently.

Valentine pulled open the door and strode through.

He was in a vestibule of some kind, perhaps a kitchen passageway, nothing a Coronal was likely to be familiar with. He walked warily through it and emerged into a richly brocaded hall, which after a moment's disorientation he recognized as the robing-room; beyond it was the Dekkeret Chapel, and that led to the judgment-hall of Lord Prestimion, a grand vaulted chamber with splendid windows of frosted glass and magnificent chandeliers manufactured by the finest craftsmen of Nimoya. And beyond that was the throne-room, with the Confalume Throne of supreme grandeur dominating everything. Somewhere in that suite Valentine would find Dominin Barjazid.

He moved forward into the robing-room. It was empty, and looked as though no one had made use of it for months. The stone archway of the Dekkeret Chapel was uncurtained; Valentine peered through it, saw no one there, and continued through the short curving passage, decorated with brilliant mosaic ornaments in green and gold, that connected with the judgment-hall.

He drew in his breath deeply and laid hands on the judgment-hall door and flung it open.

At first he thought that that vast space also was empty. Only one of the great chandeliers was lit, and that one at the far end, casting but a dim glow. Valentine looked to left and right, down the rows of polished wooden benches, past the curtained alcoves in which dukes and princes were permitted to conceal themselves while judgment was passed upon them, toward the high seat of the Coronal—

And saw a figure in imperial robes standing in the shadows at the council-table below the high seat.

15

Of all the strangenesses of his time of exile, this was the most strange of all, to stand less than a hundred feet from one who wore what once had been his own visage. Twice before, Valentine had seen the false Coronal, on that day of festival in Pidruid, and he had felt soiled and drained of energy when he had looked upon him, without knowing why. But that was before he had regained his memory. Now, in the dimness, he beheld a tall, strong man, fierce-eyed, black-bearded, the Lord Valentine of old, princely in bearing, not at all cowering or gibbering or terrified, confronting him with cold calm menace. Was that how I looked? Valentine wondered. So bleak, so icy, so forbidding? He supposed that during all these months when Dominin Barjazid had been in possession of his body, the darkness of the usurper's soul had leaked out through the face, and changed the Coronal's cast of features to this morbid hateful expression. Valentine had grown used to his own amiable sunny new face, and now, seeing the one he had worn so many years, he felt no wish to have it back.

Dominin Barjazid said, "I made you pretty, didn't I?"

"And made yourself less so," said Valentine cordially. "Why do you scowl, Dominin? That face was once better known for its smile."

"You smiled too much, Valentine. You were too easy, too mild, too light of soul to rule."

"Is that how you saw me?"

"I and many others. I understand you've become a wandering juggler these days."

Valentine nodded. "I needed a trade, after you took away the one I had. Juggling suited me."

"It would have," Barjazid said. His voice echoed in the long empty chamber. "You were always best at giving amusement to others. I invite you to return to juggling, Valentine. The seals of power are mine."

"The seals are yours, but not the power. Your guards have deserted you. The Castle is secure against you. Come, give yourself up, Dominin, and we will return you to your father's land."

"What of the weather-machines, Valentine?"

"Those have been turned back on."

"A lie! A silly lie!" Barjazid whirled and threw open one of the tall arching windows. A blast of frigid air rushed in so swiftly that Valentine, at the other end of the room, could feel it almost at once. "The machines are guarded by the people I most trust," said Barjazid. "Not your people, but my own, that I brought from Suvrael. They will keep them off until the order comes from me to turn them on, and if all of Castle Mount turns black and perishes before that order comes, so be it, Valentine. So be it! Will you let that happen?"

"It will not happen."

"It will," said Barjazid, "if you remain in the Castle. Go. I grant you safe conduct down the Mount, and free passage to Zimroel. Juggle in the western towns, as you did a year ago, and forget this foolishness of claiming the throne. I am Lord Valentine the Coronal."

"Dominin—"

"Lord Valentine is my name! And you are the wandering juggler Valentine of Zimroel! Go, take up your trade."

Lightly Valentine said, "It's a powerful temptation, Dominin. I enjoyed performing, perhaps more than anything I've done in my life. Nevertheless, destiny requires me to carry the burdens of government, regardless of my private wishes. Come, now." He took a step toward Barjazid, another, another. "Come with me, out to the antechamber, so we can show the knights of the Castle that this rebellion is over and the world returns to its true pattern."

"Stay back!"

"I mean no harm to you, Dominin. In a way I feel grateful to you, for some extraordinary experiences, things that would surely never have befallen me but for—"

"Back! Not another step!"

Valentine continued to advance. "And grateful, too, for ridding me of that annoying little limp, which interfered with some of the pleasures of—"

"Not—another—step—"

Barely a dozen feet separated them now. Beside Dominin Barjazid was a table laden with the paraphernalia of the judgment-hall: three heavy brazen candlesticks, an imperial orb, and next to it a scepter. Uttering a strangled cry of rage, Barjazid seized a candlestick with both hands and hurled it savagely at Valentine's head. But Valentine stepped deftly aside and with a neat snap of his hand caught the massive metal implement as it went by. Barjazid hurled another. Valentine caught that too.

"One more," Valentine said. "Let me show you how it's done!"

Barjazid's face was mottled with fury: he choked, he hissed, he snorted in anger. The third candlestick flew toward Valentine. Valentine already had the first two in motion, spinning easily end over end from hand to hand, and it was no task at all for him to snatch the third and fit it into sequence, forming a gleaming cascade in the air before him. Blithely he juggled them, laughing, tossing them ever higher, and how good it felt to be juggling again, to be using the old skills after so long, hand and eye, hand and eye.

"See?" he said. "Like this. We can teach you, Dominin. You only need to learn to relax. Here, throw me the scepter as well, and the orb. I can do five, and maybe even more than that. A pity the audience is so small, but—"

Still juggling, he walked toward Barjazid, who backed away, eyes wide, chin flecked with spittle.

And abruptly Valentine was rocked and swayed by a sending of some sort, a waking dream that hit him with the force of a blow. He halted, stunned, and the candlesticks tumbled clangorously to the dark wooden floor. There came a second blow, dizzying him, and a third. Valentine struggled to keep from falling. The game he had been playing with Barjazid was ended now, and some new encounter had begun that Valentine did not comprehend at all.

He rushed forward, meaning to seize his adversary before the force struck him again.

Barjazid retreated, holding his trembling hands before his face. Was this onslaught coming from him, or did he have an ally hidden in the room? Valentine recoiled as that inexorable unseen power thrust against his mind once more, even more numbingly. He shook. He pressed his hands to his temples and tried to collect his senses. Catch Barjazid, he told himself, get him down, sit on him, yell for assistance—

He sprang forward, lunged, seized the false Coronal's arm. Barjazid yelled and pulled free. Advancing, Valentine sought to corner him, and nearly did, but abruptly, with a wild shriek of fear and frustration, Dominin Barjazid darted past him and went scrambling across the room. He dived into one of the curtained alcoves on the far side, crying, "Help me! Father, help me!"

Valentine followed and ripped away the curtain.

And stood back in astonishment. Concealed in the alcove was a powerfully built, fleshy old man, dark-eyed, glowering, wearing on his forehead a glittering golden circlet, and grasping in one hand some device of ivory and gold, some thing of straps and hasps and levers. Simonan Barjazid he was, the King of Dreams, the terrifying old haunter out of Suvrael, skulking here in the judgment-hall of the Coronal! It was he who had sent the mind-numbing dream-commands that nearly had felled Valentine; and he struggled now to send another, but was prevented by the distraction of his own son, who clung hysterically to him, begging for help.

Valentine knew this was more than he could handle alone. "Sleet!" he called. "Carabella! Zalzan Kavol!"

Dominin Barjazid sobbed and moaned. The King of Dreams kicked at him as if he were some bothersome dog nipping at his heels. Valentine edged cautiously into the alcove, hoping to snatch that dread dream-machine from old Simonan Barjazid before he could work more damage with it.

And as Valentine reached for it, something more astounding yet occurred. The outlines of Simonan Barjazid's face and body began to waver, to blur—

To change—

To turn into something monstrously strange, to become angular and slender, with eyes that sloped inward and a nose that was a mere bump and lips that could scarcely be seen—

A Metamorph.

Not the King of Dreams at all, but a counterfeit, a masquerade King, a Shapeshifter, a Piurivar, a Metamorph—

Dominin Barjazid screamed in horror and let go of the bizarre figure, recoiling and throwing himself down, quivering and whimpering, against the wall. The Metamorph glared at Valentine in what surely was unalloyed hatred and hurled the dream-device at him with ferocious violence. Valentine could only partly shield himself; the machine caught him in the chest and knocked him awry, and in that moment the Metamorph rushed past him, dashed frantically to the far side of the room, and in a wild scramble leaped over the sill of the window that Dominin Barjazid had opened, flinging himself out into the night.

16

Pale, shaken, Valentine turned and saw the room full of people: Sleet, Zalzan Kavol, Deliamber, Shanamir, Carabella, Tunigorn, and he could not tell how many others, hastily pressing in through the narrow vestibule. He pointed toward

Dominin Barjazid, who lay huddled in a pitiful state of shock and collapse.

"Tunigorn, I give you charge of him. Take him to a secure place and see that no harm comes to him."

"The Pinitor Court, my lord, is safest. And a dozen picked men will guard him every instant."

Valentine nodded. "Good. I don't want him left alone. And get a doctor to him: he's had a monstrous fright, and I think it's done him harm." He looked toward Sleet. "Friend, are you carrying a wine-flask? I've had some strange moments here myself." Sleet reached a flask to him; Valentine's hand quivered, and he nearly spilled the wine before he got it to his lips.

Calmer now, he walked to the window through which the Metamorph had leaped. Lanterns gleamed somewhere far below. It was a fall of a hundred feet, or more, and in the courtyard down there he saw figures surrounding something that lay covered with a cloak. Valentine turned away.

"A Metamorph," he said in bewilderment. "Was it only a dream? I saw the King of Dreams standing there—and then it was a Metamorph—and then it rushed to the window—"

Carabella touched his arm. "My lord, will you rest now? The Castle is won."

"A Metamorph," Valentine said again, with wonder in his voice. "What could it have—"

"There were Metamorphs also in the hall of the weather-machines," said Tunigorn.

"What?" Valentine stared. "What did you say?"

"My lord, Elidath has just come up from the vaults with a strange story." Tunigorn gestured; and out of the crowd at the back of the room stepped Elidath himself, looking battle-weary, his cloak stained and his doublet torn.

"My lord?"

"The weather-machines—"

"They are unharmed, and the air and warmth go forth again, my lord."

Valentine let out a long sigh. "Well done! And there were Shapeshifters, you say?"

"The hall was guarded by troops in the uniform of the Coronal's own guard," said Elidath. "We challenged them, we ordered them to yield, and they would not, even to me. Whereupon we fought them, and we—slew them, my lord—"

"There was no other way?"

"No other way," Elidath said. "We slew them, and as they died they—changed—"

"Every one?"

441

"All were Metamorphs, yes."

Valentine shivered. Strangeness upon strangeness in this nightmare revolution! He felt exhaustion rushing upon him. The engines of life turned again; the Castle was his, and the false Coronal a prisoner; the world was redeemed, order restored, the threat of tyranny averted. And yet—and yet— there was this new mystery, and he was so terribly tired—

"My lord," said Carabella, "come with me."

"Yes," he said hollowly. "Yes, I'll rest a little while." He smiled faintly. "See me to the couch in the robing-room, will you, my love? I think I will rest, an hour or so. When was it that I last slept, do you recall?"

Carabella slipped her arm through his. "It seems like days, doesn't it?"

"Weeks. Months. Just an hour—don't let me sleep more than that—"

"Of course, my lord."

He sank to the couch like one who had been drugged. Carabella drew a coverlet over him and darkened the room, and he curled up, letting his weary body go limp. But through his mind darted luminous images: Dominin Barjazid clinging to that old man's knees, and the King of Dreams angrily trying to shake him off, all the while waving that strange machine about, and then the shifting of shapes, the eerie Piurivar face glaring at him—Dominin Barjazid's terrifying cry—the Metamorph rushing toward the open window—again and again, again and again, scenes beyond comprehension acting themselves out in Valentine's tormented mind—

And sleep came over him gently, slipping up on him as he lay wrestling with the demons of the judgment-hall.

He slept the hour he had asked, and something more than that, for when he woke it was because the bright golden light of morning was in his eyes. He sat up, blinking and stretching. His body ached. A dream, he thought, a wild and bewildering dream of—no, no dream. No dream.

"My lord, are you rested?"

Carabella, Sleet, Deliamber. Watching him. Standing guard over his slumber.

Valentine smiled. "I'm rested, yes. And the night is gone. What has been happening?"

"Little enough," said Carabella, "except that the air grows warm again, and the Castle rejoices, and word is spreading down the Mount of the change that has come upon the world."

"The Metamorph who sprang from the window——was it killed?"

"Indeed, my lord," said Sleet.

"It wore the robes and regalia of the King of Dreams, and carried one of his devices. How was that, do you think?"

Deliamber said, "I can make guesses, my lord. I have spoken with Dominin Barjazid——he is the next thing to a madman now, and will be a long time healing, if ever——and he told me certain things. Last year, my lord, his father the King of Dreams fell gravely ill and was thought close to death. This was while you still held the throne."

"I recall nothing of that."

"No," said the Vroon, "they made no advertisement of it. But it looked perilous, and then a new physician came to Suvrael, someone of Zimroel who claimed great skills, and indeed the King of Dreams made a miraculous recovery, like one who had risen from the dead. It was then, my lord, that the King of Dreams placed into his son's mind the notion of trapping you in Til-omon, and displacing you from the throne."

Valentine gasped. "The physician——a Metamorph?"

"Inded," said Deliamber. "Masquerading, by his art, as a man of your race. And masquerading afterward as Simonan Barjazid, I think, until undone by the frenzy and confusion of that struggle in the judgment-hall, which caused the metamorphosis to waver and fail."

"And Dominin? Is he also——"

"No, my lord, he is the true Dominin, and the sight of the thing that pretended to be his father has wrecked his mind. But do you see, it was the Metamorph that put him up to the usurpation, and one might suppose another Metamorph would have replaced Dominin, by and by, as Coronal."

"And Metamorphs guarding the weather-machines—— obeying not Dominin's orders, but the false King's! A secret revolution, is it, Deliamber? Not at all a seizure of power by the Barjazid family, but the beginning of a rebellion by the Shapeshifters?"

"So I fear, my lord."

Valentine stared into emptiness. "Much is explained now. And much more is cast into disorder."

Sleet said, "My lord, we must search them out and destroy them wherever they hide among us, and bottle the rest up in Piurifayne where they can do us no harm!"

"Easy, friend," Valentine said. "Your hatred of Metamorphs still lives, eh?"

443

"And with reason!"

"Yes, perhaps so. Well, we will search them out, and have no secret Metamorphs pretending to be Pontifex or Lady or even the keeper of the stables. But I think also we must reach toward those people, and heal them of their anger if we can, or Majipoor will be thrown into endless war." He rose and fastened his cloak and held his arms high. "Friends, we have work to do, I fear, and no small measure of it. But first comes celebration! Sleet, I name you the chancellor of my restoration festivities, to plan the banquet and arrange the entertainments and summon the guests. Let the word go forth to Majipoor that all is well, or nearly so, and Valentine's on his throne again!"

17

The Confalume throne-room was the largest and grandest of the rooms of the Castle, with glittering gilded beams and fine tapestries and a floor of smooth gurna-wood from the Khyntor peaks, a hall of splendor and majesty in which the most significant of imperial ceremonies took place. But rarely had the Confalume throne-room beheld a spectacle such as this.

For high on the great many-stepped Confalume Throne sat Lord Valentine the Coronal, and on a throne to his left, nearly as lofty, sat the Lady his mother, resplendent in a gown all of white, and to his right, on a throne of the same height as the Lady's, was Hornkast the high spokesman of the Pontifex, for Tyeveras had sent his regrets and Hornkast in his place. And arrayed before them, virtually filling the room, were the dukes and princes and knights of the realm, such an assembly as had not been seen in one place since the days of Lord Confalume himself—overlords out of far Zimroel, from Pidruid and Til-omon and Narabal, and the Ghayrog duke from Dulorn, and the great ones of Piliplok and Ni-moya and fifty other cities of Zimroel, and a hundred more of Alhanroel, beyond the fifty of Castle Mount. But not all this throng were dukes and princes, for there were humbler people also, Gorzval the stump-armed Skandar and Cordeine who had been his sailmender and Pandelon his carpenter, and Vinorkis the Hjort dealer in haigus hides, and the boy Hissune of the Labyrinth, and Tisana the old dream-speaker of Falkynkip, and many more of no rank higher than that, standing among these grandees with faces shining in awe.

Lord Valentine rose and saluted his mother, and rendered a salute to Hornkast, and bowed as the cries went up, "Long live the Coronal!" And when silence fell he said quietly, "Today we hold grand festival, to celebrate the restoration of the commonwealth and the making whole of the order of things. We have entertainment for you this day."

He clapped his hands and there was music: horns, drums, pipes, a lively and lilting outburst of melody, a dozen players striding into the room, Shanamir leading them. And behind them came the jugglers, in costumes of surpassing beauty, costumes worthy of great princes: Carabella first, and little scar-faced white-haired Sleet just back of her, and then gruff shaggy Zalzan Kavol and the two brothers who remained to him. They carried juggling gear of many kinds, swords and knives and sickles, torches ready to be lit, eggs, plates, gaily painted clubs, and a host of other things. When they reached the center of the room they took up their positions facing one another along the points of an imaginary star, and stood straight-shouldered and poised.

"Wait," said Lord Valentine. "There's room for one more!"

Step by step down the Confalume Throne he came, until he was three steps from the bottom. He grinned at the Lady, and winked at young Hissune, and gestured to Carabella, who flung a blade at him. He caught it neatly and she threw another, and a third, and he began to juggle them on the steps of the throne, as he had vowed to do so long ago on the Isle of Sleep.

It was the signal, and the juggling commenced, and the air glistened with a multitude of strange objects that seemed to fly of their own accord. Never had juggling of such quality been seen in the known universe, Lord Valentine was sure of that. He threw from the throne another few moments, and then he came down into the group, laughing, in high joy, interchanging sickles and torches with Sleet and the Skandars and Carabella. "As in the old days!" Zalzan Kavol called. "But you're even better now, my lord!"

"The audience inspires me," replied Lord Valentine.

"And can you juggle as a Skandar can?" said Zalzan Kavol. "Here, my lord! Catch! Catch! Catch! Catch!" Seemingly from out of the air Zalzan Kavol plucked eggs and plates and clubs, his four arms never ceasing to weave and seize, and each thing he caught he sent toward Lord Valentine, who tirelessly received and juggled and passed off to Sleet or Carabella, while the cheers of the audience—no mere flattery, that was certain—resounded in his ears. Yes! This was the life! As

445

in the old days, yes, but even better now! He laughed and caught a shimmering sword and sent it high. Elidath had thought it might be unseemly for a Coronal to do such a thing as juggle before the princes of the realm, and Tunigorn had felt the same, but Lord Valentine had overruled them, telling them with kindness and love that he cared not at all for protocol. And now he saw them watching open-mouthed from their places of honor, stupefied by the skill of this amazing exhibition.

And yet he knew his time had come to quit the juggling-floor. One by one he emptied his hands of the objects he had caught, and gradually he retreated. When he had reached the first step of the throne he halted and beckoned to Carabella.

"Come," he said. "Join me up here, and now we become spectators."

Her cheeks deepened in color, but without faltering she rid herself of the clubs and knives and eggs, and moved toward the throne. Lord Valentine took her by the hand and together they ascended.

"My lord—" she whispered.

"Shhh. This is very serious business. Careful you don't trip on the steps."

"I trip? I, a juggler?"

"Pardon me, Carabella."

She laughed. "I pardon you, Valentine."

"*Lord* Valentine."

"Is that how it is to be, my lord?"

"Not really," he said. "Not between the two of us." They reached the highest step. The double seat, gleaming in green and gold velvet, awaited them. Lord Valentine stood a moment, looking out at the throng, at the dukes and princes and the common folk. "Where's Deliamber?" he whispered. "I don't see him!"

"He had no taste for this event," said Carabella, "and has gone off to Zimroel, I think, on holiday. Wizards are bored by such festivities. And the Vroön was never fond of juggling, you know."

"He should be here," Lord Valentine murmured.

"When you need him again, he'll return."

"I hope so. Come: let's sit now."

They took their places on the throne. Below, the remaining jugglers were engaged in their most dazzling routines, which seemed miraculous even to Lord Valentine who knew the secrets of timing that underlay them; and as he watched, he felt a strange sadness come over him, for he had withdrawn him-

446

self from the company of the jugglers now, he had drawn apart to mount the throne, and that was a grave and solemn alteration of his life. He knew beyond doubt that his time as a wandering juggler, the freest and in some ways the most joyful time of his life, was ended now, and the responsibilities of power, which he had not sought but which he had not been able to refuse, were descending on him in their full weight once again. He could not deny the sorrow of that. To Carabella he said, "Perhaps privately—when the court is looking the other way—we can all get together now and then, and throw the clubs, eh, Carabella?"

"I think so, my lord. I would like that."

"And we can pretend—that we're somewhere between Falkynkip and Dulorn, wondering if the Perpetual Circus will hire us, wondering if we can find an inn, if—if—"

"My lord, look at what the Skandars are doing! Can you believe the skill of it! So many arms, and every one busy!"

Lord Valentine smiled. "I must ask Zalzan Kavol to tell me how that one is done," he said. "Someday soon. When I have time."

ABOUT THE AUTHOR

ROBERT SILVERBERG'S novels and short stories have earned him the high regard of an international audience. He is perhaps best known for his books *Dying Inside, The Book of Skulls* and *Nightwings*. Born in New York City, Mr. Silverberg now lives near San Francisco.